Martina Cole is the No. 1 bestselling author of sixteen hugely successful novels. Her most recent novel, *Hard Girls*, went straight to No. 1 on the *Sunday Times* hardback bestseller list. *The Business* was the No. 1 bestselling hardback adult fiction title of 2008. *The Take* won the British Book Aw... ime Thriller of the Year in 2006 and has ... ned adaptation for Sky One, wit... *ay* is currently in producti... & Judy as one of the Top ... of Martina's novels are ... Cole has a son and daugh...

Martina Cole is high... ard-hitting, uncompromising and haun..., as well as her incredible success.

Praise for Martina Cole's bestsellers:

'Cole has the amazing talent of making characters appear larger than life. Another fabulous effort' *Sun*

'A masterpiece of plotting, characterisation and drama . . . Terrific stuff from a terrific lady' *Mirror*

'Martina Cole writes crime novels that are intensely readable' *Guardian*

'A blinding good read' Ray Winstone

'A typical blend of *Eastenders* with the *Sopranos* and a few of the nastier moments of *The Forsyte Saga*' *The Times*

'Cole at her finest . . . gritty dialogue, shocking violence and a gripping storyline' *Daily Express*

By Martina Cole and available from Headline

Dangerous Lady
The Ladykiller
Goodnight Lady
The Jump
The Runaway
Two Women
Broken
Faceless
Maura's Game
The Know
The Graft
The Take
Close
Faces
The Business
Hard Girls

MARTINA COLE

GOODNIGHT LADY

headline

First published in 1994
by HEADLINE BOOK PUBLISHING

First published in paperback in 1994
by HEADLINE BOOK PUBLISHING

This edition published in paperback in 2010
by HEADLINE PUBLISHING GROUP

1

Cataloguing in Publication Data is available from the British Library

ISBN 978 0 7553 7407 6

Typeset in Galliard by Avon DataSet Ltd,
Bidford-on-Avon, Warwickshire

Printed and bound by CPI Group (UK) Ltd, Croydon, CR0 4YY

Headline's policy is to use papers that are natural, renewable and recyclable products and made from wood grown in sustainable forests. The logging and manufacturing processes are expected to conform to the environmental regulations of the country of origin.

HEADLINE PUBLISHING GROUP
An Hachette UK Company
338 Euston Road
London NW1 3BH

www.headline.co.uk
www.hachette.co.uk

For my sisters, Maura and Loretta. We've held each other's hands, wiped each other's tears, supported each other, laughed together even when our world had collapsed around us and enjoyed every second of it. We are grown women now, but still at heart, we're the Whiteside girls.

Remembering Jonathan Peake and Eric Lane, with love always.

Many thanks to Marlene Moore for all her help and information on Berwick Manor.

Book One

When I was a child, I spake as a child,
I understood as a child,
I thought as a child.

– 1 Corinthians 13:11

The children of perdition are oft'times made instruments even of the greatest work.

– Ben Jonson, 1637–1673

Prologue

1989

The woman in the bed was impossibly old. Her face, still showing subtle traces of a former beauty, was a mass of criss-cross lines. The thick powder she wore had cracked and flaked in the heat of the room. The red slash of her mouth was sunken and bent, emphasising her baggy jowls.

Two things were, however, very much alive: her eyes, still a startling green, despite the yellowing of her whites, and her hair. The thick redness seemed to crackle on the shrunken head, falling across bony shoulders in a shower of electric waves. It was this, and the eyes, which showed a casual observer that here lay a former beauty, a relic of another time, another era. A time when she was a show stopper, a woman of account. Now there was laughter in those eyes as she watched, beneath hooded lids, the two young nurses tidying her room.

She knew she was old and she accepted it. Death would just be another great adventure, she was sure of that. It was one of the prerogatives of great age that you made yourself ready to meet your maker. Well, she had a few things to say to him when the time came.

'She was lovely in her day wasn't she?' The blond-haired nurse picked up a photograph in a heavy silver frame. It showed a beautiful, doe-eyed woman, wrapped in fox furs, wearing a cloche hat. Her heavily lipsticked mouth formed a perfect cupid's bow. She could have been a silent-screen star.

'Yes, gorgeous. Look at all that hair coming out from underneath that hat.'

The mousey-haired girl sounded envious. What she wouldn't give for the old girl's hair, even as it was now, speckled with grey.

'Did you read about her? In the *News of the World* the other week? She had a life, she did. All those scandals in the sixties! Politicians and that, even Royalty!' The girl lowered her voice now, as if remembering the old lady was in the room.

'You don't have to whisper, dears, I'm not dead yet!'

Both nurses jumped at the sound of her voice, low pitched and surprisingly strong. She looked so tiny, so tiny and vulnerable, until she opened her mouth.

'I was seventeen when that photo was taken. I was a looker and all. Had all the men after me!'

One of the nurses sat down on the bed.

'Is it true what they said about you?'

The tiny frame shook with a deep husky laugh that turned into a hacking cough.

'Let's just say that there's an element of truth in there, shall we?'

The two nurses exchanged glances.

'Is it true that Jonathan La Billière started out in blue films?'

Briony sat up in bed and scowled. 'He's got a knighthood, you know, but he always had a soft spot for me, did Jonny. I knew many men, my loves, and I learnt one thing. Never open your mouth about anyone or anything, unless you stand to benefit by it. It's a rule I've lived by for nearly ninety years! There's things that will go to my grave with me, and there's people who think the sooner I go and take me knowledge with me, the better off everyone will be!'

She laughed again then, pulling herself up in the bed, she lit a cigarette, drawing the smoke down into the depths of her lungs.

'Well, Miss Briony, you certainly have led a chequered life!'

'How about a drop of the hard then, girls? There's a bottle of brandy over there in the dresser. I'll have a large one please.'

The blonde nurse went to the dresser and poured out the drink. The old woman sighed. This place was costing over a thousand pounds a week, though it was worth every penny. But a thousand pounds was still a lot of money, even for two of them! A thousand pounds to someone from her beginnings was a small fortune, but money was a necessity in life; without it, you were vulnerable. She sipped the fiery liquid and felt it burn the back of her throat.

'One of the perks of having money – you can happily drink yourself to death and no one gives a damn.'

The nurses smiled.

'They're making a film about me, you know? About me and my sisters. My sister Kerry was the singer. She was the youngest. Five of us, there were, but I'm the only one left. Kerry was the gifted one, and like many gifted people she used her talent to destroy herself.' Her eyes clouded over, as if she could see her sister once more in front of her.

'But they won't mention my poor Rosalee, I made sure of that, nor too much about my Eileen. I brought up Eileen's children, you know. Then there was my Bernadette. The sweetest child God ever put on this earth, unless you upset her that is! I'm the only one left out of the five of us, and I'm well on me way to the century!'

The face closed again and the old woman became lost in another world. A world that spanned many years and that seemed more real to her with every passing day.

Chapter One

Molly Cavanagh shivered underneath the sacking. It was so very cold. She could feel the earthy dampness beneath the mattress with every movement of her aching back. She shifted position slightly and looked at the children huddled around the dying fire. The eldest, Eileen, turned to face her mother and lifted her eyebrows questioningly. Molly shook her head; the child was a long way from coming. Time enough to get Mrs Briggs when it was well on.

'Can I get you a drink, Ma?'

Molly held out a dirty hand to Eileen and she came to her mother's side.

'Go down to Donnelly's and get some coal. There's a few pennies in me skirt pocket.'

The girl turned from her and Molly grabbed at her hand. 'And keep your eye on that Brendan Donnelly. Make sure he weighs it properly, last time it was all slack.'

As she spoke her breath gleamed like white mist in the dimness.

'I will, Ma.' Eileen picked up a shawl and, pocketing the pennies, she left the basement room. The four other little girls watched her go. Kerry, the youngest, got up from her place by the fender and slipped under the covers with her ma.

Molly closed her eyes. When that Paddy got in today she'd cut the legs from under him. It was always the same when he was working: full of good intentions until payday. 'We'll pay a bit off the back of the rent. We'll have a grand dinner of pie and peas and taties. We'll maybe even send the little ones to school.' Then when the first week's wages came it was straight down The Bull for a jar of Watney's, without a thought for her or his children.

Her mind was jolted back to the present by Briony, her second eldest daughter. Never a child to keep her temper long, the crack as she slapped her younger sister Bernadette across the legs broke the silence of the room.

'Ma! Ma! She gave me a dig! Did you see that, Ma? Did you see that?'

Kerry sat up in the bed with excitement. 'Will you be slapping the face off of Briony, Ma? I saw the crack she gave our Bernie . . .'

'Will you all be quiet! And Bernadette, stop that howling and jigging about before I give you *all* a crack.'

Something in their mother's voice communicated itself to the children who all became quiet at once.

After a few minutes Kerry started to sing softly to herself. Bernadette sat beside Rosalee; taking her hand, she smiled into the vacant eyes. Molly watched, and as she saw Rosalee smile back, felt a pain in her chest. Why the hell had God sent her Rosalee? Hadn't she enough on her plate as it was without an idiot? Then, seeing her chance, Bernadette leant over Rosalee and pinched Briony hard on the inside of her leg. She leapt up in the air. Pushing Rosalee out of the way, she grabbed at Bernadette's hair, dragging the now screaming child across the dirt floor, shaking her as Bernadette grabbed hopelessly at the fingers tugging her hair.

Kerry sat up again in the bed. 'That's it, our Briony. Scratch the skin from her hands . . . The dirty bitch!'

Molly dragged her cumbersome body up. With one deft movement she slapped Kerry's face. A howl went up. Then she dragged herself from the bed and set about Briony and Bernadette. Her work-worn hands found legs and arms and she slapped them hard. Rosalee watched it all in the dying firelight and her expression never changed. Three shrieking voices rang in Molly's ears. She held on to the mantelpiece for support as a pain tore through her. Bent double, she gasped and tried to steady her breathing.

'I'm giving you all one last warning,' she told them, 'I mean it. One sound and you're all out in the backyard until the birth's over. If you don't think I'd send you out in the cold, then you just try me . . . You just bloody try me!'

She staggered back to her bed. Briony tried to help her, sorry now for all the trouble, and Molly slapped her hands away.

'You, Briony, should know better. You're eight years old. You should be helping me, child.'

She dropped her eyes and her thick red hair hung over her face like a tangled curtain.

'I'm sorry, Ma.'

Molly climbed into bed once more. The bugs in it ran amok, this way and that, trying to get into the torn mattress before they were squashed by the bulk above them.

'"I'm sorry, Ma". If I had a penny for every time I heard that, I'd be living the life of Riley! One more word out of any of you and I'll let your father find you work. I mean it.'

Briony was scared now. Her father would farm them out in the morning; it was only her mother who'd stopped him until now. She took Bernadette's hand and led her to the fireside. Rosalee smiled at them both and Briony hugged her close. Molly resumed her wait. Kerry crooned softly to herself again.

'Sing us a song, Kerry.' Briony's voice broke the gloom. 'Send our Rosalee off to sleep.'

Kerry lay beside her mother, her little face screwed up in consternation as she tried to think of an appropriate song.

Her haunting little voice came slowly at first but Molly relaxed against the dirty pillows and sighed. Kerry's voice was like a draught of fresh air.

> 'In Dublin's fair city,
> Where the girls are so pretty,
> I first set my eyes
> On sweet Molly Malone . . .'

The mood in the room was once more homely. Briony smiled at Bernadette over Rosalee's short cropped hair, their earlier fight forgotten. Molly watched her children and thanked God for the peace that had descended. It wouldn't last long, she was aware of that, but while it lasted she would enjoy it.

Eileen's bare feet were frozen. The cobbles had a thin sheet of ice on them and as she walked with the bucket of coal it banged against her shins, breaking the skin. She put the bucket down and rubbed them with one hand. She could hear the singing and almost feel the foetid warmth of The Bull as she stood outside. The street lamps had been lit and they cast a pink glow around her. She straightened and pushed her thick curly hair back off her face. As she bent down to pick up the bucket once more, a man stood in front of her. Eileen looked up into a large red face.

'What's your name, little girl?' Eileen knew from his voice that he was class.

'Eileen Cavanagh, sir.'

The man was looking her over from head to foot and she squirmed beneath his gaze. He pushed her hair back from her face, and studied her in the light of the street lamp.

'You're quite a pretty little thing, Eileen Cavanagh.'

She wasn't sure how to answer the man who seemed to be dressed all in black, from his highly polished boots to his heavy cape and big black hat. He was well armoured against the weather and she wondered if it had occurred to him that she was freezing.

'Thank you kindly, sir. I . . . I have to be getting along, me ma's waiting on the coal.'

The man put heavy gloved hands on her shoulders and kneaded them, as if seeing how much meat she had on her. Then the doors of The Bull opened and a man stumbled out into the street.

Eileen recognised her da at once and called to him. 'Da . . . Da! It's me, Eileen.'

Paddy Cavanagh was drunk. Very drunk. And to add to his misery he had lost every penny of his wages on a bet. His fuddled brain tried to take in what was happening as he lumbered over to his daughter.

'Is that you, our Eileen?'

The big man smiled at her father and Eileen, for some reason she could not fathom, began to feel more frightened.

'You have a beautiful daughter, Mr Cavanagh. I believe you work for me, don't you?'

Paddy screwed up his eyes and recognised Mr Dumas, the owner of the blacking factory. Straightening up he tipped his cap to the man.

'How old is the girl?'

Paddy wasn't sure how old she was. That was women's knowledge. Women remembered everything and passed it on to other women. How the Mary Magdalene was he to know something like that?

'Tell the gentleman your age, Eileen.'

She bit her lip. Her large blue eyes were filling with unshed tears, and Mr Henry Dumas felt a stirring in him.

Patrick cuffed her ear. 'Answer the man, you eejit. You've a tongue in your head long enough to talk the legs off a donkey any other time.'

'I'm eleven, sir.'

'Old enough to be working, then. Where do you work, child?'

'She doesn't work, sir.' This was said bitterly. Paddy had wanted them all out working, but Molly had been adamant. Schooling for them all, even if it meant no food on the table.

'You don't go to work, a big strapping girl like you?'

Eileen looked down at the shiny ground, afraid to look into the big red face with the large moustache.

'I need a strong girl myself, Cavanagh. A strong young girl. I'll pay you a pound a week for her.'

Patrick's jaw dropped in shock. 'A pound a week, sir? What for?'

He looked into Dumas's face and it was written there, in his eyes and on the fat moist lips, and for a few seconds Paddy felt the bile rise in him.

Seeing the look on Cavanagh's face, Dumas added: 'Two pounds a week, then.'

Paddy shook his head, not in denial but in wonderment. He looked at Eileen: at her shoeless feet, blue with the cold, at her scrawny legs and lice-ridden hair and suddenly he felt an overpowering sense of futility. Two pounds a week was a lot of money and Mr Dumas was a very wealthy man. He could make sure that Paddy stayed employed, no matter what. As for Eileen, she would be broken soon enough, the boys around about would see to that, and then there would be more mouths to feed. Dumas was offering her warmth and comfort, and she could be the means of helping her family.

Dumas watched the man battling it out with himself. Then opening his leather purse, he took out two sovereigns and laid them in the palm of his hand. The streetlight played over them, the gold glittering in Paddy's eyes.

'I'll take her with me now, then.'

'As you like, sir.'

'What about the coal, Da? I have to take the coal home to me ma. She's waiting on it, the baby's coming . . .'

'Now shut your mouth, our Eileen, and go with Mr Dumas. You're to do whatever he tells you, do you hear me? Anything he tells you at all.'

'Yes, Da.'

The big man took her hand and pulled her away from her father. Paddy watched her go, his heart wretched. He squeezed his hand over the two sovereigns and felt a tear force its way from his eye. He tried to justify his actions all the way home. But even drunk and befuddled, he couldn't quite convince himself.

*

Eileen sat in the cab and listened to the clip-clop of the horse's hooves as it trotted through a residential area. She gaped at the big town houses in wonderment, her fear of the man gone a little now since he had wrapped her in his cloak. It smelt lovely.

Dumas studied her profile as she watched the houses. She was going to be stunning in a few years, but until then he would have her. He liked them young, very young.

Five minutes later they stopped at a small detached house. Eileen noticed the garden especially. Even in the cold it smelt of lavender. Mr Dumas lifted her from the coach and carried her up the pathway. The door was opened by a girl in her late-teens who ushered them inside. Eileen was placed on the floor in the hallway. It had carpet and she dug her toes into the unfamiliar softness.

'Get Mrs Horlock, would you, Cissy?'

'Yes, sir.' She gave a little bob and walked through a green baize door to the side of her.

'You're going to have a nice hot bath soon. Then we can have something to eat.'

Eileen didn't answer. This man was talking to her as if they had been friends for years. There was something not right here. But the thought of food cheered her.

Then someone came bursting through the green baize door. Eileen jumped with shock. Rushing towards her was a small silver-haired woman. Her teeth had long gone and her mouth seemed to have caved in around the gums. Her face was a mass of wrinkles that all seemed to criss-cross one another. Thick white hair was scraped back off her face into a tight white cap. Bright hazel eyes surveyed Eileen from head to foot.

'Cissy, take the cloak and leave it in the outhouse until we can disinfect it, then come down to the scullery and help me scrub this one.' She jerked her head at Eileen as she spoke and then pulled the cloak from her. Cissy grabbed at it and disappeared once more through the door.

Mrs Horlock sucked her gums and then felt Eileen's limbs, finally grabbing at her tiny breasts.

'Sturdy, Mr Dumas, sir. Not a bad choice, if I might say so. Got good teeth. A few good meals and she'll put some flesh on her bones.'

'My sentiments entirely, Mrs Horlock. Now if you don't mind, I'll be in the morning room enjoying a brandy. Send Cissy along with her when she's ready.'

He smiled at Eileen as he spoke and she felt terror grip her heart.

Paddy Cavanagh stood in the centre of the foetid basement room and stared around him. Rosalee awakened and began to cry. Briony immediately began to rock her gently, soothing her back to sleep. Molly stared dull-eyed from the bed, Bernadette and Kerry dozing beside her.

'The child's well on then, Moll?'

She nodded, then frowned as she saw him making up the fire. 'Where's our Eileen, Pat? I sent her out to get the coal a couple of hours since.'

He stared into the fire. Briony's eyes seemed to be boring into his.

'I met her on me way home. I'd got her a job and she went there tonight.'

Molly sat up in the bed.

'You what?' Her voice was low.

Paddy turned to face his wife, working himself up into a temper.

'You heard me, woman! I got her a job. Jesus himself

knows we need the bloody money! She'll be well looked after, she'll get decent clothes and food . . .'

'Where's this job, Pat? Come on, tell me, where is this job?'

He could hear the doubt in his wife's voice and felt a wave of anger. She did not trust him at all. Not with anything to do with the girls.

'It's working for Mr Dumas, the man who owns the blacking factory. She'll be working in the house, Moll.'

'Go and get her this minute, Paddy Cavanagh. I don't want her working sixteen hours a day, running round like a blue-arsed fly for a few pennies a week.'

Paddy stormed to the bed and slapped his wife across the face. 'I've said what she's going to do, and now it's done. I want to hear no more about it.'

Kerry and Bernadette both inhaled loudly at the slap their father gave to their mother. Kerry's mouth was open in a large 'O' and Paddy raised his hand to her before the shriek came out.

She snapped her mouth shut immediately.

'I'll scalp the bloody face of the first one to whinge in this house tonight. I mean it.'

As he turned to the fireplace, the two sovereigns slipped from his hand and landed with a gentle chink on the dirt floor.

Molly pulled herself up on the bed and stared at them in amazement. Then, as her eyes flew up to meet her husband's, realisation dawned.

'You filthy bastard, you sold her to him, didn't you? You sold my lovely Eileen to that man . . .' She put her hands to her head and began to cry, a low deep moaning that wrenched Paddy Cavanagh's heart from his body.

He tried to take her in his arms.

'Molly, Moll . . . Listen to me, she'll be living like a queen up there. Look, we'll get two pounds every week . . .'

Molly pushed him from her in disgust. 'So it's come to this? You'd pimp out your own child, you dirty blackguard!

'We had to eat, woman, can't you see that?'

'Why couldn't we eat with your wages, then? Because they all went in The Bull, didn't they? Didn't they? By Christ, I hope the priest's waiting when you go to Confession. I hope he chokes the bloody life out of you. As soon as this child's born I'm going to get Eileen, and if she's busted, Paddy Cavanagh, I'll have the Salvation Army after you, I swear it. I'll scream what you've done from the bloody rooftops!'

Molly looked like a mad woman. Her hair was tangled and in disarray, her huge swollen breasts heaving with the effort of making herself heard. Suddenly she saw her life with stunning clarity. She saw the dirt floor, strewn with debris. Saw the only chair in the room with its broken back, the small amount of tea wrapped up carefully on the mantelpiece to keep the rats and roaches from it. The smell of the sewers was in her nose continually. They ran alongside the basement, and when it rained, human excrement was forced through the iron grid in the wall. It was as if something burst inside her head.

'You brought me this low, Paddy Cavanagh, and I allowed it. I tried to stand by you, with your drinking and your whoring. Never a full meal for any of the children. But this last act has finished you with me. My lovely Eileen sold to an old man! You sicken me. Sicken me to my stomach.'

Paddy picked up one of the sovereigns and walked from the room. As he opened the door a gust of icy wind blew in.

*

Eileen was lying in a big copper bath and Mrs Horlock was combing the lice from her hair. The smell of paraffin, sickly sweet, hung over them.

'You've got lovely hair, child. Nice and thick. Once you get some meat inside you, it'll shine. Like a raven's wing, it is.'

She smiled a toothless smile and Eileen smiled tremulously back.

Mrs Horlock stood up. 'You lie there now and Cissy will bring you in some more water to rinse yourself off. The scum in the bath is as thick as me four fingers.'

She walked from the room and went to the kitchen where she prepared a meal for the girl. She shook her head. Poor little mite. Still, Mr Dumas was a rich man, and in fairness not really a nasty one. Providing the girl did as she was told, everything would be fine, and she didn't look like a fighter. Not like the last one. A red-headed bitch with a tongue that could cut glass, and a scream to match. It had taken a few good hidings from her father and a stern talking to from her mother to bring that one round, and by then Mr Dumas was fed up. The mother had finally taken her to Nellie Deakins and if she, Maria Horlock, knew anything about it, the little madam would soon wish she was back here. At least Mr Dumas would only bother her once a day. At Nellie Deakins's she was guaranteed six or seven fellows, and not all as clean and kind as Mr Dumas. Once Nellie had got the big money for the actual breaking in, the girl was worthless to her. Unless she was very young, when Nellie would use the piece of linen and the chicken blood trick a few times.

Mrs Horlock shook her head at the skulduggery of Nellie Deakins. Well, at least that little red-headed bitch would get her comeuppance there. This one though, this Eileen, seemed an amenable little thing. When she had scrubbed the child's body she had checked for tell-tale hairs around her privates but there was nothing, not even any raised follicles, so she wouldn't get anything in that department for a while yet. And a few leading questions had ascertained she hadn't started her periods just yet. Oh, Mr Dumas was going to get his money's worth with this one. The tiny budding breasts were like little plump cherries. Hard little nodules, just the way he liked them. She'd fill out though, this one, be all breasts and hips in a few years. But by that time she should have learnt enough to keep her in good stead for the rest of her life. Plus Mr Dumas always gave the girls a decent leaving present. One young lass had walked out of here with fifty pounds in her pocket!

Eileen allowed Cissy to pour the water over her body, ridding it of the residue from the bath water. Then Cissy wrapped her in a large white towel and dried off her hair. Pulling a comb through it gently, she began chattering to Eileen.

'Mr Dumas will insist you bathe every day. Me, I only have to once a week. You'll have the run of the house, but you can't go out without Mrs Horlock or one of the stable boys with you. That's not 'cos you're a prisoner or nothing, it's in case you get robbed of your togs.'

'What work will I be doing, Cissy?'

She bit her lip before answering. This one was greener than the grass in Barking Park.

'Don't you know, ducks?'

Eileen stared into the troubled brown eyes before her and opened her mouth to speak, but nothing came out.

'You're living here now, Miss Eileen, with Mr Dumas.'

Cissy threw in the 'Miss Eileen' bit because they usually liked that. It made them more amenable to their situation.

'You mean, I'm living with Mr Dumas. What as? A kind of daughter?' Eileen had heard of rich people buying children, but they were usually babies.

Cissy frowned. This one was definitely green. 'Look, supposing you was to get married, right?'

Eileen nodded, unsure where this conversation was taking her.

'Well, you'd have to sleep with your husband, wouldn't you?'

Eileen nodded again. This time a feeling of panic was welling up inside her ribcage.

'Well then, just pretend Mr Dumas is your husband, see. It's simple really, and you'll get used to it. They always do.'

Eileen began to shake her head.

'No . . . you're telling me lies. My father wouldn't do that to me.'

Cissy was losing patience now.

'Listen, miss, if Mrs Horlock gets wind of what I've told you she'll slap the pair of us from here to Timbuktu. Take my advice. Just keep your head down, open your legs and think of England. The last one we had who caused trouble was carted off to Nellie Deakins's brothel, and believe me, you don't want to end up there! The master's paid for you fair and square, your dad's already got the money and it'll come in regular every week. If you've any brothers and sisters, then they'll eat well. Look on it from that point of view and just remember what Cissy told you. Smile at the master and you'll have everything you want. Cause trouble and you'll regret it to the end of your days.'

Eileen allowed Cissy to dress her in a nightdress of white lawn and followed her meekly up the stairs and through the green baize door into the morning room. Mr Dumas stood up as she entered and smiled at her.

'Come over here to the fire, my dear. That will be all, Cissy. Tell Mrs Horlock to bring up the food.'

Cissy bobbed a curtsy and, winking at Eileen, left the room.

Mr Dumas took Eileen's hand and led her over to a large chair by the fire. She sat in it gingerly. The unaccustomed softness of the nightdress made her frightened in case she tore it. Mr Dumas took a small foot into his hand and knelt in front of her, kneading its coldness. Eileen watched him fearfully.

'Your poor little feet are frozen, my dear. First thing in the morning Mrs Horlock is going to rig you out from head to toe. You'd like that, wouldn't you?'

Eileen stared at the big man kneeling in front of her. His hands were now on her shins and she suppressed an urge to scream. Cissy's threats of Nellie Deakins had had their desired effect, though. Everyone knew about Nellie Deakins's house. Eileen wasn't sure until tonight what actually went on in there, but she knew that once girls passed through the doors they were never seen again.

The man's hands were now lifting up the nightdress and caressing her thighs. She had no drawers on and tried to squeeze her skinny legs together, but the man was parting them, gently but firmly, with his fingers. Eileen closed her eyes as his moustache began tickling her legs, its wetness roaming up her shins and along her thighs. He was lifting her off the chair now and on to the rug by the fire. She closed her eyes tightly as he began to undo the little bows on the front of the nightdress. As his cold hand enveloped one of her breasts she bit down on her lip, drawing blood.

Mrs Horlock walked into the room with a tray. Taking in the scene before her, she hastily left again, leaving the tray on the table in the hall. She smiled to herself. This one was more amenable than the last, praise God.

She was humming as she passed through the green baize door into the kitchen.

Eileen lay in a dream. Every bone in her body was aching, a fire raging between her legs. As the man pulled away from her she expelled her breath in a long sigh. She closed her eyes as he lay beside her and caressed her open body. She felt numbness invade her mind.

'There, there, my beauty, that wasn't so bad, was it? Now you're busted, it'll be easier for you in the future. I'm starving. Shall I get us something to eat?'

Eileen kept her eyes closed until he called in Mrs Horlock. The housekeeper said it had been a long day for the child and she needed her rest after all the excitement. Eileen walked from the room with the woman, feeling semen and blood running down her legs. She was tucked up into a nice soft bed, a compress of rags dipped in icewater between her legs.

Mrs Horlock spoke to her softly and kissed her sweating forehead.

Eileen didn't sleep for three days. She never said a whole sentence to anyone for six months.

Her reign with Mr Dumas lasted one year.

Chapter Two

'Briony!' Molly's voice was harsh.

Briony, who had been sitting on the steps outside the door rushed into the room.

'What's wrong, Ma?'

'Go and fetch the money from Mr Dumas.' This was said through clenched teeth. Briony nodded and pulled on her boots. Molly watched her as she rushed from the room, a coldness settling on her heart. She would have to watch Briony.

She put the kettle on for a cup of tea and sighed. It was a year since Eileen had gone and the room looked a different place altogether. It now had two proper beds, with good feather mattresses. Two brightly coloured mats on the floor, and a table and chairs somehow squeezed in. The fire was always alight, there was plenty of food in the house – and all of it stuck in Molly's throat like gall. She had saved enough to move them to a small house in Oxlow Lane, which would be a step up after this place, and still she wasn't happy about it.

It was the way they got the money that tormented her,

night after night. Her baby boy had been stillborn and Eileen, her lovely Eileen, who had been so full of life, so vibrant, was now a shadow of her old self. Withdrawn and moody, she visited once a fortnight, bedecked in her finery, her lovely face white and drawn. It was written there for all to see what Mr Dumas did to her. Eileen had been there a year and every day it broke her more.

Briony walked through the streets towards Mr Dumas's house with a shiver of excitement. She loved going there. She loved the little garden, the lovely carpets and the sweet-smelling warmth. She made her way past The Bull in Dagenham and into Barking, hurrying. She normally stayed and had a bite with Eileen, and tonight she had a little plan. She smiled and waved at people as she went, a familiar figure in her large black boots, courtesy of Mr Dumas's two pounds a week, and her long brick-red coat, courtesy of Eileen. Her red hair had as usual sprung out of the ribbon and curled around her face and shoulders.

At just gone ten years old she was a tiny little thing. Her face was open, with milk-white skin covered in freckles and green eyes that took in everything around her.

She skipped up the street that housed Eileen, her eyes taking in the lace curtains at the respectable windows, and the scrubbed doorsteps. No smelly children playing five stones out on these streets, no drunken brawling men. This was a beautiful place as far as Briony was concerned. Near to Barking Park, it exuded respectability. Briony walked up the pathway and knocked at the big green front door.

Cissy answered and Briony walked into the hallway.

'Hiya, Cissy. How's me sister?' Briony slipped off her coat and gave it to the girl.

Cissy took the coat and laid it across her arm. 'Not too good, Briony. I think she's gonna get her monthly visitor soon.'

Briony frowned and nodded. As yet Eileen had not had her period, but it was due. Her breasts and grown and she had developed pubic hair. Mr Dumas was not bothering her much these days, and it pleased Eileen but bothered Briony. Because Briony knew, through the talkative Cissy, that once his girls reached adolescence Mr Dumas wanted shot, and then the two pounds a week would dry up. She bit her lip in consternation. If the money went, then so would the food, the new house in Oxlow Lane and the schooling.

She followed Cissy through to the morning room where Eileen was sitting in front of the fire with a tray of tea and scones. Cissy gave Briony a large wink and she nodded slightly then threw herself across the room into Eileen's arms.

Her sister's long black hair was tied back off her face. She smiled at Briony tremulously.

'Sit yourself down and I'll pour you a cuppa. Help yourself to the scones.'

Briony picked up a scone and placed the whole thing into her mouth, cramming it full. She surveyed Eileen as she chewed. Her hands were shaking as she poured the tea, and Briony felt a moment's sorrow for her. She washed down the scone with a big sip of milk from the little jug and smiled at her sister.

'You all right, our Eileen?'

Eileen nodded. She handed Briony the tea and then stared into the fire.

'I'm not too bad. I keep getting a pain in me belly. I hope it's me monthlies, Briony, I really do.'

She gulped at her tea and swore under her breath. It was steaming hot.

Eileen stared at her.

'You shouldn't swear, Briony, it's not ladylike. Our mum would go mad if she heard you.'

Briony laughed. 'Well, she won't.'

Eileen laughed softly. She wished she was like her sister.

'How's Mr Dumas, Eileen?'

Eileen sighed heavily, her hands fluttering nervously in her lap.

'Oh he's all right, I suppose.'

'How's the . . . you know . . . the other business going?'

'Oh, Briony, it's horrible. Honestly, how people can do that to one another . . . It's disgusting!'

Briony raised her eyes to the ceiling in exasperation.

'I don't mean what's it like! I mean, is he doing it to you very often?'

Eileen shook her head violently. 'No, thank God.'

Briony screwed up her eyes and looked at her sister. 'That's good then.'

But it wasn't good. It wasn't good at all.

She heard the front door open and relaxed. Mr Dumas was here. Eileen stiffened in her chair and Briony winked at her.

'Relax, our Eileen, worse things happen at sea!'

Eileen stared into the fire again and Briony had to stifle an urge to get out of her seat and shake her sister by the shoulders until her teeth rattled in her head. Eileen was helping all the family and shouldn't make such a song and dance about it. That was Briony's opinion. She could be doing a lot worse things for a lot worse money. She could be up in Aldgate, in Myrdle Street, working in a sweat shop fourteen hours a day. That would soon sort her out! Let her know what side her bread was buttered. Briony knew what she'd rather be doing.

Mr Dumas walked into the room. He smiled widely at the girls and, walking towards them, kissed them both on the hand. Briony sighed with contentment. As if she was a real lady, she thought. She looked at Mr Dumas's striped tailored trousers and his single-breasted morning-coat and thought he looked like the King. She gave him her brightest smile and he smiled back. Briony slipped to the floor and sat by her sister's chair. Mr Dumas sat in her empty seat and beamed at them.

'I've ordered more tea, girls, and some more cake.' He looked at Briony as he said this and she smiled at him. He always filled her up with cake. He knew she had a sweet tooth. Eileen looked at him and his face sobered. The child's miserable face was getting him down.

'Go and get my wallet for me, Eileen, there's a good girl. Briony will be wanting your wages.'

Eileen stood up as if she had been catapulated from the chair, glad to get out of his presence. As she bolted from the room his voice stayed with her. 'And while you're there, ask Mrs Horlock what's for dinner this evening.'

She nodded and went from the room, her head down. That should give him five minutes with the little red-headed minx. As the door shut Briony stood up and sat in her sister's seat. She grinned at the man opposite.

'I love coming here, Mr Dumas.' It was said with every ounce of guile she had in her, and this was not wasted on the man.

'Do you, Briony?'

'Oh, yes. I wish I lived here, but I expect I'm not big enough yet, am I? I'm only ten.'

She fingered a tendril of red hair as she said this and sucked it into her mouth. Unbeknown to her she could not have done anything more erotic as far as Henry Dumas was concerned.

'I'd do anything to live here. Anything at all.'

The man and the little girl looked full at one another then. An unspoken agreement passed between them and the man was surprised to find such knowingness in so young a child.

Paddy Cavanagh walked into the office with his cap in his hand. 'You wanted to see me, sir?'

Mr Dumas smiled at him, a man-to-man smile.

'It's about Eileen – I think it's about time she went back home.'

He watched with satisfaction as Paddy Cavanagh's face dropped.

'What . . . I mean . . . Well, what's wrong, sir?'

His mind was reeling. How the hell were they to manage without Eileen's money? Even Molly had had to put up with the situation. For all her highfalutin talk, she wasn't backward at taking her cut from it every week.

'I feel a yen for something different, Paddy. You know how it is.'

He stayed silent. No, he did not know how it was, little bits of children had never interested him.

'Briony now, there's a beautiful child. She was at the house last night and she made it quite clear . . .' He raised a hand as if Paddy was going to stop him talking. 'She made it quite clear that she would not be averse to – how shall we say? – taking over where Eileen left off.'

Paddy licked his lips. Every instinct in his body was telling him to take back his fist and slam it into this man's face. Into his teeth. Into his very bones. But he knew he wouldn't even as he thought it. This man was gentry, whatever the hell that was. He owned factories and part of the docks. He was looked up to, made substantial contributions to all sorts of charitable causes. His wife's father was a lord. Paddy knew he was trapped. He also knew that Mr Henry high and mighty Dumas was not getting his Briony for a paltry two pounds a week.

'I thought we could maybe settle for two pounds ten this time,' said Henry persuasively.

'Three pounds.' Paddy's voice was clipped, and surprised both himself and his listener with its forcefulness.

'Three pounds?'

'That's right, sir. My Briony is worth that.'

Dumas bit his top lip and screwed up his eyes.

'It would ease the pain of her mother, sir, because she'll have a fit this night when she knows what's going on. She was bad enough about Eileen, but Briony, her Briony, she'll be like a madwoman. She was all for going for Mrs Prosser Evans over Eileen.'

Paddy had the satisfaction of seeing Dumas pale at the words. Mrs Prosser Evans was a force to be reckoned with in Barking and Dagenham, fighting for justice for the lower classes with a vigour that surprised everyone who came in contact with the tiny woman.

Paddy watched the man battle it out with himself.

Mrs Prosser Evans and a scandal, or a little red-headed child just on ten for a paltry weekly sum. It was no contest.

'Three pounds a week it is then. Bring her round to me at six this evening and you can take the other . . .' He waved his hand as he tried to think of the child's name.

'Eileen, I can collect my Eileen.'

Without wasting any more words, Paddy put his hat on

and left the office. He picked up his coat from his work-bench and walked out of the factory and along towards The Bull. Inside he ordered himself a large whisky, which he downed in one gulp. Wiping his mouth with the back of his grimy hand he laid his head on the bar and groaned out loud against the fates.

It never occurred to him not to take Briony. Three pounds a week was three pounds a week.

Molly was dishing up the dinner when Paddy rolled in the door. 'What the hell are you doing home at this time?'

Paddy grabbed her around her waist, breathing his whisky breath all over her. She drew away from him in disgust.

'Get away out of that!'

Kerry giggled. Taking the hot wooden spoon from the large earthenware pot, Molly smacked her across the hands with it. Kerry licked off the juices from the rabbit stew.

Briony sat at the table expectantly, feeding Rosalee. She was the only one with the patience. You had to force the food inside her at times.

'Bri . . . Bri.' Rosalee was catching hold of Briony's hair and calling to her gently. She leant forward and kissed the big moon face. Rosalee started clapping her hands together in excitement.

Paddy watched them and felt a tug at his heart.

'Well? Answer me, what brings you home at this time?'

'Mr Dumas sent for me.' He sat on the broken chair as he spoke.

'What about? Is it Eileen? Is she sickening?'

'No, woman. Nothing like that. Bejasus, would you let a man talk without wittering into his conversation?'

'Well, what's wrong then?'

'He's had enough of her. I'm to go and fetch her tonight.'

Molly pushed back her hair and her face, red and shiny from the cooking, looked relieved.

'I'll be glad to have the child home safe.'

Paddy got out of the chair and swept his arm out in a gesture of disgust.

'Oh, she'll be safe all right, here, 'cos this is where we'll be staying now, isn't it? She'll be safe when the real winter comes, and the shite's bursting into the room, and the cold would cut the lugs from yer. Two pounds a bloody week we'll lose, two Christing pounds! She's up there, dressed up to the nines and eating her fecking head off as and when she fancies it. Well, she'll get a shock when she gets back here, madam. She'll have to go out to work, they all will, if we're to get the house in Oxlow Lane. Even that fecking eejit.' He pointed to Rosalee.

Molly sat on the fender and tapped the wooden spoon against her hand.

'There's that to it, I suppose.' All her dreams were dissolving in front of her eyes, of a nice little house, two up, two down, with a bit of garden out the back, and no more living in basements without enough to eat. Instead it was no more boots for the girls or tea for herself, as and when she wanted it. Once going to Uncle every Tuesday with the blankets and sheets and anything else pawnable had been their way of life, until Paddy brought home some money. Now it would be again, it seemed.

'Well, woman, it's done now and I expect you've saved yourself a bit, to see us over until the spring?'

Molly didn't answer. As far as Paddy Cavanagh was concerned, the less he knew about her money situation the better.

'Yes, as large as life he says to me, "Paddy, I don't want the miserable-looking item any longer." The cheek of it!' He sneaked a glance at Molly as he enlarged on his story, building up to the point of it.

'And then, Moll . . . I was all for bashin' him, you know, except I don't want to go along the line. Anyway, then he says to me, "I'd give two pound ten a week for your Briony!"'

Molly was up in a flash.

'He what?'

'"Two pounds ten?" says I.' Paddy poked himself in the chest as he spoke. '"Two pounds ten," I says. "Not fifty pounds a week will get you another of my girls!"'

Molly nodded her head, the wooden spoon like a truncheon in her clenched fist.

'"Three pounds then," he says to me. "Three pounds and we'll negotiate again in six months."'

Paddy, warming to his story, began to embroider it freely. '"Never," says I. "Not for all the gold in London town. Be off, you bugger," I said, Moll. "Get yourself away out of that," I said . . .'

She nodded again. 'You did right, Paddy. You did right. When I think of what my Eileen's suffered this last year . . .' Her voice broke with shame and remorse.

Briony, watching the proceedings, felt her heart sink down to her boots. Trust her father to botch it up with a drink in him. He was actually believing what he was saying now. Briony was cute enough to know that her father would sell his grandmother if he thought he could get money for her. Getting up from the table, she went to her mother.

'I'll go to Mr Dumas, Ma. Think what you could do with three pounds a week. I wouldn't mind what I had to do. And . . . and our Eileen would be back home like.'

Molly put her hand on to Briony's head. 'This family has been shamed enough, child.'

Briony started gabbling: 'But, Mum, you don't understand. I don't mind going . . . Really I don't! I think I'd be good at it, what Mr Dumas wants like, and the girls can carry on at school, and you can get the drum in Oxlow Lane, and Mr Dumas said last night . . .'

Molly gripped Briony's ear hard and cracked the wooden spoon over her head.

'What did Mr Dumas say last night, child? Come on then, enlighten us.'

Briony was aware she had made a fatal error and looked at her father, her eyes beseeching him to help her.

Molly twisted her ear and Briony screamed out: 'He said that he liked me, Ma, that I could take over from Eileen because she hated it there. That I could earn more money because I was a bit more lively like.'

Molly threw her from her across the dirt floor. Briony lay still staring up at her mother. Whatever happened, she was going to Mr Dumas tonight.

'My God, you want to go, don't you? You actually *want* to go. You know exactly what you're letting yourself in for and you want to go.' Molly's voice was incredulous.

Briony stood up. Facing her mother full on, she shouted at her: 'Well, Eileen went and she didn't want to go but you still took the two quid every week! I *want* to go. I can't wait to go, and get nice clobber and decent food and sleep in a proper bedroom. I bleeding well happen to like Mr Dumas, and nothing he could do to me can be any worse than being cold and hungry and dirty and poor!'

The room was deathly silent and Briony was frightened by her own outburst, but her mother was not stopping her from going to that house tonight. She was determined. She wanted some of what Mr Dumas had on offer. She wanted regular food and warmth, and if that meant she had to touch Mr Dumas and he had to touch her, then that was fine as far as she was concerned.

'If the child wants to go, let her.'

'Oh, yes, that's about your mark, isn't it, Paddy? She's just on ten but always older than her years. A slut in the making we've got here! It'll be down to Nellie Deakins next with her, I suppose.'

'Why is it that Eileen who didn't want to go went, and me who wants to go, and for a pound a week more, can't? You tell me that, Mum?'

'You wouldn't understand, Briony, because you take after him, your father. You'd sell your soul for what you wanted. Well, you can go, girl, but I tell you now – I don't ever want you back under my roof!'

Briony looked at her mother long and hard, then at the silent girls sitting around the table.

'Well, that's a funny thing, you know, Mum, because I'll be paying for the roof I ain't allowed under. I bet you won't throw his three quid back in his face, will you?'

Kissing her sisters in turn, she put on the brick-red coat that she loved, pulled on her boots and, motioning to her father, went outside and sat on the steps to wait for him. Inside her chest was a ball of misery. She'd only wanted to help, but it had been thrown back in her face. Well, the three quid would soon soften the blow so far as her mother was concerned. But all the same, it galled Briony and hurt her too. Why was what she was doing wrong? When Eileen did it, when she didn't even want to do it, it had been right. She swallowed back a sob.

Still, she'd had her way, and she brightened herself up

now by thinking of the hot bath, the lice-free hair and nice soft nightie that was to come. She closed her mind to the other. As Mrs Prosser Evans always said at Sunday school: 'Sufficient to the time thereof.' She'd worry about that bit when she came to it.

Paddy stood in the hallway of the house in Ripple Road feeling depressed. The smell of cleanliness and the absolute quiet of the place gave him the heebie jeebies, as he expressed it. He always felt clumsy and dirty when he came to the house, and it shamed him. It shamed him that he had sold off his Eileen to Henry Dumas; it galled him now that his Briony, the only one of his daughters with a spark of real life, wanted to come here. Couldn't wait to get here. It was all she had talked about on the way. And yet, as much as he'd hated listening, deep inside himself he didn't blame the child. Not really.

Briony had always had a bit more going for her than the other girls. She was quick-witted and quick-tempered and always seemed to be a bit ahead of her years, even as a tiny child. He could understand to an extent the need in her to better her way of life. Could sympathise with her absolute single-mindedness in wanting to come to this house.

Molly had never had a lot of time for Briony, except as a helper with Rosalee. Only Briony could get her to go to bed, and stop the crying fits which at one time had been frequent. Molly was all for Eileen and Kerry – Kerry being her golden child, her gifted girl, her reason for wanting the house in Oxlow Lane. Kerry must have a good home to grow up in, never mind the rest of them. Bernadette was the odd one out of the five girls. Quiet, placid, but with a devil of a temper when roused, Bernie always looked as if she was sickening for something. As if she was just a guest who would soon leave the household. His own mother had said that the child would not make old bones, and even though she was not actually ill, there was an apathy about her that frightened Paddy at times.

He put his hands in his pockets and stared down at his old boots. This was taking the devil of a long time and he was parched. His throat was on fire with the want of a whisky. A few whiskies would be better.

He heard footsteps on the stairs and Briony rushed down to him, her face flushed and rosy.

'Oh, Dad, I'm to have Eileen's room! She's nearly packed. Mr Dumas said she can keep all the clothes and things, wasn't that nice of him?'

Paddy licked his lips. 'Aye, very kind. Tell our Eileen to hurry up, I haven't got all night.'

The morning-room door opened and Henry Dumas walked out to Paddy and gave him three pounds.

'Eileen shouldn't be long. Would you like a drink while you're waiting?'

Paddy brightened. 'Yes, thank you, sir.'

Dumas noted the civility in his voice and smiled to himself.

For the first time, Paddy went into the morning room, and was impressed way beyond his imagining. There was a good fire in the polished grate. The walls were papered in a dark blue flock, and tall green plants grew upright in painted bowls. A leather chesterfield and two winged armchairs gleamed in the firelight, and small tables held all sorts of knick-knacks and frippery, the like of which Paddy had never seen before. On the floor was a Belgian carpet that even in his hob-nailed boots felt like grass beneath his feet. He sat on the edge of one of the chairs and took the glass of whisky offered him.

No, he didn't blame his Briony at all. She had seen all this. She had been allowed a small peep into the world of the monied classes and she wanted to be a part of it. Who in their right mind could blame her? Certainly not him. Even at ten years old Briony knew what she wanted. As Paddy sipped his drink he had a glimpse of the future.

With the brains she had been given, Briony would use this place as a stepping stone. He had a feeling on him that once she tasted the delights of this house she would only want better, she would only want more, and he, Paddy Cavanagh, downed his drink in a large gulp and gave her a silent toast. May you get everything you want, my Briony, but never what you deserve.

'Oh, Eileen, fold the clothes up properly, they'll be like rags by the time you get them home!' Briony's voice was annoyed. Eileen, in her haste to get out of the house, was just throwing clothes into the leather trunk that Mr Dumas had kindly given her.

'Well, Briony, they'll be like rags soon anyway, so it doesn't really make any difference, does it? Now just help me pack and let me get out of here.'

Cissy shook her head as Briony opened her mouth to answer. 'Go down to the kitchen, Eileen. Mrs Horlock has something for you.'

Eileen flounced from the room.

'She bloody well annoys me, Cissy, ungrateful little bitch she is – all this lovely stuff!'

Cissy began packing the case properly and spoke to Briony in a low voice.

'Listen, Bri, don't be too hard on her. She hated it here. Some girls aren't made like us. We get the most out of whatever situation we're in, but other people are weak like. They don't have any bottle, see? Now help me pack and we'll get shot of her then we can get you bathed. Mrs Horlock has the water all ready.'

Briony kept her own counsel, but no matter what anyone said, she thought Eileen was a miserable wet patch. She looked around the bedroom with a feeling of glee inside her chest. It was lovely. The whole house was lovely. Soon she'd have a good scrub in the tin bath in the scullery and from tomorrow she would use the big bathroom on the landing. Oh, she thought she was going to faint with happiness. She stroked the richly embroidered bedspread gently and bit her lip. This was all hers, and unlike that scut of a sister, she was going to reign here for a long time.

No matter what she had to do.

'All done, child.'

Briony stood up in the water and held up her arms as Mrs Horlock wrapped her in a towel. The little ribcage was visible through her blue-white skin and the tiny nipples, no bigger than farthings, were hard with the cold of the scullery. For the first time ever Mrs Horlock hugged a little child and, after wrapping her in the towel, put her on her lap and cuddled her close.

Briony automatically returned the hug and made herself a friend for life. The smallness of Briony, the very vulnerability that inflamed Henry Dumas, made Mrs Horlock, for the first time, aware of what the child was to do. Maybe it was her complete acceptance of the situation that upset her, she didn't know, all she knew was that Briony Cavanagh was the smallest child yet, and no matter how much she dressed it up, it began to bother her.

But she dressed her in a white nightie and took her up to the morning room and Henry Dumas.

Henry was astounded at the change in the child. As she sat chatting with him in front of the fire, her hair began to dry. First one tight spiral of red hair sprang up on top of her head, and then another. It amazed him, and he smiled to himself. She was exquisite. Her little feet were long and thin, and what shapely ankles . . .

Briony was shocked a bit at first when he dropped on to his knees and pushed up her nightdress. Now the time had come, it seemed her big talk and lioness courage were going to fail her. But they didn't. Instead, she forced herself to relax, because Cissy told her it hurt more if you tensed up. Looking down at Mr Dumas's head, she saw her nightie all scrunched up and cried out. Henry Dumas looked at her in concern. He hadn't even touched her yet!

Jumping from the chair, Briony took off the nightdress and, folding it carefully, placed it on the chairback. Then, naked, she went and sat on his knee, slipping her slender arms around his neck. Looking into his face she smiled tremulously.

'Am I doing right, Mr Dumas, sir?' The little eager voice made him want to tear into her there and then, but he stopped himself.

Instead he laid her on the carpet in front of the fire and traced every line of her body with the tips of his fingers.

'You're doing very well, Briony, very well indeed.'

When he began kissing her body, she studied the room around her, and shut her mind off from what was happening by thinking of all the things she was going to get the next day when she went shopping with Mrs Horlock. Everything from long pantaloons to a good velvet coat. As he entered her, she bit down on her lip and closed her eyes. A rogue tear made its way down her face and she licked its saltiness with her tongue. It hurt, Eileen was right, it hurt like mad.

She opened one eye and looked up at Henry Dumas. His face was shiny with sweat in the firelight, and his tongue was poking out of the corner of his mouth. He was completely taken over by her body, and she knew it. Instinctively, she knew it. It was the mystery of men and women, and inside Briony a little bell went off. To do this to her, men would give anything. It was a revelation. She felt better now, because she suddenly realised that there had been a subtle shifting of power here tonight.

She realised that Mr Dumas wanted her very much. He wanted to do this to her much more than she wanted the nice things he could give her.

Well then, so be it. But she would make sure she got her money's worth.

Chapter Three

Molly stopped for a few seconds and rubbed her hands together. The cold had crept into her bones and pushing the handcart had skinned her fingers. She took a deep breath and resumed her task. Eileen carried a large box, while Bernadette and Kerry carried a case between them. Rosalee sat on the handcart with her thumb stuck firmly in her mouth staring ahead of her over the tables and chairs and the other items of furniture stacked up around her. Bernadette lost her hold on the case and it swung sideways and hit Kerry's shins heavily. Dropping her side of the case, Kerry, in pain and temper, pulled Bernadette's hair with all her strength, and within seconds both girls were wailing. Settling the cart once more, Molly tried to quieten them. They had just rounded the corner to Oxlow Lane and she wanted desperately to make a good impression on her new neighbours.

'Come on now, girls. Whist now, be quiet.'

Bernadette sniffed loudly and then smacked Kerry across the face with the flat of her hand.

Eileen, putting down her box, separated the two girls

who were kicking and screaming. She shook them until they quietened. Pushing her face close to theirs, she whispered, 'I'm warning the pair of you, Mum's on a short leash today and you're safe while outsiders can see you, but once in the new place she'll skin you alive if you annoy her.' She stared into one face and then the other. 'Do you two understand me?'

Both girls nodded, and picking up the case once more they trudged ahead of the handcart. Eileen picked up her box wearily and the handcart's squeaking wheel was the only sound as they walked to the cottage that was to be their new home.

Molly stood in front of the black front door and sighed in delight. They really were here, they really had this place. They finally had a proper home. Her eyes drank in the leaded light windows that only needed a good wash, the red-tiled roof and cream-painted walls. It was all her dreams come true.

The cottages had stood there since the sixteenth century and had once boasted thatched roofs and large gardens. They had been farm workers' cottages until the mid-1800s when they had been bought up and rented out to any Barking residents who could pay.

Oxlow Lane was still countrified, wide and sweeping and bordered by fields. Most of the people who could afford decent houses wanted to live near Stratford and Bow, if not in Barkingside, where the docks were. But Molly was astute enough to know that Oxlow Lane would be quiet for herself and the girls, while still close enough to East London which was only a couple of hours' walk. Rainham-on-Thames was only another hour's walk along the London Road and Molly was determined to take the girls there for the day in the summer. She had been there only once herself, when she had first married Paddy, and carried the memory with her in a kind of reverence. They'd sat on the sands as the Thames rolled by, watching the passenger ferries from Gravesend in Kent disgorge day trippers, dressed in their Sunday best. They had eaten whelks and cockles outside The Phoenix public house, and Paddy had kissed her on the beach to the scandalisation of some older women near them. Oh, she was taking the girls in the summer if it was the last thing she did!

She felt in her coat pocket for the large brass key and once more marvelled to herself. A key. For the first time they had a dwelling with a key. With a real front door. She took it out of her pocket and inserted it in the lock – then all hell broke loose. Rosalee, for some unexplained reason, decided to get herself down from the cart. She stood up amongst the furniture and somehow managed to upset the whole thing.

Eileen watched in dismay as the child was flung on to the ground with a hard thud, closely followed by the table and chairs. The door of the adjoining cottage opened and a large man rushed out. Molly saw white-blond hair and huge musclebound arms pick up Rosalee and pass her to Eileen, then the table and chairs were also picked up and stacked neatly in what seemed seconds.

Rosalee, winded from the force of the fall, gasped for breath in Eileen's arms. But she wouldn't cry, Molly knew she wouldn't cry. The last time she'd cried was when Briony left her.

'Hello, Mrs. Me and me mum's been looking out for you like,' their neighbour told them.

A little woman of indeterminate age came through the door. 'I thought you could do with a cuppa, love. I've had the kettle on all morning, waiting for you.' She looked at the four girls. Molly noticed the frown as she glanced twice at Rosalee.

'These all yourn?'

Molly smiled. 'Yes, but they're good, quiet girls.' She looked at Kerry and Bernadette who had the grace to drop their eyes to the ground. Molly so wanted to make a good impression.

The old woman opened a toothless mouth and screeched with laughter.

'I'll believe that when I hear it! I had six, four girls and two boys. He's the last one at home.' She indicated her large son with a nod of her head. 'And I'll tell you now, give me a houseful of boys any day to girlies. Fighting and arguing and moaning and crying and pinching . . . Oh, I could carry on all day. Be nice to have a bit of life up the lane again, though, not enough children here any more.'

Molly felt her heart lift.

'Now then, how about a cuppa, and what about some bread pudding for you girls, with a nice cup of weak tea, eh?'

She put out a hand, and to the astonishment of Molly, Rosalee wriggled from Eileen's arms and, taking the old woman's hand, she went into the cottage with her.

The man grinned.

'I'm Abel Jones and that's me mother. We all call her Mother Jones, me and everyone else that knows her. Now get yourselves in out of the cold and I'll get the furniture in for you.'

Molly smiled at him and followed her eager daughters.

Abel looked at her as she went through the door and smiled to himself. Not a bad-looking piece that. He wondered if there was a husband in tow. Must be to afford the rent on the cottage, but you never knew, Abel told himself. She might be free for a bit of a laugh.

He picked up the heavy wood table as if it was made of paper and walked into the cottage with it.

Briony had been living her new life for three weeks and she loved it. Well, she liked most of it, she told herself. The things that she had to do for Mr Dumas got on her nerves a bit, but she was getting to like living at the house and that was all that really concerned her. She put on a brown dress with a tiny lace collar, her walking boots and her large brown cape. Lastly she put on a straw hat with dried flowers that was totally unsuited to the weather, but she was so enamoured of it she didn't care. She walked down the stairs and went through the green baize door to Mrs Horlock and Cissy.

'Get us a cab, Cis.' Briony's voice was clear and loud in the kitchen and Mrs Horlock smothered a smile. She was a case, was this one. Not five minutes in the house and already she acted like she was born to it. If she used the toilet once a day she used it fifty times, though the novelty of the bathroom was wearing off now and she was down to only two baths a day. But Mrs Horlock was clever enough to let the child have her head, let her get used to her surroundings. If she was happy, Mr Dumas was happy and at the end of the day, that was what counted.

'You're going to your mum's then, Miss?'

'Yes, Mrs Horlock, I am. Don't worry, I'll tell the cab to come back for me at five. I'll be home in plenty of time for Mr Dumas and me dinner.'

'Shall I go with her, Mrs Horlock?' Cissy's face was expressionless but the hope behind it was evident.

'No you won't, Cissy. All the work I've got here today! Now go and get Miss Briony her cab. And hurry up!'

Cissy ran from the kitchen.

'I've made you up a hamper for your mum. She'll need it today.'

Briony grinned at the old woman. She looked stern at times, and she could be sharp, but underneath Briony liked her. She cuddled Briony sometimes of an evening when Mr Dumas went home to his real house. Briony would come out here, to the kitchen and Mrs Horlock would settle her on her lap, tell her stories and feed her hot milk and bread and butter while Cissy was ironing or baking. All under Mrs Horlock's astute gaze, of course. The kitchen fire would be roaring up the chimney and the smell of spices and baking was very welcoming to Briony. The warmth and the good smells made her feel secure.

Briony opened the lid of the hamper and saw two small malt loaves, that would be full of the raisins that Rosalee loved. A small ham and a large lump of cheese. There were also some home-made scones and a jar of strawberry jam.

'Thanks, Mrs Horlock, she'll be very grateful to you.'

The woman waved her hand at Briony. ' 'Tis nothing. There's a screw of tea on the table to go in and some sugar and butter.'

Briony put these in the hamper and then went to the housekeeper and hugged her, pushing her face, straw hat and all, into the floury-smelling apron. Mrs Horlock looked down on the flame-coloured hair that spiralled out under the hat and felt a rush of affection for the child. She hugged her back.

*

Mother Jones was ensconced by her fire with Rosalee on her lap. She stroked the downy hair and shook her head. This was a child meant for the angels if ever she saw one. Abel watched her and smiled.

'Poor little thing. Must be hard for that Molly like, Mum. Having one like her. She'll never be able to earn.'

Mother Jones sniffed. 'No, true, but she'll never leave home either, so she'll never be lonely if she loses her man.'

Abel nodded and looked towards the dividing wall. He had taken a fancy to Molly Cavanagh.

On the other side of the wall, she was busy scrubbing the floor and watching Bernadette and Kerry at their task of cleaning the windows. She had eaten two slices of bread pudding and drunk two cups of hot sweet black tea and it had fortified her for the job in hand. Mother Jones had sent Abel in to show her how to get the fire going in the range, and now she had steaming hot water as often as she wanted it. This thrilled her to bits, though coal was being burnt like nobody's business. Still, it was only for today.

'Mum, our Briony's arrived in a cab!'

Molly sighed and opened the front door. Briony got out of the cab and the driver took down a small hamper and placed it beside her on the dirt road. Molly watched her pay the man and gritted her teeth. As the horse set off, clip-clopping down the lane, Molly walked out of the cottage.

'Hello, Mum. Mrs Horlock sent you a hamper, to help you get settled like.'

Briony's voice was wary as she spoke and Molly felt a moment's sorrow for her coldness towards the child.

'Come away in, Briony, it's freezing out here.'

She smiled and followed her mother inside the cottage.

Kerry and Bernadette crowded around her as she opened the hamper and showed them what was inside.

'Where's Rosalee then?'

'Oh, she's with the lady next-door. She's really nice and gave us bread pudding and a cup of char, and her house smells really funny and she ain't got no teeth . . .'

'Shut up now, Kerry.'

Briony laughed. Trust Kerry to go too far!

She took off her coat and hat, rolled up her sleeves and, taking the chamois leather from Kerry, set about the windows.

Molly watched her as she worked away, and closing her eyes she prayed to God to give her peace of mind where her Briony was concerned. They depended on her wages, far more than they ever had on Eileen's. It was Briony who was going to keep them in Oxlow Lane, and as Paddy had pointed out, Molly didn't want to kill the goose that was laying the golden eggs, did she? Forcing herself to move, she walked to Briony and embraced the girl. Briony cuddled her back, joyful that her mother wasn't cross with her any more. For her part, Molly closed her eyes and swallowed down the disgust that touching Briony always made her feel.

Letting her go, she resumed washing the floor of the cottage and Kerry and Bernadette sorted out the bedding and curtains into neat piles on the table.

'Give us a song, Kerry.'

'What do you want, a happy one or a crying one?'

'Whatever you like.'

Kerry stopped what she was doing and thought for a second, then she began to sing. It was Paddy's favourite and Briony smiled as she began. Kerry sang this song like an angel.

'Oh Danny boy, the pipes, the pipes are calling,
From glen to glen, and down the mountainside . . .'

Next-door, Mother Jones and Abel heard the singing and both laughed as Rosalee started to clap her hands.

'They're a funny family, Mum. Another girl just arrived by cab, dressed up like a kipper. Only about ten and in a cab mind, not on foot. Where are they getting the money for cabs and the like?'

'How the bloody hell would I know! They seem nice enough, Abel Jones, so don't you go snooping round there and put them off us.'

'I'm only saying, Mum . . .'

'Yeah, well, just you say it to yourself then. It'll all come out in the wash anyway. People's business rarely stays between four walls. You'll find out soon enough, son, and when you do I hope it's what you want to hear!'

'Here's Dad and Eileen with the beds, Mum!' Kerry shrieked out the words at the top of her voice, making Molly, who was upstairs getting the bedroom floors swept, cringe. The child thought she was still in the basement where you had to shout to be heard above the din coming from the other families.

'Shall I let them in?'

Briony laughed out loud.

'No, Kerry, let's leave them out there till the morning. Of course you should let them in!'

Kerry opened the door grandly. She had been locking and unlocking it all afternoon, and the novelty of the key had yet to wear off.

Briony stamped down the stairs and, after kissing Eileen, began to help while they unloaded the beds and boxes.

Abel Jones watched the proceedings from his window, studying Paddy closely. Then a cab pulled up, and the little one with the red curly hair was kissing them all and getting inside.

He shook his head. There was something funny going on with that family, he'd lay money on it. There was only one place that child would be going in a cab and that was Nellie Deakins's house.

Rosalee sat at the table and drank her broth, Kerry and Bernadette were putting the finishing touches to their room, and Eileen was making up her parents' bed. Paddy looked at his wife in the glow of the kitchen fire and, sober for once, he felt a stirring in him. As she tended the fire he saw the roundness of her large breasts, caught a glimpse of creamy skin. She wasn't a bad looker wasn't Molly, for all the childbearing. He pulled her down on to his lap, and she laughed as the chair creaked under their weight.

'Isn't this a grand place, Moll?'

She smiled and nodded. It was her dream come true. The kitchen was also their living room, but Molly didn't mind. It meant only one fire. The table and chairs were scrubbed and clean, the mats were down, and the new chair was by the fender for when she wanted to sew or just sit and drink one of her never-ending cups of tea. Briony said she was going to get Mrs Horlock to let her have some of the old curtains packed away at Mr Dumas's. She'd fit them to the windows and the place would be like a little palace. She frowned as she thought of Briony.

She allowed Paddy to nuzzle her neck. He pulled her face round and kissed her long and hard, forcing his tongue into her mouth, and Molly, for the first time in over a year, responded. In her happiness at being in the house, she wanted everything to go well.

'Oh, Mum!' Eileen, who had walked downstairs, saw them kissing and all the revulsion she felt was in her voice. Molly pulled away from Paddy just as Eileen got to the sink and threw up, retching and hawking with the illness that engulfed her at the disgusting sight.

'Eileen. Eileen, girl.' Molly put her arm around her shoulders gently, trying to pull her into her arms.

'Don't you touch me, Mum!' Eileen pointed a finger into her mother's face. 'Don't you ever touch me after you've touched him. Not after what he's done to me and Briony. And who'll be next, that's what I want to know? Bernie, Kerry, our Rosalee?'

Rosalee, hearing her name mentioned, clapped her hands together and upset the broth.

'Bri . . . Bri.'

Bernadette and Kerry, who had come down the stairs at the sound of Eileen's voice, stood like statues staring at their mother and father, fear in their faces as they realised that something bad was going to happen, and maybe even to one of them.

Molly looked from her daughter to her husband who was sitting in the chair, his head in his hands. Then Paddy got up, took his coat from the back of the door and tried to open the front door. He rattled it hard, trying to force it open, until Kerry ran to him and unlocked it with the key, all her excitement gone now as she watched her father leave the house.

Molly pulled Eileen towards her and cuddled her tightly.

'Oh Eileen, my baby, my lovely girl. What did he do to you?'

She didn't say we – what did we do to you? – because the knowledge that she had eventually condoned what her husband had done would not allow itself to surface. She held Eileen while she cried and Kerry cleaned up the mess made by Rosalee's broth.

Henry Dumas stroked Briony's hair. It was like stroking silky springs. Briony lay beside him and let him cuddle her. She liked this bit. After all the other business was out of the way, he cuddled her and whispered things to her. She didn't always understand what he was talking about, but the tone of his voice always sent her off to sleep. She watched drowsily as he got dressed, saw him push his fat little legs into his trousers, and smiled to herself. He always looked funny undressed. But when he was dressed he was like a different person. Briony respected him when he was dressed, and didn't answer him back or make as many jokes as she did the other times.

She'd turned on her side and closed her eyes to sleep when there was a loud banging on the front door. She sat bolt upright in the bed and stared at Mr Dumas. Then she heard her father's voice, loud in the hallway, and her heart sank. He was drunk, she could hear it in every word he said.

'Where's me girl? I want me girl this minute!'

Briony heard Cissy's and Mrs Horlock's voices trying to quieten him. As Henry Dumas walked towards the door, Briony was off the bed and in front of him.

'Stay up here. I'll see to me dad.' Instinctively she knew that as her father was, if he saw Henry Dumas, all hell would break loose.

Paddy looked up and saw her walking towards him. She looked beautiful. In the white lawn nightdress and with her spectacular hair unbound, she was like a vision. Through his drink-crazed mind he realised exactly what he had done to her and to Eileen, and it made him sick inside.

'I've come to take you home, Briony, my baby.' His voice was drenched with tears.

She flicked a glance at Mrs Horlock and then back at her father.

'Come into the warm, Dad, you're freezing.'

She opened the door to the morning room and he followed her inside. Mrs Horlock lit the gas lamps and Briony pushed the poker in the fire to get a blaze.

'What's all the noise about then, Dad?'

Paddy settled himself in a chair and stared at his daughter.

'I've come to take you home, lovie. This is all wrong. Eileen's been . . . she's accusing me something terrible . . . Your ma . . .'

He couldn't get the words out to explain himself, but Briony understood him well enough.

'But, Dad, I like it here. I don't want to go home.'

Paddy blinked his eyes as if to reassure himself he had heard right.

'It's lovely here, Dad. Mr Dumas is really nice to me and I've got Cissy and Mrs Horlock looking after me, and I go out to Barking Park every day . . .'

Her voice trailed off. Her mother must have caused all sorts of trouble for her dad to be here now. Even with a drink in him, he was aware of what the money meant each week. Now they'd all moved into the new house, how the hell did they think they'd pay the rent?

'Why don't you let Cissy get you a cab home, Dad? In the morning, when everything's all right with me mum, everything will be better.'

Paddy finally understood what Briony was saying. He hadn't left her here like Eileen to make the best of it. She actually *wanted* to be here, and the knowledge hurt him far more than anything else she could have said. Even losing the house wouldn't have hurt as much as what his daughter had just said. No wonder Molly was dead set against her. Here was a whore in the making all right.

'You're coming home with me now.' His voice was harsh, and he was surprised when Briony shook her head.

'I'll not leave this house, Dad, I'm staying here whether you like it or not. You couldn't wait for me to get here not three weeks since, and if you think that I'm going back to Oxlow Lane with you, you're wrong. Dead wrong. If you take me home, then I'll just keep coming back.'

She stared into his face earnestly. 'Can't you see, Dad? I love it here. I'm happy here. And best of all, everyone benefits by it. Especially me mum. She might want me home now, but she won't when we're back in the docks, will she?'

Paddy knew when he was defeated, but at least he could tell Molly and Eileen the truth now. That he'd come to get her and she'd refused. A little while later, as he made his way home in the cab paid for by Briony, he realised something. For all the trouble he was having with Eileen, he'd rather that than have her thinking like his Briony, and that was a turn up because Briony was their golden goose. Yet Eileen, it seemed to him, was more of a decent girl than ever, for all she'd been through with that scumbag. Whereas Briony, who'd taken to it like a duck to water, had broken his heart.

Chapter Four

It was thick snow and Briony had had to brave the freezing weather to get a cab. Even in her thick coat and dress, fur hat and muff, she was still frozen. Her face was stinging with the cold and as the horse moved slowly through the icy streets she waggled her toes in her boots to stop them from going numb. It was her second Christmas at Henry Dumas's house and she was a different girl altogether to the one who had arrived there fourteen months earlier. At eleven, she had grown. Her breasts were forming and the good food had put flesh on her bones. Her face had rounded, giving her a look of a young woman already. Her hair was still a fiery red, only now she wore it in a neat chignon pinned to her head with expert precision by Mrs Horlock.

Briony had also changed inside herself. She wasn't as happy-go-lucky as she had been, and she was sensing a change in Henry Dumas as her body developed. She bit on her lip and watched the traffic in the streets, mainly pedestrians, a few ragamuffins running around offering to hold horses' bridles or carry people's shopping for a halfpenny. The majority of the people wore sacking over their clothes to try and keep the snow from freezing their bodies entirely.

As they approached Barking Broadway, the horse's pace slowed even more. Briony pushed down the window of the cab and stared out. Then she saw him.

He was a tall boy of about thirteen, dressed in ragged trousers and jacket though his heavy boots were obviously new. Brand new, not second-hand new. Briony was struck by his appearance because he had the thickest, blackest hair and eyebrows she had ever seen in her life. As she watched him from the cab she saw him stumble into a well-dressed man and apologise profusely before walking on. Briony smiled. He was dipping. She watched as another boy stepped by him and was given the wallet. It was all over in a split second and now the first boy ambled on again, safe in the knowledge that if he was stopped, he had no evidence on his person. Briony was fascinated by it all, and from her vantage point kept a close eye on him.

His next victim was to be a young docker, the worse for drink and also stumbling. She noticed the way that the pick-pocket kept his cap pulled down low over his face; his clothes, well-pressed though old, were obviously new to him. He couldn't quite carry himself in them properly. More used to being ragged arsed. Briony watched the boy bump into the docker, and then it all went wrong. The young man grabbed the boy's hand like a vice. Briony saw them start struggling and banged on the wooden side of the cab for it to stop. Getting out, she ran over to where the two men were arguing, attracting the attention of more than a few people. She pushed her way through and, without giving it a second's thought, dragged the dark boy free.

All the people there took in her clothes and assumed

she was from the upper classes. She looked it, from her well-shod feet to her fur hat and muff. She looked into the dark boy's face and in her best imitation of Henry Dumas's voice, asked: 'Have you picked up my purchases yet?'

The boy stared at her. She could see his brain seeking the appropriate answer. He was quick enough to know she was trying to help him. It was why she should that was the puzzle.

'Come on, boy, we'll go and pick them up now.' She grabbed the sleeve of his jacket and looked at the docker.

'You should not imbibe so much drink, young man, you obviously can't take it. Now get off home.'

She pulled the boy back to the cab and he helped her inside, lifting her arm and guiding her in as if he did it every day of his life. Once settled, they looked at one another.

'You didn't get to lift his wallet then?'

Briony's altered voice was such a shock the boy started to laugh.

She frowned at him. 'What you bleeding laughing at then? I just helped you out of a very tricky situation.'

The boy roared.

'It's your voice! Just now you sounded like the bloody Queen. Now you're speaking like any other street slut.'

Briony felt herself pale and this was not lost on the boy either.

'What did you just say?'

He hastened to make amends.

'I didn't mean that how it come out.'

She pushed her hands into her muff with such force she ripped the lining and the sound in the quiet of the cab was like a pistol going off.

The boy ran his hands through his hair. Realising his mistake, he tried to make it up to her.

'I'm Tom Lane, Tommy to me mates. Thanks for helping me out like. I 'ppreciate it.'

Briony looked at his handsome but dirty face, and thawed a bit.

'I'm Briony Cavanagh.'

He grinned then, showing big strong white teeth. He settled back in the cab and Briony found herself grinning too.

'Where do you live, then?'

Briony swallowed deeply before answering. 'I live in Oxlow Lane, but I work in a big house, just round the corner from Barking Park.' There was no way she was giving him an address, he looked the type to turn up there. The thought thrilled and frightened her at the same time.

'Oxlow Lane, you say? That where you're going now?'

Briony nodded. 'I'm going to visit me family.'

Tom nodded and looked her over from head to toe. A nice-looking piece, he thought, but too well dressed for service. She was on the bash or his name wasn't Tom Lane. He had two sisters and a mother on the game and neither of them had hit the big money like this one. But he didn't tell her his thoughts. He liked her, he liked her a lot, especially for saving his neck.

'How old are you, then?'

Briony tossed her head and looked out at the passing road. 'Old enough. You?'

Tommy grinned again. 'Older than that, girl.' He glanced outside and saw that they were at the Longbridge Road. 'You can let me down here.' He banged on the wooden side and the driver slowed the horse.

'Tara then, Briony Cavanagh.'

' 'Bye, Tommy Lane.'

He hopped from the cab, and before shutting the door

he winked at her. Briony watched him cross the wide road and make his way inside The Royal Oak. She saw him disappear inside the doorway and felt a moment's sadness that he had gone. For some funny reason she liked him.

Tommy walked into the public house and ordered himself a pint of beer. His eyes travelled round the crowded bar looking for a face he knew. He saw a friend called Willy Cushing and walked over to him.

'Hello, Willy, you're looking well.' And indeed Willy was looking well. He was wearing a suit more fitted to a lawyer than a petty criminal.

'He looks like a pox doctor's clerk, if you ask me.'

Willy smiled good-naturedly at the little boy sitting on the seat beside his friend.

'Me bruvver James.'

Tommy nodded at the little boy.

'He's got some trap, ain't he, Willy?'

Willy, a small dumpy boy with sandy hair and non-existent eyebrows, nodded his head vigorously.

'More front than Southend, mate, and he's only seven. Sit down, Tommy, I ain't seen you for a while.'

He sat on the wooden bench beside his friend and admired him openly.

'You're looking really prosperous, Willy, what's the scam?'

Willy took a large drink of beer and smiled. 'I'm in with Dobson's lot now. I tell you, Tommy, all the stories about him are true, but he's a good bloke if you don't cross him.'

Tommy nodded. Davie Dobson was the local hard man. He was good to people hereabouts in a lot of ways. It was known he would give money to women whose husbands had gone down before the beak, but he was also known to break a few bones when things weren't going his way. He ran most of the girls on the streets hereabouts, as far as Stratford and some up West.

'So what you doing for him then?'

'I sort out deals for him. Little deals that he ain't got the time or the inclination to bother with.'

What he actually meant was little girls. Willy procured them from the poorer families and then delivered them to Nellie Deakins's house and other establishments all over the smoke. Dobson, who was trying to make himself look respectable in certain circles, needed stooges like Willy who'd go down if they got caught and do their time without a whimper, coming home to a good few quid and a steady job. Willy was to progress soon to delivering girls to the homes of certain prominent people whom Davie Dobson would then blackmail. It was the most lucrative business, because once they paid, they paid forever.

'Could you get me in with him like, Willy? I could do with a regular job, and you don't look like you're starving from it.'

Willy swaggered in his seat.

'I'll have a word with him for you. Me and Dobson's like that.'

'You do that for me, Willy, and I'll owe you one. Now seeing as how you're in the dosh, you can get the next round in.'

Willy got up and went to the bar.

'What do you do, young man?' Tommy addressed James, who looked at him as if he was so much dirt.

'Mind your own business, you nosy bastard!'

Tommy laughed and James frowned at him. He was only three feet six inches tall and already he was a hard man. That's what life on the streets did for you.

*

Briony swept into the house in Oxlow Lane in a cloud of cold air and perfume. Molly went outside and picked up the hamper, dragging it through the door. Briony helped her get it on the table.

'Where's the girls?'

'All gone up the Lane for some last-minute shopping. Eileen's been promising them she'll take them all week. Rosalee's asleep upstairs.'

Briony removed her coat and hung it carefully on the nail behind the front door.

'How are you, Mum?'

She and Molly had had a truce for nearly a year now. It was a truce that suited them both. Molly needed Briony's wages, as they were called, and Briony had no intention of ever coming back to her mother's house. Molly had resigned herself to Briony's choice of career and now the two got on quite well.

'I wanted to talk to you, Mum, I'm glad we're alone.'

Briony put the kettle on the fire and started to make a fresh pot of tea while Molly unpacked the hamper.

'It's Henry – Mr Dumas. He's losing interest in me.'

Molly pushed back her faded blond hair and stared across at her daughter's beautiful face. Every time she looked at Briony she marvelled where she could have come from. With that red hair and white skin, she was unlike any of the others. Unlike her parents or grand-parents, though the Irish were often red-headed.

'What you going to do then?'

Briony sighed. 'I don't know, Mum, but if I get me marching orders, the wages go with me.'

Molly knew this already and it scared her.

'Have you got anything down below yet?'

'I did have, but Cissy plucked them out for me.' Briony bit on her bottom lip. 'He can't stand it, see, Mum. Once I start to develop properly, he won't want me any more. I had a show last week. The curse is on its way, I just know it.'

Molly nodded. Briony made the tea and took the steaming pot over to the table.

'What am I going to do?'

Molly sighed. 'I don't know, girl. We'll put our thinking caps on and maybe something will come up.'

Rosalee started to cry and Briony went up the stairs and brought her down to the kitchen. 'Bri . . . Bri . . .'

Briony hugged her close and kissed her. 'Yes, it's Bri Bri, and she's got a lovely present for you for Christmas.'

Molly watched the red head and the blonde together and felt a sadness in herself. Both were tainted but in different ways. Of the two she'd rather have Rosalee any day.

Paddy was drunk; not his usual boisterous drunk but a sullen, melancholic mood. He staggered out of The Bull at twenty past ten. He would have stayed longer except he'd run out of money and his friends, on whom he had spent over a pound, were now preparing to leave as well. Paddy stumbled home.

The long walk, instead of sobering him up, only made him more peevish with every freezing step he took. In his mind he conjured up all the wrongs done to him by his wife. First and foremost in his mind was the fact she'd have no sexual relations with him. He'd get the priest round to talk to her about that. Then there was the fact that she doled out the money to him. He knew she had a good wad stashed away and, on the rare occasions that he was alone in the house, had searched for it fruitlessly. Then there was her attitude with the girls. By Christ, they were grown up now, except for Rosalee who would never grow up.

He felt his eyes mist up at the thought of her. In his drunken mind, Rosalee was the fault of his wife as well. He knew she'd tried to get rid of her, he knew everything about the bitch he lived with. Then the naked white body of his infant son came into his thoughts. It was the night Eileen left to work for Mr Dumas, and somehow, in his drink-fuddled mind, he decided that Molly had got rid of his son as well. The thought induced a rage so violent he felt he could choke on it. A man was judged by his sons. Splitarses – as girls were referred to – were a slur on a man's manhood. They were no good for anything except the begetting of more sons.

As he passed by the empty streets he thought of all the setbacks he'd experienced in his life: never enough money, never anywhere decent to live. And somehow, all the blame was laid at Molly's door.

She'd never worked like other women. She used to clean doorsteps when he met her, had specialised in that. She'd been a tweenie since seven and at fourteen had begun specialising in her damned doorsteps! For a split second he saw her as she had been when he met her. High-breasted and tall, she had looked a fit mate for the big handsome Irishman he'd been. But marriage and the bearing of children had changed all that. Her and her fancy ideas about the girls going to school. Not working, oh no. Or even doing a decent day's housework until they were twelve. He gnashed his teeth in temper. With the four girls working they could have lived the life of Riley, but oh no. Not good enough for Molly Cavanagh. Her children, her girl children, were too good to slave fourteen hours a day in a sweat shop to earn their brass.

As he neared home Paddy's rage was reaching astounding proportions. He even began to blame his wife for his own drinking and gambling. If she had treated him as a wife should, he wouldn't stay out like he did, he justified it to himself. He omitted the fact he had always led the life of a single man even when married.

He opened the front door. His face was blue with the cold, but one look at his eyes and the girls saw their father was in the mood for a fight. Dressed in their Sunday best, they waited patiently for their mother to braid their hair ready for Midnight Mass at St Vincent's where Kerry had been asked to sing a solo.

Molly was busy buttoning Rosalee's dress. Hearing her husband enter, she cried: 'Where the hell have you been? You know Kerry's singing at the Mass. You promised me you'd be home early.'

She looked up into his face and her heart froze in her chest. He was drunk, roaring drunk. He wouldn't miss Midnight Mass, though. He'd stumble up to Communion like he did every Sunday, oblivious to the staring faces around him. Most of the Irishmen left it to their wives to attend church for them. It was no sin for them to sit in the pub all day Sunday, but let an Irishman's wife miss Mass with the children and she would be ostracised by all and sundry. Not for the first time the divide between men and women irritated Molly Cavanagh. Maybe it was this that prompted her to fight with him instead of ushering the children from the house to Mother Jones next door and then letting Paddy do his worst till he fell asleep in front of the fire. She resigned herself to a black eye for Christmas and decided that this time she'd get it for a good reason.

'I'll not walk in the church with a drunk, Paddy. You

can either go alone, or sleep the drink off and go in the morning.'

He pushed Kerry and Bernadette out of the way. 'What did you say to me, woman?'

Molly pulled Rosalee into her skirts and glared at her husband.

'You heard me!'

Paddy stared first at his wife then at each of the four girls in turn. Eileen gathered her three younger sisters together and, slipping past her father, took them to Mother Jones. Knocking gently on the window, she held the three white-faced girls to her. Mother Jones was in the process of tying a large bonnet of dark green taffeta on to her wiry grey hair. She opened the front door with a wide grin on her face, thinking they were all ready to go to Mass. One look at Eileen's face told her otherwise.

'It's me dad, he's drunk as a lord and about to go at me mum. Can I leave these three here?'

'Of course you can, lovie.' She pulled Eileen inside her door, closing it against the bitter wind. As they settled the children round the fire they heard Molly's scream, and a sound like splintering wood. Rosalee whimpered and the old woman pulled her on to her lap.

'There now, me pet. Everything's fine.'

Eileen stood up. 'I've got to go in there. He'll knock her from here to next week if someone doesn't stop him.'

'Stay here, child. Abel will be here soon with the cart to take us all to Mass. He'll go in.'

Eileen wiped her hand across her face.

'I've got to get their coats anyway. I'll go in.'

She left the cottage and went back inside her own home.

Molly was crying, harsh racking sobs. Eileen saw her

mother's eye already swelling and the blood from a cut on her lip. Paddy had punched her to the ground and one of the wooden chairs was lying broken on the floor. It was what her father was doing now that made Eileen pick up the iron from the fire.

He was pulling up her mother's skirts and dragging at her underclothes. Eileen knew what he was going to do because it brought back painful memories of Mr Dumas. She knew how much it hurt, and how sick and ill it made you afterwards.

Molly was staring at her daughter, beseeching her with her eyes and crying over Paddy's shoulder softly.

'No, Paddy, not like this, man! Not like this!'

Bringing back her arm, Eileen swung the iron down on the side of her father's head with all her strength. The spray of blood that shot up into the air covered both mother and daughter. Paddy slumped down over his wife, his legs twitching for a few seconds before death took him completely.

Eileen put her hand over her mouth to stem the tide of vomit rushing up inside her. Molly, with a strength born of desperation, pushed the lifeless form from her. Dragging herself upright, she put her hand to her mouth in shock. The two stood there like statues until Abel, who had arrived with the cart, was sent in by his mother.

He took one look at Paddy lying spreadeagled on the floor, his head a mush of blood and brains, and swore under his breath.

'Jesus sodding Christ! What happened here?'

Eileen began to shake. It started in her hands and travelled through her cold body until even her teeth were chattering. Abel dragged Paddy over on to his back. The unbuttoned trousers told him the whole story.

'Was he at the girl? Was he at Eileen?'

He assumed that Molly had taken the iron to him. She shook her head, and as he heard Eileen moan, Abel saw the iron still in her hand.

'He was at you, Moll?'

She nodded. Her blond hair was in disarray and her clothes were ripped. A strand of saliva was hanging from her top lip as she tried to speak.

Abel took the iron from Eileen and put it into the sink. Then he went outside to the pump and filled a bucket with icy water. He washed the iron clean of blood, talking over his shoulder as he did so.

'First I want you to get some sheets to wrap him in. Come on, you two!' His voice was urgent. 'We have to get rid of him, girls, or else one or the other of you will be before the beak in the morning.'

Molly felt his words penetrate her brain and forced herself into action. Going up the stairs, she pulled the sheets from her bed and brought them back down to the kitchen.

Abel had put Eileen in the easy chair and was pouring out a cup of hot sweet tea for her.

'We'll wrap him up tight and I'll dump him somewhere. We'll think of a story later, let's just get rid of the . . . of Paddy's . . . of his body.' There, it was said.

'Oh, Abel, what are we going to do?' Molly's voice had risen now as the shock wore off and he went to her and put his arms around her.

'Listen to me, Molly. We must get rid of him now, before anyone finds out what's happened. I'll take him down to the docks, dump him in the water. Plenty of people turn up there dead. You report him missing tomorrow and the police will assume he was set upon for his wages.'

The words were tumbling out of him. One thing was sure, he had to help Molly. Since she had moved in next-door he had grown to care for her deeply. Many was the night he'd heard Paddy going for her and had wanted to do exactly what the girl had just done. As far as he was concerned, his main priority now was to get rid of Paddy's body and keep the girls safe.

He began to wrap Paddy in the sheets, covering the broken head as best he could.

'What about Midnight Mass? Kerry's to sing there tonight!'

'The Mass has started, Moll. We'll say you was waiting for Paddy to come home. Yes, that's what we'll say. Now help me to wrap him tight, and then I'll put him on the cart and you and Eileen can get this floor scrubbed clean of blood. Come on now, Moll, or we'll all be done for.'

Eileen watched as Abel and her mother wrapped up her father's body. She felt nothing as she saw Abel put the blood-stained bundle over his shoulder and take him out to the cart.

Molly put the kettle on for more hot water and drank her tea standing up by the fire, waiting for the kettle to boil. She was suspended between two feelings. One of shock at what had happened, and the other a drive for self-preservation. The world now consisted of herself, Eileen and Abel Jones. Because Abel had involved himself for her, and she knew why. Though Paddy's passing was shocking, it was also a passport to a better life for her and this thought kept her going through the gruelling night ahead.

Abel went in to his mother before he took Paddy's body off in the cart. She had put the children to bed in her own room and he explained what had taken place to her in hushed tones. Being a sensible woman she didn't moan or wail, but nodded at her big handsome son and then began to talk.

'Take him to Dagenham Docks, son, but don't put him in the water wrapped in the sheets. Bring them back and I'll burn them. Empty his pockets. Street thieves take everything, even a good coat, remember that. If his boots are in good nick, take them off and we'll get rid of them too.' She racked her brains for what else she should tell him.

Abel kissed her on the forehead and tried to wink at her.

'You know you'll hang if this is found out?'

He nodded. 'I know that, Mum. But if you could see those two in there . . .' His voice trailed off.

'You're a good boy, Abel. Too good sometimes, I think.'

On this he left the kitchen and, taking the blanket off the horse, covered the body with it and clip-clopped down Oxlow Lane in a light flurry of snow.

Briony turned up at nine on Christmas morning, laden with food and presents. As soon as she walked into her mother's house she knew that something had happened. The three younger girls ran to her and she kissed them, pushing gaily wrapped presents into their hands. The smell of roasting duck was heavy on the air, but her mother's wan, swollen face and the absence of Eileen told her that something was afoot.

'Where's Eileen?'

'She's lying down, Briony. Come upstairs and see her.'

Briony followed her mother up to the bedroom without even removing her coat. Once inside the tiny room, she gasped. Eileen was lying in bed staring at the ceiling.

'What's wrong with her, Mum? And where's me dad?'

Molly bit on her swollen top lip.

'Eileen . . . she hit him last night. He was drunk and trying to . . . Eileen saw him and something snapped inside her, girl. She hit him with the flat iron.'

Briony stared into her mother's face.

'Where is he then? In the hospital?'

Molly shook her head.

'He was dead, Briony. Stone dead. And Abel . . . Abel . . .' She swallowed back tears. 'He dumped him in the Thames. In the docks. She'd have been taken away otherwise.'

Molly's voice was rising and Briony put her arms around her. 'All right, Mum. All right. You did the right thing. What's the next step?'

'I'm going to report him missing like, this afternoon. I'm going to pretend that he stayed out often all night and that if he's been picked up drunk then they can keep him. Abel . . . well, Abel says that's the best way. More natural like.'

Briony nodded, seeing the sense of what was being said. The police in this area were used to women like her mother who brought up families on the money they could slip from a drunken husband's pockets. But if they came to Oxlow Lane then they'd wonder where the hell the money came from for the house. Briony felt no loss at the death of her father, he had been like a thorn in all their sides. All she had ever known was either the back of his hand or his drunken caresses. She was more interested in looking after Eileen and her mother.

'If they question you about this place, then you tell them about me. I'll deal with them when and if I have to, all right?'

Molly nodded. Briony went over to the bed and stared down at her sister's face. It was white and pinched. Her eyes, normally so blue and clear, looked dull. Eileen stared back at Briony and her lips trembled.

Kerry and Bernadette burst into the room, both waving pairs of shiny new leather shoes.

'Oh, Bri, they're lovely, thanks, thanks!'

Briony turned and hugged them, while Molly hastily wiped her eyes.

'Keep your noise down now, Eileen's not feeling well.'

Kerry jerked her head towards Eileen and frowned. 'Will I sing you a nice song, our Eileen? To cheer you up.'

Eileen nodded weakly, trying to smile.

Kerry put her new shoes on the bottom of the bed and, pushing back her thick black hair, began to sing.

Chapter Five

Isabel Dumas watched her husband closely as he cosseted his niece. He had pulled the little girl on to his lap and was caressing her blond hair as he whispered endearments to her. Isabel felt a sickness inside herself as she watched him. She glanced at her husband's sister and saw that she was smiling benignly at her brother and daughter. Isabel dragged her eyes from the scene and, excusing herself on the pretext of seeing how dinner was progressing, went up to her room.

Standing in their brand new bathroom, a marble and brass affair that she thought vulgar in the extreme, she splashed cold water on to her face and looked at herself in the mirror. She was twenty-five years old and had been married to Henry Dumas for seven years.

Her dark brown eyes took in the slight droop of her generous mouth and premature lines under her eyes from sleepless nights. Nights when she tossed and turned until she saw the daylight creep under her heavy bedroom curtains and intrude on her private world. She had long thick brown hair that had lost its gleam; her whole appearance was dull. It broke her heart every time she looked too closely at herself. She fancied sometimes that she was getting so sad and grey that eventually she would pass through the world completely unnoticed. Her mind went back to her husband caressing his five-year-old niece and she felt a wave of nausea engulf her.

It was true about Henry, she knew it. There was nothing for her with him any more, she couldn't hide from that fact. Her marriage was a lie, a blatant lie that she was beginning to regret with all her heart. All the long, lonely nights!

After their marriage her fine new husband had taken her up to bed and, after kissing her perfunctorily, had left her. She had assumed he was being kind, thinking of her, of how it was all new and the wedding had been tiring, and at first she had actually felt a surge of happiness to have such a thoughtful husband. But as the months passed it had become a nightly ritual. Henry pecked her on the cheek and went straight to his own room or left the house altogether. She had begun to think that something was dreadfully wrong with her. How was she to get a child if he never came near her? The worst of it all was that it was not something she could discuss with anyone. Her mother would have a fit of the vapours and be taken to bed for the day with a liberal supply of brandy if Isabel so much as mentioned it to her. So she had kept it to herself, and every month the strain was telling on her more. As friends had babies and talked of their husbands' indelicate appetities she felt like screaming, because everyone assumed her childlessness was her own fault.

'Oh, Isabel must be barren.' She knew what was being said after seven years of marriage, and the sympathy all went to Henry. Poor Henry. To be saddled with a barren wife. She gritted her teeth together and pressed her forehead on the cool glass of the mirror.

After a year of marriage, one night she had brushed out her long brown hair and, when she was sure the servants were all in bed, crept surreptitiously to her husband's room wearing just her chemise. She was a buxom girl with large firm breasts, and had slipped into bed beside Henry, thinking that maybe he was shyer than she was. She had put her arms around him and tried to draw him to her. In his sleep he had put out his own arms and then, opening his eyes, had recoiled from her.

She would never forget the look of horror and repulsion on his face. He had stood by the bed and upbraided her soundly on the wantonness she had displayed. He had reminded her that good women from good families did not lower themselves to the same level as harlots. Isabel had sat up in the bed white with shame and shock and listened to him. But after that night a hatred for him had begun to grow in her.

Isabel wanted a man, and she desperately wanted a child. The two went together. But as the years had gone on she had despaired of ever getting what she wanted. Her father would not hear of divorce, and so she was stuck. Sometimes she daydreamed that Henry got hit by one of the new motorcars and died, or that he fell under a train. She knew these thoughts were wicked but his dying was the only way she could escape from this life.

She closed her eyes to stop the tears from falling.

'Isabel! Are you staying in here all night? My sister has come all the way to visit us and bring the children and you're not even trying to be entertaining.'

She faced her husband.

'I see you're quite enamoured of your little niece, Henry. You take no notice of the boy.'

Husband and wife looked each other in the face and both felt the subtle threat. Henry had the grace to lower his eyes first.

'She's a very engaging child. Now come along, Isabel.'

She followed him out on to the landing and persisted with her conversation.

'And you like engaging little girls, don't you?'

Henry turned to her on the stairs and whispered under his breath: 'I've been a very good husband to you, Isabel, never raised my hand to you, but you're sorely near to that now. Now come along, and forget this nonsense.'

Isabel followed him down the stairs and was surprised to find she was smiling. She knew a lot about her Henry, but it could wait until after Christmas.

Molly stood in Barking police station with Briony. Her hands were trembling. A man with large handlebar moustaches who had told them he was Sergeant Harries was writing down the description of Patrick Cavanagh. Briony watched him closely for any tell-tale signs that he was suspicious, but his eyes lingered sympathetically on Molly's black eye and swollen lip. Sergeant Harries had always had a loathing for wife beaters, even though it was a pretty common occupation. His own mother, God rest her soul, had always told her son that women were like flowers, gentle and fragile, and that they needed careful tending. He smiled at Molly.

'Was it a bad fight, madam?'

Molly nodded.

'And had the gentleman been drinking?'

She nodded again, afraid to speak.

'I take it your husband's Irish?'

Molly nodded once more.

'Have you thought of getting the priest out to him? I know many women in your position who've got the priest out, and their husbands haven't raised their hands to them ever again.'

Molly looked at the man in front of her as if he had just arrived from another planet. It was on the tip of her tongue to shout: 'Are you sure?'

'I'll . . . I'll try that, officer, when he comes home.'

'Good, good. Now where does he normally go like?'

Briony answered for her mother, her voice low. 'My father will go anywhere there's a drink. He'd been drinking all day yesterday and came home like the devil was in him.'

She had guessed the policeman was Temperance and embroidered her story with that in mind.

'Without a drink he's the most mild-mannered man in the world, but with it . . .' She rolled her lovely green eyes. 'He's like a demon.'

The policeman nodded his head sagely.

'So he could be anywhere then?'

Molly and Briony nodded vigorously.

'Once he didn't come home for a week, and then he couldn't remember where he'd been!'

'That sounds a familiar story, ladies, if you don't mind me remarking. Well, we've got his description and if he turns up we'll let you know. How many children did you say you've got, Mrs Cavanagh?'

'Five, sir. Five girls.'

'Well, you get home to them, and if we hear anything, we'll be in touch.'

*

It was three days after Christmas that Briony went with her mother to identify her father. He had been found by a man walking the shoreline looking for driftwood. His boots were gone as was his jacket and Molly and Briony were told that he had probably been set upon by thugs and robbed. He was to be given a funeral courtesy of the parish and Briony and her mother hoped that that would be the last of that.

Molly hurried home to tell Abel the good news and Briony made her way back to Barking with a dragging feeling inside her. Since her show the month before she had been expecting a period, and when none had come she had felt euphoric, though her breasts were still sore and tender. On this particular day she was expecting Henry at five-thirty and as he had lately taken her straight upstairs she was not expecting a long evening.

She was to be proved wrong, however.

While Briony had been identifying her father, Henry Dumas had been dealing with a crisis of his own. After taking a light tea with his wife, he had got up as usual to get his hat and coat. He always made a point of being very civil and kind to his wife whom he saw as an ornament rather than anything else. Today, however, as he had stood up to leave her as usual, Isabel put her hand on his arm.

'I don't want you to go tonight, Henry. I think we should talk.'

He had looked down at her and frowned. But he had resumed his seat, and that in itself gave Isabel courage.

'I know this is a delicate subject, Henry, and believe me when I say I don't like discussing it any more than you do, but I feel we must get this thing sorted out. I want a child, Henry, I want a child desperately.'

She saw the look on his face and felt a knot of anger begin to form inside her.

'As you know only too well, Henry, it takes two to make a baby, and I think that you should give this some thought.'

Henry stood up, gave her a cold glance and left the room. A little later she heard the door slam as he left the house.

Isabel stared into the fire. She would endure Henry's attentions to get a child of her own. She was trapped in this marriage whether she liked it or not. She knew that a lot of women took lovers but those opportunities never presented themselves to her, and as she was still a virgin she had no idea of the wiles women used to inaugurate such affairs.

In order to forget his wife's unpleasant suggestion, Henry went straight to Briony. She was playing with her kitten in front of the fire in the morning room, her hair braided into two plaits. She was wearing a simple lemon-coloured dress with matching socks and hair ribbons. When he was due she made herself look as young as possible.

'Hello, Henry.' Her voice was high and girlish.

Henry smiled at her wanly. She really was a pretty little thing and her beaming face when she saw him always made him feel better. With this child he was in control, master of everything. He sat himself in a chair and patted his lap. Briony picked up the kitten and went to him. She slipped on to his knee and kissed him chastely on the cheek. She knew exactly how to act with him. He rubbed her thigh under the silky dress and felt the first stirrings inside him.

'How's my best girl been?'

Briony dropped the kitten gently on to the carpet and put her slender arms around his neck.

'I've been good. I've been a very, very good little girl. You can ask Mrs Horlock.'

Henry grinned and felt the tension seeping out of him. He rubbed at her little breasts with his large hand and

Briony stared at an oil painting over his shoulder. It was of a ballerina and she loved the brightly painted scene. Henry nuzzled her neck.

'Shall we go upstairs and play some games?'

Briony rolled her eyes at the ceiling, then putting her face in front of his, smiled engagingly.

'That would be lovely.'

As she followed him up the stairs to her bedroom she saw her father's face as it had been that afternoon, and tried to blot it out.

Inside the bedroom a small fire blazed in the grate. Briony went through the usual routine of letting Henry undress her, then in nothing but her long socks she sat on the side of the bed while he undressed himself, carefully folding his clothes and putting them neatly on to a chair. Once he was naked he went to sit beside her on the bed. Taking her tiny hand, he placed it on his member and Briony gently massaged it the way she knew he liked her to. He closed his eyes and let out a heavy breath. She looked down at what she was doing and saw that her breasts were much more prominent than they had been. Then she sighed. Her body was letting her down.

As Henry pushed her backwards on to the bed, she played her own personal little game. In her mind she was grown-up and famous, with lovely clothes and a lovely house and lovely friends.

Henry Dumas, unaware of his charge's lack of enthusiasm, drove her hard that night before leaving. But although her body ached with his roughness, Briony's mind stayed crystal clear and untouched.

It was two-thirty in the morning when she felt the first pain. It shot through her like a red hot knife, waking her from her sleep. She pushed her knees up to her chest in an instinctive move to stop the pain. But it came again a little later. It was like a cramp inside her. Pulling herself from the bed, she made her way to Mrs Horlock's room. Shaking the old women roughly awake, Briony explained what was happening to her.

Mrs Horlock leapt from the bed in her haste, her old bones forgotten as she took the terrified child back to her own room. It must be her period coming. The old woman went down to the kitchen and made her a hot drink of milk with a touch of whisky in it.

'There, there now, me pet. You'll feel better soon.'

But when Briony vomited and the pains got worse, Mrs Horlock woke Cissy and went for the doctor. Mrs Horlock was very worried. The child looked as if she was about to give birth! She held her hand until Dr Carlton arrived and then thankfully gave way to him.

Dr Carlton was in his fifties and, though he was a respectable practitioner in many respects, was also known for his attendance on people with money who could afford to pay for medical services with no questions asked. He helped gentlewomen who, for one reason or another, needed an abortion, usually because the child wasn't their husband's. He also helped men who had contracted certain diseases and were worried they had passed them on to their wives.

Dr Carlton examined Briony with practised hands and then, after giving her a draught to make her sleep, stepped outside to Mrs Horlock and Cissy.

'You called me just in time, madam, the girl was about to miscarry. I can't guarantee she won't lose the child, the next couple of days will be crucial, but if she keeps taking the draught I've prescribed and sleeps as much as possible, she may give it a chance of survival. She must not be distressed under any circumstances. At this stage it's crucial she rests in bed. I can't emphasise strongly enough, madam, the need for peace and quiet.'

He looked at the old woman as he gave his speech. Always a lover of drama, he injected it into his work as often as possible. He was nonplussed at the old woman's look of utter astonishment.

'How old is the girl, by the way?' he asked in a whisper. He could smell a rat before it was stinking, he prided himself on that. It hadn't occurred to him at first that the patient was a young girl, he didn't really take much notice of women as a rule, but something in the housekeeper's face alerted him.

'She's just twelve, sir. We thought it was her periods like.'

Twelve! He had put her at about fourteen or fifteen.

'Only twelve, you say? Where's her mother and father?'

Mrs Horlock bit her lip and thought for a second before she spoke.

'Cissy, go down and make up the fire in the morning room. Dr Carlton, can I get you a hot drink or a whisky?'

He sniffed loudly.

'A Scotch would be agreeable, madam.'

'Then follow me, sir.' Cissy was already down the stairs and rekindling the fire with the poker when they came in.

'Make me a pot of tea, Cissy, and bring it through here. Please sit down, Doctor.'

Mrs Horlock poured him a large Scotch. The redness of his nose and the broken veins on his cheeks told her he liked his whisky and when he swigged it back in one go she replenished his glass without a word.

'I look after the girl, sir, for my employer. She's a

distant relative of his, you understand, and her mother was just a bit beyond the pale. From a very good family, mind, but she run away when young and the child was the result of an unhappy union.'

She once more refilled the doctor's glass. 'I don't know how this could have happened. As for Mr Dumas – well, he'll be broken-hearted.'

At the mention of Henry's name the doctor's eyebrows rose. So, he thought, the child was his. Henry Dumas was married to a peer's daughter and was respected in the local community, indeed in the whole of London. He was wealthy, from an impeccable family, and would be able to pay well. Extremely well.

'What a wicked, wanton child, madam! Like her mother, I'd say. I can well understand the need for secrecy. Such a scandal! Not a word of it will pass my lips, madam, I do assure you, and you can pass that on to Mr Dumas as well.' He tutted. 'Poor Mr Dumas, to have his kindness repaid like this.'

He shook his head for maximum effect. 'Well, I have done all I can. I'll return in the morning to see her once more. I'll say goodnight to you, madam.'

Mrs Horlock saw him to the door and then went back into the morning room where she helped herself to a large whisky. The child was pregnant. She had another drink to help her think. Well, maybe she'd lose it tonight. Then they'd all be able to get back to normal.

'I'm what!' Briony's voice was incredulous.

She looked from one face to the other. Cissy's looked as shocked as her own, but Mrs Horlock's face was closed.

'I can't be, there must be some mistake.' Briony was close to tears and Mrs Horlock took her into her arms.

'There's no mistake, my love. You must have fell just as your body was coming to womanhood, I've heard of it before.'

She didn't say she'd experienced it before and had helped get rid of the offending child. She knew Briony's temperament too well to say anything like that.

'What am I gonna do?' It was a childish wail.

'Now don't you worry, my angel, I'll sort it all out for you.'

This was comforting to Briony and she settled back against the pillows plumped up around her and held tightly on to Cissy's hand. For the first time in her life she was frightened, really frightened.

They heard the front door shut and Mrs Horlock smiled at the two girls and left the room. The sooner Henry Dumas knew what was happening, the better. He looked up at the old woman as she descended the stairs.

'What's the to do, Horlock? Is the child ill?'

He'd been dragged from his place of work by a note twenty minutes earlier and now he was worried.

'In a manner of speaking, sir. Would you join me in the morning room? I took the liberty of getting a tea tray ready, I'll just get the hot water.'

Henry went into the drawing room where there was a trolley full of tea things, cakes and sandwiches. He picked up a paper-thin paste sandwich and popped it into his mouth, carefully avoiding his moustache. He wished the old girl would hurry up, he was due home for dinner. His wife's father was coming today and he wanted to be with Isabel when he arrived. She was acting very strangely lately, and he was concerned about what she might hint to her family. Luckily Lord Barkham was not a listener to women's gossip, having no time for his wife or indeed his daughter. Henry was pretty certain he would pooh-pooh anything she said. Nevertheless, he would like to be there during the visit.

Mrs Horlock came in with the freshly made tea and as she sat down Henry smiled at her faintly.

'Well, what's going on?'

'It seems Miss Briony is pregnant.'

'She's what!'

'She's pregnant, sir. I've had the doctor in and he's certain.'

'God's teeth, woman, how did that happen?'

Mrs Horlock suppressed a smile. If you don't know, she thought, I'm not about to enlighten you.

'It'll have to go, Mrs Horlock.'

'My sentiments entirely, sir.'

'And so will the blasted baby!'

Mrs Horlock looked hard at him and he felt a flush of shame.

'With all due respect, sir, it's not Briony's fault, now is it?'

Her own words shocked her. Never before had she reproached the man for anything. She had always been a willing accomplice to his schemes, but Briony Cavanagh had got under her skin and into her heart. Oh, Maria knew the child was a mercenary little bitch, but she did what she did more for her family than herself, and for her corrupter completely to disregard the child after all she done for him over the last sixteen months brought a feeling akin to anger. Briony was the child she had never had. The girl trusted her, and there had been more fun and laughter in her life in the last year or so than ever before.

'Really, Mrs Horlock, I think you're forgetting yourself. Something like this is not to be taken lightly.'

Mrs Horlock smiled grimly and interrupted him. 'I understand the situation, sir, better than you think. I will arrange with Dr Carlton for the removal of the . . . of the baby. I don't think Briony would want to have it at her age. Then we'll have to get our thinking caps on about the best thing to do once it's all over.'

Henry relaxed then, and sipped his tea.

'Of course, Mrs Horlock. I'll leave it all in your capable hands.'

She smiled at him. Thinking to herself all the while: Don't you always leave your dirty work to me?

Five minutes later Henry was on his way back to his house, his wife and her father. This couldn't have come at a worse time. Damn and blast the little guttersnipe to hell!

Isabel sat with her father and mother in the drawing room. Her father was telling one of the long-winded stories that required no answers, just an expression of rapt interest. Her father's stories always entailed a long boring account of how he had done someone down, as he put it. He had no time for the King, the army, suffragettes, or anything else that might be a topic of conversation in more moderate households. Any mention of suffragettes would indeed result in a long diatribe on the failings of womanhood in general going back to Eve, the mother of all sin. Isabel noticed that her own mother had dropped off to sleep in front of the fire.

She was almost pleased when Henry came into the room. He walked across to her with his usual beaming smile and kissed her on the cheek. Getting up stiffly, Isabel excused herself and went down to the kitchen to see how the food was progressing, feeling the tightening in her chest. It was a feeling of complete hopelessness.

How long must I endure this existence?

O Lord, how long?

*

Briony lay back against the pillows and waited for her mother to arrive. She had insisted to Mrs Horlock that her mother be sent for as soon as possible and eventually, after some cajoling and a few tears, Mrs Horlock had reluctantly sent Cissy to collect her in a cab. Briony looked around the little room with wide eyes. Her longing for this comfort had brought her to this. She was just twelve and now she was having a baby.

A tiny part of her was thrilled at the thought. Having lived around babies all her life they were not an unknown quantity. But with all the upset over her father, and Eileen's involvement in it, she knew that this was not a time for anything like this to be happening. It would have been bad enough at any time, but now . . . She bit her lip.

She heard her mother arrive and watched the door with trepidation. Molly came into the room like a whirlwind.

'Are you all right, child?' Cissy's arrival had frightened her more than she liked to admit. Briony, who had been fine up until seeing her mother, promptly burst into tears.

'Oh Mam, Mam!'

It was what she had called her mother as a small child and Molly was reminded of the tiny red-headed baby she'd loved so well.

She pulled her child into her arms, the first time she had touched her without shrinking for over a year.

'There now, me pet, what's wrong? Have you a pain?' Cissy had told Molly nothing other than that Briony wasn't very well.

'Oh, Mam, I'm going to have a baby!'

Molly pushed her back against the pillows and stared into her face. 'You're what?'

Briony nodded, her little face streaming with tears.

'Dear God in heaven, save us!'

Briony threw herself into her mother's arms, a child once more despite the life inside her. Suddenly, faced with her mother, the enormity of what had happened over the last few days hit her.

'Me poor dad. Me poor dad. I want me dad.'

Molly held her close, fear replacing the anger and shock. All she needed now was Briony to blurt out the whole sorry business with Eileen and her da.

'Hush now, Briony. You're not ever to tell about that. Promise me?'

She looked into the fear-filled face. 'Promise me, Briony?'

'I promise, Mum. Oh, what am I gonna do?'

'We'll think of something, Briony, I promise you.'

As she spoke Mrs Horlock brought them all in tea and for the first time the two women came face to face.

'Mrs Cavanagh.'

Molly curled her lip in distaste at the older woman, who was to her mind no better than Nellie Deakins.

'Mrs Horlock.'

The old woman gave Briony her tea and, looking at Molly, said gently, 'I think me and you should have a talk.'

Molly nodded, running her tongue around her teeth. 'I think we better had. The sooner the better, to my mind.'

Both women having established exactly what they thought of the other through a few choice words, they retired from Briony's bedroom and went down to the kitchen for the first battle between them.

It was a battle neither could win without Briony's say so, but they enjoyed it nonetheless.

Chapter Six

Henry Dumas had been watching his wife carefully during the meal. As usual the table was impeccably laid. In fairness to her, he conceded, Isabel really was an exemplary wife in some respects. The crystal gleamed, the cutlery was of the very best, and the food was well above par. Once Isabel lost these notions she had begun to acquire, she would once more be his meek and obedient wife.

He had just taken a slice of apple pie when his wife spoke to her mother loudly.

'Mama, are you still working in the East End? I understand they have just opened another home for wayward girls there?'

She glanced at Henry as she spoke and then looked immediately back to her mother.

Venetia Barkham nodded.

'Yes, God knows they're more in need than ever. Some of the girls are only twelve or thirteen.' She lowered her voice as she leant across the table towards her daughter. 'It's a scandal, Isabel, what some men will do!'

Lord Barkham, who approved of his wife's charitable

works because she mixed with the cream of the aristocracy, nodded sagely.

'My dears, you don't understand the lower classes like I do. Some of those girls could turn a veritable saint's head. They're evil, preying on men who are otherwise exemplary.'

Isabel looked at her father, avoiding Henry's warning glance. 'So, Papa, am I to understand that men cannot help these appetites? Even men of good birth?'

Lord Barkham began to choke on his apple pie.

'Don't be silly, Isabel. A doxy's a doxy, whatever her age. There's many a good man who's been taken in by a pretty face. These girls, some of them little more than children as your mother pointed out, are natural sluts. It's inbred in them. A woman of good birth never acts the strumpet. You wouldn't understand, Isabel. You see, my child, men must be iron-willed and have faith in God and their own constitution. Look at me.' He waved his arms expansively. 'I attend church regularly, and even in the thickest snow I never wear a heavy coat. It's in the constitution, you see? Sound in mind and body, I am, and always have been.

'The namby-pamby men who get involved with these chits are obviously mentally unstable. They have no place in civilised society. They can't resist temptation, just haven't the willpower of stronger, more intelligent men, and these chits know it.'

'Thank you, Papa, for explaining it so eloquently. I really do understand exactly what you mean. Don't you, Henry?'

Henry paled and cleared his throat before answering. 'I think it's hardly a suitable subject for discussion in front of ladies.'

Immediately he realised his mistake. He had just implicitly criticised Lord Barkham.

Barkham glared at his son-in-law, a milkwater sop if ever he'd encountered one!

'How are your own charitable works, my dear?' he asked Isabel.

She looked at him and smiled. This was going even better than she'd expected. She knew her father was only asking her the question to force the issue with Henry.

'I still work with Mrs Prosser Evans, of course, though I am thinking seriously of joining Mother's Little Band of Helpers. I feel that the child prost – I mean, the poor children, really need a guiding hand.'

Molly and Mrs Horlock had finally agreed and both women were relieved. After the initial bout, where each woman had carefully sized up the other, they had realised their common goal and were now co-conspirators.

Both had one end in mind: the removal of Briony's child. Molly pushed her hair back from her flushed face and drew her legs away from the kitchen fire so she could face the older woman head on.

'But isn't that dangerous? I mean, Briony wouldn't die or anything?'

Mrs Horlock shrugged her shoulders. 'There's always the possibility of death, Mrs Cavanagh. Even if she went through with the birth. But Dr Carlton has been used by the richest in London. We're not talking about a filthy back room and an ignorant old woman.'

Molly nodded. 'I suppose you're right, but it seems so brutal somehow. Briony's only a child herself.'

Mrs Horlock smiled slightly.

'And a very lovely child she is too. She's a credit to you, Mrs Cavanagh.'

Molly took this compliment with a nod of her head.

'It was her father who brought her here, you know. And my Eileen. I was against it from the start . . . When I think of my poor Eileen, how she's suffered . . .'

Mrs Horlock put a hand on her arm, and squeezed it gently. 'Would you like a drop of the hard? I keep some down here for emergencies.'

She got up and, taking a bottle of whisky from the pantry, made two strong hot toddies. Molly watched her spooning in sugar generously and decided she could like the older woman, given more time.

'So I'll talk to the master tonight then?' Mrs Horlock's voice broke into her thoughts.

Molly sipped her drink. 'Yes. Do you think I should take her home with me?'

Mrs Horlock shook her head.

'No. Definitely not. The master needs to be reminded of his obligations, if you get my drift. I wouldn't advise taking the child from under his nose just yet.'

Molly and the older woman found once more they were in accord and, raising their glasses, pledged a silent toast.

Henry looked down at the child in the bed and felt a sickness in his stomach. Suddenly, her little elfin face had taken on harsh lines and her abundant red hair seemed vulgar in the extreme. His father-in-law was right in one thing he had said earlier: these children would turn the head of a saint. Now, with all the annoyance from Isabel too, he was faced with this. It took all his willpower not to raise his fist and strike the girl in the bed, venting his frustration on her for all his troubles, real and imagined. Instead he forced himself to take the tiny hand in his and smile at the child. He saw the swelling of her breasts and shuddered inwardly. In his eyes she was a woman now, and women had never been of interest to him.

'Dr Carlton is coming tomorrow to look at you, Briony, and then all your troubles will be over.'

She stared at him with a puzzled expression.

'What's gonna happen, Henry?'

He gritted his teeth at the use of his Christian name. Out of bed he was Mr Dumas. This really was a liberty! But he overlooked it this time, afraid of upsetting the apple cart.

'Oh, nothing for little girls to worry about. I'll be in to see you after he's been.'

Briony licked her lips and looked at the man beside her. Since the news of the baby, she had felt a change inside her. She knew what was happening to her, had seen births enough times, even helped her mother with a couple, including the birth of her dead brother. It was as if all this had turned her into an old woman. She no longer felt the childish exuberance that shielded her from the horror of nights spent with this man. Now every little thing they had ever done stood out in her mind with stark clarity. She felt his revulsion towards her, saw it in his eyes and felt it in his touch. She knew with an inner certainty that she was dead already as far as this man was concerned. That her child, the little life he had sparked, was also dead. That he wouldn't rest until it had been dragged out of her. She also knew that she was not having any part of it.

'I want to see Eileen and me sisters, please. Could you arrange it?' Her voice was low but strong.

Henry cleared his throat and was about to protest when she spoke again.

'I couldn't understand what was wrong with our Eileen for a long time, but now I understand exactly, Henry. No amount of money is worth all this, is it?'

It was said so simply, so honestly, that he didn't have the guts to answer her. Instead he walked from the room.

Dr Carlton had imbibed a generous amount of whisky and was waiting now in the morning room for a light lunch to be served before the serious business began. The old woman, Mrs Horlock, was like a cat on hot coals. He sighed. It was never a nice business this, but needs must when the devil drives. The older woman should be hardened to it by now. He remembered her from years back when she'd worked for a much more illustrious client. She'd had no qualms about holding the chit down then, while he saw to the business in hand. Got softer as she got older probably. Well, she'd need her wits about her today. He'd have a quiet word with her before the off. The girl would be nervous enough without the old woman frightening the life out of her.

He hated these jobs, but twenty pounds was twenty pounds, and who was he to sneeze at it? He got out of his seat with difficulty and poured himself another whisky. Just to fortify him. His hands were shaking again this morning, and he wondered, as he did every morning, if he was coming down with a cold.

Cissy saw his bloated, red-veined face and breathed in the whisky fumes on serving his lunch, and went straight down the stairs to give the information to Mrs Horlock.

'He's drunker than a Saturday night sailor! Bleeding old git!'

Mrs Horlock sighed. 'Maybe the food'll soak it up a bit.' She didn't hold out much hope. 'Mr Dumas will be here soon anyway.'

She wiped her hands on a clean cloth and looked at the clock. It was just twelve. He was due at one and she'd made up her mind. Hadn't she done enough to the Cavanagh family, what with Eileen and now Briony, without being part of murder as well? She was going to talk him out of the abortion.

Isabel, sitting outside her husband's house in Ripple Road in a hired cab, was also waiting for him to arrive. Her hands were trembling at the thought of what she was going to do, but she took deep breaths and channelled her mind on to the job in hand. She was going to wait all day if necessary and then surprise him with her presence. She had convinced herself that by doing this, she could achieve some kind of power over him. Force him to give her a child. She had considered going to her father with her information and demanding he do something about it, but she knew it would be futile. He would never countenance a scandal of any kind. And a divorce? She laughed ruefully to herself. It would be unthinkable. His own sister had been married to a brute who had attacked her on more than one occasion. Isabel could remember, as a child, a badly beaten woman arriving in a governess cart of all things at nine in the morning, her face a bloody pulp. Her father had ordered a doctor, then given her aunt a dressing down for being a slovenly wife who had obviously asked for her husband's hand and had got it.

No, she would have to deal with Henry himself, threaten him with her father. It was a threat that would frighten him out of his very wits. She knew her family's social status gave her a small hold over him, and it was a thrilling feeling. If only she could control her own fear! With Henry, it did not do to let him know you were afraid of him, or indeed of anything. He hoarded that type of information away like a squirrel, dragging it out of its hiding place when the time was ripe. Oh, she'd learnt a lot from Henry Dumas. An awful lot.

She saw his cab arrive and braced herself. She would give him fifteen minutes before she entered the house.

Henry looked at the doctor in dismay. The man was drunk!

'Shall we adjourn to the bedroom, Mr Dumas?' Carlton's voice was slurred.

Henry looked at the man quizzically. 'Why on earth should I go up there?'

Carlton waved a hand at him. 'Sorry, Dumas old chap, got meself a bit puddled there. Always the same with this kind of job. Nasty business.' He'd remembered at the last minute that Henry was only there to pay him. Imagine asking him if he wanted to be there! In his drunken state this struck him as hilarious and he laughed aloud.

A silent Henry watched the doctor walk from the room with exaggerated care. He poured himself a brandy and sat down to wait. Upstairs Briony, Mrs Horlock and her mother were arguing furiously.

'I'm not gonna let them do it, Mum. It's wicked!'

Briony's face was white. The strain was beginning to tell on her and Molly felt her heart go out to the child.

'Oh, Briony, you don't understand! What are we gonna do with another child in the house? Now your father's gone, and your wages too . . . we'll end up back in the dockside slums.'

'No, we won't. I'll think of something, Mum. Won't I, Mrs Horlock?'

Briony turned pleading eyes on her in the hope she'd come up with something. Briony was frightened of having the child, but she was more frightened of the alternative. After Carlton had saved her from a miscarriage, it seemed evil to take the child now, why couldn't her mother see that? And her a good Catholic as well. 'I mean it, Mum. I'll not let that doctor near me, I'll . . . I'll scream the bloody house down!'

As she spoke he lurched into the room with his big black bag and three pairs of eyes looked at him.

All three registered the fact that he was roaring drunk.

'Jesus in heaven, save us!' Instinctively Molly crossed herself.

'You're drunk, man!' Mrs Horlock reproached.

Carlton stood on his dignity. 'Madam, I am never drunk. I had a medicinal whisky for medicinal purposes. Now if you'd be so kind as to hold down the patient, I shall begin.'

He opened up his bag and began taking out his instruments. Briony's eyes widened to their utmost and she began to scream – high piercing screams that went through the doctor's skull like a drill.

Both Mrs Horlock and her mother put out their hands to try and calm her. Briony, thinking they were going to hold her down, kicked out and, leaping off the bed, ran across the room, Carlton grabbed her flying hair as she passed him, and she screamed again as she was yanked backwards.

'Let go of me, you old bastard! Let go of me, I say.'

Twisting around, she bit his arm. He let go, she opened the bedroom door and, running out, flew straight down the stairs and into the arms of a plump dark-haired lady who was standing in the hallway with Henry.

'Oh, please don't let them hurt me, missus! Please!'

She clung to the newcomer as her saviour. She looked kind, with those big brown eyes in a white face. Please God, Briony prayed, let her help me.

Isabel wrapped the child in gentle arms. Looking first at her husband, then at the two women and the obviously drunk man standing at the top of the stairs, she said, 'What on earth's going on here?'

Henry's shoulders slumped and Briony heard a terrible groan come from him. It was as if he had been punched in the stomach with an iron fist.

Briony was sitting on the nice lady's lap being petted, her mother and Mrs Horlock telling Isabel everything she wanted to know. Henry was sitting by the window on a straight-backed chair, biting his knuckles.

Isabel listened to the two women with growing amazement, every so often looking down at the fiery head laid against her breast. She knew this child should repel her, but all she felt was motherly concern. That the girl had been coerced into her situation, she had no doubt. This beautiful child with the porcelain white skin and the glass-green eyes should be outside in the air playing games, not sitting in this overstuffed morning room waiting to find out if she was going to be allowed to give birth to a child she should not be carrying in the first place. Isabel looked at her husband and felt an urge to rise from her seat and fell him to the floor with one heavy blow.

What he had done here was disgusting and cruel. And all the more so because this child had been handed to him on a plate by a father who needed to feed the rest of his family. Henry played on people's poverty, the big Bible-thumping bully!

'What do you want, my dear?' She looked down at Briony's face, her voice gentle.

'I want to have the little baby, missus. I don't want that doctor near me.'

Isabel nodded. 'But who will look after the baby when it arrives?'

Briony sat up straight on her lap and grinned. 'Well, I suppose I will. I know a lot about babies, don't I, Mum?'

Molly nodded, defeated by all that had happened.

'That's settled then.' Isabel's voice was brisk. 'She'll stay here, of course, until the baby comes, and then we'll sort something out. Henry will pay the bills, don't worry about that. I'll see to it personally.' Her voice was getting stronger. 'I shall undertake to oversee everything myself. Mr Dumas will not be visiting here any more, so any belongings of his should be packed and ready for him to take with him as he leaves.'

Briony looked at her saviour's face and smiled shyly. God had answered her prayers in the shape of Mrs Henry Dumas. Mrs Prosser Evans had been right. God was good. God was very, very good.

Henry waited until he knew Isabel had retired for the night before going to see her. He had eaten dinner at his club, trying to decide how to face the situation in hand. A few large brandies had given him the courage he needed but it was already failing as he listened at his wife's door.

Isabel was humming. The annoyance he felt at the sound was so profound, it made his hands tremble and his heart beat a tattoo in his chest. She was laughing at him. In his own house, dammit!

Isabel, brushing her hair in front of her dressing-table mirror, turned in her seat to face him as he strode in without knocking. She was wearing one of the lacy chemises that had come with her trousseau. Her large breasts spilled out of the tiny garment, showing dark pink nipples. She smiled at her husband. She had been expecting him and had purposely waited up until he showed himself. She watched the flicker of disgust as he eyed her bosom, and her smile widened.

Raising one eyebrow, she spoke softly.

'Why, Henry, this is the last place I expected to see you.' The inference wasn't lost on him.

'I want to talk to you, Isabel, and this place is as good as any.'

She interrupted him easily.

'No, Henry, you'll hear me out. You picked this room because it's farthest from the servants' quarters, so what we have to say you do not want overheard. Well . . .' she spread her hands, 'what I have to say had best be stated in private anyway.

'From now on there will be some changes in our marriage. We will still function outwardly as man and wife, I expect your full support when socialising. In public we shall carry on as the devoted couple.' She allowed herself another smile at that. 'But inside this house I do not want to see you unless I absolutely have to. You disgust me, Henry. When I think of that child . . . the position she's in because of you. Well, I intend to look after the girl, and when the time comes I want the baby. I think the mother will be happy, and the child will have every advantage here with us. It's your child after all, Henry Dumas, and your child should be brought up in this house, as you were.'

Henry's face was white with shock and disbelief. He

took a step towards her and she slipped from the chair and picked up a large cut-glass perfume bottle.

'If you make one move to stop me, I shall go straight to my father and Mrs Prosser Evans, I swear that to you. If you touch one hair on my head, or indeed Briony's, I will bring such trouble to your door your life will never be the same. I want a child, Henry. I want a child so desperately I am willing to take on a street urchin's brat. So now you know what's going to happen.'

Henry watched his wife, breasts heaving as she spoke. The vehemence in her voice was more frightening than anything he had ever experienced. He realised belatedly that she had an iron will, stronger even than his own.

Briony was looking forward to seeing Mrs Dumas; she liked her. She liked the softness of her hands and the nice smell that enveloped her. At breakfast today Briony had eaten two boiled eggs, with thick bread-and-butter soldiers, and washed it all down with a whole pot of tea. She had woken from her sleep ravenous, content in her child's mind to let Mrs Dumas take over her life. Her belly was much better, and the reality of the child inside her had yet to hit home. Her mother was still to get her money, Henry was already a distant memory, and her sisters could all stay at Oxlow Lane. Her three main worries were over.

Mrs Dumas arrived promptly at ten-thirty. Briony stood up as Isabel entered the room, smiling widely.

Isabel looked into the deep green eyes and smiled back. The child was far too knowing already, but whose fault was that?

'Hello, Briony dear.'

Briony waited for her to seat herself before sitting down

too. 'I've ordered some tea. I thought that today we could get to know one another better.'

Briony readily agreed. As Isabel listened to the child's chatter about her earlier life, about her ambitions and dreams and hopes, she felt herself relax. She would enjoy looking after the girl, seeing that she rested properly and ate well. Her health was to be watched with the utmost care.

Isabel passionately wanted this child's baby.

Chapter Seven

Briony was five months pregnant and she looked blooming. Her face and body had filled out becomingly and today she looked a picture of health and prosperity, her hair tied back into a neat chignon and her feet encased in kidskin boots with tiny pearl buttons. She wore a blue velvet dress with a lace cape around the shoulders.

She was sitting on a bench by the boating pool in Barking Park, lifting her face to the weak spring sun. She closed her eyes as her mind drifted off to another place. Mrs Dumas had generously allowed her this hour's freedom every day. A cab waited at the entrance of the park for her so she had no fears about walking home alone. Briony liked Mrs Dumas, or Isabel as she now called her, but this hour every day was Briony's favourite time. Oh, she loved living in the house with them all, she loved Mrs Horlock and Cissy, but she craved her own space more and more as the days passed. The child had become more real to her, and she guessed, rightly, that it was the reason behind Isabel's kindness to her. Because of the child she could have anything she wanted, and, being Briony, she used this to the full.

Hence the afternoons in the park without Mrs Horlock, Cissy, or that awful boy Mrs Dumas had employed to run messages. Briony shuddered as she thought of him, with his forever running nose and his big bulbous eyes. She had made Cissy get him a pair of boots because the sight of his callused feet sickened her. She knew she was being unfair to the boy. He was no more than eight, and his mother was probably glad of the few pennies he made a week, but Briony hated him. He was a reminder of where she came from, what she could be again, and he disturbed her for that reason.

She sat back on the bench and let her whole body relax. The child within her quickened and unconsciously she put her hands to her stomach. A tiny smile still playing around her mouth, she jolted upright as a familiar voice broke into her thoughts.

'Hello again. I thought it was you.'

Briony opened her eyes to see Tommy Lane. He grinned as he saw her obvious surprise at his changed appearance.

'Well, sod me! Ain't you going to talk to me?'

His voice was deeper than she remembered. He sat beside her and looked her over, his eyes staying just a second too long on her bulging stomach. He took out a small cheroot. Briony watched as he lit it. He certainly looked different. He was dressed in a checked suit and wore a rather natty bowler hat. He was clean, shiny clean, and his hair was cut close to the head, with just the right amount of hair tonic on it. She was impressed. He was a very handsome boy.

'Look, are you going to sit there gawping or are you going to talk to me?'

Briony grinned back at him.

'You gave me a shock, Tommy. Last time I saw you, you was trying to save your arse. Now you look like . . .'

He took a puff on his cheroot and then clamped it between his strong teeth.

'What do I look like, eh? A man of substance and fashion? At least, that's what these togs are supposed to make you look like. The geezer in the shop said so.'

Briony relaxed once more and laughed.

'Well, let's just say you look all right, shall we?'

Tommy surveyed her once more through a haze of cheap tobacco smoke.

'Looks like you got caught then?'

He motioned with his head towards her swelling waist and Briony put her hands to it.

'Yeah, that's about the strength of it. I'm going to be all right though, I'm being looked after by a nice lady who wants the baby when it comes.'

Tommy pricked up his ears.

'I hope you've made a good deal for yourself? Nippers is worth a fortune. Especially if the mother's a looker and ain't got the clap.'

Briony looked so shocked Tommy felt guilty and tried hastily to make amends.

'I didn't mean that how it came out. But you're obviously on the bash . . .'

Briony sat up straight. 'Listen here, Mr Tommy whatever your name is, don't you come and sit here and speak trouble into my face, I won't have it! My business is my business, and I think I've said a bit too much to you already. If I want your advice, I'll bleeding well ask you for it. Until then, either go away, or keep your trap shut!'

Tommy looked away. His face had reddened and he

smoked his cheroot in silence. She was a funny little thing. He should clout her across the lug for talking to him like that, but for some strange reason he liked her. He had liked her since she had saved him from a nicking, and for that reason he would swallow her words.

'Who's the father then?'

Briony looked at him and sighed. He really was the nosiest person she had ever met.

'A man.'

Tommy threw away the cheroot and laughed.

'No! I'd never have guessed that! I mean, who is he?'

'Never you mind. What about yourself? You're looking prosperous, what work are you doing now?'

Tommy flicked an imaginary speck of dirt from his trousers and sat back in his seat.

'I'm working for Nellie Deakins now . . . I was working for some bloke – a right villain he was and all. But Nellie asked me to work for her exclusively, and so I do.'

Briony was intrigued. Nellie Deakins's brothel was something she'd heard talked of since she could remember. It was a standard threat to most of the children roundabouts. 'You do that again and I'll cart you off to Nellie Deakins.' But she had never spoken to any one who actually worked there.

'What's it like?'

Tommy grinned.

'It's not so bad really, Briony. She gets a raw deal, old Nellie. The girls are looked after, she gets a quack to them if they're feeling a bit rough. My job's delivering them around London to private parties and that. I only deal with the women though, not the little girls.'

His voice was thick as he said the last sentence and looked back across the park at the people strolling around the boating pool feeding the ducks. Tommy had hated the job he had first taken with Davie Dobson. It had sickened him to be expected to drag kids, some no more than six or seven, around London. Boys as wells as girls. Then taking the poor little blighters back again, their faces filled with fear and their sobs reproaching him. He'd kissed that job goodbye without a backward glance. He had gone to Nellie's on spec, and with one look at the big strapping lad, she had employed him there and then. He had given Dobson the bad news through his friend Willy and had not looked back since.

Briony bit her lower lip. She decided that although he got on her nerves, she liked Tommy.

'My dad took me to the house I live at now. Me sister went first and then me. I like it there, I've always liked it there.'

Tommy nodded as if he understood. And the funny thing was, he did. He understood only too well what an empty belly and a dead fire could cause. People sold their only assets, whether it was a woman going on the game or a man selling off a child. It was some people's only way out. It had been his mother's and his sisters'. He smiled at Briony and she smiled back. They were both aware of the other's way of life and it bonded them together. Standing up, Tommy held out his arm and Briony took it. Together they strolled around the park and chatted. More than one pair of eyes strayed to the well-dressed young couple. Briony, with her brazen hair tied back, looked older and more mature; Tommy, with his new clothes and confident gait, led her around with the pride of ownership.

He looked down on to the china-white face and felt a lurch inside his chest. Her green eyes were so trusting as they looked into his, he felt a swelling of his heart.

He gleaned from her that she came to the park every day for an hour, and decided there and then that he'd make a point of being here when she arrived.

Isabel poured herself a cup of tea. She had arranged dinner with Mrs Horlock and had set Cissy the task of hemming the remainder of the baby garments that she herself had made. She sipped her tea delicately, breathing in the aroma. Briony joined her a few minutes later.

'I really feel well, Mrs Dumas.'

Isabel smiled. The child did look well. The walks in the park were obviously doing her the world of good. Her white face had taken on a rosy glow and her body, nicely rounded now, looked more supple somehow, more relaxed.

Briony took a noisy sip of tea and ate a sandwich. 'I'm hungry all the time lately.'

'It's the baby, Briony. You're eating for two.'

She nodded and ate another sandwich. She had been meeting Tommy every day for a month now, and had gleaned a mine of information from him. Although she was shrewd in her own way, Tommy had first-hand knowledge of the world and relayed this knowledge to Briony in plain and simple language. She took a deep breath and spoke to Isabel Dumas.

'You want this child, don't you, Isabel?'

The fact she had called her 'Isabel' spoke volumes. The older woman looked into Briony's face, searching for the reason for the question.

'I do.'

Briony smiled widely.

'You can have it. I can't look after it properly, me mum's got enough on her plate as it is, so I think the best thing for everyone would be for you to look after it.'

Isabel swallowed hard. This girl-woman sitting opposite had answered all her prayers and she felt an urge to kiss the white face and embrace Briony in her arms. Instead, she nodded.

'Thank you. I do want your baby, I want it very much.'

Briony, in her youth and her naivety, just smiled. 'That's that, then. If you have it, I can see it sometimes, can't I? Not every day like, but now and then?'

Isabel nodded again. 'Of course you can, and my husband and I will see to it that you benefit by giving us your baby.'

Briony patted her stomach and said, 'I wish I didn't have to leave here. I love this house, and Mrs Horlock and Cissy . . . And you.'

It was a simple statement of truth and Isabel took it as that, but still she said, 'I'll give you this house as a gift once you're delivered of your child. I'll also arrange a substantial sum of money for you to live on.'

Briony's face opened like a book.

'Really, you really mean that?'

Isabel smiled. 'Yes, I do. It's the very least we can do for you.'

Briony jumped from her seat and flung her arms around Isabel, hugging her tight. Isabel hugged her back, breathing in the smell of her, feeling a surge of love and sadness for the girl as she held her. Knowing that she was taking from her an integral part of her life.

Abel looked at Molly's frightened face and sighed.

'How long's she been gone this time?'

Molly bit her lip before answering him.

'Well, since this morning. Oh, Abel, she worries me!'

He pulled out a chair and sat Molly down, then, chucking a solemn-faced Rosalee under the chin, poured Molly a large mug of black tea.

'Well, don't worry, Moll. I'll get out the cart and go looking for her. She'll likely be up on Rainham Marshes again.'

Molly nodded, dull-eyed, as he walked from the cottage. Rosalee, sensing that something was wrong, pulled herself up from the cracket and went to her mother, pushing her bulky body between her legs. Instinctively, Molly pulled the child's head to her breasts and stroked the short-cropped hair.

'Oh, Rosalee, Rosalee. Where's your sister?'

She hugged her mother back and said, 'Bri Bri.'

Mother Jones bustled through the door then, all energy and common sense. Molly smiled weakly at her.

'Now stop your worrying, Molly. Abel's off looking for her and I'll sit with you till he comes back.'

She didn't say 'comes back with Eileen', because it was Mother Jones's opinion that the girl was a few farthings short of a penny, and that what she needed was to see a doctor. If Eileen was to jump in the cut, it wouldn't surprise her. That dirty blackguard of a father had seen to her ruin and now it was just a matter of time before she went completely off her head.

Eileen stood alone on Rainham Marshes. The sun was warm on her face, though the wind was cold. She took a deep breath and looked around her. She felt cleanliness envelop her when she was here. Here there was no one, no one and nothing. Just her, clean and pure. She loved it. She began to walk down towards the dirt track that would lead her through the marshes to the little hamlet of

Rainham itself. Sometimes she ventured that far and sat by the big pond, watching the people come and go. People she didn't know and who didn't know her. The anonymity pleased her.

Every time she stood in her mother's kitchen, she saw once more the flat iron coming down on her father's head. She blinked back the picture in her mind and unconsciously walked faster, as if she could outwalk the picture, run away from it.

In the distance she saw a hare, leaping in the long grass. She walked towards it. In the sunlight its coat had a red tinge and she saw Briony then. Briony lying in the big bed with Henry Dumas; Briony with her tiny hands and feet and her head of red hair. Eileen felt the familiar heaving of her stomach and swallowed hard. She hadn't eaten again today. She never had an appetite, and the more her mother went on at her about eating, the less appetite she seemed to have. She had taken to forcing down an evening meal and then, when no one was looking, forcing it back up, up and out of her body. Enjoying the emptiness once more. Hating the feeling of being replete, of being filled with the food her sister's degradation bought. It was evil food, bought with evil money.

She was walking fast again and the hare, seeing her approach, skittered away with wide, frightened eyes. A man was walking nearby with his dog. He noticed the girl and nodded at her. He frowned as she turned abruptly away from him. His dog, a small black mongrel, ran to her, jumping up at her dress in excitement and muddying the ragged hem with dirty paws. The man walked towards her and, pulling the dog away from her with one hand, put out the other to steady her.

Eileen saw his hard work-worn hand on her flesh and

looked fearfully into his face. Pushing his hand from her, she backed away from him, eyes wild.

The man stared at her, puzzled. Thinking that the dog had frightened her, he walked towards her to apologise, to make amends, when Eileen opened her mouth wide and began shouting. She was threatening him, mouthing obscenities the like of which he had never heard before from a woman, let alone a young girl. She stumbled away from him, her arms outstretched, her face screwed up with hatred.

It was then that Abel came upon her. He had witnessed the scene and as the man saw the huge musclebound individual put his arms around the shouting girl, he felt fear overwhelm him.

'I swear I never touched her, mister. I never touched her! The dog was jumping at her, that's all. She just went mad, stark staring mad . . .'

Abel held tightly on to Eileen. Strangely she never tried to fight him off but held on to him, sobbing into his barrel chest.

'He touched me, Abel, he was touching me.'

'I know, Eileen girl, I know. Calm down and I'll take you home to your mother.'

He motioned with his hand to the man to go away and leave them. He grabbed his dog by the scruff of its neck and almost ran in his haste to escape.

Slowly Abel led Eileen back to the road and his cart. He lifted her up tenderly and placed her on the seat, all the time talking to her softly, calming her down.

'He was touching me Abel, look at my arm. Look where he touched me, on my arm . . .'

Abel looked at the arm and nodded at her. She kept up a conversation with herself in low tones all the way home, rubbing furiously at the arm as if it was covered in filth.

It wasn't the first time she had wandered off and it was not to be the last.

Briony and Tommy sat on their usual bench. As the weather was warmer they had both begun to bring picnics with them. Today, Tommy had brought some tongue sandwiches and a small stone flask of lemonade. Eating the sandwiches, they put down crumbs of bread for the ducks, laughing at their antics as they fought over the tiny morsels.

'How are you feeling in yourself, Briony?'

She patted her stomach and smiled. 'Not too bad. I've only a few weeks to go now, and I can't wait until it's all over.'

'Has that woman, that Mrs Dumas, said any more about giving you the house?'

Briony nodded. 'Oh, yeah, she's like a nervous wreck waiting for this baby.'

Tommy nodded solemnly.

'Well, you just make sure you get it all in writing. You're thirteen now, aren't you?'

'Yeah, I'm thirteen in a few months, why?'

'Well, you might have to get it put in trust for you or something. With your mum. Either way, make sure you take any papers they give you to a good brief. I know a bloke who's well up on all this kind of stuff, I'll arrange for you to see him.'

Briony screwed up her little face.

'Mrs Dumas wouldn't tuck me up. She's lovely.'

Tommy swallowed the last of his sandwich and threw the crust to the ducks.

''Course she's lovely, she wants your baby. Once it's born and she's got her hands on it, you might as well piss in the wind with all the legal jargon they'll baffle you with. You just listen to me, Briony, I've got contacts that could help you. You must look out for number one. If you don't, no one else will.'

Briony digested this bit of logic and shrugged. She trusted Isabel Dumas with her life, but she didn't trust Henry. Though he was never mentioned by Isabel, Briony sensed his baleful influence. What Tommy said made sense, and when the time came she would take his advice and see his lawyer friend.

'Thanks, Tommy, I'll keep that in mind. Now tell me some more stories about Nellie Deakins's place. They make me laugh.'

He poured her another glass of cool lemonade and handed it to her.

'First of all you tell me what's been happening with you. Have you seen the doctor this week?'

Briony sighed and began telling him everything he wanted to know. Tommy relaxed on the bench and watched her tiny rosebud mouth. He could listen to her and watch her all day. They chatted until her cab driver came for her and then, after promising to see him the following day, Briony went off. Tommy watched her go. As she reached the park exit she turned and waved and he waved back, feeling low now she had gone. They had met nearly every day for over three months. In that time he had felt a closeness spring between them that was not just friendship. He found himself thinking about her at odd times of the day and the evenings. He would not call what he felt for her love, because in his youth he wasn't sure what love was.

But whatever it was he felt for Briony, with her little button nose and that crackling red hair, he liked it.

He liked it, and he wanted to keep it.

Isabel was staying in her own home tonight. She made a point of staying two nights a week, eating dinner, seeing to her household bills, ordering the different cuts of meat and overseeing the general upkeep. The rest of the time she stayed with Briony.

As she sat in her room, she brushed out her long brown hair and was delighted to see the firelight pick out golden highlights. Her skin looked creamy in the triple mirrors on her dressing table and she smiled at herself. Since the night she had rescued Briony Cavanagh, her life had taken on a different slant. Her depression had lifted, and even the thought of being married to Henry didn't stop her from enjoying herself. Briony had given her a new zest for living, and now she was certain to get the child, she couldn't be happier.

She glanced at her heavy breasts in the mirror. Their rosy nipples peeping out from behind the thin lace brought a momentary return of her old longings. She quickly pushed these thoughts from her mind, concentrating once more on the coming child. She hoped it looked like its mother. That way she could guarantee it would be a beautiful child. If it looked like Henry and it was a girl child . . . She picked up her hand cream and began the laborious nightly ritual of softening her hands.

Henry walked in the room without knocking.

Isabel looked at his red face in the dressing-table mirror and saw at once he had been drinking.

'What can I do for you?'

He sat unsteadily on the edge of her bed and looked at

his wife. In his drunken state, he noticed everything about her as if for the first time. Her high breasts and slim waist, the length of her legs, her well-turned ankles. The dark brown hair that tumbled across her shoulders and down her back. And suddenly, all his hatred of her dissolved. He saw her for what she was in other men's eyes. To any other man, she would be a desirable companion, a good wife. She was pleasing in face and figure, intelligent and well educated. She could talk on almost any subject and could also listen exceptionally well. He could almost pity her for being married to him.

'It's about the child, Isabel.'

He watched her smile as she turned to face him.

'What child? The one you got pregnant? Or the child of the child?' Her tone was sarcastic and Henry closed his eyes.

'You're still intent on bringing it into this house then?'

'I am.'

He shook his head.

'What about the talk it'll cause?'

Isabel laughed now.

'There's always talk, Henry. I am seeing my father tomorrow and telling him I'm barren. We both know that's not true, don't we? I will tell him that you have a mistress, a respectable widow of the lower middle classes who has found herself in an embarrassing predicament. You wish to take the child and bring it up as your own and I have agreed to it. My father will set the rumour abroad and everyone will think you are a rake who has taken on an illegitimate child because your legal wife can't produce one. You'll come out of it as rather a colourful character, a man with many women. I'll come out of it as the poor barren wife taking another woman's leavings. So don't worry about the talk, Henry. It will all be grist to your mill really. Who would ever think that a rake like that really liked little girls?'

Henry sat still under the onslaught of his wife's tongue, and as they stared at one another felt an urge to confess his feelings to her. To tell her about the demon that drove him to little girls. But even as he thought it, he dismissed it. She wouldn't understand.

'What if your father refuses to allow you to take on the child?'

'Henry, I'm not going to ask his permission, I'm going to *tell* him. I don't care what he thinks. All he is to me is a means to an end. I'll talk him round, don't worry. Now if you don't mind, I want to get into bed.'

She was dismissing him and they both knew it.

'I am the man of this house, madam. It would behove you to remember that.'

Isabel stood up and her laughter caused her breasts to shudder.

'If you were the man of the house, Henry, indeed any kind of man, we would not be having this conversation!' With that, she walked past him and opened the door wide.

'Goodnight, Henry. I'll keep you informed of what's happening.'

He walked from the room. As he sat on his own bed drinking a large brandy, it occurred to him that she had won again. She would bring the gutter brat's child into his home and he was powerless to stop her. Her strength of purpose was terrifying to him. Never had he felt so powerless, so utterly powerless.

He lay back and closed his eyes. Seeing Briony in his mind, he shuddered. He would not be in this predicament if it hadn't been for her. Well, he had a long memory and a lot of money. He would wait for his chance and get his own back on her eventually.

Happier now he had a fixed goal in mind, he waited for a drunken sleep to claim him. But the light was already sneaking in at the chinks of the curtains before it came.

Chapter Eight

Briony sat on the park bench waiting for Tommy. She shifted her position slightly as she had a dull ache in her back. The child had dropped inside her and her stomach felt as if it was lying on her knees. She was wearing a large silk cape to hide the enormous bulge that seemed to be quivering and turning constantly. She took a deep breath as she felt a stabbing pain go through her body. She closed her eyes until it passed. Isabel had been right, she should not have left the house today. But the thought of seeing Tommy had been too much of a draw for her and after nearly having an argument with the nervous woman she had finally got her own way. Now, though, she wished she had heeded the advice and stayed home. The last couple of days she had been possessed of a great energy, feeling as if she could climb a mountain if she wanted to. In the space of an hour that feeling had been replaced by one of a dull lethargy.

She felt Tommy sit beside her and opened her eyes.

'You look ill, girl. Are you all right?'

Briony stared into his face and shook her head. 'I think it's on its way.'

Tommy saw her eyes widen as she sat forward, clasping her stomach with both hands.

'Oh Tommy . . . Tommy . . . I've wet meself!'

The boy jumped from his seat in panic. 'Stay there and I'll get someone . . . I'll get the doctor!'

Briony laughed despite the pain. 'Just get me to the cab and back to the house, as quick as possible.'

Her voice had a strength in it that calmed the youth in front of her.

'Here, give me your arm and walk me to me cab.'

Tommy helped her up and they walked slowly towards the entrance of the park where her cab waited. In ten minutes they were outside her house. Tommy helped her down while the cabby knocked at the door. Pandemonium erupted.

Mrs Horlock and Cissy took Briony up the stairs while Mrs Dumas sent the cabby for the doctor. Tommy stood in the hallway watching in amazement. Isabel turned to him as she went to walk up the stairs and looked at him as if just seeing him for the first time. She unconsciously took in the neat suit and the well-cut hair. His penetrating blue eyes stayed her and she walked towards him.

'I'm so sorry, young man, thank you for bringing my charge home.'

Tommy looked at her, decided he liked the look of her and smiled.

'I'm a friend of Briony's actually.'

The woman stood stock still.

'Really? I can't say she's ever mentioned you before.'

'Well, she's mentioned you, Mrs Dumas. My name's Thomas, Thomas Lane.'

He held out his hand and Isabel took it before she had time to think.

'How do you do, Mr Lane?'

'If it's all right with you, I'd like to stay for a bit, see that she's all right like . . .'

Isabel was nonplussed for a second. She wasn't sure what to say to the boy. She was saved from answering by Cissy running down the stairs.

'She wants her mum, Mrs Dumas. She's insisting on having her mum here.'

Tommy stepped forward. 'Tell me where she lives and I'll go for her.'

Two minutes later he was rushing from the house and on his way to Molly's.

Briony felt as if her whole body was being rent in two.

'Oh, Mam, Mam . . . it's hurting me . . . it's hurting me!'

Her voice was high and filled with terror.

'Calm yourself, child. Would you calm yourself . . . It won't be long now.'

Molly looked at the doctor and he nodded at her, confirming her own opinion.

Briony twisted her head on the pillows. Her whole being was filled with pain. It seemed to her at that moment that even her teeth ached with it. Molly stared down at her child and felt such love come over her she would gladly have borne the pain for Briony at that moment. The doctor suddenly pushed past Molly.

'This is it, it's coming.'

Molly stood by, helpless, as the top of the child's head appeared. She watched the opening of her daughter's body stretch and the tiny head, that looked so small and vulnerable to her and felt so big and cumbersome to Briony, push its way out into the world. Then its shoulders appeared and it slipped from its mother and into the doctor's arms where the baby immediately began to cry, big, gasping, lusty cries that made Molly smile in delight. The child had a reddish tinge to its downy hair and its face, unlined and smooth, had a peach colour to it that denoted health and strength. Looking at it, she felt a stirring inside her. This was wholly Briony's child, that much was evident.

Briony lifted her head from the pillows and tried to glimpse the baby, but she could see nothing. Then the doctor put the child on her now blessedly flat stomach and she looked into the sea-green eyes of her son. He looked at his mother and his crying ceased immediately. It was as if mother and child sized each other up for a few split seconds.

Molly saw Briony smile at him and felt a great sadness for her. It would be hard to give up a big beautiful child like this, but give it up she must. Instinctively she grasped her daughter's hand as the doctor finished cutting the cord and Mrs Horlock swaddled the child. She kissed Briony then, tenderly, in a way she had never kissed any of her children before. It was as if she and Briony had become sisters, sharing now a common bond: the pains of birth and of motherhood.

Isabel was sitting in the morning room with Tommy Lane. They had hardly spoken to one another. Both sat silent, straining their ears to hear what was happening upstairs.

Tommy noticed that the woman was wringing her hands together. He watched her ample bosom heave as she waited for the outcome of the birth. Then they heard the long low shriek and the sound of a child's crying.

Their eyes met and of one mind they stood up and

went to the door. They met Molly on her way down the stairs.

'It's a boy child. A big, lusty boy child.'

Isabel lifted her skirts and ran up the stairs like a girl, her face glowing with happiness and expectation. She burst into the bedroom where Briony lay in the bed with her son in her arms.

Looking down into his face, Briony experienced a feeling like looking forward to ten whole Christmasses rolled together. Like the excitement caused by a very high place or the opening of a large present. She traced his every feature with her eyes, drinking in the smell of him, the size of him, the shape of his jaw.

She lifted her eyes to Isabel Dumas, and saw mirrored there the same expression as her own. But she also saw the raw longing, the gnawing want that would never be fully assuaged.

Holding out the child to her, Briony smiled widely. 'Look at him, Isabel, he's beautiful.'

She took the child and sat on the edge of the bed with him.

Mrs Horlock watched the exchange and felt a surge of relief go through her. She had convinced herself that Briony would not let the child go. She bustled from the room taking Cissy with her, on the pretext of making Briony a strong cup of tea. The doctor patted the mother's hand and walked from the room, ready to get his money and depart.

Alone together, Briony and Isabel looked at one another.

'He's beautiful, Briony.' Isabel's voice broke and Briony placed her hand over Isabel's so both of them were holding the child. He stirred in Isabel's arms and settled himself more comfortably. Staring at the two faces above his. Trying to focus on one and then the other.

'You'll look after him, won't you?'

Isabel smiled and nodded her head vigorously. 'I'll look after him all my life, I promise you that. Thank you for giving him to me, Briony. Thank you.'

Satisfied, she lay back against the pillows, her face white and drawn. She felt so tired and so sore all she wanted to do was sleep.

Tommy waited until he was sure that Briony was safe and then left the house, telling Cissy he would be back the next evening.

Molly was the next to depart, then Mrs Horlock and Cissy both drank a large hot rum to celebrate the safe delivery.

Briony awoke at eleven in the evening, after sleeping for nearly two hours. Cissy was sitting by her bed and as soon as Briony was fully awake, went for Mrs Horlock.

The old woman brought Briony up a simple meal of coddled eggs and broth, knowing that hunger would have made itself felt by now. After a few sips of the broth, Briony looked at the wizened old face and smiled.

'I feel much better now. Where's the baby?'

Mrs Horlock put the bowl of broth on the bedside cabinet and sat beside Briony on the bed.

'He's gone to the mistress's house, Briony.'

She sat upright in the bed, her face a study in disbelief.

'What? Already? But I only saw him once. I want to see him again. Now!' Her voice had taken on a strident quality and Mrs Horlock pulled her into her arms.

'It's no good, Briony. If you see too much of him at first you won't be able to let go. I know, I've seen it happen before.'

Briony felt a hotness behind her eyes.

'But he's my baby, Mrs Horlock. I want to see him.'

She started to cry then, her little shoulders heaving inside the nice white lawn nightdress with the pink bows that she had been so delighted with, had loved to think she owned.

Mrs Horlock held her while she cried bitter tears. When she quietened, the old woman went from the room to make her a strong hot whisky with lots of sugar in. She would ensure the child slept. It was a great healer.

Alone in the room, Briony looked around her. At the brocade curtains and bedspread, the carpeted floor, and the pictures on the walls. Above the bed was a tapestry, worked by her own hands in the long afternoons of her pregnancy. It was a proverb from the Bible and read: 'For whom the Lord loveth, he correcteth.' It was one of Mrs Prosser Evans's sayings and Briony had always remembered it. Now, though, she knew exactly what it meant.

All that she now had – this house, the money that was being given to her, the fact that her mother and sisters would benefit from her giving away her little child – meant nothing. All the nice clothes and all the good food and all the warmth would never replace the feeling she had experienced when she had looked at her son.

Her son. He was her son, her son and Henry's.

But he would live with his father, a man who only wanted little children. A man who had taken Briony and abused her, tempted her with his promise of luxury and warmth and three pounds a week.

Now he had everything and she had nothing.

She had lain racked with pain, had pushed a life into the world, and at the end of it all she didn't even know what they were going to call her son.

She didn't even know his name.

*

Isabel looked down at the well-shaped head in the crib and sighed with contentment. The baby moved, snuggling into the warmth then, snuffling through his button nose, drifted back off to sleep again. Sally, his nurse, looked on and smiled to herself. Her own baby, born two months previously, had died after a week as if he just couldn't be bothered to breathe in the slum he'd been born to. She had made sure of keeping her milk by letting her sister's children suckle her, now she was ensconced in this lovely house, had been bathed and given two uniforms. She had her own room with three guaranteed meals a day, and milk and beer as and when she fancied it. Even if talk in the house was rife, if they did say that the child was the master's by a whore, what did she care? As long as she kept her position she would look after the child of the devil himself.

Isabel was beside herself with excitement. She had a child, a dear and blessed little child, and felt as if she had been touched by the good Lord himself. Unable to sleep with excitement, she watched the wet nurse feed him, watched his strong lips find the nipple and suck on it hungrily, and wished fervently that she could do that particular job herself. She was gratified that he looked like his mother, that he would be a handsome boy. He was big, so big. She had not been prepared for the sheer size of him. For the force of love the baby would awaken in her. Already Briony was all but forgotten.

Hardly able to contain herself, Isabel took the child from the wet nurse as soon as he was replete and, taking him back to her own room, sat in front of the fire and just looked at him.

She held him in her arms and drank in every part of

him. He grasped her finger and she laughed out loud in the silent room. He was strong and he was hers.

Her son, Benedict Dumas. All the frustrated longing and the unrequited love she possessed would be channelled into this boy. He would be loved, cared for and educated. He would have everything that money and her influence could give him. He was, from that day on, her boy.

Her darling boy.

Henry walked into Isabel's room as she sat with the child. She heard the door open but was unable to take her eyes from the child long enough to see who it was.

Clearing his throat, he walked across the room and stood behind the chair, forcing himself to look. He was unprepared for the sheer beauty of the child in his wife's arms. He saw the strong hand holding on to his wife's fingers. Saw the perfectly shaped lips and the button nose that were wholly his mother's. He saw the startling green eyes and caught his breath in his throat.

Looking down on to the wide awake infant he felt a revulsion inside him that was so acute he could almost taste it. It was as if every nightmare he had ever had was there, in that body on his wife's lap. It was his flesh and blood, he knew that, but he wanted no part of it. No part of it at all.

Molly arrived at nine the next morning and was closeted with Mrs Horlock for a good hour before she ventured up the stairs to her daughter's room. She looked around her as if seeing everything for the first time. It amazed her that her daughter of only thirteen owned this house. Owned everything in it. That her child was now a woman of property.

She walked into the bedroom and forced a smile on to her face. Briony lay in bed, pale and wan. Her usually animated face was drawn and dark circles were visible under her eyes. Molly could see the expert bindings around her breasts through her nightdress, and the sadness in her daughter's drawn face.

'Are you feeling all right, Briony?'

She looked at her mother and sighed.

'She took him, Mum. Isabel. She took him home with her.'

Molly sat on the edge of the bed and grasped Briony's hand. 'Of course she did, love. It would do you no good to see too much of him.'

Briony pulled her hand from her mother's and her face set in a pout. It made her look very young and very spoilt. Seeing the look, Molly herself sighed. Briony was the only one of her daughters who had never been biddable. She had always gone her own way. Even as a tiny child, when Molly had chastised her for something, Briony had taken the punishment and then gone and done exactly what she wanted to. It was this trait in her daughter's character that was evident now. Briony was quite capable of getting out of bed and going to Isabel Dumas's and taking the child. Molly tried a different tack.

'Look, Briony, Mrs Dumas can give the boy everything. He'll be educated, he'll be well looked after, with all sorts of people seeing to his every whim. He'll grow up with all this –' she gestured around her '– as part and parcel of his everyday life. Would you honestly take that chance from him and bring him up in Oxlow Lane? Because if you take that child now, you can kiss goodbye to this place, and the three pounds a week, and everything else you ever wanted. If someone had come and asked me for any one of you, I'd have given you up, and gladly. This is like a gift from the gods, girl. Your boy's being offered the chance to be somebody. Don't ruin it for him.'

Briony let her mother's words sound inside her head. It saddened her that she was in such a position. It was as if the three pounds a week to keep her mother and sisters at Oxlow Lane was the most important thing in the world. And the worst part of all was, she knew it was important. It was Briony's sole responsibility to keep them where they were now accustomed to being. How could she take Eileen and Kerry and Bernie and Rosalee back to the dockside slums? Eileen would never be fit to work again so it would all fall on Briony's shoulders and her mother's while the two younger girls would be left to look after Eileen and Rosalee. Their lives would all become set into a pattern that they'd never be able to change.

'Shall I get you a nice cup of tea, love?'

Molly's voice broke into her thoughts and she nodded. Unknown to her, all her thoughts were plain to her mother. Molly had deliberately set the chain of thought in motion and now she wanted to leave Briony alone for long enough to think through the consequences of any foolish action. No rash decisions must be allowed to wreck an otherwise harmonious arrangement.

Briony didn't watch her mother leave the room, just waited with bated breath until she was alone once more. It was the first time Briony had felt the full force of the responsibility she had assumed. When it had all been a childish game, when she had dreamt of being a lady in the eyes of the world, looking after her family and taking over where her father had left off, it had all seemed glamorous somehow. Now, after the birth of the child, her child, who was even as she lay here being looked after and fed by a stranger, the sheer enormity of her own actions bore down on her, leaving her feeling crushed and afraid. She could no more ask Isabel for her son than she could ask the good Lord himself to take her to tea at Claridges. It was out of her control now.

What was it Tommy had once told her? Possession was nine-tenths of the law? Well, the Dumases had the law on their side and she knew that if they chose to use it, she would have nothing at all. No child, no house and no money.

She saw her baby again in her mind's eye. His big long body, the red tinge to his downy hair, and knew he was still hers in so many ways.

Biting her lip, she made a pledge to herself. She could do nothing about her son now; she was too young, too vulnerable and far too poor. What she would do was to let herself heal physically and then work out a plan of action. If it rested with her she would never be vulnerable again, never be in a position to be overlooked by anybody, least of all Henry and Isabel Dumas who had both used her.

For different reasons maybe, but they had used her just the same.

Isabel had left the child sleeping and made her way up to Briony's bedroom with light feet. She had not felt happiness like this for years. The sheer act of looking at the child made her into a happy carefree woman. She bounded through the bedroom door with a large grin on her face.

'How are you feeling, Briony?'

The girl in the bed turned to face her and immediately Isabel's expression changed. Briony looked ill and drawn. Her eyes were dead and even that glorious hair, which usually crackled with a life of its own, looked dull and flat.

Isabel went to her and embraced her, all concern.

Being taken into the arms of the woman who now had her child made Briony's shoulders heave. Tears seemed to burst from her eyes. These hands, so soft and gentle, the hands that had held her and petted her throughout her pregnancy, were the same hands that would caress and protect her son. Would hold him when he cried, would rub a sore knee better. The very touch of the woman whom Briony both loved and despised brought out the tears that needed to be shed.

Isabel held Briony tightly to her. She stroked the hair that her son had inherited, whispered endearments. She realised that in her own excitement, in her own longing for a child, she had forgotten the very person who had made all her dreams possible.

It would take all her tact and diplomacy now to right the enormous wrong she had done. But one thing was for sure: Briony Cavanagh would not get her child back. Isabel could no more part with him than she could cut out her own heart.

When the crying subsided, she kissed Briony's cheek and under pretext of plumping up her pillows, tried to be as normal as possible.

'Are you feeling better, dear?' Her voice was all kindness and sympathy.

Briony nodded.

'I have heard tell that many women get crying fits after a birth. It's natural.'

'How's the child?' Briony's voice seemed harder than Isabel remembered it.

'Oh, very well. A big healthy child. Briony, how can I ever thank you for what you've done for me? I look at him, and everything in my life has taken on a new meaning. I'll give that boy the earth if he wants it. I'll give him everything he wants and more. Much more.'

Briony nodded, gratified to hear that. She could hear the love and the want and indeed the need in the other woman's voice as she talked of the child, and already it seemed he was long gone from her.

'Is he a good baby?'

Isabel heard the little tremor in her voice and found it in her heart to pity this girl-woman in front of her.

'Oh, he's a perfect little boy. Sleeps on his tummy, as young as he is. Not a day old! He pushes his arms from the swaddling and turns himself on to his stomach. He's a baby who knows his own mind already. Like his mother, I would say.'

Her voice was jocular, and it pleased Briony to hear that, as Isabel knew it would.

'And Henry, what does he think of the child?'

Isabel took a small breath.

'Henry wants what I want. His opinion is nothing in this.'

Briony nodded again. It was as it should be. If Isabel had said that Henry was pleased with the child it would have troubled her. If the child was to stay with the Dumases, as it was, she didn't want Henry Dumas to stake too large a claim. For the child's own safety.

Isabel swept the hair from Briony's forehead and smiled. 'I know it's hard to give him up, dear. If I had birthed him, it would break my heart to give him up. But it's all for the best. After all, what would you do with a child, no man and no money? What would your mother and sisters do?'

Even as she spoke the veiled threat, Isabel felt a disgust with herself that was forced down by her need to keep what she had taken. It would do no harm to remind Briony of the consequences of any rash actions.

'I have arranged for two thousand pounds to be made available to you. Once you're up and about I shall take you personally to see the banker and to find out how to write cheques. The house is going into your name as well. You'll be a woman of substance and wealth. The next child you have will be born to something better than you were. The world's out there waiting for you, Briony Cavanagh, and I have no doubt, no doubt at all that, you'll be someone in it!'

Briony didn't respond. She was more than aware of what all this talk was really about. It was about Isabel's having the child in exchange for giving Briony comfort and money. The two things that had brought her to this house would now be used to trap her.

'Thank you very much, but I just want to get back on my feet for now. I'll think about the future then.'

'As you wish. I've arranged all your menus for the next few days and I'll pop in again tomorrow to see you.'

Briony knew the woman wanted to get away from her. Knew that she wanted to be back in her own home with the child.

Isabel kissed Briony's cheek with hot feverish lips. Suddenly, she had to get out of here and away from this creature in the bed. Even as she thought it she knew she was being unfair. But like everything that is used for the wrong reasons, Briony was a source of annoyance. Isabel admitted to herself that a large part of her feelings was of guilt. As she walked to the door, Briony's voice stayed her.

'What did you call him, Isabel? What's his name?'

She turned once more and smiled gently. 'He's Benedict. Benedict Dumas.'

Briony nodded and looked out of the window where she could see the roofs of the houses opposite and an expanse of blue sky.

She heard the door shut behind Isabel and clenched her fists together on the counterpane.

Benedict. Benedict, my son.

My flesh and blood.

It was not a name she would have chosen herself. It was a name for a child of the Dumases. Somehow, even the name made the gulf between Briony and her child wider.

Tommy Lane had had a good day. He was happy as he made his way up the path to Briony's house. In his hand he carried a bunch of flowers. Red carnations, blood red. He knocked at the front door with a flourish. He was looking forward to seeing Briony. The door was opened by Cissy, and he took in the split second hesitation as she looked at him and deliberately walked back into the hall. He smiled at her.

'I've come to see Miss Briony Cavanagh.'

'Well, I didn't think you'd come to see me, lad.'

Her sharp cockney accent made Tommy smile.

'I'm not sure what Mrs Horlock's going to say about this, I'm sure.'

'I'm not too worried about Mrs Horlock, love. You go and tell Briony that Tommy Lane's here and wants to see her.'

Mrs Horlock appeared as if from nowhere.

'You're not seeing anyone, young man.'

Tommy sized the old woman up and decided she sounded more ferocious than she looked.

'As I was just remarking to this young lady, you go and tell Briony that Tommy Lane's here. I think she'll see me.'

It was said with an air of confidence that made Mrs Horlock bristle.

'She's only just out of childbed. It ain't seemly!'

Tommy rolled his eyes and started walking up the stairs. Cissy watched Mrs Horlock dart up behind him and threw her apron over her head in shock, closing her eyes tightly. The cheek of him!

Brushing Mrs Horlock off like a fly, he opened all the doors he came to until he found Briony. Holding out the flowers at arm's length, he walked over to her with Mrs Horlock soundly berating him as she chased in behind.

'It ain't right, Miss Briony! This lout here needs a clout round the earhole. Pushing his way in and upsetting the whole house. Suppose the mistress had been here? What would have happened then, I ask you?'

Briony took the carnations and held them under her nose. She breathed in the scent of them and smiled. Her first real smile. Pointing them at Mrs Horlock, she snapped: 'In case it's escaped your notice, to all intents and purposes *I'm* the mistress here now! So take these flowers and put them in water, and then bring us some tea.'

Tommy stifled a grin at the look of utter shock on the old woman's face. But she did as Briony asked her, taking the flowers with a snatch of the hand and a glare in his direction, before stamping from the room, slamming the heavy door behind her.

'You look ill, girl, and I'm not surprised with that nutty old cow looking after you!'

He went to the window and opened it wide. 'Get some air in here, for Christ's sake.'

Briony watched him and felt a stirring inside her. She had needed a pick-me-up and it had come in the shape of Tommy Lane.

'So how are you then?'

Briony smiled at him. 'Not too bad, Tommy.'

He sat on the end of the bed and grinned at her. He knew instinctively that the child wasn't in the house. There was no evidence of it anywhere. He took in the white face and the bound breasts and his heart went out to the girl in front of him. He immediately launched into a convoluted story that made Briony laugh despite herself and forget her own worries for a few moments. Mrs Horlock, bringing up the tea tray, heard the laughter coming down the stairs and decided that she would not press Briony about the boy. If he could cheer her up, he could move in for all she cared! She brought in the tray of tea, and a little while later a tray of sandwiches and cakes, without being asked. As Tommy ate another sandwich in one gobble, Briony grinned.

'That means she likes you really, you got her angel cake.'

Tommy laughed. 'I don't care whether she likes me or not. We're friends, ain't we? Why can't I visit a friend?'

He finished his sandwich and then asked Briony the question that had been in his mind since entering the house.

'Where's the baby?'

She sipped her tea delicately and the natural grace as she did this made Tommy want to grab her and hold her to him. To look after her.

'Isabel – Mrs Dumas – took him last night.'

Tommy nodded.

'Well, it's for the best, girl. You're only thirteen, you don't want a nipper hanging around your neck at your age. Not only that, they can give him much more'n you could even if you had a man. Get yourself better, get yourself up and around. Start over again.'

Briony nodded at him, her face sad.

'Come on, Bri, you don't want to go worrying about what's done. You just start worrying about what you're going to do next. Now then, has she signed the house over to you?'

'Oh, yes, and she's put two thousand pounds away for me.'

Tommy gave a low whistle. What he couldn't do with that! He had the lowdown now on how to run a good 'house'. Once he had the capital, he would buy a place and run his own. He wouldn't stay the rest of his life at Nellie Deakins's. He looked at Briony and a glimmer of a plan formed in his mind.

'Would you care to invest five hundred in a little business venture with me, Bri?'

She was intrigued.

'What kind of business venture?'

Tommy took a deep breath and began to speak. And as Briony listened to him, to his plans, to his dreams, she felt a faint stirring in herself.

Chapter Nine

Briony looked around her and took in first the high ceilings, then the grey and gold flock on the walls, and lastly the rather garish chandeliers on the ceiling. She looked at Tommy who smiled at her. She nodded her head, smiling back.

The small stocky man with the handlebar moustaches, Mr Tillier the builder, grinned at them, showing pointed teeth.

'I knew you'd like it. I ain't overdone it, see? Now Nellie's place is nice, but it ain't got no class. All that red and burgundy, it looks what it is. This place, it's got a bit of class, and as you're having only a select clientele, well then, Bob's your uncle.'

He watched the young couple as they walked from room to room. The boy, or man as he tried to think of him, was cute. Cute as a nine-bob note, and as bent, but the girl – and she was a girl – was a completely different kettle of fish. He'd put her at no more than seventeen or eighteen, though he had heard through the grapevine that she was only coming up to her fourteenth birthday. Well, he mused, she must have pleased someone into giving her the money that she'd been spending like water. Her voice was nice, she spoke well, but it was forced. She still slipped in a 'bugger' or a 'bleeding' when she spoke to the young man.

He watched her climb the staircase. He was proud of the staircase. It curved round, and any of the ladies who walked down it would be shown to their best advantage. The chandeliers above it were of real crystal, their light giving off a bluish hue that made even the worst skin look good. As toms grew older it seemed the skin was the first thing to go with most of them, so good lighting was a priority for a class house.

He followed them up the stairs and into the first bedroom. This was done out in deep blue and peach, the bed a large fourposter with deep blue velvet drapes around it. Hanging up on the wardrobe door was a woman's wrapper of the same colour, as sheer as a spider's web. This would be called the Blue Room. Briony checked that everything was to her satisfaction and, seeing a pair of ornate cherubs over the fireplace, their features picked out in gold leaf, shook her head decisively.

'They'll have to go, Mr Tillier. I don't like them. A big mirror would be much more appropriate, I think.'

He nodded and wrote in his little notebook. She was cute all right. He'd thought they were a mistake himself. Although the walls to either side of the bed had large mirrors running the length of the panels, he thought that another mirror would not go amiss, especially when you thought of what the room was to be used for.

Both men followed Briony through the rest of the house. Each of them seemed to expect her to give the expert opinion and this she did, in a low voice that brooked no argument. There were now ten bedrooms of different sizes. The original six had been divided and rearranged and now there was plenty of room to accommodate ten men at a time. Briony walked down the stairs and through the hallway to the small offices set aside for herself and Tommy. Unlike the rest of the house these rooms were plain with good solid furniture. These were working rooms, and they looked it. Briony sat herself behind a mahogany desk and gently fingered the inkwells and the leather blotter in front of her. She was raring to go. In forty-eight hours she was opening the doors to the most select clientele she could gather. Thanks to Tommy's knowledge of Nellie Deakins's customers, they had arranged discreet invitations to the cream of London's society. Briony looked at her tiny fob watch and stood up.

'I have to go, Tommy, I'll leave the rest to you. I want the cherubs gone by this evening, Mr Tillier. I'll wish you both good day.'

She left them. Both men looked at one another and smiled.

'How about a glass of madeira, Mr Tillier?'

'That would be most excellent, Mr Lane.'

He took the proffered drink and was sorry the young lass had gone. She would have had the sense to offer him brandy.

Isabel sat in the park and chatted to Benedict in baby talk. She made a point of sitting away from the nannies and they allowed for this. Initially, they had praised the child and tried to strike up conversations, but once they found out who Isabel was, they respectfully kept their distance as they realised she did not want company. Then the chatter about Mrs Dumas had reached their ears, through a grapevine of scullery maids, tweenies, and finally cooks and butlers, until the knowledge that Henry Dumas had saddled his barren wife with the child of an unmarried woman, supposedly a widow of good standing, had resounded around London. Now they watched her carefully, seeing her obvious love for the child, and were frankly amazed by it.

Briony got out of her cab and told the cab driver to wait for her. She walked into Barking Park with a feeling of excitement at the prospect of seeing Benedict. She was dressed all in lilac, her hair pinned up in glorious tendrils under a matching hat. She walked with a dignity that was envied by most of the women who saw her, and her small-breasted figure looked just right for the fashions of the day.

Isabel saw her walking towards her and smiled widely. Benedict noticed her and started to clap chubby hands together, crowing with excitement. Briony sat down on the bench and looked into green eyes so like her own.

'How is he?'

'Thriving. Look at him. He doesn't stop eating and poor Sally is run off her feet looking after him. How are you?'

Briony peeled off her gloves and took her son's hands in her own.

'I'm OK. We open up soon, so I'm really busy.'

Isabel just nodded at this. The fact that Briony was to open a bordello shocked her more than she liked to admit.

'How's your mother?'

'Funny you should ask that, I'm going to see her today. Eileen's bad again. It's a shame because she started to get well for a while. Kerry and Bernie are fine as usual, and poor Rosalee . . . well, Rosalee never changes except to get heavier.'

'Did your mother take Eileen to the doctor I told you about?'

'Oh, him, yes. He wanted her put away, but we'll never allow that. We'll look after her.'

The two women were quiet now, both admiring the child in the perambulator.

'His hair's getting darker.'

'Yes, but he's still got your red highlights. I think he'll probably be a dark brown, like me.'

Briony nodded. She'd noticed that Isabel often tried to point out likenesses to herself in the child and far from being irritated by it, felt sorry for her. If poor Isabel had had a normal man and her own children she would have been an exemplary mother, her treatment of Benedict proved that.

'I have something to tell you, Briony. I've been trying to find the words . . .'

She was alarmed at Isabel's tone.

'What? Is – is Ben . . .'

'Oh no, nothing to do with him. Well, not directly anyway. We're moving up to the West End. Henry's bought a house in Belgravia and we feel it's about time we moved away. This house is far too small really, and my father would see more of Benedict . . .'

There, it was said. She didn't add that this monthly visit from Briony was worrying her. That she was frightened that now Benedict was getting older he might become too attached to the young redhead he saw in the park. That she was secretly jealous of the time he spent in his mother's company.

She could not look into Briony's eyes and see the hurt and confusion she knew she would find there. Instead she busied herself picking up the child and settling him on her lap. She kissed his downy head and hugged him to her. Briony watched as her son put his fingers up to Isabel's mouth and she kissed them, pretending to bite them gently and making the child laugh. Briony felt as if a stone had been placed inside her chest. A big solid weight that would eventually drag her down.

'I see.' But she didn't see. She didn't see at all. She was shrewd enough to guess what was really behind the action. She wondered who wanted the move most, Henry or Isabel.

'When will I see him then?'

'Oh, we'll sort that out in due course. I think it's best if the visits are cut down anyway. He's as bright as a button and might start saying your name, or when he's talking he might tell someone about you. That would not be good for any of us, let alone the child.'

Briony licked dry lips.

'But I must see him, Isabel. I have to see him sometimes.'

'And you shall see him, I promise. Only we have to be careful. If Henry knew he was seeing you now . . .'

She left the sentence unfinished.

Briony put her hand out to the child and he grasped her slim fingers, bringing them to his mouth to chew on them. Briony felt the tiny needle-sharp teeth as he gnawed and the familiar love for him overwhelmed her. If she was denied access to him she would die inside. Not an hour of the day went by but she thought of him. Everything else in her life was as nothing compared to this child.

'But I have to see him, Isabel.' Briony's voice was louder than she'd intended and Isabel put her hand on her arm.

'For goodness' sake, keep your voice down. Do you want all the nannies to know our business and take it back to their houses with them?'

Briony shook her head and Isabel settled the boy once more in his carriage and stood up.

'I really have to be going. I'll be in touch soon.'

Briony nodded weakly as she watched her son being pushed away from her. Her eyes blurred as tears stung them and she stared after Isabel and the child until they disappeared out of the park gates.

Molly was force-feeding Rosalee when Briony arrived. Rosalee was going through one of her not-eating phases. She swung between a state of constant hunger and one of not eating a scrap. Either way she still got heavier and heavier. Briony walked in the door and, kissing Rosalee's face, took the spoon from her mother and began to feed her sister. Molly watched as Rosalee ate every morsel Briony gave to her.

'You've certainly got a way with her, Bri. I wish to God I had it.'

Molly poured out two mugs of tea as Briony finished feeding Rosalee, then, taking off her hat, perched it on Rosalee's head and grinned at her.

Rosalee, looking ridiculous in the lilac confection, grinned back, saying her only words, 'Bri Bri' and clapping her hands together.

Molly tried to grab the hat off Rosalee's head but Briony stayed her hand.

'Oh, leave her alone, Mum, it's only a hat.'

'A hat that cost a small fortune.'

'So what? I don't mind, and it's my hat, so why should you care?'

Molly sipped her steaming tea and shook her head.

'I just saw Benedict. Isabel and Henry are moving up West with him. I think the days of letting me see him are numbered.'

Molly put a hand over her daughter's and said, 'Well,

what did you expect, love? They won't want you around now, will they? And it's better for the boy.'

'But I'm his mother, Mum. Me, not her!'

'I know that. But, Briony love, he's better off where he is and you must accept that. He's their child now. Theirs. Not yours. You just try and remember that this way he will have everything he ever wants out of life.'

Briony nodded. She knew that what her mother said made sense, but when you loved someone as she loved Benedict, it didn't make any difference.

'That Kerry is getting to be a handful, Briony. She was caught singing in the pub again. I've scalped the arse off of her but it's no good.'

Kerry, now twelve, was uncontrollable. She would sing in a midden if someone would listen.

'Where is she now?'

'She's out with Bernie and Mother Jones. They're pea picking.'

Briony was glad of the change in the conversation. She knew that her mother was all for Benedict being with the Dumases and it would only cause more rows if they discussed it further.

'Pea picking? Well, she can sing to her heart's content there.'

'True, and she will, knowing her. When's the house opening?'

'In a couple of days. It's finished, the girls are all interviewed and ready to go, and Tommy is sorting out the last few details today. We'll need a few more strong men like Abel to keep a modicum of peace.'

Abel was now one of the men employed to dress in dinner suits and mingle with the guests. If there was any trouble they would deal with it as quickly and unobtrusively as possible.

Molly shook her head and smiled.

'Imagine you owning two houses, I can't believe it.'

Briony smiled despite herself. Her mother had changed her opinion of Nellie Deakins and the like when she had found out how much money was involved in the business. Also Abel, whom Briony knew to be her mother's beau, had been offered a job at twice his old money and that made Molly happier still.

Kerry and Bernie burst through the door, bringing the smell of the open fields with them.

'Hello, Briony!'

Both girls kissed her and then Rosalee was clapping her hands together to show her excitement. They both screamed with laughter as they saw the lilac hat perched on her short-cropped hair.

Molly busied herself making them some tea and a bite to eat. Kerry sat opposite Briony and grinned at her.

'This house you're opening up, will you have any entertainment there?'

Molly looked at Briony with raised eyebrows. 'There'll be plenty of entertainment there, girl, don't you worry about that.'

Kerry sighed loudly. 'I don't mean *that* kind of entertainment. I mean, will you have a band there playing music or anything?'

Briony shook her head. 'No.'

'Then you should. It'll make it a bit different, wouldn't it? From what I've heard, the people what go there have a drink and a natter first. Well, why not give them a bit of entertainment like?'

'Such as, Kerry?'

She stood up and opened her arms wide.

'Like me, of course! I know all the popular songs and I'd only need a piano player like. I don't need no orchestra nor nothing. I can sing everything, you know that, Briony. It'd be good for you and good for me. I don't want to end up in Myrdle Street in some sweat shop, I want to be a singer.'

Briony laughed at her sister's outrageous suggestion. Kerry singing in a bordello? It was absurd.

'Oh, come on, Bri. You know I could do it. Just give me one try and if it don't work then that's that . . . Oh, Briony, answer me then!'

Kerry's voice was sharp now. She wanted this so badly she could practically taste it.

'Look, you're twelve years old . . .'

Kerry interrupted her.

'I want to sing, Mum, I don't want to work there as a doxie, do I? I will put on a nice dress and hat and just do a few lively numbers to get everyone in a good mood. That's all. Abel will be there to keep his eye on me, and Briony and Tommy. Where's the bleeding harm in that?'

Striking a pose that looked ridiculous in her pea-picking clothes, she began to strut up and down the kitchen, singing:

'Jeremiah Jones – a ladies' man was he –
Every pretty girl he loved to spoon.
Still he found a wife, along beside the sea,
Went to Margate for the honeymoon.'

Briony and Molly creased up with laughter as Kerry began. Coming to the chorus, she swept out her arms and roared at the top of her voice:

'Hello, Hello, who's your lady friend?
Who's the little girl by your side . . .'

Molly wiped her eyes with the back of her hand. As much as she scolded Kerry, she had to admit that the girl was talented and could be hilarious when the fancy took her.

Kerry knelt down in front of Briony and implored with her eyes. 'Oh, come on, Bri. Give me a chance.'

Briony grinned. She had needed a bit of fun today and should have known it would come from Kerry.

'I'll talk to Tommy about it. But that's all I can do, so don't get your hopes up.'

Kerry cuddled her sister close and shrieked out loud in excitement.

'Oh, thanks, Bri. Thanks. You won't regret it.'

Briony looked at her mother. 'What about you, Mum? What do you think?'

'Abel will be there as she says, and you and Tommy. It can't do any harm.'

None of them had noticed a jealous Bernie slip from the room.

Eileen came down the stairs and smiled at everyone and Briony looked at the thin vague-faced girl who had once been her bright and chatty sister, and felt depression descend again.

Sometimes life stank. And the worst of it all was, hers had hardly even started.

She tried to make conversation with her sisters for the rest of her time there, but her mind was on Benedict once more.

Briony had taken Kerry out shopping and bought her a green, high-necked, natural-waisted dress. It suited her perfectly and was respectable enough to please not only Briony but her mother and Abel as well. It had long sleeves with hanging three-quarter flounces in black lace. She had her black hair piled high on her head, and wore a large-brimmed black and green silk hat over it. She also had a green silk parasol which finished the outfit, and black button boots.

Briony stared at her, amazed. Kerry looked much older than her years, being taller than Briony already. She had on a small amount of make-up provided by Lil, one of the 'girls', and waited eagerly for Tommy to announce her.

'Oh, Briony, I'm so nervous, I could get tom tick!'

Briony laughed. 'Just relax. You're the one who wanted this, remember. Now just stay here until you hear the piano start and then make your way out.'

She kissed her on the cheek and left her in the small anteroom behind the main lounge.

Briony herself, dressed all in lemon, looked a picture. She had deliberately worn a close-fitting dress that accentuated her slim frame while revealing nothing. That much would be left to the working girls, who were all dressed in little more than stays and wrappers. The air was thick with cigar smoke and as Briony looked around her she felt a thrill of anticipation. It was their first night and the place was packed out.

She knew that most of the gentlemen normally went to Nellie's or other such establishments and wanted them to have such a good time here that they would come back again and again. Once more she blessed Tommy for arranging such a guest list. There were no Two Bob Joes in here, only men of means with respectable reputations. She was sure that the offer of a bit of entertainment would go down well, as the men liked to get a bit drunk before they retired to the bedrooms upstairs.

She made her way through the crowded room to the double doors where Abel stood surveying the room with a serious expression. A good-looking man grabbed her arm and tried to pull her to him. Briony shrugged him off good-naturedly and he grinned at her. Tommy, seeing the exchange, came over and introduced Briony to the man as his future wife. The customer apologised profusely before being dragged off by Tilly Rowlings who rolled her eyes good-naturedly at Briony as she did so.

'I'll just introduce Kerry and then I'll be back, OK?'

Briony nodded at Tommy and smiled. She watched him stand on the tiny makeshift stage and call for quiet. Everyone looked at him expectantly and he cleared his throat and introduced the new singing sensation, Kerry Cavanagh.

Kerry came out on to the stage, her face white with worry but, hearing the clapping and cheering from the men, she seemed to take on a different persona. A saucy wink at her audience and putting all her weight on to the parasol, she stuck out her behind. After nodding at the pianist who started to play her first number, she wiggled her rump, much to the merriment of the audience, and began to sing 'Hold Your Hand Out, Naughty Boy.'

Briony was laughing with the rest when she turned her head and her heart froze inside her chest. Standing at the front of the little crowd was Henry Dumas. She could see him perfectly, and as she watched him looking at Kerry she felt the bile rise inside her. He would like Kerry, she was just his type. No more than a child.

Briony grabbed Tommy's arm and pulled him from the

room and through the hallway to the offices. Closing the door with a quiet thud, she faced him.

'What's Henry Dumas doing here, Tommy?'

He saw the whiteness of her face and shook his head.

'I don't know, he must have come with one of the others. Look, Briony, I'll go out and keep me eye on him.'

'I want him out of here now, Tommy, I mean it.'

'You what? Our first night and you want me to sling someone out? Let me find out who he's with first.'

Briony could feel her hands shaking.

'You find out then, and after you find out, you give him the bad news. I don't want him in this house. Not now, not ever.'

Tommy walked over to her and grabbed her arms.

'Listen, Briony, you're only a girl for all your grown-up looks and ways. If any of them knew you owned the best part of this place, there'd be trouble. As it is now they think I've got a sleeping partner. I let the word go round that it's one of them, a rich bloke who's invested in me. If I go out there and rock the boat with Henry Dumas, he could fuck all of this up for us. Get it? Do you understand what I'm saying?'

Briony saw the earnest expression in his eyes and felt the futility of it all. What Tommy said made sense. If Henry decided to make trouble for her then he could ruin them, and she knew he was capable of it. She heard Tommy leave the room and sat in the chair, staring at the blotter in front of her without seeing it.

You had to be rich as Croesus before you didn't have to worry about anything. You had to be as rich as Solomon to know that you could do anything you wanted. Until then you had to keep your head down and kowtow to everyone and anyone. It was like gall to her, this knowledge. Henry Dumas had taken her childhood and her child. And still she had to pander to him. Indirectly, he still ruled her life.

Well, one day she would finish him. One day she would get even.

She would not venture out of the night. She did not know what she was capable of if she came face to face with him. On top of everything else they were taking her child to live far away from her. It was this, more than anything, that broke her heart.

Henry watched Kerry singing and was enthralled by her. He had had a lot to drink and now he felt a rosy glow enveloping him.

He walked unsteadily towards the stage and clasped his hands as the girl sang. She was singing a slow song now, and all the men and women around him were listening to the haunting voice, enjoying the sound and the timbre of it. Her little elfin face was captivating to him. He saw the jet-black silky hair that framed it and felt a stabbing pain in his heart. She was exquisite.

As Kerry finished her last number, she bowed to the audience who clapped her whole-heartedly. She was as good as any of the singers at Drury Lane, or indeed at any music hall. And she was no more than a child. A large man in the front of the audience, loving the ballad she sang, took out his purse and threw a sovereign on to the small stage. The other men in the room, not wanting to be outdone, did the same and Kerry scrambled around the floor in all her finery, picking up the coins.

The pianist began to play a solo number and Kerry picked up her money as fast as she could, amazed at the reception she had received and the generosity shown her.

As she picked up the last coin, a plump hand covered hers and she looked into the face of Henry Dumas.

'Hello, my dear. You really are a very good singer.' In his drink-fuddled brain he knew she reminded him of someone but he couldn't quite place who.

Kerry, though, knew him and, pulling her hand from under his, said: 'Hello, Mr Dumas.'

Standing up, she walked across the little stage and back into the ante-room. She placed all the coins on the small table by the door and, taking off her gloves, began to count them. Henry Dumas followed her a few seconds later. Opening the door, he popped his head around it playfully, moustaches quivering in anticipation.

Kerry backed away from him.

'How did you know my name, dear?'

Without thinking, she said: 'I'm Briony's sister.'

She watched him sober immediately as he registered exactly what she had said.

'You're Briony Cavanagh's sister?' His voice was full of surprise. As she opened her mouth to answer, he grabbed her arm in a vice-like grip.

'Where is she? Is she here? Answer me, girl, where is the bitch?'

Kerry pulled away from him, rubbing her arm.

'You touch me again, mister, and I'll scream the bleeding place down!'

As she spoke Tommy came into the room.

'I think you'd better leave the young lady alone, sir. Come along, I'm sure we can find you someone more suitable.'

He took Henry's arm firmly and led him from the room. Kerry watched them go and bit her lip. How did he get in here tonight? Surely Briony hadn't invited him?

She looked at the pile of coins but the excitement had gone from her now. She leant against the table and absent-mindedly rubbed her arm where he had touched her.

Henry was so deep in drink he didn't care any more. He had arrived at the stage where a shock or a loud noise can cause one of two reactions, maudlin sadness or great rage. Unfortunately for him, he felt great rage. As he walked through the room he tried unsucessfully to shrug off the iron grip of the young man escorting him. He saw his friend John Dennings embracing a young woman in a blue gauze wrapper, her huge breasts spilling out from white silk corsets. It made him feel sick.

All this flesh around him! He could smell cheap scent and fresh sweat. He could see garishly painted lips and eyes. He could feel the sexual charge of the men around him as they feasted their eyes on a bevy of young girls. But not young enough for him. They were women in his eyes, with breasts that jutted from their clothes in a disgusting fashion, hair between their muscular thighs and under their arms.

Tommy dragged him into the hallway, trying to prevent the trouble he knew was imminent. Without thinking, he pushed Henry into Briony's office and the two came face to face for the first time in eighteen months.

Briony stood up, shocked, and as they looked at one another, Henry seemed to grow before her eyes. He stood erect and stared into the sea-green eyes that his son had inherited. He laughed, a deep bitter sound that cut into her.

'So, the slut is working, is she?'

Tommy watched the two warily. It was as if an electrical charge had been placed between them and he stared, fascinated as Briony stalked around the desk.

'If I'm a slut, Henry Dumas, what does that make you? I can't think why you're here tonight. After all, the men who come to houses like this function normally. I wonder what they would say if they knew you were fancying a little girl – the girl they all clapped and cheered, without a bad thought in their heads towards her? Eh? Well answer me, Henry. If I remember rightly, you used to have a lot to say, most of it filth!'

'I'll finish you, Briony Cavanagh.'

She laughed at him now, her fear of him suddenly gone as she saw him for the pathetic fool he really was.

Her laugh goaded him. She was the cause of all his trouble. The reason for his wife's mutiny; for his father-in-law's happiness, that must therefore be Henry's apparent happiness. Here was the mother of the child he hated and despised because he had fathered it, because it had sprung from his loins and been birthed by the slut standing before him, laughing. Laughing at him. Well, he'd soon put a stop to that. He swung back his arm to strike her and she picked up one of the heavy inkwells.

'I'll split your head open without a second's thought, Henry Dumas! You think long and hard before you ever threaten me because I don't frighten so easily these days.'

Tommy grabbed at Henry and put his arm up behind his back.

'Come on, you, out! I don't think we want your sort in here.'

As he was pulled to the door, Henry faced Briony once more.

'I'll finish you, Briony Cavanagh. You and that bastard you saddled me with!'

She laughed again, louder this time, and it was as if the sound sent him into a frenzy. He threw Tommy from him and made to run at Briony. She stepped sideways and he hit the corner of the desk with all his weight behind him, sending him to his knees.

Grabbing his hair, Briony looked down into his face. 'You get out of here, you hear me? You get out of here because you don't know what I'm capable of where you're concerned.'

She looked at Tommy and waved her hand at the man on his knees before her.

'Take him away.'

Tommy did as she bade him. Dumas was quiet now. Tommy walked him out of the house and put him in his cab.

'You're not welcome here, keep that in mind. If I ever hear that you've tried to cause any trouble for her, or anyone to do with her, I'll see you dead. As rich as you are, as influential as you are, don't ever make an enemy of me, mate. You'll regret it to your dying day.'

Later that night, Tommy tossed and turned in his lonely bed. He knew that Briony had needed to face Dumas, it was something that had to happen eventually, and now it was over and done with. The rest of the night had gone well; they had pulled in over two hundred pounds. He shook his head in the darkness as he thought about it. The place was a success. All they had to do now was save up enough money to open another.

Briony had a natural talent for figures which amazed him. She had taken over the ledgers and the financial side of the business. Kerry too had been offered a regular job, her innocent little act having gone down very well with the men.

He turned over in bed. By rights he should be out

celebrating the success of his new venture, but he knew that the only person he wanted to celebrate with was Briony. He was nineteen years old, soon to be a man of real wealth and property. He had worked all his young life with these goals in mind and they had been put within his reach by a little girl called Briony Cavanagh. He knew now that he loved her, really loved her. He turned over in the bed again. The pillow felt as if it was stuffed with stones and he was too hot. As tired as he was, he couldn't find it in him to sleep.

He had moved into Briony's house a few months previously, because with all the preparations to be made, they could not be parted for any length of time. They had spent long evenings together discussing everything from the decor to the clientele. During this time he had consciously endeared himself to Mrs Horlock and Briony's mother Molly. Cissy, he was aware, was half in love with him so she liked him no matter what he did. It was Briony he wanted, though. Briony with her outrageous hair and her deep green eyes. He had fallen asleep many times in the last few months with the picture of her milky naked body lying beside him, his large rough hands caressing the tiny breasts. He turned once more in the bed.

As he closed his eyes tightly and tried to sleep, he heard the creak of the door opening. He sat up in bed as Briony, in a white nightdress, her red hair unbound, crept into his room with a candle in her hand.

'Are you asleep, Tommy?'

He was too astounded for speech.

Briony walked towards him and placed the candle on the night table. In the flickering light she smiled at him. He watched with fascination as she took the hem of her nightdress in both hands and pulled the garment over her head, revealing her body slowly and tantalisingly to him. She dropped the garment on to the floor and he pulled back the covers of his bed so she could slip in beside him.

He made love to her gently and firmly, taking in every part of her body with his hands and his tongue. It was like a dream come true to him. She had walked out of his mind and into his bed.

Briony for her part enjoyed the petting and the feel of him near her. She had needed someone after the events of the evening. She had needed strong arms around her and had got them the only way she knew how.

Tommy was not to realise that the feeling of closeness was the only part of sex that Briony enjoyed. So carried away was he in his own excitement he did not notice her mechanical responses. But that night, it didn't matter anyway. It sealed their fates. The coupling of their bodies was just an extension of their partnership.

At least, that was how Briony saw it.

Book Two

My sister and my sister's child,
Myself and children three.

– William Cowper, 1731–1800

With affection beaming in one eye and calculation shining out of the other.

– *Martin Chuzzlewit*
Charles Dickens, 1812–1870

Chapter Ten

1925

'Oh, for Christ's sake, Tommy, what the hell has got into you?' Briony's voice was hard and Tommy clenched his fists in an effort to keep his temper.

'I don't like it, Briony. For one thing it's expensive, for another you can't guarantee you'll make any money out of it.'

Briony laughed out loud.

'Oh, can't I? Listen here, Tommy Lane. On the continent these pictures are all the rage, mate. The French are shipping them over here like they're going out of fashion. Private viewings are bringing in a fucking fortune! I've more than looked into all this, believe me. That "useless ponce", as you call Rupert in your more friendlier moments, is the goose that's going to lay us some golden eggs. Tomorrow I put up a quick grand, then we sit back and rake the money in. We can show the films in the houses, have our own private screenings. We can get in on the bottom of the market before it takes off. And quite frankly, Tommy, whether you come in with me or not, I'm having some of it. It's the thing for the future, it'll make us untold money, I guarantee that.'

Tommy looked at the girl opposite him. Her face was alight, as it always was when she was talking about money. In fairness to her, he knew she had really done the groundwork on the films, she was too astute not to, but the thought annoyed him. Inside himself, Tommy actually found the thought of filming couples having sexual relations distasteful. He voiced this.

'I think it's perverted.'

Briony really did laugh now. A contemptuous sound that grated on him.

'Oh, Tommy, you're priceless, do you know that? Of course it's perverted! That's what makes the films a guaranteed money-spinner! Think about it. There've always been dirty pictures, silly naughty postcards with half-dressed women, that sell for a small fortune. Our boys even took them off to war with them. Where's the harm? In our houses we have paintings everywhere of couples having it off, they're part and parcel of the fixtures and fittings, so it seems logical to me to take it one step further. Moving pictures are what people want. All it takes is some girl flashing her clout and some bloke enjoying himself, and we're made. It's no different to what we do already.'

Tommy could see the logic of her argument, he was honest enough to admit that. It was more the fact Rupert Charles had approached Briony direct, as opposed to himself, that was the bug bear. But whatever way he looked at it all, the pictures – well, they didn't seem right.

Briony watched him battling it out with himself and felt

the familiar annoyance. Every time they ventured into a new area it was the same unless: Tommy thought of it first, then she was expected just to nod and go along with whatever he decided. When she thought of something it was days of discussing the pros and cons, Tommy humming and hahing, working out the costs, the overheads, the benefit it would be to the business. She knew that at times she made him feel inferior. She didn't mean to, but the fact would always remain that she was much quicker on the uptake than he. He would be the eternal heavy. She was the real brains behind them. Artfully, she tried a different tack.

'Listen to this, Tommy.' She picked up a newspaper beside her and began to read: ' "Josephine Baker, the sensational nineteen-year-old dancer of *La Revue Nègre*, is the talk of Paris. Her Charleston, slapping her buttocks in time to 'Yes Sir, That's My Baby!', and her bare-breasted mating dance, wearing nothing but strategic circles of coloured feathers, arouses audiences to frenzy. Colette calls her 'a most beautiful panther', Picasso calls her 'the Nefertiti of today', and Anita Loos speaks of her 'witty rear end'. Poiret and Schiaparelli are designing clothes for her, painters are begging her to sit for them and the Folies Bergères are wooing her to join the show . . ." '

Tommy interrupted her.

'What's she got to do with all this?'

'On the continent they're more relaxed about sex and anything to do with it. The sodding can-can was performed originally by women with no drawers on! This is 1925. People want more. They aren't as shocked as they once were. We have a whole band of punters out there with money to spend and not enough to spend it on. They can either go to Paris for a bit of a thrill, or we can provide it for them here. Once this filming is off the ground, I'm going to open more houses. Places where people, men and women, can get exactly what they want. Fuck Paris, mate, we'll have it all here in London! We've the contacts and the clientele. We can have private screenings of the films and then live entertainment. Live shows . . .'

'You're deadly serious.'

Briony grinned.

'Too right I am. Now, I'm doing this whether you come in or not. I mean it, Tommy. The filming first and the houses after. I want to own every decent house in London, and I will.' She stood up. 'I'll get us some more coffee.'

She left the room, giving him time to think.

Tommy watched her leave. She was, as always, beautifully dressed. At twenty-two she was glorious. Thank God she hadn't succumbed to the Eton crop which most women now sported. Her hair was still elaborately dressed with pins, but her clothes were up to the minute – up to the second, in fact. She wore the drop-waisted dresses with a jaunty air, showing wide expanses of milky white arms and legs. She plucked her eyebrows and drew them back on in wide, painted arches, and she wore deep red lipstick, painted on to her lips in a perfect Cupid's bow. She was the epitome of the new modern woman and sometimes, like now, it broke his heart.

She was right in all she said, he conceded that. She was always right. Maybe that was why she annoyed him so much. Like the jazz club she had insisted on opening, this very night in fact. Now it was up and off the ground she wanted another project as quickly as possible. And the pictures and the new houses were to be those projects. Oh, he had no doubt she would make a success of them, she always did. But he wished sometimes they could lead a calmer, more normal life.

He smiled to himself at the thought. Nothing about Briony Cavanagh would ever be normal. She was a law unto herself, had been from a child and, if he knew her, would be till the day she died. In fact, at times she wore him out with her endless enthusiasm. It wasn't natural to be driven like she was.

She wouldn't marry him, she was adamant about that. He had stopped asking her. But she slept with him, she ate with him, she dressed with him. That was as far as it went. She wanted no more children, she had made that as plain as day. In fact, it was only her sporadic visits to see her son that revealed any kind of human warmth or feeling in her. Then he saw the girl he had known before, the child, the Briony with whom he had fallen hopelessly in love. Her son, her sisters and the girls who worked for them were her whole life now. She looked after them all like a mother hen.

He knew she loved him in her own way, cared about him deeply, but not in the same way he loved her. Even knowing this, he couldn't leave her. He knew he would take whatever she offered him and be grateful, because he couldn't live without her. Acknowledging this to himself, he knew his course was set.

Briony walked back into the room with the tray of coffee and smiled at him, her tiny hands holding the tray steady. Placing it on the desk between them, she picked up the coffee pot. 'Shall I be mother?'

'You can be mother. And yes, Bri, I'm in on the new deals.'

She slammed down the coffee pot and rushed around the desk to plonk herself none too gently in his lap.

She kissed him hard on his lips and laughed.

'You won't regret this, Tommy. We'll rake the money in!'

He smiled and kissed her back.

'I know we will, Bri. We always do.'

He held her to him, feeling the smallness of her, the tiny waist, the firm breasts that poked through the thin material of her dress, and breathed in the scent of her. If only once he could spark some life into her sexually, he would be a happy man. He wanted to throw her to the floor and make love to her there and then, to make love to her and have her respond, just once, with the same passion he felt for her.

It was her total passivity that ensnared him, he knew. If he pushed her to the floor now, she would allow him to undress her, caress her body and make love to her as hard or as gently as he felt he wanted to. Then, when he was spent, she would get up, dress herself and smile at him, as she always did. He would not have touched her mind.

Instead he kissed her and petted her, the way he knew she liked, and held himself in check.

If she would only respond to him in bed . . . but he knew she never would. Though every time he touched her, he lived in hope.

Briony walked into her club The Windjammer at two-thirty in the afternoon. She smiled at the people milling around, putting the finishing touches to the place. As she passed the hat check girl she was amazed to see her bob a small curtsy. It made Briony smile widely. She walked into the club itself and eyed the room, taking in everything from the fresh flowers to the newly laid carpets. Briony was pleased. In the dimness she saw Kerry and Bernie on the small stage, talking to the piano player and saxophonist. She saw the excitement on her sisters' faces as they turned at the sound of her clattering heels on the wooden dance floor.

'Hello, Bri. I'm just going over the final numbers one more time. Want to hear them?' Kerry called.

Briony nodded and took a seat at one of the tables at the edge of the dance floor. She glanced around her as Kerry sorted through her music and was once more assailed with a feeling of happiness. She was more than satisfied with the place. The decor was brilliant: the walls painted a very pale gold and adorned with photographs, head-and-shoulders shots of the most beautiful women of the day. The largest was of Anna Pavlova, her eyes staring out across the room. Briony had also had musical scores framed and hung on the walls. The tables all had white cloths of pristine Irish linen and the glasses that sparkled behind the long carved wood bar were all good quality crystal.

It had cost a small fortune, but one of Briony's main beliefs was that you got what you paid for. Well, this was a jazz club, one of the first in London, and she had planned it on a grand scale.

She had hired a quarter of black American musicians who were thrilled to work at the new club, and even more thrilled with their wages. She dragged her eyes back towards the stage as she saw Kerry walk forward. She noticed the eyes of the pianist, Evander Dorsey, watching her closely. Their whites seemed to glow with the look and she smiled to herself. If he liked Kerry he would play even better. Everything had its good side for Briony. The fact he was black and looking at her sister did not shock her as it would have done others. She took everyone at face value. Always had and always would.

Kerry cleared her throat, and as the first few bars of the music struck up, Bernie slid into a seat beside Briony.

She watched the instinctive swing of Kerry's body. Unlike herself, Kerry was buxom and small-waisted. Her breasts looked too big for the fragile ribcage. She was also tall, her height giving her the grace to carry off the figure God had given her. Her short black hair, freshly bobbed, framed her face to perfection. Briony looked at her younger sister with a mixture of admiration and pride. Pride because it was she, Briony, who had made her sister's career possible. And it was she, Briony, who had looked after Kerry until now when she was making a name for herself with this new music called jazz. Unlike the majority of white women singers, Kerry could sing the blues, and everyone who heard her was spellbound. Briony knew that she was going to be big, much bigger than anyone had thought possible, and the knowledge was like balm to Briony.

Kerry's voice when she began to sing was as clear and haunting as the words of the song she sang about lost love.

The deep soulfulness of the voice carried across the room. Briony watched as the pianist shook his head in wonderment and delight and knew then that tonight her sister's career would be made. Her success was assured, and along with it the success of the club. Kerry would be their draw.

Ginelle Carson walked as if she owned the world. In fact, she felt as if she owned a small part of it. Ginelle was now a main attraction at Briony's top house. She had appeared in a couple of Briony's films and now her notoriety added to her value as a good-time girl. She was dressed in a long brocade evening coat and silver high-heeled shoes. She pulled her shoulders back as she stepped off the kerb and tottered slightly. A large arm came out and steadied her. Ginelle turned to face the man and smiled at him professionally. Her lips were a deep orange crescent and her eyes heavily made up, her youth hidden beneath a veneer of sophistication. She automatically put a hand up to her short cropped hair and patted it unnecessarily back into place.

'Thank you.' Her voice still held its East End sharpness, but she was working on it. The man gave her a smile that quickly faded.

'We're going for a little walk, love.'

Ginelle stopped dead and looked at him closely. Something in his voice made her heart beat faster. She tried to pull her arm from his but it was held in a vice-like grip.

'Here, leave go! Give over!' Her voice was rising and there was no trace of her refined tones now.

The man frog-marched her across the busy road and towards a waiting car. He bundled her inside without ceremony and the car pulled away from the kerb.

Ginelle had regained her composure by now.

'What the bleeding hell's going on here? Stop this car and let me out now!'

Her abductor turned to face her. Slapping her hard across the face, he said: 'Shut your trap before I punch your head in now instead of later.'

It was said in a low voice, completely devoid of emotion. Ginelle stared into the hard face and felt a sinking sensation somewhere in the region of her bowels.

But she shut up.

One thing in Ginelle's favour, she was clever enough to

know when she was in trouble and knew instinctively that tonight she was in the worst trouble of her life.

The thing that puzzled her was, why? What on earth had she done? She racked her brain for the remainder of the journey, staring vacantly at the red neck of the large man in front driving the car.

Ginelle was dragged from the car on the quay of the East India Docks. She stood in her ridiculous heels as various foreign sailors walked past, all looking at her with admiration tinged with fear, because of the two large men beside her.

They walked her between them, towards a small cabin that smelt strongly of molasses. Tearing her arms away, Ginelle began to run, her shoes giving the two men an unfair advantage.

The bigger man laughed as he caught up with her. He dragged her roughly back towards the cabin. By now she was shouting and screaming. Something inside Ginelle told her that if she entered that cabin it would be the end of her, and with a strength born of desperation she fought the man, her crimson-tipped nails flying dangerously close to his face. Taking back a large hairy fist he dealt her a blow to the side of the head that left her sprawling on the floor in the dirt and the mud, her ears ringing.

Men were watching the proceedings with shining eyes. Her dress had risen up in the tumble and her stocking tops were exposed; her silk drawers, freshly washed and pressed, smeared with dirt. Picking her up by her coat, the big man half dragged, half pushed her towards the cabin.

Ginelle was looking around her at the sailors, beseeching them with her eyes. She realised in a daze that some of the men were London dockers, all watching her and not one doing anything about it. They thought she was a dockside harpy. They didn't realise she worked for one of the most exclusive houses in the smoke, Briony Cavanagh's Mayfair house. That Tommy Lane was her boss along with Big Briony, as she was known, even though she was so tiny. That she commanded a fortune from men because she was a star of certain films shown to a select clientele, men who paid money to see her, and afterwards to bed her. She was someone of account, she was not a sailors' darling, she was important, important enough to be on first-name terms with her employers.

She opened her mouth to shriek these facts to the spectators, but a filthy hand closed over her mouth and she was dragged struggling inside the cabin. The men watching all went on their way, the pretty young girl gone from their minds already. A prostitute being beaten by her pimp was an everyday occurrence here, part and parcel of dockside life.

Inside the cabin it was dim. Ginelle registered first the smell, the deep scent of molasses, and underneath another of dankness and dirt, that brought back the filth and squalor she had been brought up in. It was a slum smell, a sweet, bitter, cloying smell that stuck to the clothes and never entirely left the nostrils.

Sitting behind a small wooden crate was a man whose face was lost in layers of fat. His eyes were like slits. Ginelle felt a final sinking of her heart as she realised who he was.

Willy Bolger was a pimp with a reputation for nastiness, violence and his perverted sense of humour. He was obese, his arms and legs looking too short and feeble to be any use, yet he was surprisingly fast with a knife. His teeth were pristine white, small and pointed as if he had chiselled them into shape. Now he smiled at Ginelle, who shuddered.

He shook his head slowly, languidly, as if he had known her for years, as if she was a recalcitrant child. The smile even displayed a sort of affection.

'Please, sit down.' He looked at the big man. 'Get the lady a chair!' The word 'lady' was said with exaggerated politeness. The big man dragged up a small three-legged stool and slammed Ginelle down on to it hard, jarring her already bruised spine.

'Forgive Seamus, he's no manners at all, my dear.'

Ginelle sat there, her hands icy cold, even in the foetid warmth of the cabin.

'What do you want with me?' Her voice was small. She sounded like the child she was for all her expensive clothes and make-up. Willy linked his fingers together on the crate in front of him and grinned again.

'I am going to hurt you, my dear. Nothing personal, believe me. But I want to get a little message over to a certain lady, and you, so to speak, are going to be my messenger. Hold her there, Seamus.'

He held Ginelle's shoulders in his vice-like grip, but there was no need. She had collapsed with fright, her body held up only by Seamus, because as Willy had spoken he had unlaced his fat fingers and picked up a large knife.

Willy walked towards her and tutted. He had hoped she would have stayed conscious long enough for him to hear her scream at least once. Sighing hard with disappointment, he picked up a wooden pail which was used by the night watchmen to relieve themselves and threw it into her face.

Ginelle spluttered to life, the urine stinging her

eyes. Then, humming softly between his teeth, Willy started cutting, and was pleased to hear her scream, not once but many times as he removed first her nose, then her ears.

Seamus watched the proceedings with a bored air. His eldest daughter was getting married and he had to take her to see the priest later that day. Now he'd have to go home and change first, Blood was an absolute bastard to get out, and his wife would have his guts.

Ginelle slumped to the dirty floor, her clothes staining crimson, the brocade of her coat soaking it up like a sponge.

Tommy looked around the club and smiled. The Windjammer's first night was better even than they had hoped for. It was packed to the rafters with people, the atmosphere was electric and the cash was pouring in over the bars. Tommy lit himself one of the cheap cigars which he still had a penchant for, and smiled delightedly.

The whole place stank of money and he loved it. He nodded and waved to different people as he made his way through the tables. The resident band, which was to play between Kerry's sets, had struck up with the 'Black Bottom'. Girls – some debs and some shopgirls – leapt on to the wooden dance floor and began to jiggle around, their dresses shimmering in the lights. There were more than a few bright young things, hanging off the arms of young men who had been boys in the war and were now the new monied generation. If nothing else the war had taken down a few of the class barriers, but Tommy knew with his latent shrewdness that it was only a beginning.

He scanned the room again and saw Briony. She

looked stunning in a gold sheath dress that emphasised her fashionably boyish figure and was the exact shade of the walls. The glorious hair, that he loved to caress in the darkness of the night, was piled on top her head. She looked beautiful to him. She would always be beautiful to him.

He frowned as he saw who she was sitting with. Jonathan la Billière was an actor, or so he said anyway. Tommy had never heard of him. He was one of Rupert's little band, which meant he must be as queer as a fish.

Rupert Charles was the typical bad boy, handsome and rich. His father had died in the war, leaving a fortune to Rupert's mother, a ridiculous woman much given to wearing clothes too young for her and with an appalling taste in men, and to Rupert, a rather spoiled young man who had never had anything to do with the actual making of money, only the spending of it. Now he financed movies as he liked to call them, and everyone thought he was quite the thing, and fought to claim friendship with him. Rupert in turn loved the notoriety of Briony and fought to become a crony of hers. It made Tommy smile sometimes, the double standard, but not tonight, because Jonathan was watching Briony with an intent gaze. It seemed he wanted her. Perhaps he wasn't queer after all. Tommy could see the tell-tale expression. He knew it well. But Jonathan wouldn't have her. Even if she succumbed and slept with him, he wouldn't have her. Not in the way he wanted. Knowing this pleased Tommy.

He dragged his eyes from them and made his way back to the offices. He wasn't in the mood tonight for all that theatrical old fanny. He needed a couple of stiff drinks.

*

Being a Friday evening, the Mayfair house was packed. The girls working nights started at six-thirty at weekends. Many men arrived at six, retired to bed at six-thirty and arrived home to take out their wives around nine-thirty. So at seven-thirty the house was already buzzing. Winona, the head girl, was counting out money in her office when a repeated ringing on the bell brought her out personally to answer the front door. Heidi, the young girl paid for this job, was at that moment helping one of the 'young ladies' to brush out her hair. Winona opened the large front door wearing her plain black dress and professional smile. It died on her lips as she saw a crate left on the doorstep and no one in sight.

She walked out of the house and down the front steps, searching the street for a messenger or someone who could have left the heavy crate. The street was as usual quiet and empty, except for a few motorcars. Turning, she walked back up the steps and sighed loudly. She called down the back stairs for two of the men who worked there, and between them they hefted the crate through to the offices. Winona finished counting her money before she once more turned her attention to the crate. There was no address on it, no message, nothing. Briony had not mentioned any deliveries. She frowned in consternation. The new club was opening tonight so Briony wouldn't thank her for calling her away over a crate, but something wasn't right here.

Winona had a long nose – her mother had always said it was long enough to pick a winkle – well, that nose was quivering now, scenting trouble. She went to the crate and looked at it just as Heidi, the young maid, walked through the door.

'There's a Mr Blackley up top, wants to know where Ginelle is. Says he'd arranged to see her tonight.'

Winona turned, pulling herself up to her full height. 'How many bloody times do I have to tell you, girl, knock before you enter a room!'

Heidi blinked rapidly, a nervous habit that drove Winona to distraction. 'And for fuck's sake, stop blinking blinking!'

Heidi, all of eleven and looking nine, blinked even harder. 'Me mum says if you shout at me it won't get any better, it's me nerves like.'

Winona raised her eyes to the ceiling.

'Tell Mr Blackley that Ginelle will be along shortly, then nip round her mother's and see if she's there. Since she became Briony's blue-eyed girl, she's really started pushing her bleeding luck! Well you tell her that she can get her arse round here, she still works in this house as a whore no matter what else she might be involved in, and I run this place for Briony Cavanagh. I am the head girl, and I ain't putting up with tardiness!'

'With what?' Heidi's voice was incredulous.

'Just go and do what I say, will you!' Winona made a conscious effort to keep her voice down, but this child really was the limit.

After that, Winona was called on to sort out more than one petty drama, so she didn't open the crate until nine fifteen. It was an act she was to regret all her life.

Briony watched with shining eyes as Kerry came on stage. The lights were dimmed and Kerry looked much too pretty and much too young to be a real singer, but the audience were with her, Briony picked that much up from the atmosphere.

The first few bars were played by Evander Dorsey then Kerry began to sing.

The people who had still been chatting paused to look and listen properly. The whole club seemed to quieten and Kerry, feeling the reaction, put more and more emotion into the song.

As the last few bars were played, she was greeted with a standing ovation, drinks were raised and feet thumped on the wooden floors.

Briony laughed with delight. She had known this was going to happen, she had counted on it.

She was still clapping and smiling when Tommy came to the table and whispered in her ear.

Jonathan, clapping and smiling himself, was shocked to see Briony's face drain of all colour. She got up from the table, smiled half-heartedly, said her goodbyes then immediately left the club.

Jonathan la Billière watched her leave. There was trouble brewing there, he would lay money on it. Well, he was seeing her next morning, and he was looking forward to that. He was looking forward to it immensely.

He turned his face back to the stage where Kerry had just started singing a lively number. He enjoyed the rest of the set. But the memory of Briony's white face stayed with him.

Tommy and Briony arrived at the Mayfair house just after eleven. They walked into its pink warmth, slipping off their coats as they entered the front door. Heidi took the coats without a murmur, her eyes blinking in overtime now with the shock the house had had. Briony and Tommy went through to the office where Winona was sitting at her desk, her face grey, hands clutching a large glass of brandy.

'She's dead, Bri . . . But it's Ginelle, all right.'

Tommy lifted the lid of the crate and stared into it. Ginelle, minus nose, ears and breasts stared up at them. Her hands were fingerless, bloody stumps crossed over her body in some grotesque parody of the funeral rite.

Briony felt first the burn of bile as it welled up inside her throat, then she felt rage, a white rage that there was no reasoning against. Ginelle was just eighteen years old. She kept her mother and her younger sisters on what she earned. She was a nice girl, a kind girl. Whoever did this had better start saying their prayers, because she, Briony Cavanagh, was going to have their balls on a plate!

'Who knows, Winona? Who knows in the house?' Briony's voice was hard and brooked no nonsense.

'Heidi knows. She came in just as I opened the crate. Denice knows and Lily. They're keeping it quiet. I told them not to alert the rest of the girls.'

'Good . . . good. You did the right thing.'

Briony looked at Ginelle again and then at Tommy. Her voice was shocked and disbelieving as she spoke.

'Why would anyone do this, Tom? Why?'

It was the first time in years he had seen Briony shaken, and it saddened him.

'I don't know, Bri. But I have a feeling we'll find out soon enough, love. This is a message of some sort. What we have to do is find out who sent it.'

She nodded and stared at Ginelle's remains again, remembering the girl's laughter of the week before, remembering when she had come to her for a job in her ragged dress and her mother's shoes. Remembered her chatter, her unaffected pleasure in life, and felt rage once more for the destruction of a young life.

'Yeah, Tom, we'll find out who sent the message and

then I'm gonna muller them. Me personally. No one, but no one, touches me or mine . . . So whoever sent this so-called message better start saying their prayers because, as Christ is my witness, they'll need all the fucking prayers they can get!'

Chapter Eleven

Molly was brushing out Rosalee's hair. Unlike years before, when it had been cropped to keep the lice at bay, Briony had insisted on having her sister's hair left to grow. Now Rosalee sported a mass of thick blond curls.

'Would you keep still, Rosie darlin'!' Rosalee was fidgeting, moving her head from side to side and making low guttural noises which annoyed the life out of Molly.

Eileen walked into the kitchen and Molly smiled, a real smile that encompassed the girl from head to foot.

At twenty-eight Eileen was much better. Her nerves were still bad, but she had stopped her wandering and the nonsensical conversations were long gone. She even had a beau of sorts, a friend of Abel's who took her for long walks and listened avidly to all her chatter. He was a good deal older than Eileen, but Molly wasn't against that. Eileen needed a man who was settled. A man who would look after her.

'I've had a really good time, Mum. Joshua took me to Bow. We shopped in the little market and stopped for pie and mash. And I bought some material, I thought I might make meself a dress.'

Molly was amazed at those words. Although Eileen was clean, God knows she was forever washing, she still had that unkempt look about her. The shapeless garments she wore were such a part of her that the thought of her wearing anything even remotely nice was like music to her mother's ears.

'But Briony is always offering you money for clothes and you turn it down.'

Eileen faced her mother.

'I don't want anything from Briony thank you very much. I know she means well, but the thought of wearing anything bought with the money she makes . . .'

'Oh, all right, Eileen love, leave it, leave it. You make yourself something nice if that's what you want.'

Molly sighed heavily. It was still a sore point with Eileen about Briony, and Molly, who had once been her daughter's most ardent opponent, was now her most ardent supporter. The girl had taken the bit of money from the Dumases and turned it into a small fortune. Also, Molly could deny no longer her own involvement in both her daughters' downfall. Though the word 'downfall' was certainly not how she would describe Briony's life.

'Kerry's not been then?' Eileen tried to make amends.

'To be honest, I don't think she remembers where she lives!'

This was said with pride and without any malicious feeling against Eileen who didn't work, let alone keep herself. It was this fact that galled Molly most about her eldest daughter. She balked at accepting Briony's money but had no intention of going out and earning any for herself. Molly didn't say this though, because now

Eileen was back on her feet she didn't want to rock the boat.

Bernadette came down the stairs and both women smiled at her. 'Did our Kerry come home, Bernie?'

'I ain't her keeper, Mum, only her dresser. She probably stayed overnight with someone.'

She poured herself some tea and smiled craftily to herself. She knew who Kerry had stayed with all right, but she'd keep the knowledge to herself a while longer.

'How did it go last night? Was it a success?'

'Oh, yeah. Kerry went down a storm. Everyone was raving about her. But it's funny, Mum, Briony was called away quick like. She looked rough I can tell you. I reckon there was hag at one of the houses.'

Molly put down the brush and went to the table to pick up her mug of tea. 'What do you mean, trouble?' Her face was clouded.

'What kind of trouble do you normally get in those places?'

Eileen's voice was low and Molly stopped herself from clouting her. Sometimes Eileen's holy Joeing, as she called it to herself, really got on her nerves.

Bernie laughed.

'Look, stop worrying, you know our Briony. If there's trouble it will be sorted by now. It was a shame really because she missed most of the opening. Oh, Mum, you should have seen some of the people there! Really rich like, their clothes . . . Even the air in there smelt nice, with all the perfumes and that.'

Molly nodded, pleased. This was more like it, this was what she wanted to hear. 'Were there any titles there?'

Bernie pushed her face close to her mother's and smiled. 'The place stunk of titles, Mum, it was really, really impressive. Our Briony is gonna make a bloody fortune.'

Molly sipped her tea and grinned.

That was more like it all right. She lived now in Briony's shadow, loving her notoriety, enjoying the stir her daughter created. People spoke about her in tones of awe. She was both loved and feared, and that, as far as Molly was concerned, was exactly how it should be.

Evander looked down at the girl asleep in his bed and felt his heart constrict. What the hell had he done? She was no more than a child really, for all her body and her incredible voice. She was a white woman. He had spent the night with a white woman.

Now hold on, a voice whispered at the back of his mind. You ain't in the States now.

But if certain people knew about them, it would be like the States all over again. There was something about a black man and a white woman that incensed people. Women as well as men. He had grown up under that cloud and had thought to die without ever knowing the pleasure of a clean white woman. Oh, he had slept with white women before, poor white trash who had gone to the bad and were thought diseased so sold their body only to the black boys.

All this talk about niggers over here . . . about how niggers could dance, niggers had natural rhythm. They liked your music and your soulful songs, they liked to be seen with the black musicians, it made them look very hip, but if they thought you were sleeping with one of their women they'd turn like a pack of bloodhounds. What was it that Shakespeare guy had said? There's an old black ram, tupping your ewe? Well, that was exactly what Evander had done. And he had loved every second of it!

Kerry was worth anything they might throw at him, though. The smell of her, the feel of her silky black hair, was like nothing he had ever experienced before. And she had been a virgin, that was the most fantastic part! A virgin. In the darkness of the night before he had been too carried away with wanting her to think of the consequences. Now, as she lay asleep and the sun burned through the dirty windows, the thought made him feel physically faint though he was aroused again.

'Evander, my love. Come back to bed.'

He looked at her face and saw her staring at his enlarged member with the same fascination as he had stared at her. He watched as her long thin white fingers caressed him, running down the length of him and caressing his genitals, and groaned out loud. He knelt beside the bed and caressed her large white breasts with their pink nipples, and knew he was lost then. Any sensible thoughts were gone now, completely overshadowed by the milky-white skin and the wet pinkness between her legs.

Briony and Tommy were sitting down to lunch but Briony just pushed her food desultorily around her plate.

'Last night was a resounding success anyway, Bri.'

She nodded.

'Good. Kerry went down well.'

'Look, Briony, worrying about it ain't gonna make it go away.'

She shook her head.

'I tell you, Tommy, every time I think about Ginelle, I feel a rage in me. I can't stand this hanging around, waiting for the next move. Suppose they touch one of the other girls?'

'We've got them all watched. Fuck me, Bri, even King

Street Charlie couldn't get in one of the houses at the moment.'

'I think we should tell the girls. They have a right to know.'

Tommy pushed his plate away in temper.

'Oh, yeah? Start a general exodus, why don't you? The less the brasses know the better. They've got mouths like the parish ovens. It'd be all over the smoke by tonight. "Briony and Tommy have got trouble. Big trouble." Once word like that hits the pavements every little ponce with dreams of the big time will be out mob-handed. We've gotta play this one close to our chests, wait and see what develops. If it was a loony, say a bloke with a grudge, he wouldn't have had her delivered to the house, would he? That was personal.'

'Did it ever occur to you that it could be a customer? A bloke who's got a grudge all right. It's all right for you, ain't it? You ain't gotta go round and give Ginelle's mother the bad news, have you? You ain't gotta go round and tell her that her daughter's died. I've got to make up a story that she had an accident or something. How can I tell the woman that her daughter, her main bread winner, was cut up like a fucking piece of meat on a butcher's slab!'

Briony stared at Tommy hard then. Something in what she'd said had sparked off a train of thought. Now it had gone. Disappeared as quickly as it had come.

'What's the matter, Bri?'

'Just then something came to me mind, and went again.'

Tommy got up from his seat and walked around the table to her. Putting an arm around her, he pulled her to him.

'Look, love, just try and relax. As soon as we get word, whoever it was is history.'

Briony nodded sagely.

'Oh, they'll be that all right, Tommy. I'm gonna pay this one back myself. Personally.'

He held her close. Never had he seen her so intent on anything in her life. It was as if Ginelle's death was a personal affront. As if the girl was a daughter or a sister. Tommy would never realise the feelings Briony had for her girls. She loved them. Each and every one.

'It had to come now, didn't it, when we was branching out? I'm supposed to be seeing Nellie Deakins this afternoon. If word's got to her ear then I'll be a laughing stock.'

Tommy kissed her cheek, a wet smacking kiss.

'Nellie's an old has-been, Bri. Christ, I used to work for her meself when I was a boy. No one will hear anything about any of this, I guarantee that. We have to sit on it, just be patient. Then once we know what we're dealing with, everything will come right. OK?'

She nodded. But the thought of Ginelle wouldn't let her rest.

Mariah Jurgens was a big woman. Her grandfather, it was said, had been a large and troublesome Swedish sailor; her mother and grandmother were what was termed Bog Irish. Her father unknown. Mariah had the white-blond colouring of her grandfather and the Irish temperament of the women in her family. Six feet tall in her stockinged feet, she had a body the like of which was rarely seen. Twenty years before she had been a highly sought-after courtesan. Her huge breasts and tiny waist, coupled with her sheer height and unusual colouring, had been prized by rich men. She had known her high price was for her sheer novelty value and had enhanced it with a pair of shoes especially made with high heels so that she looked even taller than she actually was. The fact that the majority of her clients were small men had made her laugh as she salted away the guineas; as she felt like laughing now, at the little man in front of her. She watched him take a pull on his cigar. It smelt expensive and was nearly as big as the little man himself.

'So, Mariah, what do you say?'

She spat into the fire and shrugged nonchalantly.

'Let me think it over, I'll get in touch with you tomorrow.'

She watched the man frown and felt the urge to laugh again. 'You do realise what I'm offering you?'

She nodded, serious once more. 'I do.'

'So what's to think about?'

'Mr Bolger, I always think over everything before I commit myself. It is, to my mind, the only way to do business.'

'As you wish, Mariah. I will expect your answer in the morning.'

He stood up to leave and she stood too. Towering over the man, she put out a large hand with fingernails painted bright red and grasped his tightly, emphasising the size and strength of her own. He left the room and Mariah rang her bell. It was answered by a young blonde, at whom Mariah smiled sweetly.

'Bring me some decent brandy and something to eat.'

'Yes, ma'am.' The girl was nervous. Mariah changed with the weather. From being a big cuddly woman she could turn into a demon from hell in an instant. Mariah was known as a woman who could 'turn on a coin', so unstable was her temper. It was something she nurtured in her madam's role, a trait that was mandatory in her profession.

She relaxed back in her seat, her mind racing. Bolger was as bent as a two-bob clock. So he was, in reality, offering her something he eventually wanted to take back from her. She had settled that in her mind immediately. He wanted something that Briony Cavanagh had, and that meant he was willing to take on Tommy Lane. That in turn told Mariah he had a lot more backing than usual.

Bolger was just a small-time pimp, really. He now had visions of hitting the big time, and this could only be brought about by an alliance with someone else. An original thought in Bolger's head would die a slow death from loneliness. No, there was a bigger fish involved in this, a much bigger fish, but who? The girl came back with the brandy and food. Thanking her, Mariah told her to send in Big John. While she waited for him she wrote a note to Briony Cavanagh, asking her to visit her establishment at seven that evening. Two bitches had always had more going for them than one dog, and she had heard through the grapevine that Briony Cavanagh was as sharp as a razor.

Sandy Livingston walked along the Caledonian Road with his youngest son, Pete. The boy was so like his father it was startling to see them together. Pete was only fifteen, but already he was as tall as his father. Both men had watery blue eyes, ruddy complexions and the sandy hair and eyebrows that gave the older man his nickname. Pete loved his father. He knew he was notorious as a heavy, that he was paid huge sums to hurt people, and looked forward eagerly to the day he could join Sandy in the family business. His eldest brother Joseph was already making a name for himself, as were Martin and Eddie, his other two brothers. The Livingstons were a force to be reckoned with around Silvertown, or anywhere in the East End in fact.

Sandy saw the woman approach out of the corner of his eye. He automatically faced her and nodded in a friendly fashion.

'Hello, Miss Cavanagh.'

Briony smiled lazily.

'Hello there, Sandy. Come inside a moment, I want to see you.'

Sandy looked surprised at the request but followed Briony into the tiny terraced house without a thought. He knew Tommy and through him Briony Cavanagh. He respected her, a thing that was previously unheard of as Sandy Livingston had never respected another woman in his life, not even the wife who had borne his sons with the minimum of fuss and then looked forward to nothing but the back of his hand at least once a week.

Pete followed his father into the tiny house with exaggerated nonchalance, hands pushed into the pockets of his trousers in a parody of his father and brothers. Inside the house they were startled to see Tommy Lane and two big Arabs standing in the front room.

'Hello, Tommy. All right?'

Sandy looked around him, a trickle of fear running up the base of his spine.

Pete watched as the two large Arabs grabbed his father and pinned his arms to his sides.

'What's going on here? You leave my old man alone!'

Pete was frightened now. His big dad, whom he took such pleasure in bragging about, was scared – and this fact terrified the boy. Briony pushed him out of her way and dismissed him.

'Shut your trap and you'll be all right.' She looked at Sandy. 'He's like the spit out of your mouth, ain't he, Sandy boy?' Her voice was low now, even friendly.

Sandy licked his lips with a yellow-coated tongue.

'Look, Miss Cavanagh, I don't know what's going on here, but I swear, whatever I'm supposed to have done . . . well, I never done it!'

Briony and Tommy laughed. Briony slipped her hand into the waist of Sandy's trousers and took out the large boning knife he kept there. She took it out of its leather sheath and stared at it for a few seconds before placing the tip at Sandy's throat.

'You could do a lot a damage with this, Sandy, cut someone to pieces. But then, that's what you do best, ain't it? Cut people? For a sum of money?'

'I swear on my boy's life I ain't cut no one you wouldn't want cut . . .'

'Shut your mouth and listen! I'm gonna ask you something and if you lie to me you're dead, Sandy, dead as a doornail. I ain't joking.' Briony held a finger up to his face. 'Did you cut one of my girls, Sandy? The truth now, I want the truth. A little blonde bird called Ginelle. As God is my witness, you lie to me and I'll cut your fucking throat meself.'

Sandy looked down at the tiny woman in front of him. He met her hard green stare and swallowed deeply before he answered.

'No. I ain't cut no brasses. I swear to you I ain't cut no brasses! Not for yonks.'

Briony nodded slowly, watching his fear and sniffing it into herself, trying to assuage the rage inside her.

'Then who has, Sandy? All you cutters know one another, you all talk. Who is cutting up my girls? You give me the name and I'll see you all right, boy, but I must have a name.'

Pete watched his father battle it out with himself. He knew that grassing was the worst thing a cutter could do. Because cutters were the bad men, the really bad men, and they were the hardest. Hard men did their time, kept their heads down, and emerged from prison with their reputations intact, happy to take on the mantle of hard men once more. He held his breath as he watched his father.

'I heard a whisper that Willy Bolger done a brass yesterday, down the docks. It was just a whisper, mind, from another cutter. I don't know the strength of it like . . .'

Briony sighed heavily.

'That's all I wanted to know.'

She nodded at the two Arabs and they let Sandy go. Briony handed his knife back to him and smiled.

'No hard feelings, Sandy, this was just business, boy.' She looked at Tommy. 'Give him a monkey, he's working for us now. Exclusively.' She faced Sandy and smiled. 'That OK with you?'

He nodded furiously. 'Yeah, I don't mind. I'm ready when you are, girl.'

'Then you can go.' As Pete and Sandy were leaving the room, Briony shouted after them.

'One last thing, Sandy. I don't want any mention of what took place in this room, from either of you. Otherwise I would be very annoyed, you see, and let's face it, Sandy, there're more than a few cutters around, aren't there?'

He nodded again, his face serious.

Outside on the pavement he walked along with his son,

quiet and subdued. 'Little Pete', as his mother called him, searched his father's face and swallowed down his disappointment. His dad was a grass. The knowledge broke his heart.

Even worse, though, was the fact that his father was frightened of a tiny little lady with red hair and green eyes and the smallest feet he had ever seen. Even surrounded as she was with big men, little Pete had felt the fire from her, had felt the menace, and as upset as he was, felt a tremor of pity for whoever had angered her so much. If she could frighten his father, she could frighten old Nick himself.

'Well, you was right, Bri. But it wasn't Sandy. I heard a whisper a while back that Willy was branching out, but I didn't dream it was in our game. He's more a heavies' heavy, if you know what I mean. He pimps, but not for our kind of girls. He's always dealt exclusively with the rough trade.'

Briony nodded, her face set in a frown that etched deep lines on her forehead.

'I have to scoot in a minute, I have to see Nellie Deakins and then Mariah Jurgens. I wonder what Jurgens could possibly want? I have a feeling in me boots she's involved in this somehow. It seems more than coincidence that she wants to see me after one of my girls gets topped.'

'There's no harm in Mariah, I knew her years back. She was always straight, Bri, always fair.'

Briony laughed bitterly.

'Tell that to Victoria Staines's mother. Her daughter still carries the scars of her run-in with Mariah to this day!'

Tommy sighed. 'You'd have done the same, Briony. If

a girl is thieving you got to put the hard word on them, otherwise before you know it all the brasses are having a field day.'

'I can see you like her. Well, I promise to be very, very nice, unless she upsets me. I'll hear her out. But if she tries to cross me, I don't care how big she is, I'll wrap her from one end of London to the other! I ain't in the mood for fun and games at the moment.

'Now, you find all the cutters in town, and see if they're working for Bolger. I'm going to see him, but first I want to know exactly how much muscle he's got. He's more slippery than a greased eel, but he's made two bad mistakes. One, he touched something of mine, and two, the bastard has the audacity to think he can frighten me. Me, Briony Cavanagh! Well, he's got the shock of his fucking life coming to him. I'll pay him back tenfold for Ginelle, and for taking the piss.'

Tommy looked at her with awe and a tinge of respect. Never before had he seen her like this, and much as it troubled him, he was happy to know she would always look after herself and her own.

'*We'll* get him, Bri. We as in us.' His voice was low.

Briony went to him then and he pulled her into his arms. 'Yes, Tommy boy. We'll get him.' She looked up into his face and tried to smile. 'But I'll cut the bastard, you owe me that. I'll be the one to cut him.'

Tommy nodded almost imperceptibly. It was what he had expected.

Nellie Deakins had grown big over the years. Now she was ponderously fat. Her neck, which had once been long and smooth, sported several chins. Her eyes were embedded in the fat of her face. She looked constantly as if she had just run a considerable distance, though she rarely left her chair. She puffed herself through each day, and even her girls had begun remarking on the unsavoury smell emanating from her.

Nellie had always ruled by fear; nowadays she relied heavily on her reputation from her younger days to keep order in her house. Nellie had once beaten a girl nearly to death, her crime to tip her hat at one of Nellie's boys. As Nellie had grown older she had taken an undue interest in young men. Big handsome young men whose only duty was to treat Nellie with a bit of respect, light the cigars which she smoked constantly and hold doors open for her. It was the illusion of youth and desirability that Nellie still fostered, even though the illusion was nowadays quite incongruous. Nellie wasn't really a jealous woman; she had beaten the whore for the simple reason that, if you let them get away with the little things, soon they'd try for bigger. Nellie had lived by that adage all her life. Until now, that is. Nellie was only sixty-two years old, not a great age for a madam. But she was so fat and lazy that the day-to-day running of her establishment had become something of a bind to her. She knew, deep down, that she had lost the urge to keep the place going, keep outwardly respectable and, worst of all for a madam, the urge to look out for her girls.

Now she had that young scut Briony Cavanagh coming to see her. Nellie pursed her lips to stop them twitching into a smile. She was a clever girl, that Cavanagh. Clever, good-looking and sensible. A lethal combination for a madam. Opened her first house with Tommy Lane when she was just a little girl, a greenie. Now the word on the street was that Briony was branching out into all sorts of skulduggery, legal as well as illegal.

Nellie sat back in her well-padded chair and absent-mindedly unwrapped a sweet. Popping it into her mouth, she waited patiently for Briony Cavanagh to arrive and say what she had to say.

Briony walked into Nellie's house with barely concealed shock. The door had been opened by a girl of about nine who had sniffed loudly as Briony introduced herself and said at the top of her considerable little voice: 'You'd better come in.'

She had then been left in the hallway a good ten minutes before she realised the little minx had forgotten all about her. Briony was usually calm and fair in her dealings with children, but today she felt she had taken just about as much as she could stand.

She walked unannounced into the large main lounge and surveyed the room and the girls in it while she pulled off her gloves. The room had once been beautiful, if overdone. The crystal chandeliers were now hung with cobwebs, and the floor covering was bare in places. Around the room were girls and women, smoking and chatting. They glanced at her and resumed their talking. Briony breathed in the foetid stench of unwashed bodies and lavender water. Nellie's establishment had gone down even further than she had anticipated. The girls sprawled around this room would have been long gone from one of her own houses. She guessed they were lice-ridden and shuddered inwardly.

'Where can I find Nellie?' Her voice was loud and all the girls turned to face her with raised eyebrows.

'You a new girl?' This from a thin whore with non-existent breasts.

All the occupants of the room were taking in Briony's

pale green dress and coat and costing it in their minds.

'What's your name, girl?' Briony's voice travelled across the room and hit the skinny one full on.

'You what?' The voice was belligerent now.

'I said, what's your name? Not too difficult a question, is it? I presume you know the answer.'

The others laughed and this put the girl in a terrible dilemma. She either fronted the red-headed cow in front of her, who though small looked like she could handle herself, or she answered the question and lost face in front of her friends.

'I'm Jinny Collins. And who are you?' It was said without any respect whatsoever and Jinny was pleased with herself. She had answered the question and asked one. To Jinny this showed considerable wit.

Briony let her eyes travel the length of the girl's body before she said: 'I am Briony Cavanagh, and you, Jinny Collins, had better start talking to me with a bit of respect!'

Briony nearly smiled at the different expressions on the girls' faces. They ranged from fear to a healthy curiosity which she noted with pleasure.

'I am here to see Nellie, and one thing I'll say to all you girls before one of you kindly shows me where she is, is this. You stink! All of you stink, and you're lousy. You're also ignorant. I could have been anyone coming in here, and you let me. If one of my girls did that, I'd scalp the bitch. My advice to you lot if you want to carry on working here is this: get washed and get your miserable little lives sorted.' She pointed to the skinny girl.

'You, Jinny, show me where I can find Nellie. Now!'

She practically jumped from her seat.

'Yes, miss.'

They all watched as Briony followed Jinny from the room. So that's Briony Cavanagh, each thought, and then cursed themselves. Briony Cavanagh was the person to work for and they all had inadvertently buggered it up for themselves. It was quiet after she had left them. But the room was filled to the rafters with regrets.

Jinny showed Briony into Nellie's office.

'It's Miss Cavanagh to see you, Nell.' Briony noted the use of the Christian name and sighed inwardly. This place was really run down.

Nellie watched Briony dust off her chair before sitting on it. She noted everything about her, from the perfectly arranged hair to the pale green suit that was plain and simple yet screamed of money. She decided she liked the look of the girl. The only thing that threw her was the fact that Briony Cavanagh, the big Briony Cavanagh, was small. 'Petite' the French would call her. Nellie decided she would rather describe her as scrawny.

'Now then, what can I do you for?' Nellie wheezed with laughter at her own joke.

'I think it's more a case of what I can do for you. I am looking for some more houses. I want established businesses, like your own.' She held up her hand as Nellie's mouth opened.

'Just hear me out, Nell, then answer me. I walked in here today to a bunch of filthy dirty brasses, the place is in tatters and looks unkempt – like its workforce. You are obviously losing heart in the place. I know that, in your day, you were one of the best madams this side of the water.'

She saw the woman respond to the compliment.

'Now what I want from you, Nell, is to buy this house

outright, but I would still want you to run it. I will have a big say in what happens here, I admit, as will my associate, Tommy Lane. But you will be our mouthpiece, Nellie. I'll clear this place of crooks and vagabonds and wandering thieves. I think the house is in a prime location, it's big, and all it needs is a few quid poured into it to make it one of the best houses in the business once more. Now then, Nellie, what do you say?'

Nellie looked at the girl, because Briony was only a girl for all her sophistication and expensive clothes, and felt a grudging respect and admiration for her. She had simply and firmly stated her case which Nellie was shrewd enough to know she would carry, with or without Nellie's co-operation. Briony Cavanagh struck her as that sort of person. What she offered was fair, and was also exactly what Nellie had dreamt of in her darker moments. She would have the status of head of the house without the real aggravation. It was a dream come true.

'I'll tell you what I think, little lady.'

Briony raised her eyebrows.

'I think you should go to the cupboard over there by the door and get out a bottle of my good brandy. Then we can toast our partnership.'

Briony grinned and did as she was told.

A little while later they were both pleasantly discussing the influential customers Nellie had had over the years, when Briony said: 'What about Willy Bolger, Nellie? You ever had any dealings with him?

Nellie waved her hand dismissively.

'He's a ponce of the worst order, Briony, but I know one thing about Willy that's always served me in good stead with him: he's a coward. He'd cut a brass or a bloke, but only mob-handed. Get Willy on his own and he shits bricks. He was in here not a week back telling me he wanted this, that and the other, but young Barry Black was in here. I've been hiding him up because the Old Bill's after him for that jewellery robbery over in Kent. He saw Willy off, no trouble. Willy reckons he's got a right royal backing now. I nearly laughed me head off! I mean, who in their right mind would back William Bolger? I remember him when he had no arse in his trousers and an empty stomach.'

Briony smiled and changed the conversation again, listening with half an ear to Nellie telling her about Lord this and Lord that who'd frequented her house over the years. But her mind was on Bolger, and on Mariah Jurgens who was next on her list of things to do.

It stood to reason Willy had backing, but from whom? That's what she had to find out.

Chapter Twelve

'You're what?' Molly looked at Eileen as if she had never before clapped eyes on her.

'I'm getting married, Mum. Joshua asked me today and I said yes.'

Molly grabbed her daughter in her arms and squeezed her tight. 'Jesus, Mary and jumping Joseph! This is the best news I've heard for many a long day, and aren't you the dark horse! I never guessed it was gone this far. All your gallivanting around and never a word! Oh, Eileen, I could shoot meself with happiness! You've made a good choice, child, a good choice!'

Molly's voice was loud enough to carry through the wall and beyond. Her pleasure was written all over her face. Rosalee, picking up on this, grinned widely and clapped her hands together.

'Your sister's getting married, Rosie darlin', now isn't that something!'

Eileen smiled at her mother's obvious happiness.

'Wait until I tell the others!' Molly sat herself down by the fire and carried on making the tea. 'Now then, first things first. He's Catholic, thank God, so we'll have to see the priest and put the banns up. Our Briony will have to be told first, though.'

'What's Briony got to be told first?' Bernadette's voice wafted in at the front door as she pushed herself in laden down with packages. Eileen took them from her and, blushing furiously, said: 'I'm getting married, our Bernie, to Joshua.'

Bernadette screwed up her eyes in wonder and said loudly, 'You ain't? But he's an old man!'

Molly, seeing Eileen's face drop, gave Bernadette a stinging blow across the face and shrieked: 'Shut your mawing, you jealous bitch! Your turn'll come, if you can keep that galloping trap of yours shut for five minutes!

'Our Kerry will walk down the aisle fastern'n you because she only opens her mouth to a bit of singing.'

Molly's hard eyes stared into her daughter's with a warning and Bernie shook her head hard before saying, 'Our Kerry won't be walking down the aisle, as you put it. Our Kerry just might find herself getting a bit of a shock . . .'

She stopped herself from saying any more because of the look on Eileen's face. Even Rosalee seemed subdued now. Bernie realised that, as usual, she had walked into a merry situation and ruined it. It was a knack she had acquired as a child. Everyone was now angry or depressed on the day Eileen had announced she was getting married. For one of the few times in her life, Bernie felt ashamed. Poor Eileen had been so unhappy for so long, and now she was taking the shine off the news. She rubbed at the handprint that was glowing bright red on her cheek and grinned ruefully.

'I'm sorry, Eileen, it's great news. The best news ever!'

She kissed her sister on the cheek and in all the consequent excitement and chattering about the big day, Molly ignored the quip about Kerry, but it stayed in the back of her mind nevertheless.

Briony stood outside Mariah's house in Hyde Park and gave the large imposing building the once over. It really was a lovely old place. Painted white, the four-storey edifice blended in perfectly with its neighbours. It was class, and Briony felt a grudging respect for the woman who owned it.

She walked up the flight of scrubbed stone steps that led to the front door and rang the bell. The door was opened by a finely muscled young man in his early twenties dressed in the scarlet and silver livery that, Briony was to learn, was worn by all Mariah's staff.

He took her through a large entrance hall and into the office area of the house. He asked her politely to sit while he summoned his mistress. Briony was now impressed beyond her wildest imaginings. She might have been calling on Isabel Dumas. She sat herself in a leather winged chair and pulled off her gloves, her eyes greedily drinking in her surroundings.

Mariah was like her; where she worked was obviously important to her. Briony scanned the rows of bookshelves along the far wall and smiled to herself. Other than the copy of *Fanny Hill*, she guessed correctly that none of the books had ever been opened. Nevertheless they gave the room an air of respectability that Briony admired. She would angle for a look around the house if she could. It was always good to get a look at what the opposition was offering, and Mariah was her only serious opposition as far as the houses went, which was why she had never tried to take over any of her properties. There was room in London for both of them, providing Mariah didn't blot her copybook with Briony personally.

Her mouth settled into a grim line as she thought about this. She would make that point clear enough. Mariah might have requested the meeting, but Briony had only deigned to come because she had an ulterior motive. No, Miss Jurgens didn't scare her at all. Big as the bitch was, and as hard a reputation as she had, it would take more than a whore to frighten Briony Cavanagh.

She settled herself in the chair and resumed her neutral expression.

'Well, you're a runt and no mistaking!' Briony heard laughter in the big woman's voice and said, 'Yeah, and you're a big bastard. So that makes us quits.'

Briony's voice was hard, her face set. She stared up at the huge woman in front of her, her heart beating a tattoo in her chest. Briony consciously kept her eyes away from the massive clenched fists of her rival.

Mariah watched her and felt a flicker of respect. As small as she was, and God knows this girl was small, she wasn't afraid. In front of Mariah that took great courage. Men who were feared across the smoke were wary of her, she knew this and used it to her advantage. Yet this little thing was actually fronting her. She sat behind the desk with as much dignity as she could muster and said, 'Anyone else said that, I'd brain them, but I invited you here today for a good reason. Are you after my houses? I know you're after Deakins's place. Old Nellie is a bit long in the tooth these days for rowing, but I ain't. So I want a straight answer from you. Whether I brain you or not depends on what you say.'

Briony took a deep breath. The woman in front of her was renowned for her size, her strength and her temper. Well, Briony could match her in two of those attributes. But Mariah was also known to be fair. Briony decided to tell her the truth.

'It had crossed my mind, as you must have guessed. But no, I don't want to take over your houses. Unless you want to sell them, of course? Is that all you wanted me for?'

Mariah sat back in her chair and sucked on her teeth. Her white-blond hair framed her face becomingly and for a second Briony got a glimpse of the woman she had once been, breathtakingly beautiful.

'I was sorry to hear about Ginelle, she was a good kid. Now then, before you leap out of your chair and start shouting your mouth off, hear me out. I know everything that goes on in this town, I make it my business to. I can find out anything about anyone. Now I had a visitor here, but I need to know a bit more about what's going on before I tell you who it was and what they wanted. I ain't known for sitting on any fences, unless it earns me money or peace, so let's cut the fucking crap and get our cards on the table. What exactly happened with Ginelle, and what threats have you had? Is this all about you taking over other houses or what?'

Briony was having difficulty controlling herself. She knew about Ginelle, this woman knew, and now she wanted to know the score! Briony knew she was trapped. She would have to come clean and hope for the best.

'How do you know about Ginelle, Mariah? I need to know.'

'Let's just say a little bird told me. It's enough that I know. Now tell me the honest truth and I'll come out into the open. I think that you and me could do each other a favour here. Let's see, shall we?'

'Nellie's house is in the bag. The death of Ginelle had nothing to do with that, as far as I know. She was delivered in a crate minus parts of her body. Bolger is behind it, but I need to know who's behind him before I can make a move. And I swear to you now, I take oath, that bastard is living on borrowed time! No one, but no one, touches my girls. Whoever is behind him had better start saying their prayers.'

Mariah smiled then. A real smile. She had heard what she wanted to hear. This little woman was a madam of the old sort. No milkwater sop who would run at the first sign of trouble. Mariah decided she could even get to like the skinny little bitch, given time. She stood up and, going to her drinks table, poured out two generous measures of brandy. Giving one to Briony, she resumed her seat and said: 'Bolger's been here, offering me the earth and other things besides. I don't like him but that's neither here nor there, I don't like a lot of people I do business with, but worst of all I don't trust him. He's a two-faced ponce, a violent two-faced ponce. He cut Ginelle up, and I won't forgive him that one. The girl was nothing to do with anything. Then he came here and offered me your houses. He wants me and my muscle on his side. Personally, I don't want to get involved, but I have to. Because otherwise eventually he'll want what's mine. I think I can find out who's backing him, then together we can wipe them out. Now, what do you have to say?'

Briony smiled at Mariah.

'I think, Mariah Jurgens, between us we could frighten the life out of the little shit!'

That was exactly what Mariah wanted to hear.

'I'm going to tell Bolger that I want to meet the man behind him, otherwise no deal. Bolger is a showman, a show off. He'll enjoy setting up the meet and letting me see how much he's come up in the world. I'll relay the information to you and Tommy. Then we decide what to do next. How's that?'

'That will suit me fine. Tommy is as anxious to sort this out as I am. We've got some pretty impressive muscle on our side.'

This was a threat to Mariah who took it how it was intended. But she didn't say anything. Briony was giving her fair warning, exactly what she would have done herself.

Raising her glass she said to Briony: 'I don't know, girl, what the fuck are we breeding these days? People like Bolger are getting thicker on the ground. Sometimes I hanker back to the good old days when you worked your girls, you took the money, and all the house owners met socially. There's a new breed out there now and we've got to stick together to fight the fuckers at their own game.'

Briony raised her own glass and said, 'My sentiments exactly.'

The two women sipped their brandy for a while, lost in their own thoughts. The groundwork was done. They had called a truce, felt each other out, and now they would work together to find a solution to all their problems.

Evander's friend and confidant Glennford Randall shook his head as he looked at his friend.

'I'm telling you, man, that girl spells trouble for you. No white meat ever tasted any different to black. You're gonna get hurt, I know it.'

Evander sighed heavily, his deep black skin shiny in the lights of the club.

'Kerry's different, man. She's real, something special.'

Glennford laughed. 'She's got a pair of tits and a splitarse, she ain't no different to any other woman in the world! She can get pregnant and, boy, if she does, you're a dead man.'

Evander watched his friend walk away, his long rangy body loping across the wooden stage. Kerry came out of her dressing room and smiled at him.

'Why so sad? What are you thinking about?'

Evander looked into her lovely face and felt the familiar tightening in his guts. She was exquisite, she was young, she was exciting, and she was milk white. It was a heady combination.

'I wasn't thinking about anything in particular, baby. Are we still on for tonight?'

'Yes, and I have a surprise for you. Bernie's staying at my mother's so we have the flat to ourselves. You can stay till the morning.'

Evander went to touch her arm when Tommy Lane came bowling up to them.

'All right, Evander? Listen, Briony's going to be a bit late tonight but she wants the sets a bit longer. Another couple of numbers in each one, could you manage that?'

Evander and Kerry nodded. Tommy was too caught up in his own affairs to notice the redness of Kerry's face and neck.

'The punters like a dance so we thought a few more lively numbers wouldn't go amiss. Now before I forget, there's a men's outfitters in Dean Street and the bloke's going to measure you boys up for some new stage clothes. At the moment you're all a bit bland, you know? We thought a nice deep green or a deep blue, whatever. You see the bloke and choose for yourselves. We'll be picking up the tab so don't go overboard!'

'Yes, sir, Mr Lane.' Evander's voice held the bland neutrality inherent to a black man and Tommy whacked him on the shoulder and said, 'For fuck's sakes, call me Tommy. All this Mr Lane and sir is going to me head!'

He ambled off to find a drink and Evander looked at Kerry. She saw the stark fear in his eyes and felt a lump form in her throat. He was scared of Tommy, was scared of all white men. They slapped you on the back one minute and put you in your place the next. She knew what he was thinking and felt a great sorrow for him.

'Tommy's all right, Evander. He means what he said.'

'I ain't never met a white man yet who means anything, Kerry. I call him Tommy boy tomorrow in front of his fancy friends and he'll try and break my head! Believe me, I know.'

'Not Tommy Lane, Evander, you're wrong.' Her voice was soft and reproving and for a second he felt the terrific pull of her, and at the same time was reminded of just what trouble this relationship could bring him. Tommy Lane slapping you on the back and buying your clothes was one thing. Tommy Lane with the knowledge he was sleeping with Kerry would be a different matter entirely.

'I'll see you tonight, Evander, won't I?'

He looked into her little face, full of yearning, and he smiled.

' 'Course you will, sweetheart. Now let's get on stage before the crowd gets restless!'

Kerry put on her widest smile and walked on to the stage. Evander followed but his smile didn't quite reach his eyes.

*

Rupert Charles sat with Jonathan la Billière and a rather pale young man called Dorian. His face lit up at the sight of Briony walking towards his table.

'Briony darling! Where have you been? We've missed you, haven't we, boys?'

Jonathan stood up as Briony sat down and he winked at her.

'How did the filming go?' she asked them. 'I couldn't make it, I'm afraid, but I have a lot of faith in you, Rupert.'

She took out a cigarette and placed it in a long black holder. Dorian struck a match and lit it for her. She blew the smoke out into his face and smiled her thanks.

'Dorian darling, this is Briony Cavanagh. Briony, this is Dorian Carnarvon, the Duke of Tenby's only son. A darling boy with the most delightful grey eyes, don't you think?'

Briony smiled absently at the boy and concentrated on Jonathan, the male star of the film.

'So what's the score?'

Jonathan grinned and, losing his gentlemanly manner for a moment, said, 'The girl was young, plump, and knew all the right moves. There's a reel of film in your office waiting for you. Have a look and tell me what you think.'

'Is it as good as the other films? The truth now.'

'Honestly, yes! It's not bad. We know all the pitfalls now. You have a look and you'll be pleasantly surprised.'

Briony nodded, satisfied.

'What happened to you anyway, Briony? I was looking forward to seeing you. I was going to take you out after the shoot.'

Her eyes scanned the club around her as she answered.

'I had a bit of trouble, but it's sorted now. Do me a favour, set up another session and I'll put up the money. I want this pukkah, I want it right.'

He laughed.

'Do you only ever do business, Briony? Don't you ever relax?'

She looked into his face and he saw the fine lines around her eyes and mouth. It occurred to him then that this woman had a lot on her mind of which he knew nothing. For the first time she frightened him. Her reputation had preceded her, yet on his first meeting he had been pleasantly surprised. Looking at her now, he was convinced she was capable of anything.

Chapter Thirteen

Briony woke up to a terrific thumping on her bedroom door.

'What's going on!' Tommy opened his eyes and stared at her.

'It's your mother, Briony, she's downstairs with Rosalee.' Cissy's voice was loud and Briony screwed up her eyes and groaned.

'All right, tell her I'll be down in a minute.'

'Your mother's like a bleeding jinx, always around when no one wants her.'

Briony laughed gently.

'Tell me about it.' She pulled herself out of the bed and, going to her wardrobe, took out a wrap of heavily embroidered Chinese silk. Her long hair was hanging down her back in tangles and she began to brush it furiously to try and tame it.

Tommy got out of the bed and scratched his belly while he stretched. 'I feel knackered.'

'Stay in bed. I'll get Cissy to bring you up some tea.'

'Nah, I've got to see some people today.' He sat on the side of the bed and closed his eyes.

'Who have you got to see?'

'Oh, no one in particular, just a few mates. Tell Cissy I'll have that tea now, if you don't mind. And tell your mother not to get me up in future.'

Briony grinned.

'As if she'd take any notice!'

'What kind of time do you call this, still in bed at ten-thirty in the morning. My God, child, you must be raking it in.'

'And good morning to you and all, Mum.' She knelt down and kissed Rosalee's face. 'Hello, Rosie darling.'

Rosalee clapped her hands together and said: 'Bri, Bri.'

Molly tutted loudly and poured her out a cup of tea Cissy had brought them. 'I don't know, Briony, you're a lady of leisure, sitting in your dressing gown like Lady Astor, and the day nearly over.'

'Oh, Mum, put a sock in it, for Christ's sake! My clubs don't shut till three in the morning, then I have to do the takings among other things, so please give me five minutes' peace. Now what do you want and how much is it gonna rush me?'

Molly screwed up her eyes and gritted her teeth. 'What makes you think I'm after something?'

Briony did laugh then, a real laugh that burst out of her tiny frame and caused Rosie to laugh with her.

'If I see you and her before noon, then you're after a few quid. Tell me what you want and let's . . .' The sentence was lost in a long loud yawn.

'I came here this morning to tell you that Eileen's getting married.'

Molly had the grim satisfaction of seeing Briony's eyes

widen. 'There, I thought that would put a stop to your gallop! Joshua's popped the question and she's said yes. I thought me and you could have a little chat about the do. That's all.'

'The do?' Briony's voice was puzzled.

'The reception! For the love of Mary, would you pay attention, girl! She's getting married and I want it to be the biggest thing this side of the water. I want her to go off in style. The way you lot are going, she'll be the only one of my daughters wedded and legal.' Her voice became wheedling. 'I want me eldest girl to have a good weddin', Bri. I want her to be set up like a queen.'

'Our Eileen getting married? Bloody hell! Who'd have thought it.'

Molly wiped Rosalie's face with a hankie and said, 'I'll never marry off this one, will I? And you living over the broom, and our Bernie without a man in sight. As for Kerry, well, she would marry her voice if she could. I want our Eileen to have something special. After all that happened to her, and all her troubles . . .'

Briony put up her hand for silence.

'Look, Mum, she can have whatever you like, so drop the sales pitch. You book it and I'll pay for it. In fact, if you like we can have the reception here, I don't mind. My garden's huge, we could easily get fifty, sixty people here no trouble. Mrs H can do the food and Cissy can bring in a few girls to help serve. What do you think?'

Molly smiled smugly.

'You're a good girl, Briony, you're a kind and decent girl. Only a saint would look after her sisters like you do.'

Briony drank the rest of the tea and poured herself another cup before she said, 'Why do I get the feeling, Mother, that you've just mugged me off?'

*

Kerry was lying in bed with Evander, at the quiet stage after lovemaking. When the only thing needed, or indeed wanted, is to feel your lover's heart beating with your own. He stroked her belly with soft fingers and Kerry groaned. The bedclothes had fallen to the floor and the remains of a bottle of wine and a platter of bread and cheese stood on the night table. They had yet to sleep, and were both dozing when they heard the sound of a key in the front door.

Evander sat upright, and Kerry hastily jumped from the bed and pulled a sheet around her when they heard Bernie's voice.

'Hello, Kerry, it's me!'

Kerry and Evander looked at one another and Kerry, putting a finger to her lips, went to the door and slipped through it out into the hallway. Bernie was hanging up her coat. She smiled.

'Morning, Kerry.' She looked her sister up and down and raised one finely plucked black eyebrow.

'What has the wicked witch stumbled on here then? Could you have a man in there!'

Kerry licked her lips nervously.

'What you doing back here so early? I wasn't expecting you until this afternoon.'

'Our mother's took Rosie and gone on the ponce round Briony's about the wedding – Eileen's wedding actually. So I thought I may as well come back here and get started on your dresses for tonight.'

'Eileen's getting married?'

Bernie walked through to the kitchen and started to fill the kettle.

'How many cups of tea shall I make, two or three? Or would the chap in there prefer coffee?'

Evander's love of coffee was common knowledge around the club. He had tried tea and it had made him violently sick. Suddenly it was crystal clear to Kerry. Bernie knew everything and she was going to use it against her. That had been her way since childhood. She looked for a handle on people then used it for her own ends.

Kerry drew herself up to her full height and walked into the bedroom.

'Get up, get up now!' Evander looked at her in shock. She threw the sheet from her own body and pulled on a dressing gown. Then she stormed from the room.

Bernie was getting the cups out of the dresser when Kerry stamped back into the kitchen.

'You bitch! You nasty, vindictive cow! You know exactly who I'm sleeping with. Well, yes, you *can* make him a cup of coffee. You can also pack your bags and get the hell out of here and back to Mum's. I don't need you on my back, Bernie Cavanagh, I never did and I never will. Take yourself and your arseholing ways back home to Mum!'

Bernadette turned to face her sister and her mouth opened twice before she could form any words.

'What? What did you say?'

Kerry snorted through her nose.

'You heard. What? You deaf now as well as stupid? I said, you can get the hell out of here. I know your game, mate. Well, you tell who the fuck you like. It won't make no difference to me. I ain't ashamed of anything where that man's concerned, I love the bones of him. So now you know.'

Bernie's mind was working overtime. If Kerry slung her out now she would be back home permanently; she would also be without a job. As Kerry's dresser she got a good wage and did nothing really to earn it except iron her dresses or alter them if necessary. She was well set up nowadays and it was all thanks to Kerry and Briony. She also knew that no matter what Briony's opinion of Evander Dorsey might be, she would not like the fact Bernie had tried to deck one over on Kerry. She wouldn't like that at all.

'I don't know what you mean, Kerry. I guessed ages ago about you and Evander, saw you looking at each other. I knew what the outcome was going to be. If I was going to say anything I would have said it by now. I'm pleased for you. I'm glad you've found someone!'

'Oh, pull the other one, it's got golden bells on! I know your game, Bernie, you've always been the same . . .'

Evander walked into the kitchen. He had pulled on his trousers and vest. Bernadette looked at his muscled torso and his handsome face and found it in her heart to see just what had attracted Kerry.

'Stop all this shouting, ladies. It's wrong for you two to fall out over me. Now let's have a cup of coffee and try and talk this out.'

Bernie saw that his eyes were wary and her heart lifted. He was scared of her, of what she could say, of who she could tell. Unlike Kerry, he was more than aware of what the outcome could be if she walked from this house. After all, no one would physically hurt Kerry but he would be lynched.

'She's a vicious cow, Evander, you don't know her.'

Bernie was shocked at the vehemence in her sister's voice.

'Oh, come on, Kerry, what have I done to deserve that? I wouldn't do anything to hurt you, I swear. I'll keep this as close a secret as you. After all, if it got out . . .'

She left the rest of the sentence in mid-air and Evander

bit his lip. The kettle boiled and Bernie busied herself making the drinks. Kerry stood with her back against the table and her arms tight across her chest. Unlike Evander she knew what Bernie was capable of, though unlike Evander she wasn't as aware of what would really happen should the affair become public.

Bernie gave everyone their drinks. Putting her arm on Kerry's, she said sweetly: 'I don't want to fall out over this, Kerry. You're my sister and I'll keep this a secret for as long as you want. I mean it. If you're happy then I'm happy. If you really want me to leave I will. I won't stay where I'm not wanted. But even if you ding me out, I won't say a dicky bird to anyone.'

Kerry looked into the face so like her own and felt the sting of tears in her eyes.

She knew that Bernie was staying whether she wanted it or not, Evander's reaction had seen to that. But it saddened her that she could never trust her sister, or indeed understand the hatred in her. It had always been the same. Since they were babies Bernie had always had a vicious streak where she was concerned. It was jealousy, and jealousy made people do evil things. For the first time Kerry was really frightened, not for herself but for Evander.

Molly was putting the finishing touches to the lunch she had prepared for Joshua O'Malley and his mother. She swept her eyes around her house to make sure everything was gleaming. Satisfied, she went to the fireplace and, taking up a large brick, banged it on the back of the grate three times. The banging was answered by two knocks from the other side of the wall and two minutes later Mother Jones came in at Molly's front door.

'Oh, Molly, it looks a picture. Beautiful. Even that old bitch won't be able to find fault.'

Molly smiled in satisfaction. Elizabeth O'Malley was the only fly in the ointment as far as Eileen's wedding was concerned. Hated by everyone in Dagenham and Barking for her vindictive tongue and her holy Joeing ways, she was now to become a member of the Cavanagh family, and as much as the thought distressed Molly she would take a lot to see her eldest daughter happily married, even take on Elizabeth O'Malley if necessary.

'The food smells beautiful, now stop your worrying. Did I tell you what I heard the other week?'

Molly busied herself tidying Rosalee's hair and said, 'No, what?'

'It seems Mrs O'Malley was cleaning out St Vincent's Presbytery when who should come in but Jean Barlow. The woman's got a tongue like an adder! Well, poor Father McNamara was nearly shitting himself at the two of them in the same place. I mean, their hatred of one another goes back years! Barlow was knocking off O'Malley's man just before he died. Well, this is the rub. Barlow asks the priest if he could set the banns up for her next weddin', looking at O'Malley all the time like, trying to annoy the life out of her. So O'Malley says all innocent like, "Aren't you a bit long in the tooth for getting married, Mrs Barlow?" And that mare turns on her and says: "There's no set age for getting married, or indeed falling in love. Why, Mr O'Malley could have told you that, dear." '

Molly gaped. 'She didn't mention O'Malley's man?'

Mother Jones roared with laughter.

'She did! Well, the priest, God love him and keep him, had to separate them. Mrs McAnulty his housekeeper threw a bucket of water over them in the end. Like alley cats, she said they were, and the language! The priest was red-faced for days after!'

'Well, good for Barlow, I say. It's about time someone gave that bitch one in the eye. No one split on her old man because they were glad to see someone getting one over on the old cow.'

As she said that Eileen walked through the front door with the woman in question and her son, and Molly, being Molly and a mother who wanted her girl wed, held out her arms and said: 'Come away inside, Mrs O'Malley. This is indeed a pleasure!'

Tommy Lane and his close friend and minder Jimmy Reynard walked into the lunch-time crush of The Two Puddings in Stratford. They pushed their way through to the bar and Tommy ordered two pints of best bitter. He noticed he was being observed by a huge bald-headed man called Boris Jackobitz. Tommy looked the man in the face and, raising his pint, motioned with his head to the back bar. Boris nodded almost imperceptibly and five minutes later slipped through the curtained doorway at the back of the pub. Tommy and Jimmy followed.

Their disappearance went unnoticed by the clientele who were waiting for the result of a horse race. This was the place for betting. It was crowded out day and night with punters. From well-to-do middle-class shopkeepers to run-of-the-mill petty criminals and local hard men, all had one thing in common: a love of the horses. It was the main topic of conversation and the only interest of most of the clientele.

Boris employed runners from the age of seven to fifty, and was the foremost bookie in London. He chased his bets like the fillies chased the Cheltenham Gold Cup:

conscientiously and without ever letting up. If you couldn't pay Boris it was time to leave the country.

He closed the heavy wooden door behind the thick curtain and motioned for Tommy to sit. He didn't extend this courtesy to Jimmy because a minder should always stand and remain alert. Jimmy leant against the wall and crossed his arms, watching Boris all the time.

'So what can I do for you, Tommy Lane? Long time no see.' Boris's deep and throaty voice was accompanied by a chuckle. Tommy smiled and crossed his legs. Pulling out one of his cheap cheroots, he lit it before saying: 'You're looking well, Boris me old mate. Prosperous and happy. That's what I like to see.'

Boris shrugged his shoulders and clenched his fists, emphasising his muscular torso.

'I have to keep well, Tommy, there's so many people wanting to come up in the world over my back. And yours, I don't doubt. I keep my place with fear and a little bit of respect. Now, we've had the polite chit-chat, what's the rub? I'm a busy man.'

'You know just about everything that's going on. People owe you money, and when they can't pay they trade information. What's been going on in the streets that would interest me particularly?'

Boris digested Tommy's words and, opening a drawer in the table, took out a bottle of red-eye whisky. Pulling the cork out with his teeth, he took a long drink before offering it to Tommy. He took the bottle and swigged from it, wiping his hand across his mouth afterwards.

'Is what you have to tell me so bad I'll need a stiff drink first?'

His voice was jocular and Boris, noted for his dry sense of humour, laughed out loud.

'Maybe, Tommy Lane. Maybe. It's Bolger you're interested in, isn't it? Well, I heard a whisper – only a whisper, mind – that he has been seen with Isaac Dubronsky. He's well in with the Jews. Now they've always stuck to trading and loan sharking, but I understand Willy wants them to branch out into the cat business. Never had no time for whores myself, prefer my females to have four legs and a good pedigree. But it's funny, you know, Tommy, you coming here, because I was going to see that woman of yours, Briony. It seems she's the one he's gunning for. He's been asking all over town about her. It sounds more a vengeance thing to me. You know, I wondered if she'd had a word with him at sometime, a run-in like? Because he was asking about her in Stratford not a week since. And around Barking. About her family. You might not believe me but I was going to see the lady in question myself, especially after that young girl was cut.'

Tommy stared at Boris with awe. There was nothing that escaped his notice. He rarely used his information, it was more of a hobby to him.

'You know about Ginelle?'

Boris grinned. 'Listen, Tommy, I know everything about everyone, yourself included. But I don't use anything unless it benefits me. If you have a handle on someone it brings in unpaid debts a lot faster than a hiding. Also, if I hear of a robbery and one of the people involved owes me money, I can collect it quickly and cleanly. But this Bolger I don't like. He cut a friend of mine a few years back, a young tom who liked a bet. He cut her face. I went to see him myself. That's where Willy got the scar across his back. I done him with a razor and Willy, being Willy, let me. That was why I wanted to see young Briony. I like her. I liked her when she was a child and her father used to send her with a bet. Tell her from me, whatever happens, I will be on her side.'

'Thanks, Boris, I appreciate that.'

He smiled, showing black teeth, and shook his head. 'I always was a gentleman. Whatever my reputation, I would never hurt a woman. Bolger has made a career of it. The sooner he's cleaned off the pavements, the better.'

Tommy stood up and held out his hand. Boris grasped it and squeezed it tightly.

'Go and see Dubronsky. If I know him he's in over his head. He's strictly small-time.'

'I will.' Turning back at the door, Tommy said, 'I'll tell Briony what you said, Boris. She'll really appreciate it.'

He grinned.

'She's a good businesswoman, clear-headed and sensible. Most women are when you get to know them properly. I think they could even run the country one day!'

Tommy laughed at the incongruity of the statement and left. He made his way with Jimmy to Petticoat Lane, stopping to pick up two hand guns on the way. When you visited the Jews on their own territory it was just as well to go there with a little bit of insurance.

Kerry sat on her bed staring at the pile of clothes on the floor, trying to summon up the energy to get herself dressed. Evander had left and she could hear Bernie humming to herself as she prepared some food. She gritted her teeth together, making a grinding noise. Why did she have to be plagued like this. She wanted Evander Dorsey so bad she could taste it.

It was all she thought about, all she wanted to think about. If he had been a big blond Swede, no one would have said a word. But he was black, and because of that fact, he and Kerry had to skulk around like criminals. Now Bernie knew about them and that was the beginning of the end. Instinctively Kerry knew this.

In France she could live openly with Evander. They were artists, and as such would be forgiven much. Here, and in America, if she publicly proclaimed her feelings they would be ridiculed. Hated. It was so unfair. Her mother would go mad if she heard about Evander. You could be a twopenny whore and get more respect than a woman who went with a black man.

It was so unfair. So very, very unfair.

Bernie bustled into the room with a hot drink. She looked at Kerry and smiled sadly.

'Come on, Kel, get yourself sorted.' She began to pick up the clothes on the floor and Kerry leant forward and grabbed her wrist. Bernie looked up into her face, stunned.

'If you try and bugger this up for me, Bernie, I'll kill you! Do you understand me? I'll kill you with my bare hands.'

Bernie nodded, her eyes filling with tears. What really hurt her was the fact that Kerry knew her so well, knew exactly what she was capable of. She could see through her like a pane of glass.

'I won't, Kerry. I promise.'

Kerry pushed the offending arm away from her and said, 'Too right you won't, because I won't let you!'

The two sisters stared into each other's eyes, and it was Bernadette who looked away first.

Chapter Fourteen

Brick Lane market was packed. The stall holders were shouting out their wares in loud voices. Children ran among the stalls, looking for a chance to swipe the nearest thing to hand. Old women and young mothers stopped for a gossip or to scour the second-hand clothes stalls, of which there were plenty. Barrow boys stood by with apples and oranges piled high, their dirty hands grasping money and weighing up their produce quickly and efficiently, always underweighing when possible and keeping up a stream of talk as they did so, chatting up customers, young and old.

The shops were open. Gold was displayed behind metal grilles, diamonds sparkled, and furniture was displayed outside on the pavements. It was the era of the never-never and the Jews cashed in on this. They had always been the Uncles, the moneylenders, they were established and commanded respect because of this. They were rich, owning property in Brick Lane and roundabouts, but lived in Golders Green, respectable lives, with respectable families. Many of the men started out making a small fortune from the cobbles, a term for boxing without gloves. They fought all comers at Victoria Park and when they had a stake eventually made their way into the garment or gold industry, always lending money as a sideline. The easy atmosphere belied the real dealings that went on here. The lane was open till late at night. The smell of gefilte fish and blintzes vied for a place among the smells of rotten vegetables and the ever present smell of steam from the hoffman pressers. Tommy walked along with Jimmy until he came to Dubronsky's small pop shop. 'Pop' was the term for pawn. It was not unusual for a woman to take her husband's good suit in on a Monday and get it back out Saturday, ready to be worn on Sunday. Pawning was a way of life for most people. It was the only way to stretch meagre pennies, and to keep children's bellies full. Inside the shop, Tommy closed the door and put up the 'Closed' sign.

The small Jewish man behind the counter smiled at him.

'Tommy, my boy. What brings you here?'

Dubronsky's exterior did not kid Tommy one iota. He knew the little man could blow his head off at a whim; his meek and engaging exterior covered a calculating brain and a violent streak. Until now, Tommy had always got on very well with him. He used this fact as he ambled over to the counter.

'I hear you've been making friends with the pimps? Is this true?'

Dubronsky shrugged.

'Since when have I had to ask you who I can be friends with? What are you, Tommy Lane, an Irish rabbi, that you come here on to my premises and question me about my likes and dislikes?'

Tommy grinned then.

'Jimmy, have a look out the back, would you?'

He walked through, slamming up the flap of the wooden counter noisily and walking through to the back of the shop. He emerged with a girl of about eighteen. She had thick black hair and a large nose. Dubronsky's daughter Ruth, the likeness was unmistakable.

'Leave my daughter be, Tommy, she's only a child helping her father.' Tommy detected the worry in his voice. Jimmy was well known for his vicious ways and his non-existent brain. Dubronsky knew that if Tommy nodded, Jimmy would just batter the girl without a second's thought. But Tommy was piqued that the man thought so little of him.

'I wouldn't hurt your daughter, you should know that. I want to hurt Willy Bolger. I don't want to fall out with you or anyone else for that matter, but I will if needs be. Bolger has upset me, and now he has to pay the price. If you protect him, I'll raze this fucking place to the ground! I mean it. So you give him a little message from me. Tell him I'm looking for him, and I'll find him eventually. So he can make it a lot easier on himself if he makes a point of coming to see me. If I have to look for him, it will be worse on him and any of his so-called friends. Do you understand me?'

'Perfectly. Now if you don't mind, I have work to do.'

Tommy stared at the man for a few seconds, battling the urge to attack him. It seemed that whoever was behind Bolger was a bigger fish than he'd first thought, otherwise why would Dubronsky be so cavalier? Walking around the counter, Tommy grabbed the little man by the scruff of his neck and frog-marched him out to the back of the shop. Kicking open the toilet in the yard, he pushed the man's head down the pan, using all his considerable strength.

The toilet, though well used, had not seen soap for many years. The smell of dank urine and mould hung in the air. Someone had used it a while before and the urine was deep orange, an oily film floating on it. He held Dubronsky's head under until the man's body began to sag, then he dragged his head up and threw him on to the ground outside the toilet door. He proceeded to kick him ferociously, concentrating on the chest and back.

Dubronsky lay on the ground heaving. Eventually he turned on his side and a trickle of blood-stained mucus came from his mouth. Tommy knelt beside him and grabbed his face, squeezing it.

'Don't you ever mug me off again, you ponce! Not ever! Now, you're going to tell me who's backing Bolger or I'll drown you in your own piss. Believe me when I say you've pushed me too fucking far. Out with it. I want a name and I want it now!'

The man looked up with fear in his eyes. In all his years of knowing Tommy, he had never seen him like this. It began to dawn on him that he had written Tommy Lane off too soon. The boy, and he was still a boy for all his grown-up looks, was a person he should not have underestimated. Like the Cavanagh girl, he was part of the new breed, and the prospect of what they could be capable of was frightening. All Bolger's big talk was suddenly forgotten in the face of this boy's wrath.

'Tommy, leave go of me! Let's talk.'

He laughed low.

'I've had it with talking, you short-arsed runt! Now tell me who Bolger's new friends are, and me and you will get on a lot better.'

'I don't know, I swear. All I know is that Bolger came to me and a few others with a proposition. He has a lot of money at his disposal, and a lot of manpower has been bought and paid for. Believe me, Tommy, it was nothing personal, just business. But I swear to you I don't know who's behind him. He said once it was a businessman, a big businessman. That's all. He won't let on who it is to anyone.'

'You expect me to believe that and all, don't you?'

Tommy's voice held an incredulity that was forced. Dubronsky would save his daughter's arse if not his own. But he had to be sure the man didn't know.

'Tommy, listen to me, I don't know. Before God, I swear to you I have no idea . . .'

He let go of the man's face. Livid white fingermarks were indented upon it. Tommy wiped his wet hand on the man's shirt.

'Where will I find him? He ain't been seen in his drum for a while so where's he hiding out?'

The little man squinted. Without his glasses he was nearly blind.

'He's staying with the Olds brothers down by Upton Park. But I warn you, Tommy, he's well protected.'

'How much muscle has he bought? Who are they?'

Dubronsky coughed and spat the mucus out on to the ground before answering.

'The Olds, the Campbells, the Dennings. Not to mention a lot of the Jewish muscle as well as Maltese. The Marianos are considering his offer and I tell you now, he's spending money like water.'

Tommy ground his teeth together. Poking his head at the man before him, he said: 'I don't care if he's bought the whole of the smoke. He's a fucking dead man. And if he's dead he can't pay anyone anything, can he. I'll piss all over his fireworks, you see if I don't.'

Standing, Tommy walked through the back of the shop to where Jimmy was standing with Ruth. The girl's sallow complexion was now white. Nodding to her, Tommy walked through the shop and out of the door with Jimmy. Outside he took a deep breath. Picking up a metal dustbin from the gutter, he threw it with all his strength through the shop window. People watched the spectacle with bright eyes. Dubronsky was not well liked, the Uncles never were really.

Jimmy smiled as they walked towards their car. Sometimes he wondered why the hell Tommy wanted him along. He was quite capable of taking on anyone by himself.

In the car Tommy said, 'Home. Me and you are going to see the Olds tonight. There's a bundle tonight at Victoria Park, and if I know Ronnie Olds, he'll be there.'

Willy Bolger nodded at the man sitting behind him in the car. His face was set in a neutral expression and he coughed gently before he spoke.

'Look, trust me. I'm not afraid of Briony Cavanagh or Tommy Lane. They're history. Soon they'll be out of the picture for good. Between us we'll run their businesses. In six months' time they'll be folklore.'

The man in the back of the car whispered: 'They'd better be. I'm paying you a lot of money to get this off the ground. I want Briony Cavanagh wiped off the face of the earth. I want everything she owns, and I want her out of the way once and for all.'

Willy grinned, showing his tiny pointed teeth. 'It's as good as done.'

The man slipped out of the car and walked along the Bayswater Road where he hailed a cab. Willy watched him go with contempt. What a fool. He'd handed over large sums of money and Willy had taken it without a second thought. If the man had had any sense he would just have had them taken out. It would have been cheaper. But for some reason best known to himself he wanted Briony Cavanagh stripped of everything she had first. Willy pocketed the wad of money the man had passed to him at the start of their meeting and smiled again. Who gave a fuck? he thought. So long as the money kept coming he could do what he liked. As he drove towards Hoxton he daydreamed of being the Baron of the East End. The first Baron who was also a pimp. He would be in control of just about all the women who worked the streets. The prospect pleased him. It was his dream come true. Plus he would enjoy taking out Miss Cavanagh, the feisty bitch! She needed knocking down a peg and he was just the man to do it.

He had heard the whispers that Lane was looking for him. Well, let the fucker look. There was no harm in that. But he wouldn't find him. Tommy would see him when the time was right, and then he would be the last person Tommy Lane saw in his life.

Briony had just finished drying herself when Tommy came into the bedroom. She stood naked, her tight belly emphasising her small breasts, and Tommy dived across the room and grabbed her. His hands were freezing and Briony screamed. He picked her up and carried her to the bed. Laying her down gently he kissed her mouth tenderly.

'You still look like a kid, especially with that mad hair all over the place.'

'Well, I don't feel like one. Let me up.'

Tommy leant on her with all his weight, pinning her to the bed.

'No. Why should I?'

Briony laughed. 'Because I'm bleeding well freezing that's why! Cissy never even bothered putting a fire up here today.'

'I'll warm you up, girl.' He felt Briony consciously relax and stifled a sigh. It was always the same. She would allow him inside her, that was all. He felt an urge to bite her, make her feel something if only pain. As if she read his thoughts, she whispered to him. 'I'm sorry, Tommy.'

The tiny voice was desolate and he pulled her to him, breathing in the mingled scents of soap and perfume.

Pulling himself back, he looked into her face. The deep green eyes had golden flecks that made them luminous. They were framed by deep, long black lashes, that were a startling contrast to her hair. As she was now, scrubbed free from cosmetics, with her hair tumbling around her, she looked good enough to eat. She looked like the girl he had fallen for. Only a few lines around her eyes betrayed her troubles and her age.

His eyes roamed over her body to the fine white lines just inside the pubic hair, the only evidence of womanhood she displayed. Her small breasts were unmarked, as were her thighs, but a few rogue stretchmarks glistened on her stomach and Tommy loved her more for them. Because they reminded him, as they did her, of what she had given up. Had had taken from her.

Briony ran her slim fingers over them tenderly.

'Sally's coming on Saturday, I'm going to arrange to see Ben if I can.'

Tommy nodded solemnly. Sally was Benedict's nurse. After Isabel Dumas had stopped Briony seeing the boy, she had cultivated his nurse. Briony now saw him only from a distance but it helped to soothe the ache inside her.

Lowering his head he kissed her belly tenderly.

'I love you, Bri.' His voice was husky with pent-up emotion and Briony pulled him on top of her and kissed him, her fingers expertly unbuttoning his trousers. As she caressed him he became hard. He pulled off his trousers and lay beside her, kissing her breasts and neck, murmuring his love for her. Briony slowly unbuttoned his shirt, running her nails gently across his back, feeling the goose bumps appearing on his skin. As he entered her, he groaned. She gripped him with her vaginal muscles, pulling him into her expertly, cold-bloodedly, like one of the girls who worked for her. He felt the familiar feeling of sadness envelop him. He rode her hard, thrusting himself inside her until he was spent. Then he collapsed on top of her, and she loved him then. Kissing him gently, whispering endearments. Enjoying his nearness. And as always he forgave her for his hurt. The feeling he was using her and being used in return. Because he knew that Briony was incapable of the feelings she generated in him, and the saddest part for him was what she was missing. But he petted her as he knew she liked, and kissed her.

They lay together for nearly an hour, both lost in their own thoughts. Both wanting to speak of their real feelings and both lost for words.

Finally, Briony stirred. Slipping from under him, she put on a silk wrapper and built up the fire. It was early evening and the sun was slowly disappearing. She put on the bedside lamps and smiled down at Tommy.

'What have you been doing today?'

He stared up at her and smiled.

'To be honest, Briony, I've been chasing up Bolger.'

'What's the rub? Have you found out who this mysterious backer is?'

Tommy shook his head. 'Nah. It seems our Willy is staying round with the Oldses. Ronnie Olds hates him, I know that for a fact. He's always hated ponces. Ronnie's strictly robbing and villainy. But here's a lot of dosh being spent, and I'll be honest, Bri, it's beginning to worry me. Someone wants us out of the picture for good. We're not talking healthy competition here, my love, we're talking death and destruction. Namely, mine and yours.'

She sat on the bed and put her hand over Tommy's. 'You're really worried, aren't you?' Her voice was shocked.

Tommy bit his lip and nodded.

'To be honest, girl, I am. There's something going down here and I can't get to the fucking bottom of it. I've been tramping the pavements like a madman and I can't get nothing from no one.

'Whoever's backing Willy is very shrewd, and I think we already know that, and he's arsehole fucking lucky. Because Willy ain't mentioned him to anyone. Also, whoever it is ain't a villain, because Willy's buying up anyone who's anyone.'

He sighed and wiped his hand over his face. His thick hair was tousled. Looking at him in the firelight, his face drawn, a feeling of fear stole over her. If Tommy Lane was scared then there was definitely something to be nervous about.

'So what's to do? Do we sit here and shit ourselves or do we go out and find the fucker? You tell me.'

Her tone was aggressive as she wanted it to be. She was frightened now herself, really frightened, and she didn't like it. She didn't like it at all.

Despite himself, Tommy laughed. Only his Briony would be prepared to go out looking for someone who could be the death of them. She'd pick up a chair and fight anyone!

'Tonight there's a fight over at Victoria Park. Olds will be there, maybe even Willy. I don't think we can wait for Mariah to have her meet. I think we need the element of surprise, don't you?'

Briony nodded and grinned.

Tommy leapt from the bed and lit one of his cheap cheroots. 'Ring for a bit of scran. Bacon and eggs will do, anything. I'm starving. Then I'll round up all the boys and tool them up. We'll go there tonight and give them a run for their fucking money. If I'm going down, I intend to take a good few with me.'

Briony rang the bell.

'I'll get myself washed and dressed. I think we should get there as the first fight comes on. That way we'll slip in easier.'

Tommy looked at her and shook his head.

'Oh, no! You're not going. That ain't no place for you, or any woman come to that. You're staying here. Sort out the clubs, the houses, anything. But you ain't going near the places tonight!'

Briony faced him. Putting her hands on her hips, she said: 'And who's gonna stop me?'

Tommy walked to her and pushed his face close to hers. 'I ain't never raised a hand to you, Briony, nor to any woman, but I'll give you the leathering of your life if you set one dainty foot near that place tonight!'

Tommy rounded up twenty of his best men, including Abel Jones and Jimmy Reynard. In the basement of a slum in Wapping, Tommy displayed his arsenal and the men each picked out a weapon and secreted it on their person.

Knives, guns and coshes were the order of the day, and as they all left to go to the fight there was a general air of excitement. Most of the men had grudges against the Oldses and the Campbells, so were looking forward to the fight. Tommy smoked cheroots one after the other as the cavalcade made their way to Hackney. They arrived just after nine.

The first fight was already taking place and the park was literally packed out. Tommy and his men pushed their way through the crowds, looking for Ronnie Olds. He would be made to tell them where Bolger was hiding out, even if it meant losing his testicles during the conversation. Tommy was now acting on pure adrenaline. His heightened awareness made him more aggressive than ever and he pushed through the crowds with a grim look on his face. He wanted this sorted once and for all. The chance was he would end his life here tonight but it was a chance he was prepared to take. Tommy noticed Jimmy and another man buying themselves roast chicken from a vendor. Walking over to them, he grabbed Jimmy by the throat.

'What's this then, Jimmy, a fucking night out or what?'

Jimmy put the piece of greasy chicken back on the barrow and followed Tommy sheepishly. He was starving. Unlike Tommy he hadn't eaten since the morning and his stomach was gurgling now, with only a few pints of Watney's inside it.

Tommy walked along, keeping up a stream of abuse.

'I don't fucking believe you, Jimmy! What next? Shall we have a break and watch the poxy find-the-lady bloke? Or, I know, how about we go and have our fucking fortunes told?'

They were approaching the area where the fighters

were; a ring had been roped off and the money men were milling around. Tommy spotted Ronnie Olds by a small marquee. He signalled to his men and they all surged forward together. Ronnie was busy taking bets and didn't see Tommy till it was too late. Tommy was beside him with a false smile on his face and a dangerous grip on Ronnie's arm. Looking at the old woman who was trying to place a bet, he said, 'Sorry, love, this bookie just closed. You'll have to go somewhere else.'

The woman, a known penny lender, looked at Tommy in temper and said: 'Balls! I wanna place a bet. I've been queueing for half an hour!'

Tommy looked down at her and said between gritted teeth: 'Fuck off, Grandma, or I'll shove your money right up your arse!'

People began to move away then, guessing there was trouble afoot. It was Ronnie Olds' trouble and not theirs. The old woman contemptuously spat at Tommy's feet and went along to the next bookie, complaining loudly.

Tommy pushed Ronnie into his marquee and the two men faced one another.

'You're out of order, Lane. You've no business coming here and pushing me around.'

'Bollocks, Ronnie. All I hear lately is you and the Campbells and that slag Bolger. Well, tonight's the night I pay my fucking debts, and I'm starting with you, matey.'

Ronnie Olds was a big man, big and cumbersome. Tommy knew this and had planned accordingly. Pulling a boning knife from his waistband, he slashed it across Ronnie's beer belly. The blade went in about an inch. Ronnie watched in dismay as blood began to seep out. The boning knife was so sharp he hadn't even felt any discomfort. But he was cute enough to know the pain would come. He held his stomach with both hands, unsure whether the knife had cut deep enough to spill out his guts. Once they left the body you were dead. White-faced, he staggered back, his heart beating too fast, sweat appearing on his forehead.

Tommy slashed him again, lengthwise this time. Making a red cross on his stomach.

'You fucking ponce! You thought you could fuck me up, didn't you? You thought that Bolger was the dog's bollocks. Well, he ain't, mate. He ain't, but I am. You want violence, I'll give it to you. I'm gonna take out every one of you, even your fucking drunken old man. You want fear, well, I'll make sure you get more than you ever dreamt of in your poxy little life!'

He took the knife and wiped it across Ronnie's face. Slicing through the skin until the cheek flapped down exposing the bone.

Both men stared at Briony as she walked into the tent with Mariah Jurgens.

'Hurts, don't it, Ronnie? Stings I should imagine. Well, thanks to you one of my girls was tortured like that by your mate Willy Bolger. Now, where is he? Tommy's mob-handed and so are we. Me and Mariah just picked up every piece of shite in the Arab quarter of the docks. So you'd better start talking or we'll just round up your brothers and cut them till they tell us what we want to know. Won't we, Tommy?'

He stared in amazement at Briony and Mariah. They stood there, dressed up to the nines without a flicker of fear on their faces. Mariah grinned maliciously.

'By the way, Ronnie, we've rounded up Micky Campbell too. He's outside in my car now with Marcenello, the Maltese hero. An Arab friend of mine is watching them for me. You know big Kousan, don't you, Ronnie? He's the one who chased you off his manor with a meat cleaver not six months ago when you was trying to get into the dock industry. Well, he don't like you and I think we can safely say, you don't like him. So tell us where Bolger is.'

Ronnie looked at the three people in the room. He was gradually feeling a faintness stealing over him. Not just from the loss of blood but at the realisation that here were three people who could not let him live after this night's work. It was all Bolger's doing, with his packed wallet and his smarmy tongue. He was as good as dead, and he knew it. Being a nasty man, if he was going he wanted to take as many with him as possible.

'He's round Valence Road. Bethnal Green. He's staying with a girl of his, Gilda the Pole. You'll find him there. But he's well protected. The Jews are seeing to that.'

Outside the fight was in full swing and the crowd screamed for blood. That meant an opponent was down. Briony, Mariah and Tommy left the tent without a second look at Ronnie who was still trying to hold his guts inside the large gaping hole across his belly. Ronnie Olds had lived by fear all his life. He was a known villain who dealt out death like other people dealt out cards. Now he was coming to the end of his life, inside a marquee in Victoria Park, a pile of money in his wallet and a bottle of whisky in his pocket. He slumped to the floor and, pulling out the whisky bottle, drank from it eagerly.

He died as he had lived, violently, and there was no one to mourn his passing.

Pushing through the crowds who were eagerly shouting encouragement to the two fighters on the stage, Briony fought down the urge to vomit. As bad as Ronnie

Olds was, the sight of him bleeding like that made her ill.

She breathed in the stench of the unwashed bodies around her, the old sweat mingling with the new, the heavy aroma of food cooking on braziers, and the sweet smell of candyfloss and rock, and she emptied her stomach just as she approached her car. As she heaved, Mariah rubbed her back gently.

'Listen, Briony, if he had his way, he'd have stood and watched you die in agony. I know Ronnie from the old days. Put it out of your mind. He deserved it. And if Tommy hadn't done it, someone else would have.'

Briony slipped into her car, aware that Tommy had not spoken a word to her which was a sign of his anger. Closing her eyes she sat back in the car as they all made their way to Valence Road. Ginelle's face danced in front of her eyes, in her ridiculous cloche hat and her silk flapper dresses. And that imitation posh accent she had tried so hard to acquire.

By the time she reached her destination she felt infinitely better, her resolve strong in her once more. She had to frighten people enough so that nothing like this ever happened again. She lived in a violent world where the law of the street was the only law you could live by and survive. Well, she'd made up her mind that was exactly how she would live from now on. She would rule through fear. No one would ever touch her or anyone to do with her again.

At the entrance to Valence Road Briony, Tommy and Mariah directed their respective men. Jimmy Reynard and two others, Abel and Kevin Rafferty, were to watch the back entrance to Gilda's house. The men rushed off to take up their positions. Micky Campbell and Marcenello sat terror-stricken in Mariah's car. Kousan, the undisputed leader of the Arabs, sat smiling at them, his huge head seemingly split by a wide grin. His men had stayed at Victoria Park and were rounding up the men belonging to Olds, Campbell and Marcenello. It was a well-planned and well-executed operation.

Mariah and Kousan were old friends and old adversaries. But he had listened to Mariah and Briony and had been persuaded into taking part in this war because he trusted them. It benefited him to have a good relationship with whoever ran the East End. No one, but no one, got near the docks unless he allowed it. Anything that went missing off the ships went to him; he had no interest in prostitution whatsoever although a few of the dock dollies were under his protection. That was because they were with Arab men, or had given birth to Arab children at some point. He would enjoy having a good relationship with this Tommy Lane and Briony. It could only benefit them all.

An added bonus was that he could pay back a few debts of his own tonight, starting with Micky Campbell. He hated the Campbells and they hated him.

At this moment Micky was terrified because for the first time ever he was on his own, without a weapon, his brothers or his formidable mother, who was the real brains behind the Campbell businesses.

He and Marcenello watched as Briony, Tommy and Mariah walked down to Gilda's little terraced house. Gilda the Pole was a woman of uncertain age with a pronounced limp who catered to the lower echelons of the docks, the African sailors and the Chinese. She was a small woman with a beautiful peach skin, and the worst temper this side of the water.

She was called 'the Pole' because she'd had polio which had left the limp, and had no other known last name.

The women's heels tapped on the pavement and Tommy heard the sound with his temper bubbling up inside him. When he got Briony home he was going to slap her face for her, hard. When she had walked into that marquee he had felt such a fool. So annoyed he could easily have throttled her.

This was men's work, they were dealing with the lowest of the low, and as much as he respected her cunning and her bravery, he couldn't forgive her for turning up there with those Arabs and that bleeding lanky bitch Jurgens! It made him look soft. As if he held on to her apron strings. His temper was so hot he nearly knocked Gilda's neat green front door into the hallway when he hammered on it.

Willy had seen their approach through the small front room window, and taking a gun he ran out to the kitchen, telling Gilda to open the door and try and stall them.

As she opened the front door, she flicked her head and said: 'He's trying to do a poodle out the back door. He's got a gun, and the hump. What more can I say?'

Outside in the yard Willy looked at the three men waiting for him and, hearing Gilda's opening words at the door, knew he was finished. He was supposed to have an armed guard here and there was no one but Lane's men. He looked around in the hope a couple of his minders would appear from the woodwork, but he knew instinctively that they were long gone. He didn't hold out any hope that any were sitting outside or watching from the road. The Jews had abandoned him. They obviously knew something he didn't. He could try and shoot his way out but he would be dead in seconds. It was the end of the line and he knew it.

He had been so close to achieving his aims! So very

close. Now it was all falling down around his ears. The thought amused him even in his terrified state and he began to laugh. As Tommy appeared at the back door, he grinned at him.

'Hello, Tommy boy. I hear you've been looking for me?'

Then, as Tommy watched, he put the barrel of the gun in his mouth, curling his tongue around the metal and still laughing as he pulled the trigger.

He had cheated them of his death and they were still none the wiser as to who had been backing him.

Going to the lifeless form, Tommy began to kick it in his rage. Briony and Mariah walked out with Gilda. Turning to Briony, Tommy bellowed: 'You lot had to stick your beaks in, didn't you? Well, he's brown fucking bread now, so that's an end to it. If you don't mind I'll sort out Campbell and the others. Or do you want me to put me hand up and ask permission first?'

With that he pushed through them and went out through the house. Jimmy and Abel looked at one another, eyebrows raised, before they left.

Mariah put her hand on Briony's arm.

'He's upset.'

Before Briony could answer, Gilda shouted: 'So what? I'm upset! That fat bastard was paying me a small fortune for staying here. Now I've got to get the Old Bill and report a fucking suicide!'

Looking at the little woman in front of her, standing awkwardly with all her weight on her good leg, Briony started to laugh. A laugh that rapidly turned to tears. Taking her by the arm, Mariah walked her back to her car.

Pulling away from Mariah, Briony went to Tommy and

said in a low voice: 'All right, big shot, so you're annoyed, but think on this. Where the fuck are the Jews? They were supposed to be protecting him, remember? Someone got here first, mate. Bolger thought he was running out to help and security. There wasn't a soul there but us. Think about it. Come on, Mariah, we'll leave the big boys to their little games.'

When the women left, Tommy got into Mariah's car. It was being driven by her minder, Big John. Nodding at Kousan, Tommy said to the men: 'As you can probably see, I'm fucking fuming so don't bugger me about because I ain't in the mood. I've got two dead men and no explanations. So have a good think before you open your traps!'

Campbell and Marcenello had no intention of aggravating Tommy Lane any more than was necessary.

They both began to talk at once.

Chapter Fifteen

Ma Campbell was sixty-eight, with a face like a walnut, and black hair liberally sprinkled with grey worn piled up on her head in a neat French pleat. As always she was in a shapeless grey dress, covered over by a large apron which crossed over her pendulous breasts and was tied in a neat bow around her waist. Her feet were swollen, and bulged out of carpet slippers cut at the side to allow her bunions free rein. She had just made her husband and herself a ham sandwich, and was settling by her kitchen fire waiting for her boys to come home and tell her the evening's doings.

As the door knocker was slammed against the wood she heaved herself out of her chair. Walking along her hallway, she bellowed: 'All right, all right, for fuck's sake! I ain't deaf!'

Pulling open her front door she closed her gaping mouth as she saw Mariah Jurgens and Briony Cavanagh standing there. She drew herself up to her full height and stood aggressively before them.

'Well, well, well, if it ain't the bleeding Tarts' Society on me step!'

Briony and Mariah pushed her into her hallway in a flurry of bad language and shoves.

'Who you bleeding pushing, you pair of whores? My boys won't take no sodding nonsense, mate. They'll cut your tits off if you touch me.'

Briony grabbed the woman by her immaculate French pleat and practically ran her into her kitchen.

'Shut up, Ma, before I lose me rag. Your Micky is at this moment in a car with Kousan the Arab and Tommy Lane, and I don't hold out much hope of him coming home.'

Da Campbell, as he was known, carried on eating his sandwich without glancing at them.

'Everyone knows you're the brains, Ma, so why don't you just calm down and tell us what we want to know? Believe me when I say we've had enough for one night and we're rapidly losing our patience.'

Ma Campbell was so incensed her face was a bright red and her hands were visibly shaking.

'I don't know fuck all! Now get yourselves and your cheap perfume out of my clean kitchen.'

Mariah slapped her across the face, hard, making her head roll back on to her shoulders.

'You bitch! Raise your hand to me, would you?'

As Ma made to grab at Mariah, Briony took hold of her arm and twisted it up her back.

'Shut up, Nancy!' Da Campbell's voice was loud in the room and the three women stared at him.

'You bastard! You'd do a deal over your boy's life, wouldn't you? Wouldn't you?' The last two words ended on a scream.

Taking another bite of his sandwich, Da wiped his hands over his mouth and said through the food: 'If Kousan's got Micky, he's a dead man. I told him to steer clear of the screaming Ab Dads but he wouldn't listen. It's the other four boys I'm worried about now. What's gone on tonight?'

Briony pushed the old woman from her and shoved her into a chair. The tiny kitchen was silent as she began to talk.

'Ronnie Olds is dead. So is Willy Bolger. Me and Tommy come out in the open tonight, and believe me when I say we ain't having any more nonsense. This is our manor from tonight. There's no room any more for wasters or ponces. Anyone wants to work the East End, they've got to come to us. One of my girls was cut up and I ain't taking that lying down. No one touches me or mine and that goes for your precious fucking sons. It's all over, finished with, but I have to know who the big man was, who Bolger was cultivating, because I won't rest easy until I've cut the bastard. You understand me? I want him, and I'll trade the rest of your boys for him.'

Da Campbell nodded, it was what he'd expected. Unlike his wife he had no personal feelings about anything. His boys were an extension of him and his own quest for survival; he was quite happy to sacrifice Micky for the good of the rest. Kousan had been one of his son's biggest mistakes and without doubt his biggest enemy. He had a grudging respect for these two women because to get the Arabs working side by side with you was an achievement.

Da Campbell swallowed the last of his food. Standing up he went to the fireplace. He picked up his pipe and tapped it against the bricks.

'I saw Bolger about a week since. He was with a gentleman, and I mean gentleman. I worked for him once – around the same time as your old man Briony, actually.

Do you know, I remember you when you had the shit still running down your legs! Always had that flaming red hair though, even as a baby. Who'd have thought you'd have turned out like you did?'

Briony wasn't listening now. She knew who he was talking about but until she heard him voice the name she wouldn't rest.

'Who was the man? Tell me his name.'

'It was Henry Dumas. I was going down the Old Kent Road, up by The Apples and Pears. You can put on a good bet in there without the hag of getting paid out with an hammer. I saw them together. Now what would them two want with one another? I thought. But I knew straight off. My Micky was a prat. He should have taken Bolger's money and wasted the little shit. Never liked ponces, never. Dirty two-faced bastards, the majority. Whoring's a woman's game, the money's too easy. Bad as my boys are, they don't live off no tarts. You ladies know the game better than any man, I'll bet. And you've got the muscle behind you.'

Ma Campbell listened to her husband and then turned on him viciously.

'Hark at him! The bleeding oracle. By Christ, Da, you've sunk low before but, dear God, tonight you've sunk to the depths. Your son is sitting somewhere with that Arab bastard and you're telling this pair of whores what they wanna know!' Her voice was drenched with tears. Micky was her first-born, her baby. She knew he would never walk in her house again, never be there when she woke up, never speak to her again, and it broke her heart. Mariah patted her shoulder gently.

'Don't you touch me! I'll never forgive you for the news you brought here tonight. My boy's dead. My beautiful boy . . .'

Briony stared at the woman before her, at the tears bubbling out from underneath her closed lids, and felt a stirring of pity inside her. If her son was to die, was to die in fear and terror, without her near to try and help, to try and protect him, she would feel the same as this old woman before her. As bad as Ma Campbell was, and God himself knew she was a vicious woman, she loved her children. She had robbed, schemed and threatened to give her boys what she considered a good life. That meant plenty to eat, good clean clothes on their backs, and shoes or boots on their feet. Unless you were born as low as them, you couldn't understand in a million years what an achievement that was.

'You'll see me other boys come home, won't you now?'

Briony nodded at the man, who bit his lip and half smiled. 'Then there's nothing to do now but wait for the body to turn up.'

Mariah touched Briony's arm and silently the two women left the house, the only sound the heart-wrenching sobbing of Ma Campbell, which followed them out into the night.

Briony sat in her bedroom with a large glass of brandy in her hand and a cigarette dangling from her lips. She looked ugly and full of hate. Since finding out about Henry Dumas, she had felt a canker growing inside her. With every second the clock ticked, the feeling grew. She was now full of it, it consumed her until she was ready to burst. Everything she had ever suffered at his hands was there in front of her eyes in crystal clear detail. His flabby body, his roughness as he took her, the putrid stench of his breath on her face.

She'd been a child, and she had thought as a child. She

had thought to save herself and her family from poverty by letting him have her. But he should have known how wrong he was, her father should have known! How could she have realised what she was doing? All she had wanted was the warmth of the house, the good food, the cleanliness. She had wanted it for herself and her sisters, and Dumas had made use of that. But what a price she had paid, still paid.

He had taken her child, and before that he had taken her very heart. Had helped strangle every natural instinct she possessed. Until now she was empty.

But she would pay him back. Dear God, she would pay him back tenfold, a hundredfold for what he had done to her. What he had tried to do to her.

She heard Tommy enter the house and held her breath. The front door was banged hard; she could even hear him throw his coat across the banisters, the buttons making a snapping sound as they hit the wooden balustrade. She heard him stamping up the stairs, heard Mrs Horlock's light tread on the landing and her voice as she spoke to him.

'What's all the noise? What's going on? Briony's not fit for man or beast, like a madwoman . . .'

'GO TO BLEEDING BED!' Tommy's voice echoed around the hallway, sending the old woman scurrying away.

Briony tensed in her chair, waiting for the onslaught that was to come. Tommy opened the bedroom door and it banged against the dado rail with a sickening thump.

She watched him as he walked into the room, his face set, his hair standing on end as if he had received a massive shock.

'You mare! You showed me up tonight, Briony. Never have I felt so embarrassed, so small. You charged in there like I didn't mean anything, I was nothing! I don't work for you, madam, let's get that straight. We're a partnership! A partnership. I ain't your fucking lackey, I ain't no one's lackey.'

He pushed his face close to hers. She could see the tiny veins in his eyes and almost taste his breath as he bellowed. 'You ever do that to me again, put yourself in the frame like that, and I'll give you the biggest slap you've ever had in your life. Do you hear me?'

Briony took a long drag on her cigarette and blew the smoke into his face.

'Yes, Tommy. I can hear you, mate. The whole of Barking can hear you.' She pushed him from her with a strength that surprised him. Standing, she pointed at him with the cigarette.

'All I ever hear is *you*. You, me, I – sodding Tommy Lane! Well, for once I ain't interested. I've got a bit more on my mind than your stupid fucking worries about saving face. As you just said we're supposed to be a partnership so that gives me the right to do what I want, go where I want, and have a say in what I want too! *That's* a partnership, boy. Not sitting home like a fucking wife while you run around being the hero!

'And while you was ducking and diving tonight, running round like a blue-arsed fly, I went round and saw Ma and Da Campbell. It's Dumas we want, Tommy. Henry Dumas. Da Campbell saw him and Bolger having a meet and put two and two together. So why don't you calm yourself down and use your head instead of your arse for once? Only I would be interested to know what the other half of this so-called partnership has to say about that?'

Even in her grief she was secretly pleased to see Tommy deflated by her words.

He was shaken and disturbed.

'Dumas?' His voice was low, incredulous.

'The very one.' She stubbed out her cigarette and immediately lit another, pulling the smoke into her lungs with a ferocity that stunned him. 'I want him. I want that bastard once and for all. I don't care if he has got a father-in-law who's a fucking lord, I couldn't care less if he is the Prime Minister or fucking King Street Charlie, I want that bastard cut!'

'Oh, Briony, come here, love . . .'

She screwed up her eyes and clenched her fists, her whole body tense.

'Don't try and make it right with me, Tommy, please. I don't want a cuddle or kind words, they don't mean nothing. I want that bastard prostrate in front of me. I want to pay him back for me, for my emptiness, for Ginelle, and most of all for daring to try and tuck me up.'

She looked at him and he couldn't meet her eyes. Couldn't acknowledge what he saw there: the pain and unhappiness. And the lust for revenge. She wanted revenge and he knew she would get it, with or without him. All the anger seemed to seep from his powerful frame in seconds. Compared to what she had suffered at that man's hands, his own feelings were as nothing.

'We'll get him, girl. Between us we'll get him, I promise you that.'

It was what she wanted to hear. The burden of her thoughts was lifted, shared now and taken on by Tommy. Walking to him, she let herself be pulled into his embrace. Over his shoulder she watched the cigarette smoke curling up in tendrils in the empty air and saw the faces of Ronnie Olds and Willy Bolger. Tomorrow Tommy and she would be the undisputed King and Queen of the East End, and the knowledge made her feel sad and bitter. It was a title she had never craved, wanting respectability through her clubs and money-making schemes. Now she would have to keep the title and fight for it, otherwise Dumas and people like him could get to her once more. Could try and force her back to the gutter she had crawled out of. Sometimes things were forced on you, and you had to bear the consequences. It was the story of her life.

Finally, after what seemed an age, she cried.

Benedict Dumas watched his father's moustaches quivering as he sat in his chair reading his daily paper. He pushed his own food around his plate, unable to stomach the kidney and scrambled eggs. He liked a boiled egg and bread and butter, his father knew this, but forced the kidneys on him every morning and waited until he ate them.

'What are you staring at, boy? Eat your food.'

'Yes, Papa.'

Henry clenched his teeth in anger. Every time the boy called him 'Papa' he fought the urge to beat him. He had to acknowledge the child. His father-in-law doted on him, his wife adored him, even the blasted servants pandered to him. Henry hated the sight of him. Hated what he represented.

Banging his fist down on the table he shouted: 'Eat your breakfast, boy!'

Isabel walked into the room with the mail and the atmosphere immediately lightened. Benedict smiled at his mama, and she kissed him on his cheek lightly.

'Your grandpapa is coming today to take you to see the trains at Paddington. Then, I believe, he is taking you to the zoological gardens!'

'Oh, Mama, how splendid! I'd better not eat too much breakfast as he always buys me an enormous lunch.'

Henry gritted his teeth and carried on with his pretence at reading the paper.

'No, darling. Leave that now and run up to your room and get your lessons prepared for Mr Bartlet. He has kindly allowed you to miss French today, but you must make up for it tomorrow.'

'I will, Mama.'

Isabel's eyes twinkled as the boy looked at her with the special conspiratorial look reserved for when Henry was near them. Already Benedict knew the set-up in the house. His father was a terror to the face, and a joke behind his back.

Isabel watched her husband as he tucked into his bacon, eggs and sausages. She had aged a great deal since the arrival of Benedict in her household. At first Isabel had been shunned by her so-called friends and contemporaries. But as her father had become besotted with the child and rumours had begun circulating that the child was actually his and not Dumas's, people had begun to call again and life had resumed its normal pattern. Isabel adored the boy; she saw him as the only thing in her life she actually possessed wholly. He was also a stick to beat Henry with and she took delight in this, surprising herself with the keenness with which she pitted her wits against her husband.

Now the child was ten, he ate with them, as a boy was expected to at a certain age, was allowed to greet company, and was being trained in the niceties of being a young man of wealth and good family. The latter made her smile in her darker moments, knowing his stock so well: a father who was enamoured of little girls and a mother who was a whore of the first water. She shunned Briony now, hated thinking about the girl who had borne him. He was her son, wholly her son.

Henry's fork crashing on to his plate distracted her from her reverie and she looked at him, the animosity between them tangible in the confines of the room.

Folding up his paper, he stood and left the room without a word or a backward glance. Pouring herself more coffee, Isabel smiled and mentally chalked up another victory to herself.

Joshua was eating his lunch at The Chequers Inn. As always he had a pint of brown ale, and pie, peas and mash. He was swallowing down the last of his peas when his friend Billy Buggins started chattering about events of the previous night.

'Anyway, seems that Tommy Lane went to Victoria Park and caused all sorts! I heard this morning that Ronnie Olds is dead, Micky Campbell, Marcenello and Willy Bolger! Though no one's gonna miss him! Cut Ronnie Olds up right under his brothers' noses they did. The Old Bill has been crawling around like maggots on a bit of rancid bacon. Well, they ain't gonna find out nothing, are they? No one's gonna put their face in the frame for the likes of them, I ask you. That Briony Cavanagh was there by all accounts, with the big Swede Jurgens. Now there's two women I wouldn't fancy . . .'

His voice trailed off and Joshua wiped his tongue around his teeth before saying: 'Go on, Billy. Finish what you was going to say.'

Billy was terrified – not of Joshua, he had known Joshua for years. He was terrified of the fact Joshua was soon to be a part of that set-up too. He was marrying Briony's sister.

'Say what you was going to say, Billy, I ain't going to have a go nor nothing. I want to know what you was going to say.'

Billy was as red as a beetroot, even his neck was flushed. 'I never meant nothing by it, Joshua, everyone knows Eileen's a good kid. I mean, she can't help her stock, can she? Can any of us?'

This was a veiled reference to Joshua's father and he digested the words before he said: 'In future, Billy, think before you open your mouth. I'm a peaceable man but my wife's family is soon to be my family and I can't listen to anyone bad-mouthing them, can I?'

Billy shook his great head furiously. 'No, Josh . . . You're right, I was out of order.'

Joshua smiled and carried on eating his food.

But he was worried. Eileen's sisters had not really played a part in his life, not yet anyway. But all he had heard this morning was how Briony and Tommy Lane had taken on the hard men and won. It was just occurring to him that his sweet-faced Eileen, with her angelic face and compliant nature, might be more trouble than she was worth.

Bernadette and Kerry were sorting through a pile of clothes together. They'd had a truce since Kerry had made it plain she would brook no trouble. Bernie for her part was frightened of her sister now. Besides being her employer, she was Bernie's ticket out of the East End. Evander was not discussed by mutual consent and they played a game that everything was as it had been, though both knew that to regain their old easy footing would be impossible now. They walked around each other carefully, weighing up their words and phrases. It was exhausting for them both.

Now, though, they had a subject they could discuss freely: the events of the night before in Victoria Park.

'Our Briony's got it all now, Kerry. She's number one, the business as they say.'

Kerry nodded. 'Yes, our Briony is up there with the hard men. Jesus wept, I never thought she'd stoop to murder! I thought she was strictly a good-time girl, a madam. Oh, Bernie, what on earth will all this come to?'

She shook her head.

'Our Briony was always a law unto herself, you know that. It's why she got as far as she did and took us with her. We'll just have to hope she can take on contenders for her crown, because there'll be plenty of them, once the novelty wears off. She'll spend her whole life looking over her shoulder now.'

Kerry looked down at the dress she was holding and bit her lip. If Briony looked over her shoulder and saw Evander, what would happen then?

Chapter Sixteen

St Martin's Church was full. Ginelle's coffin was closed, the lid screwed tightly down. Briony stood at the front of the church with Tommy, Ginelle's mother and her elder children taking the second pew. Briony's eyes strayed constantly to the coffin, knowing exactly what was inside it. She heard the muffled sobs of her girls, and the vicar's droning voice.

Unlike a Catholic Mass, with its pomp and ceremony, the Church of England service seemed very shallow and unfeeling to Briony. The vicar, a dour man in his sixties, kept referring to Ginelle as 'the young lady', as if frightened to admit any kind of association with her. There were no hymns, no real prayers, and as far as Briony was concerned, no emotion. She grasped Tommy's hand for warmth. He squeezed it tightly, as if knowing the battle raging inside her, the guilt she felt. Ginelle's death was her fault. Ginelle had become a valuable asset, appearing in the films with Jonathan la Billière. She had been the girl of everyone's dreams. Bolger had killed her because she was worth money to Briony, a lot of money. If Briony hadn't decided to branch out into the films, Ginelle would have still been just a Tom. Would still be walking around with her phony accent and her outlandish clothes.

Recognition of this caused her a great deal of concern. Though Briony had fought for Ginelle, and now guaranteed her girls a much safer life, she still couldn't rest easy in her bed. Not even with the reassuring presence of Tommy beside her. Because in her mind's eye, in the dark, she once more saw Ginelle in the crate. Smelt the sticky blood. Saw the terrified face on the dead girl. Now there were other faces too. Bolger's, Marcenello's, Campbell's and Ronnie Olds'. Ronnie holding his guts inside the gaping hole of his belly. As soon as this service was over, and Ginelle had been laid to rest, she was going to go round and see the bastard who was behind all the carnage, and the death. She forced herself to concentrate and began praying.

Tommy watched as her lips moved in silent prayer, not at all sure what exactly he was doing in this church, burying a working girl. He sighed heavily. Briony gave him a quick look out of the corner of her eye and, feeling ashamed, he tried valiantly to remember a prayer from his childhood. As he began his 'Our Father' he smiled to himself. Only Briony could get the new governor of the East End to a whore's burial. But that's what he had always loved about her: her dogged determination to do what she considered right and just.

He finished his prayer and hastily blessed himself, feeling a glow of righteousness go through him. Then, bored once more, he concentrated his thoughts on Henry Dumas, and contemplated the vicar who was saying nothing and taking far too bloody long about it.

*

Henry sat in his office and looked over a pile of papers. His secretary, Miss Barnes, a recent acquisition, stood nervously by waiting for his approval. Henry took his time, enjoying her discomfiture. He had no real need of a woman in his workplace, but it was now the done thing. She stood there in front of him in her long grey skirt, high button boots and a sensible white blouse, her brown hair tied at the back with a black velvet ribbon, her hands clasped demurely together. At least she didn't smoke. He couldn't abide seeing women smoke.

'They'll do, Miss Barnes.' He held the papers out for her without looking up and the girl hastily took them and departed. Henry rested his elbows on his desk and glanced at the heavy mahogany clock on the wall. It was a quarter to five. He grinned to himself, contemplating the little girl waiting for him at a small house in Upney Lane. He decided to leave early and walk to his destination. It was only fifteen minutes from the dock offices. Nodding at Miss Barnes, he left the building.

Briony and Tommy watched him leave, buttoning his coat. They watched him walk down to the corner of the street and walk into a small shop. He came out five minutes later with a brightly coloured box of sweets. Briony felt her heart stop dead in her chest.

It was as if she was a child again and Henry was coming to visit her, with his little treats and presents. She gripped Tommy's hand on the steering wheel and whispered: 'Follow him, let's see where he's going.'

He shrugged and started up the car, the urgency in her voice communicating itself to him.

'He's got a girl, Tommy. The bastard bought sweets, and from what Sally's said they're not for Benedict. He can't stand the sight of the child. He used to bring me bits and pieces. The bastard, the dirty bastard!'

They followed him, matching his brisk pace. As he turned into Upney Lane, Briony held her breath inside her chest until it hurt. Henry's pace quickened and when he opened a small wooden gate and practically danced up the path, she felt the rage build inside her. The front door was opened by a young woman. Briony squinted. She looked familiar. The woman greeted Dumas effusively, and when the door shut behind them, Briony and Tommy emerged from their car on to the dirt road.

'I'll kill him, Tommy. I swear to you, I'll kill him!'

'Calm down. We'll go in and find out the score. There'll be no killing here today. If we top him it'll cause us too much trouble. It's a warning we're here to deliver, right?'

Briony stared into his face and the misery she displayed made Tommy want to wring Henry Dumas's neck.

'I hate him! I hate him from the very bones, do you know that? Even Olds, as bad as he was, deserved to live over that bastard. Had more right to life.'

Pulling away from Tommy, she walked over to the house purposefully, banging open the little wooden gate and tramping up the neat path as quick as her legs would carry her. Tommy followed her, a feeling of foreboding inside him.

This was more than revenge. Briony was facing her own personal demons today, he understood that, and as the front door opened, he put his hand inside his coat and caressed the policeman's truncheon he had placed there earlier. He had a good few scores to settle this day himself.

Christine Howell opened the door smiling, her big moon face split in a grin that rapidly disappeared as she saw the two people standing before her.

'Where is he?' Briony's voice was tight.

'Who?' Christine's voice was high. Fright mingled with confusion making her panic.

'Who? Who do you fucking think! That nonsense who just walked in here!'

Pushing past the terrified girl, she opened the first door she came to. Bursting into the room, she stopped dead. Sitting by a blazing fire, his face drained of colour, was Henry Dumas, on his lap a little dark-haired girl of about nine. Her hands were still clutching the box of sweets, her face a mask of dismay.

As if just realising the child was there, Dumas pushed her from him as if she was red hot, emptying her from his lap on to the carpet with a thump.

'What are you doing here?' His voice was high and incredulous. His mouth moved again, but this time no sound emerged. Henry Dumas was literally lost for words. As his eyes burned into Briony's he became aware of Tommy Lane picking the little girl up and leading her from the room. Heaving himself from the chair, he stood up, shoulders back, and in his most commanding voice, shouted: 'Leave that child alone! Now take yourself and this . . . this . . . slut back where you came from!'

His voice and demeanour triggered a reaction from Briony. He dared to shout at them? He dared to stand there in this house and order them out?

She flew at him, hair and nails flying. Instinctively she went for his face, dragging her nails through the soft plump skin of his cheeks, feeling it tear, a superhuman strength flowing through her body. As small as she was, she forced him to the floor. His utter shock at being attacked gave Briony the edge over him. As Henry hit the carpet, his hands trying desperately to hold her clawing fingers away from him, Briony kicked him in the stomach.

He let go of her to hold himself and she picked up the poker from the embers of the fire and brought it crashing down on to his head, the smell of his singeing hair permeating the room. Raising the poker up over her head again she brought it down on to his shoulders and back, again and again, every blow easing the pain inside her until, spent, she looked down on to his bloody face and dropped the poker with a dull thud. She closed her eyes tightly, savouring the moment.

In the recesses of her mind she heard him groan and was aware he was still alive. Her breath was coming in deep gulps, a hoarse whisper escaping from her lips with each gasping breath. Her chest hurt, her arms ached, but she felt a sort of peace descend on her body as she stared at the man before her.

'You'll never do to anyone what you did to me, are you listening?' Her voice was low in the room. The three people at the door watched her in the firelight with a strange fascination. 'You tried to ruin me, Henry, and you failed, you'll always fail, because as God is my witness, the next time I have any dealings with you, you'll die. Ronnie Olds is dead, so's Bolger. You've no one and nothing on your side now. All you have left is me, and I'm gonna watch you from now on, mate. If you so much as shit I'll know what colour it is. That will be my revenge on you, boy. I'll see you never play your little games again.'

Henry looked up at her, and even through his pain he realised that in trying to destroy her, he had inadvertently destroyed himself.

'You so much as breathe at Benedict and I'll hear about it. I've eyes in your house and in your workplace. My boy is all I have in the world, and thanks to you and Isabel I have to look after him from afar. Well, you'll toe the line after tonight, Henry big man Dumas. You'll be a proper father to him. If you so much as look at him out of place, I'll ring your fucking neck. Do you understand me?'

He looked up at her, his face and mouth bleeding profusely.

'DO YOU UNDERSTAND ME?'

Her voice echoed around the room and Henry nodded, the action making him wince.

'You sicken me. You make me hate like I've never hated before. You made me what I am today, and I'll never forgive you for it.'

She turned from him and walked to the door. Looking into Christine Howell's face, she sneered, 'I know you.' She looked at Tommy who was still watching her with awe. 'We went to school together, we was in the same class.' Then, taking back her arm, she slapped the woman a heavy blow to the side of her face.

'You dirty bitch, you'd give your little child to him? Your own flesh and blood!' The little girl, her face pressed into Tommy's thigh, began to whimper. Briony shook her head in wonder.

'She's a beautiful child, and you'd let him touch her! You'd deliver her to him on a plate. Well, your game's over now. You and that child are leaving this drum tonight. I don't care where you go or what you do, Christine, but I'll keep my eye on this little girl. I'll make sure you look out for her or you'll answer to me. By Christ, you'll answer to me!'

Kerry watched Evander talking to Glennford. She smiled over at them and waved. They waved back and grinned at her, but Glennford's grin was forced.

'I'm telling you, Evander, you're in over your head, boy. From what I have been told, her dear sister, our employer, is now some kind of gang boss here. Her and that Tommy wasted four men the other night! They're bad people to mess with, and you're sleeping with her kid sister.'

Glennford's face was covered with a thin sheen of sweat. Since hearing the talk about Briony and Tommy he had become very worried for his friend, and not a little concerned for himself and the other members of his band. Mud tended to stick in his experience, and the mud would be flying in all directions if Evander's association with Kerry Cavanagh came to light.

'I'll sort it out, don't worry.' Evander's voice was low. His athletic body moved away with speed and easy grace. Glennford stared after him, a feeling of foreboding inside him.

Evander walked to Kerry and smiled at her.

'You look beautiful.'

Kerry smiled up into his eyes and gave a low throaty chuckle.

'So do you.' Without thinking what she was doing, Kerry put up her fingers and touched his face gently.

Glennford watched the exchange and felt the feeling of foreboding once more.

'You look as white as a ghost, Briony. Are you drinking enough milk?'

Molly's voice was beginning to annoy Briony. Taking a deep breath, she said: 'Give it a rest, Mum. It's been a hectic few days.'

Molly wiped Rosalee's face with a handkerchief and grinned. 'It has that, child. Oh, you should have seen the way I was treated down the Lane. Like visiting royalty. "Yes, Mrs Cavanagh. No, Mrs Cavanagh. And how's the girls, Mrs Cavanagh? Give Briony my regards, Mrs Cavanagh." Huh! The two-faced bastards. I can remember when I couldn't get a fecking smile outa them. When I had a shilling on a piece of string to see me through the week. Collecting the rotten veg from the gutters as they packed up for the day to keep you lot fed. While that drunken sod of a father pissed away the money in The Chequers . . .'

Briony put her hand up to her head and groaned.

'Oh, Mum, we're not going through all that again, are we? You're all right now, aren't you? You've got plenty of money now. Don't I see you all right?'

Molly looked at her daughter with concern.

'Jesus and Mary, you're a daughter any woman would be proud of. Look at the way you handle your businesses. But sometimes, when I remember how it was, how it could have been, I feel the old sadness creep over me. It's hard to see your babies hungry, you know. To hear them cry themselves to sleep. It's a sound that never leaves you. You hear it sometimes on the wind when it's whistling around your house. It still taps on the windows, taunting you in the cold weather.'

Briony smiled a smile she didn't think she had in her.

'Well, stop remembering! The old man's dead, and we're all alive and kicking. We've plenty. Even if I never made another penny we'd have enough to keep us all for the rest of our days. So stop worrying. Now, what's happening about Eileen?'

'Well, we thought we'd have the wedding in six weeks' time. I've booked the church, and she's waiting till you've a minute to yourself to help her pick the dress. You, Kerry and Bernie and Eileen can all go out together one day. What do you think?'

'That would be lovely. I know a dressmaker in Bond Street who'll knock her up a stunner. Real silk and all. She makes my clothes.'

Molly felt as if her heart would burst. Wait till she bragged about this to everyone! A real seamstress making Eileen's dress. She'd knock their eyes for them.

'I don't think it'll be long before our Kerry's giving us a bit of news. She's got a man or I'm Anne Boleyn. Do you know who he is, like?'

Briony shook her head.

'It's news to me. I've never seen her with a bloke. No one in particular anyway. There's a young fellow at the club . . . he's an earl's son. A second son mind, so he won't get the title, but he's besotted with her. Moons over her all the time. But so far as I know he ain't got anywhere. She's a dark horse, old Kerry. She'll do her own choosing, her, and once she chooses, that'll be it.'

Molly smiled and nodded.

'An earl's son. Oh, that would be nice, that would.'

'Anyone you think is gentry, as you put it, would do for you, wouldn't it? Even if he had a hump on his back and a club foot! Mum, believe me, they're no different from us. They eat, sleep and shit, same as we do. They just do it in nicer surroundings!'

Molly flapped her hand at her daughter and laughed out loud. 'I'd rather my girls did it in nicer surroundings as well. When I think of what we came from and where we are now. Well, I tell you, girl, it does me heart good. Even my Rosie looks a different girl.'

Rosalee, hearing her name, grinned and clapped her hands together.

'Bri, Bri.'

'She loves the bones of you, Briony. You've done so well, child. I couldn't have been happier at the way you've turned out. You lot could have been living in the basements now with four or five children hanging round your necks and the back of some bastard's hand round your lug on a Friday. But not my girls! I can look people in the face now and say: "Not my girls." My girls are women to be envious of, and believe me, people are envious of you. That Nellie Flanagan – well, it's like a poker up her arse to think of you lot and what you've become!'

Briony laughed despite herself.

'I hope you won't use expressions like that if Kerry does bring home an earl's son!'

Molly grinned back and said in her best imitation of a posh voice: 'I'd say poker up her behind if I was in good company!'

They laughed together loudly, Briony's laugh bordering on the hysterical.

Molly wiped her eyes with the back of her hand and said seriously to her daughter, 'You're all right, Bri, aren't you? I mean, now you're like you are. It's what you wanted, isn't it?'

Briony felt an urge to tell her mother everything in her heart, but she knew Molly wouldn't want to hear it. So instead she lit herself a cigarette and said brightly, 'Of course I am! You're looking at the first female Baron of this town, and I intend to keep me title, Mother, no matter what. Me and Tommy have this place sewn up.'

Molly laughed in delight. That was exactly what she wanted to hear. After experiencing life with an influential daughter, a really influential daughter, she couldn't bear the thought of having her new position taken from her.

To Briony, this knowledge was just another cross to bear.

Briony walked into the warmth of The Windjammer and listened to the sounds of conversation and glasses rattling. Giving her coat to Donna, the hat check girl, she smiled at her briefly before entering the club itself.

It was full. People who couldn't find seats were standing around in small groups, breathing in cigarette smoke and perfume. She pushed through the throng, greeting people as she went. Not stopping to chat, she made her way to the small dance area, scanned the tables, and was surprised to see Tommy sitting with Rupert and Jonathan. She saw his flushed face and guessed he had been drinking. Jonathan noticed her and waved her over. His face was flushed and sweating too. Briony walked across the small dance floor and deliberately ignored the people watching her. She felt as if she was in a glass bubble, on show to the world. She sat beside Tommy and he kissed her on the lips.

She had dressed in a deep crimson dress which accentuated her white skin and green eyes. She looked startling, almost too bright. The colour gave her a brittle quality, her rouge a deep stain on her cheekbones, her lips a deep crimson to match her dress. Tommy eyed her for a few seconds before kissing her again, this time on her cheek.

'Hello, darlin'. Have a glass of champagne.'

She took the fluted glass from him and sipped the cold liquid. Then, tilting her head back, she drank it down, holding the glass out again for another drink.

Five glasses later she was having a friendly argument with Jonathan about the films they were going to make. He wanted art, she decided to be contrary and insist on porn. Tommy sat back and listened to them with a smile on his face.

She was holding up. He had counted on that. While she was sorting out her mind, coming to terms with herself and her actions, he had been organising their protection and their new workforce. Tommy had no qualms about what he had done. It was over with, finished, done. Briony was a different kettle of fish; she needed to adjust to her new status. But he knew that once she did, the two of them would be a dynamite team, and nothing and no one could ever stop them.

People dropped by their table to pay their respects. Men who would not normally have been seen dead in their club had made a pilgrimage to the West End to offer their support and friendship, and Briony gave them just the right amount of her time and her interest.

Tommy sat back and relaxed. She was holding up all right, as he had known she would. By the time Kerry had finished her second set, Briony looked positively relaxed.

Chapter Seventeen

Briony lay in the bed alone, her head thumping. She closed her eyes tightly to stem the pain. She could hear the sounds of the household coming from below, the heavy tread of Mrs Horlock on the stairs, and the rattling of crockery. Her bedroom door was pushed open and the tray of tea was placed on her night table. Without a word the older woman went to the heavy curtains and opened them, letting in the weak sunshine.

'What do you think you're doing?' Briony's voice was low and angry.

'What's it look like? You deaf now as well as stupid?'

Mrs Horlock bustled to the bed and began pouring out the strong tea. Kitchen tea, thick and black, which she knew Briony loved.

She squinted up at the woman and said: 'What did you just say?'

Mrs Horlock laughed loud. 'So, the dead arose and appeared to many! My God, you look terrible. Worse than a Saturday night whore on Monday morning. How long are you going to keep this up?'

Briony was blinking her eyes rapidly and straining to keep her temper.

'Keep what up?'

'Drink your tea.' She thrust out the white china mug, spilling a few drops on the bedspread.

Briony sat up in bed and, taking the mug, slammed it down on to the bedside table.

'Keep what up, I said? Answer me, woman!' Raising her voice made her wince and she held on to her head gently. 'Oh, piss off, I ain't in the mood.'

'Look at you, Briony. You look a disgrace. You've bags under your eyes big enough for me to get me weekly shopping in. Your skin's in a terrible state, no doubt due to your drinking like a fish and eating like a bird. You was thin before, fashionably thin, now you're like a scrawny cat! Even your hair's in rat's tails. And don't think you can talk to me any way you like because you can't. I've put up with your bad mouthing for the last month, and all I can say is, grow up!'

Briony sat up in the bed, stunned.

'How dare you . . .'

'I dare, young lady! I dare. Because you might be Miss Big out there, but to me you'll always be a child. You've drunk yourself stupid now for over a month. Out till all hours, coming in roaring drunk and upsetting the whole house. Arguing with Tommy like a demented woman.'

'This is my house . . .'

Mrs Horlock stuck her face close to Briony's and cut off her tirade.

'Well, you might just find yourself all on your own in it if you're not careful. Because you pull another stunt like you did last night and we'll *all* bugger off!'

Briony racked her brains to remember the night before.

'What happened last night?' Her voice was low now, bewildered.

'Huh! Last night you picked a fight with your new minders, Jimmy and David Harles. You woke up first the whole street, then the whole household, and you told Cissy to fuck off out of it at three o'clock this morning. You took a swing at Tommy, which is why he's not in bed beside you. I don't know where he went, but if it was to another woman, who could blame him.'

Briony groaned, it was all coming back to her slowly, in crystal clear pictures.

'My God.'

'Well, I'm glad you think of him as yours because I've a feeling on me you just might need him. What's wrong with you, girl? You've been like a bear with a sore arse for weeks.'

Briony shook her head and said sadly, 'I really don't know. I feel like I'm going to explode or something. Since we had all the carry on with Olds, we've had people constantly sitting outside the house. I can't shit but I have to have a minder with me! I feel as if my whole life's in everyone else's hands but me own. Even the clubs had to tighten security, the houses have more locks on them than Fort Knox! The girls treat me differently. It's "Miss Cavanagh" this and "Miss Cavanagh" that. I feel like a freak.'

'Oh, my heart's bleeding for you. Don't give me all that old fanny, Briony. You made your bed, as the saying goes. And there's another saying might interest you: Don't play with the big boys unless you know the rules to their games.'

'Oh sod off!'

'Drink your tea and get washed, you smell like a

drayman's cart! Then get yourself out of that bed and come and eat something. Your mother will be here soon, about the wedding. Not that you've shown much interest in that either this last few weeks!'

The old woman took the mug of tea and thrust it into her hands.

'Get that down your neck and I'll run you a bath, then you can apologise to Cissy and the minders as well. No one, no matter who they are, is above common courtesy. Remember that, young lady.'

She flounced from the room and Briony closed her eyes and sighed. The truth hurt, but sometimes it was a welcome pain. She drank her tea.

Molly sat with Eileen and Rosalee, her face dark. Briony walked into the room and smiled widely, ignoring the pain thumping in her head.

'Hello, Mum, Eileen.' Kneeling down she kissed Rosalee's face. 'Hello, Rosie.' Rosalee hugged Briony to her.

'This is a fine time to crawl out of bed, I must say, and your sister getting married.'

Briony laughed.

'What? You getting married today then, Ei? Have I missed the service?'

Eileen burst into tears and Briony realised something had gone drastically wrong.

'Sorry, Ei, I was only joking.' She put her arm around her sister's shoulders.

'It's that eejit Joshua. He wants to postpone the wedding now. It's that scut of a mother behind it, I swear. He turned up last night all sweetness and light, saying they should wait, it was all a bit quick, and he thought they should have a bit longer together courting. The bastard of hell! And there's me, making them tea and leaving them together while I went in to old Mother Jones's. When I came home I found this one crying and your man nowhere to be seen. I'd have scalped the face of him if I'd have seen him.'

Briony knelt before Eileen and said: 'Has he mentioned anything before now? Anything that would make you think he'd changed his mind?'

Eileen shook her head. 'He hasn't said a word, but he's been funny for weeks now. For the last month. It's as if I got the plague overnight or something. And his mother, she cut me dead the other day at Mass . . . She doesn't like me, Bri. I don't know why.' She dissolved into tears again.

Briony's face took on a hardness noticed by Molly. Both women were thinking the same thing. Joshua and his mother didn't want to be related to her, Briony, in her new role. It was bad enough when she owned the houses, though her offer of help in buying Joshua his own home had been gratefully accepted. But now they were actually frightened of becoming involved with the Cavanaghs whose name was synonymous with violence. Well, Joshua O'Malley would find out what violence meant before he was much older! Briony determined she would see to that personally.

Elizabeth O'Malley shook her head at her son. 'Sure, you're better off home with me. That Eileen was a pasty-faced bitch if ever I saw one. Not a spark of life in her at all. Jasus, she'd breed you mewling brats.'

Joshua stared into the fire. It was Eileen's passiveness that had attracted him, but his mother was right on one thing. The Cavanaghs were not a family to get tied to. Not now anyway.

'That Briony . . . a murdering hoor if ever one was born! Your father must be turning in his grave. All those girls with skirts up their nostrils and legs bare to the world!' His mother blessed herself fervently.

According to her, Joshua thought, his father must be like the Spinning Jenny in that grave of his. Yet he himself had been a rake who had been finally driven from the house by the harridan standing before Joshua now. His mother's first sight of Kerry and Bernadette with their lipstick and bare-legged mode of dressing had incensed her, especially the short Eton crop worn by Bernie.

'To think you would have been a part of them! You're well out of it, son. You're a young man with your whole life in front of you. There's plenty of girls who'd be grateful to you for taking them on.'

'Mother, I'm thirty-eight years old. Hardly a boy. And in case it's escaped your notice there hasn't exactly been a stream of women beating a path to my door.'

'Men are fools! They shouldn't marry till they're in their forties. Even then they have to be careful. A pretty face can hide a multitude of sins, you know. You have to look at the stock they come from. If that Briony Cavanagh comes around here shouting her mouth off, I'll fill it for her meself. I'm not scared of her, or any of them for that matter. Let them come and see what I'm capable of! My son will marry who he bloody well wants and it won't be a Cavanagh. Over my dead body! You hear me, over my dead body!'

Elizabeth O'Malley was in full swing when Briony walked in at the back door of the tiny terraced house in Longbridge Road. She stood in the scullery for a few seconds before she made herself known. As she stepped into the kitchen Elizabeth O'Malley nearly jumped from her skin in fright. Holding her hand over her mouth, she whispered: 'Jesus cross of Christ!'

Briony smiled widely.

'I take it you wasn't expecting me then? Well, you should have been. You should have been sitting here with locked doors pretending you was out like I was the tally man coming for me money. Only unlike the tally man, the chances are if I don't hear what I want to hear, I'll break your fucking necks! Starting with you first, Mrs O'Malley.'

Joshua stared at the little woman in awe.

'Shut your mouth, Joshua. You look like you should be on a slab at Billingsgate market. What's this I hear about you dumping me sister after promising to marry her?'

Joshua just stared at the apparition in front of him.

'What my sister sees in you I don't even pretend to know, Joshua. But she wants you so she's going to have you, see. Because you strung her along, you asked her to marry you, and now I'll see to it personally that you do. You are going to get washed and spruced up, you're going round my mother's at seven-thirty tonight, and you're going to tell Eileen all that old fanny you gave her was just wedding nerves. Do you understand what I'm telling you?'

Joshua nodded.

'And you're going to do what I say?'

He nodded again.

'Good boy. Now another thing while we're on the subject. I don't want you, Mrs O'Malley, within a ten-mile radius of my sister. If I find out you've even touched her without Eileen's express permission, I'll rip your ugly head off your shoulders and give it to me henchmen to play footie with.' She smiled at them. 'Well, I'm glad we had this little chat. It's good for families to talk and get things sorted, don't you think? Now if you'll excuse me, I am a very busy lady and you've caused me enough trouble for one day.'

Tommy sat in the Dickens Club in Soho nursing a large Scotch. He had earlier met a man called Siddy Trundley, a small Jew who took the bets for the traders in Soho Market and aroundabouts. He was hoping Tommy would come into his business with him so he could have the protection of Tommy's men and also some extra capital. Tommy had been agreeable, seeing the chance to expand the business and double the turnover. He would give one of his more intelligent minders the job of managing it for him. That way everyone was happy. Now he sat thinking about Briony and the night before. She had gone off with Jonathan and Rupert again and got roaring drunk, coming home in the small hours causing havoc. It was becoming a regular occurrence. He was wondering whether to chance giving her a right hander, as he put it to himself, when her voice startled him out of his reverie.

'You gonna drink that drink, Tommy, or get engaged to it?' She sat beside him, smelling of musk and orange flower water. 'I've been looking for you.'

'Really, Briony, what for? To call me a prickless wonder again? Or to try and scratch me eyes out? Only your histrionics are beginning to get on my tits, know what I mean?'

Briony licked her lips and opened her eyes wide. 'I'm sorry. Honestly, Tom, I'm deeply ashamed of what I did last night.'

He looked into her innocent face and barely controlled his desire to slap her.

'You're mugging me off, Bri, and I won't have it. It's

not funny. Sitting there all wide-eyed and trying to make me laugh won't work this time. You have been pratting about for a month. You ain't done a full day's collar in the houses or the clubs since we took out Olds. Either you sort yourself out or me and you are finished, over with. I mean that.'

Briony sat up straighter in her chair.

'You're right. I have been pratting about but it's over with now. I took a while to adjust to our new position but I think I've sorted meself out now. Come to terms with it like. I don't want you to leave me, I don't want to break up the partnership. I love you, Tommy, more than you will ever believe.'

For Briony to say she loved him in broad daylight in a crowded place spoke volumes to Tommy. Kissing her hand softly, he smiled at her.

'What's really wrong, Bri?'

'I don't know, Tommy. I found it all a bit scary, I think. Taking out Olds and Bolger, all that with Dumas. Everything just got on top of me and I couldn't cope with it.'

'And you can cope with it now?'

She smiled brightly. 'Yes, I think I can. I've come to terms with meself, with what we did.'

Tommy squeezed the tiny hand in his and smiled gently. 'I'll look after you, darling, you should know that.'

She smiled and nodded. Tommy knew that Briony wasn't as hard and calculating as she liked to make out. That she was just a young woman, for all her talk and her business acumen. She had taken the death of Ginelle hard, and the consequent deaths of Olds and Bolger and the others had given her many a sleepless night. He would stick by her, support her, and take the pressure off her for a while. She was his woman, his love, and whatever the rights and wrongs of their life, he loved her desperately.

Briony pulled her hand from his. 'Have a guess what I just done?'

'What?'

She told him of her visit to Joshua and his mother, making it sound amusing, playing on the comic aspect instead of the real, frightening part of it. As they laughed together Tommy was aware that Briony's laughter was a bit too high, her gaiety too brittle to be true. He would keep his eye on her. In fact, he'd watch her like a hawk.

Chapter Eighteen

Henry Dumas sat up in the bed and made a pretence of reading the paper. Isabel watched him as she fussed around the room. His whole countenance was different, even his mouth had lost its arrogant sneer.

'Anything interesting in the paper, Henry?'

He shook his head. 'Not really.'

Isabel tidied the counterpane. 'What about this new thing, sending people to Australia? I think it's a wonderful idea.'

'If it gets rid of the working class, then it can only be good.'

Isabel sighed. A livid scar travelled up from the top of Henry's cheekbone and disappeared into his hairline. It was a startling white and when he was angry, as he was now, it seemed to raise itself from the skin around it. He also had scars on his shoulders and back. Whoever had attacked him had really meant to do him harm. She'd wondered at first why his attackers had not taken his wallet and watch. But the police said that maybe the men had been disturbed, it often happened in daylight robberies.

Now her sympathy, and she had been surprised to feel any at all, was slowly disappearing. As he was getting better, he was getting back to his old self. Never an appealing prospect at the best of times.

'You're a very difficult man, you know. Since you were attacked you've changed. You haven't left this bed. God knows, you were bad enough before but now you're impossible. Even the doctor is getting worried. Your wounds are healed, you're fit and well enough to get up. So why don't you come down today, have your meal in the library? The garden looks lovely.'

'Isabel, do me a favour and leave me alone. I still feel unwell and if I choose to stay in bed that is my prerogative. I do not want to sit in the library or look out on the garden. I have no interest in the doings of little people who want to go to that Godawful continent Australia. I don't care what we're having for dinner or lunch. I don't care what you're doing or what your blasted father's doing. In short, you bore me. Please go away and leave me alone.'

Isabel pursed her lips and stood up. As she walked from the room, Henry called her back.

'And keep that child and his confounded dog away from me!'

As she opened the door, Nipper, a large German Shepherd, leapt into the room, closely followed by Benedict. Nipper bounded on to the bed and began a ferocious licking of Henry's face and balding head. Muddy paws ripped into his copy of *The Times.* He pushed the animal away with all his strength, knocking it on to the floor.

Nipper was an amiable animal. He was still young, and even though Henry Dumas had never given the dog a kind word the animal lived in hope. Jumping on to the bed once more, he resumed his frantic ministrations.

Benedict stood at the door, his face alive with fun, and called the animal loudly.

'Nipper, Nipper! Come here now. Leave Papa alone. He's not well!'

Isabel bit back a laugh as Henry's face appeared above the mass of fur and said through clenched teeth: 'Get this dog off me!'

Benedict pulled the dog from the bed bodily, heaving him on to the floor where Nipper sat with his huge tongue hanging out of the side of his mouth, panting from exertion.

'I'm sorry, Papa, but he likes you. I try and keep him out of your way . . .' His voice trailed off and Benedict hunched his shoulders in exasperation.

Henry looked at the boy closely. Other than those startling green Cavanagh eyes, it could have been his own mother standing there. Benedict had unconsciously used a movement of his mother's. She would tilt her head to the side and smile at him, hunching her shoulders, exactly as Benedict had, when she couldn't answer his constant questions. For the first time ever, he felt a flicker of interest in the boy.

'Do that again, boy.'

Benedict shrugged.

'Do what, Papa?'

Henry parodied his action and Benedict laughed. He held out his hands, hunched up his shoulders and did as his father asked him. For the first time ever, Henry smiled at the boy, a genuine smile.

'Isabel, get my albums from the bottom drawer in my dressing room.'

Amazed, she did as she was told. Benedict stood by the bed and stroked Nipper's ears absently as he waited for his father to speak again. He was unsure what he should do. His father actually having a conversation with him was so rare. It normally only came about when his school work was not up to par. Then he was upbraided soundly.

Henry laughed again, a wide open laugh that showed his teeth. 'Here it is, look! Look at that, boy.'

Benedict took the photograph from his father's hand and looked down at a woman dressed in black bombazine. She had white hair and a sad smile on her face.

'That's my mother, your grandmother.'

Benedict looked into his father's face and said: 'She's very pretty.'

Henry nodded sagely. 'She was very pretty. Too pretty, some thought. But I always loved her dearly, she was a good woman.'

Isabel stood in absolute shock and amazement as father and son chatted for the first time ever.

'What happened to her, Papa?'

'Oh, she died when I was a lad. Not that much older than you. She had many children but they all died. My mother died because of that. Because she was too gentle, too fine-boned to have children. She was like a child herself. Her laughter was so beautiful . . . she was a generous woman, and doted on me of course. We would play hide and go seek and blind man's buff with my old nurse Hattie.'

He stared into the distance as if seeing them all again. Benedict looked at the old sepia photograph with interest. 'Have you any more photographs, Papa? I'd love to hear about my grandmother. I've seen the painting of her in the drawing room so many times and I've often wondered about her.'

Henry looked at him again, a piercing look. It was natural the boy would want to know of his background. He smiled then, a cruel smile. His mother would be a revelation to him if he knew.

'Come and sit on the bed with me and I'll show you all the photos I have. I've only one of my father, but his portrait is up in the attics. He was painted in his full dress uniform. He was a lancer.'

'Did you like him, Papa?'

Henry laughed at the childish enquiry and shook his head. 'No, I didn't, actually. He was a nasty-tempered man.'

Benedict bit his lips and stared trustingly into his father's face. The sentence hung on the air.

'You're thinking I take after him, aren't you?'

Benedict shook his head furiously, unwilling to break the friendliness of the moment; it was so rare to speak to his father like this he couldn't bear for it to end.

Henry sighed heavily. 'Maybe I do, boy. You inherit things from your parents, you know. I inherited my father's bad humour. I wonder what you'll inherit from me and your mother?'

As he spoke he looked at Isabel and she felt herself sinking inside at the expression on his face.

Briony awoke the morning before Eileen's wedding in high good humour. In the weeks since her showdown with Tommy and Mrs Horlock, she had gradually become more like her old self. Only now she had a touch of hardness to her that was not apparent before.

She opened the bedroom curtains herself and frowned

slightly at the two men lounging against their Cowley motor car, smoking and chatting. She still hated to be watched like this. To have minders everywhere. They never did a real day's work and they ate their heads off. Tommy laughed at her complaints, telling her that if they ever had any serious trouble, the men would more than earn their dinners. But it galled her just the same to have those two standing around constantly, have them follow her everywhere she went, and even vet visitors to her home. It was necessary, but that didn't mean she had to like it.

'Come back to bed, Bri, it's too early to get up.'

Briony smiled. 'Listen, Tommy, I have a full day ahead of me. The final preparations for Eileen's wedding, plus a meeting with Mariah, and on top of all that I have a special date this morning.'

He pulled back the covers and Briony saw he was aroused. 'You can have a special date now if you like!'

'Oh, Tommy, you're terrible! I have to get bathed and dressed and off to Regents Park for ten-thirty.'

Tommy pulled the covers back over himself and said, 'Do you want me to come with you?'

Briony was nonplussed for a moment. 'Would you like to? Only you haven't really seen him, have you? He's beautiful, Tommy . . .'

'I know that, Bri, you tell me often enough.'

'Sally's taking him to the park, and while he runs his dog we chat. If Isabel knew there'd be murders, but what she don't know can't hurt her. Sometimes I feel like just taking him, you know? He's ten now, he's growing up, and he doesn't even know I exist. It hurts, Tommy.'

He took her small hand in his and kissed it.

'We go through this every time. He don't know you,

Bri, he's happy with them. Well, with Isabel anyway. He'll have everything we never had, he'll have the right friends, go to the right schools. Fuck me, Bri, he's got it made! I wish my old mum had given me to someone like that.'

'But I could give him all that now.'

Her voice was small, distressed.

'Oh, Bri, don't go queer on me again. You can offer him money, but you'll always be Briony Cavanagh. You're not even married. He'd just be an illegitimate kid. This way he's someone, someone important. He'll go to one of them university places, then he'll inherit all that old goat's money. Don't balls it up for him, Bri, because he won't thank you for it. Watch him from a distance, watch over him like that. When he's a man, then tell him the truth. Who knows? Maybe he'll find out himself. But for now, don't rock his boat, love, you don't know what the upshot might be.'

Briony's radiant face had paled. 'Tommy Lane, the voice of reason.' The words were bitter.

'Yeah, well. I'm only trying to do what's best for that boy. Think with your head, Bri, not your heart. Now then, let's get ourselves suited and booted and off out! I'll treat you to a nice Jewish breakfast in Brick Lane before we go to Regents Park, how's that? I ain't had no lox or bagels for ages. What do you say?'

'Who you got to see at Brick Lane?'

Tommy laughed.

'You always outthink me, don't you? I have to see Solly Goldstern. He owes me a whacking great sum of money and today I collect.'

'All right then, Tommy. I'll get Cissy to run the bath.'

As she busied herself getting ready, she daydreamed of having her son back home with her. Of her dressed in her best walking him to school. Dreams were free, and no one could stop you having them.

That was why, for Briony, they always had the edge over real life.

Solly Goldstern was thin to the point of emaciation. He was sixty-seven years old and was a gold merchant. A gold merchant in the East End bought for peanuts from the Jewish immigrants who were trying to get a start and a new life, and sold for a small fortune to the wealthier jewellers in Hatton Garden and roundabouts.

Solly had borrowed a large amount of money off Tommy to buy a ruby tiara from an old Russian woman. She was shrewd, knew her tiara's worth and stuck out for fifty per cent of its real value. Solly had borrowed the money from Tommy, made the purchase and then sold it on for a huge profit. All was good, until his daughter's husband, Isaac, had taken the money, left his forty-year-old wife and five children, and run off with a little cockney girl called Daisy. The funny thing was, Solly was more annoyed about Daisy than anything. Isaac had run off with a *goy*, an English girl. His daughter's shame was worse because of this fact.

He had tried to locate the errant husband without any success whatsoever, and now Tommy Lane was coming for his money and soon it would be common knowledge. His daughter and grandchildren would be shamed, he would lose the respect of his usual clientele. People would think he was old, foolish, that if his son-in-law could rob him, he was easy prey. He knew exactly the East End mentality. It was what had shaped him from his first arrival in this country, when he still spoke Yiddish and had only his quick brain and business acumen to help him along.

He felt the sting of tears in his watery blue eyes and hastily blinked them away. He caressed the handle of the gun before him and bit his lip till it bled, licking at the salty droplets of blood. He tasted his own misfortune and felt the urge to cry again.

He had borrowed a lot of money for that tiara, and now he was expected to pay it back. He had nowhere near the amount Tommy would want. With the ten per cent interest and the five per cent handling charge Tommy had insisted on, Solly was just about broke already. Like a cornered rat, he was thinking in terms of death.

Vita, his daughter, came into the room with a glass of tea, her harassed face more deeply lined than usual. She had wanted Isaac desperately as a young girl. She had got him, thanks to her father and a good sum of money, had borne his children and loved him. Now he had betrayed her, and not only her but his children and her father. She felt responsible for her husband's actions and as she looked at her father's grave countenance her heart constricted. She had brought him this low. Had been the instrument of his downfall. He owed money everywhere now, and it galled him. Soon the talk would start, and in the Jewish community that was fatal. If you had no money, you had no power.

'Drink your tea, Father. Tommy Lane will be here soon. He's a reasonable man, a decent man. He'll understand.'

'So, my daughter, you want me to beg to a street urchin, is that it? Me, the chief gold merchant in the East End, whose credit was always the best?'

'If he was good enough for you to borrow his money, the least you can do is give him the benefit of your honesty, Father. Who knows? Maybe he'll take an offer of so much a week until you're better fixed.'

Solly laughed nastily.

'Tommy Lane isn't a tally man. He won't want his five thousand pounds back at a rate of fifty pounds a week, for God knows how long! He'll want the lump sum, plus the ten per cent interest and the five per cent handling charge! Now leave me alone, for the love of God. Take your wittering somewhere else.'

Vita stared stonily at the gun in front of her father. He was still touching it and she shook her head.

'As if we haven't enough troubles, you want to give us more! Isaac has gone, your money's gone. We have to try and sort this thing out.'

'If he was here now I'd shoot him like a dog.'

She snarled through clenched teeth: 'If he was here now, I'd shoot him myself!'

The shop bell rang and Tommy's deep booming voice followed it into the back room.

'Hello, Solly me old mate!' As he walked into the room with Briony behind him he stopped dead. 'What's going on here then?'

Briony's eyes opened wide at the sight of Solly Goldstern waving an antiquated gun in front of him.

'Have you gone mad, Solly?' Tommy's voice was low now. He put his hand behind him and pushed Briony gently away. She stood in the tiny shop front, her hand to her mouth. She heard Tommy's voice as he tried to reason with the old man.

'Give me the gun, Solly.'

Solly's hand was shaking and Vita walked over to him and took the gun gently from his fingers.

Tommy said dryly, 'I take it you ain't got me money then? Or do you always try and top people as they come in here?'

Vita gave Tommy the gun. 'He's out of his mind with worry. We've had a lot of trouble . . .'

'Don't tell them anything, Vita! Let Tommy do his worst. You can't get blood out of a stone.'

The old man's voice, full of dignity, made Briony intervene. 'Look, Mr Goldstern, you remember me, don't you?'

His face softened. 'Of course I do. Every Monday regular you brought in your mother's wedding ring to pop. I gave you seven shillings and you brought back nine shillings on the Saturday. Briony Cavanagh . . . my wife Etta thought you were the most beautiful child she had ever seen.'

Briony sat beside the old man. Smiling at him she said to Vita, 'Make a cuppa, girl, we'll all have a little chat.'

Vita went to make the tea and Tommy pulled out a chair and straddled it, the old silver-handled gun still in his hand.

'By rights, Solly, I should knock you from here to Kingdom come for the stunt you pulled on me.'

Solly's face was grey. His skin seemed to become baggier by the second. Briony had thought of him as an old man all her life, it was the way when you knew people from childhood, but he seemed to be ageing in front of her eyes.

'Shut up, Tommy, let him talk.'

Solly shrugged his shoulders and held out his hands helplessly.

'Vita's husband Isaac, he worked for me. I borrowed the five grand off you, Tommy, to buy a particularly nice tiara from an old lady. Beautiful workmanship, white and yellow gold, with diamonds and rubies. It was one of the finest pieces I've ever seen.'

'All right, Solly, we get the picture. What happened?'

'Well, Isaac, he has five children by my daughter Vita. I had him work for me because he couldn't keep a job down. Here I could watch him. Make sure the children were fed. You know the score.'

Briony and Tommy nodded.

'He waited till I resold the tiara to a jeweller up West who had a buyer for it. Then in the night he came and took the money, also every bit of the cash I'd saved over the years, and – even Vita doesn't know this – all my Etta's jewels. They were to be hers one day, Vita's. He had taken up with a young girl, a slut of the first water, a *goy*! We haven't seen him since.'

Briony laid her hand gently on the old man's arm, her heart going out to him.

Tommy on the other hand said waspishly: 'You was gonna top me over that ponce Isaac!'

Briony shook her head at him. 'Look, Mr Goldstern, listen to me. We'll sort something out, all right?'

'Huh! What, my little love? I am finished. I can't even scrape up enough to start my business again. I'm at rock bottom. I have Vita and her children to look after. Her eldest son is fifteen now. I have so much responsibility and I haven't the capital. I'm even behind on the rent for this place!'

Vita walked into the room with the tea as her father broke down crying. Placing the tray on his desk, she went to him, taking him into her arms.

'It's pointless beating him. He can't pull your money out of thin air. It's been preying on his mind for days.'

Briony began to pour out the tea. Giving everyone a cup, she smiled at Vita. 'Sit down and let's try and make some sense out of this. We'll look for Isaac, see if we can recoup any of your money, right? He's the main holder of the debt now so if he's still in the smoke, he's as good as crippled. I'll arrange for three hundred quid to be delivered here first thing in the morning. You owe me then, Mr Goldstern, not Tommy. You pay me back at a pony a week, restart your business from scratch. I'll want a twenty per cent return on me dosh. What about that?'

Solly looked at the girl in front of him and had a sudden vivid memory of her father. Paddy Cavanagh had even brought in his children's boots to pawn for a drink. He was a waster, a schmuck, yet he had bred this beautiful girl with a kind heart. She had known only poverty and hardship. His own daughter, who had had everything a girl could want, had taken up with Isaac. Solly had bought and paid for him so she would once more have everything she wanted. It was a strange world when the girl with the least became more of a woman than the girl with everything.

His eyes were wet again. Unable to talk, he grabbed her small hand in his and kissed it.

Vita sipped her tea, her eyes watching the changing expressions on Tommy Lane's face. She guessed, shrewdly, that Tommy wasn't at all pleased at having his five grand scrubbed in such a cavalier fashion by Briony Cavanagh. But she also guessed that Briony generally got what she wanted, regardless of who she upset in the process.

Twenty minutes later, in Tommy's car on their way to Regents Park, Briony took the brunt of his tongue.

'I don't fucking believe you! Why didn't you offer to put him in your Christmas club? Five poxy grand down the crapper, and the old bastard had a gun! You've no right to countermand me like that, Briony, you was out of order.'

She smiled to herself. 'Shall I tell you something,

Tommy Lane. When I was a kid I hated having to pawn me mother's wedding ring. I hated it. That "old bastard", as you call him, never once made me feel like the dirt I was. He always called me Miss Cavanagh, as young as I was, and he always gave me a sweet.'

Tommy stopped at a junction and shouted to a barrow boy: 'Oi, got any hearts and flowers on there?'

With a laugh, the boy watched him turn the corner.

'Very funny, Tommy. Why don't you do a turn at the club? I'll tell you something now, for nothing. It hurt me seeing him brought so low. Even when he was on top – and he was, Tommy, he was the business as far as fucking gold was concerned – he still had the decency to treat me with a bit of respect. I owe him for that. After years of being treated like Irish shite, it was a welcome change!'

Tommy shook his head, and Briony watched him battle it out with himself. She knew exactly how he was feeling. She knew him better than she knew herself. Every mood swing, every nuance of his personality. He was fighting within himself now, because one half of him wanted to muller her where she sat, and the other half of him understood what she was saying, because being treated with respect was what they'd both fought so hard for. If you had money you automatically had that respect, even if only for the fact you were well heeled. To be treated with respect when you were no one, with nothing and no visible means of ever getting anything, counted for a lot.

'So old Goldstern gave you a sweet, and because of that you let him get away with pulling a gun on me? It's nice to know you care so much!'

'Oh, balls! That gun was so old it was positively ancient, it would have backfired and killed him, not you!'

'Oh, so now you're a firearms expert as well?'

Briony started to laugh then, a rollicking boisterous sound. 'Give it a rest, Tommy, you would have done the same.'

'Yeah, maybe. But I didn't get the chance, did I?' This was said seriously and Briony kept her peace. He was five grand down, and she knew when she had pushed her luck to its extreme.

Sally sat in Regents Park watching Benedict as he played with Nipper, rolling around the grass in his good trousers and shrieking with suppressed energy. She would spend the best part of the evening sponging his clothes down so all the tell-tale evidence of his supposedly sedate walk would be cleaned away. She didn't care, she loved him. Only with her could he be a boy, a real little boy who jumped and played. Even Isabel, who loved him dearly, Sally conceded that, tried to make him into a little gentleman. Well, in Sally's opinion, there was plenty of time for that.

She saw Briony walking towards her with Tommy Lane and signalled with her head towards Benedict.

Briony and Tommy settled themselves on the wrought-iron bench beside Sally and started chatting. To passersby it looked innocent enough, their subject matter would be unheard and their interest in the little boy was cleverly disguised.

'Hello, Sal. You know Tommy, of course?'

She nodded.

'How's me boy?'

'You can see for yourself, Miss Cavanagh. Healthy as hell, eating like a horse, and more energy than a lightning bolt!'

Briony laughed. This was what she wanted to hear. 'How's things at the house?'

Sally looked her straight in the eye. 'Well, that's a funny thing, Miss Cavanagh. It's been strange since the master was attacked.'

Tommy pushed his face towards Sally and said, 'What do you mean?'

Sally shrugged.

'Well, lately he's took to playing with the boy like. Taking him out and that. The master wouldn't leave the house for weeks, then all of a sudden it's "let me take you here, let me take you there".'

'And how's the boy responding to it all?'

'Well, Mr Lane, he loves it. They play chess together, and you want to hear them laughing! It's like someone's switched masters in the night like. One day he was a miserable old fucker, the next all sweetness and light. It was strange, I can tell you, and the mistress ain't happy with the change. She don't like it one bit!'

Briony nodded, thinking. 'Well, she wouldn't, would she?' She wasn't sure she liked it herself. But hadn't she told him to be nice to the boy? Was this his way of doing what she'd said? 'Benedict's happy enough, though?'

'Oh, bugger me, yes! Never seen him so happy. He's been a little darling. Not that he was ever any trouble before, mind, but now he's got his old man behind him, it's put the icing on his cake if you see what I mean.'

Benedict ran and Nipper jumped up, sending him sprawling on to the grass. Briony nearly got out of her seat, thinking he was hurt, when high-pitched laughter floated over to them.

Sally grinned. 'He's a hard little sod, Miss Cavanagh, take more'n a tumble to set his waterworks off!'

Benedict ran over to Sally, holding out his sleeve. 'Oh Sal, Sally! Look what I've done to my jacket!'

'Come here, let me look.'

Briony felt the tightening in her chest as he approached. He smiled at her and Tommy before he held out the offending arm to Sally.

'Mama's going to trounce me, Sally.'

Briony and Tommy's eyes both opened wide at the expression.

'Now, young man, don't you be using those words in front of your parents! Your mother would have my guts for garters if she thought I was teaching you words like that!'

Benedict smiled craftily. 'As if I would, Sal! But look at it, it's covered in mud.'

'It'll clean, lad. You go and play with your dog.'

Nipper, deciding he liked the look of Briony, jumped up at her, putting his muddy paws on her coat.

'Nipper! Get down! I'm sorry about that . . .'

As Benedict looked into the lady's face his words dried in his throat. It was like looking in a mirror.

'Hello, Benedict. Your nanny was just telling me all about you. What a wonderful dog.' Briony's voice was quavering with emotion. It took every ounce of her will-power not to grab hold of him and crush him to her chest.

Benedict stared into the green eyes so like his own and said, 'Yes, he is a wonderful dog. Excuse me, but do I know you?'

Briony shook her head and answered, 'No, you don't know me.'

'How strange. I feel as if I know you from somewhere.'

Briony and Benedict locked eyes. Tommy watched them as they sized each other up. Benedict was so like her it was uncanny. The same heart-shaped face, the same high cheek-bones, and the same green eyes. Benedict was like the spit out of her mouth, as his mother would have said.

He was going to be handsome, and if he had his mother's nature as well as her looks he would be one hell of a man. Looking at Briony and Benedict together, he felt the pull that Briony must experience and understood then exactly what kept her going in life. She looked after everyone, even old Solly Goldstern, but the one person she really wanted to take care of was out of her jurisdiction. She couldn't put him to bed, wipe away his tears, or hold him in her arms. No wonder she had gone for Dumas as she had. At the end of the day, he had got everything and she had got nothing.

'Would you like an ice cream, son?' Tommy's voice broke the momentary closeness.

'Oh, yes please.' Benedict's eyes were bright.

'You take him, Bri, I'll chat to Sally for a while.'

Briony stood up and walked with Benedict to get the ice cream. He held on to her arm and they chatted together. Sally watched them go with fear in her heart.

'It's not a good idea, Mr Lane. He's at an age when he'll talk about things, in company like.'

Tommy lit himself a cheroot and shook his head in dismissal. 'Who gives a fuck. Certainly not me, love. She's every right to see him if she wants.'

Sally kept quiet but the thought scared her.

Briony and Benedict chatted together and enjoyed themselves. Briony listened to all his boyish talk and drank it inside herself. Benedict, guessing he had a sympathetic ear, poured out all his doings, good and bad, with a fervour.

When he was walking home with Sally later in the day he said, 'I don't think I'll mention the nice lady to Mama, she'd think she was a bit common. But I liked her, didn't you, Sal?'

Sally smiled in relief.

'I think you're right there, young Master Ben. Your ma or your pa wouldn't like her one bit. But we can keep her friendship our secret, can't we?'

'Do you think we'll ever see her again, Sal?' He stroked the dog's coat as it walked beside him.

'Oh, yes, young Benedict, I have a feeling we'll see her again. In fact, I can guarantee it.'

Chapter Nineteen

Briony liked Mariah and liked the way she ran her houses. Both women were fighters and survivors which gave them a bond, something neither had expected. But now they owned just about every house in London between them, they were also adversaries. Although both worked their respective patches it was only natural that they would at certain times poach one another's girls or customers. It was an unwritten rule of business.

Mariah wanted to cement their newfound friendship with something tangible. Not just because she liked Briony, though she liked her a lot, but because Briony's newfound status with Tommy Lane also made her a threat in certain ways. If push ever came to shove, Briony could take what was Mariah's at the drop of a hat. She was certain that Briony was too straight and fair for such skulduggery, but there was nothing in Mariah's book like an insurance policy. A guarantee. Which was the reason Briony was sitting in her house now, with a cup of tea and a slice of Battenberg.

Briony wiped her sticky fingers on a napkin and grinned

at Mariah amiably. Her afternoon with Benedict had made her happy with the whole world.

'Now then, we've had the tea and cake, you've offered me a stiff drink, which I declined, and we've run out of chit-chat. So come on then, girl, spit it out, what's the rub?'

Mariah laughed with her.

'I have a proposition to put to you, Briony, which, if you agree, will really bring us in money.'

Briony lit a cigarette. Blowing out the smoke in a large billowing cloud, she said, 'Go on.'

Mariah sat back in her chair, her large breasts heaving under the strain of her tight bodice. Briony wondered briefly if they would escape their confines and burst out into the warmth of the room.

'There's a house up for sale, Berwick Manor. It was used through the war as a hospital. The place is in a right mess. It's going for a song, and I mean a song. The thing is, between us we could restore it. It's perfect for what we'd want. It stands in its own land, it's big, it's got plenty of rooms. We could really make it pay.'

Briony nodded.

Mariah took a deep breath. Briony was not making this easy for her.

'If we both invested equal amounts of capital in it, we could make it a showplace. Private functions, our best girls working there, catering for the elite. I know you have a few faces. Well, so do I. We could double up our clients *and* our takings. It's a good investment.'

Briony smiled slowly.

'I know the old manor. Who don't? We walked past it often enough when we was kids pea picking. Kerry used to say, "I wish I lived there!" It's a nice property, you're right. It's in a good location, too. We could cater to the London mob without them having to go too far. We could have weekend parties like, theme parties. Ancient Greece, French nights!'

Briony's enthusiasm pleased Mariah who knew now that the idea was sold. All she had to do was collect the collateral.

'Yeah, we could start them Friday and they could go on till the Sunday night. There's a banqueting hall there where the punters could eat, plus plenty of outhouses for livestock and that. It could pretty much be self-contained. The grounds are enormous, acres of fields, even the old Berwick pond, ducks and all! It's very picturesque, perfect for the monied man. Near to London and discreet. Just the place for a weekend in the country.'

'How much is this going to rush me then? Only if it's going for a song, it must need a lot of work on it.'

'Oh, it does, Bri. I'm not gonna try and spin you about that, girl. It needs a major redec for a start, from carpets to curtains. It ain't been touched since 1919, then it was boarded up and put on the market. In the last six or seven years it ain't even seen a broom. But think of how it could be!'

Briony grinned. 'I am. I know just the girls to work it, too. Young, pretty, wanting to make a quick few grand to set up on their own. It would be so easy. So how much money are you looking at?'

'Off hand, Bri, I'd say about ten thousand each. To get it off to a good start. By my figures we'd recoup that within the first three months of opening.'

She passed over a book where she had broken down the costs. Briony scanned the pages for ten minutes while Mariah smoked a cigarette.

Briony was impressed. Mariah had even allowed for an odd job man. It was well thought out, and it was viable. Two things Briony found hard to resist.

'Shall I tell you something, Mariah?'

She smiled. 'What?'

'I'm in. I'm in up to me bleeding neck! This is going to be a real money spinner. It's class, Mariah, real class.' She shook her head in wonderment.

Mariah clapped her hands together in excitement.

'I'm glad, Bri. I think me and you could make a good team.'

'Plus, together as working partners, we can't tread on each other's toes, can we?'

Mariah saw the crafty look on Briony's face and knew she had been rumbled. Sobering now, she said, 'Well, Briony, there's that to it as well, I suppose.'

'Oh, don't take on, Mariah. I admire your foresight. I'd have thought of something like this in your position. But I can tell you now, I wouldn't turn on the hand that fed me. When we had all that business with Henry and his mob you was a good mate. I'd never forget that. Friends abound in our position, but good mates are few and far between.'

Mariah's face softened and Briony saw a glimmer of the girl she had once been. Big, beautiful and innately nice. Mariah was a nice person, except it seemed too small an epithet for her huge frame.

Rupert and Jonathan were roaring drunk and the noise was beginning to disturb the other customers. Tommy watched them without intervening. He thought they were ponces, though he had given up arguing the fact with Briony. He watched her, dressed in a cream sheath dress, walk over to their table and cajole them into quieting down. He shook his head and walked behind the bar to pour himself a decent Scotch. When the punters first arrived, they were given real drinks. When they were drunk, they were served from the 'cottage' bottles, the watered-down versions. They paid top price and Tommy's excuse was, he was doing them a favour.

As Briony walked towards him he motioned with his head for her to the offices. Briony followed him, stopping at tables to chat for a few seconds and waving at other customers. In the office the thumping beat of the Charleston reverberated through the walls.

'How'd it go round your mother's?'

'It's like a mad house, but Eileen's all right. She seems happy enough. Tomorrow it will all be over!'

'You look really lovely tonight, Bri. Really beautiful.'

She kissed him. 'You don't look too bad yourself.'

He poured her a drink and she sipped it gratefully.

'That Ben . . . he's like you, Bri. I don't just mean in looks but personality. You had the same naivety when I first met you.'

'When I saved your arse, you mean?'

Tommy laughed, remembering.

'He is a lovely boy though, Bri.'

She pushed her hair into place with one hand and nodded. 'I know. It takes a lot for me to leave him. I feel like picking him up and taking him away. But even as I am now, with all my connections, my so-called friends, I know I couldn't do it. If push came to shove the courts would take that bastard's side.'

Tommy pulled her into his arms.

'You'll survive, Bri. That's your greatest talent. You see him, you watch him from a distance. He'll be all right.'

Briony looked up into his face and he saw the hurt she felt.

'Sometimes, in the night, I see him. I wonder if he's ill or feeling frightened, you know? And I'm not there to comfort him. To see he's all right . . .'

'Look, whatever you think of Isabel Dumas, she loves the boy. She loves him with all her heart.'

'But she's not his mother, is she? His real mother. I am.'

'And you're a good mother, in your own way.'

Briony pulled away from him and laughed scornfully. 'Oh, yeah, I was a great mother, me. I let them walk off with him. Take him from me and bring him up, a pervert and a frustrated spinster! Because that's all she is, she's only married in name, no other way. He couldn't get it up with a woman, she told me that herself. I must have been stark staring mad!'

'Not mad, Bri, young. Young and foolish. But think about it. Without him, you have all this.' He swept his arms out to encompass the whole room.

Briony nodded slowly.

'Yeah, I have everything and nothing. Because without my boy, this is sweet fuck all.'

Tommy shoved her hard in the chest, sending her drink flying everywhere.

'Oh, save me the self-pity, for Gawd's sake, Bri. You can't have him and that's that! You have a lot more than anyone of our station could even dream of. You could have more children, but you won't. Don't you think I might want a baby, a child of me own? No, of course not. You only think of yourself. Sometimes, Bri, you really wind me up, do you know that? I sometimes dream at nights of a son or a daughter, our child. OURS, not fucking Dumas's.

Mine and yours! A red-headed little girl I could take out, could love, or a boy with your eyes and my hair, a boy we could bring up together, could give everything to. So don't try and put your silly poxy self-pity on to me all the time. I'm sorry, right, heart sorry. But don't you ever put down my achievements like that again. We worked hard to get where we are and if you would rather give it up for that boy, you're a fool. Because with him, you'd have been scratching in the dirt, his arse would be hanging out of his trousers, your sisters would be in sweat shops working for a living and the bleeding wedding wouldn't be taking place tomorrow, because you couldn't buy your sister a bridegroom!'

Briony stood stock still. Tommy had never spoken like this to her before. It was a shock and a revelation. Suddenly she saw the real loneliness in his face. The sadness in his eyes. He was right, of course, in everything he said. But being right didn't mean she had to stand there and take it. He had embarrassed her with what he said, stung her to the quick, humiliated her. She felt her face burning and before she could think the words tumbled out of her mouth.

'I'll never give you a child, Tommy Lane, you or anyone else. So think on that! You crawl all over me, night after night, and I hate it. I hate everything about it. I allow you to use my body, that's all. I feel nothing for you physically, and you know it. You've always known it. But still you want it, still you're there, night after night, with your stupid pawing and your wet lips. You sicken me! You're no better than Dumas, no better than the men who come to our houses. Your prick rules your head.

'But, not me, mate, not me! I have a child, and if I can't have him, I don't want any! Not by you or anyone else.'

As soon as the last words were out of her mouth she wanted to retract them. Wanted to tell him that it was sheer temper talking, that she was upset. Instead she stood silently as he recovered from the blow he had received.

'You bitch, you fucking bitch of hell.'

Taking back his arm he slapped her across the face, sending her flying across the office on to the desk. The inkwell crashed to the floor. In the silence, Briony pulled herself to her feet.

'I've tried, Briony, to be a good man to you. I've put up with things off you another man would have scalped your arse for, and this is how you repay me, is it? Well, we're finished, girl, after tonight. I know exactly where I stand now, don't I? We'll sort out the pennies and halfpennies another day. For now, I have to get as far away from you as possible.'

Briony went to him, her eyes beseeching.

'Tommy, Tommy, listen to me . . . I didn't mean it.'

He held up his hands.

'Don't touch me, Bri. Not now, not ever again. You've finished anything we ever had between us. You always had the gift of the gab, didn't you? Talked us in and out of every situation. Well, you talked yourself out of me! I sat back today while you talked me out of five grand, lady. I've always listened to you, let you have your head, and all the time you had no more feeling for me than a mad dog. Talk about a fucking eye opener, eh! Get out of me way.'

Briony held on to him, grabbing the sleeve of his jacket.

'Let go of me, Bri, or I'll knock you out, I mean it.'

She held on harder, beginning to cry now.

'Please, Tommy! I never meant it, any of it, I was hurt!'

Putting the flat of his hands on her chest, he pushed her with all his considerable strength. She flew backwards against the wall, the force knocking the breath from her body. She crumpled down on to the floor, her back aching with the blow.

'Good night, love. See you around.'

She was crying hard now.

'Tommy, I'm begging you . . .'

He looked down at her and laughed.

'I've got to hand it to you, Bri, you never did know when to give up, did you? Your big trap will still be moving when they put you in the ground.'

He walked from the office and Briony sat on the floor and cried bitter lonely tears.

Tommy walked from the club and out into the evening air. He pushed his hands down into his pockets and walked quickly towards the East End, his motor car left behind.

He felt the sting of tears and blinked them back. All around him London was quieting for the night, the streets empty and void of life. He had loved her so much, so very very much. She had been like a beacon to him, calling him home to her. She was his other half, his second skin. In her, he'd had a deep abiding friendship and a love he thought could rival any in the world. He had been such a fool, a stubborn fool, not to see what was under his nose all the time! Well, they were finished, finally and irrevocably. He couldn't think what the upshot was going to be now. He still loved her dearly, despite what had happened this night. All he knew was that this was the end of the road for them. The final parting. He never wanted to look at her lovely face again.

In his mind's eye he saw her as she had been all those years ago, with her belly high in pregnancy, her blue velvet suit, her stunning hair. Even then, she had had something special about her. He saw her when they opened their first house, her face serious and exquisite. What was it that made one person more to you than another? What was the magic chemistry that made only one person your life, your love? Why was he plagued by her day and night, year after year, when there were women aplenty in the world? Other women as beautiful, with better bodies and sweeter natures. Why was he cursed with wanting her? Because he still wanted her, even now. After all that had happened, he still wanted her.

It was this that hurt him more than anything. Where Briony was concerned, he had no pride.

Well, he decided, he would find the pride. Nothing would induce him to have her back after this night's work. Not even her tears. From tonight, Briony Cavanagh was on her own.

And a little voice at the back of his mind said: So are you, Tommy Lane, and you'll be the lonelier in the end.

He stood on London Bridge later that night, and watched the traffic on the water, the boats' hooters sounding ghostly in the light of the dawn.

It was then, cold and tired, that Tommy decided just what he had to do.

Briony could hear the preparations for the wedding from her bedroom. She was sorry now she had decided to have the reception at her house. It meant she had to be nice to everyone, talk and chat and be the good hostess, when all she wanted to do was tell them all to bugger off out of it. Go away and come back another day.

It was overcast, and Briony hoped the heavens opened

so the reception would be cut short. She looked in the mirror and groaned. Her eyes were swollen and red. Her face grey-tinged.

She knew that she had blown it with Tommy, that what she had said would always be between them. It was her wicked vicious tongue that had taken her over. It was not even the truth. Just words spoken in temper, a temper brought on by hearing the truth. She felt the useless tears again and swallowed them down. She had no time for tears now. But, oh, she was hurting inside, she was in an agony of pain.

The door was opened and Mrs Horlock bustled into the room. Briony looked at her with new eyes, saw the aged look of her face, the way the skin had sagged, the heavy jowls and ruddy complexion, and suddenly it occurred to her that years were passing with a sameness that was startling.

'Come on, girl, get yourself up and eat this toast! I'll cook you a proper breakfast later when the main work's done. The bloody help is no good at all, a couple of nervous children! By Christ, you get what you pay for these days all right. Still, they'll have to do and they're showing willing so I mustn't be too hard on them.'

She dumped the tray of tea and toast on a small table beside Briony's bed.

'Your mother's arrived, by the way, sticking her great galloping oar in where it ain't wanted!'

Briony ignored the tirade and sighed gently.

'Look, lass, I don't know what happened with you and your man, but he's sent a message for his bags to be ready to be picked up first thing tomorrow morning. Now I know you've had a fight, but this is your sister's wedding day and you've got to show willing. You and him have always fought like cat and dog. But he'll be around with his tail between his legs as usual, and everything will be all right.'

Briony shook her head. 'No, he won't, Mrs H. This is the finish.'

'Oh, Briony girl. Listen to me. Whatever has happened with you and your man, it'll all be resolved before you know it . . .'

'No, that's just it, Mrs H. Things were said last night that can never be retracted. Can never be forgotten. I blew it with Tommy. I pushed him too far this time.'

Briony started talking again, babbling, her words running into one another as she tried to make sense of them herself. 'It was seeing my boy, it was seeing him. Being near him. I couldn't get the thought from my head that if things had been different we would have been together. I could have looked at him every day. I hate the thought of him with them. It grieves me, it kills me. It should be me, not her. Then Tommy said we could have children and I said . . . I said no. Never. And I meant it. I realise now I really meant it because I only want my boy! Benedict. My son. Any other child would be like second best, you know?

'Tommy deserves better than that. And knowing all that, I still want him. I would have fifty children if it kept Tommy here, but now it's all too late. Too fucking late to try and make any sense of it all.'

'Then don't. Don't try and make sense of it. Try and pull yourself together, child, for God's sake. There's a whole army arriving here in a few hours and you've got to greet them with your sister. It's her day, not yours. It's Eileen's day. And let's face it, Briony, she deserves some happiness, doesn't she? Think of Eileen and your sisters and your mother. Everyone will be expecting you to be the life and soul of this gathering.'

Briony looked into the lined face and before her and sighed heavily.

'That's been the trouble, hasn't it? It's all always been for everyone else. Never for me. For me mum, me family. I even frightened Joshua into marrying Eileen. What about me? What about what *I* want?'

As she walked down the stairs forty-five minutes later, she was a semblance of her old self, a veneer of the old Briony that pleased everyone. They all looked at her and she could read in their eyes the same thought.

Briony was here, she would take over, and everything would be fine.

Only she knew that nothing would ever be the same again.

But Briony, being Briony, played the game she had started so long ago, the game where she set the rules and never told anyone else what they were. Least of all Tommy Lane.

Chapter Twenty

Briony stood in Saint Vincent's church with her mother and sisters, waiting for Eileen to walk down the aisle. She knelt down and made the sign of the cross, giving an offering prayer of two Hail Marys and an Our Father. As she kissed the cross of Christ on her rosary beads she noticed Kerry staring at her and dropped her eyes. Only Kerry had noticed something wrong with her, only Kerry had realised she wasn't her usual self. Kerry was to sing today, at her sister's wedding. It was a family day all right, and even though Joshua was giving Eileen his name, O'Malley, it was still a Cavanagh day.

Rosalee, dressed in a silver-grey dress and coat, looked at her and clapped her hands together. Briony smiled at her. Rosie was enormous now. Her flat face, so adorable to Briony, still made people stare at her. She trotted alongside her mother wherever she went, and was well known to all the shopkeepers. Her vocabulary was still limited to 'Bri, Bri'. It was the only word she had ever spoken, though Briony guessed she would talk more if she really wanted to. Briony straightened up the black silk headscarf Rosalee wore and gave her a little kiss. Bernie was tapping her foot against the wooden floor. She looked agitated and Briony didn't bother acknowledging her. She couldn't bring herself to have a whispered conversation, just wanted to take Rosalee and walk from the church, from all this pretence, but knew she couldn't. Instead she smiled wanly at her mother.

No one as yet had asked after Tommy, Briony's demeanour had made sure of that. The fact he had ordered his clothes to be packed was common knowledge, though, thanks to Cissy. Dressed in an outrageous red silk suit, she was already crying before Eileen even walked down the aisle.

Kerry slipped from her pew and walked up to the altar. She knelt and blessed herself before taking up position at the side, ready to sing. Eileen had let her choose the hymns herself.

Joshua waited patiently for his bride. His new suit looked and felt incongruous. He had never owned anything so fine in all his life. He was frightened of all this sitting down because he didn't want to crease it. It had been provided by Briony, which he hated, but he consoled himself with the thought it would last him the next thirty years if he watched his weight. It was of good material and fully lined, a fact that had him swinging between pride and a kind of shocked wonderment. It was a suit you could take to Uncle's and get a good price for, and as it was no shame to pawn things, he was actually looking forward to doing so. It would only get damp or smoke-damaged hanging up in the house, depending on what time of year it was, and where the hell would he wear it, except maybe to weddings and funerals.

He bit his thumbnail, and quickly chastised himself.

No biting nails in church, no crossing of legs or arms in church, and never, ever was one to think a bad word or thought in church. He concentrated on the pink roses on the altar. The church looked lovely. His mother and Eileen had dressed it early that morning. It looked a picture.

He smiled nervously at his friend Harry Higgins, and Harry patted his pocket to let him know he had the ring safe. The news Joshua was marrying Eileen, one of the Cavanaghs, had spread through the East End like wild fire. For the first time in his life he was treated with the utmost respect. Yet he wasn't sure he even wanted to be here. At first Briony getting the better of his mother had pleased him. He had been forced into this marriage, and being a weak man, there was a kind of pleasure in that fact. Always living by his mother's lights, he had exchanged that for living by Briony Cavanagh's. But Eileen now, she was a different kettle of fish. With Eileen he would rule the roost and she would let him. That fact pleased him enormously. He had a fleeting vision of her naked before him and squeezed his eyes closed. After this day, he could take her any time he wanted to. He would be master in his own house, and master of her.

Everyone looked towards the back of the church when Eileen began the walk down the aisle on Abel's arm. Kerry began to sing, low at first, her voice rising as she picked up the organist's tempo:

> 'Amazing grace, how sweet the sound.
> That saved a wretch like me.'

People sighed with contentment as she sang. Eileen looked at Joshua, and even the stern old priest, Father

McNamara, smiled, shaking his head in wonder at the sound of her voice. As he thought to himself, the way some of the eejits in his parish murdered the good God's hymns, it was a breath of fresh air to hear that one sing them.

He opened his bible and blessed it. He was ready to begin.

An hour later Joshua kissed his bride and they went through to sign the register, everyone following, happy now the deed was done and all that was left was the merry-making.

The sun had come out, and Briony was pleased. She was sorry for her churlish thoughts of the early morning. The heavens had not opened and the garden was jam packed with people.

As Joshua stood with a jar of ale in his hand he was more than pleased with the reception. There was a large four-tier wedding cake, and food the like of which he had only dreamed of. A large ham, turkey, chicken, beef. There were all sorts of salads and cold vegetables. He had even eaten curry for the first time, amazed at the skill of Briony's cook, Mrs Horlock.

He watched as his friends relaxed in the grand surroundings and sampled the fine foods and the plentiful drink. All the children had little cakes thrust into their hands and one of the men had made a swing on a large tree at the end of the garden. He looked over to where his wife was talking to her sisters and suddenly felt an enormous burst of pride. She was actually his, now, his wife. She looked beautiful and he knew this was being remarked on.

A normal East End Irish wedding reception consisted

of some currant cake and a barrel of holy water. This was home-made Scotch, or poteen as they called it. Then the next day there would either be a big joke, such as, 'Someone forgot to book the fight!' Or the talk would be of an actual fight that had ensued at some point in the drunken proceedings. Not on his wedding day, though. People were enjoying tasting a bit of the high life, as they would put it to themselves. They'd talk for years about this day, the only chance many would ever get to stand in a garden like this, with drinks and food, and not be either working there or watching from a vantage point. Joshua knew that the general consensus was he had done well for himself, and basked in his newfound status.

Eileen smiled at him tremulously, and he smiled back. Her tiny waist was emphasised by her ivory satin wedding gown, and he told himself that soon she'd be sporting a belly full of arms and legs. He couldn't wait to start the ball rolling. Tonight couldn't come quick enough for him. He'd drive her hard, by Christ, because after all, she was his wife, wasn't she? And a man was allowed to be a man in his own home, surely?

Eileen and Joshua were in their small terraced house in Bow. It had been presented to them a week earlier by Briony and now Eileen stared around her in wonder. It was hers entirely. In her name, in fact. She didn't even have to pay rent.

She had been all for refusing the place, her horror of how Briony accumulated her money still fresh. But Joshua had said it would be churlish to refuse such a magnificent gift, so she had acquiesced. Now she stood in the kitchen, with the freshly leaded range and the smell of lavender polish and coal, and continued to gaze about her in wonder.

It was fully equipped, she didn't even have to supply a tablecloth or a tea towel. Everything was already there.

Joshua put his arm around her waist and she pulled away from him as if she'd been burnt.

'Shall I make a cup of tea?'

Joshua smiled. 'It's not tea I want, Eileen love. You just get yourself upstairs and get into bed. I'll sit here for a while and have a smoke. I'll be up soon.'

The words were heavy with emphasis and innuendo and Eileen licked dry lips and nodded.

Upstairs she stared around her at the bedroom. The bed looked very big all of a sudden, and the lights from outside seemed to give the room shadows and dark corners previously unnoticed. She didn't want to turn on the light though, the thought of Joshua seeing her in the light frightened her. She sat on the bed and bit her lip. Unsure now why she had been so keen to get married. She liked the thought of having her own home, and cooking meals and looking after children, but that was all daytime stuff. She had not allowed herself to think of the nights. They were like her times with Henry Dumas, to be pushed into the furthest recesses of her mind. Only now, here she was married, and the night was here, black and ominous and threatening to go on forever.

She started to unhook her dress, unable to reach the tiny pearl buttons with her trembling fingers. She covered her face with her hands, seeing another bedroom, warm and pretty, and herself lying in bed terrified in case Henry came in and woke her. It was the fear of the unknown that frightened her so. Would Joshua want what he'd wanted? Would he want her to put her hands and lips in secret places that made her feel faint just thinking about them? Would he want her naked and open, kneeling on the bed, her tears seeming to spur him on. Was that what the priest meant when he said children were born through pain? The pain of rough hands and humiliation and fear?

She searched the room with wild eyes, as if expecting a doorway to appear so she could run through it and escape. She closed her eyes tightly and tried to stem the burning tears that were filling up her eyes. Tried to stop the erratic beating of her heart. She could smell her own fear and it spurred her terror on to new heights.

She heard him tapping out his pipe in the fireplace, the rat-tat-tat like an explosion in the silence. She held her breath, ears straining to pick up the sounds as he shut the kitchen door and made his way up the stairs. His tread was heavy, new shoes creaking with each movement of his feet. The breath was hurting her chest and she let it out noisily. A fine layer of sweat was covering her body. The armpits of the dress were wet now. As the bedroom door swung open she groaned in fright. Her whole body seemed to be stiff and unyielding, her legs rooted to the floor.

'Come on, Ei, aren't you undressed yet?' The words were low, spoken in a cajoling whisper.

Her face, strained and white, devoid of colour, stared at him in dumb terror. He unbuckled his trousers, a loud belch escaping from his lips. The trousers dropped to the floor and he stepped from them.

'Let's get some light in here.'

As he turned to put the light on she croaked out through stiff lips: 'No . . . No, please, Joshua. I'm frightened.'

He turned to her, a smile on his lips.

'I'm sorry, Ei, I'm forgetting it's your first time.' He sat beside her on the bed, taking hold of her hand. 'Stop your shivering, girl, we'll soon warm each other up.'

Eileen saw his face in the dimness. He had drunk too much and his face was ruddy. His thick lips gleamed and his eyes looked empty. Like vacant sockets. She pulled her hand from his and stood up.

'I can't, Joshua, I can't . . .'

He pulled her down on to the bed. Lying on top of her, he began pulling up her wedding dress. Feeling for her underclothes, he kissed her – wet, tobacco-tainted kisses that made her whole body shrink. She pushed his chest, feeling the roughness of his shirt on her palms. He laughed. Hitching himself up, he pulled off her drawers, tearing them with the force he used. Dragging them down her legs while his mouth sought her again. She tried to put her head on to her shoulder, the panic welling up inside her. Wanting to be anywhere but in this room. She saw her father trying to take her mother, Henry taking first herself and then Briony. All the pictures ran through her mind and merged, until all she could see was Henry, her father and Joshua, all naked, all trying to pull at her, touch her. With one almighty push, she forced him from her.

She heard his muffled curse as he landed on the floor. Before she could pull herself from the bed, he was up, dragging at her dress. She could hear the material tearing, the pearl buttons coming apart with ease. She hooked her hands and tried to tear at his face, arms flailing in the darkness. He grabbed her wrists and a searing pain shot through her arms. Then he slapped her hard, across the face, knocking her head sideways with the blow. She lay then, stock still, looking at the man who loomed over her.

He pulled her clothes from her then in silence, meeting no resistance, his hands rough, his mouth spewing out reprimands and curses. He looked down on her nakedness, her heavy breasts and tiny waist, and felt the full force of his want. Kicking her legs open with his knees, he held on to her waist and roughly entered her, jabbing himself into her, careless now of her pain, of her fear. Enjoying the sensation of being the master of the situation. As he entered her he suddenly stayed still. Buried inside her, he looked down at her in confusion. There had been no resistance in her at all. He had slipped inside her, even as she was, dry and terrified, and had met nothing. He took her hair in his great fist, pulling it hard.

'You've been busted.' The words came out low and deep.

Eileen stared up at him, her mouth moving in prayer. She wasn't aware that he had spoken. She lay there staring up at him in terror, her mind blank except for the prayers that were crowding into her mind.

Joshua began to lose his erection, all desire for his virgin wife leaving him. In his drink-clouded brain he saw her as she had been when he met her. Never a real kiss, never a touch, nothing. And all the time she was busted, had been used. No wonder that sister of hers had been so quick to marry her off. Had threatened him. Some other man had known her, had touched her. They must all be laughing up their sleeves at him, like it was one big joke.

Eileen, realising that he had stopped, assuming it was all over, tried to rise. It was as if this action, the way she tried to get up, get away from him, finally finished him. Shoving her down by her shoulders he pinned her to the bed and began to ride her hard, thrusting himself inside her with every ounce of energy and strength he possessed.

He wanted to kill her, wanted to slip his hands around that slim white throat and squeeze the breath from her body. But he couldn't. Even in his rage he remembered she was the sister of Briony Cavanagh. Well, he decided, there were other ways to skin a cat, and by Christ he'd use everyone of them. Eileen O'Malley, as she now was, would never know another day's peace.

Chapter Twenty-One

Mariah looked at Tommy with shock tinged with well-concealed annoyance. She put her hands together and tapped her two forefingers against her lips. 'And what has Briony to say about this?'

Tommy shrugged nonchalantly.

'They're my halves of the businesses, I can dispose of them where I want.'

Mariah shook her platinum-blond head, a smile playing on her lips as she answered him.

'I don't see it that way, Tommy, and I have a feeling on me that Briony won't see it like that either. Now then, I don't know what has brought all this on, what's transpired between you, but I know this much. You're not using me to get a sly dig in. Me and Briony get along very well, we're going into business together on a house actually, and I have no interest in making an enemy of her. Not now, not ever.'

Tommy was surprised to hear about their business deal and looked at his hands, clasped together in his lap, while he digested the news. Briony had said nothing about it to him. Nothing.

'I see.'

Mariah grinned. 'No, you don't, Tommy Lane, and I think you should be ashamed of yourself. You walk in here, like the big "I am", offering me your half of Briony's businesses when they're hers really. Briony's the one who built up the houses while you concentrated on chancier deals. I know about your bookies, I know everything about everyone. I've made a career out of it. If you want shot, as you so eloquently put it, of any connection with her, my advice is to let her buy you out.'

Her voice softened and she leant towards him. 'Listen, Tommy mate, I don't know what's happened between you, but this ain't like you. Trying to tuck her up! Whatever she's done to you, remember the past. Remember when it was good and then decide on big things like the partnership. You might be having a nasty half-hour today, but think, will you still feel like it a month from now, or a year?'

'To tell you the truth, Mariah, I can't face her. This ain't nastiness. I thought you'd be the best bet for a partner. You're alike, so bloody alike! But I can't face her meself. I'm sorry, I don't want to clap eyes on her now or ever. I don't really want to do her down, I swear that. But I have to sever the ties.'

'Do you need the money?'

Tommy shook his head.

'No. I don't need the money.'

'Then write to her, tell her from now on you're a sleeping partner. To bank your half of the profits. That way, you don't cut all your ties – you might be sorry you did one day – and also you don't have to see her until you feel you can handle it. And I'll give you some more free advice. Don't try and sell your half to anyone without consulting her first. That's taking the piss and you know it. If she done it to you, there'd be murder done. Try and keep an element of friendship there, Tommy. Give her first offer, then if she refuses, be a sleeping partner. But don't make things worse than they are. Trouble comes without you going out looking for it.'

Molly was shocked at the sight of Eileen. She had left the newlyweds for a week, restraining herself from going to the house, telling herself they would want a bit of time on their own. Finally, she had made the long awaited trip and now she sat in the little kitchen with Rosalee chewing on a slice of bread and wasn't sure what the hell she had stumbled into.

Eileen was as quiet as a church mouse, her face pinched and drawn. She was preparing her dinner, and such was her lassitude, even peeling the carrots was a long-drawn-out operation. She had made a pot of tea and had not opened her mouth since. Molly had talked about all her own doings, until now there was an absolute quiet that hung in the air like a silent cloud.

'Is everything all right, Eileen? You don't look yourself, girl.'

Eileen looked at her, her face strained. Molly felt a sinking feeling at the sight. Please don't let Eileen's nerves get the better of her now, not when she'd been better for so long. Holy Mary, don't let her be going off her head again, please.

'I said, are you feeling all right, Eileen child?'

She nodded.

Molly sighed loudly, wondering what to say.

'Is everything all right with you and Joshua?'

Eileen cut the carrots up, the scrape of the knife against the wooden chopping board the only sound in room.

'For the love of Christ, Eileen, will you bloody well answer me?'

Molly's loud voice made Eileen and Rosalee jump.

Eileen stared at her mother from fearful eyes. Molly noticed that in the week since the wedding her shoulders had acquired the old drooping look of before. Her face seemed to be on her collarbones instead of her neck.

'What do you want me to say?'

Molly closed her eyes. At least she'd answered, she wasn't entirely gone.

'Tell me what's wrong with you, girl? I'm worried about you. For a woman who's been married a week, you look suspiciously like one who's been married forty years, when the novelty's well and truly worn off! Is it Joshua? Is Joshua not nice like . . . You know. Is he doing something to upset you?'

Eileen shook her head, terrified, thinking of the taunts he constantly gave her, the way he asked her to tell him in detail what her seducer did to her, as if this spurred his own sexual appetite on. Telling her he would tell the world about her killing her father, and about Henry Dumas. How the police would dig her father up, and how she'd have to go to court . . .

'Is it that fucker of a mother of his then? Has she been at you? Because if she has, you tell me and I'll wipe the floor with her!'

Eileen shook her head.

Molly gritted her teeth. She'd get to the bottom of this if she had to throttle Eileen with her bare hands.

'Is it the bed like, the nights, love? Is that it?'

Eileen put her hand to her mouth and nodded furiously and Molly sighed with relief.

'Listen, Eileen, I remember me own mother telling me on me wedding day: "There's some that like it and there's some that don't." I was an in-between meself. I liked it at first but once you lot arrived, I soon went off it.'

Eileen didn't answer and Molly spoke again, her voice gentle. 'Look, Eileen, it's a part of marriage we all have to put up with. It's the only way you'll get babies, and believe me, when you have a little one on your breast, you'll see it was worth it. Do you understand me?'

Eileen looked away and nodded.

Molly watched her as she made the dinner, and crossed herself. She wouldn't like the bed part, that stood to reason, she'd bad memories of it. But if she could get a child, then that would straighten her out. Once you had a few babies, you didn't have time for worrying about your troubles, and Eileen had had far too long to dwell on hers. Joshua was a good man, he'd see her all right. Molly consoled herself with that thought.

It had been over a week, and still Briony hadn't heard from Tommy. She had sent three messages, and he hadn't answered one. He had not tried to get in touch about any of the businesses, or about their new ventures in the East End. It was as if he had never existed. A young fellow had picked up his clothes from the house and had refused down and out to tell Briony where he was taking them. That had hurt desperately. Now she was to go and look at Berwick Manor with Mariah, and pretend everything was still tickety boo.

She felt the sting of tears. Well, he had to get in touch soon, even if it was just for the businesses, if she could speak to him once, she'd be all right. She'd convince him of how sorry she was, how much she missed him, loved him . . .

The door of her office swung open and Briony groaned as Bernie breezed into the office.

'What do you want?'

Bernie laughed. 'Oh, you're pleased to see me then!'

Briony half smiled. 'Sorry, that came out a bit vicious, didn't it? I'll start again. What can I do for you, Bernadette?'

'Nothing really, I just thought I'd pop in and see you, that's all. I've hardly seen you at the club and I thought, I know, I'll go and see her. See how she is like.'

Briony was inordinately pleased that Bernie, selfish, sharp-tongued Bernie, who could start a fight with her own fingernails, should be thinking about her.

'I'm all right, Bernie.'

'No word from Tommy then?'

'Nothing, not a whisper.'

'He'll be back.' Bernie's voice was strong.

Briony laughed. 'I hope so, Bern, but I have a feeling that this time he won't be coming back. Not now, not ever.'

'Balls to him if he don't, Bri, it's his loss not yours. Sod him, that's what I say. He was at the Ninety-Eight Club last night, Fenella told me. You know Fenella, the big girl with the huge buzumbas!' Bernie held her hands out from her chest to emphasise what she said and Briony laughed.

'Was he on his own?'

'What do you think? 'Course he was. Pissed out of his head and all, according to her.'

'No Kerry today?' Briony wanted to change the subject. Tommy going to the Ninety-Eight Club had upset her. He was going out then, even if he was getting drunk. She had waited in last night, as she had every night, for him to come round.

Bernie shook her head.

'Our Kerry is sleeping, she had a heavy night last night.' Her voice was heavy with sarcasm.

'What's that supposed to mean? She got a bloke then? It's true, is it? Me and Mother wondered. Who is it?'

Bernie smiled craftily.

'I've been sworn to secrecy about him, Bri, I can't even tell you. I'll give you a hint though. It's the last person in the world you'd expect.'

Briony picked up an air of malice in Bernie's voice and it troubled her.

'Is he married, is that it?' She was all concern.

Bernie shook her head. 'I don't know, do I?'

Briony stared at her for a long moment before she said, 'What's going on here, Bernie? You ain't come here to be Miss Nice Sister, you've come here to cause a bit of hag. Now if you've got something to say, spit it out, or else shut up.'

Bernie sat down and grinned. 'I ain't saying nothing, Briony. If you think there's something funny with our Kerry, you ask her yourself. You'll find her at home in bed about now. She don't get up till five these days. Like living with Dracula it is. Up all night and asleep all day. Even the cleaning woman asked if there was a coffin in her bedroom!'

Briony laughed and shook her head.

'You're a bleeding wind up, Bernie, do you know that?'

Bernadette smiled.

'Now, how are you really, Briony? We've all been worried about you.'

Her voice was so sincere, Briony left the subject of Kerry and started to reassure her sister that she was fine, knowing it would all go back to her mother. But what had been said about Kerry stuck in the back of her mind.

Kerry was not lying in bed, she was sitting in her small kitchen with Evander eating toast and drinking strong black tea, full of sugar. Evander was wearing just his trousers and shirt, Kerry was in a silk dressing gown.

'Tell me about Alabama, Evander, please? You never really tell me anything about America.'

Evander chewed on his toast slowly, deliberately annoying her. He knew that Kerry was impatient. Pulling his arms open, she sat on his lap.

'Come on, Evander, don't annoy me.'

He kissed her on the lips.

'There's nothing to tell, Kerry, really. Nothing that would interest you anyway.'

She took a bite of his toast. Licking the butter from her lips, she said: 'I'm serious, I want to know about your life there.'

Her voice had lost its jocularity now and Evander hugged her to him.

'Look, Kerry, let's just say it's very different from England.'

Kerry pulled herself up and looked at him sternly. 'For crying out loud, I'm not a kid, Evander! Stop treating me like one. If I ever go there, I want to know what to expect.'

He placed the remains of the toast on his plate and carefully wiped his hands on a napkin. This was becoming a regular occurrence. Kerry had a mad idea that they could go to Paris and live there, eventually going to America. No matter how hard he tried to dampen her enthusiasm, she would brook no argument on the subject. Looking at her now, standing with her hands on her hips, he knew the time had come for the real truth. He had to tell her everything. And somehow he had to explain to her exactly why they could never really be together. Not as man and wife.

'Sit down, Kerry. Sit down and keep your peace, woman. I'll tell you what you want to know.' His voice was low. Sitting herself in a chair opposite him, Kerry picked up her tea and waited, her face bright, as if lit from inside.

'Go on then.'

Evander wiped his mouth with his napkin and began to talk in a low sing-song voice.

'I was born in 1896 in a small place just outside Birmingham.'

'We've got a Birmingham here!'

Evander nodded and held his hand up for quiet. Now he had decided to tell her his story, he wanted her to hear it all.

'My father was a drifter, he was half-white. My mother, Liselle, lived on a small farm with her father. My three elder brothers were her father's children.'

Kerry screwed up her eyes at this and Evander could practically hear her mind clicking as she worked out the relationships.

'In Alabama, the blacks were treated worse than the animals. If a black man worked on a farm, then the horses and livestock would get priority over him for food, warmth and shelter. Most niggers slept in an outhouse. Some brought up whole families scratching in the dirt, working on a small place for food and maybe a few clothes.

Children there worked from the time they could walk and feed the poultry. It's hot in the summer and cold in the winter. But it's hotter'n hell for a nigger come summer-time and colder than an icebox for a nigger come fall.

'So, my mother picked up with a half-chat called Rusty Dorsey, a big, smooth-talking man. I can't remember him too well, but I can remember his voice. Like brown molasses, sweet and thick and syrupy. My mother bred four children in three years to him. I was the first. My sisters came after. He worked around, had a trade kind of, good with wood. My mammy always said that he could make a piece of tree bend itself whichever which way he wanted it to. Well, he left. We woke up one mornin' and he was long gone. Liselle, my mammy, broke her heart, and lived in hope of his coming back. Never did, of course, 'cept he'd turn up when he was rock bottom and then drif' off again after a while.

'My granddaddy liked him. They were both hard-talking, hard-drinking men, 'cept my granddaddy had the religion as well. We all lived in one small shanty, but it was ours. There weren't no bedrooms or toilets or nothing like that. You saw and heard everything about everyone. No privacy at all, but then children don't need none.'

Kerry nodded then, remembering the basements. The squalor, the tightly packed bodies in the beds.

'When I was five, I went to work with my mother at a white lady's house. She had a man servant called Tobias, a big nigger. More a field hand really, than a lady's servant, but the woman, Miss Gloria Day . . . she was older than him, she was really old, you know. But she weren't ready to lie down, at least not in the ground anyways. Land's sakes, I watched her a watchin' him with that look!'

He laughed and Kerry smiled to hear him. Her eyes were boring into his face.

'Yes, sir! She liked black meat did Gloria Day! And Tobias, well, he was good to her. Anyway, Tobias took a liking to me. He knew I loved to hear the piano. Miss Day would play and I'd listen, getting a whipping for not sweeping the porch or cleaning the floor, whatever I was supposed to be doing. Well, Miss Day called me in and said to me – she had a high voice, kind of sweet but bitter, you know? – she says, "Evander, you like my piana playing, boy?" And I says real cute, "Yes, mam."

'So she shows me the scales. Anyway, for some reason she decided to teach me to play. I'd spend hours with her, listening to her. I could listen to her all night and day. She was an interesting person, you see. My mammy said, "Evander, she gonna get fed up soon so don't you be breaking your heart over it if she does."

'But God was good, and she began to teach me Chopin. Well, I picked it up real quick, and it pleased her. When I'd play, she'd laugh her head off. That went on for five years. The best five years of my life. By the time I was ten, I could play any damned thing she asked. Somehow, I think now, looking back, I was like the child she never had. She even tried to get me into a school, but the authorities wouldn't even listen. But I'd already accepted that so when she told me, I wasn't too disappointed.'

'It sounds wonderful. You had a great childhood . . .'

Evander laughed out loud.

'No, Kerry. That part of it was good, sure, but I was a nigger, and niggers don't have no childhood! You're a man from the first time you hold you own pecker and pee! Anyway, one morning we goes there and Miss Day is sitting on her porch, looking real bad. Her face was whiter than I ever seen it, and she was white you know. White skin, white hair, white clothes . . .' He swallowed hard and took a sip of his cold coffee.

' "Look round the back, Lissy," she tells my mammy. "Look what they done." '

He looked down at the table for a few seconds.

'Who are "they", and what had they done?' Kerry's voice was serious now. She was frightened of what he was going to say, but had to know.

' "They" were the white men. They'd come late at night. Around the back of her property was an orchard. I'd spent many hours picking the fruit in the summer. There was a large oak tree. It had stood ever since I could remember. I'd climbed it so many times, chasing the coons. Well, hanging by his feet on the oak tree was Tobias. Only I didn't realise it was him at first. They'd burned him, burned him alive, but first they'd beaten him with sticks, kicked him with their boots. His face would have been unrecognisable anyways. They'd castrated him at some point, and pushed his pecker in between his teeth. That was the weird part, you see, because he was charred all over, his clothes were gone, everything, but that was still recognisable. You could see it hanging down.'

'Dear God, I feel sick . . . Really sick!'

Evander smiled.

'I got sick. I looked at that body and I brought up my grits like a hand was pushing up inside my stomach and forcing the food from me. My mammy was crying, she was crying hard, snot hanging from her nose and spittle hanging from her mouth. I ran back to my granddaddy and finally he came with Tobias's father and they cut him down.'

'What about the law, the police?'

'Honey, that *was* the law. It's still the law even now, all these years later. The law says a black man can't look at a white woman. If a white woman thinks a nigger is looking at her in lust, then he can be hanged. Someone at sometime had guessed about him and Miss Day. They didn't care that she wanted it, that she liked it, that she paid him! They wouldn't touch her, her family had been there for years. She had the security of money. So they touched the next best thing – Tobias. Black and white don't really mix, girl, and it ain't no different in France. It's no different anywhere. You've got to understand that sometime.'

Kerry stared across the table at him. She saw his hair like coiled watch springs, his chocolate-coloured complexion. She wanted him so badly she could almost taste it.

'What are you trying to do? Why are you telling me this? You think I don't know about poverty, is that it? Believe me, Evander, I grew up in a slum, the worst kind of slum. We're Irish trash, we're paddys, even though me and my sisters were born here. Why are you trying to scare me, make me listen to such stories? If you don't want me, Evander, just come out and say it, because if you're waiting for me to finish with you, don't hold your bleeding breath, mate.'

Her voice was high, scared. The depth of feeling for him in it made him want to cry out at the injustice of it all. He went to her and knelt before her. Framing her face in his big hands, he tried to reason with her.

'I love you, girl. God help me, I worship you. But you don't understand what I'm trying to say! If anyone ever found out about us, you can't even begin to guess what trouble it would cause. I'm scared. Not for me, for you! You!'

Kerry tried to pull her face from his hands and he held her hard, digging his fingers into the white flesh.

'Listen to me. You think that love conquers all. Well, it don't. When me and you were living hand to mouth, you'd hate me, and if we had children, eventually you'd hate them too. We can't ever believe, either of us, that this is forever, because it's not, it can't be.'

Kerry began to cry then, her eyes filling with tears, blurring his face as she stared at him. Her whole body ached with the want of him, and the harshness of what had happened to them. He held her close, smelling her perfume, her hair. The gentleness of his touch was her undoing, and she cried bitter tears. Hard sobs that made her shudder, and soaked his shirt

'I should never have let it go so far, girl. I was wrong. But believe me when I say I love you, all of you, and I'd do anything at all so we could be together always. But, Kerry, there's just no way. I've lain awake night after night, trying to think of a solution to our problems, and there ain't one.

'I'm going back to the States. I know a guy who can give me a job, I'll go and you'll forget all about me.'

'No . . . I won't, I'll never forget you. I'll follow you . . .'

Her voice was thick with tears. She knew she was babbling and couldn't stop herself.

'We'll find a way, I know we will.'

He held her away from him and looked into her face. Shaking his head, he said: 'I'm gonna leave you, baby, but I'm leaving my heart right here. You gotta accept that, Kerry. This ain't about what we want, it's about what we can and can't have, and we can't have our love. Not now, not ever. Maybe one day, who knows? Maybe one day it'll be different. But not in our lifetime, you can be sure about that.'

'But I love you so much, so much!'

He smiled, grateful for her undying love, even though he knew he should never have sought it.

'I love you too, baby, more than you'd ever dream. I want you so much. I've never had anyone like you before and I never will again. But let's be strong now. It's time for us to grow up and be big people. Big enough to finish what should never have been started and can only end in heartbreak. I'm going, girl, I'm finishing out my contract and then I'm off.'

'So all we have left is a month right? Just four weeks?'

He nodded, sorry to the heart for the sadness in her face, her voice, her whole being, but at the same time he was proud to know that she did love him, really love him. It was like a soothing balm to his wounds. It was sweet to know that he was the one finishing it with her, and he could finish with her for all the right reasons and come out of it with his dignity and his pride intact. He was, for the first time in his life, in charge of a white person's destiny. He was telling this lovely white girl enough was enough. It was a heady feeling.

Kerry sniffed loudly, her face still streaming with tears. 'Then we'd better make these four weeks the best of our lives.'

Evander kissed her then, pulling her face down softly on to his lips.

'We will, baby. Now that, I *can* promise you.'

Chapter Twenty-Two

Briony watched the flickering screen with interest. Despite herself she was impressed with the way Rupert had made use of the girl and the camera angles. Jonathan's face was always obscured in some way, which was good, because the men who watched these films would want a faceless man. It stood to reason.

The girl was typical, which disappointed Briony. She had platinum hair, huge breasts, and a tiny waist. Briony detected an air of boredom emanating from her, but she knew that only she would notice that, and maybe the girls who worked for her. The men couldn't see it in the flesh and blood girls they bought and paid for, so a screen beauty would be no different.

The sex on the screen was hot and heavy, the girl's face expressing faked wonderment and lust. At one point she looked at the upright phallus in front of her and, staring directly into the camera, put a well-manicured hand over her mouth and opened her eyes to their utmost. It was what the punters would want, and exactly what Briony had invested in. As the girl turned over on to her stomach and stuck a perfectly rounded bottom into the air, Briony actually laughed out loud. Jonathan, naked except for a cape, entered her roughly, holding on to her hips. Tommy would hate it . . .

The thought brought Briony back to earth and her face clouded over. Tommy wouldn't even see it. It was ten days now since he had left and she had heard nothing, nothing at all. Oh, she knew he'd been out and about, she had heard that much, but he had not even had the decency to get in touch. Well, she wasn't going to get in touch with him again. He had ignored all her letters and messages, the ball was in his court now! Rage was getting the better of misery and she was glad. She preferred to be cross with him, it made his absence more tolerable. But she was getting worried. If they were still partners that meant she was still half-owner of the East End and she was acting accordingly. If Tommy didn't come back soon, then the rift would be open, really open, and that left her dangerously exposed. At the moment she was still protected, but if he left her high and dry, she would have to fight to regain credibility, and fight she would. No one, but no one, was going to pull her down or take what was hers. Not even Tommy Lane.

The two people on the screen began to flicker and dissolve. The film was coming to its conclusion and she forced her mind back on to the subject matter. She had to OK it with Rupert and Jonathan. She watched it end and then put the light back on.

It was good enough for what they wanted, it would do. She stared around the room for a moment, taking in the furnishings which she hadn't really looked at for a long time. A picture of Benedict stood in a silver frame on the mantelpiece. This was her private room. Only people who were specially invited ever came in here. It was her own private domain. Even her mother wasn't allowed inside. It was where she did her thinking, where she and Tommy had once planned and schemed. That seemed so long ago now. It was as if he had always been gone.

There was a photograph of her and Tommy too. It had been taken the day they had gone to see Charlie Chaplin in *The Kid.* They had loved little Jackie Coogan, loved the film. Both were smiling widely, her face partly obscured by a large hat. Briony picked up the photograph and stared at it, trying to remember everything about that day, every nuance, every moment. If only she had realised sooner how much they had meant to one another.

But that was the trouble, she never did think. Tommy had been there for a long time, she had thought he always would be. She had not realised you had to keep people. She collected people like others collected luggage, and kept them with the minimum of trouble. Her family, for example. But Tommy had needed more and she had been too wrapped up in herself to notice that. She sighed heavily. If Tommy truly abandoned her now, she was back where she started: a madam, a club owner, nothing more and nothing less. If Tommy wasn't there she would look after herself.

She placed the photograph back on the mantle, picking up the one of Benedict. He was grinning. Dressed in a dark suit, he leant against a pillar. It was a good photo, had caught his laughter. Sally had taken him to have it done, telling him it was for herself. He thought Sally looked at it in her room, never contemplating the fact it could be for someone else.

Her face broke into a small smile. Ben looked like her. Even in the sepia-coloured photo where you couldn't see the green of his eyes or the red tinge to his hair, he was wholly her child.

She felt the familiar tug of him, the need of him, inside herself. Replacing the photograph carefully, she walked from the room. She had to go to her mother's today. Another crisis in the family was beckoning. Sometimes she wished they'd all disappear down a big hole and leave her alone. She wasn't in the mood for trouble, she had enough of her own. But no one was to know that, of course. Briony had to be strong, morning, noon and night. It was the law of the Cavanaghs, and she wished with all her heart she hadn't been the instigator of that law.

Molly waited in Eileen's kitchen for Briony. She had left word for her to go straight there, threatening Mother Jones with death, pain, torture and destruction if she made her a cup of tea and delayed her. Elizabeth O'Malley sat wide-eyed, staring into the fire, her face swelling where Eileen had smacked her in the eye.

'Briony was coming to see me today anyway, I was going to tell her that Eileen wasn't right. I blame you and that son of yours, you bitch of hell! Torturing the poor girl out of her mind!'

Elizabeth O'Malley shook her head slowly.

'That girl is as mad as a March hare, you know that in your heart. You were here, you saw what happened. She attacked me for no reason at all. I only came to see how she was.'

Molly made a grunting noise of disbelief.

'That's what you say! You come here day after day. Oh, don't think I don't know. Driving my girl to fecking distraction with your mawing and your jawing! You think you had a smack off our Eileen? Wait till my Briony gets here, she'll wipe the fecking floor with you! And as for that great galloping eejit of a son of yours, my Eileen's never known a minute's peace since she walked down that aisle with him. Not two weeks wed and she's like a poor distracted maniac. He's like your husband, madam, one of them sex fiends! Everyone knew about O'Malley. By Christ, as long as it was breathing, he'd bed it!'

Elizabeth O'Malley's mouth stretched to its fullest. 'YOU BITCH!'

'Yeah, I'm a bitch, but you're a vixen of the first order and my Briony will take the jump from your gallop, by Christ she will. She'll maul the face off you!'

Briony walked in at the back door just as they started fighting properly. Separating the two women, she looked at them both in disbelief and said: 'What the hell is going on here?'

Molly pushed her rival in the chest, sending her careering across the kitchen and into the dresser, the plates and mugs dropping to the floor with a resounding crash.

'That whore of hell there, Bri, *her*, she's the blame. Her and that boy of hers. Call himself a man! Huh! I've seen better men laid out in coffins!'

'Where's Eileen?'

'She's upstairs, and if you ask me she needs to see a doctor. She's out of her mind and my boy ain't responsible for a madwoman, no way. She's your bad blood, not ours. Yours!'

Briony looked into Elizabeth O'Malley's face and said low, 'If I was you, old lady, I'd keep my trap shut. Only I ain't in the mood for hag, and I'm that far from losing me temper.'

She held out a finger and thumb to emphasise her point.

'That's it, Bri, rip the cheeks from her . . .'

'MUM! Will you give it a rest and let me see Eileen? You two can fight and argue the day away, but for fuck's sake take it out into the street. This is neither the time nor the place.'

Both women shut up then, though both would fight till the cows came home left to themselves.

'That's better. Now make a cup of tea, I'm gasping, and keep it down. I'll go on up and see what I can do.'

She made her way up the stairs with a heavy tread. The two older women were still arguing, but softly now, in vicious whispers. Rolling her eyes at the ceiling, she went into Eileen's room. What she found there shocked her to the core. Her sister was curled up on the floor, the quilt from the bed over her, a corner in her mouth pushed in as if to stop a scream from escaping.

'Eileen, Eileen! Are you all right, love?'

Briony knelt down beside her, her face and voice concerned. Eileen stared from pale blue eyes, as if unsure of who she was.

'It's me, love, Briony. Are you all right, what happened? Tell me what happened?'

Eileen's nose was running, and taking a hankie from her coat pocket, Briony wiped it gently. Then she pulled the quilt from Eileen's mouth, wiping the spittle away.

'I can't take any more, Bri. They fight all the time, the two of them. Shouting at me and at each other. Joshua won't leave me alone, see. He won't ever leave me alone. Night after night. I don't like it, Bri, I don't like him. He's nasty to me he is, makes me tell him things, and I can't stand it.'

Briony looked down at her sister, her elder sister, and shook her head, trying to comprehend what was going on.

'What do you mean, tell him things? What things?'

Eileen swallowed hard.

'You won't let on I told you? You mustn't let him know I said anything, see. Because he said if I told anyone, he'd kill me.'

Briony screwed her eyes up and said, 'Oh, he did, did he? Well, I won't let on, darling. You tell me and I'll see what I can do. How's that?'

Eileen grabbed Briony's hands in hers, relief flooding her face. Briony saw the fear there, and the worry. She felt an urge to take Joshua and throttle him with her bare hands for putting that terror there in the first place.

'Come on, Eileen, you tell Briony. I'll look after you.'

'He made me tell him about us, Bri. About me dad, and Henry Dumas . . . He knows everything. About the boy, about me dad, what I did to me dad. He says he's going to tell the police. And he makes me do things to him. Awful things. I don't know why he's doing it. He was nice to me, Briony, always nice. He never hurt me before . . .'

She started to cry harder. Briony stroked the fine dark hair gently.

'Come on, up you get, I'll help you undress and put you to bed, then we'll sort all this out once and for all.'

Eileen sniffed loudly and allowed Briony to help her up. As she slipped her dress off, Briony saw the bruises and scratches on her body and clenched her teeth. She made the bed and helped Eileen into it, smoothing the covers over her with kind hands. Eileen's face, so white, so pinched, broke her heart. Briony felt responsible for all that had happened. Kissing her sister on the forehead, she left the room.

In the kitchen Molly and Elizabeth O'Malley were sitting at the scrubbed table, tea cups in hand, mouths clamped shut. Briony walked in and shut the kitchen door behind her.

'What's been happening here?'

Elizabeth O'Malley shook her head. 'I don't know. I came today to see her like and then your ma arrived. We had a row and Eileen just went mad. Attacked me. And her language!'

'She must have learnt that off your son, our Eileen never said a bad word to my knowledge all her life.'

'My Joshua is a decent man, I'll have you know . . .' Pride in her son overrode any fear of Briony Cavanagh.

Briony poked her face into the older woman's.

'Your son is an animal, and that's what's turned our Eileen's head. Now get up off your fat arse and go and get the doctor. Then go home, go anywhere, but get as far away from me as possible. Oh, and another thing. Your son won't be living here after today, so expect him home at some point.'

Molly grinned in anticipation of all that was to happen in the next few hours. Her Briony would sort it all out, she knew that without a doubt. When Elizabeth O'Malley had left, she smirked and said:

'That told her. If you'd have heard the carry on here today!'

'Shut up, Mum! You're as bloody bad, coming round here tormenting the life out of her. Eileen's ill. She's ill in the mind, Mum, and if you hadn't got me round that ponce's house to marry her, none of this would have happened. She should never have married anyone, not after what happened to her. Dad taking her to Dumas broke her; the day the old man died finished her. Remember when she used to wander off? How she couldn't cope with anything? Well, I think now she's gone over the edge and you can thank yourself for that, not the O'Malleys, mother or son. Yourself.

'Now listen to me and listen good. In future you leave everything be, and keep that big galloping trap and hooked nose out of other people's business, right? Because I blame you for all this today. You and myself. I should never have listened to you.'

Molly's mouth dropped open. That Briony could talk to her like this spoke volumes. Molly felt the first twinge of shame envelop her.

'I'll tell you something else, Mother, he knows all our business. About the old man, Dumas, my boy, everything. He made her tell him, been torturing the life out of her with it. How's that for the icing on the fucking cake!'

'NO! She told him? Dear God in heaven, the stupid, stupid girl.'

'Not stupid. Frightened, terrified, mentally ill, lots of things, Mum, but not stupid. We were the stupid ones to countenance the marriage in the first place. I'll see Joshua O'Malley meself, and shut his trap up once and for all if he ain't careful. He needs knocking down a peg and I'll see to it myself!'

Kevin Carter, Briony's driver, was surprised by the look on her face when she emerged from her sister's house. Her usual good nature seemed to have deserted her and her face was a mask of anger. She got into the back of the car.

'Elizabeth O'Malley's, pronto.'

Without further ado, he drove. Briony sat in the back. Wrapped in her coat, she stared out of the window at the passing streets. Children played on the pavements, men lounged against the lamp posts. It was like going back in time. The streets were no different from how they had been when she was a child. Since the war times had changed. Only the people in these streets had been passed by. They still lived in the same back-to-backs, soot-blackened and small. They still kept a few chickens if they could afford it, or a rabbit or two in a hutch knocked up out of a jerry crate. They still lived hand to mouth, still had that look of hopelessness about them.

The car pulled up outside Elizabeth O'Malley's and Briony got out slowly. It was seven-thirty, still light enough to see everything that was going on around her. A group of ragged children hunched around a doorway, their game of five jacks forgotten as they gazed at the lady in the deep green coat who owned a car. One little girl scratched at a festering flea bite on her ankle and broke the skin. She dabbed at the blood with dirty fingers.

Briony saw curtains twitching, and a mother with a young child on her arm stopped where she was and stared at her. Briony recognised her: Lily Bains, a girl she had gone to school with. She smiled and nodded and banged on Elizabeth O'Malley's front door. The knock resounded through the house and instinctively Briony knew no one was there.

'Lily, do you know where she is?'

Lily stepped back a pace, unsure whether to talk to Briony, a woman who was spoken of in hushed whispers these days; the girl with whom she had once played Tin Pan Alley and shared some childish dreams.

Briony walked towards her. 'Come on, Lily, cat got your tongue? Where's the old bitch O'Malley? Have you seen her son?'

Lily heard the gentle tone and shook her head. 'They went out about an hour ago. I think Mother O'Malley was moving because they had some bags. I hope she was, I can't stand the old cow.'

Briony forced a smile.

'Any idea where she could be moving to? Has she anyone who'd put her up like?'

Lily shook her head again and the child smiled. Briony saw the caries in the child's teeth already; he was no more than a year old.

'The only place she's welcome is the church, and I don't think she's really welcome there. How are you, Briony? You look really well. Really smart.' The last was said with admiration.

'You look well and all, Lily. This your boy?' She stroked the child's face with soft hands. He chuckled. Lily puffed out her cheeks, aware that they were being observed. Now Briony had singled her out for attention, she could brag about how she had grown up with her and people would be impressed.

'I've got four, this is me youngest. I married Danny Little, remember him?'

'I remember him, he used to show us his birds' eggs.'

Briony knew the O'Malleys were long gone, and somehow she was reluctant to leave Lily, a reminder of times past. Of her real youth.

'He still collects them, Briony. Knows all about birds does Danny boy.' Lily's voice dropped. 'I heard you're doing well. I'm glad, Briony. I'm glad you got away from here. You was always a clever girl, always had your eye to the main chance, you did!'

Briony smiled. 'That was me, all right, Lil. It was lovely seeing you. You must know where I live. Come round one day and we'll have a cuppa, talk about the old days.'

'Maybe I will and all.' Both knew that she wouldn't, that her children were infested with lice and she wouldn't have the guts to take them to Briony's house, but it was nice to be offered and she respected Briony for that.

Opening her bag, Briony took out all the money she had in it, about eight pounds, and pushed it into Lily's hand.

'No! No, Briony, I can't take that! No, it was lovely to see you, and talk to you. I don't want your money.'

Briony laughed then.

'Well, you're the only one who don't! But you're the only person I really want to have it. Take it, there's plenty more where that came from!'

Lily looked at the money in wonder.

'I won't say it won't come in handy, girl!'

'Listen, Lily, if ever you need anything, you come to me, right?'

She nodded, tears in her eyes.

'Thanks, Bri. It's funny but we was at rock bottom today. Danny got laid off at the docks. This'll keep us going for a good while.'

Briony and Lily embraced, the child between them crushed by their bodies. He shouted to remind them he was there.

'Tell Danny to go and see Bobbie Phillips tomorrow at the Royal Albert. He'll have a job, I'll see to that.'

Lily nodded, her throat constricted.

'Tara, mate, see you round.'

'Tara, Bri, and thanks again.'

Inside the car Briony was aware of Kevin Carter looking at her as if she'd gone mad.

'Saint Vincent's church, Kevin.'

Her face looked more relaxed than it had earlier and she waved at her friend until they turned the corner of the street.

Father McNamara was not surprised to see Briony Cavanagh in his hallway. He smiled at her and showed her into his library.

'Now then, Briony, what can I do for you?'

'I'm looking for Elizabeth O'Malley and her son, Joshua.'

The priest nodded. 'I see, and why would you be looking for them. You're related now, aren't you? Didn't I see him married to your sister not two weeks since?'

Briony smiled.

'You did, and now he's left her. I want to have a little talk to him. Only I can't find him, or his mother.'

The priest lit himself a cigar and puffed on it for a moment to get it fully alight.

'That woman is like one of the deadly plagues, a mouth on her like nobody's business. Has she put you out like?'

'You could say that, Father. Now have you seen them?'

'No, I haven't seen them.'

Briony stood up.

'Thanks anyway. I'll just keep looking. Do you know if they have any relatives at all? Someone they could go to?'

The priest looked at the girl before him, weighing up in his mind whether to speak out or not.

'Sit back down and tell me what's happened. Then I'll answer your question.'

Briony sat back down and told the priest about Eileen, a carefully edited version, leaving out the juicier bits.

'So Eileen's in a terrible state and he's to blame. I want to see him and set the record straight once and for all. I think I owe him that much.'

'Poor Eileen. She was never right, that one, I saw the change in her myself, God love her and keep her. Didn't she used to work for that feller with the moustaches who owned the blacking factory and half the dock properties?'

Briony screwed up her eyes to slits and nodded. 'As I did, Father. I worked for him as well.'

'Ah, that's right indeed.'

Briony and the priest looked at one another in unspoken communication.

'She wasn't right, poor girl. Maybe the work was too hard for her? I remember your father taking Communion afterwards every week, regular as clockwork.'

Briony didn't say a word. If you took Communion, you had to have your Confession heard. She knew the priest was telling her he knew exactly what was wrong with Eileen and still she didn't speak.

The priest sighed. He had hoped to trade information. This girl and her family intrigued him.

'Well now, if I remember rightly, Elizabeth O'Malley has a brother in Islington. He's a bit of a demon by all accounts, another one with religious mania. I don't think they really get on, but that's not surprising, is it? You ask around Islington and I'm sure you'll find him.'

Briony nodded and stood up.

'Thanks, Father.'

'Would you like me to go and see poor Eileen?'

'My mother would like that, Father. There's just one thing, before I forget.'

'What's that, my child?' The priest looked up at her with his hands clasped together on his lap, cigar clamped firmly between his teeth.

'Don't ever try and find out my business or my family's again. What you guess and what you know is up to you. But in future remember where the money comes from for your expensive cigars and whisky, because there's plenty of other churches who'd welcome me with open arms. No questions asked.'

She left the room, leaving a stony-faced Father McNamara whose Havana cigar had suddenly lost its expensive taste.

Chapter Twenty-Three

Eileen was tucked up in bed in the house where all her troubles had started. Cissy and Mrs Horlock fussed over her, Molly stared at her in bewilderment, and Briony soothed her. But inside her head nothing was right. Her thoughts seemed to run off on tangents; she wasn't sure what was fact and what was fiction. She stared vacantly around her, smiling at times but always quiet. Too quiet.

Briony left her in Mrs Horlock's capable hands and she and Molly retired downstairs to the library to talk.

'You're good to have her here, Briony.'

Molly's voice was stiff. She was still upset about what Briony had said to her, and wasn't sure how to approach her daughter now. Briony turning on her had shocked her more than she cared to admit. Molly liked to think that everything was fine, that the horrors her daughters had experienced were now relegated to the back of their mind, as they were to hers, but Briony had brought them all back. She had reminded Molly that in her own way she had played an integral part in their unhappiness, that in effect she had condoned what her husband had set out to do. Molly lost no sleep any more over Paddy's demise. In fact, since then she had experienced a measure of freedom which would have been unheard of had he still been alive. Now she had to try and ingratiate herself once more with this powerful daughter.

'I think I'll get another quack in to our Eileen in the morning, Mum. There's a bloke from up West, Scottish name, treats Lord Palmer's son for shell shock. He's the best in his field for mental illness.'

Molly nodded but kept her peace. Only rich people could afford nerves and mental illness. She believed still that the devil made work for idle hands. In Molly's eyes a good day's work looking after a few kids and a husband and house was more than sufficient to keep a woman from thinking. Thinking was a bad thing. Too much time for thought and you started sickening.

'I've asked around and about. It seems Joshua has an uncle in Islington, I'm going there later. Kevin Carter's out now with a couple of others tracking him down. If he's there we'll find him. I've got to shut his trap up in some way. But the main thing at the moment is our Eileen. Getting her better if we can. Though I think, eventually, she'll have to go away.'

Molly nodded again.

'Oh, for fuck's sake, Mum, have a go at me, fight me, but don't keep being so bloody passive, it don't suit you. If you've anything to say, any thoughts on all this, say them! I can't stand you quiet, it's unnatural!'

Molly opened her eyes wide and nodded once more, infuriating Briony even further.

'God give me strength!'

'Oh, he's given you that, Bri. He's given you enough already for ten men.'

Briony laughed gently.

'Oh, it can speak then?'

'I can. It's whether or not you're interested in what I have to say?' There was a semblance of Molly's old spirit as she spoke and Briony was pleased.

'Mum, think about this. When did any of us ever listen to you anyway? That never shut you up before, did it?'

Molly grinned then. Briony was joking, she was over the worst, the sun was out and everything was going to be all right. Briony would look after them all. The weight was lifted from Molly's shoulders and she could relax again.

Kevin stood uncertainly in front of Tommy Lane.

'If she knew I knew where you were, Tommy, there'd be murders.'

'I know that, Kev, and I appreciate you telling me everything. Is Briony all right like, in herself?'

'Oh, yeah. Well, I mean, she seems all right. But I think all this with her sister has shocked her more than she'd ever admit. You know Briony, she's more close-mouthed than the government.'

Tommy smiled in spite of himself.

'True. So Joshua has something over her, has he? Well, ain't he the brave bastard! Milk and water, I booked him. Wouldn't say boo to a mouse on a mortuary slab. Well, we live and fucking learn, don't we? Still, don't worry, Kev, I'll find the ponce and sort him out. In fact, me and you can go and see this bible basher now. Maybe I'll get a bit more out of him than you did.'

'Suits me, Tommy. I just want to give Briony a break. Her sister's bad, I saw her meself. She's ill, mate. That bloke's worked her over and all, black and blue her arms were. But he never touched her boat race. Well, he wouldn't, would he? What a turn up, eh?' He shook his head in silent disgust.

'Sit down and I'll get changed. Help yourself to a drink.'

Tommy left the room and walked up the stairs of his new house in Stratford. As he entered the bedroom a female voice said, 'Are you coming back to bed, Tommy?'

Shirley Darling, as she was called, held out one long slim arm towards him. He smiled.

'Sorry, Shirl, but business beckons. Get yourself dressed and trundle off now. There's a good girl.'

Shirley sat up in bed, the sheet dropping away to reveal enormous breasts. 'Oh, Tommy! Can't I wait for you to come home later?'

'Nope! Dressed and home for you, young lady. I'm busy.' He pulled on his clothes with a nonchalant air.

'You're a wanker, Tommy Lane!'

He laughed out loud. 'Very ladylike, I must say.'

Shirley, who really liked Tommy, had always liked him and had been over the moon to climb into his bed, was upset that he was dismissing her like a two-bob tart. Her eyes screwed up and she said, 'You *are* a wanker. As for me being ladylike, I'm no more ladylike than Big Briony, as they call her. They also call her the Poison Dwarf, did you know that? What's the matter, Tommy? Frightened she'll find out I've been here and little Tommy Lane's been a naughty boy? Scared of her, are you?'

She froze as he yanked her from the bed by her arm. He ran her across the room and into the dressing room where her clothes were neatly folded on a chair.

'Get dressed and fuck off. As for Briony, you ain't even fit to walk on the same bit of pavement as her. Now take your stuff, take your big fucking trap, and piss off!'

Shirley sat on a chair naked, and rubbed at her arm. 'You hurt me!'

Tommy made a tragic face. 'NO! I never, did I? If you're not careful I might just tell Briony what I've been doing all afternoon. Now if she frightens me, what must that thought do to you, eh?'

He left the room but as he walked down the stairs felt a wave of temper wash over him. So people thought he was scared of Briony, did they? Then he smiled. The Poison Dwarf! Briony would laugh if she heard that one. Collecting Kevin, he left the house, Shirley never once entering his thoughts. Unlike Briony, she was over and done with.

Padraig O'Connor was a thin wiry Irishman with burnished red hair, a red bushy beard, and large rough hands. Not a tall man, only five foot four, he gave the impression of great strength in his compact, tightly muscled body. His deep-set blue eyes had the glint of a man on the verge of religious mania.

Padraig went into the lowest of pubs and drinking establishments, giving out the word of the Lord. He knew his bible backwards and forwards, believing in the pure and simple sanctity of living your life by the word of God, the ten commandments and *Leviticus*. He drank only water, Adam's Ale, and ate simple foods. He also worked hard as a coal man, delivering the sacks everywhere, his hands and back ingrained with coal dust, a sign to the world that he toiled hard at good honest work. Drunks, women of the night and local priests ducked into corners and under hedges when they saw him coming. As Father Kennedy had once remarked, the man could make a top of the morning sound like a declaration of war.

Padraig was in The Green Man, his bible open at *Leviticus*, regaling the rather drunken customers with the Lord's words on bestiality.

'"Thou shalt not lie down with the beasts of the field."'

A big burly docker shouted out, 'I'll agree with you there, mate, but what if your old woman looks like the fucking back end of a bullock? What then, eh?'

Everyone laughed. A tiny man with horn-rimmed glasses, carried away with drink and camaraderie, shouted out: 'Your old woman *sounds* like the back end of a bullock! She's got more mouth than a cow's got . . .'

The docker stopped laughing immediately and, turning to the man who'd insulted his wife, said: 'Do you want a bunch of fives or what?'

The little man's head disappeared into his glass of ale and the docker looked around him for anyone who fancied having another go about his wife.

Padraig O'Connor carried on regardless, his words delivered in a loud voice, his whole demeanour taut and intense. He believed every word he said and couldn't for the life of him understand how no one else could gain the enjoyment from the Bible that he did.

The smoky atmosphere was burning his eyes and throat. He coughed loudly and the barman pushed a pint of beer on to the counter.

'Go on, man, drink that. It'll cool you down.'

Padraig shook his head.

'A glass of water will be sufficient, thank you.'

The barman got him his water, and handing it to him, said, 'Drink that and go. They're laughing at you, can't you see that?'

Tommy Lane and Kevin Carter walked into The Green

Man. One look at the man at the bar drinking down a glass of water and they knew they'd struck gold. They stood watching as he started his preaching once more.

' "Thou shalt not lie with mankind as with womankind, it is abomination!" I see this all the time. Round the docks, men dressed as women, men looking for other men, like painted harlots!'

Tommy looked at Kevin and made a face. 'Fuck me, he's as mad as a hatter!'

Kevin laughed.

'Shall I get him outside so you can talk?'

'Yeah, I think this lot will probably be grateful to see the back of him.'

Kevin walked over to Padraig. Whispering in his ear, he half dragged and half cajoled the man from the public house. To the amusement of everyone there, the docker shouted: 'Oh, leaving so soon? And we hadn't got to the bit about whoredoms yet! Well, don't hurry back, mate.'

Outside Tommy looked at the man before him with sorrow. In his own way Padraig was a good man, only like most people who were too good, he got on the nerves of lesser mortals like Tommy himself.

'Hello, Mr O'Connor. I'm Thomas Lane, and I'm looking for your nephew Joshua.'

Padraig stared at Tommy intently, his hard blue eyes seeming to bore into his face.

'My nephew is no concern of mine, or yours come to that.'

Tommy smiled widely then, opening his coat, waited until O'Connor was watching this action before punching him with all his might in the solar plexus, driving the man on to his knees. Dragging him up by his shirt, he looked once more into his face and said: 'If you know where your nephew is, you'd better fucking tell me because the wrath of God is nothing compared to mine.'

Padraig weighed up his chances. His bible was lying in a small puddle, the pages open and getting soaked with dirty water.

'I've nothing to say to you.' Tommy began working him over then. Kevin held Padraig's arms behind his back and Tommy pummelled him in the stomach and head. Five minutes later, his face was bloody, his eye swollen.

Tommy looked at the man's destroyed face and said, 'I can keep this up all night if needs be. It's no skin off my nose. Now then, where's your nephew? He's hurt a woman I care about deeply. Sent her off her head, in fact, beaten her up and broken her heart. You're not telling me you'll hide someone like that?'

Padraig was shocked at the charges against his nephew. He had never cared for his sister much. They had tried to outdo one another on the religious front since childhood, but her husband had been a fornicator and a drunkard. Now it seemed the son was the same.

'Hurt the woman you say? Beat her?'

'Black and bleeding blue. I'll take you to her, if you like?'

'No . . . no. Joshua is at my coal yard in Shepherds Bush. At the corner of Scrubbs Lane. They're both in the shed at the back.'

Tommy smiled then, sorry for what he'd had to do.

'Thanks, mate. You can get on with your holy work now. We won't keep you a moment longer.'

Padraig wiped a hand across his mouth. 'The Lord is

slow but he's sure, young man. "What ye sow shall ye reap."'

'God also has another little saying. It's: "An eye for a fucking eye." Well, tonight your nephew's going to find out exactly what that means.'

With that Tommy left the man and climbed into his car. He saw Padraig pick up his bible and wipe the pages lovingly before walking back into the foetid warmth of The Green Man, and in a funny way Tommy couldn't help but admire him and his principles.

'Come on, Kevin, let's get moving. All this do-gooding is making me feel ill!'

Joshua was chewing his thumbnail, a habit that had always annoyed the life out of his mother.

'I blame you for all this. I've had to leave me home, everything, because you brought the Cavanaghs into our house. Two weeks you've been married, two weeks! And now we're hiding out in my brother's bloody coal yard! Me, a respectable widow, reduced to this!' She felt a terrific urge to brain her son where he sat. 'Will you stop chewing your fingers to pieces!'

'Listen, Mother, I can sort all this out. I have something Briony Cavanagh wants, in a manner of speaking. I'll get us the money to start up again somewhere else. Now, for goodness' sakes, give it a bloody rest!'

Elizabeth looked at her son, a weak man like his father. A weak and cowardly individual who had been both the pride and bane of her life.

'What have you got exactly that's so important?'

Joshua shook his head, annoying her once more. 'Nothing for you to worry about. Let's just say I have certain information that could help us, both physically and financially.'

As what he said sank in, Elizabeth O'Malley felt her legs begin to give way. She sat down abruptly on an old chair, glad of its support. Her voice low now, she said: 'You fool of hell! You stupid foolish boy. You're not seriously contemplating blackmailing the woman, are you? Jesus wept! She'll take you by your balls and hang you from the highest lamp post she can find, and she'll do it in public and all, because there's none will ever split on her. That's what this is all about, isn't it? You've found out something. This isn't over Eileen really. Tell me what you know now, before they find us.'

Joshua licked dry lips and swallowed hard. He was in over his head and he knew it. Now, worst of all, his mother knew it too.

'It's Eileen and Briony . . . they were both whores of Henry Dumas as children. Their father took them as little girls. Eileen attacked her father with the flat iron, and killed him stone dead . . .'

'Jesus fecking cross of Christ! And you thought you could use that to get us out of this trouble? You're even more stupid than I gave you credit for.' Joshua saw the fear on his mother's face and felt the heat of terror enveloping him, making him sweat.

'Briony Cavanagh kept that a close secret, boy, so do you think she'll ever rest easy again, knowing we have her marked down? Do you really think that? Could you be so bloody stupid! That Eileen, as mad as she is, was at least a decent wife in that she was quiet. Amenable and easily handled. You could have kept us both up there, living the life of Riley, but you had to push the girl. I can see now you pushed her over the edge. You've signed your own death warrant. Briony and that Tommy Lane rule the roost and, let's face it, there's more than a few people who'd like to see us out of the way. They'll have all the help they need to find us.'

Joshua jumped from his seat.

'Will you shut up! For once in your life, shut that great big gob of yours! If it hadn't been for you, I'd have married Eileen fair and square. But no, you didn't want me married, not to her or anyone. Well, she was a slut like her bloody sister. Can't you see, I can get us enough money with this knowledge to set us up anywhere we want to go?'

For the first time ever Elizabeth O'Malley was lost for words. This great big son of hers really thought he could get away with threatening Briony Cavanagh.

'You're mad, son, stark staring mad if you honestly believe that. Briony Cavanagh will tear London apart looking for us. You have nothing on her, nothing at all. Because she'll see you don't live long enough even to breathe a word of what you know.'

Tommy Lane walked into the tiny cabin then and said: 'I couldn't agree with you more, love.'

Joshua felt a sinking sensation in his bowels as he looked at Tommy Lane's smiling face.

Elizabeth O'Malley took her son's arm, pulling him to try and get him to move.

'Come on, Joshua. At least walk out of here under your own steam.'

He allowed himself to be led from the cabin. Tommy walked beside them, his hand on Elizabeth's arm. The vicious-tongued old woman beside him looked very small all of a sudden, and very vulnerable.

Gritting his teeth, he helped her into his car. This one was for Briony. He owed her this much at least.

*

'Who's at the door?'

Cissy marched across the hallway in her dressing gown. 'How the bleeding hell do I know? See through solid wood, can I?' She opened the door wide and gasped.

'Hello, Tommy . . . Briony's in bed.'

Mrs Horlock smiled as he walked into the entrance hall. 'I'll go up to her then.'

As he disappeared up the stairs, Cissy and Mrs Horlock clasped one another in glee.

'He's back then, I knew he would be!'

The two women smiled conspiratorially.

'Briony will be sleeping in, I'll bet!'

Cissy pushed Mrs Horlock in the shoulder gently. 'Oh, you're terrible you are!'

Tommy walked into Briony's bedroom, shutting the door gently behind him. Briony lay asleep, her hair around her head like a deep red halo. She had on a small night light which flickered as the door opened and closed, giving her milky skin a luminous glow. She turned on to her side, giving him a tantalising glimpse of breast, then as she began to burrow under the covers, she froze. Opening her eyes in alarm, she realised someone was there.

'All right, Bri, calm down, it's only me.'

She lay on her back once more, staring up at him in wonderment.

'Tommy?' She blinked her eyes a couple of times as if unsure what she was seeing was real.

Sitting up in the bed, her face glowing, she hugged her knees through the blankets.

'You came back? Oh, Tommy, it's good to see you.'

She flung her arms around his neck, pushing her body against his and feeling the comforting warmth as he hugged her back.

Tommy remembered the love he had had for her, felt the pull of her. He disengaged himself from her arms with difficulty.

'I'm not back for good, Bri, let's get that straight now.'

Her face darkened. 'What do you mean?' He could hear the confusion in her voice.

'What I say, Bri. We're old news, love. I came to tell you something important, something that has to be said face to face. Joshua and his mother are gone. They won't be back again. What he knew about you and Eileen is as safe as houses.'

'How did you know . . . How did you know he'd found out? No one knew, no one except me and me mum and our Eileen . . .' She was stammering.

'I found them tonight, and heard everything they said. At least his mother had the sense to know he'd gone too far. Well, I've shut the pair of them up, permanently.'

Briony's face dropped. Her whole countenance seemed to crumple before his eyes.

'You don't mean . . .'

He nodded.

'You didn't have to do that! I could have shut them up. Fear would have shut them up, Tommy, plain and simple fear. I wanted to kill them myself, but I know I never would have. It was just temper. I could have shut them up by myself!' She pushed him away from her then. Getting out of the bed, she pulled on a wrapper and began pacing the bedroom floor as she tried to comprehend what Tommy had done.

'My God, Tommy, you'd kill anyone, wouldn't you? Without another thought? I admit I could have wrung his bloody neck, and a good hiding would have been compulsory, but I'd never have topped them. They weren't worth topping. They were nothings, no ones. Shit on my fucking shoes! How dare you do that without telling me? How dare you take something like that on yourself and expect me to be grateful!'

'Well, that's rich, Briony, I must say. Here's me trying to help . . .'

'Don't give me that old bollocks, Lane. You wanted an out. Well, you've achieved what you set out to do, you've got your out, and your big fucking finale into the bargain. Only don't expect me to drop to me knees with thankfulness. It ain't gonna happen.'

Tommy stood up.

'Before I go – about the businesses. I'm staying as a sleeping partner. I'll send you details of where to bank me money.'

Briony cut him off. 'Sleeping partner? More like a fucking coma victim! You never ran the houses or the clubs – *I* did. And I didn't feel the urge to kill all and sundry while I did it. You know something, Tommy Lane? One day you'll go too far. You always did before. It was me who was the sensible one, the voice of reason. Remember that next time you feel the urge to batter someone's brains out.'

'Well, then. We know where we stand, don't we? I'm off.' Tommy walked to the bedroom door. 'Goodbye, Briony.'

She watched him leave the room, then sat on the edge of the bed, her face buried in her hands, tears forcing their way through her fingers.

Tommy was gone, she was really alone. Empty at last of any real feeling, she dried her eyes. She herself was the only person she could ever rely on from this day forward. It was Briony Cavanagh against the world, and this Briony was a harder, sleeker version than the previous one. Because she had no one at all now except herself.

Tommy drove himself home, his heart light inside his chest. He had achieved what he had set out to do. Briony would be fuming with him for what she thought he'd done. But her mind would be at rest with the thought that her secrets were safe. She had broken with him, and so he would try and make a life of sorts without her. His need for her was as strong as ever, but he had to try and live without her.

As he parked outside his house he glanced at his watch. At this moment Kevin Carter was driving Elizabeth O'Malley and her son to Liverpool. They were frightened out of their wits, and both knew better than ever to open their mouths about Briony.

Tommy opened his front door, frowning. It annoyed him that she thought him capable of killing an old woman, even if the old woman was Elizabeth O'Malley!

As he climbed his staircase though, he felt a sort of lightness come over him. He was young, he was unattached, and he was a man of substance.

He had severed his ties with Briony, even though they were still partners. He would still look out for her, no one would hurt her while he breathed, but now he'd look out for her from afar. Her status in the East End wouldn't change. Briony would still be the force she had always been, only now she would be on her own.

Chapter Twenty-Four

Delilah Glasworthy was fifty-five years old and looked good on it. Her hair was still thick and dark, with only a sprinkling of grey, her eyebrows lustrous and finely shaped and her deep-set brown eyes were humorous. She was tall and slim with long shapely legs which she did not try to hide. A widow for over twenty years, she owned a house in Stepney, in East Street, and let it out to boarders – gentlemen of good standing, civil servants, engineers, and others of that ilk.

She looked down her nose at the people around her, watched young mothers giving their windowsills what she called a 'cat's lick', tutted over children with dirty knees and snotty noses. But in general she kept herself to herself. Today, though, she was sitting in Molly Cavanagh's kitchen drinking a cup of tea and trying her hardest to pluck up courage to talk frankly to the woman in front of her.

'You look great, Delilah, your hair is beautiful still. You always had the hair, even as a child.'

Delilah smiled tremulously. She had known Molly

Cavanagh from childhood. Their mothers had known each other in Cork; their fathers had both been seamen, then dockers. Of an age, the two women found it easy to pick up exactly where they left off, even though they might not see one another from one year to the next.

'I still board, Molly. I have some lovely gentlemen at present. Refined types, you know.'

Molly stifled a grin. Refined my arse! she thought, but she nodded pleasantly anyway.

'But East Street! Molly, it's gone downhill, I tell you. We have some horrible characters there now. The young women of today. Make-up in the middle of the afternoon! Tally men banging their doors down at all hours, men coming home to ructions and fighting. It's a disgrace, I tell you. And over the road to me, well, they take blacks now. Nanny Carpenter lets to blacks!'

Molly looked suitably scandalised.

'Nanny Carpenter! Why she was always the one for respectability!'

Delilah raised her plucked eyebrows and said: 'You can charge them double, see? It's a terrible thing really because the poor people have no choice, do they? It's robbery. And the men seem quite refined and well dressed. In fact, I heard they work in your Briony's club. Must be her band, eh?'

She gave a tinkling little laugh that she thought sounded very ladylike, and which she practised when she was alone.

Molly's face dropped now. If they worked for her daughter they were her property, so to speak. Briony was responsible for them. Her eyes narrowed and she said, 'Charging the poor buggers double, is she? Why, them boys of Briony's are cleaner than most whites, my Kerry told me that herself! Works with them, doesn't she? She should know, it stands to reason. Can't stomach the buggers meself.'

'I've seen Kerry there, actually, Moll. A few times, in fact. That's what brought me here today. I don't want to gossip or cause any trouble, you know, but a girl's reputation is her greatest asset . . .' She foundered under Molly's direct gaze.

'Go on then, Delilah, spit it out.'

'Well, people have noticed. Look, Molly, I'm here as a friend so will you stop staring at me like that? You're making me nervous!'

'Are you saying what I think you're saying? That my Kerry's black man's meat. Is that what you dolled yourself up for today, to come and bring lies and filth into my home?'

Delilah stood up abruptly.

'I'm sorry, Molly, I thought you'd want to know. If it was my daughter . . . I mean, I'm not saying that anything's going on, but she picks him up from there in a car, they chat and talk like . . . well, like people who are more than friends. I'm telling you before anyone else does.'

Molly chewed on her bottom lip, her face a mask of dismay.

'I'll see myself out, Moll. 'Bye, Rosalee love.'

She kissed Rosalee and left hurriedly, rushing up the lane as fast as she could. Sorry now for interfering.

'They chat and talk like people who are more than friends . . .'

Kerry had no place being friends with blackies, that was what was bothering Molly. True, she was a singer, a bit bohemian, but that was Kerry. But Molly uneasily remembered her sitting in this kitchen one day and arguing the toss about black people when her mother had made some disparaging comments. She'd been defending her man, the big mysterious man they'd all assumed was married or, as Molly had thought, a man of substance, gentry, a lord. When all the time he was a black man, a dirty stinking black man!

Her disgust knew no bounds. That Kerry, her talented, beautiful Kerry, could sink to that level, broke her heart. Jumping from her seat, she pushed and pulled poor Rosalee roughly as she got her coat on her, dragging the protesting girl from the house on their way to Briony's.

She would know what to do.

Andrew McLawson held Eileen's hand. He had taken her pulse, checked her over physically, and now he sat looking at her, puzzled.

'Are you going to talk to me, Eileen?'

She opened her eyes and smiled tremulously.

'Come on, tell me about yourself.'

He watched the changing expressions on her face and sighed. He had seen people like her before though not many times, he admitted. But he had seen the same haunted look, the same fathomless eyes, the same symptoms. Yet this wasn't a family who would terrorise a child, or at least they didn't give that impression. He had a girl at his nursing home, Sea View, who was the product of a very Victorian father and a weak-kneed mother. The girl had had all the life drained from her. The lust for life, the wanting of it, had been gradually beaten from her. Oh, not with fists, though this girl was still carrying the remainder of bruising on her arms and back, but with words and harsh behaviour. She'd been told she was worthless, and now she believed it. Quiet as a church mouse, she sat out her days, looking at the sea and drinking tea, constantly drinking tea, her hands clumsy and shaking. McLawson would lay money that the father had sexually abused the girl, he knew she wasn't a virgin. But the father was a man of wealth and position, and the doctor was employed to hide people's mistakes. 'Bad nerves' had become a catchall phrase for all the illness of the mind. At Sea View he had men, young virile men, who were still shell shocked from the war. He also cared for old spinster aunts or eccentrics without the private means to keep themselves who were shunted into homes like his by their uncaring relatives. Now he was to have this girl. The Cavanaghs were working-class, the voices betrayed that. But Briony Cavanagh seemed to have an inexhaustible supply of money, judging from this house. He shrugged. How she'd come about it was her business, but her concern for her sister was genuine enough. It was that concern which had prompted him to leave Sea View and travel up to this house to see Eileen O'Malley. Now he knew he would take her. She was like a poor broken bird. He'd take her to the home and try to look after her, but there was something her sister should know first.

Briony walked into the room. 'Everything all right, Doctor?'

He smiled. His dark eyes were sad and his thick dark unruly hair stood up as if he'd been out in a gale, though this was the result of his constantly running his hands through it.

'Sit down so we can talk.'

Briony sat beside the bed in a large leather chair. Andrew McLawson was surprised to see how tiny she was. Her feet were so small in her little white shoes they looked like a child's. And all that hair, that beautiful red hair, with those startling green eyes. She was a lovely girl all right.

'As you know, your sister's not well.' He looked at Eileen as he said this and smiled. 'I think we could accommodate her at Sea View, but I really have to know all the details of your sister's illness first. Everything. If I'm to help her at all.'

He noted the whitening of Briony's face and looked at Eileen pointedly. He smiled at her gently. Briony was surprised to see Eileen smile back. She liked him.

'If you would like to follow me down to the drawing room, I'll tell you what I think you need to know.' Her voice was hard and for a fleeting second the man felt that this little woman could be dangerous. The feeling passed as quickly as it had come and he stood up to follow her.

'Anything you tell me will be in the strictest confidence, Miss Cavanagh.'

She looked into his face and said, 'The name's Briony, and some of the things I do aren't strictly legal. In fact, they're highly illegal. What do you say to that?'

Andrew McLawson picked up his bag.

'I am in the business of keeping secrets, Miss Cavanagh. Many of my patients are from the cream of this country's aristocracy. I want to help people, not hinder them.'

'Then you sound like just the man for me.'

The fact that he had first called her 'Miss Cavanagh' pleased her, and he wanted to keep everything businesslike, which could only augur for the good.

'That is a very tragic story you told me there, Briony. I think your sister has had a very very sad life.'

She nodded. 'My father brought her here to this house. He brought me a year later. Only I was stronger, I survived it all. I'm now a very influential woman in my own right, Dr McLawson, and what I want, I generally get. If something upsets me, I leave no stone unturned to sort out the problem.'

The doctor laughed out loud.

'You're threatening me!'

Briony smiled now, but it didn't reach her eyes.

'Not threatening, Dr McLawson, making you a promise. I have been very candid here today. The knowledge you now possess is because I want what's best for my sister, but it has never been discussed with outsiders before. I want to make sure it stays that way.'

'It will. Your father was a very wicked and evil man . . .'

Briony cut him off.

'My father was a very poor man, a totally uneducated man, a man at the end of his tether, in fact. Born into the same circumstances, who knows what you would sell to keep your head above water?'

'I wouldn't sell my children.'

Briony smiled again. 'You don't know what you'd sell, young man, in the same position. You'd be surprised what I could get for you round the slums for five shillings. Every sexual act under the sun. It's some people's only saleable commodity. So don't be too harsh on them. If I can find it in my heart to forgive my father, I'm sure you can.'

Andrew McLawson bowed then to a will much stronger than his own. This was a strange household, with strange secrets. He was beginning to be sorry he had ever entered it.

'I'll bring my sister tomorrow and stay till she's settled in.'

'As you like. I really must go now, to meet my train in time.'

'My driver will take you to the station.'

'Thank you, that's very kind.'

He shook the tiny hand that fairly glittered with jewels. This was a strange household indeed. Thank goodness he'd left by the time Molly arrived, breathing fire and fury.

'Mum! Will you calm down?'

'Calm down, she says! Calm down when that black-headed whore has been running round with a black man!

Briony stared at her mother in wonderment. 'What! What did you say?'

'That Kerry, she's been running round with a mystery man all right. A fucking big darkie from her band! Oh, the shame of it! How will I ever hold me head up if this gets out?'

Briony managed to laugh.

'You'll manage somehow, Mother. If you could live down me and Eileen and the old man, you'll live down Kerry. Now how do you know this is true?'

'Because Delilah told me. She has a boarding house in Stepney. Well, your woman has been seen there, picking him up and dropping him off, as brazen as you like!'

'She might just have been giving him a lift. You've no proof that anything's going on. Bloody hell, Mum, you know what people are like. They're still reeling from the disappearance of O'Malley and his mother. Don't tell me they've time to talk about Kerry and all!'

'Listen to me, Briony, I've had a feeling on me for a long time there was something not right with Kerry. Then the other week, I said something about blacks and she went mad. I should have guessed then. If she was here now I'd rip her sodding head off her shoulders, I would that! The thought of her and him . . . him touching her with his black hands.'

Briony saw the disgust on her mother's face. Going to her, she sat her on a chair.

'Calm down, for crying out loud.'

'You've got to do something, Briony. Smash him up! Smash his bloody face in! Teach him a lesson he won't forget! You have to put a stop to it – now.'

'Hello, Bernadette. Sit yourself down.'

Bernie sat opposite Briony in her office. The door was closed but they could hear Kerry's voice as she sang.

'Sounds well, don't she, Bri?'

'She does that. In fact, she sounds just like a girl who's getting a regular portion off a big black man. Am I right? Is Kerry having a fling with someone in the band? Because they ain't likely to be getting engaged, are they?'

Bernadette's face was a bleached white.

'Who told you?'

'Never mind who told me, it's enough I know. You were obviously in on the big secret. You even tried to hint to me about it, didn't you? Is it that Evander then, the one she's so sure is talented and clever? Is it? Well, answer me then, you two-faced cow!'

'I ain't two-faced! I never said a word to anyone.'

'That's just the point, ain't it? Normally you've a mouth big enough to get your foot in it, both your feet, in fact. Why keep quiet about something like this, eh? Is it because you thought that once the shit hit the fan Kerry would be finished, is that it? You sat and watched your sister bugger up her life and didn't even try and do anything about it? You should have come to me, told me as soon as you knew or even guessed. Now I've got the job of getting rid of the ponce ain't I?'

'He's going back to the States anyway at the end of the month.'

'Oh no he ain't, love, he's going tonight. And he's going with a flea up his arse. Rupert Charles knows a bloke who wants to record our Kerry. He thinks she's going to be big, very big, and so do I. Unlike you, Bernie, our Kerry has a brilliant future ahead of her – and a black piano player ain't in the picture anywhere! Tonight, after work, you keep her in the club. Evander and his merry little band are going to leave tonight, leave this place permanently, back to the good old US of A.'

'But, Briony, they're going at the end of the month anyway. What difference does a few weeks make?' Bernie was amazed at her own argument for Kerry and Evander, but now the cat was out of the bag she genuinely felt sorry for them.

Briony shook her head in amazement.

'Can't you see? She's been tumbled. Someone came and saw the old woman. It's common knowledge, Bernie. We have to get shot now, as soon as we can. He has to leave with the knowledge that, if he ever comes back looking for her, there'll be big trouble.'

Bernie looked at her hands clasped in her lap. 'This will break her heart, Bri, she's mad about him. Honest, she really loves him.'

As sorry for her sister as Briony felt, she had to be hard, and when she answered Bernadette, she meant every word she said. 'Then that's more fool her, ain't it? But one day she'll thank me for this. One day she'll see the folly of what she's been doing. Can you imagine what the upshot would be? Can you? If this was public knowledge Kerry would be an outcast. No. Her voice is the biggest thing she's ever likely to have, and if it rests with me, she'll use it to its fullest potential. I'll see she don't fuck up. I'll see to that much personally.'

Bernadette stared at her sister for a long while before she said: 'Do you know something, Briony? It must be great being you. You just barrel through life organising everything and everyone. You play God, and we all play your disciples. Well this last lot stinks. I admit, I wanted to see Kerry get her comeuppance. Talented, marvellous Kerry, the girl with the golden voice. But now I'm not so sure. Because I'll tell you something for nothing – she loves the bones of that man, and you can send him off on his bike, do what you like, but you can't change people's feelings. I'd have thought you'd have appreciated that fact better than anyone? Look at how you feel about Benedict, and look who fathered him. You can't help where your feelings lie, Bri. Not you, not me, not Kerry. Not even poor old Eileen.'

Briony leant across the desk, knocking her glass of whisky flying.

'You've got a big mouth, Bernie, it's always been your downfall. From a kid that trap of yours has always got you into bother. Well, let me tell you something, girl. I ain't in the mood for you tonight. I don't want to hurt Kerry in the least, I want what's best for her. You're the one who wanted her to be hurt. Whatever you say now, the fact you kept that big mouth of yours buttoned speaks volumes to me. So you'll do what I tell you. You'll keep her back tonight, and if you let on about any of it, I'll wring your neck. Tonight this lot is finished and Evander Dorsey is history.

'Now piss off out of my sight, Bernie, before I forget you're my sister.'

Chapter Twenty-Five

Kerry had promised Bernadette that she would have a quick drink with her at the bar to hear all the latest news on Eileen. The night had been a big success, the last of the stragglers were leaving and Kerry stood with a glass of champagne. She sipped it, and catching sight of herself in a mirror, automatically straightened up. Julian the bar manager watched her and smiled sadly. Kerry liked him, he was usually fun.

'What's the matter, Ju, you look miserable?'

'Well, to be honest, dear, your sister isn't exactly the happiest soul in purgatory tonight, know what I mean?'

Kerry laughed.

'She has a lot on her plate now, what with Tommy taking on more outside business . . .' Her voice trailed off. It must be common knowledge about Tommy and Briony, but it wasn't going to come from her. She knew that the word was Tommy was expanding, which was the reason he wasn't at the club any more. But people weren't stupid. She had heard herself he was chasing every bit of skirt that passed his way. You couldn't say that to Briony, though.

Kerry was sorry for her sister, what with all that trouble with Eileen and Joshua, and now the split from Tommy. Their relationship had been so well established, it must be hard to live something like that down.

Evander walked past her and shouted, 'Goodnight, Miss Cavanagh.'

She smiled and said goodnight to him, keeping up the big pretence even though she was aware that Julian had guessed months before about them.

'Goodnight, Evander dear, see you tomorrow!' Julian's voice was high and Evander smiled as he left the building.

'Very nice chap that. I like him a lot.'

Kerry smiled and sipped her champagne. Where the hell was Bernadette? Evander would have to wait for her on the corner now until she could pick him up in her car.

She swallowed down the champagne.

'Another?'

Kerry nodded, and studied herself in the mirror once more. She was looking forward to seeing Evander tonight, she had some news for him. A club owner from France had heard about her singing and had offered her a spot with her band in his club, the *Joie de Vivre*. She had told her agent she was very interested. It was the break she had been praying for. She had convinced herself that France was the place where she and Evander could be together. The French were much more open-minded. Somehow they would be all right there, if only they could get away from London. She felt a small shiver of excitement in her breast. Her main aim in life was to stop him going back to the States. Stop him from leaving her. And now she had the handle she needed. She was surprised to find her champagne glass was once more empty and, turning to Julian, said: 'Do you know where Bernadette is?'

He smiled and said, 'She left about an hour ago.'

Kerry frowned.

'Are you sure? Only we were supposed to be having a drink before we went home.'

Julian shrugged.

'Perhaps she forgot.'

Kerry smiled, but she was puzzled. Bernadette had been very insistent.

'Maybe. Goodnight, Julian.'

'Goodnight, Miss. You sang like a little bird tonight. It was a pleasure to listen to you.

'Thanks. See you tomorrow.'

Kerry left the club. Five minutes later she was on the corner of the street where she normally picked up Evander. He was nowhere to be seen.

She waited ten minutes and then drove herself home.

Evander was sitting in the back of a large car between two men he had never seen before. Kevin Carter, Briony's driver, was in the front. No one had said a word since they'd bundled him inside. He could feel the sweat rolling down his forehead and into his eyes. Evander was a big man, and strong, but there was no way he could hope to fight his way out of this situation. Knowing this, he became calm inside. He knew what they were going to do to him, he knew they were aware of his relationship with Kerry Cavanagh. He knew the time had come to pay the piper.

'Can I smoke?' His voice, he was glad to hear, came out strong, without a trace of terror.

'Only if I set fire to you.' Kevin Carter's voice was hard, but the other two men laughed as if it was a big joke.

'That's what happens to blokes like you in the States,

ain't it? You get burnt alive on crosses. I read about it in the paper. The Ku Klux Klan, they're called, ain't they?'

Evander felt a return of the terror he had so valiantly suppressed. These men were no different from their American counterparts. No different from the people who rode up in the night and burnt out black shanties. Their sort was the same the world over. Red necks with cockney accents. He smiled in the darkness, watching the streets pass by, trying to figure out where he was.

'I wonder what that means?' Archie Tubby's voice was genuinely interested.

'What? Ku Klux Klan?'

'Yeah, funny name, ain't it?'

'It's Greek. It comes from the Greek, Kukos, meaning circle. Klan is from the Scottish clan. The first four Klansmen were confederate soldiers, descendants of the Scottish settlers.'

'How do you know that?' Tubby's voice was nasty now. He couldn't write his own name. A black man being educated was alien to him.

'A white lady told me, a long time ago when I was a child. I just never forgot it.'

Kevin Carter laughed.

'You won't forget tonight, either, you black ponce. What the fuck did you think you was playing at, dipping your wick with a white girl? You're scum, you're shit beneath my shoes, you're nothing. And you thought you could take a decent white girl and soil her? Well, you're going to learn a big lesson tonight, mate.'

The mood in the car was ugly, the atmosphere heavy with malice. Kevin Carter stopped the car in the East India Docks. They walked a now terrified Evander into a small warehouse. Kevin Carter picked up a large pickaxe handle, and when the two Tubby brothers had forced him to the ground, proceeded to beat Evander mercilessly across the back of the legs. Finally, when he was unconscious, they broke every one of his fingers. An hour later, they were banging on Glennford's door. When it was opened they threw Evander's bloodied and bleeding form on to the bare floor.

'Here's your tickets, you lot fuck off tonight! You're to be gone by the morning or there'll be more trouble.'

Glennford nodded, wanting to fight but knowing since his years of childhood and manhood it was a fight he could never win. Instead, he did as he was bidden.

They were all gone by first light.

Briony was impressed by Sea View. It was a large rambling Victorian house on the seafront at Southend. It had two large turrets either side of the roof, which provided bedrooms with windows that looked over the Thames estuary towards Kent. The round bedroom to the right of the building was to be Eileen's.

As Briony unpacked her sister's things, she noticed that Eileen was sitting on a window seat gazing out to sea.

'It's beautiful here, isn't it, Eileen?'

She nodded, her feet tucked underneath her. She looked like a child again.

'I like it here, Briony, it smells nice.'

'That's the salt, Eileen. Remember when Mum took us to Rainham on Sea when we was kids? And we sat on the beach and paddled in the water?'

Eileen nodded, smiling at the memory.

'We had jellied eels and whelks for supper and Kerry got sick everywhere on the way home.'

'That's right, Eileen.' Briony was pleased she was

talking, pleased she seemed to like this place peopled with nuns and patients who seemed to move about as silently as the nuns. It was peaceful, though, with only the sound of the tide coming in. Briony sat on the seat beside Eileen. A few lone fishermen sat on the small quayside. It was overcast and they wore their oilskins and wellingtons with a jaunty air. This part of the coast was called Thorpe Bay. All along this road were large houses, imposing residences owned by people with money and position. She gazed out over the estuary, seeing the silent movement of the ships as they passed one another. It was a calm and beautiful place. It would do Eileen good. Make her happier.

A ship's hooter blasted and Eileen jumped. Briony laughed and put her arm around her shoulders, pulling her sister's head next to hers.

'Everything will be all right, Eileen, I promise you.'

'What's happened to Joshua, Bri? Where is he?'

Briony took a deep breath. 'He's gone away, love. He can't hurt you any more.'

'Will he come back, do you think?' Her voice was low.

'No, he can't come back, darlin'. Not where he's gone.'

Eileen relaxed against her.

'Good, I'm glad. I can't face him any more, Bri, any of them. Keep Mum away from me for a while, will you?'

Briony started. 'Mum? Why don't you want to see Mum?' This request shocked her.

'I can't face anyone but you, not for a while. She bosses me about, you know that. Tells me to pull meself together. I wish to Christ I could, Briony. But I have those feelings again, like I had before, remember? Sometimes I don't know for sure who I am or what I'm doing. I hear things, Bri . . . People keep talking to me, all the time. I know there's no one there really, but I have to listen to them. If

I don't, then I feel like something bad will happen.'

Briony hugged her close. Her voice was thick with tears as she said: 'Nothing bad is ever going to happen to us again, not me or you or the others. I promise you that.'

'I really like it here, Briony, I feel safe.'

'You are safe, Eileen, as safe as houses.'

'And you'll keep Mum away, just for a little while, until I get settled?'

'Of course I will. Anything you want you can have.'

She looked at Eileen, but she was gone again, to wherever it was her mind drifted to. She pulled herself from Briony's arms and looked out at the seascape before her.

She didn't say another word the whole time Briony was there.

Kerry woke up alone. She stretched in the bed and put out her arm to a cold empty space. Opening her eyes, she remembered that Evander had not been there when she had got home the night before. She turned over on to her back and sighed. She had got used to having him beside her, having him there when she opened her eyes. Her neighbours were faceless people who kept office hours so she rarely saw them, and the fact that she was a singer, one who was becoming well known, gave her the perfect excuse to have a black musician with her. Now she wanted that black musician and he wasn't here.

She looked at the clock by her bedside. It was nearly ten-thirty. She sat bolt upright in bed. She had slept later than she had for a long time. As she pulled a dressing gown around herself, she heard Bernie's key in the door.

'Hello, Bernie, where've you been all night?' Kerry walked out into the hallway as she spoke, tying the sash of the dressing gown. The sight of Bernadette's face made her stop in mid-sentence.

'What's wrong? Is it Eileen?'

Bernadette shrugged off her coat and dropped it unceremoniously on the floor of the hallway. Then, yanking off her cloche hat, she dropped that on to the untidy pile as well.

'Come through to the kitchen, Kerry. Nothing's wrong with Eileen but there's something I have to tell you.'

'What? What's wrong, Bernie?'

Bernadette picked up the kettle and banged it down on the hob. She lit the gas then, satisfied it was fully alight, looked into her sister's face and said: 'He's gone.'

Kerry screwed up her eyes in disbelief. 'Who? Who's gone?'

'Evander. The whole band, in fact. Mother tumbled you, Kerry, she was told about you and him. Briony had him driven out last night.'

Kerry put a slim hand to her throat. Holding on to the table with the other hand, she whispered: 'He ain't dead?'

Bernadette, after a sleepless night with her mother who'd been cursing her errant daughter up hill and down dale, finally snapped.

'Oh, don't be so bloody dramatic! They got shot of him, that's all.'

Kerry sat on a wooden kitchen chair, her face grey now. 'Don't be dramatic, you say! She made short bloody work of Ronnie Olds, to name one of many! Dear God, my poor Evander. They must have taken him last night. I waited for him, but he didn't come.' She jumped from the seat and ran through to the bedroom.

Bernadette made the tea. She was bringing in a cup when Kerry emerged from the bedroom, dressed.

'Where you going?'

Kerry looked at her in amazement. 'Where the hell do you think? Stepney.'

Bernie put the cup of steaming tea on the small hall table. 'He won't be there.'

'How do you know? He might not have gone yet, she might have just told him he had to go, maybe he'll still be there, he might have left a message for me.' Kerry knew she was babbling.

'Calm down, will you? You'll have the whole place on the knocker in a minute.'

Pushing Bernadette out of the way, she grabbed her bag and keys and left the flat. Bernadette followed her out on to the stairwell.

'For Christ's sake, Kerry, it's pointless going there, can't you see that? Please come back inside. We'll talk about it, try and sort something out!'

Kerry laughed nastily. 'You and me, talk? You must be joking! Who told on us, eh? I bet it was you. You vindictive cow! I bet you loved every second of it. I wouldn't put nothing past you. Nothing!'

Outside on the street she tried to unlock her car. Her hands were trembling so much she dropped the keys. Kicking them across the road in a temper, she flagged down a passing cab. 'Stepney, East Street. Quick as you can.'

The cabbie laughed.

'What's the matter, darling? Your old man doing a moonlight flit?'

'Just drive the sodding cab, mate, and shut your mouth up! If I wanted a fucking comedian I'd have arranged to have Stan Laurel drive me!'

The cab driver shut up. Dressed like a lady and with the

mouth of a dockside harpy. Now he was sure he'd seen everything. She jumped from the cab at the top of East Street, throwing the man ten shillings as his fare. He took the money and saluted her like a general before driving off.

Kerry walked down East Street. She was dressed in a deep red brocade evening coat, with fur collar and cuffs. The coat swung as she walked, displaying a suit of pale pink wool that hugged her ample figure. She wasn't wearing a hat but her hair was fresh-looking, swinging healthily with each step she took.

East Street had once been a nice area. It had large imposing four-storey houses, with steps leading up to the front door. Years before these steps had been scrubbed every day; now the majority were filthy and chipped. Rubbish was strewn in the road – vegetable peelings, soiled rags and human waste where the children dropped their pants and defecated where they played. It smelt like the basements, only every now and then a billow of fresh air whipped through, giving the residents a welcome change. The breeze smelt of coal from the factories around and about. The houses were covered in soot. At eleven-fifteen in the morning the tally men were on the knockers, the children were out in force, and women were gossiping among themselves. Or rather the women who weren't trying to avoid a tally man, or the rent collector.

Kerry was aware of hostile eyes watching her as she approached the house where Evander and his band had lodged. Outside number two was a young boy of about sixteen. He looked her up and down with a surly leer as she stopped beside him.

'Would you like to earn a shilling?'

'Doing what?' His voice had a thick twang, affected and very unpleasant.

'I want a message taken to a Mr Dorsey in there.' She jerked her head towards the front door of the house.

'Cost you a bit more than that, darling. Messages for blackies is double.'

Kerry swallowed down the retort that came to her lips and nodded.

'All right then. Two bob. I want you to knock at his room and tell him that Miss Cavanagh is outside and wishes to speak with him.'

'Gis the money then.' He held out a dirty hand. Opening her bag, she took out a half crown.

'That's all I've got, I haven't anything smaller.'

'Well, I ain't got any change, girl, so it looks like the price just went up again, don't it?'

With that he disappeared up the step and into the house. Kerry stood uncertainly outside, wishing she had not worn such a striking coat. Wishing Evander would come out so they could get away from this place. Hoping against hope that he would tell her everything was all right and it was just another of Bernie's nasty jokes.

A figure appeared at the top of the steps and Kerry's heart sank.

'You've got a bloody nerve, I must say, you trollop! Coming here for your bleeding black fancy man!'

All the residents in the street looked in the direction of the loud strident voice. Kerry felt her heart sinking. The woman was old, her huge pendulous breasts hanging down to her waist beneath an old wrapover apron. On her feet were an old pair of men's issue army boots, minus the laces, and her stockings hung around the tops in wrinkles. Arms like meat cleavers were crossed before her and her face was screwed up in disgust.

'He left here in the night, love, they all did, owing me

a bleeding week's rent! Someone must have tumbled your game, darling, because he was dripping blood. All down the stairs it was this morning! Up me bleeding walls, everywhere! My God, you've got a Christing nerve coming here to a respectable woman and looking for your darkie! Your black man!'

A few men emerged from doorways in their vests, obviously just woken by the harridan's voice and coming out to see the uppity bitch in the red coat get her comeuppance.

Kerry turned away and started to walk down the street, her heels clattering on the pavements, her head hanging down on to her chest.

'Gerroutofit, you whore of hell! Before I stick me boot up your arse! Black man's darling, are you? Go on, piss off!' The man disappeared into his doorway after shouting at her and Kerry began to walk faster.

A woman with a young child on her arm walked across the road. Hawking deep in the back of her throat, she spat in Kerry's face, the spittle running down her cheek and on to her fur collar.

'You filthy bitch, coming here for your darkie! Don't think we never saw you.'

Kerry was waiting for the woman to move when the man who had shouted at her came out of his house carrying a chamber pot. He threw the contents towards Kerry. A small amount hit the bottom of her coat and her shoes. Looking into the man's face, seeing the hatred there and all around her, she began to run, dropping her bag on to the pavement as she went. Never before had she felt such malevolence. Never before had she experienced anything so utterly shaming and humiliating. She ran until she was in the High Street, staring around her like an animal being chased by a pack of hounds, her eyes wild. She carried on running until she came to Victoria Park.

Sitting on a bench, she cried, bitter tears that seemed to wrench her whole frame in two. Wrapping her arms around herself, she caressed her belly underneath her ruined coat.

She had had such good news for him, such a secret. Now she could tell him nothing because he was gone.

Bleeding and beaten he had left, but if he was bleeding he was still alive. This thought, amongst so many other bad ones, comforted her.

If he could bleed, he was still alive.

At that moment in time, she hated Briony more than she had ever hated anyone or anything in her life.

It was late and the journey home from Southend-on-Sea had tired Briony out. Sitting alone in her small sitting room, she sipped a steaming cup of tea. She was supposed to go to the club tonight, she was supposed to go to the houses, and she was supposed to be seeing a man called Joey Vickers about some very cheap liquor. Eileen's blank face was haunting her. She looked at the photograph of Benedict. Bernadette had been right in a lot of respects. You didn't know where your heart was going to lie. The fact that his father was Henry Dumas, a skunk, a piece of filth in Briony's opinion, didn't stop the feelings she had for the son she'd borne him.

How many times had she heard people say, 'If I could have my time again, I'd do it all differently'? Well, she wouldn't really, because as bad as it all seemed now, it had been the means of her son coming into the world. Of Benedict's very existence. Although he was away from her, was in a different house, living a life she could only glimpse through Sally, he was still her boy. One day he would know that, when the time was right.

She drank her tea and poured herself another cup. The room was quiet, the house too. She was enjoying the peace when Cissy tiptoed into the room.

'Can I get you a bite?'

'No, thanks all the same. Sit down a second, Cissy. Take the weight off your feet.'

Cissy sat beside the fire and glanced ruefully at her swollen legs. 'Look at them, like legs of pork!'

'If they're bad, you should take the doctor's advice and keep off them now and then. There's plenty of help coming in now. You don't have to take the brunt of the work any more.'

Cissy blew out her red mottled cheeks, making a rude noise. 'What's that silly old bugger know, eh? I can't sit around all day, I'd go off me head . . .' She bit her lip. 'I'm sorry, Bri, that just came out.'

Briony laughed. 'You don't have to watch what you say to me, Cis, I was just thinking about her meself.'

'How was she? All right?'

Briony nodded. 'Yeah, she seemed to like it there. It's really lovely, Cis, the view from the place is gorgeous. I've never really seen so much water before. I know we used to swim in the cut when we was kids, but this was different. Clean-looking and deep green. It was lovely. And the smell! I tell you now, I felt like staying there meself. Getting away from it all. Never coming back here.'

Cissy made a loud noise.

'I can just see you now, in an early dotage, sitting on the prom in a bleeding bathchair. Listen here, Briony, you've got a lot of bother at the moment, I know that. You ain't been yourself since all that with Ginelle. That threw you. I watched you change. But even if you did leave this place, left London even, you'd soon be back. You're a woman who needs aggravation, you bloody well thrive on it. Otherwise, why the hell would you have opened up your houses? Look at this week. You've had no Tommy to back you up yet you've sorted out Eileen, in between running your clubs and your houses, of course.'

Cissy's voice was full of admiration. 'Me, I couldn't organise the proverbial piss up. Don't sell yourself short, and don't get maudlin. Get drunk if you want, let off a bit of steam, but don't let it all get you down now. I don't like seeing you depressed. Somehow, if you're not right, then the world around you don't seem right.'

Briony looked into the face of her old friend. Cissy was only a few years older than she, yet she looked ancient. She was a workhouse child, had known nothing but hard work all her life. Without it she was like a fish out of water. That's why she couldn't bear to let a younger girl take on any of her work. She had to be needed, to earn her keep. It was something that had been drummed into her at a very early age.

'I'm all right, Cissy, but I have a lot to think about these days. There's been trouble with Kerry. I don't think she's exactly going to love me for a while. I had to do something that won't make me the most popular sister in the smoke.'

'What happened then?'

Briony shook her head. 'I can't say, Cissy love. I think that's something best left between me and Kerry.' And me mother, she thought, because Molly was adamant that Kerry was never to darken her doors again.

Chapter Twenty-Six

Briony had dressed carefully for her meeting with Mariah, the two women were going to look at Berwick Manor and decide if it was a viable business. Briony already knew the answer would be yes, because Mariah was shrewd. All they would do today was put Briony's stamp of approval on it and make an offer.

She put on a deep cerise suit, the skirt full, the waistband tight. As she walked it clung to her silk stockings. The jacket was long and shapeless, cut with a square neck, and she pinned a lizard-shaped diamond and ruby brooch on to the shoulder, giving the whole outfit a touch of class. She pulled her erratic hair up into a tight chignon, pinning it carefully, though tendrils of hair escaped, framing her face with their curls. Sighing, she gave up hope of getting it smooth and put on her make-up. Finally she buttoned up her shoes and looked at herself in the full-length mirror by her dressing table. She would have to do.

It was as she was sorting through her large black handbag that she heard the commotion in her hallway. Kerry's voice, loud and strident, and Bernadette's more modulated tones. With a grim face she left her bedroom and walked to the top of the staircase.

'So you're here then? I was expecting you sooner.'

Kerry stared malevolently up at her sister.

'You bitch! You bloody cow! You think you're so clever, don't you?'

Briony walked down the stairs. Cissy and Mrs Horlock watched with interest, Bernadette with fear.

'I tried to stop her coming here, Bri, she's out of her mind. Don't take any notice of her . . .'

Kerry looked dreadful. Her clothes were mud-stained, the hem of her brocade coat looked as if it had been dragged through the dirt. Her legs were filthy, her white stockings black and laddered, her hair uncombed and tangled. She turned wild eyes on Bernie and shouted: 'Oh, don't try and smooth this over. This can't be forgotten, swept under the carpet like the old man's death! This is my business, mine! So why don't you piss off out of it? Keep your nose out where it ain't wanted!'

Briony walked down the stairs. She looked at Cissy and Mrs Horlock and said calmly, 'Make some tea.'

The two women left the hallway through the green baize door, but Briony knew they would stand behind it listening. There was no way they would want to miss all this. Kerry tensed as Briony walked over to her, but Briony passed by and opened the door to the lounge.

'Come in here and do your talking. And I mean talking, not shouting. I've got a headache actually, and your voice is going right through my head.'

Kerry stood uncertainly. She had expected a lot, but not this. The calmness of Briony threw her, as Briony had known it would. Kerry watched Briony disappear and had no option but to follow, with Bernadette hot on her heels.

Briony was standing by the fireplace, her immaculate clothes and hair making Kerry more annoyed with each passing second.

'Look at you! I suppose you've got a red hat and all? What's the saying, Bri? Red hat, no drawers? That certainly sounds like you, don't it?

'Tell me, who beat up Evander? You? I wouldn't put it past you. You're like a man, do you know that? You think like a man, you act like a man, no wonder Tommy Lane dumped you. It must have been like living with a queer. Two men together, only one wore a dress.'

The barb about Tommy struck home as Kerry knew it would. As she'd wanted it to. She wanted Briony to hurt, as she was hurting.

'You're quiet all of a sudden, normally your mouth's going like the clappers. What's the matter? Truth hurts, does it?'

Bernadette tried to take Kerry's arm but she shrugged her off.

'Leave me alone, you!'

'Sit down, Kerry. Sit down, for Christ's sake.'

Briony's voice, so calm, so clear, jolted something in Kerry's mind.

'Don't you tell me what to do, you vicious bitch! You've ruined my life. Me and Evander was going away. I had a job lined up in Paris, I was going to tell you to stick your club right up your arse. We would have been all right there, me and him. But no, you had to have him removed, taken away, like so much rubbish. Well, let me tell you something else, Briony Cavanagh, I'm pregnant!' She laughed at the look of shock on her sisters' faces.

'Yes, thought that might give you a start. I'm in the club, up the duff, by a blackie. And shall I tell you something? I'm proud of it. I hope it's as black as night! I hope it's so black it shines! So what are you going to do about that, Bri, eh? How are you going to sort this out? You know, all your threats and all your money and all your trapping can do nothing at all because I want it. I really, really want it. Especially now you've driven my Evander away. It's all I'll have left of him, ain't it? All that remains.'

Briony heard a loud sighing noise, and it was a few seconds before she realised it was coming from herself. It was as if Kerry had stuck a pin in her chest and she was deflating slowly.

Kerry laughed at her sister's reaction.

'That's pissed all over your fireworks, hasn't it?' She rubbed her belly gently. 'Never banked on that one, did you?'

Briony pulled herself up to her full height and, walking across the room, slapped Kerry hard across the face. Then she grabbed her arm roughly and shouted: 'You stupid little bitch! You stupid little cow! You think this is funny, clever, do you? You think you've got one over on us? What are you, on a death wish or what?'

She threw her on to the chair by the fire, then leaning over her, screamed, 'You've ruined your life, you silly mare, if you could only see it! Pregnant? I could cheerfully throttle you!'

She began to slap Kerry around the head and shoulders, holding back the urge to punch her, rip at her hair, tear her skin with her nails.

'My God, girl, you've really done it this time. You're right, I can't help you. No one can help you now. You wonder why I stick my nose in your business? I'll tell you why. Because if it was left to you lot, you'd fucking crumble. You're all as thick as shit! You especially. You've got a talent, a voice, you had something going for you, and now that's nothing, that's all finished, because the day you give birth, you're a second-class citizen.

'I liked Evander, believe it or not, I liked him a lot. But liking him ain't enough. With him you would have been ostracised, shut out, people would have looked at you like you was dirt! Now you've got all that coming anyway, and for the rest of your life. And you have the cheek to come here and tell *me* what *I've* done wrong. It was a pity you didn't think of that when you was counting the cracks on the ceiling, on your back for Evander bloody Dorsey!'

Kerry looked fearfully into Briony's face. All the dark thoughts that plagued her in the night were being spoken out loud. The truth, as she had pointed out only minutes before, did hurt. It hurt a lot.

Briony paced the room, her hands shaking in temper. Bernadette lit her a cigarette and passed it to her.

Briony pulled hard on the cigarette. By now Kerry's white face and dishevelled appearance were making her feel sorry for her sister, despite herself. She wanted to take her in her arms and tell her everything was going to be all right. But how could she? Nothing was ever going to be all right for Kerry Cavanagh again.

'Are you sure you're pregnant? I mean, are you really certain?'

Kerry sat hunched in the chair. She looked very small and forlorn, her face stained with tears and dirt. She nodded her head.

'How long gone are you? I mean, is there still time to do something about it?'

'I don't know, I'm over three months.'

Briony closed her eyes and stubbed out the cigarette, immediately lighting up another.

Sitting down on the chesterfield, she looked at her sister, now bowed down not just with the pain of losing the man she loved, but with the knowledge she also carried his child. A child that would be spurned because of its colour. In her heart of hearts, Briony felt a glimmer of compassion for the poor unborn child, nestled so cosily in its mother's womb. But she had to try to save the situation.

'I'll arrange for you to see Denice O'Toole, all my girls use her. She's clean and she knows what she's doing.'

Kerry looked up at her sister. Her face crumpled then, tears gushing from her eyes, a terrible low keening sound issuing from her open mouth. Briony went to her and pulled her into her arms, hugging her close, stroking the dark head, and murmuring words of endearment.

Later on that afternoon, when Briony had left Kerry in Mrs Horlock's capable hands, she and Mariah walked round Berwick Manor with Mr Jackson, the solicitor instructed to sell the property. He was a tall thin man with iron-grey hair and a small moustache, perfectly waxed. He blew his nose often, to the amusement of Mariah who rolled her eyes at Briony, making her smile.

They toured through the rooms, taking in their size, the high ceilings and old fireplaces. There were four large reception rooms with huge windows which looked over the Essex countryside. There were two large kitchens, with pantries and what would once have been the butler's and the cook's sitting rooms. There was a huge cold store, with marble slabs to keep butter and milk cool in the summertime.

A large sweeping staircase led up to a galleried landing. Off this were eight bedrooms, and above these a rabbit warren of servants' rooms. More stairs, steeper and narrower now, led up to the attics.

Briony saw the dilapidated state of the property, but she could also see its potential. From the upstairs bedrooms the whole of Essex seemed to have been laid out before them. The Berwick Pond Road was quiet, unsurfaced, and would ensure they kept their privacy. The outbuildings were still in a decent state. Even the stables were still usable. It was only the inside that had been allowed to deteriorate. The soldiers who had convalesced there after the war had used and abused the rooms terribly. Wood panelling was wrenched off the wall, the carpets were worn, and the curtains, once beautiful Austrian silk, were in tatters. Mr Jackson, to give him his due, pointed out the finer points as best he could. But even his powers of persuasion flagged as he surveyed the interior.

'Of course, ladies, the outside is still very much as it was before the war. A very picturesque property, don't you agree?'

Briony walked over to the inglenook fireplace and stared at the remains of a fire. It seemed the paintings and the furniture had eventually ended up as kindling.

'It needs a lot of work to bring it back up to scratch, Mr Jackson. It's Tudor, isn't it? Do the cottages at the beginning of the lane form part of the property, and if so are they occupied?'

Mr Jackson was in a terrible quandary. The big blonde woman was intimidating enough, but this little redhead was worse. He wasn't sure which question to answer first when Briony began talking again.

'Also, the stables will have to be turned into garages. Neither myself nor my colleague ride. So that will be an added expense if we do decide to purchase. Also the kitchens need refitting and I notice that electricity hasn't been installed. Another expense. How long has the house been up for sale? Since 1919? So it's been empty for six, nearly seven, years. I should imagine the damp's got in by now.'

Mr Jackson leapt to the house's defence. 'The roof is in perfect condition, madam, I can assure you of that.'

Briony wiped her fingers daintily on her handkerchief and said sweetly, 'I'm glad to hear something is.'

Mariah grinned.

'If you would be so kind as to leave my friend and myself alone for a few minutes, Mr Jackson . . .' With a last trumpeting blow of his nose, he left the room.

'I shall wait outside by my vehicle until such time as you have concluded your business.'

When he had gone, Mariah said, 'Well, conclude, Briony, conclude!'

'Is he all the ticket, Mariah?'

'I don't know about that, Bri, but if he blows his nose once more I'll scream!'

Briony grinned. 'It is a bit disgusting.'

Mariah looked around the large drawing room and said, 'So? What do you think?'

Briony looked at her friend and smiled.

'I think it's perfect. We can do a lot with it. I thought upstairs we could really go to town, you know? There's so much scope for the bedrooms, and even the servants' rooms could be made up to accommodate customers. It's exactly what we want.'

Mariah relaxed. 'I knew you'd like it. It's like a shit-house at the moment, I know, but that's to our benefit. It'll get the price right down, but think how it could look, eh?'

'I think I'd like this room in dove grey and deep burgundy, it would look stunning. We'd easily accommodate thirty or forty men here at any given time. If the cottages aren't part and parcel of the deal, we'll buy them somehow. They're too close for comfort. The people who come here want guaranteed privacy and we'll make sure they get it.'

Mariah laughed in delight.

'So shall we put in the offer today or let Mr Jackson and his client sweat it out?'

Briony shrugged.

'We'll put in an offer. Now let's get going, I'm dying for a cup of tea.'

They left the house, happy now they were both in accord. Mr Jackson watched them emerge and sighed. They were not ladies, not by any standards. What was the world coming to?

Kevin Carter was at home having his dinner. He had three young daughters, all with dark hair and brown eyes. His wife Annie was a small girl with black hair and a small, pretty face. She opened the door to Briony and smiled widely.

'Hello, Miss Cavanagh. Kevin's just having his dinner. Come through, I was making a cup of tea anyway.'

Briony walked into the house and down the tiny hallway into the dining room. Kevin saw who the visitor was and stood up. 'Sit yourself down and finish your meal, I'm ready for a cup of tea anyway.'

She sat on a large overstuffed chair by the doorway. Three identical little faces looked up at her hopefully. Carmel, the eldest, said shyly: 'Have you got something nice for me?'

Briony laughed, and opening her bag took out three mint creams in bright green paper.

'You shouldn't ask, Carmel!' Kevin's voice was loud.

Briony flapped a hand at him and said airily, 'Leave her be, Kevin. If you don't ask, you don't get!'

Ten minutes later she sat in her car, with Kevin driving her to the house in Barking.

'By the way, Kevin, I want you to go and pick up a bloke for me today. Marcus Dowling. He's interested in becoming one of the team.'

Kevin whistled softly.

'He's getting a name for himself, is Marcus.'

Briony cut him off. 'When I want your opinion, I'll ask for it.' Her voice dripped ice and a shocked Kevin turned slightly to look over his shoulder.

'Drive the car, Kevin, that's what you're paid for. And one last thing. If I tell you to frighten someone, that's what you do, get it? If I want him cut, I'll tell you. Evander Dorsey was bleeding. I never asked you to do anything but scare him. You ever take something like that on yourself again, and you'll feel the full force of my anger. Do I make myself clear?'

Kevin nodded almost imperceptibly.

'Yes, Miss Cavanagh.'

'Good, now we know exactly where we stand, don't we?'

Kevin didn't answer, but Briony had not expected him to.

Briony could hear the new band through the walls of her office. The Velvetones were good, but they weren't Kerry. Bessie Knight, the singer, had a good voice, but it was Kerry people came to see. She sipped at a glass of brandy and lit herself a cigarette, dispensing with the holder while she was alone. She heard a small tap on her office door and bellowed: 'Come in.'

Jonathan la Billière walked into the office with a wide beaming smile on his face.

'Someone upset you, Briony?' His thick eyebrows rose quizzically and she smiled.

'I'm feeling a bit fragile to say the least.'

Jonathan sat on a chair and, crossing his legs, said jocularly, 'Drinking alone? Shouting? All the symptoms of an old maid, my dear. Be careful, you have been warned!'

Briony laughed gently.

'What can I do for you?'

'I want to ask a favour actually. We're filming again in two weeks. Now I have a little girl in mind to star with me, but Rupert's not too happy about her. He has another one lined up and quite frankly, Briony, I couldn't fancy her baked, fried or boiled! In fact, I want to concentrate more on a real acting career, you know. I've been asking around and I think I may be in line for a part. But it's Rupert . . .'

His voice trailed off and Briony nodded at him, and smiled.

'He's mad about you, Jonathan, you knew that at the start. What you're saying is, now you have someone else who can help you, you want me to give Rupert the bad news. Am I right?'

He had the grace to look a little ashamed.

'Well, I wouldn't put it quite like that . . .'

'Of course you wouldn't. But I would, because I always say what I mean.'

Jonathan squirmed in his chair.

'Look, Briony, the deal was a couple of art pictures then he'd consider me for something serious. And that isn't happening. Now you hold all the cards in your hand, he'll listen to you. In fact, you're the only person he *will* listen to, period. I deserve a break . . . just one break. I can act, I'm good. And I look good on film. I don't want to spend my life at Rupert's beck and call.'

Briony stubbed out her cigarette.

'Can I ask you something?'

Jonathan spread his arms.

'Of course, anything you like.'

Briony took a deep breath. 'Are you really the son of an impoverished vicar? Only, now and again you sound very South London to me.'

Jonathan looked at her for a second, his piercing blue eyes boring into her deep green ones, then he laughed.

'How long ago did you suss me out?' He'd dropped the affected accent slightly and Briony warmed to him then.

'From about five minutes of meeting you, actually. Look, Rupert will keep his side of the bargain, I know he will. You have to learn how to handle him is all. Drop a word here and there about your other offer. Don't tell him anything concrete, just hint. He is serious about going into the legitimate film business. As silly as he acts at times, he's shrewd. It's only with the young boys he loses his head. But I expect you've noticed that yourself?'

Jonathan rolled his eyes.

'You're telling me! Honestly, Briony, how he hasn't been locked up, I don't know. He sails really close to the wind at times. Now he's gone on Lord Hockley's boy, and I mean this kid wears full make-up! I've told Rupert to be careful, the boy's father's up in arms about it, but they're seen together everywhere. That's what bothers me, I don't want to be tarred with the same brush. In fact, Briony, he's never been near me. I wouldn't want that. I am mercenary, I admit, I want to get on, but not that way. So far I've kept him at arm's length, and young Peter Hockley's keeping him occupied. But now I want out.'

'I'll see what I can do. But keep your eye on him and the boy in the meantime. That kind of thing could bring us all down. Lord Hockley's got a lot of sway in this town. He's rich and influential. If he decides to do something about his son, it could affect us all. Me as well as you. Does the boy know much about our business dealings?'

Jonathan nodded vigorously.

'He knows it all, Briony. I warned Rupert to keep quiet but you know him after a drink, and the cocaine doesn't help. The other morning I found them both lying on the floor naked with a couple of Arab boys. It made me realise just how low Rupert was sinking. I mean, he's not even trying to hide his preferences these days. It's as if he wants everyone to know. When it was just him, it was all right, but now that young Peter's involved, it could all end in tears. The boy's only nineteen. I don't think he even shaves. But he's hardly as sweet and innocent as he makes out. It's him who arranges their little diversions. Frankly, Briony, it's like a three-ring circus in that house some nights. Even you would be shocked at the goings on.'

She frowned.

'It's really worrying you, isn't it?'

'It should be worrying you, too, because he knows enough about you and me and Tommy to get us all up before the beak. Hockley threatened Rupert only a week ago because of Peter. He's not a man to cross, Briony, yet Rupert refuses even to countenance not seeing the boy. Peter seems to find it all exciting. I think he's enjoying the stir he's creating.'

'I'll keep an eye out, all right? But if I was you I'd take up that other offer, Jonathan. The way things are going, you might be glad you did.'

After he had left she pondered the situation. If Lord Hockley caused a ruckus then it would be a big one. He was a leading industrialist, owned a newspaper, was a member of parliament. All in all, a man to fear. If only Rupert could see that. Hockley's son's sexual preferences would be hidden, no matter what it cost. Hockley had the money and the influence to ensure that.

Chapter Twenty-Seven

As Denice O'Toole opened the front door of her semi-detached house in East Ham to Briony and Kerry, her face was beaming smiles. 'Come in, my dears, I've just made a pot of tea.'

Briony and a white-faced Kerry were ushered through to a small overstuffed parlour that was far too warm and far too full of knick-knacks.

Kerry sat down on the edge of a chair, and Briony settled herself at a small table.

Denice bustled about pouring the tea, pouring milk and enquiring who took sugar and who didn't. Kerry felt as if she was stuck in some kind of bad dream. This was the last thing she'd had expected. In her mind's eye she had pictured a dim dirty room, with an old wizened hag holding a crocheting hook. Somehow that picture seemed more fitting for what she knew was going to happen.

Denice smiled at her in a friendly fashion.

'Don't you worry, my dear, everything will be all right, I promise you.'

Briony sipped her tea. The atmosphere in the room was

one of gentle conviviality. Her girls had never seemed to mind coming here. Briony always asked them if they would like to keep their child, and was always amazed at the number who said no. A clear and categoric no. For them the child inside them was just a nuisance, a problem to be solved by Denice and her ministrations. It was their body and their life. Now she sat here with her sister who did not class her pregnancy as an occupational hazard, something to be sorted out like the laundry or a little domestic problem.

Denice stood up. Her attempts at conversation were falling on deaf ears.

'If you would care to follow me, we'll get down to business.'

Kerry looked at Briony wild-eyed. Taking her sister's hand, she pulled her gently from the chair.

'Come on, Kerry love. Soonest done, soonest mended.'

It was a saying from their childhood. Kerry stood up uncertainly, her hands icy cold. She felt sick with apprehension.

They walked slowly from the room, through the narrow hallway and up the stairs to the back bedroom.

Kerry hesitated at the doorway. The white room looked forbidding in the bright light. Briony pushed her gently through the door. Inside there was a large table, covered in newspaper, and a chest of drawers with all sorts of instruments and padding set out neatly along the top.

'Hop on the table, my love, and let me have a quick feel.'

Briony helped Kerry off with her coat, and in a dream she pulled herself on to the table top, her legs feeling like jelly, her hands trembling so she found it difficult to use them. She lay back slowly, her head touching a soft pillow.

'Relax yourself, dear, so I can have a good mooch around!'

Denice's voice was loud. It echoed in the hollow confines of the room. Unlike the rest of the house, this room was bare. No knick-knacks of any description, it was like a doctor's surgery. Even the blinds on the one window were plain black. They were pulled down and the artificial light cast shadows on the white walls. Kerry closed her eyes.

Denice pulled up her dress and began to feel around her stomach, digging her fingers into the softness of her belly.

'She's well on, Briony, over three months. It'll be the hook, I'm afraid.'

Briony licked dry lips. Kerry's face was as white as the walls around her. Her eyes strayed to the implements on top of the dresser, and one large imposing piece of metal with a hoop on the end made her feel faint.

'Kerry . . . Kerry love, are you all right?'

Kerry opened her eyes and shook her head. Then, sitting bolt upright, she was sick. Briony stood by shocked as Kerry threw up, over and over again.

Briony went to her sister. 'All right, all right, Kerry. Relax, love, take deep breaths.'

Kerry looked at the instruments again and once more started heaving.

'Get . . . Get me out of here, please, Bri . . . I can't breathe, I can't breathe!'

Denice ran through to her newly installed bathroom and began to fill the bath, shouting, 'Bring her through, Briony, she's in shock I think.'

All the time she was praying that Kerry Cavanagh would not be sick again on her new lino or all over her new bathroom suite.

Briony put Kerry's arm over her shoulder and helped her to the bathroom. There she sank down on to her knees, her whole body shaking with fear.

Between them Briony and Denice stripped her of her clothes and placed her in the hot tub. She lay back in the hot water, breathing deeply, her breasts heaving with every breath she took.

'Feeling better, Kel?'

She opened her eyes slowly. 'I'm sorry, Bri, but I can't go through with it. I can't.'

Briony smiled half-heartedly. '*You* can't! *I* can't go through with it and it's not happening to me! You just relax. We'll get you home soon and then we'll talk. We'll think of something, love, I promise.'

Kerry grasped her sister's hand, all animosity forgotten in the closeness of that moment. Kerry and Briony had accepted the child. Between them it would be all right, no matter what else happened.

'What about me mum? She'll go mad,' Kerry whispered after a minute.

Briony sighed heavily.

'You leave her to me. Now come on, sort yourself out. This place is giving me the heebie jeebies!'

Kerry laughed, a choking, throaty sound that was heavily tinged with relief.

As she dried her sister's milky body, Briony felt as if someone had stepped on her grave. She fancied they were being watched by the ghosts of hundreds who had never had a chance of life. Denice O'Toole's calm and collected manner now seemed chilling. Briony was amazed by the way she'd never really thought like this until it directly affected her or her family.

Kerry's baby was going to cause trouble, she accepted

that, but anything, no matter how bad, had to be better than the alternative offered by Denice O'Toole.

Molly's eyes were bulging out of her head in temper.

'You what? You're telling me you brought her back home here with the child? Are you stark staring mad?'

Molly started to pace the room in a blinding rage, her heavy body tense and erect.

'Sit down, Mum, and for once in your life think of someone else.'

Molly marched towards Briony and bellowed in her face: 'All I can think of is that my daughter is going to give birth to a blackie! Jesus suffering Christ! I could brain the bitch, I could. I could rip the hair from her bastard head. How will I hold me own head up once this gets out?'

Briony pushed her mother none too gently in the chest, sending her flying back across the room.

'All I ever hear in this family is me, me, me. How are *you* going to hold your head up? The same way you did when me dad died, and the same way you did when me and Eileen were whoring for you, and the same way you are now, with our Eileen in a nut house! Jesus Christ, this baby will be a godsend in some ways, give them something else to talk about at last.'

Molly's face was twisted with temper.

'Every time I think of her . . . with a black man . . . it makes me stomach turn. The whore! She's nothing but a dirty stinking whore!'

Briony's face went a dull white.

'Then she's in good company, isn't she? Because, quite frankly, give me a good whore any day of the week to a hypocritical old woman who jumps into bed with the man next door. Abel won't even marry you. And why should he, eh? Talk about having your cake and eating it! He's got his mother runing round like a blue-arsed fly after him in one house and you on your fucking back in the other! I don't think you've got much room to talk. You was at it with him before the old man was cold!'

Molly laughed nastily.

'At least he's white. I didn't drop me drawers for the first eejity blackie I laid me eyes on.'

'You know I have to laugh at you at times, Mother. As Irish Catholics we're the lowest of the low round here, always have been. Old shawlies shouting in the street – your own mother was one. Men who drink hard and work as and when it suits them. Evander Dorsey was a talented man, an intelligent man. Kerry's only mistake was falling for someone like herself, a kindred spirit. I can see that, so why can't you? I got rid of him before I knew what the full score was. I knew she was going to come a cropper, Mum. I knew that because there are far too many small-minded people like you around. Christ, you make me laugh. You was up in arms last year because Jenny O'Leary was marrying a Protestant, a ranter. You hated *him* and he had blond hair and blue eyes! Your prejudice knows no bounds, woman. That little child is the innocent party in all this. It's your grandchild!'

Molly grabbed at her daughter's hair, tearing at it as she pulled her across the room, her great bulk giving her added strength. Briony elbowed her mother hard in the stomach, making her double over in pain as she gasped for breath.

'You . . . you bitch! That child is nothing to me! Do you hear me? Nothing. It should be dead, I hope it's born dead. I hope she loses it now, while there's still time. I never want to clap eyes on it! If that whore has it, me and her are finished for good. And I mean that. She'll not drag this family's name through the dirt. No way. I'll disown the bastard first.'

Briony started laughing, a high vicious sound.

'Drag this family's name through the dirt! Well, that's not hard, is it? We're only accepted because I keep this family's name spoken with respect. Through fear, Mother, plain and simple fear. People are scared of me, Briony Cavanagh. They tolerate you because I do. If you disown our Kerry, then I will disown you and I mean that, Mother. Let Abel poxy Jones keep you in the manner you've become accustomed to. Let him pay your bills and put the food on your table. We don't need you, woman, we never did. You needed us more. You couldn't keep a sheep in wool and you know it! You've never got up off your arse and done a real day's work in your life! You swan around Brick Lane market like the fucking Queen of Sheba. Well, in future you'll swan around on Abel's money. Disown us, go on, disown the lot of us. See how far it gets you. You'll need us before we'll ever need you, I can guarantee you that.'

Molly stood and stared at Briony, the daughter she had found it increasingly difficult to like as a child yet the one who had grown into a woman of substance, a woman of renown. All Briony had said was true. Molly was respected only because of this daughter. Because she was a force to be reckoned with, a woman no one in their right mind would cross. Except, of course, her mother. Now Molly had crossed her, and had had her answer. Well, she had a trump card still and she played it.

'Take your money, see if I care. Me and Rosalee don't need it, we can get along by ourselves.'

She looked at Briony shrewdly, sure that she would not want to think of Rosie going without. But Briony had outthought her and answered equally craftily.

'That's all right then. You and Rosie fend for yourselves. You do what you have to. But that little child is here whether you like it or not. So if you disown us, do it now because I have a lot to do today.'

Walking past her mother she left the room. Upstairs Kerry was lying on the bed, the screaming and swearing from below barely reaching her. Bernadette sat beside her holding her hand. Briony breezed into the room and said, 'How are you feeling in yourself?'

Kerry shrugged. 'All right, Bri, I suppose.'

'I'm very pleased to hear that, love, because you're going back to work tonight. You're not ill, you're pregnant, and we're all going to brazen this out. So get rested and bathed, and later on dress yourself up to the nines. My club is waiting for you, love!'

Bernadette laughed with glee. This was more like it, this was Briony at her best.

Waltzing from the room, she said nonchalantly over her shoulder, 'Oh, by the way, I've some news for you. Mother has seen fit to disown us. Personally, I couldn't give a toss!'

Bernadette was once more Kerry's dresser. In the few weeks since the run-in with their mother, everything had calmed down. Molly had kept a very low profile, and Briony had made a point of sending a cab to the house to pick Rosalee up for her visits to her sisters. Molly had been all for stopping her going, but had thought better of it. Rosalee came back flushed, excited, and full to the brim with dainties. Eileen could only be visited by mutual consent. If Briony was going, Molly kept away and vice versa. Bernadette had not been near or by her door which galled her, as it seemed three of her daughters had now formed some kind of unholy alliance, Briony and Bernadette both protecting Kerry.

In fact, it seemed to Bernadette that the three of them were getting on better than ever before. Briony was even talking about having Eileen home for a visit. Kerry didn't look pregnant to outsiders, so the secret was still closed. It would come out eventually, but they had an unspoken agreement that until it did, they would put it out of their minds. Kerry had a glow to her skin that gave her looks an added lustre. In fact, she had never been healthier, had never enjoyed her singing so much. She lost herself in the words of the songs, and gave them an added meaning.

Pieter Delarge, a small dark-headed man with a beaked nose, had been in the club frequently of late, and now, on a cold October evening, he sat opposite Briony in her office, drinking coffee laced with vodka and chattering amicably.

'Come on, Pieter, what are you really here for? I know it's not to talk about the weather or your health.'

Briony smiled to take the edge off her words.

Pieter shrugged expansively.

'I've come to ask you about your sister Kerry. I know through the grapevine that she's had an offer from Templar Records.'

He blew out his lips dismissively as he said it. 'I'm here because I can make you a better offer. A much better offer.'

'And what might that be?'

'I want to sign her for Campion Records. They're new, but they're going to be big. We want her to do four recordings over the next three months. We shall promote her well, her name will be everywhere. Even the music sheets would carry a picture of her, as well as her name in large letters. We want our own Billie, our own Ella. In short, we want a white singer for this new music. We want her to be the first big performer of this new age. We also want to pay her a great deal of money.'

Briony looked at the little man with shrewd eyes. 'A percentage of the royalties as well? That's what Templar have offered.'

'Then of course that would be fine by us. The girl has something about her . . . youth, talent. My God, such talent! She also has a presence lacking in so many artists today. I have watched her, seen how she plays to her audience. The girl's a natural.'

Briony nodded in agreement. Her eyes were burning with ambition for her sister, with the knowledge that this little man with the bad breath and cocky manner could make Kerry into a star.

'Tell your lawyers to contact mine with the contracts. We'll talk again next week. How's that?'

Pieter smiled.

'That suits me down to the ground, my dear.' He stood up. 'I will leave you now. Thank you for the coffee, and I look forward to seeing you one week from today.' Clicking his heels together, he left the room.

Briony relaxed into her chair. She would get Kerry signed, sealed and delivered then they would drop the bombshell about little junior. If she went into recording, they could keep her from the public gaze for a few months, once the pregnancy became noticeable. Then, once the child arrived, they could get someone to mind it. It was the only solution. She knew through Jonathan that a lot of the stars in movies these days were hiding a multitude of sins. He was one of the few outsiders to be told about Kerry's child, and had been very supportive, telling Briony that he would do anything he could to help.

It seemed that his first legitimate acting part had made him overnight. He photographed well and looked the part of the movie star, even though he was far from being one yet. She would do the same thing with Kerry. Let her sign the contracts, get a few records under her belt. Become a known name and face. Then once the child was born, they would go on from there.

She had promised Jonathan that once Berwick Manor was underway, she would allow him to hold a big party there, a great big madhouse party, with her girls and his friends. Female as well as male. It would be a wonderful advertisement. The rich and famous gravitated towards one another.

Marcus Dowling, now her number two, walked into the office and Briony jumped. She'd been so deep in thought she hadn't heard him knock.

'Marcus! You made me jump!'

He smiled. He was big, blond and devastatingly handsome. He sat down opposite her and grinned, showing perfect white teeth.

'I'm sorry to barge in like this, Miss Cavanagh, but I needed to talk to you.'

Briony poured them both a drink.

'Go on.'

'Well, it's about the men you intend to employ at the Berwick.'

'What about them? I picked them all myself.'

Marcus smiled.

'Well, going over the lists, I found some of them were well-known nancies.'

Briony giggled. This man was so finicky it made her want to roar with laughter.

'Listen, Marcus, those men are part of my staff, not yours, love. They'll be working there just like the girls. You just worry about the heavies. Anyone else is my business, OK?'

Marcus relaxed visibly.

'Thank Gawd for that! I didn't really fancy keeping *them* in order. Give me a big burly docker any day of the week. Every place I've worked with them, they're murder.'

'Not all of them, love. Most are no different to me and you. They just have a different outlook on life, that's all.'

Marcus raised his eyebrows saucily and said, 'Well, I agree with you there anyway. Everything's running smoothly, I saw Mariah earlier, the work is nearly done. Another week or two at the most. The plasterers are finished. Soon it'll be ready for the redecoration.'

Briony nodded.

'Me and Mariah have that all in hand. By the way, I wanted to ask you something personal.'

Marcus scowled.

'What's that, Miss Cavanagh?'

'Next time you give my sister Bernadette a lift home, turn your engine off, would you? Only you kept half the bleeding street awake last night, and the night before.'

Marcus reddened and Briony laughed gently.

'Surely you didn't think you could keep that a secret, did you? Everyone knows. I was told about you and her within minutes of you being seen together. I look out for my sisters, you see, I take a deep interest in what they're doing.'

It was a veiled threat and he knew it.

'I happen to have a very high regard for Bernadette, but we've only been seeing each other a week. So it's early days yet. We're friends, that's all.'

Briony nodded.

'Well, she's a big girl now. How's the recruiting going for the bar staff at the Manor?'

Marcus relaxed, back on his own territory once more.

'I've decided on the men. I thought the heavies could be incorporated better as barmen, etcetera. Then, they'll be there all the time, should any trouble arise. I'll suit and boot them up, give them a good talking to beforehand, and hopefully they'll blend in with the wallpaper.'

Briony grinned.

'I can't see Big Denny Callaghan blending in with pale grey walls somehow, can you?'

Marcus also laughed.

'Big Denny is on the door, Briony. It's the only place for him!'

'Good. Well, you seem to have everything in hand. I want you to take over a lot from me, Marcus, as you know. I want you to run the Manor, do all the heavying so to speak. But any major decisions will be mine.'

Marcus Dowling smiled.

'Of course.'

'And Mariah's. Who could forget Mariah!'

Marcus relaxed in his chair, crossing his legs.

'But, one day, I take over everything properly?'

Briony took a pull on her cigarette before she answered.

'Providing me and you don't have any major falling outs, that's about the strength of it, yes.'

'I'll go a good job, Briony. In fact, I'll work like a nigger for you!'

The smile faded from his handsome face at the look Briony gave him.

Chapter Twenty-Eight

Tommy Lane was tired out. His face was aching with the cold and his hands were frozen. He turned to face the wind, his eyes immediately stinging with tears. He sank his hands deep into the pockets of his coat, wishing now he had put on his gloves. He saw a car coming towards him, its headlights bright in the darkness. He could see his own breath as he exhaled in relief. The car slowed and he walked to the passenger side and slipped inside.

'You're late.'

Marcus Dowling looked at him, a cigarette dangling from his bottom lip.

'Sorry, Tommy mate, but Briony kept me late then I had to take Bernadette home.'

Tommy nodded in the dimness of the car. He lit himself a cigarette and said seriously, 'I've had word that there's trouble brewing for Briony with the Ricardos, the Maltese ponces.'

Marcus scowled, his usually open face troubled.

'They've been in The Windjammer a few times, haven't said a word to anyone that I know of.'

'They think that now me and Briony are history, they can have a crack at her. Well, me and you are going to pop round and visit the old man, let him see a show of solidarity. He should be at his gambling rooms in Soho about now. So let's get going, me balls are nearly frozen solid.'

Marcus drove towards the West End. He was quiet for a while. Then: 'They've got a fucking nerve 'ain't they?' He spoke incredulously. 'I mean, Tommy, even if you're off the scene as far as they know, Briony's no pushover and she's got me as her number two now. Her workforce are hardly bumboys, are they?'

Tommy laughed gently. His taut face relaxed. 'Listen, Marcus me old mate, I never met a Maltese yet who had an ounce of brain in their thick skull. She's a bint, so she's a prime target. As far as they're concerned she's got above herself, see. And if they think so, everyone else will, so tonight me and you put them all out of the ball game. I've got a shooter in me coat. You came tooled up, I take it?'

Marcus nodded. 'Of course.'

'Good. How is Briony?'

Marcus shrugged lightly.

'All right. Eileen's still bad, they've got to go and see her tomorrow. Kerry's getting heavier, but she don't look pregnant. Briony still ain't having none of it with her old woman, and Rosalee . . . well, Rosie's Rosie, if you know what I mean.'

'And how's Bernadette?' Tommy's voice was full to the brim with innuendo.

'Bernie's doing all right, thank you very much.'

Tommy laughed heartily.

'Touchy, ain't we?'

Marcus swerved round a corner fast, and Tommy held on to the dashboard to keep himself upright.

'All right, Marcus, I can take the hint.'

Marcus slowed down, his face grim now in the dimness.

'I don't know why you don't just keep in touch with Briony. I mean, you've me and Kevin Carter watching out for her, and reporting back to you. Wouldn't it be easier if you just kept up a full-time partnership?'

Tommy shook his head.

'No. It wouldn't.'

Marcus heard the hard edge to Tommy's voice and dropped the subject.

Tommy stared out of the window in silence, thinking of Briony. He had had to leave her, to save himself. Briony was just too much, she had too many complications in her life. But that alone would not have been enough for him to have left her. He had left because, much as he loved her – and he did love her, deeply – she could never give him more than she had already.

But that didn't mean he couldn't look out for her, and he always would. No matter who he married, or who was the mother of his children, Briony would always occupy a big place in his affections. Without her, he would have had a much harder road. He owed her, and Tommy Lane always paid his debts.

Although he wouldn't admit it to a soul, he missed her at times so much it was a physical pain. If only they could be friends. But their relationship was such that that would be impossible. He either had her, one hundred per cent, or he had nothing of her.

At this moment in time, nothing seemed the better choice.

*

Victor Ricardo was a Maltese immigrant. Born in Buggiba, a small fishing village, he had come to England in the late 1800s bringing his fifteen-year-old wife, Maria. He had settled in Stratford where his wife had given birth to six sons in quick succession – all big-nosed, with deep-set dark eyes and thick unruly black hair. He loved to look at them, they were like his doubles. His only daughter, Immaculata, was tiny, pretty, and had the same modest demeanour as his highly religious wife.

Immaculata went to Mass, she cooked, she kept her lovely hair covered, and never spoke unless spoken to. She would not marry until her brothers had left home, as she was a great help to her mother with all the cooking and cleaning for the seven men of the household. Victor already had his eye on a husband for her, a Maltese baker who ran a bookie's on the side and had buried his wife a year before. He was older than Immaculata, but that was good. A man should be older than his wife. Women needed to be looked after. They had no right to opinions other than their husband's, and needed a man to guide them and their children. He himself was twenty years older than his wife and it had been a satisfactory arrangement.

He watched his eldest son Mario eject a troublesome man from the club, and smiled to himself. Mario was a good boy. Big and strong, he was not the most intelligent of Victor's sons, but his physical prowess was legendary around the East End.

Victor's little Soho club was in Greek Street. It was a basement really, but he had made it into a gambling house ten years before. He also allowed certain girls to work his place for a small percentage of their earnings. He treated the toms with contempt, not being a great lover of the female sex.

Tonight his eyes scanned the basement room with interest. The smoky atmosphere and constant buzz of conversation gave him a thrill every night of his life.

Victor poured himself a small medicinal brandy, staring at his bulbous hands which were becoming stiff with arthritis. Sighing, he went to his office and sat behind his desk. In front of him were the ledgers, telling him who owed what, and how long the debt had been outstanding. He would go through them tonight, then in the morning one or another of his sons would chase up the late payers. It was a good arrangement. He was toying with the idea of starting a protection racket in the West End. Now Tommy Lane was seriously East End, and his relationship with Briony Cavanagh was over with, Victor felt the time was right to make his own mark. He already collected from Maltese and Italian businesses in Soho. Now he felt he could extend his operation to the clubs. If he could get a madam like Briony Cavanagh to pay up, the others would rapidly follow. She was a woman without the guidance of a man, and no matter what anyone said about her, she was only a woman. He would prove that she was not indestructible, he and his sons would be the men to make her pay what she should have been paying for years – protection money.

Victor smiled to himself as he thought about it. The Irish were scared of her, the Jews were scared of her, even the German and Russian immigrants were scared of her. The Italians paid whoever asked them, so it was down to the Maltese or the Arabs to take advantage of this situation. It seemed the Arabs weren't going to, so that left the door open for him.

Victor sipped his brandy slowly, savouring the taste as it slipped down his throat and warmed his belly. He looked up as the door of his office opened, and swallowed heavily as he saw who was standing there with his son Mario. A very subdued Mario.

'Hello, Victor, how are you?' Tommy's voice was friendly and calm. 'Do you know Marcus Dowling at all?'

Victor stood up slowly and nodded at Mario who shut the door and stood in front of it, trying to look menacing. Tommy turned and faced him, saying loudly, 'Fucking hell, you two are so ugly you even look alike! Sit down, Mario, before I box you down. I ain't in the mood tonight for anyone trying to annoy me.'

Mario stayed put and Tommy shook his head at Marcus. At the signal, he pulled a gun from under his coat.

'Sit, Mario, or I'll blow your legs from under you.'

A white-faced Victor rushed around the desk.

'Mario, for God's sake, sit down!'

Tommy pushed Victor back towards his seat and, looking at the two men, said loudly, 'Did I ever tell you that I had a run-in years ago with Maltese Jack? Do you remember Maltese Jack, Victor? A big ugly bastard, a bit like you actually. He had a big hooter and all. Well, he tried to tuck me up so I shot him. No kidding, I shot him in both his feet. Now in the East End, if you shoot someone in the plates, it means they've tried to run you out of your business. You've trod on their toes, like. Do you get my point? So in a minute, I'm gonna shoot you both in the feet, then everyone will know you tried to take what was rightfully mine.'

Victor shook his head.

'I swear, Tommy, I have tried to take nothing of yours . . .'

Tommy laughed gently.

'But you have. Because me and Briony Cavanagh are partners still. I've left the running of the businesses to her because I have other fish to fry. So if you go to her for protection money, indirectly you're stepping on my patch. Now my Briony would have sorted you, because she isn't as easygoing as I am. She would have got this young man here to blow up your club, or maybe even your house. Because she hasn't got the patience I have. She's much more quick to anger than I am. Which is why I trust her to run my places. But me and Marcus here, we thought to ourselves, we'd better go and see Victor before Briony does, because me and you have known each other a long time, haven't we?'

Victor nodded slowly, his dreams and his hopes fading before his eyes.

'So when we shoot you in your feet, you'd better thank us, because we saved your lives.'

Mario looked at his father in shock. He tried to raise himself from his chair and Tommy shot him at close range in his right foot, shattering the ankle bone and the shin.

Mario dropped back in his chair, his devastated foot hanging loosely on to the floor.

All were aware that the hubbub in the club outside had dwindled into silence.

Tommy poked his finger in Mario's face.

'So, what do you say?'

Mario groaned with pain, and Tommy screamed at the top of his voice: 'What's that? I can't hear you, Mario. Did you say, "Thank you, Mr Lane"?'

Victor saw his son's face, the sweat standing out on his brow, the trickle of mucus running from his nose.

'Thank him, Mario. For God's sake, thank the man and get this over with!'

'Th . . . Thank you.' Mario's voice came out stronger than he'd expected.

'Thank you, Mr Lane.' Marcus's voice was high-pitched, as if talking to a child.

'Thank you, Mr Lane.' Mario's voice had tears in it now.

Tommy grinned. Then, shooting Mario in his other foot, he said, 'You're welcome, my old son. More than welcome in fact.'

Victor looked at his child, his first-born son, and a seething hatred for Tommy Lane swept over him. He swiftly opened his desk drawer. Marcus aimed his gun at the older man and shot him full in the chest.

Victor slumped over the desk, his body twitching uncontrollably in the throes of death.

Tommy tutted loudly. Walking to the man, he turned him over. In the desk was a small revolver. Tommy took it and slipped it into the pocket of his coat. Then Marcus and he walked slowly from the office, and through the hushed crowd outside in the club itself.

As they drove the few streets to The Windjammer, Tommy was humming to himself. Marcus, on the other hand, had not reached the point where the use of a gun didn't bother him at all. But he was determined he would get there, in the end.

'You really expect me to believe that?' Briony stubbed her cigarette out with such force she pushed the ashtray across her desk. Only the quick action of the girl before her prevented it from crashing to the floor.

'Honestly, Miss Cavanagh, it's the truth.'

Briony walked around the desk and held up a finger. Pointing it into the girl's face, she said slowly, 'You ever try and muscle in on another girl's customer in my club again, I'll have your guts. Do you hear me?'

The young girl opened her eyes wide in alarm and once more tried to deny everything.

'But I never . . .'

Briony stared into her face, her green eyes glittering with malevolence.

'Are you calling me a liar? Because I was watching you, love. You waited for the girl to get up and go to the powder room. Then you sauntered over there like butter wouldn't melt and tried to muscle in. I saw you! Now I couldn't give a toss, but Betty wasn't having any of it. You two were fighting in my club.' She poked herself hard in the chest. 'My club! You hear what I'm telling you, girl? You don't fucking cause hag in my place. Now get your bag, and get your arse out of here. If I ever see you or your lousy mate on my premises, I'll see you never work the smoke again. Do I make myself clear?'

The girl nodded, her face frozen with fear at the change in Briony Cavanagh. Only a week before Briony had stopped by her table and said a friendly hello. It was silly to underestimate her, it was foolhardy. Now she well and truly had her card marked, and all over a punter who was only good for a fiver, top whack. She could cheerfully kick herself.

Picking up her bag, she left the room. Her face was drawn and her shoulders drooped.

Briony watched her leave and sighed heavily.

Brasses weren't worth the hag half the time. She was happy for the girl discreetly to ply her trade. It didn't bother her in the least. She was clean, well dressed, and blended in with the clientele. But two of them arguing the toss over a man was a different ball game. It lowered the tone of the club, and that was the last thing Briony wanted.

The door opened once more and she turned away in a temper. 'I don't want to see or hear any more about it, Julian!'

Tommy's voice was soft as he said, 'Hello, Bri. All right?'

Turning back, her jaw dropped with the shock.

'Tommy? Oh, Tommy.' Her voice was thick with pleasure.

'Can I sit down then, or is everyone getting a bollocking tonight?'

Briony laughed at his jocular tone.

'Oh, Tommy, you're the last person I expected. Sit. Sit down and let me get you a drink.'

She poured him a large Scotch, her brain whirling with the implications of having Tommy Lane in the club, in her office, chatting to her as if nothing had happened.

He pulled off his heavy coat and slung it casually on to the floor. Then he sat down and opened the cigarette box on her desk. He blew out the smoke heavily, a large grey cloud forming around his head.

'Jesus, Briony, what's in these fags? Camel shit?'

She placed his drink in front of him.

'Could be, they're Turkish!'

'You're supposed to give this kind of crap to the punters and smoke the usual Gold Flake yourself! Now then, how are you?'

Briony sat down opposite him; and gazed into his eyes. 'All the better for seeing you, Tommy.' Her voice was soft, gentle.

Tommy looked at her for a long moment. Smiling, he said, 'How's the family?'

As she spoke of her sisters and her mother, he felt the familiar pull of her. But he also reprimanded himself for being weak enough to come and see her. She was like a dainty piece of Dresden china: her milky-white skin so flawless, her deep red hair emphasising the green glint of her eyes. Her mouth looked too good to be on a mortal woman. He could hear the deep longing in her voice, see it in the depths of her eyes, and just for a second he wondered if he had come here deliberately. To show her he could walk away from her again, maybe even to show himself.

'So Eileen's getting better? I'm pleased to hear that, Bri. Really. She had a rough deal, did old Eileen. I'm glad I got rid of the pair of ponces.'

Briony smiled. 'So am I.'

Tommy sipped his Scotch.

'Actually, Bri, I helped us both out tonight. That's why I'm here. Maltese Victor was all for blowing this place up! Can you credit that? He wanted protection. Anyway, I heard a whisper so I got your new bloke, Marcus, and me and him went round to see the old bastard and gave him and his son the bad news.'

Briony's eyes had widened to their utmost.

'He was going to do what?'

'Give this place a quick singeing. Cheeky bugger! Anyway, everything's sorted now. That's why I came round.' He looked at his watch ostentatiously. 'I have to run in a minute. I have to see a man about a dog.'

Briony sat back in her chair heavily.

'I beg your pardon?' Her voice sounded small and hurt. Tommy found he couldn't look at her. 'You mean, you've come here to let me know you've slapped Vic the Maltese, and that's all?'

'I did a bit more than slap him, love. I shot Mario the wonderboy in his feet and Marcus shot the old man through the heart. I expect the Old Bill is having a field day about now. It's only round Greek Street, ain't it?'

Briony nodded, her mouth twisted in a grim line.

'Oh, I get it now. You had to show a front. You still own part of the clubs so you wanted to protect your investment. I'm sorry, Tommy. I thought maybe the years we spent together might have brought you back round here, but I was wrong. I won't make that mistake again in a hurry.'

Standing up she snatched his glass from him and slammed it down on the desk. 'Well, you've told me your bit of news. Exciting as it is, I think I have the details now. So why don't you piss off to wherever it is you're going? Or more precisely, whoever.'

Tommy stared at his empty hand, then picking up the glass he drained his drink in one gulp. Standing, he picked up his coat from the floor and walked towards the door.

'You dirty bastard, Tommy! You came here to see how the land lay with me. You're laughing at me, aren't you?'

He faced her then.

'No, actually, I'm not. You're still a big part of me, Briony. But I'll tell you something for nothing, love, something I've told you many times before – your big mouth and your attitude will always be your downfall. You couldn't swallow could you? Just for a few minutes. I always had to do what *you* wanted. Well, if you want me back, I'm sorry. Because at this moment I wouldn't have you gift wrapped.

'You're too demanding, Bri. You have to take the lead. You have to be in charge. Well, you don't pay my wages, love, and you never have. I do what I want, when I want, and that includes visiting you or any other woman in the smoke as and when it suits me.'

He poked himself hard in the chest as he said the last word and Briony fought back tears of frustration and rage.

'Well, you don't visit no other woman while you're with me, I won't stand for it!'

Tommy laughed then. 'But we've already established I ain't with you, am I? We're partners, Briony.'

'Yeah, silent partners, and that suits me right down to the ground. In future *I'll* sort out Vic the Maltese or anyone else who wants to muscle in, all right? You sort yourself out. I still own the lion's share of this place, mate.'

Tommy smiled sarcastically.

'Of course you do. You always owned the lion's share of everything didn't you? Well, now I've been put well and truly in my place, I'll fuck off.'

As he walked out of the door Briony threw her own glass of Scotch at the door. It smashed into thousands of tiny pieces. Tommy shut the door quietly behind him without looking back. Briony sat down at her desk, the tears running down her face. How could he have done this to her? How could he have walked in here, all sweetness and light, and then dumped her back down on the ground so wickedly? She had felt so euphoric at seeing him, telling herself he could not live without her the same way she couldn't live without him, and all the time it was just business. Plain, simple business.

Stalking across the room, she opened the door. Spotting Julian, she bellowed, 'Get Marcus Dowling, now!'

Julian winced visibly as the door was slammed. Walking through to the club itself, he spied Marcus at the bar with Bernadette.

'Briony wants you, now. And I do mean now. She's rather upset.'

Briony was standing by her desk when Marcus walked into the office. 'Oh, so you've come then? I understand you did a bit of business with Tommy late tonight. A bit of business you should have consulted me about?'

Marcus licked his lips. 'That's correct. I did a bit of business. But I didn't see fit to bother you with it, Miss Cavanagh. After all, I am your number two. It's what I'm paid for. I deal with things as and when they come up.'

'Did Tommy Lane approach you?'

'Yes . . .'

Briony cut him off.

'You've been reporting to him, haven't you? Now don't lie to me, Marcus.'

He sighed. 'I have never lied to you, Miss Cavanagh.'

'No, you ain't lied, you just ain't said nothing. Well, I'm telling you now, as the person who pays your wages, you owe *me*, not Tommy Lane, your loyalty. He's a sleeping partner. I am the main owner of this place. I don't employ dogs and then bark myself. Do you get my drift?'

Marcus nodded. 'Yes, I understand. But we was trying to protect you . . . We was just . . .'

Briony flew across the room and grabbed his shirtfront. Shaking him hard, her tiny body possessed of the strength of great anger, she screamed: 'I don't need anyone to protect me, especially not a slag like Tommy Lane! Me and you could have sorted that out. Me and you! That's why you're my number two. How's it going to look now, eh? Tommy Lane still fighting my battles. Well, I can fight me own battles, and if you still want to work for me, you'd better get that into your thick head!'

Marcus grabbed her wrists and pulled her hands from his clothes.

'I'd thank you never to drag at me like that again. I know you pay my wages but I was doing my job. Believe me when I say tonight was well thought out and well planned, Miss Cavanagh. I am known to be your number two, and me and Tommy showing up like that only made you look stronger. More in control. Now calm yourself down. You're not acting rationally. I've never seen you like this before.'

His deep gentle voice was her undoing. Leaning against him, she began to cry, a high sobbing that wrenched at his heart. Putting his arms around her, he held her close, letting her cry herself out. He could feel her body shuddering with each breath she took, and for the first time ever he felt a twinge of sympathy for her. She seemed more human now than at any time before. Gone was the work machine. The hard-nosed businesswoman. In her place was a Briony Cavanagh who could be hurt, who was human and cried because she was hurting inside. All that he saw was pain, and an intense loneliness that made him ashamed of all his previous feelings about this little woman.

In the space of five minutes, he knew her better than he would ever have believed possible.

He held her until she had cried herself out. Then he lit her a cigarette and poured her a drink. Leaving her sitting at her desk, he went back to Bernadette, knowing in his heart of hearts that neither he nor Briony would ever mention this night again but that it would always be there between them. It would anchor him to her. Because it was proof that Briony Cavanagh could feel. Something he would have found very hard to believe had he not seen it with his own eyes.

Chapter Twenty-Nine

Kerry sat beside Eileen, her hands resting on her belly. Her pregnancy was not yet evident to outsiders but her spreading waistline was now obvious to friends and associates. Kerry poured out the weak tea and, mustering up her best voice, said gaily: 'How do you fancy a nice cup of tea, Ei?'

Eileen smiled dreamily. Her deep blue eyes drooped as if she had just woken from a long sleep.

'A cup of tea would be lovely, thanks.'

Kerry gave her a cup, stirring it solicitously.

'You're putting on a bit of weight, Eileen. You look much better for it.'

Eileen nodded. She was staring out of the window at the sea.

'I like the ships, Kel. I like to watch them. They blow their hooters so loud. Sometimes I can almost feel the spray of the salt water on my skin. I wish I could be on a boat. I watch the sailors pulling up the rigging, or getting the little fishing boats off the sand. It fascinates me how you can live on the sea, be a part of it, and yet only a few miles away we had no real inkling of it. I wish I'd been born here. Born on the sea. It's clean here. Even the sailors' breath on cold mornings looks clean. Sister Mary Magdalene says you have to respect the sea because it's a stronger force. It can be calm and friendly one moment and like a raging tyrant the next. Her dad died on a ship, he was a merchant seaman.'

Kerry sat amazed at Eileen's monologue. Personally she couldn't give a tinker's cuss about the sea, but obviously Eileen had taken a fancy to it and that was good.

'It is very pretty here. That view. I suppose that's what it's named after. I expect you watch the boats all the time?'

Eileen nodded and resumed her contemplation. Kerry smoked her cigarette. She wished Briony and Bernie would hurry back from seeing the doctor. Eileen gave her the heebie jeebies these days.

Briony and Bernadette were sitting in Andrew McLawson's office, looking stunned.

'Are you sure?' Briony's voice was incredulous.

The doctor nodded seriously. 'I'm sure. Your sister knew, in fact. She's four months gone.'

'Bloody hell!' Bernie shook her head in shock. 'Does my mother know? Has she been told?'

'She was informed three days ago. She was very pleased, in fact. Over the moon. I was quite surprised, considering her daughter's illness. Personally, I'm not sure it's a good thing.'

'Do you think Eileen will be able to cope with this pregnancy?' Briony sounded agitated.

McLawson shrugged.

'I really can't say. Your mother thinks it will be the making of her, but in truth I'm not so sure. Your sister is physically very weak, has to be forced to eat. We have a nun here, Sister Mary Magdalene, who seems to be the only person your sister will do anything for. They have a very close friendship. Sister Mary is a very kind girl, only twenty, with a very deep vocation. She loves Eileen dearly. I think maybe she could see her through this pregnancy, but we have no facilities here for children. I'm afraid you'll have to make alternative arrangements. We'll keep her here until she's ready to give birth, then she'll have to leave. Once she's delivered of the child, if you can get someone to care for it, Eileen can come back. We all feel she's doing very well.'

Briony sighed. 'But not well enough to look after her own child?'

'Good God, no! I would be very surprised if Eileen ever went back into the real world. I think your mother will probably take on the child. At least that's the impression I got anyway . . .'

Briony interrupted him.

'Over my dead body! She ain't getting her hands on it, or my Eileen. She'll drive the girl stark staring mad, as if she ain't doolally enough as it is! I wish you hadn't told her, Dr McLawson, she is a very determined woman.'

Andrew McLawson smiled once more.

'I think it runs in your family, Miss Cavanagh.'

Molly was making a large loaf. Her huge arms were stretching and pulling the dough into shape, kneading it to give it a nice crisp lightness as it cooked. Her front door opening was nothing to her, she didn't even bother to look round.

'Come away in, woman, and make yourself a cup of tea.'

She expected to hear Mother Jones's voice. Instead she was surprised to hear Bernadette's.

'Hello, Mum.'

Molly swung around to face her. 'Well, if it's not one of me daughters. What do you want?' Her floury hands on her ample hips, she looked formidable. Bernadette swallowed hard.

'I've come for Rosalee.' She smiled at her sister as she spoke.

'Oh, you have, have you? Well, maybe I might not let her go today. It's very cold out.'

Bernadette raised her eyes to the ceiling. 'Don't start, Mum. Our Briony's expecting her, and you'd better not cause any hag. Marcus is keeping the engine running, so I've got to go.'

'How is Marcus? When am I going to meet him properly?' All her animosity was forgotten at the thought of Bernadette's beau. She was ecstatic at the thought of one of her daughters having a man, a decent man.

'He's fine, Mum, now can I please take Rosalee?'

Bernadette was already putting Rosalee's coat on. Molly watched her without speaking.

'Kerry's fine, Mum, if you're interested.'

Molly went back to her task of making bread, not even acknowledging her daughter's words.

Bernadette swallowed down an angry remark and instead said, 'I'll bring Rosalee back tomorrow afternoon, OK?'

'If you like. And tell that Briony she's not to stuff her on cakes and sweets, she's a big enough lump as it is.'

'Okey doke. Come on, Rosie darling, we're going in the car.'

Rosalee grinned and said, 'Bri, Bri.'

Bernadette kissed her face and said, 'That's right, Rosie, we're going to see Briony.'

Molly wiped her hands on her apron and kissed her daughters on their cheeks.

'Watch her now, she's got a cold coming on.'

'See you tomorrow, Mum.'

Molly walked out to the car with them. Smiling widely, she waved at Marcus Dowling. She approved of this big man with his blond good looks.

Marcus waved back. Once Rosalee was settled in the back of the car with Bernadette beside her, holding her hand, he drove away. Molly waved until they were out of sight, then Mother Jones came out of her front door.

'He's a fine-looking specimen and no mistaking.'

Molly nodded in agreement, then in a jocular voice said, 'I wouldn't mind his boots under my table meself!'

Mother Jones cackled in agreement.

Rosalee and Briony were sitting on the hearth rug before a roaring fire. Briony was shelling monkey nuts and Rosalee was opening her mouth at regular intervals to eat them. Kerry sat on the settee, her knees drawn up under her, and Bernadette sat on a chair by the fire, her feet resting on the polished brass trim of the hearth.

'She eats so much, Briony, we should cut her down. Mum said she was getting too heavy for her to lift.'

Briony laughed. 'Mother always says that, then she feeds her a great slice of apple pie.'

Kerry was at the sleeping stage of pregnancy. At five and a half months, all she wanted to do when she relaxed was have a quick nap. She yawned widely, making a throaty noise. Briony laughed.

'Keeping you up, are we, Kel?'

'Oh, Briony, I feel so tired. I'll have to have an early night tonight.'

Briony was immediately concerned. 'Look, I think you should cut the club now until after the birth. Concentrate on your recording. I reckon that's where you'll be best off. The contract's signed and they can't do nothing. You just get that out of the way. Bessie Knight can do two spots at the club, she'll be glad of the dosh anyway.'

Kerry nodded lazily. 'I like Bessie, I like all the Velvetones. She goes down well and all, don't she? With the punters. Very good-looking woman.'

Bernadette said, without thinking, 'Marcus said she ain't bad looking for a . . .' She stopped speaking and the room went very quiet. 'Oh, Kerry, I'm sorry.'

Kerry pulled herself upright, awake now.

'For a what, Bernie? A blackie? A soot? What did the marvellous Marcus Dowling say then?'

Briony knelt up and put her hand on Kerry's leg.

'Come on, Kel, she never meant nothing by it. Let's not let this ruin a nice evening. It's bad enough we ain't got our Eileen here. Let's not have any rows. Not tonight anyway.'

Kerry made a moue. 'Well!' Then, her voice lowering, she said: 'I'm shitting myself about having this baby, Bri, I don't know if I'm strong enough to face what it's going to bring.'

Bernadette leant forward in her chair and said firmly, 'Don't you worry, Kel, we'll weather anything. That baby is going to be the best looked after kid this side of the water.'

Kerry smiled.

'I wonder what I'll have. And what Eileen will have. Mother's over the moon about Eileen's baby at least.'

Briony blew out her lips in a very unladylike way.

'It's your baby she should be pleased about, if anyone's. Eileen won't be able to cope.'

'Mum wants it, don't she?'

Briony laughed. 'Well, Mum ain't getting it! Eileen's coming here. Once she's delivered safely, we'll see how the land lies. If she still ain't all the ticket, she can go back to Sea View. I'll have the child.'

Bernie and Kerry both heard the deep aching longing in her voice and exchanged glances.

'You!'

Kerry's voice was loud and Briony looked her full in the face. In the firelight Briony's hair looked redder than ever, her eyes for once a glittering black.

'And why not? I'll get a wet nurse in to do the business with the feeding, and I'll oversee its upbringing. What's so bloody strange about that?'

Kerry shrugged. 'Well, ain't you got enough on your plate? In a way I think Mum would be the best bet. Let's face it, she's sod all else to do all day.'

'She's also got Rosalee and her life with Abel, such as it is. She's too old for a baby in the house. Not only that, I can give it more, give it a better start in life.'

Kerry sat back on the settee. 'I suppose so. Bri?'

'What?'

'Can I ask you something, without you getting all aereated?'

Briony grinned. 'Of course.'

'You really miss Benedict, don't you?'

Briony's face dropped. She bit her lip before answering.

'Shall I tell you something? I miss that boy with a vengeance. I'll be walking down the road, happy as a sand-boy, and then I'll see his little face. Wonder what he's doing, who he's talking to. Whether or not he's happy.' She stared into the fire then, watching the flickering of the flames.

'In the dead of the night, I daydream. I imagine how it could be, you know. I imagine me and him living here, Tommy and me married and looking after him. Tommy taking him out to play in the garden, a swing for him, a rabbit. You know, things children like. I see him asleep in bed, and me kissing him goodnight, ironing his little clothes meself, ready for the next day. I see me combing his hair, smoothing it over his forehead. I miss him all right, Kerry. I miss him so much it's like a physical pain. Especially on his birthday or Christmas, because I can't ever really touch him, or smell him, or talk to him. He's my child and I have no contact with him at all.'

Her voice trailed away and Bernadette patted her shoulder. Rosalee leant towards her and kissed her, a whacking wet kiss that sounded loud in the quietness of the room. Briony hugged her sister close, smothering her with the little dry kisses she knew Rosalie loved.

'I think you're right, Bri. I think Eileen and her baby will be better off here. At least you'll really love it.'

Briony looked at Kerry and said: 'And I need a baby to love, don't I?' Her eyes were full of tears.

'You can have my baby and all if you want.'

Briony coughed to give herself time to recover.

'I'll love your baby, Kerry, I'll love it and care for it. I swear that to you.'

Kerry smiled. 'I feel just like you do, about Evander. I think of him in the night. It's as if the darkness makes you think more somehow. I imagine me and him married, and everyone pleased for us . . .'

Briony nodded. 'I know. I'm sorry I chased him away, Kerry. Honestly. If I could put the clock back, I would.'

Kerry answered her bitterly, 'But I don't want him back, that's the funny thing. Because it's only now, with this baby, that I realise I was chasing a big dream. A pretend life. Because I'm not strong enough to live a life with him. I know that now. This baby has taught me that much.'

Bernadette said softly, 'Are you going to keep the baby after you have it, Kerry? Have you decided yet?'

She shook her head vigorously.

'Ask me again after the birth. One minute I want it, I love it to death. The next the thought of its colour and the effect it's going to have makes me feel faint. I can't answer you, Bern, 'cos I don't know the answer meself.'

'Well, whatever you decide, I'll stand by you. And so will you, Bernie, won't you?'

Bernadette nodded her head. 'Of course. There's a girl at the club, her baby's with a woman in Devon. She travels down every couple of months to see her. The baby's father is a married man, and she can't hack the thought of people knowing she has an illegitimate child. She says the arrangement works well, 'cos the father coughs up the money like.'

Kerry sighed. 'I don't know if I could have the baby too far away. Oh, to be honest I don't know what the fuck I want. I don't know whether I want a shit, a shave or a shampoo, as the old man used to say.'

They all laughed then, the atmosphere lightening. Rosalee pulled on Briony's sleeve and she said to her, 'What, darling, what do you want?'

Pointing to the nuts, she opened her mouth, opening it as wide as it would go.

Bernadette and Kerry both started screeching with laughter, Kerry's with a tinge of hysteria to it.

Briony picked up the bowl of nuts and said seriously, 'Of course, madam. If madam wants the nuts, madam must have them, tout suite!'

Rosalee closed her mouth and Kerry shook her head slowly. 'At least she knows what she wants, Bri, which is more than I do. Ain't that right, Rosie darlin'?'

Rosalee clapped her hands together and made the deep-throated gurgle that meant she was happy.

Chapter Thirty

Briony ran through her front door like a lunatic. Pulling off her coat, she raced up the stairwell, shouting to Cissy over her shoulder.

'Tea, hot and steaming. I'm freezing.'

Cissy picked up the full-length silver fox coat and tutted to herself as she went through to the kitchen.

Briony went into Kerry's bedroom where the midwife was making Kerry comfortable.

'How are you, Kel, all right? I came immediately.'

Kerry lay against the pillows, her face shining with sweat. 'I'm all right, Bri.'

The midwife wiped her face with a damp cloth. 'This is a quick birth, I've seen the type before. One lady I had was up and over it all in less than three hours! She won't go long. The doctor's seen her and he's coming back later, he's got two emergencies. Christmas is always the same.'

Briony smiled at her. 'Go down and get yourself a cuppa, I'll stay with her.'

The woman left the room gratefully. Briony Cavanagh was paying her a lot of money to deliver this child and keep it quiet. She had no intention of blotting her copybook, not where Briony Cavanagh was concerned.

Kerry moaned as another pain shot through her. 'Imagine, a Christmas baby, Bri. In another half an hour it's Christmas Day!'

'And what a present, eh? A baby.'

'Now I know how poor old Mary felt!'

Briony laughed, pleased at how well Kerry was coping.

'At least she had a husband, Bri, that's one thing in her favour.'

Briony sat on the bed and said, 'Yeah, but he wasn't the father of the child, was he? Poor old Joseph got all the hag and none of the pleasure!'

Kerry grinned, scandalised. 'If Mum was here, she'd flatten you for that remark.'

'Yeah, well, she ain't, is she? And it's only the truth anyway. How are the pains?'

'Let's just say they're there, shall we? Give me a drink of water, Bri, I'm parched.'

She doubled up as another pain shot through her. The sweat was standing out on her brow and Briony picked up the cloth and wiped her sister's face gently.

'Oh, that's lovely, Bri.'

'Here you are, have a drink of water.' She held the heavy crystal glass to her sister's lips.

Kerry gulped at the water, the coolness easing the burning of her throat.

'Have a guess what I heard today, when I was shopping.'

'What, a bit of scandal?'

Briony grinned. 'No, nothing like that. I heard your record being played in all the music shops. It's selling wonderfully.'

'Oh, good.' Kerry had a lot more on her mind at the moment and sighed.

'I wish this bloody baby would hurry up and come, I'm starving.'

Briony laughed.

'Bri, would you do me a favour?'

'Of course, anything.'

'Get me Mum, would you? I want me mum.'

Briony heard the hurt in her sister's voice and said calmly, 'Of course I will, love.'

Standing up she walked to the door, saying over her shoulder, 'I'll send the midwife back up and go and get the old woman meself. Be back soon, all right?'

Kerry nodded, panting in the aftermath of a pain.

Briony ran down the stairs and through to the kitchen. 'Can you go back up, I have to go out.'

'I've just made your tea!'

'Then drink it yourself, Cissy. Mrs H, make Kerry something light – she's starving. Coddled eggs will do. Where's me coat?'

Cissy went to the scullery where the coat was hanging up, dripping water from the snow. Shaking it, she took it out to Briony.

Dragging it on her slim frame, she smiled at everyone. 'Be back in two ticks. I'm going to get me mother. Keep your eye on Kel for me, all right. And if Bernie rings, tell her to get herself home, though with a bit of luck Kevin Carter will have tracked her and Marcus down.'

'All right, Bri. Get yourself off. And drive carefully, the weather's atrocious.' Mrs Horlock's voice was concerned.

Briony felt a glow come over her. Kissing the old woman's wrinkled cheek, she said, 'Look after Kerry, won't you?'

Mrs Horlock smiled. 'Of course I will. Now you get going before this snow gets worse.'

After Briony left the kitchen, the midwife said: 'She's a lot nicer than you'd think, isn't she?'

Cissy nodded. 'Yes. But if anything happens to Kerry, you'll see a different side to her, so get yourself back up the stairs.'

The woman didn't need to be told twice. She left the kitchen in double quick time.

'If Molly comes, I'll be very surprised.'

Mrs Horlock shook her head sagely.

'If Briony wants her here for Kerry, then she'll come. Briony will see to that.'

Cissy poured herself a cup of tea and in her mind admitted to the truth of that statement.

If Briony wanted her, she'd get her.

Molly was trimming the small tree with Rosalee passing her the ornaments as she always did. Marcus and Bernadette had brought round presents for them both, and Molly looked at the gaily wrapped parcels with sweet anticipation. Briony's presents to Rosalee were with them; Rosalee's was a new coat of deep red wool that would keep her as warm as toast. Bernadette had told her that earlier. Briony had also bought Rosalee a collection of hand-made animals that she could put on to her dressing table. They were carved from hard wood and Rosalee would be unable to break them.

'This cake is lovely, Mrs Cavanagh, did you make it yourself?' He knew Molly had, but he also knew she liked to boast about the fact.

'I did, it's me own recipe. Boiled fruit cake it is. Quick and tasty, with just enough cinnamon to give it a kick.'

'And a drop of brandy as well, Mum, if I know you.'

Molly laughed.

'Of course. A drop of the hard doesn't go amiss with dried fruit. They complement each other.'

The feeling in the house was festive and cheery. It was into this happy warmth that Briony came, bursting through the doorway in a flurry of snow.

'Briony!' Bernie's voice was high with shock.

'Hello, Bernie, I've been trying to locate you all afternoon. Kerry's in labour.'

Rosalee had set up a screeching from excitement, her huge cumbersome body rocking itself in her chair by the fire.

'Hello, Rosie darlin'.' Briony kissed her sister who pulled her into a hard embrace.

Molly watched with contempt. So that whore's time was on, was it? Well she hoped she had a dead child. That would make Molly's Christmas.

Briony extricated herself from Rosalee's arms and said, 'She wants you, Mum.'

Molly carried on fiddling with the tree.

'Oh, she does, does she? Well, she'll have to know what it's like to want then, won't she?'

Briony stood up, staring at her mother with eyes narrowed dangerously. Bernadette closed her eyes. Marcus, on the other hand, watched in fascination as Briony went to her mother and said: 'I don't think you realise, Mum, but you haven't got any say in it. You're coming if I have to drag you there myself.'

Molly looked down at her tiny daughter and smiled grimly. 'I'd like to see you try, madam.'

Briony lifted her arm and Bernadette jumped from her seat. Pulling Briony away, she said, 'Come on, Mum. How long can you keep all this up? It's Christmas. Poor Kerry's got enough on her plate as it is. Try and have a bit of Christian spirit, you're always going on about it.'

Molly sneered at her daughters.

'That bitch of hell can go and die for all I care, that child is a stain on the earth. It's . . . it's an abomination! She wants me – me! – to go to her in her labour. Well, she can want all she likes, the whore. I couldn't care if Christ himself or the angel Gabriel appeared in me kitchen this second, I still wouldn't go.'

'You're a vicious old cow, Mother. Come on, Bernie, help me get Rosalee's coat on.'

Molly stood in front of Rosalee and shouted, 'She goes nowhere.'

Briony laughed. 'Oh yes she does, because this house is still in my name. I put you down as the lodger, Mother. I handed it to you only as a lodger. You won't own it unless I die before you. It was my way of keeping Abel's hands off it. So if I'm going to put you out – which I fully intend to, legally mind – then Rosalee is homeless, isn't she? I don't suppose they'd welcome her and all next-door. Also, the allowance stops so you'll have to live off Abel who gets a good wedge from me, by the way, for doing fuck all! Or you'll have to get yourself a job.'

Molly's face paled.

'You wouldn't do that to me? You wouldn't use your money to force my hand, surely?'

Briony smiled nastily. 'Wouldn't I? You don't know me very well, Mother. In fact, you don't really know me at all. You get your coat on, or me and you are really finished, Mum, I mean it. Not another penny do you get. I'll make it my business to let everyone know me and you are old news. That anyone giving you a kind word will answer to me.'

Picking up her mother's coat from the peg behind the door, Briony threw it across the kitchen at her. Molly instinctively caught it.

'Come on, Kerry is well on her time and you must be there to greet your grandchild.'

Rosalee stood by the door, her huge bulk blocking it. She smiled at everyone with her wide grin and Marcus smiled back at her. He liked Rosie, which endeared him to Bernie and her sisters. It was not a fake liking. He genuinely accepted her.

'Come on, Rosie, you come with me and your mum in my car. Bernadette, you go with Briony.'

She could have kissed him. He was trying to defuse the situation.

Walking out of the door, he took Bernadette and Rosalee with him. Briony and Molly stared into each other's face. Molly was amazed at how beautiful this child of hers was. The white skin, standing out in contrast to her hair, and those deep green eyes really made for a beautiful woman. Yet at this moment she felt nothing for her except contempt. A deep-rooted contempt, because she was owned by this girl, owned by her own flesh and blood. Now she had to go to her whore of a daughter, the one daughter she had truly loved and who now disgusted her, or else give up her easy way of life.

Molly was an intrinsically selfish woman, and the decision once made was easy to accept.

She followed Briony from the house and out to her car.

Kerry was in pain, a deep racking pain that surprised her with its ferocity. Nothing had prepared her for the sheer agony, the feeling of having her body split into two.

'Oh, it hurts, Bri. It's a fucking nightmare!'

Briony smiled. 'I know. I remember me own labour. Not the pain, you forget the pain. But the memory of being a part of something bigger than you doesn't ever fade.'

'Never again, I'll never do this again.'

The midwife laughed now. 'If I had a penny, love, for every time someone said that to me, I'd be a millionaire!'

Kerry grimaced as she was once more torn in two. 'I want to bear down. It's coming. I can feel it.'

Molly sat in a chair by the window looking out at the snow which was now a blizzard. A thick whiteness covered the roofs of the houses and all the gardens looked beautiful. She heard the grunting of her daughter as she pushed and bit on her lip.

'Please, dear Mary at the throne of Christ, don't let this child breathe. Let it be born dead.'

The prayer came from her mouth in a whisper. She heard her daughter grunting again, remembered her own births, particularly the dead boy. She wished now he had lived. He would have been coming up to manhood. A big strong son, with her blonde good looks and his father's strength.

Kerry's breathing changed and the midwife pushed everyone away. Pulling back the covers, she exposed Kerry's bottom half. Her legs wide open on the bed, she lay back against the pillows and began to push.

Briony stared fascinated as a darkness appeared between Kerry's thighs. A deep blackness. Briony shrieked with delight.

'Its head's here, I can see its head!' She laughed out loud in excitement.

At the window, Molly closed her eyes, her prayers intensifying.

'Dear God, in all your wisdom, take the child from her. Don't let it ruin the rest of her life. Make it go away. Take its breath as it comes into the world.'

Kerry had her sweating face on her chest, a deep animal-sounding moan escaping her lips as she gave another great push.

Her whole body screamed out with the pain inside her. In her mind she begged God to take the child from between her legs before she fainted away with the pain!

Briony and Bernadette both clapped their hands in excitement as the baby pushed its head out from inside its mother.

The midwife looked at its face and stood stock still. It was so dark. Its skin was dark. Then, her natural instincts taking over, she said, 'It's got the cord caught. The cord's around its neck.'

Hooking her little finger underneath the cord, she pulled it over the child's head.

'Now come on, Kerry, give one more push. It's nearly over, love, nearly over . . . Come on, push.'

Kerry answered crossly, 'I am pushing for fuck's sake.'

Then, after one more almighty push, she felt a queer sensation come over her body. The child slipped easily from her and she felt a great peace. Relaxing back on to the pillows, she let out a deep-throated, heavy sigh.

Briony looked at the child on the newspapers underneath Kerry's buttocks. It was covered in blood and vernix. It was not very dark! It was the cord around its neck that had made it look so black. It was nearly white. Foreign-looking, but not black.

'Oh, Kerry, she's beautiful. Gorgeous!'

Kerry pulled her head and shoulders off the bed and laughed delightedly.

'Is it a girl? Let me have a look then!'

The midwife cut the cord and the baby gave a lusty cry. Over at the window, Molly felt the sting of tears. It was alive then, this baby. It lived.

Briony picked up the precious bundle and gave it to Kerry, Bernadette was crying softly, and Briony, Kerry and Bernie all bent over the tiny scrap of humanity and admired it.

Kerry's voice was incredulous. 'Briony, she's nearly white! Look at her, she looks white!'

Molly heard the words and turned from the window.

'Mum, Mum, look at her. She's beautiful. Oh, she is beautiful.'

Kerry's voice had the tired pride of many a woman before her. The midwife carried on cleaning her up, acting deaf as she heard the exclamations around her about the lightness of the child's skin. So that was what all the secrecy was for. The big wad of money she had been promised. Kerry Cavanagh had stepped way out of line if the father was a black man. Well, the child was dark enough to cause comment. Not that anyone would say a word to their faces, of course.

Molly stepped gingerly towards the bed, and as she caught sight of the child, let out a long slow breath. It was dark, but it wasn't black. It could be a Jewish child, or an Italian. She nearly smiled at the grim irony of an Irish Catholic over the moon for a child that looked like a Jew. But that's how desperate she had become.

'She's lovely, Kerry, a very beautiful child indeed.' Molly's voice came out much happier than she had expected. It was the relief. The relief of seeing a nearly white child that had done it. And the little girl was beautiful, she was one of the most beautiful children Molly had ever clapped eyes on, and when Kerry pushed the child towards her she took it instinctively.

But as she looked down on the baby's features, the child yawned, its mouth a pink hole in its dark face, and the revulsion she felt was almost tangible. So deep was her dislike for this innocent child, it took all her might and willpower not to throw it from her physically. Instead, she passed it to Briony who took the small bundle tenderly. Laying it on the bed beside its mother, she unswaddled it from its blanket and kissed the tiny hands and feet, even though they were still bloody.

'Oh, Kerry, I love her to death already. She is beautiful, wonderful. I could kiss her and eat her!'

Bernadette and Kerry laughed.

'You're bloody mad! Oh, Kerry, she is lovely though. Look at those great big eyes, she'll break a few hearts when she grows up.'

The child's deep black eyes reminded everyone of what she was and the room went quiet. Kerry pulled her baby to her naked breasts and said softly, 'Oh, Briony, I never believed I could love something so much. But I do. Oh, God help me, I do.'

Briony smiled down at her sister and put her hand on top of hers where it held the child's head.

'I told you, didn't I? And I'll tell you something else. That feeling never goes away. I know that myself. Isn't that right, Mum?' All the animosity had gone from Briony now as she looked at her mother, and Molly, feeling a great big lump in her throat, said: 'No, Bri. You never lose that feeling for your children. No matter what they do.'

Even as she spoke the words, she knew they were lies. Kerry was nothing to her now, and this grandchild was even less. The knowledge, accepted and admitted, was nevertheless true. And like most truths, the knowledge ripped her apart inside, because it hurt.

It was Christmas Day. No one had slept, but the dinner was still festive and gregarious. Molly was drinking heavily, and no one minded. The whole house was full of good will and camaraderie. Molly sat in the kitchen with Mrs Horlock, who was also full of beer, and the two women discussed the situation in the house in hushed tones.

Mrs Horlock could sympathise with Molly, even though she couldn't totally agree with her. The new child had been adopted by the whole household. Briony and Bernadette could not bear to be away from her for any length of time, and they all talked about her incessantly.

Upstairs in Kerry's room Briony looked at the baby for the thousandth time and said, 'She is the best Christmas present ever. All we need now is Eileen's little baby and we'll have a whole new generation of Cavanaghs under one roof.'

Kerry got upset, knowing that Briony was thinking of her own son who was enjoying his Christmas Day with others.

'Thanks for standing by me, Bri.' Her voice was thick with tears, the enormity of what she had done just now hitting her. Bernadette and Briony cuddled her as she wept.

'I don't know why I'm crying, I've never been so happy in me life!'

Bernadette laughed out loud.

'You're just tired, that's all. Mum always cried after a baby.'

Briony nodded in agreement.

'Mum cried because she wasn't sure how she was going to afford the new arrival. Well, Kerry ain't got no worries on that score.'

'That's the truth. Come on, Kerry, drink your glass of port. The midwife said it will build your blood up, whatever that means!'

Bernadette held the glass to her lips and Kerry sipped the thick red liquid as she had been told.

She wiped her eyes with her fingers. 'How's you and Marcus, Bern?'

'We're all right. He's getting me a ring after Christmas. At least, we've talked about it anyway.'

Briony made a face, making Kerry laugh through her tears. 'That should please Mother, a respectable married woman in the family. Good luck to you, Bern, he's a nice bloke.'

'Give me the baby, Bri.' Briony picked up the child and placed her in her mother's arms.

'What you going to call her?'

Bernadette cried: 'How about Noel, as it's Christmas?'

Briony tutted loudly.

'Don't be stupid, Bernie, that's like naming her Turkey.'

They all laughed.

'How about Christine then, the feminine of Christopher? Bearer of Christ? It is Christmas after all, the birthday of Christ himself. Christine.' She tried the name again. 'That's a nice name.'

Kerry shook her head.

'No, I know what I'm going to call her.'

Briony and Bernie stared at her.

'Well, bleeding tell us then!'

Kerry smiled down at her daughter and said, 'Liselle. It

was Evander's mother's name. It's all I can give her of her father.'

Briony nodded.

'It's a beautiful name for a beautiful girl. Look at that hair! It's already long and curly.' She poked her face down at the child. 'Lissy, Lissy Cavanagh, can you hear us, eh? We're all talking about you. You're the only little girl in England, in the world in fact, with three mums!'

They all laughed again.

'Lissy! Her name's Liselle.' Kerry's voice was indignant.

'Oh, come on, Kel. It's a bit of a gobful, ain't it?'

Bernie agreed. She stroked the little girl's hair and said, 'Lissy is nice, it suits her. It's soft somehow. She'll be Lissy to me, I think.'

Kerry grinned.

'Oh, all right! Lissy it is. I wonder how Eileen will get on when her time comes?'

Briony shrugged.

'She'll be all right. I hope she has a boy, then we'll have one of each! You're still coming tomorrow, aren't you, Bern? Only I was worried about driving down on me own in this weather.'

'Marcus will drive us, he's coming later anyway. By the way, have you opened your presents? I mean other than this big present here!'

They both shook their heads and Bernadette ran from the room to get all their presents from under the tree.

Liselle snuffled into her mother's breast and, looking down at her, Kerry felt a rush of protective love.

'I'm glad Mum came. I didn't think she would. Did she take much persuading?'

Briony shook her head, saying lightly, 'Nah, in fact I got the impression she was glad to be asked, you know?'

Kerry grinned.

'Love her, I bet she was relieved all the hag was over.'

Briony got off the bed and walked to the window. 'Look at that weather. I'm looking forward to seeing Eileen tomorrow, I hope the weather don't stop us.'

Kerry pushed herself painfully up on the pillows. 'I shouldn't think it'll deter you, Briony. I like it to snow at Christmas. It's fitting somehow.'

Briony agreed, glad the conversation had veered away from their mother.

Bernadette came in with her arms full of presents. Kerry gave the baby to her and she and Briony began opening theirs.

Briony picked up a small present wrapped in gold paper. She opened it carefully, a deep abhorrence of wasting anything stopped her tearing the paper apart. Inside was a small velvet box. She opened the lid and gasped.

Lying on plush red velvet was a choker. It was a large diamond-studded B with either side a thick black ribbon with which to tie it around her neck.

Kerry and Bernadette both gasped along with her.

'Bloody hell, Bri, that's some present! Who's it from?'

Briony shook her head. 'I don't know, Kerry.'

Bernadette smiled then, taking a small envelope from her skirt pocket, gave it to Briony.

'Marcus was asked to deliver it, here's the card that went with it.'

Ripping open the envelope, Briony pulled out the card. It had a silhouette of a woman against a gold background. Opening it, she read: 'Happy Christmas, Briony. I saw this and I had to buy it for you. Because you are a B, in the nicest sense of the word. Be happy, Tommy.'

Briony's eyes burned with tears. He hadn't forgotten

her, and even if they weren't together, as she wanted, he was saying he still cared about her. If he still cared enough to do this, there was hope for them yet.

Briony fingered the beautiful choker with wonder. What with the birth of Liselle, and the present from Tommy, a present that said though they were no longer a couple he still thought of her, still admired her, this was a better Christmas than she could ever have anticipated.

Chapter Thirty-One

'So what do you think then? It's March now, we could have the opening night for the Manor in ten days. Make it a Friday night and we can cater to the clients for the weekend. Those who want to stay on, of course.'

Mariah watched Briony from under heavy lids. 'If you want the opening then, that's fine with me. It was you who delayed it to build a swimming pool.'

Mariah had been set against the pool, the conservatory to house it had cost a small fortune on its own. That was without getting the pool dug, and the mosaic tiling which Briony insisted had to be the best. She hoped it wasn't going to be a big white elephant.

Briony smiled. 'Listen to me, Mariah, I know one thing, and that is you have to spend money to make money. Men are going to pay a small fortune to use that house, and you get what you pay for. It's a good excuse for the girls to be undressed as well. I think women walking around half-naked in a house like that doesn't really give the right impression. We can dress them in wonderful costumes. They can skinny dip, cavort all night in six feet of water, I don't care. But it adds to the value of the property and it's something different. Most large estates are having pools put in, along with tennis courts. It's a sign of wealth and also a sign of the times. It will pay for itself in six months.'

Mariah lit another cigarette and pulled on it hard. 'You do realise there's a depression out there?' She pointed at the window.

'Depressions only affect the little people, never the big ones. And we are big people, don't ever forget that.'

Mariah shook her head. 'What about all this talk of more strikes . . .'

Briony interrupted her.

'I ain't interested in all that. Let them strike till the cows come home. It don't affect us, or the people we deal with. I have five cabinet ministers champing at the bloody bit to get into the Manor. I've made sure it's talked about in my houses, as I hope you have and all. The rich are like the poor, they'll always be with us, and if I can remove a portion of their wealth, and ding it in me own pocket, I will. I don't know what's got into you lately, Mariah, you're like a bear with a sore arse!'

She laughed.

'I don't know, Bri. There's trouble brewing in this country . . .'

Briony cut her off impatiently.

'Then let it brew. Once it affects my businesses, I'll take an interest. My betting boys have never done so well, so there's money somewhere. But then there's always money for a bet, even when there ain't none to feed their kids. That's my working class, Mariah. A pint of Watney's, jellied eels or pie and mash, and a bet on a Saturday night. The old woman in best bib and tucker down the local with the old man, a few gins, a good row or a good fuck, depending. Those are the people you're talking about. Christ almighty, what do you want from me? I ain't interested in those people. I give to charity, I do me bit for the orphans, and I also make sure no one on my manor goes too hungry. That is it. I ain't old JC himself, and quite frankly, I don't want to be. So drop all your bleeding hearts' speeches and let's get the bloody Manor up and running.'

Mariah nodded in agreement. 'All right, I was only saying! How's Kerry and Lissy, by the way?' Mariah's voice was genuinely interested. Lissy had captured the heart of everyone she came into contact with.

'Oh, she's great, my Lissy. You want to see her now. She's growing by the day. Her eyes are like dark pools. Honestly, Mariah, she's exquisite. Clever and all! She pulls her head up to look round. Now would you credit that, not four months old yet?'

'She's strong, I felt her grip last time I saw her. She'll be a beauty and all. That long black hair. I've never seen such hair on a child.'

Briony smiled widely.

'And how's Eileen faring?'

Briony's smile faded.

'She ain't right, Mariah. Due any day, too. That nun's coming tonight, Sister Mary Magdalene. I think she'll be a great help. Eileen really thinks the world of her, she can get through to her. But she's so thin! No matter what you give her to eat, she don't put on a pound. All she has is this great big belly, and her arms and legs are stick thin! She looks weird.'

Mariah nearly said 'She is weird', but stopped herself. She couldn't take to Eileen but could never tell that to Briony.

'What's the doctor said?'

Briony shrugged. 'Not a lot. Just that her nerves are not all they could be. She drinks port wine every day for her blood and eats plenty of liver, once more for her blood, and takes a lot of rest. In fact, she ain't got out of bed this last three weeks. I reckon she should be made to have a walk or something. The room stinks of her. I know that's horrible but it's a bitter smell. It's in her sweat, I think.'

Mariah grimaced.

'I've heard her talking to herself and all. That's how she was before, when it all started. She's definitely out of her tree. I don't know what's going to happen once the child comes. I'll look after it, and she'll have to go back to Sea View, I suppose. I feel like shaking her sometimes, telling her to pull herself together, but of course, I don't.'

Mariah sighed softly.

'It must be hard, Briony.'

'It is. Watching someone you love going down hill by the day, and unlike the doctor I don't think it's the pregnancy that's making her ill. I remember her as she was before. It's a symptom, but not the whole reason, if you know what I mean. I don't think the pregnancy's helping, but I think she wants to die. Honestly, that's the conclusion I've come to.'

Mariah got up and put her arm around her little friend's shoulders.

'You can't know that, Bri. No one wants to die.'

Briony smiled grimly.

'I know Eileen. She's weak, God love her, and too much has happened to her. She ain't like us, Mariah. She's different. Highly strung, me mum calls it. "Sensitive" the doctor calls it. I call it plain and simple nuttiness. She's as daft as a yard brush, and that's the truth of it. I only hope this nun coming will snap her out of it for a while.'

Sister Mary Magdalene cast a shadow over the house for the first few hours after her arrival. Everyone, including Briony, was watching their language, watching what they spoke about, and all were acting completely out of character. Kerry was terrified the nun would find out Liselle was illegitimate, Molly was terrified she'd find out Briony owned brothels. And Bernadette had told a rather subdued Marcus that he couldn't stay with her while the nun was under their roof. Cissy took to curtsying at her every time she laid eyes on her, Mrs Horlock avoided her like the plague, and only Eileen acted natural around her. Natural only in the fact that she was the same as she was every day, except she smiled every now and then at the young nun.

Sister Mary Magdalene, for her part, felt the different tensions in the house but was more concerned for Eileen, who looked dreadful. The doctor visited every day, she knew, and was the best money could buy, and yet Eileen looked like a dead person already. Her face was covered by thin stretched skin, and her bones protruded through it. Her stomach was huge, a great lump that made her arms and legs look painfully thin in comparison. Even her hair looked dead, no lustre or sheen on it. Her blue eyes were flat, the colour of slate. They moved in her head slowly, as if the action was painful. The nun started praying within minutes of walking into Eileen's bedroom.

Later, as she sat down to eat with Kerry, Bernadette and Briony, she said: 'This is a lovely piece of beef. I like good food. Though I suppose I shouldn't, being with the Sisters of Mercy!'

Briony smiled at her. She had a wonderfully soft voice, an Irish lilt that held authority and carried without her having to raise it.

'How do you find Eileen, Sister Mary Magdalene?'

The young nun flapped her hand at Briony.

'Sister Mary will be fine, or just plain old Mary. I was lucky, my name was already Mary. We've a nun at Sea View called Sister John the Baptist! Now that's a mouthful, and she insists on it all as well. Behind her back, I call her JB.'

Bernadette and Kerry laughed, scandalised.

Briony smiled.

'You haven't answered my question, Mary?' It felt strange to address a nun thus and Briony wasn't at all sure she liked doing it.

'Shall I tell you the truth? I think she's dying.'

Hearing the words so plain, so true, threw Briony. She dropped her fork with a loud clatter on to the parquet flooring of her dining room.

'Well, you did ask. I've never seen a person so ill-looking in all my life. God love her, she's had more than a body can cope with.'

Bernadette put down her cutlery. Kerry just sat staring at the tiny Irish nun. She was sure the sister was about to get a slap across her wimple from Briony for daring to say such a thing.

Briony stared as well. She held back her natural urge to give this chit a piece of her mind because she knew the girl was merely stating a fact, a fact Briony also knew to be true. Instead she said, 'I've thought that myself. Tell me, Mary, what can we do? What can we do to make her better?'

The little nun finished chewing her piece of beef and said truthfully, 'All we can do is pray. Pray that the child's safely delivered. We don't want to lose them both, now do we? If she survives the birth, then I think she'll be fine. But there's not an ounce of meat on her, and worst of all she's lost the will to live. You only have to talk to her to realise that. Who's been emptying her chamber?'

Kerry looked startled at the question and said, 'I have, we all have, why?'

'She's sicking up her food, I've seen it before. Is the chamber covered with a cloth or paper?'

'Of course it is, we ain't going to walk round with a big Richard, are we!' Bernadette's voice was high and Kerry kicked her under the table.

'I thought as much. She's been emptying her stomach after every meal. That's why she's no weight on her. I only hope the child's been nourished properly.'

Briony licked dry lips. All along she had guessed at something like this.

'I make sure she drinks her milk and her port wine. I give her that myself. The doctor also prescribed a tonic, she takes that regularly. She has warm milk with honey in it before she sleeps, and one of us sleeps in the room with her so she must be keeping that down.'

The little nun nodded.

Bernadette started to cry.

'Don't you be crying now. We'll all work together to get her over the birth. I'll stay up at nights with her, as well as during the day, and we'll see she can't get rid of any more food. She'll have to keep it down if we're watching her, won't she? Then, once she's safely delivered, we'll see about getting her properly well. So she can look after her child.'

Briony nodded. 'Maybe the baby will give her the will to live again?'

The nun nodded and cut herself another slice of beef.

'I'm starving! Look at me, eating like a battalion!' She carried on eating her meal, but didn't answer Briony's last question because she didn't want to say out loud what she really thought. It was the child that was killing Eileen Cavanagh.

Jonathan la Billière and Rupert Charles were enjoying themselves immensely. Kerry was up on stage belting out a fast number, the club was buzzing. Everywhere people were chatting, dancing or drinking. The air was thick with cigarette smoke, and the atmosphere was genial. Jonathan and a young lady called Helen were holding hands. On the left of Jonathan was Rupert and his amour Peter Hockley, also holding hands. More than a few people who saw them gave a second glance in their direction. Peter was wearing make-up: his eyes were lined with kohl and his lips stained ruby red. He had on a man's suit and open-toed sandals with his toenails painted the same colour as his lips. The effect was startling.

Jonathan was drunk, and quite oblivious of the stares they were gathering. His film *The Changeling* had been a success. He was now famous and many people gave him a second look. Now that Hollywood was calling, this was his farewell party, given by Rupert for his old friend. Everything had been provided by him, including the young and attractive Helen. Now Jonathan was out of his head, on a mixture of cocaine, brandy and champagne that made him ignore the stares and jibes around them.

Peter jumped from his seat, a cigarette in a gold holder dangling from limp fingers.

'Oh, come on, let's dance!' He was an exhibitionist who loved to shock, loved being stared at – half the reason for his garb – and also loved to irritate. He was like the child to whom a smack is as good as a kiss. He walked unsteadily to the dance floor where, lurching sideways, he careered into a table full of people. There was a loud crash. A woman shrieked as an ice bucket hit her lap and a large man stood up. Angrily picking up Peter by the scruff of his neck, he threw him towards Rupert, shouting, 'Take this disgusting excuse for a man home! You should be ashamed of yourself, walking in here with this creature! I've a good mind to call the police.'

Two bouncers appeared as if by magic and the table was righted, the champagne replaced and the man soothed by promises of a free night at the club.

Peter laughed out loud, but his expression changed when Briony appeared. Her face was stark white, two large red spots of anger standing out on her cheekbones.

'This is it, you're finished here, Rupert. I want you out now! You can either walk out under your own steam or I'll have you all thrown out!'

Jonathan shook his head and looked at her blearily. He seemed unaware of the recent scene.

'Hello, Briony. How are you?'

She sighed heavily. Looking at her men, she said: 'Get rid of them, now.'

Rupert stood up and said loudly, 'Madam, no one speaks to me like that!'

Briony looked him up and down and said scathingly, 'Why don't you just piss off before I really lose my rag?' Her voice was low and menacing.

All around people were watching the spectacle. On stage Kerry had started another number, her voice straining to rise over the hubbub. People were muttering among themselves and Briony, seeing the ruin of a good evening, was getting more annoyed by the second.

As Rupert and Peter were ejected from the club she said to Jonathan, 'I can't believe you could still associate with those two! You're the one who told me they were on a downward slide. Now go home and sober up, man. You sicken me like this.'

Jonathan bowed low, his drink-fuddled brain unable to comprehend what had taken place around him.

When they had left, Briony apologised personally to her customers, and told the doorman that under no circumstances were Rupert and Peter ever to be allowed entry into the club again.

Briony arrived home at just after four in the morning. She was tired out. In her Hyde Park house there had been trouble. A valued customer had contracted syphilis and Briony had had to tell the girl responsible. She had gone mad, saying the customer had given it to her. After what seemed an age, Briony had finally sorted out the situation. The girl's working life was suspended until a treatment of arsphenamines was working. The man in question, not a very amiable person at the best of times, was a well-known industrialist who had lost two wives through his philandering and was now eager to get into parliament. A scandal was not in his best interests but nevertheless the man raged and blasphemed until Briony felt an urge to slap his face for him. Instead she had smiled, and smoothed everything over. When she finally got home she was fed up, tired out and in need of a good night's sleep. Peter was bad enough, but the trouble at the house had made a bad evening even worse.

She poured herself a large brandy and tiptoed up the stairs to her bedroom. As she undressed, she heard a tap on the door.

'Come in.'

It was Sister Mary Magdalene.

'I'm sorry to disturb you, but I think you'd better come and look at Eileen.'

Briony sighed heavily. Pulling off her dress, she grabbed a wrapper and followed the nun from the room. In Eileen's bedroom she froze. Her sister was lying in bed wide awake. Her eyes were bright and she was smiling.

'Hello, Bri. Come and talk to me for a minute. You look all in.'

Briony smiled in wonder.

'Eileen? How come you're all bright eyed and bushy-tailed at this hour?'

Eileen shrugged.

'I feel fine. I was just thinking about when we were kids. Sit down for a while. I feel the urge to talk to you. You've been very good to me, Briony, you know that, don't you?'

She sat on the bed, her tiredness forgotten, and took her sister's hot hand in hers. Close to, in the lamplight, she could see the feverish glow to her sister's face.

'I'll go down and make us all some tea, shall I?' The nun's voice was low.

'Please, Mary. If you don't mind.'

'I could drink a gallon of tea. I've got a thirst on me, Bri. A real thirst.' Eileen's voice was stronger than Briony could remember for a long time.

When the nun left the room, Eileen said: 'Remember when Kerry used to put on her shows down the basements? All her rude songs! Then when the priest come she'd change to a hymn and we'd all join in?'

Briony smiled, remembering.

'Yeah. I remember. We had some good laughs.'

'I liked living in the basements. I wish we'd stayed there, Bri. We were much safer in a lot of ways. Remember how cold it used to get in winter, though? The walls would freeze up inside.'

Briony frowned. 'How could I forget?'

Eileen nodded seriously.

'Mrs Jacobs' baby froze to death one Christmas, remember that? And they had to put it outside in the snow till the ground was soft enough to bury it.'

Briony squeezed her sister's hand tightly.

'Don't think about things like that, Ei, just think of the nice things. The summer days when we'd all swim in the Beam river, or walk out to Rainham and go pea picking.'

'I liked the basements. It was when we left them, or when I left them, that all my troubles started . . . I don't think I was ever meant to be happy, Bri. But I was as a little kid. Dad used to make us laugh, didn't he, sometimes?'

Briony swallowed hard.

'Yeah, I suppose he did.'

'I never meant to kill him, you know. It was an accident. Here, I'll make you laugh. Do you remember Sally Connolly and her talking dog?'

Briony laughed, remembering.

'Yeah, she could make that dog do anything. It was a big bastard and all, weren't it? I can still see the day it bit her dad for smacking her one.'

Eileen grinned.

'That's right. She'd given it half her dad's dinner and he went garrity, and when he smacked her, the dog went for him. It had to sleep outside after that, and anyone who walked past their house got growled at.'

'It wouldn't let her dad in unless they got Sally up to calm the dog down!'

They both laughed together, remembering happier times. Eileen grimaced and Briony was immediately concerned.

'You all right, Ei?'

She nodded. 'Yeah, the baby's moving, that's all.'

'You looking forward to having it?'

Eileen wiped a hand over her face and ignored the question. 'I was thinking the other day about when Bernadette was ill that time. Do you remember? You was only small yourself. She had the whoop. I sat up all night with her because Mum was flat out herself. I sat with her little head over a bowl of hot water. I really thought she was going to die. But the next day she was all right. The doctor gave me a sweet. Said I was a good girl.'

'I was the one going out in the freezing cold to fill the kettle, how could I forget that? I was only a kid meself.'

'You was five and Bernie wasn't even two. Dad wouldn't go out any more. He said he had to sleep to get up for work. Mum was just plain knackered. I hated him for that because you know something, he wasn't working, Bri. He lied, said he had a day's work but he never. You walked in and out all night filling that bloody thing.'

Eileen's voice was sad now and Briony kissed her cheek. 'Don't get maudlin.'

'I was eight years old. That was the year of Mr Lafferty's party. That was a great day, weren't it? Two barrels of beer, and all the faggots and peas you could eat! He won a big bet, a really big bet, and blew nearly the lot on that party. The next day he lost the last of it on another bet!'

Briony grinned.

'That was Mr Lafferty all right. His daughter married a Salvation Army geezer, and he disowned her.'

'I always liked her. Mrs Lafferty was down the pop the day after the party to get enough money to feed her brood. Mum was scandalised that she hadn't had the sense to raid Mr Lafferty's pockets while he was drunk and salvage a few bob!'

Sister Mary Magdalene came in with the tray of tea and Briony poured them all a cup.

Eileen drank her tea scalding hot, gulping it as if she was dying of thirst.

Putting down her empty cup she grinned, and the sight made Briony want to weep. Her face was like a living skull.

'I needed that. It's funny, you know, but I feel a lot better. Much better, in fact.'

The nun patted her hand.

'You're looking and sounding better, if I might say so.'

'Mary? While you're here can I ask you to do something for me?'

The nun nodded. 'Of course, anything.'

'When my baby's born, if anything happens to me, will you be a witness that I want Briony to have it? You would have it, wouldn't you, Bri? Don't let Mum have it. I don't want me mum bringing it up. I want you to. You and Kerry and Bernie. Promise me?'

Briony nodded.

'Of course I promise, but nothing's going to happen to you. You'll get better. You're better already. Look at you, nattering on. You're halfway there already. So don't think about anything like that. Now do you want another cup of tea?'

'Please. Mary, I was just talking to Briony about when we were kids. I helped deliver Briony, you know. I was only three, but I was the one who held her head while me mum pushed her out. The midwife was late, and me and me mum delivered her between us. After it was over me mum sat me by the fire with Briony in me arms while she burnt the rags and the newspapers. I was just coming up four, but I can remember it clearly.'

Mary smiled.

'Well, you would, something like that.'

'I loved Briony more than the others, she was like my baby after that. The others came thick and fast, a few dead ones and a few misses, as me mum called them. But Briony was special to me. I'd helped her into the world, as if I'd given birth to her meself.'

Briony felt an absurd lump in her throat hearing her sister talk. A great rush of love for Eileen washed over her.

Eileen grimaced again, and her tea spilt into the saucer. She made a grunting sound and Mary and Briony both looked at one another in alarm. Taking the cup from Eileen, Briony pulled back the covers of the bed. Lying between Eileen's legs, unmoving, was a tiny baby. She dropped the cup to the carpet with shock.

'Jesus save us! Mary, get the doctor! For goodness' sakes, get a doctor!'

Eileen lay back in the bed, a triumphant smile on her face. Briony stared down at the child. It looked like a skinned rabbit. Then it moved, its small hand making a fist, and mewled like a newborn kitten.

'It's alive! Oh, thank God, it's alive.'

Sister Mary pushed Briony out of the way and took over. It was Briony who telephoned the doctor, Kerry and Bernie were outside on the landing and Mrs Horlock and Cissy were inside helping.

Briony pushed through the door, her heart beating like mad, her face flushed.

Cissy held the little boy in her arms by the fire, and Mrs Horlock pushed down on Eileen's stomach.

'What's going on?'

Mrs H flapped a hand in front of her face and resumed her pushing.

'There's another little bugger in here or I'm a Chinaman. Come on, Eileen love, push!'

Eileen lay in bed, her face screwed up in concentration. Briony watched entranced as another head appeared. The child slipped from its mother without a sound then set up a lusty wailing as it hit the cold of the air.

'Twins! Oh, Eileen, you've got twins!'

Kerry and Bernadette burst into the room at this and both began doing a little dance.

Eileen lay back, her face wet with sweat. 'What are they?'

Mrs Horlock smiled at Eileen and said, 'They're boys. Two boys as identical as your own two hands!'

Sister Mary looked the children over and grinned. 'They're small, but they're healthy. Who would have credited that, eh? Two of the little buggers!'

Kerry, Bernie and Briony, along with the other occupants of the room, all stood open-mouthed with shock as they heard the little nun swear.

She laughed with delight, her relief at the birth being over making her excited.

'I think the Good Lord will forgive a bit of overexuberance at a time like this, eh?'

Eileen was cleaned up and both her sons placed in her arms at her request. She looked down into their tiny faces and smiled.

'My sons, my boys.' Her voice was thick with emotion.

Cissy and Mrs Horlock disappeared to make them all

some breakfast. Bernadette and Kerry got dressed. Bernadette was going to fetch their mother and Kerry had to feed Liselle who had set up a wailing of her own. Briony hugged the tiny nun and hugged Eileen.

'They're beautiful boys, Eileen. And what a night! Why didn't you let on you were in labour?'

Eileen smiled and said softly, 'I wasn't sure, to be honest. Take these two for me, Bri, would you?'

She took one baby and Sister Mary the other. As they unswaddled the babies and began to wash them, Eileen gave a long sigh.

Briony smiled at the nun. 'She must be tired out, bless her.'

The nun placed a baby back against her chest and said sadly as she walked to the bed, 'I think she's been tired for a long time, Briony. She's gone.'

Briony walked to the bed, one tiny baby snuggled into her breast, and as she looked at Eileen's serene face, gave a loud cry.

The doctor arrived five minutes later, but he was too late. As Briony remarked to Sister Mary, he was fifteen years too late.

Chapter Thirty-Two

Briony stared down at the two children lying side by side in their cots. Each slept on his stomach, tiny hands clenched into fists as if they were born to fight. If one moved, the other moved. Just three days old and so alike it was impossible to tell them apart. As Briony looked at them, she was filled with love. Eileen had known what she was doing when she gave these boys to her. They filled a deep gaping void in her, that had been growing bigger and bigger in the years since she had handed over her own child. Now these two motherless boys assuaged that grief.

Briony had found two wet nurses, Lily Nailor, whose own baby had died a week before, and Carol Jarret, whose child was off the breast and being cared for by her mother. Needless to say, only Lily lived in. The two boys had already become the focal point of the house, along with Liselle. It seemed that after years of being peopled only by adults, the house was now full of babies. Everywhere Briony looked was evidence of them.

Molly was prostrate with grief. Even Briony had warmed to her at this evidence of her love for Eileen. She was taking the death of her child badly, and when Sister Mary had told her of Eileen's dying wish that the twins should go to Briony, had acquiesced without a murmur. Briony felt already as if the boys were her own.

She stroked the two downy heads. They were so alike it was startling. Both had the same burnished copper hair that was already darkening, eventually to become a deep chestnut-brown, and both had deep-set blue eyes. They had nothing of their gentle mother in them, though Briony could see nothing of O'Malley in them either. She was glad. These were Cavanaghs, and would be called Cavanagh. She would see to that.

Jonathan la Billière awoke, a pain shot through his skull and he groaned. He looked at his watch, and groaned again. Sitting up in a strange bed, he was relieved to find himself alone. He had been partying with Rupert and Peter for three days solid and now he had woken thirsty, hung over, and stinking. Catching a glimpse of his reflection in a mirror opposite, he pushed his hands through his dark hair in consternation. He had deep shadows under his eyes and needed a shave badly. He lay back in the bed as he felt giddiness coming over him again. He was finished with drink, he promised himself that. He was due in Hollywood in less than a fortnight and had a lot to do before then.

He smiled at his own good fortune. *The Changeling* had shown everyone what he had always known: he was a damned good actor. The story was a melodrama about a man who comes back years later to claim his inheritance, after an evil housekeeper switches her child for the rightful heir. It was a stupid storyline, but he had made it work. He *was* the Changeling and he had given the part all he had.

The film was a success, and now offers were pouring in thick and fast. He was pleased with himself, pleased at how his life was going. The boy from the South London backstreets, still alive in him, though carefully submerged these days, kicked himself each day to make sure it was all true.

He walked out on to the landing and realised he was in Peter's house. He opened a door nearby, looking for a bathroom of some description. No luck. It was as he approached another door that he heard the noise. He stood still and listened carefully.

It sounded like someone crying.

Walking towards the sound, he opened Peter's bedroom door. It was an act he was to regret all his life.

Peter was sitting on the floor naked; the whole room seemed to be covered in blood. It was even on the ceiling, great red splashes vivid against the white paint. The bed was one deep crimson stain, and on it lay a young man Jonathan could not remember seeing before. Beside him, sitting with his head in his hands, was Rupert.

Peter looked at Jonathan over his shoulder and said brokenly, 'It was only a game, a silly game . . . I never meant it.'

He started crying harder, his face a mass of make-up and tear stains.

Jonathan put his hand to his mouth to stop the tide of sickness rising up in him. The fresh smell of blood was cloying, sickly sweet on the air. Staggering from the room, he ran down the stairs. He picked up the phone and dialled Briony's number. She was the only person he could think of who would be able to sort out a mess like this.

*

Briony was at the house in twenty minutes. She walked through the door with her usual air of capability and common sense. The first thing she did was to give Jonathan a large Scotch, then she went up and looked at the damage for herself.

Staring at Peter and Rupert, she shook her head in disgust. She didn't bother checking if the boy on the bed was still alive. It was obviously far too late. He was no more than sixteen, she saw. His hands were tied behind him, and his legs were manacled to the bed. His throat had been cut from ear to ear. When she forced herself to look closely, she found that his head had been practically severed from his body. Nowhere in Briony's wildest imaginings could she envisage a sex game resulting in this. And she knew more about the sexual wants of people than most. But this was out of her territory.

Peter was crying again. His face had two long glistening trails of mascara down it. Briony stifled an urge to let him feel some pain and scratch his eyes out.

Leaving the room, she went down to Jonathan. 'Any servants here?'

He shrugged. 'I have no idea.'

'I should imagine Peter has someone come in. With his lifestyle, he wouldn't want anyone living here, would he? It stands to reason.'

'What are we going to do, Briony? I didn't know who to call. If this gets out, my career will be over before it's even fucking started.' Jonathan clenched his teeth. 'Why, oh why, did I ever take up with Rupert again? I must have been mad. The two of them were getting out of hand, and this is the result. You don't know the half of it . . .'

He was nearly hysterical and Briony said, 'Oh, shut up, Jonathan, let me think.'

She paced the room for a while.

'I'm going to ring Mariah. She'll help you get away. The main thing is to remove you from here. OK?'

Jonathan nodded. 'You're so good to me, Briony! I knew you'd know what to do.'

'Go upstairs and get dressed. I have a couple of calls to make. Come on, get your arse in gear!'

She rang Mariah then picked up Peter's telephone book and dialled Lord Hockley's number. She spoke to him personally and afterwards sat smoking till Mariah arrived. Her driver took Jonathan home and the two women waited in silence for Lord Hockley. Both knew that this was something they could use to their advantage, though neither voiced the thought out loud. Briony, herself, was numb, Eileen's recent death still an open wound. When Lord Hockley arrived she had the grace to feel deeply sorry for the man.

She walked wordlessly up to the bedroom and opened the door. Lord Hockley, who had fought in the Boer War and had witnessed first hand the tragedy in the trenches of the Great War, took one look at the naked boy on the bed and, putting his hand to his heart, made a deep moaning sound that seemed to be pulled from his strong barrel chest.

Then, entering the room, he took the knife from beside his son and threw it at the wall. Its bone handle made a loud cracking sound as it broke under the blow. Then he began to belabour Peter, pulling him up by his short-cropped hair and slapping him across the face, the shoulders, anywhere on the boy's body he could make contact. He finished by kicking him in the chest.

'You animal! You filthy little animal! Is this what I brought you up for? This – carnage!'

Rupert watched the scene through glazed eyes.

Lord Hockley turned to Briony and said: 'And where do you fit into all this, eh? Only I've washed my hands of the blighter if you're thinking of getting money out of me. I want no more to do with him. This is the end! The finish!'

Briony said in a low voice, 'I want nothing. I was called here by a mutual friend. I thought that as this Peter was your son, you'd better sort it all out. I want nothing from you, nothing. Except for you to finish what your son started.'

She saw Hockley deflate in front of her eyes. His whole body seemed to sag.

'Come on, let's go downstairs, get out of this. It's up to you now. But if I was you I'd try and help your son, because that boy is dead and nothing is going to bring him back. He's more than likely a pick up, so I shouldn't imagine anyone's looking for him just yet.'

Briony's sensible words penetrated the man's distress. But an innate sense of justice fought with his natural instinct to protect not just his child, but his family's good name. He followed Briony down the stairs.

Mariah poured them all a drink and Hockley swallowed his straight down and held out his glass for more.

'I gave that boy everything, but even as a child . . . His mother encouraged it, you know. She's the real culprit. Should have let me send him overseas, put him in the army like his forebears, but no. Her darling boy had to be encouraged, he was artistic. Artistic, my eye! He's plain unnatural, an offence to the eyes of God. My only son, can you believe that? My only son. And look where he is now . . .'

Briony heard the sorrow in his voice and felt an urge to

flee. To get away from this house and its occupants. She had enough to think about as it was. Her Eileen was dead, and Peter Hockley was alive. It was so unfair.

'Shall I call the police then?' She hoped he would say yes. She wanted Peter Hockley to pay the proper penalty for the ending of that young life. But she knew that even if she telephoned the Chief Inspector, it would be hushed up, because Hockley was a newspaper baron and he had clout. A great deal of clout. He shook his head slowly.

'No. I will make sure everything's taken care of. By the way, who was the mutual friend you spoke of?'

Briony shook her head.

'That's for me to know, and you to find out. If you'll excuse us, Lord Hockley? It's been a long night and I have a feeling it's going to be a very long day.'

Mariah finished her drink. As they went to leave, Lord Hockley's voice stayed them.

'Why didn't you phone the police?'

Briony looked back and answered truthfully. 'Would it have made a difference? Let's face it, there's no way this is ever going to come to light is there? You might be angry with your son now but you won't want him banged up, no more than I would my child. No matter what they'd done. But I trust you remember in years to come that we kept quiet about this, Lord Hockley. That we didn't go to the other newspapers, the ones you don't control.

'Now, if you'll excuse us, we've done our bit. The rest, I'm afraid, is up to you.'

Briony was still thinking of the scene she had witnessed earlier in the day as the priest spoke his last words over Eileen. Kerry and Bernadette held Molly between them, and Briony stood away from the small group alone.

Eileen's death heralded an end of an era. Never again would the five sisters be together. She heard Rosalee crying and felt the sting of tears herself. Marcus was holding Rosalee to his chest. No one was ever sure exactly how much she understood. If they cried, she cried; if they laughed, she laughed. Today she was breaking her heart.. Maybe somewhere in her mind she realised what was going on. Or maybe she just felt the deep unhappiness around her.

Sister Mary Magdalene was also crying; her young face, so soft and virginal-looking, seemed out of place here.

So many people had turned out for the funeral, Briony had found it hard to believe at first. It seemed that every woman in the East End of London had gathered at The Chase graveyard to mourn her. The Chase was on the old Romford Road, surrounded by countryside. Eileen would be pleased to be laid to rest here, Briony was sure of that.

The cortège had grown longer and longer as people joined it all along the route until now there was a large silent crowd. Briony knew it was their way of lending support. Their way of looking after one of their own.

She swallowed down the hot burning tears with difficulty. She felt a soft touch and looked round to see Tommy standing beside her. Biting her lip, she held on to him, feeling the strength of him through her coat, feeling a peacefulness settle over her.

Father McNamara blessed the coffin, Briony threw in the first lump of dirt and a single white rose. All the sisters followed suit, even Rosalee. Molly had to be taken from the graveside, her wailing becoming hysterical.

As Briony stood by her sister's open grave people filed past her, murmuring condolences. Everyone knew she had taken on Eileen's boys. It was common knowledge, and proved once more that Briony Cavanagh was one of them, for all her money and her businesses. Local hard men paid their respects to her personally, looking out of place in their suits and clean shirts.

Tommy finally walked her from the graveside and over to his car. He drove her back to her house himself. In the car Briony shed the tears she had been holding back. Tommy let her cry, knowing it could only be for the good. Briony bottled up too much. She needed to let off steam. Then outside her house he took her in his arms and comforted her.

Briony, smelling the familiar smell of him, allowed herself to be held. Never had she felt so alone in all her life, and never had she been more grateful for Tommy's company.

Molly was drunk, stinking drunk. She was so drunk she could barely move in her chair. Briony got Marcus and Tommy to carry her mother up to bed. She stripped Molly with difficulty and slipped the quilt over her. As she looked down on her mother's swollen face she felt a tremor of love for her. Abel had taken his mother home earlier. Mother Jones would always come first with him, and Molly knew that and was hurt by it. Even at her daughter's funeral, his mother had taken first place. Briony felt her mother's pain as surely as if it was her own.

As she walked from the bedroom she saw Tommy standing on the landing, leaning against the wall.

'Thanks for coming, Tommy, I appreciate it.'

He smiled, his familiar little grin, and Briony felt her heart lurch.

'Would you like to see the boys?'

Tommy nodded and followed Briony into their room.

He looked down at the two babies and laughed aloud. 'Oh, Briony, ain't they small?'

She nodded, placing a finger in each child's right hand. 'But they're strong. They've got a good grip. Poor Eileen. Two beautiful children and she'll never see them grow up . . .'

Her voice broke and Tommy put an arm around her shoulders. 'Who'll bring them up now? Your mum?'

Briony shook her head furiously.

'No way. I'm going to bring them up. They're my boys now. Mine. Daniel and Dennis Cavanagh. Aren't you, my lovelies?'

She bent closer to them and Tommy sighed softly. 'They're O'Malleys, Briony. Eileen was legally married, remember?'

Briony shook her head.

'No, you're wrong. These two are Cavanaghs. Eileen gave them to me. I'll be their mother, I'll bring them up, and they'll be brought up as Cavanaghs. That's an end to it. I have great plans for these two young men, Tommy. Great plans.'

'I'm sure you have, Briony.'

She was unaware of the undercurrent in Tommy's voice.

'They'll have everything. Liselle will be like a sister to them. She's a beauty, too. They're the next generation of Cavanaghs and all living under one roof. I'll make sure they have the world on a plate. The best education, the best of everything. I promised Eileen I'd look after them and I will.'

The bigger of the babies turned himself over and Briony picked him up tenderly.

'Look at your Uncle Tommy, Boysie.' She looked at Tommy and said: 'We call him Boysie because he's the bigger one. I don't know why but he looks like a Boysie, don't he?'

Tommy smiled and nodded agreement.

Briony kissed the child softly on his tiny rosebud lips. 'Who's their mummy's little babies then, eh? Who's my beautiful boys?'

She placed the child back in his crib tenderly and then picked up the other. Daniel snuggled into her arms naturally, used to the feel and the smell of her.

'Oh, Danny Boy.' She looked at Tommy again. 'This one is the quieter of the two. As alike as they look, they're different in many ways. Boysie is much louder. Danny Boy, well, he'll be a thinker, I reckon. He's the quiet one.'

Tommy watched her look at the child intently, practically drinking him in with her eyes.

'They're lucky to have you to look out for them.'

Briony shook her head and said truthfully, 'Oh, I'm the lucky one, Tommy. It's me who's the lucky one. I can give these boys so much. And in return it'll be like having my own boy back. Like having two Benedicts to care for. I owe it to Eileen and to myself to make sure these two little spats have the best that money can buy. And I'll see that they do.'

He touched the child's downy head and said, 'Money can't buy happiness, Briony. You more than anyone should know the truth of that.'

She pulled the child from him and said tartly, 'Well, at least I can be miserable in comfort, can't I? Which is infinitely preferable to being miserable as well as cold and hungry. Why must you always put the mockers on everything, Tommy? Why can't you just once say something I want to hear? These two little boys deserve to be happy and I want to make sure they are. And the kind of happiness I want for them takes a great deal of money.'

Tommy sighed and said in a low voice, 'Don't try and *make* them happy, Briony, let them *be* happy. I often think you don't know what real happiness is. All the years I've known you I can honestly say, hand on heart, I don't know of one time when you was ever really happy.'

Briony put the child back in the crib. Facing Tommy, she looked into his eyes. The sight of her long neck and Titian hair enflamed him, she was so beautiful, so alluring. Her eyes were like emeralds glittering in her head. Her mouth was trembling as she said, 'That, Tommy, is because I have never really been happy. Not since the day I gave up my boy. But now I have a second chance, and Eileen's boys are that chance. She wanted me to do my best for them, and I swear on her grave that I will do just that. I'll look out for them, and love them, all the days of my life.'

'That's very noble, but what about you, Bri? What about you having happiness? Don't you want to be happy, inside yourself? Don't you want to feel the same happiness you're so determined to give to these two children?'

Briony shook her head in confusion.

'But don't you see, Tommy? I *will* find that happiness now. I'll find it through them. With them. Because of them. Even today, when I've buried my Eileen, I feel a certain happiness, because I have these boys. Can't you understand that?'

Tommy shook his head.

'No. Frankly, Briony, I can't.'

She watched him walk from the room. Then, sighing heavily, she turned back to the boys.

*

Tommy let himself out of Briony's house. Getting into his car, he drove away from her. Inside he was in turmoil, because that last conversation had proved, as if he had not already known, that with the advent of those children he had finally lost her for good. She had not had much to give him before. Now she would have even less.

He acknowledged, bitterly, that he was jealous of Eileen's boys, two little motherless boys. He was. Because today he had decided to take Briony back, and had found that she had even less need of him than before. It was ironic that after leaving her, after convincing himself he was better off without her, he had found out too late just how wrong he had been.

He felt a burning need to cry because he had just left behind the only woman he would ever care about, the only one he would ever want or need.

It was this knowledge that hurt him more than anything. Because he, himself, had broken the bond between them, and enjoyed himself while doing it. He had broken Briony's heart and all along had been setting himself up for more misery than he had dreamt possible.

Briony had her sisters and those children. Now he was the one left with nothing. Because he wanted nothing else, and so nothing else would do.

She probably didn't even realise he was gone.

St Vincent's church was once more packed out. The new priest, Father Tierney, looked over the sea of faces and smiled. It did his heart good to see so many people here, men as well as women. It was the christening of the Cavanagh boys, as they were being called already. The highlight of the christening was seeing the film star Jonathan la Billière stand as their godfather, with Kerry as godmother to Daniel and Bernadette to Dennis. As he poured the holy water over the boys' heads they both set up a wail that could be heard outside the church. Briony and Bernadette quietened the boys as Kerry sang. The church was hushed as her voice came out low and sweet:

> 'Swing low, sweet chariot, coming for
> to carry me home . . .'

Everyone stood in silence as she sang. More than a few people would remark on the strangeness of the song and the way she sang it. And more than a few would also remark later behind closed doors on the dark-haired little girl who had sat up bright-eyed and alert as she viewed the proceedings from Cissy Jackson's lap! She was darker than was natural, everyone tacitly agreed, but no one said it anywhere near the Cavanaghs.

Briony smiled at Jonathan and he grinned back. He was more than grateful to her for sorting out the business with Peter and Rupert. He had made a special journey back from America for this christening and the stir it had caused had been worth every mile of the journey. On that dreadful morning he had believed his whole career was over. When Briony, despite all her own troubles, had told him that it was sorted out, he had felt a deep, abiding thankfulness. He would do anything for her now. Anything.

Back at Briony's house there was plenty to eat and drink. All the remaining sisters, together with Molly, Jonathan and Mariah, were sitting in Briony's lounge chatting between themselves. Marcus came in with two bottles of expensive champagne.

'This was Jonathan's gift and I thought we'd open it now.'

Everyone took a glass and toasted the infants.

'To Danny Boy and my Boysie!' Briony's voice was filled with love.

'To the boys!'

Kerry sipped her drink and placed a crawling Liselle on the floor. Lissy, as she was now called by everyone, tried to pull herself up using Molly's skirt as an anchor.

Kerry smiled at her mother who strained to smile back. Liselle stood up uncertainly then dropped down on to her bottom with a thud. She set up a wail and Briony scooped her up off the floor and hugged her close.

'What's wrong then, Liselle Cavanagh? You'll be walking soon enough. Kerry, this child is so intelligent I don't know what to do with her! Look . . . It's as if she knows exactly what I'm saying.' She kissed Liselle's mouth and said, 'Have you been here before, madam?'

Liselle grabbed Briony's hair and pulled on it hard, laughing as Briony made a mock stern face.

Molly got up and walked away from the scene. No matter how often she saw the child, she still felt a deep dislike for her. The whole idea of the child's father and the fact that he had lain with her daughter disgusted her.

She smiled, though, as she looked at the twins. Now there were two boys to be proud of! Her grandsons, the light of her life. In them was held out the hope of greatness. She knew that Briony would see they got everything befitting two such handsome lads. Who knew what they might become?

Kerry watched the change in her mother as she bent over Eileen's boys and forced down the hurt she felt inside. Since the birth of the twins, Lissy had been left out in the cold. Oh, Briony still made a fuss of her, as did

Bernadette. But the boys were the real focal point. They were twins for a start, so that made them special, and they were white. Wholly white. She tried to keep these thoughts from invading her mind, but still they plagued her at all hours of the day and night.

She drained her glass in one swallow and went to get herself another. She had seen the looks today, outside the church. The peering looks at Lissy as Kerry had stood, head high, with her daughter in her arms. People guessed, she knew that, but Lissy was her true love. She worshipped her daughter even while she resented the feelings the child produced in her at times. She poured herself another drink.

More Dutch courage. She found she needed it more and more as Lissy was growing up.

Briony saw Kerry toss back another drink and made a mental note to have a word with her. She was drinking a lot lately. Her eyes strayed to Marcus and Bernie. Now there was a match made in heaven if ever she saw one. They'd be married before long. She smiled as she thought of it.

Molly was still cooing over the twins and Briony smiled again. It was six months since Eileen had been laid to rest and the boys were now two fat healthy babies. The hurt of bereavement had lessened with them in the house. Briony had opened the Manor, which was going great guns, and now she smiled at Mariah as she thought how lucky she was. She had her health and she had money, plenty of it, and was making more by the day. She also had two little boys to care for, and if at times like this she thought of another little boy, it was now a bitter-sweet remembering. Danny Boy and Boysie had done a lot to assuage her guilt and hurt. But one day she would have Ben too, she was determined on that. One day he would know who she was.

Cissy came into the room, flushed and excited. 'The *Barking and Dagenham Post*'s outside. They want a picture for the paper!'

Briony laughed as they all put on their hats and coats and trooped outside to her front garden.

The photographer lined them all up, with Briony in the centre, the two boys asleep in her arms. Her face was almost obscured by a large-brimmed hat. Beside her stood her mother on one side, and Jonathan, the real reason for the photograph, on the other. The rest of the family, including Mrs Horlock and Cissy, gathered around them. Kerry, also a celebrity, stood smiling while trying to hold a struggling Lissy in her arms as the flash went off with a loud crash followed by a blinding light.

The picture was the talk of Barking for a long time, and Briony kept a framed copy on her mantelpiece for the rest of her life. Every time she looked at it she would smile sadly. The only person missing was Eileen.

Briony laughed and joked through the rest of the day. Late in the evening, though, as she sat with Jonathan, she heard the twins cry. Leaping from her seat, she bolted from the room, leaving Jonathan staring after her and Bernadette and Marcus laughing.

The pattern was already set. The twins called, and Briony came running.

[illegible] the room flushed and excited. [illegible] and [illegible] Party Outside. They went [illegible] return for the paper.

[illegible] laughed [illegible] and [illegible].

The photographed of them all [illegible] in the [illegible]. [illegible]

[illegible]

[illegible]

[illegible]

Book Three

Out of the crooked timber of humanity no straight thing can ever be made.

– Immanuel Kant, 1724–1804

He that maketh haste to be rich shall not be innocent.

– Proverbs, 28:20

Believe me! The secret of reaping the greatest fruitfulness and the greatest enjoyment from life is to live dangerously!

– Friedrich Nietzsche, 1844–1900

Chapter Thirty-Three

1947

'I swear to you, Boysie, I ain't done nothing! Danny, Danny Boy, tell him for Christ's sake!'

Dickie Lawson watched as two identical faces peered at him through the gloom.

'You're a liar, Lawson. You tucked us up and we ain't having it.'

Boysie grabbed him around the throat with one large fist. Tiny Dickie Lawson looked at him with terrified eyes.

'Now I'm going to hit you, see, hit you so hard even your grandchildren will have an headache.'

Daniel stood by while Boysie began pummelling Lawson with his fists. As the man dropped to the floor, Daniel kicked him once in the stomach.

The twins looked at one another and smiled. Then, checking their suits to make sure they were still in pristine condition, walked out of the alleyway and along the Barking Road.

'Little ponce he is! I tell you now, Danny, he better

have my winnings by the end of the week or I'll muller him. Mind you, after tonight I think he'll be paying us out all right. Quick smart.'

Boysie looked around him as he walked, taking in everything and anything. Convinced that people were looking at him, admiring him. He had an air of arrogance that tended to draw people's attention. Daniel on the other hand kept his eyes straight ahead. Of the two boys he was the quieter, the one who did the thinking, the one who was the planner. Unlike Boysie, who lost his temper in an instant and was just as quick to forget a fight, Daniel was unforgiving. He had to have a reason to resort to violence but when he did, he never forgave, ever.

They got into their car in Marlborough Road and made their way towards Manor Park where they lived.

Barking and Dagenham were still showing the signs of the war in great empty spaces filled with rubble. Dirty children were playing where terraced houses had once stood. The Becontree Estate was underway, new homes, shops and new churches to go up upon the rubble and ashes of the past. The spirit of the people, though hungry, homeless and drained by a war that left many of them without men or a place to call their home, was as it always had been. They'd won, and if the price they had paid was high, it was for King and country – though the wags said for a King they hardly saw and for a country that was going to the dogs!

It was the joke of London when Buckingham Palace was bombed and the King said he now felt like a Londoner. The silly old bugger should have been in the East End during the blitz, stepping across gaping holes in the road with electricity cables and gas mains open to the elements; he should have heard the screaming of the women and children as fires raged and people tried frantically to find relatives and even family pets. Suddenly even a scabby old cat was important.

Still, it was over now, the building had begun and a new breed of youth was emerging. The wide boy arrived in 1945 and was to become a role model for the children growing up. The country had undergone a change, a big change. Old values were slowly disappearing, the King and Queen were no longer just to be obeyed and worshipped from afar, the young ones wanted none of what their parents had endured. There was more work and money to be spent.

Women who had never been outside the home before had been earning good money in the war, and had enjoyed their independence. Now the ones with husbands back home were adjusting once more to being 'the wife', or 'her indoors', and the widows were keeping their heads above water as best they could. It was a sad woman who didn't have a full belly once her husband was demobbed. Children were being born left, right and centre, the new generation that was to change the world. Or so they thought.

As for Danny and Boysie, they had lived through the Blitz, seen bodies dug out of mounds of steaming rubble, and witnessed all the horrors of the war from the home front. They were changed as a result. Like many young men they had an outlook on life that shocked the older generation.

It was survival of the fittest now. That was the law of the streets where Boysie and Danny were about to make their mark.

As the twins drove home they chatted.

'Shall we go up the club later? After the bit of business.'

Danny nodded as he drove. 'If you like, Boysie. We've

got to see The Aunt beforehand, though. I'll drop round Auntie Bernie's so we can get spruced up first.'

'I can't wait for tonight. It's like a dream come true, ain't it? I'm so excited inside.'

Boysie's euphoria made Daniel laugh.

'Just remember, after tonight, there's no going back.'

Boysie shrugged. 'I don't want to go back, I can't wait to get started.'

Bernadette and Marcus lived two doors down from Briony in Manor Park. The road they lived in was tree-lined and contained fifteen houses, all large and rambling, all with half an acre of gardens, and all looking very well kept. Bernadette's still had the leaded lights from the original windows and the house was gabled. She lived there with Marcus and their two young daughters, Rebecca and Delia. The names were hated by the rest of the family, but as far as Bernie was concerned, they were classy. Bernie, as the years went on, had become obsessed with being classy. She opened the door to the boys herself and grinned at them widely.

'Hello, me ducks. In you come. The bathroom's free!'

Boysie grinned back at her. She was a bit of all right was Auntie Bernie. Both boys went up for a quick wash and brush-up and came downstairs to a large mug of tea.

Becky and Delia sat on the floor in front of the fire and gazed up longingly at the two big men in their front room.

Every time Bernie clapped eyes on her nephews, she felt an overwhelming feeling of love and pride. They were so handsome, and so huge! Both stood tall at six foot, both were well built. They had the same blue eyes, the same thick eyebrows, and the same brown-red hair. Boysie had a thinner face than Daniel though it was only noticeable to people who knew them exceptionally well.

In turn the two boys loved their aunts to distraction. Briony was referred to as 'The Aunt', though they called her Mum when they were with her. Bernie was next best; living so near and doting on them, it was inevitable. Then came Auntie Kerry, the singer, the famous one of the family who lived in Knightsbridge with their cousin Liselle. Then there was Auntie Rosie, or 'poor Auntie Rosie' as she was known, whom the boys had always adored uncritically. Their granny, Granny Moll, also worshipped them. In short, they felt quite at home in a family of women.

Nothing they did could ever faze 'The Aunt'; everything just washed over her. Even when they'd set fire to the house in Barking by accident, she'd eventually laughed it off as a boyish prank. When the house had been bombed in the Blitz she'd laughed about that too, moving them all to Manor Park without any fuss. The boys had missed being called up by months, their Auntie Briony keeping them from going with a mixture of backhanders and chats with influential friends. Now they were just reaching manhood, voting age, the time to strike out on their own, and were still inexorably tied to 'The Aunt', though neither realised this fact.

They always dropped in on their Auntie Bernie to clean up properly before they went home. It had always been that way. The Aunt only ever saw them looking perfect. Even as little boys they had done it. Filthy rotten, they'd drop in on Bernie and she would spruce them up. It was their mark of respect for the woman who had brought them up and whom they loved wholeheartedly.

The clock chimed six and of one mind they rose to leave. 'Thanks for the tea, Auntie Bernie.'

Bernadette kissed them both. Delia, the younger cousin

at eight, held her arms up for a kiss and Boysie threw himself on the carpet, holding his leg.

'Oh . . . Oh! Help me, I got a bone in me leg, maybe two!'

Bernadette, Delia and Rebecca laughed at his antics. Bernie dragged him up.

'You are a case, Boysie. Here, let me brush your coat down.' Out in the hallway she took a clothes brush from a hook by the coatstand and brushed at his coat. Smoothing the shoulders with her hands, she said, 'There you go, son. All ready for Briony.'

The two boys kissed her on her cheek. 'Thanks, Auntie Bernie. See you tomorrow.'

Leaving their car in her drive they walked to their own house.

Briony was writing some letters when she heard the front door open. As always, she felt a rush of pleasure at the thought the boys were once more in the house.

'Hello, boys. What's to do?' she greeted them.

She had asked them this same question every day of their lives from young babies and somehow they expected it, welcomed it, and always answered in the same way.

'We're doing all right.'

Briony rolled her eyes in mock annoyance. ' "We're doin' all right"? Is that what that bleeding poncey school was costing me the national debt for!'

Both boys grinned sheepishly.

'Come here and give me a big kiss.'

Standing, she hugged them, looking even smaller between the two big hulking men.

'You in for dinner?'

'Yeah. Then we're off to a club.'

'Right then, I'll let Cissy know. Pop in on old Mrs H, will you? She loves seeing you both.'

As they left the room she smiled to herself and went back to her letters again. The boys were home, the house was alive and everything was well once more.

Mrs Horlock, now in her eighties, was bedridden. She had shrunk till all that was left was a frail old body and a wispily covered skull. Her teeth were long gone and she sucked up stews, broths, and bread and milk noisily. Her mind, though, was still as sharp as a knife. As the two boys entered her bedroom she treated them to a gummy smile and patted her bed.

'Hello, you pair of 'andsome little gits! Come and see your old Auntie H!'

They sat either side of her on the bed and took a thin hand each.

'Hello, Auntie H. How you feeling?'

'With me bleeding hands as always! What you two been up to then? Been fighting?'

'Her shrewd eyes scanned the two of them and they smiled. 'Got me winnings have you?'

'The end of the week.' Boysie's voice was tight.

'That scut Lawson's tucked you up, ain't he? Well, listen to me. When people tuck you up and get away with it, it's like they won, see?'

'I gave him a dig. If he ain't got the brass at the end of the week, I'll slaughter him.' Boysie's voice was matter-of-fact.

'Good boy. Now there's another fight this week in Bethnal Green. I want you to put a tenner on for me. It's Jimmy Sands and Michael Derry. Put a tenner on Derry for me, he'll piss it.'

Daniel laughed.

'I'll see Tommy Lane about putting the bet on for you. Might have a monkey on him meself. Do you want us to get you a drop of the hard, Auntie H?'

The old woman cackled. 'What do you think? 'Course I do. You off out with the birds tonight, I suppose?'

'Something like that.'

'Oh, Danny Boy, the girls who get you two will be lucky!'

They kissed her and made their farewells.

Cissy was big. Over the years weight had piled on her. She now ran the house in between carrying on relationships with different men, from American airmen of indeterminate age to the coal man who had a wife and thirteen children. She was as ugly as the day was long but her ample breasts and cheery manner helped enormously, coupled with the fact she wasn't too fussy. She would say to Briony: 'If they've got their own teeth and a bit of hair, that's good enough for me.'

To which Briony always replied. 'Cissy, they only have to be breathing to be good enough for you!'

This reply always sent Cissy into gales of laughter. She said the blackout was the best thing that had ever happened to her and Briony was inclined to agree. Like a lot of unmarried women, and a good few married ones, she had had what was termed 'a good war'.

Tonight the boys sat down to a large dinner. They started with a nice slice of home-made chicken liver pâté with hot toast. Then they devoured a large roast chicken and finished off with a slice of apple pie. They had never known anything about shortages. In Briony's house there was always plenty of butter, milk, eggs and meat, and the boys never questioned this, just took it all as their due.

Both of them held their stomachs with their hands and declared at exactly the same time, 'That was handsome, Cis.'

Cissy swelled with pride, holding back an urge to take a bite out of them.

Briony laughed.

'You two can certainly eat! Cissy, love, bring the coffee through, and a cup for yourself.'

Cissy did as she was told and they all sat chatting for a while. Both boys lit up cigarettes and Briony watched them through half-closed eyes.

'What's this I hear about you two being over Bethnal Green way, in a drinking club?' She had chosen her moment carefully and was gratified to see them start.

'Oh, I hear everything, my loves. Now listen to me. I give you a lot of freedom, but take this bit of advice. You only play with the big boys when you're big enough to win. You get my drift?'

Both boys nodded and Briony smiled at them. Relaxed now, they smiled back. Daniel and Boysie looked at one another and raised their eyebrows. They were being given permission and they both knew this.

'Listen, Mum, we want to start up our own business but we aren't really sure yet in what way. We went to the club in Bethnal Green just to feel the place out like. We're going to another tonight in Canning Town. There's a lot of money to be made with these clubs. People want a bit of life after the war. *We* want a bit of life, don't we, Boysie?'

'Too right we do!'

'Well, just as long as you know what you're doing. If you need anything, you only have to ask.'

They each grasped one of her hands.

'We know that, Mum.'

Briony nodded but her heart ached. Here they were surrounded by people who loved them. She corrected herself, women who loved them. They had been fawned over and petted since birth. Briony knew that it was a harsh world out there and wanted to protect them from it. She knew they were spoilt rotten, she knew that they had been given more than was good for them, but they were fine boys nonetheless. A bit wild at times, she had had the police round on more than one occasion. But somehow she had always got them out of it, and knew she always would. They had become her life and the habit of loving them would have been too hard to break, even if she'd wanted to.

'I set the plans for Berwick Manor in motion tomorrow. You want to see the state of it! Jesus, they wanted it for a hospital. Well, all I can say is they must have had sick pigs in there, it's like a bleeding shithouse! Still, we all had to do our bit for the war, I suppose. There's plenty of work ahead if I can get the wood. Luckily I have a friend who can get me all I want.'

'At the right price?' Boysie's voice was jocular.

'Of course. You don't have a dog . . .'

Both boys interrupted her.

'. . . and bark yourself!'

Cissy shook her head. 'As clever as a bag of monkeys, these two, Bri. They'll go far.'

Briony laughed and said, 'That's what worries me!'

Boysie stood up. 'We'll never leave you, Mum.'

'Nah, we know when we're well off!'

The place the boys were going to in Canning Town was a snooker hall. It was tucked away in a little turning just down from The Bridge House pub. They had dressed carefully for their evening out and both wore black suits, white shirts and black ties. Their hair was Brylcreemed back and they wore light beige camel-hair coats.

The October wind was biting as they slipped through the little doorway and entered the snooker club. It was nearly empty, as they knew it would be, and walking up to the tiny bar they ordered large whiskies. The man behind the bar surveyed them warily. He knew who they were all right, the Cavanagh twins. This was the first time he had ever seen them in his establishment and it worried him. Wherever the Cavanaghs went, trouble followed.

They were a pair of little fuckers in his opinion, but what could he do? Their aunt was Briony Cavanagh.

The twins drank their Scotch and looked around them. The place was dim. Four men were playing a desultory game of snooker, watching the boys surreptitiously as they chalked their cues. Eyeing one another with unspoken questions.

At just after eight-thirty three more men walked in. The proprietor smiled at them eagerly but the snooker players kept their distance. Everyone including the twins knew who these men were. The McNees were well known in Canning Town, all over Silvertown for that matter. They were three lunatics who took protection money from little clubs such as this and played the heavy for the bigger villains who couldn't be bothered to do their own dirty work. The eldest, Seamus McNee, was hoping to become the torturer for the Rileys eventually. It was his only aim in life. They clocked the twins immediately and nodded in their direction. The twins nodded back, smiling cheerfully.

'Fancy a drink, Seamus?' Boysie's voice was loud and jocular. 'Another round here, mate, and whatever the McNees want.'

The proprietor heaved a sigh of relief. He had been worried that there was going to be trouble with them all.

He set about pouring two large Scotches and three pints of Guinness with whisky chasers, the McNees' trademark.

'We'll have a drink with you.' Seamus sounded like he was doing them a favour. He saw Boysie's face harden and clicked his fingers at the owner.

'Ain't you got something for us?' He held out a large meaty paw.

'Of course I have, Mr McNee, I ain't never let you down, have I?' His voice was nervous. The feeling of foreboding was back. Declan and Porrick McNee smiled at the twins in a friendly manner and Seamus rolled his eyes.

'All right, Declan? How's it going, mate?' Daniel's voice was low.

'Oh, not too bad. What one are you? I always get you two mixed up.'

Boysie laughed as he watched the owner hand over a roll of cash to Seamus.

'That's because you're as thick as fucking shit.'

Seamus turned to face them, dropping the money into a pool of beer on the bar.

'What did you say?' His voice was outraged.

The twins laughed together.

'What, you deaf as well as stupid?'

Seamus stood erect, his face growing red with temper. As he drew back his fist the twins looked at one another and stepped away from him, then together they put their hands inside their overcoats and took out sawn-off shotguns. The four men playing snooker all dropped to the floor.

Boysie took the money off the bar and laughed as he put it in his pocket.

Then he pointed the gun at Seamus McNee's legs and pulled the trigger. The explosion as the gun went off shook the small club. The owner crossed himself before running out through the back of the bar and locking himself in the toilet. Declan and Porrick looked at their brother writhing on the floor in agony as if they had never in their life seen him before. Boysie and Danny laughed out loud.

'Get your brother to the hospital, lads. I think his little legs is hurting him.' Then they tossed back their drinks and walked towards the door.

Daniel stopped and looked back. 'Oh, by the way, tell Seamus we'll be picking up all your rents in future, OK? And if he causes any more bother, the next shot goes right into his head. Tara.'

Porrick, never noted for his brains at the best of times, waved and said tara back.

Outside, the twins laughed and joked with each other all the way to the car. They were high on adrenaline, both feeling the rush of pure pleasure that their violent act had produced.

The story hit the streets within hours.

The Cavanagh twins were well and truly on their way.

Briony was with Mariah, sorting out how best to get the Manor back up and running. It had always been their most lucrative house, and now the war was over and everyone was getting on with their lives, they wanted to get it back in business. Mariah had been all for refusing to let it be used as a hospital but Briony had stood firm. It was the least they could do for the war effort. She had been so patriotic that everyone had been amazed. Once the Blitz started Briony had arranged for a soup kitchen, and for clothing and soap to be supplied to bombed-out people. She had doled out money, taken people in until they found alternative shelter, and had won the hearts of even the most hardened charity worker. And if she had also been the instigator of a thriving black market, she felt that her efforts to help far outweighed any of the shady things she'd done. Now all she wanted was to get on with her old business.

The call came for her at ten minutes past ten. Mariah handed over the phone while Briony was laughing about something. Her face sobered up almost immediately and Mariah watched in amazement as she had slammed down the phone and poured herself a large Napoleon brandy.

'I'll kill those two little fuckers! By Christ, I'll kill them!'

Mariah looked at her friend and shook her head.

Briony was still a very good-looking woman even though she was well into her forties. Her figure was slim, and her face barely lined. The new fashions suited her and her spectacular hair was worn in a chic French pleat. It was only her voice that betrayed her. Until she opened her mouth, people always assumed she was from the upper classes.

'You'll never guess what the twins done tonight?'

'What?' Mariah's voice was shocked. Briony never spoke about the twins like this. Usually she spoke of them as a mixture of the Pope and God himself.

'They only shot bleeding Seamus McNee in the legs. In a snooker hall in Canning bloody Town. The stupid little gits! Wait till I get my hands on them. It's all over Silvertown so you can bet it'll be everywhere in the morning. And as for the Rileys, well, I just heard they're not too happy about it. The McNees worked for them.'

'Oh, for Gawd's sake!'

Briony swallowed the burning liquid and shrugged.

'Oh, sod the Rileys, they don't bleeding well scare me. It's the audacity of those two little sods. They sat in that house tonight like butter wouldn't melt! They must have been planning this . . . You wait till I get my hands on them.'

Mariah took a deep breath and spoke.

'Listen, Bri, me and you go back a long way, girl. Let me tell you something now. Those two boys are out of control. Look at last year when they had that fight at the fair in Victoria Park. They crippled that bloke, remember? Even as little kids they had a violent streak. This is the culmination of it. You've got to put your foot down once and for all. Stop bloody well getting them off the hook.'

Briony closed her eyes till they were slits and looked at the big woman in front of her. Mariah bleached her hair and still wore dresses that were too tight; she plastered the make-up on these days but she looked her age: sixty-two. It suddenly occurred to Briony that out of everyone she knew, Mariah had never been one to sing the boys' praises. She had always pointed out their shortcomings. Even though at heart Briony knew that what her friend said was true, hearing her pulling her boys to pieces went against the grain.

'So that's your opinion, is it?'

Mariah shrugged. 'For what it's worth. It's about time someone told you the truth of it. You and your family treat them like visiting royalty. Well, look where it's got them. They've kneecapped a known villain in a dirty snooker club. I bet you're really pleased about their good education now, ain't you! And another thing while we're about it . . .'

Briony held her hand up to stem the flow.

'I think I've heard enough from you for one night,

Mariah. I never realised before that you didn't like my boys. But I think I get the picture now, thank you very much.'

She started to pull on her fox fur coat and Mariah grabbed her arm.

'I love those boys, Briony, but unlike you I can see their faults. They play you, girl. They get all spruced up round Bernie's before they darken your door, then they sit and smile – and I tell you now, girl, they're taking the bleeding piss! Oh, I don't dispute they love you. No . . . they worship you. But all the same, they know what you want from them and they deliver it. This is the proof of it. You told me tonight that they were thinking of getting a little business. You was pleased as bloody punch. Finally settling themselves, you said. And what is this business? Collecting fucking rents! It's villainy they want, girl. They want to be like the Rileys. Like . . .'

Briony pushed Mariah in her ample breasts, shouting, 'Go on, say it! They want to be like *me* . . . me and you. Because you're in all this up to your bloody neck too!'

'I know I am, but unlike your bloody boys, me and you don't heavy people. We don't shoot stupid bloody thugs in dingy little clubs. Can't you see that if you don't put a stop to their gallop, they'll end up dead or locked up?'

Even though Briony secretly agreed with everything Mariah said, her deep-seated loyalty to her family got the upper hand.

'They're my boys and I'll deal with them.'

'Well, you do as you see fit. But don't say I didn't try and warn you!'

Briony opened the door and snarled back, 'Don't worry, I won't.'

Slamming the door behind her she stormed out of

Mariah's house. She was even more annoyed with the twins now because on top of everything else they'd caused her to row with her best friend. All the way home in her car, she had a pain in her chest.

It was true what people said: the truth hurt. It hurt a lot.

Danny and Boysie came in at two-thirty. After the snooker club they had gone to The Two Puddings in Stratford and had a quiet drink. Watching the Rileys' counterparts, the Moneys.

Michael Money was the leader and Boysie and Danny had made a conscious effort to ingratiate themselves with him. He was unaware that he was next on their list. Then at ten-thirty they had gone to a drinking club in Frith Street owned by Tommy Lane. There they had gradually come down from their earlier euphoria. As they walked in at the front door of their aunt's house, the drawing-room door opened and Briony stood there waiting for them.

'Well, well, well, if it ain't Frank and Jesse James!'

Despite themselves they smiled. Only their Aunt Briony would talk to them like that.

'Get in here, you two. Now!'

They walked into the drawing room behind her. Both stood in front of the blazing fire and looked at her.

Even in her rage she was overcome by the sheer power and magnetic quality of the two men in front of her. The two viciously handsome faces were turned towards her. The boys' eyes and bodies were fiercely alert.

'I want to know what happened tonight in Silvertown.'

'I think you already know, Mum.' The way Boysie called her 'Mum' tugged at Briony's heart. They were her boys, her big boys now. Her Achilles heel.

'I know enough to realise you two must be off your fucking rockers!' Her voice filled the room. 'Shooting people in front of witnesses. Carrying sawn-off shotguns. What next? You going to go in Scotland Yard and rob their payroll? You must be stupid. You *are* stupid. The Rileys will come after you hammer and tongs. Seamus was to be their next torturer, they worked for the Rileys, all the McNees, and what do you do? You go and shoot them. Jesus wept.'

Boysie and Daniel looked at the little woman in front of them.

'We ain't scared of the Rileys, or the McNees, or the Moneys. We know what we're doing, Mum, so just calm yourself down. Gordon Bennet, anyone would think we'd done something really wrong!'

Daniel's voice was jocular and suddenly Briony saw them both as plain as day. They'd always been the same, even as children. If they wanted something, they asked, then they asked again more pointedly, and finally they demanded it. She had always seen that they got what they wanted. She'd wanted to make up to them for not having Eileen, not having a father. She'd wanted her boys to have everything. Now the upshot of all this was standing in front of her. They wanted what the Rileys and the McNees and the Moneys had, and they would get it, she had no doubts about that at all. They'd get it.

They walked towards her and kissed her, as they always did, one on each cheek, and Briony was undone. Nothing she could say now would do any good. She had to retreat or she had to fight with them, and she wouldn't fight with them. She couldn't because then she knew they'd leave her, and if they left her she'd have nothing. Nothing at all. She had to go along with them, had to accept it. Deep inside herself, though she wasn't aware of it, she was secretly proud of them. They wanted a life of villainy and, being her boys, had started at the top. At the pinnacle. If they took the Rileys out of the game they were set up for life.

'Oh, boys. You do worry me. What can I do to help you with the Rileys? Do you want me to smooth it over?'

Boysie laughed.

'The Rileys don't trash you, do they?'

Briony shook her head. 'No. Not really.'

'Well, they don't trash us either. Me and Danny Boy know what we want from life.' He walked to the window and pulled back the heavy velvet curtains.

'There's a big old world out there, Mum, and me and him, we're gonna be the kings of it. Ain't that right, Danny?'

He nodded.

'We want to make our mark in our own way. Without you, Mum. We're men now, and we're men who know what we want. And nothing and no one's gonna stop us.'

Briony knew it was a threat and finally saw what Mariah meant. They were saying: 'We'll do it with you. Here in this house. Or we'll leave and do it on our own.'

Briony went to them both and hugged them to her.

'It's also a dangerous world out there, full of people like the Rileys and the McNees and the Moneys. Don't you ever forget that, boys.'

They smiled at her then, two identical smiles with identical white teeth.

'We won't.' It was spoken in unison and Briony nodded at them. The course was set.

Chapter Thirty-Four

'Come on, Mum, get up! It's after ten.'

Liselle pulled the covers back from her mother's body and sighed.

'Please, Mum, you're recording at eleven-thirty.'

'Leave me alone, Liselle, I'm tired.'

Kerry's emaciated body was curled in a ball. Liselle put her arm under her mother's head and pulled her forcibly to a sitting position. Then, half dragging and half carrying her, she pulled her from the bed, across the bedroom and into the shower. Kerry felt the cold water hitting her body and began to gasp for breath. Liselle laughed.

'That'll teach you to tie one on! I'm getting sick and tired of having to do this. Now, when you're awake come down and have something to eat and a cup of coffee. I'll drive you to the studios.'

Kerry stuck two fingers up at her daughter's retreating back and turned on the hot water. Five minutes later she emerged from the shower and wrapped herself in a towel. Then, going back into her bedroom, she opened the dressing-table drawer and took out a bottle of pills. She swallowed five without the aid of water and slipped on a dressing gown. Downstairs her daughter was waiting for her.

'You look like you've been done and left!'

Kerry smiled. 'I feel like it, love. Where's me coffee?'

She poured out the coffee and they drank in silence. Liselle studied her mother. Kerry was working late in the clubs singing, she was cutting an album, and she was also taking far too many pills. What really annoyed Liselle was that her mother looked so bloody good on her way of life. Anyone else would have been burnt out, looked terrible, but not Kerry Cavanagh. She seemed to thrive on work, work and more work. Even during the war she'd travelled all over the world singing to the troops and had come back raring to go. It was the pills that bothered Liselle, those and the vodka.

At twenty-one she was her mother's full-time minder. She wasn't sure exactly when this had come about, but it had. It seemed to Liselle that she had spent her life looking after her mother instead of the other way round. She even signed all the cheques these days because her mother was either unavailable or stoned out of her brain. Now Liselle froze off reporters, she confirmed Kerry's singing dates, checked that her clothes were all looked after, that her mother remembered to eat, hid as much drink as she could, and all in all made sure her mother was presentable for her public engagements. It was getting harder by the day. As Kerry's eyes began to glaze again she sighed mentally. At least she could sing OK on the pills. It was when she had had the drink that it got difficult, though her mother's reputation was well known in the business.

'Come on, Mum, eat a bit of scrambled egg.'

Kerry made a face.

'I wouldn't eat that crap if you paid me! I've had a bit of toast, that'll do.'

'Well, go and get dressed then, we've got to go in a minute.'

Kerry stood up.

'You're a right old bossy boots, Liselle, do you know that?' It was said in a jocular manner but it hurt Liselle nonetheless.

'Someone's got to get you sorted out. If it was left to you . . .'

Kerry sobered up immediately. 'I know. I know, love.'

Liselle watched her mother walk from the room and wished she could bite her tongue off. Her mum was a difficult charge, she really was. But Liselle loved her.

Going out to the hallway she looked in the big mirror by the phone. The face that stared back at her had deep circles under the eyes and her full lips were painted with a deep red lipstick. Her deep brown eyes were heavily made up and her thick blue-black hair pulled up on to her head. She often wondered how she had got so dark, her mother would never tell her about her father, only that she had loved him very much and he had left her. She'd daydreamed as a child that he was a Spaniard or an Italian. Her granny always said they had Basque blood in the family, maybe it had come from there? It was strange not to know your beginnings and lately it had bothered her very much. But it was pointless asking her mother or her aunts, they all clammed up as soon as it was mentioned.

She heard her mother's footsteps on the stairs and picked up the keys to the car. It would all come out in the wash as her granny always said when gossiping about someone when she didn't know the full story. It would all come out in the wash. Smiling at her mother they left the house.

Kenny Riley was so annoyed his face was coming out in red blotches. His breathing was painful and his fists ached from clenching them. He looked at his right-hand man, Michael Money, and sighed.

'I want those Cavanaghs given a lesson they'll never forget, do you get my drift? I think they're a pair of little piss-takers who need to be taught a few manners!'

Michael Money nodded. He was still reeling from the shock of the shooting himself. The fact that the twins had turned up at the pub after and had chatted to him as if nothing had happened scared him. Scared him very much. Boysie was a nutter, a temper merchant, but Danny now, he was a different ball game. He was cute, he was clever, and by Christ if he was the brains behind the two, then they'd all better watch their backs. He didn't say this to Kenny Riley though, he knew when to keep his peace. At the moment Kenny was on a short fuse and anyone who lit the match under it was guaranteed a long stay in the Mile End Hospital.

'What about their aunt, Kenny? She ain't exactly Snow White.'

Kenny clenched his teeth and said sarcastically in a high voice: 'Oh, are we frightened of women as well as children now then? Shall I run home and get me old Mum to sort it all out for me? Eh? Shall I, Micky? Or how about me and you make some jam sandwiches and go for a nice picnic in Victoria Park, and when we come back all the naughty boys might be indoors having a bath and eating their tea! Bollocks to Briony Cavanagh! Bollocks to all the Cavanaghs! Go out and get them and bring them here to me. I have a few words to say to them that might just frighten the little fuckers enough to make them leave me and mine alone.'

Michael Money nodded his head furiously and backed out of the room. As he looked around the crowded offices of Riley and Co. in Bethnal Green, at men, some too old to be villains really, some far too young, at the caches of guns and other paraphernalia garnered over the years, he felt a feeling of foreboding. Young the Cavanagh twins were, but frightened? Not a chance. Especially not Boysie. Boysie was a bona fide nutter, that was well known. Now he had the task, the frightening task, of telling them that Kenneth Riley Esquire wanted to see them. He didn't know at that time who he was the more scared of, the Rileys or the Cavanaghs.

He soon found out.

Boysie and Danny had been up since seven. They had as usual eaten a large breakfast cooked by a very subdued Cissy who had heard the news and was torn between a natural hatred of violence and shock at thinking her twins were even capable of it. But as the meal had worn on their usual bantering had won her over and she consoled herself with the fact that the boys must have been driven to such a desperate act. Finally, by the time she had washed up their plates and made them another pot of tea, the McNees were the undisputed villains of the piece in her mind.

By eight-thirty Bernadette and Granny Moll were also at the house with Auntie Rosie in tow.

Molly, to everyone's shock, was absolutely made up over what the boys had done. Briony sat and listened in amazement as her mother hugged them and kissed them and told them they were good sensible boys who knew what they wanted and went after it. Her mother's easy acceptance of it all shocked Briony and Bernie to the core. Watching the boys' performance, and Briony was honest enough to admit it *was* a performance, she felt a grudging respect for them even though they had shot a man. Mariah was exactly right in what she had said: they did play her and their aunts and their granny. The twins were what you wanted them to be, even when you knew darned well they weren't! They still kept up the illusion of being her boys, her good boys.

Only the boys were now men, dangerous men, and the worst part of it all was that she still loved them with every ounce of her being. No matter what they did.

Rosalee was sitting on a chair and Boysie was helping her drink her tea. The gentleness of him as he wiped her chin with his clean white handkerchief and kissed her wet lips made Briony's heart ring with love. Danny brought her another cushion and placed it at the small of her back, making sure she was comfortable.

Molly watched them with Rosalee and felt her heart swell with pride. These were men to be proud of – unlike her husband who had allowed life to get the better of him, who had sold his daughters off for the price of a drink and a good meal, these two here would always look after their own. The women who got them wouldn't scratch in the dirt for a living, wouldn't have to rifle through pockets in the dark, feared of waking the drunken tyrant in the bed beside her, to salvage a few shillings of their wages. Oh, no. These were men who'd bedeck their women in finery, would provide for their children, and love and respect their women. After all, weren't they brought up by a houseful of women? Even Briony, the bastard of hell as

Molly sometimes still thought of her, had made sure the boys respected women and had given them an insight and knowledge into women's lives.

Oh, they were good boys, good men, and if they shot the legs off that scut McNee, who really cared? He was a dirty torturer, could do things with a pair of pliers that would make the Borgias sick to their stomachs. Now her boys would become the Barons of the East End and the streets would be safe and she could carry on holding up her head with pride.

The twins, for their part, accepted their granny's adulation as they had always done: with wide smiles and plenty of hugs. Briony, watching, was impressed in spite of herself. Eileen's boys would go far all right.

It was just a case of whether they went too far.

Kenny Riley was waiting for Michael Money to arrive back with the twins. All day he had been thinking about what they had had the temerity to do. As he had looked around him at his crew, as he thought of the main men who worked for him, the earlier rage had worn off slightly and he was suddenly left wondering if maybe the Cavanaghs would indeed become a force to be reckoned with. With hindsight he remembered they were closely linked to Tommy Lane, onetime Baron and an old favourite of their aunt's. Tommy, still a bachelor for all his womanising, was not a fool, and the boys would get plenty of support there. Also there was Marcus Dowling who worked for Briony and was a hard man himself. Briony Cavanagh was a hard case too. It was said years before that she was in on the disappearance and murder of Willy Bolger, Ronnie Olds and one of his minders. She and Mariah Jurgens were both shrewd enough to woo the right people, and they not only courted villains like Tommy Lane but also befriended high court judges and members of parliament, to name but a few.

By lunchtime he was beginning to sweat and regretting his earlier impulsive behaviour. He should have had the twins gunned down and then made his peace with the families. That was the usual way of the East End. Once they were dead there was nothing anyone could do. The McNee brothers wanted vengeance, his own brothers wanted vengeance, he wanted vengeance. But it was vengeance with a bitter taste. He had seen the worry in Michael Money's face and Michael wasn't easily scared.

Neither was he, for that matter, but the motley crew outside, much depleted by the war, seemed to him all of a sudden like a Darby and Joan club. Old lags and young tearaways were all he had now. Fuck the war! It had been hard in that department. Some of the best minders had joined up and died, while less patriotic counterparts like himself had gone on the trot and sat the fighting out from pub basements and other such places, building an empire that was now there for the taking by people like the Cavanagh twins.

He lit himself a Lucky Strike and pulled on it deeply. Life was a bastard sometimes, it really was.

Michael had tracked the twins down to their aunt's house and sat just down the road from it in his Ford Deluxe station wagon, waiting for them to emerge. He loved Manor Park, it was a very desirable area. He approved of Briony Cavanagh's house, which must be worth all of twenty thousand pounds. In fact, this was the sort of life he thought he could get used to.

Michael Money was clever and he knew it. He had had

no formal education to speak of, but he'd had the education of the pavements and the streets, which to his mind was all he needed. He was debating whether to make an alliance with the Cavanaghs and help wipe out the Rileys when the twins pulled out of the driveway in an Aston Martin.

Turning on his engine he decided to follow them, until he plucked up the courage to put his money where his mouth was and make a decision on whether to try and take them to Kenny or try and do a deal. He realised almost immediately they were going to Bethnal Green.

Boysie was humming in the car, enjoying the ease with which they travelled. They passed a police car and Boysie, being Boysie, waved at the occupants.

'How do you think The Aunt took last night, Boysie?' Danny's voice was worried.

'All right. She's a game old bird, she knows the score.'

Danny turned a corner and looked over his shoulder. 'We're being followed by Michael Money in his stupid fucking car with the wood all over it.' His voice was disgusted.

'Let him follow, he'll know the score soon enough. They all will, The Aunt included. Don't worry about her, Danny. She's shrewd and she's crooked, like us. She'll come round once today's over and all this is finished once and for all.'

Danny carried on driving while Boysie made sure he had everything they needed for the final part of their exercise.

Briony went to the house in Hyde Park where she knew she would find Mariah. As she walked into the offices behind the main part of the house, Mariah raised her head and the two women locked eyes.

'Hello, Mariah. I've ordered us coffee.' Briony's voice was normal. It was her way of saying sorry and Mariah knew this.

'Great, I could do with a cup. We had a good night last night in all the houses. I had the receipts brought over this morning and I've been going through them.'

They chatted about business until they had their coffee in front of them, then Mariah spoke.

'What happened with the boys?'

Briony smiled brightly, too brightly.

'Not a lot. They shot McNee all right, today they're going after the Rileys and the Moneys. But apart from that they're great.'

'I'm sorry, Briony.'

'What for? They're nearly twenty-one, old enough to look after themselves now. I mean to say, if you're big enough to shoot a known lunatic with a sawn-off shotgun, you're old enough for anything, ain't you?' It ended in a question and Mariah went round the desk and put her arm around her friend's shoulders.

'Do you think they can handle it?'

Briony nodded. 'Oh, they can handle it, all right. I think that's the trouble.'

'Come on, drink your coffee. Like you say, they seem to know what they're about.'

Briony sipped the coffee and put the cup back in the saucer with a clatter.

'You know what really bothers me about it all? What Eileen would have thought. She entrusted them boys to me, on her death bed. "Look after my boys", those were her words. I feel that if she could see them now, she'd be disappointed. You knew our Eileen. She hated any skulduggery. She was straight as a die. You know, I see her in them sometimes, the movement of their heads or an expression when I talk to them. She wouldn't have allowed them a free rein like I did. She would have chastised them more. Seen to it they kept up their schoolwork. I protected them from so much . . .'

She put her hand up to her brow and leant her elbow on the desk. 'I don't know what to think now. In a way I expected something like this, I think. Only not so soon. I wanted to hand the clubs over to them, the nightclubs, and I wanted to expand the other businesses. I wanted them legit, you see. Now they've taken matters into their own hands and I can't do a thing. Only sit back and help them if I can.'

Mariah poured a large Scotch and gave it to her. 'You did your best, girl, you can't do no more than that. Some people have it built into them. That's what I think, anyway. Look at them American boys, what's their names, who committed that murder back in the twenties? Leopold and Loeb, that's it. They were sons of millionaires and they went off the straight and narrow. All you can do now, as you say, is let them get on with it and pick up the pieces if it goes wrong.'

Boysie and Danny slowed the car down as they approached the headquarters of the Rileys. They had taken over a vacant house in Shoreditch after it had been bomb damaged and now they ran their various businesses from there. Kenneth Riley himself still lived in Bethnal Green.

Michael Money watched aghast as he saw Boysie get out of the Aston Martin in broad daylight and pull the pin from an American-issue hand grenade. As he threw it through the window of the building, Michael put his hands up to his face.

The Aston Martin sped away and Michael Money sat in shock and disbelief as the building and surrounding area was rocked by the explosion. Then he turned on his ignition and drove home to tell his brothers the news.

The King was dead, long live the Cavanaghs.

Liselle loved to hear her mother sing. As she sat in the recording studio and watched Kerry talking to the musicians, explaining what particular beat she wanted and whether any musician could have a solo, Liselle always felt proud.

She asked politely, as always, if any of the technicians wanted a coffee and then went in search of a cup for herself. The technicians always said no. She guessed, rightly, that like her mother they preferred a drop of the hard stuff but she asked anyway. It was good manners. Her mother had already topped herself up with a few large vodkas provided by her current amour, Victor Sanderson. Liselle didn't particularly like him, but he owned Badger Records now and had taken more than a shine to Kerry Cavanagh, one of his star artists.

Where her mother's love life, or more correctly sex life, was concerned, Liselle stood back. Her mother had always gravitated from man to man, never staying with any of them longer than five minutes. Her temper when in drink generally put them off. But this didn't seem to deter Victor, which was one thing in his favour with Liselle. As she walked out of the studios in Abbey Road and went over to the coffee shop opposite, she bumped into a big black man.

'I'm sorry, I didn't see you there.'

The man touched his cap and walked on. Liselle forgot about him and carried on over the road to get her coffee.

She didn't see the black man get into a large black Roadster just down the road and carry on watching her from there.

Kerry began to sing. Everything was quiet, as if a funeral was about to take place, and as she sang the opening bars of her song, Victor Sanderson sighed with contentment.

This was talent on a grand scale.

Kerry still sang the blues with a deep throaty voice, but had emerged with a sound all of her own over the last twenty years. She was up there now among the greats and her voice was a guaranteed seller. When people thought of singers, great singers, they thought of Ella, of Billie, and of Kerry Cavanagh. Her voice had wafted through dusty dance halls and expensive night spots all through the war, and she had emerged bigger than ever. Now Victor Sanderson was going to see that she didn't go the way of Billie Holiday and her counterparts. He was going to watch her like a hawk, an investment that would make him more money than he dreamed of. On top of all that, though secondary to it, she was a great looker, and great in bed when she was sober enough. It was no hardship to him, looking out for her.

If only she could be made to go to America where her records sold like hot cakes, they would be set. But nothing he or anyone else said would get her there. She'd go to France, anywhere in Europe, but never to the States. Jonathan la Billière had tried to talk her into going over to Hollywood for a holiday, but she had flatly refused. That had fazed even Victor. Jonathan la Billière, the biggest movie star in the whole world, and Kerry had turned him down! Even a pretend romance would have hit all the papers, Victor would have made sure of it. He'd have personally written the copy! La Billière was an old family friend; they went back years apparently. Unlike most women who would have shouted this fact out straight away, he had found it out through a mutual friend. But the fact remained, Kerry would not go anywhere near America and if you wanted a fight with her, you just tried to force that issue. They had been offered a staggering fifty thousand pounds for her to appear at Madison Square Garden and she had coolly declined. Victor could have cried.

He had even tried to speak to that sister of hers, the one who ran the whorehouses, but she had politely told him to get on his bike. Oh, in nicer words than that, but that had been the general drift.

Still, he consoled himself, Kerry was being good at the moment, she was turning up at the right places at the right time and she wasn't always plastered. Her daughter played a big part in that. She watched her mother like a hawk. Between them they'd see her all right, and maybe get her overseas one day.

Dickie Lawson found the twins in Soho. It was early evening and they were having a drink in Tommy Lane's club, The Bolthole. Dickie looked at the two of them and took a deep swallow as he plucked up courage to go over to them.

The club was small and select and it cost a fiver to get in. The people who used The Bolthole wanted to be somewhere where the police, wives, girlfriends, or even Military Police during the war, couldn't get to them. Dickie had paid over his fiver, signed himself in and now he had to walk into the lion's den.

He could have kicked himself for trying to tuck the

twins up with the bets. He felt faint every time he thought about it. Everywhere he went they were being talked about. Anyone who'd shoot a McNee in the legs and blow up Kenny Riley was guaranteed to frighten Old Nick himself, let alone a small-time hustler like Dickie Lawson. Plucking up courage, he went over to them. Boysie and Danny watched him approach them in the bar mirror. He stood behind them uncertainly for a few seconds before he spoke.

'All right, lads?' His voice was strangled-sounding, as if one of the twins already had a hand around his throat.

Both of them turned around at once.

'Well, well, well, if it ain't Dickie Lawson. Come to buy us a drink and pay over our winnings, have you?' Boysie's voice was loud, jocular, and Dickie took heart.

'That's right, lads, what you having?'

He took a brown envelope out of his jacket pocket and slipped it on to the counter. Danny picked it up and opened it, counting the money.

'There's only a hundred quid in here, Dickie boy.'

He bit his lip and then licked his lips which had dried in record time with fear.

'That's what I owed you, lads . . . hundred quid.'

Boysie snapped his fingers and the barmaid sloped over and smiled at them.

'What can I get you?'

'Two very large Scotches, my love, a half of bitter for me little mate, and whatever you want of course.'

The barmaid set about getting the drinks and Boysie turned back to Dickie who was now a deathly shade of white.

Danny laughed.

'What we want, Dickie, is our rents. As you probably

know, poor Kenny Riley is well out of the ball game now, through explosives like. He left us everything he owned. And that, I think, includes yourself.'

Dickie, seeing the light, the crystal clear, plain as day kind of light, nodded his head furiously.

'Of course . . . Of course, lads.'

He slapped his sweaty forehead with a sweaty palm and, taking out a roll of money, paid up without a murmur.

Boysie poked Dickie in the chest none too gently.

'A word in your shell-like. We ain't your lads, see? We are Mr Cavanagh to you. Do you think you can remember that?'

Dickie was once more nodding, harder now.

'Yes, lad . . . I mean, yes, Mr Cavanagh!'

Boysie and Danny laughed out loud.

'Good lad! Now pay for the drinks like a good boy and then piss off. You're beginning to annoy us. We'll see you next week, Dickie. You won't have to look for us, we'll find you. All right?'

Half an hour later they were on their way to meet two girls, both good Catholics, both definitely virgins. Both waiting to be plucked like nice ripe gooseberries.

All in all, life couldn't be better for the Cavanagh twins.

Liselle sat in The New Yorker, Briony's latest club, with her mother and watched her get roaring drunk. She was the life and soul of the place, as usual, and eventually got up and sang a few numbers to the delight of the audience. Bessie, who now sang there with the Velvetones despite periodic threats to go home to the States, stood in the wings and smiled. Until she turned and saw the black man standing by the stage door. Then her heart began to hammer in her ears and she closed her eyes tightly.

When she opened them again the man was gone.

It was the lights playing tricks on her, that was all, but for one moment she could have sworn she saw Evander Dorsey standing there. Fatter, greyer, but Evander all the same. As Kerry called her out on stage she put a smile on her face and stepped into the lights, but the niggling thought that she had seen Evander spoilt her evening.

As they sang together, that old favourite 'Summertime', she looked at Liselle sitting at the table, drinking soda and looking dead on her feet, and felt foreboding wash over her.

That girl wasn't a child any more and soon, very soon, she'd need to be told the truth. She didn't look Negro at all, at least she didn't to the British, but in the South she would be known immediately for what she was, and Bessie knew from experience that the girl could give birth to children as black as the African slaves who were her forefathers.

Oh, the girl needed to be told all right, and Kerry wouldn't be the one to do it. Kerry had enough difficulty just getting through an average day. Someone else would have to tell her, but who?

As the song finished she bowed and held on to a rather drunken Kerry, stopping her from falling over.

It was seeing that black guy that made her think these morbid things, that was all.

A little later Liselle helped her mother from the club and got a taxi to take them home. Tired out as she was, she didn't notice the black man standing in the doorway at the side of the club. If she had, she wouldn't have realised he was the man from earlier in the day.

Evander watched his daughter get into the taxi. He walked to the Roadster once more, and the three white men sitting in it.

'Yeah, that's her all right. I had to be sure.' He lit himself a cheroot with crooked and deformed fingers. 'Tha's my girl, no mistakin'. Looks jes like my sister.'

The three white men in the car nodded.

Evander smoked his cheroot and nodded to himself as if carrying on a conversation. Only no one was interested in what he had to say. He pulled out a hip flask and took a deep draught of cheap brandy.

He laughed softly to himself. Liselle! That bitch had named her for his mama.

Chapter Thirty-Five

It was two months since the twins had taken over the East End of London. Briony had adjusted to the fact that the boys were now men, that she had very little say in what they did or, worse still, how they did it. Instead, she threw herself into the re-opening of Berwick Manor. The Manor represented a lot to her, it was the pinnacle of her achievements. She had had just about everyone who was anyone in there, and wanted it like that once more. She wanted it lit up like a beacon, with all the old crowd, and some new faces.

As she stood alone looking over the place she felt a tiny thrill of anticipation. The damage wasn't too bad when you got used to it. Mainly the carpeting and the wall coverings. Most of the original mouldings were still in perfect condition. In the top bedroom, where prominent cabinet ministers had spent many a sleepless night, she found a letter wedged between the windowsill and a walnut dresser. Briony picked it up and glanced at it.

It was for a Flying Officer Byron, from his wife Juliette. She smiled as she read the endearments from her. The longing for her husband's return home. The little anecdotes about the children. It was a lovely letter written in graceful handwriting by a woman whom Briony visualised as neat in body, mind and home. She hoped that Flying Officer Byron had made it home, she really did.

She sat on the bare mattress, clutching the letter. Trying to imagine what it must be like to love a man like that. To have his children and look after his home and just dedicate your life to that one person and their progeny. It was a strange thing to her, this being married. It was something she couldn't for the life of her imagine. Bernadette had married her Marcus and overnight she'd turned into a household drudge. Oh, she enjoyed it, Briony knew and respected that. But there was no real reason for it. She had had the girls and now took care of them, Marcus and the home. Bernadette was happy just overseeing her family. Making sure meals were prepared on time, that the house ran smoothly.

Well, Cissy did all that for Briony, and before her Mrs H had done it. If she had had to stagnate in a house just waiting for a man to breeze in and out as it suited him she'd have gone mad. Stark staring mad.

She glanced down at the letter again. The sender's address was in Northumberland. She pushed the letter into her pocket. She'd mail it to this Juliette Byron, whoever she was. Maybe she'd want it back. Especially if Flying Officer Byron hadn't made it home.

She wandered out of the room and looked out of the window at the greying skies. The view from the Manor had always entranced her. From one side of the house were wide sweeping fields that in the summer glowed yellow with corn. From the front of the house the view was of Rainham marshes, and from the top window you could see right up Upminster Road North to the church with its clocktower.

She heard a noise and turned from the window. Standing at the top of the stairs was a man. In the dimness brought on by the overcast skies she couldn't make out his face. As he walked towards her she put her hand to her chest in momentary fright.

'My God! It's you.' Her voice was a whisper.

'Surprised to see me?' His voice was the same as always and Briony was transported back over the years to her first sight of a young boy in a new suit that looked too big, with a voice that had just broken properly.

'Tommy. Tommy Lane. You're the last person I expected to see.'

He smiled then, that easy smile that she remembered so well. Even though they had spoken by phone over the years, they had met only twice, by accident. Then they had been chillingly polite to one another. Now he was here, in the Manor, and she knew it was for a good reason.

'They don't call me Bad Penny Lane for nothing, you know!'

Briony smiled. 'Come down to the kitchen and I'll make us some coffee.'

They walked down the stairs in silence, both aware of the attraction still between them. The gathering storm overhead served to make the atmosphere even more charged.

Briony put the kettle on the range and turned to face him. 'Black coffee, I'm afraid, there's no milk.'

Tommy sat down at the scrubbed table and looked at her as if drinking her in. Despite herself, Briony blushed at his scrutiny and Tommy laughed out loud.

'Now I've seen everything. Briony Cavanagh blushing? That's a turn up for the book, I must say!'

She grinned.

'It's the shock of seeing you, I think, Tommy, after all this time. I take it this is a friendly visit?'

His face sobered at her words. Standing up, he went to her and put his hands on her shoulders. Looking down into the deep, green depths of her eyes, he said, 'As friendly as you want it, Briony.'

She felt the confusion in him, in herself. Suddenly she wanted Tommy Lane like she had never wanted anyone or anything before. He was here, a reminder of her past, her youth, her old life. He was like a big present, waiting to be opened. All she had to do was tear away the wrappings.

A new feeling swamped her body as the first slap of thunder trembled overhead. It started in her groin and its warmth spread gradually up into her stomach and breasts. She found, for the first time ever, that she couldn't even talk, couldn't speak to make her feelings known.

As she parted her lips, Tommy took her into his arms and kissed her hard. Bruising her mouth, he forced his tongue into her mouth, exploring her with it. Briony felt the feeling swamp her then, and she kissed him back, hard kisses, as they rubbed against one another's bodies, discovering each other for the first time in over twenty years. They finally came together up against the scrubbed pine table, Briony hooking her slim legs around his waist and grinding her hips into him as she finally felt the sensations that had always been denied to her. Never had she expected to feel this passion in her lifetime.

She ground into him, crying out into the silent kitchen. A flash of lightning lit up the kitchen and they saw each other properly then. The feeling was enveloping her now, she was dying to capture it properly, and he was carried along with the want in her, now in him. She heard him groan and her heart raced. Don't let this stop, she thought. Don't cheat me now. And it didn't. She felt the first tentative throes of orgasm, felt the hardness of Tommy inside her, and it was enough then. It was finally enough. Clutching at his hair she jerked in his arms, pulling him deeper and deeper inside her until there was nothing. No thunder, no storm, only the two of them. Together they shuddered and moaned and finally were spent. Briony felt the sweat on her brow, the dampness of her body. He held her to him, gently, firmly, and they felt the thundering of each other's hearts.

Briony kissed his face. Little kisses over his eyes, his cheeks, and on his mouth. She held his face between her tiny hands and she knew, at last she knew. The mystery of man and woman. What had driven Kerry and Bernie, and what had driven Juliette Byron to write such a letter to her absent husband. She felt a flicker of jealousy for the women who had found this out when young, when well able to follow their star. She was forty-four years old and felt like a newborn.

The kettle was screaming on the hob and the rain battering, against the windows. Pulling away from one another, Briony and Tommy smiled at one another shyly. As if they had just met. Briony looked down at the lacy scrap of underwear on the stone floor and giggled. Her cami-knickers were torn beyond repair. Tommy had his trousers around his ankles and looked ridiculous, but handsomely ridiculous. She pulled down her skirt and rebuttoned her blouse quickly with trembling hands. Taking the kettle off the range, she made the coffee, listening to his movements. Frightened that he might leave her now, and never come back.

As she turned to face him, she swallowed deeply. Then

slowly, squeezing out of her eyes as if unsure what they were doing, the tears came. Hot stinging tears. Tommy went to her and took her in his arms, whispering endearments, stroking the erratic red hair that had escaped from the confines of its French pleat.

'I never knew, Tommy. I never knew you could feel like that. I've been only half alive all my life. Only half alive . . .'

Tommy held her tightly. If anyone had told him that his coming here would have brought this on he'd have laughed aloud at the very thought. But it was as if today they had reached their turning point. She had been there in front of him, his girl, his Briony. His best friend for so long. And fate had decreed that today was to be the time for them. The time for them to get together properly. As they should have done years before, when young and eager.

'I know, Bri . . . I know, my love.'

And he held her while she cried. There was time enough to tell her why he had followed her here, why he had waited to see her alone. For the time being they had one another and that was enough.

God knew, he had waited long enough for her. Even if he hadn't fully realised that himself until today.

It was Sunday and Liselle slept in till ten-thirty, secure in the knowledge that her mother had nowhere to go today and she could let her sleep. They'd go to evening Mass with Granny Moll as they did every Sunday, then out to dinner. The drinking would start about eight-thirty, and her mother would set herself up for the week.

Lying in bed listening to the sounds of the radio, Liselle sighed. She lifted one slim arm to turn the radio up slightly. The darkness of her arm against the white chest of drawers made her stare. Pulling the covers from herself, she looked down at her body. Even her nipples were black. She remembered at school, all the other girls had had tiny pink nipples, and they had all laughed at her brown ones, brown ones that were now nearly black. She frowned. Her pubic hair was jet black, tiny black spirals that seemed to grow prolifically around the tops of her legs. Yet she knew she was attractive. Men looked at her twice. It had always been that way.

She had developed earlier than her friends, having large heavy breasts by the time she was twelve. Her school friends had been envious of her, but she had shrugged it off. Her mother said all the Cavanagh girls had been early developers and she had been satisfied with that explanation. But lately, she had wondered about herself. During the war, a black airforceman had smiled at her. She had smiled back, naturally, as you did to anyone who smiled at you in a friendly manner. Her Granny Moll, seeing the exchange, had gone mad. She had gone for the man in the middle of Brick Lane, bringing the eyes of passersby on to them. Going to her granny, Liselle had pulled on her arm, shame and hurt welling up inside her.

'Granny . . . Gran, leave it be!' she'd cried.

The man had looked at her and said, 'She's your granny, girl?' His voice had been incredulous. She had nodded, humiliated. But the exchange had stayed with her, bringing all sorts of fancies into her childish heart. Now at twenty-one she remembered the long buried incident and it troubled her.

Sitting up in bed, she clasped her knees. She would ring the twins and arrange to see them. They always cheered her up.

When Kerry got up, she found Liselle's note. She went into the lounge in a green silk wrapper and poured herself a large vodka and fresh orange juice. She drank it straight down and immediately poured herself another. Then sitting down she picked up the Sunday paper and lit herself a cigarette. She was reading the *News of the World* when the telephone rang.

Leaning out of her chair, she picked it up, the smell of Mrs Harcourt cooking her some eggs making her want to gag.

'Hello.'

'Is that you, Kerry girl?'

She dropped the phone on to the beige carpet, staring at it as if it was a demon. Scrambling from the chair, she picked the receiver up once more and held it tentatively to her ear.

The line was dead.

Placing it back in its cradle she stood there staring at it, willing it to ring.

She knew that voice. That deep brown voice.

It didn't ring again. Kerry sat all day, with the bottle of vodka by her side, waiting. Still it didn't ring. She spent the rest of the day lost in a drunken world of jazz music, smoky clubs, and the arms of a big handsome man called Evander Dorsey.

Molly stood outside St Vincent's church with Rosalee. Both had on their best hats, coats and gloves, though Rosalee's gloves were grubby where she had insisted on picking privets all the way to the church. Molly pursed her lips and shook her head. Abel was asleep in bed, getting ready for his night's work at the club in Soho that Briony now owned. It was his way of getting out of going to Mass, she knew that. She saw the twins and Liselle get out of the boys' Aston Martin and her heart swelled with pride. They never missed Sunday evening Mass with their gran.

As they walked into the church and genuflected before the Cross of Christ, Molly felt as if her whole life had been worth it for this. Boysie helped Rosalee into the front pew, which was now reserved especially for them, and the others filed in beside her. All knelt and said the regulation prayers, then sat back in silence, waiting for the priest and, hopefully, Kerry to arrive. Liselle watched the back of the church anxiously every time the doors opened. Her mother had better turn up. If she didn't it meant she was too drunk, and Liselle hated her mother when she was really plastered.

Father Tierney walked down the church and everyone stood up. Boysie looked around the church as the service started, automatically making the responses in Latin as he always had. Boysie and Danny liked Mass. They always had from little children. They liked the feel of the church and they respected its sanctity. They believed in God as they believed in themselves. As the Mass drew to a close and the priest asked for prayers for the sick and the dying, the twins sat happily with their gran and their aunt and cousin Liselle, and enjoyed the feeling the church always created in them.

In there, with its high ceiling and its quietness, they could really believe that there was peace on earth and all was well with man.

Well, with these two men anyway.

The twins dropped their granny off at Briony's and then took Liselle home. As they walked into the large house they heard the housekeeper, Mrs Harcourt, a widow of uncertain age, shouting.

Liselle rushed into the lounge where her mother was lying unconscious on the floor, the phone beside her.

'Oh, Miss Liselle! I can't wake her up. She's been drinking steadily since she got up, wouldn't eat a blessed thing, and now she's unconscious!'

Liselle turned on the woman, saying sharply, 'Well, shouting at her when she's like this isn't going to help, is it? Go and make a pot of coffee.'

Danny and Boysie looked at one another. Of one mind, they picked up their aunt and carried her up the stairs to her room. Plonking her down on the bed none too gently, Boysie threw a cover over her.

'She should be put away, Liselle, as much as we all love her. She ain't doing herself no favours with the drink.'

Liselle sighed heavily.

'She won't go. I've tried all that. There's a place in Surrey where they dry you out, but she goes mental if you even mention it. Sometimes I feel like buggering off out of it, I really do. Just leaving her to it. I've got no life to speak of. I just watch her day and night. Look what happened when I went out with you today. All this.'

Danny felt an enormous surge of affection for the cousin who was more like his sister. Their situation while growing up had been so similar, no father and their Aunt Briony being the main person in their lives, even Liselle's.

'Come on, she's out for the count now. Let's all go out together, we know a terrific little club!'

Boysie joined in. 'Yeah. Come on, Lissy, she'll be out till the morning. Even black coffee won't help her now.'

Hearing the name they had called her as a child made Liselle smile. 'All right then. I suppose you're right. She won't wake now for about twelve hours.'

'There you go then. Get dressed up and we'll be your dates tonight.'

Boysie spoke in fun but Liselle looked at him and said seriously: 'Boysie, you two are the only dates I've ever had.'

As she left the room the twins looked at one another sadly. Poor old Liselle, stuck looking after their Auntie Kerry who could sing, who could do anything as long as it was musical, yet couldn't leave the drink or the drugs alone.

As they went to leave the room Kerry stirred and opened her eyes. Looking at the twins she said: 'Evander?' Then closing her eyes she was gone again.

Boysie said, 'What did she say?'

Danny shrugged. 'Something about lavender, I don't know. Come on, let's go downstairs, this place gives me the creeps.

Liselle got changed and walked out of the front door as if the weight of the world had been lifted from her shoulders. When her mother was unconscious, like now, at least she knew where she was, and how long she was going to be there. That in itself was a result.

Molly had kissed her grandchildren then, taking Rosalee by the arm, walked up the drive to Briony's house. Rosalee was slow and Molly had to fight an urge to drag her along. At forty, Rosalee had lasted a lot longer than they had expected. Her weight was enormous, but she waddled through life happily enough and everyone doted on her, especially the twins. As they walked through Briony's front door, Ciss, hardly able to contain herself with excitement, whispered: 'Have a guess who's here, Moll? Tommy Lane!'

Molly's mouth dropped open. 'You're kidding?'

Cissy shook her big fat face till her cheeks wobbled. 'I ain't. He's in there now with Briony, Bernie and Marcus, as large as life!'

Molly divested herself and Rosalee of their coats in double quick time and, taking Rosalee's hand again, went into the drawing room.

Tommy and Briony were sitting on the chesterfield by the French windows, and Bernie and Marcus were in easy chairs either side of the fireplace. Rosalee, waddling in behind her mother, looked at Briony and as always clapped her hands together and said in excitement: 'Bri, Bri.'

Briony got up from her seat. Kissing her sister, she led her to the chesterfield, placing her between herself and Tommy. He took Rosalee's hand and squeezed it.

'Hello, Rosie love.' He was genuinely pleased to see her.

Rosalee for her part smiled a huge toothless smile and said, 'Tom.'

Everyone in the room was absolutely amazed.

'Jumping Jesus Christ, did you hear that!' Molly's voice was low with shock.

As if showing off, Rosalee said once more, louder than anyone had ever heard her speak before: 'Tom.'

Marcus shouted, 'Well, I'll be buggered!'

And Briony, quick as a flash, shouted back, 'Not in here, you won't!'

Even Molly laughed then.

'Didn't I always say she could talk more than we thought, Mum, didn't I?' Briony's voice was so happy even Molly was gladdened at the sound of it.

'You did that, Briony. You did that. Now I think I'll have a drop of hot rum to celebrate. Would anyone like to join me?'

Briony felt as if her ship had indeed come in. Rosalee was more animated than she had ever seen her, she was drinking without help, and Tommy was sitting so close. She couldn't wait for night to come so she could leap into bed with him and experience again the things she had felt that afternoon.

'How's herself?' Molly's voice was confidential as she enquired after Mrs H and Bernie laughed.

'We've been up to her. She's as right as the number ten bus, Mum.'

'I'll pop up to her meself in a minute. Poor old soul she is.'

Bernie got up to replenish Marcus's glass and Tommy saw that she was now a middle-aged woman. Her figure was fuller, her waist long gone. He was sad for a second as he visualised her as she had been when he'd first known her.

As she placed the glass in her husband's hand Marcus winked at her and Tommy smiled to himself. They were happy, that much was evident. He knew that Marcus was one for the ladies, it was well known in their circles. Obviously Bernie knew nothing about it, which was good. A wife, a good wife, was worth hanging on to. Bernadette sat down and crossed her legs demurely. Her ankles were fat, and Tommy looked at them in consternation. When a woman aged, a beautiful woman, it was like the destruction of a beautiful painting.

He let his eyes roam to Briony. In the firelight, with only the lamps on, she looked exactly as she had the last time he'd seen her. Oh, the fashions had changed, but she was still the woman he had known, only now she was a real woman. In all respects she was a woman. And he intended to keep her like that. For as long as he could. He had wanted to see her about the twins, but that could wait now. He would pick the right time to talk about them.

'Did the twins go to Mass with you, Mum?'

'They did, God love them. Liselle came too, as usual.'

Briony frowned slightly. 'What, no Kerry tonight?'

Bernie sighed. 'Probably drunk out of her head. She really worries me, Bri. The other day I rang her up and she could barely talk. It's not fair on Liselle. That poor girl has to cope with everything now.'

Briony said after a few seconds' thought, 'Kerry has a lot of responsibilities, you know. I asked her to cut down on the concert dates but she didn't want to. I might go and see Victor. He manages her well, I admit, but I think he pushes her too hard at times. A friendly word might be in order there.'

Molly made a disgusting noise with her lips as she let her breath out and said nastily, 'Send the twins round to see him. They'll make sure my Kerry's not overworked.'

Briony laughed. 'If you had your way, the twins would be threatening everyone who ever drew breath! For God's sake, Mum, Kerry has always pushed herself, you know that. She's more famous these days than the bleeding Pope!'

Molly loved her daughter's fame, like she loved the twins' newfound notoriety.

'Well, all I'm saying is, she should have a bit of rest like.'

Marcus joined in. 'She should be dried out really. One of the barmen at The New Yorker said she done a bottle of vodka in an hour the other night. She won't last long drinking like that.'

'I always had a lot of time for Kerry, you know that, but if her drinking is as bad as you say, something should be done. I watched my old mum's liver give out through the drink. She went bright yellow one day, and within a week she was dead.' Tommy's voice was low.

Bernie coughed slightly and said, 'I think he's right.'

Briony nodded.

'Well, we'll have to put it to her. If she won't go we'll have no alternative but to have her committed.'

Molly felt her face stiffen. Another daughter sent to a mental home. 'Oh, she's not that bad, for goodness' sakes. She's not mad, for crying out loud, she just likes a drink.'

'Oh, Kerry likes a drink all right, a bottle at a time. When she was in France, just after the war, Bessie told me that they had to sober her up every night before her performance. I don't think it's so much the drink as the pills she drops with it.'

Molly, her own tongue loosened by drink, said, 'She's never been the same since she had that child. That's what sent her on the drink. Not the singing.'

Unbeknown to her, the twins and Liselle were in the hallway, having let themselves in with a key. They had decided to see if Briony wanted to come out with them. Molly's voice floated through the door to them and all three stiffened as they heard it. Unaware, Molly carried on.

'An illegitimate child's bad enough, but one like that? I ask you?'

Liselle was so still, she looked like a statue made of bronze. Boysie and Danny watched her fascinated.

Briony's voice broke through their grandmother's. 'Shut up, Mum. You're always the bleeding same with a drink in you! Kerry loves that girl, we all do. No matter where she came from. Now just leave it, all right. Just bloody well leave it!'

Molly stood up. 'I've every right to speak me mind where me own child's concerned.'

Bernie was trying to placate her. 'Mum . . . Mum . . . Sit down. Let's leave it now. It's in the past.

Briony walked over to her mother and poked her in the chest. 'Why do you always do this? A couple of bevvies and you get stroppy. The world according to Molly Cavanagh. You've never had any time for Liselle, we all know that. Well, listen to me and listen good. Our Kerry was a fucking saint to keep her, you should be proud of her. Anyone else would have got rid of her quick smart.'

All Molly's feelings burst like a cancer inside her. The strong rum toddy made her tongue run away with her. Forgetting everything, where she was and with whom, she bellowed: 'And that's what Kerry should have done! You should have made her do it. You could have talked her round. But no, not you. Not bloody Briony the marvellous wonder woman Cavanagh. You welcomed her in here with open arms. Knowing she'd slept with a bloody bl—'

Danny burst into the room and everyone stared at him. A second later the front door slammed and they heard Boysie calling Liselle's name as she ran up the drive.

'She heard you, Gran, she was listening to you! You nasty old bitch! What's she ever done to you? What's all this about? You been drinking as usual? Is that it? I'll go and help Boysie find her and you'd better be gone by the time we get back, Gran. I ain't in the mood for you tonight.'

Tommy watched the drama unfold before his eyes and sighed. But the way Daniel had spoken was like listening to Briony. Earlier that day she had said 'They're my boys', and Tommy was inclined to agree with her. Well, if they had some of their natural mother and some of Briony in them, they couldn't be all that bad. No matter what he had heard.

Briony said slowly, 'Go home, Mum. Just go home.'

Marcus got up and took Molly's arm.

'Come on. I'll take you home, love.'

Molly stared at Briony, her face troubled. 'I didn't know the child was listening, I swear. I wouldn't have hurt her for the world.'

Briony laughed bitterly.

'Of course you wouldn't. You've never wanted to hurt anyone, you. But Christ himself knows, somehow you always bleeding well manage to!'

Boysie caught up with Liselle at the bottom of the street. She was crying, really crying, and he held her to him, stroking her hair and whispering endearments.

Danny arrived a little while later and they tried to take her back to their house but Liselle refused.

'I don't ever want to see me gran again! Ever.'

Danny wiped her eyes with a clean white handkerchief and smiled crookedly.

'You know Gran. When she's had a drink she's always stroppy. Look at last Christmas when she started on poor old Mrs H, accusing her of all sorts. Forget it.'

Liselle looked up into his face and said through her teeth, 'If she'd said about you two what she's just said about me, would you forget it?'

Boysie and Danny both looked away, knowing they wouldn't.

'Whoever my father was, he seems to have made quite an impression on everyone. I wish now I'd listened to the rest of it, I might have found out just what was so very wrong with him.'

'Come on, girl, we'll get the car and take you home.'

Boysie and Danny had guessed that Liselle had what was termed 'a touch of the tarbrush' in her. But how could they tell her that if she didn't even guess it herself?

Chapter Thirty-Six

Tommy and Briony sat up waiting for the twins to return. Bernadette had left shortly after Marcus had taken Molly and Rosalee home. Sitting in her warm lounge with the fire roaring and Tommy Lane by her side, Briony finally felt the enormity of what had taken place. Her anger against her mother grew virulent.

Tommy grasped her hand in his. 'She should have been told, Bri . . . before now.'

Briony nodded and swallowed hard. Her face white and earnest, she looked at him. 'I know that, Tommy, better than anyone. But how? How do you tell a girl something like that? Especially at this time, with all the black servicemen who were over here in the war? The feeling against them by men in particular? Black people live under a stigma. It's wrong, we know it's wrong. But not everyone's us, are they? Christ himself knows I wanted to tell her, I wanted to tell her when she was fifteen. But when she don't look black, it seemed unfair somehow. Now bloody Mouth Almighty's started a chain of events that can only lead to trouble. Oh, Tommy, sometimes I could wring my mother's bloody neck!'

'Well, the twins will see Liselle all right.'

Tommy kissed the palm of her hand. Briony smiled crookedly and touched his face with gentle fingers.

'I'm so glad you came to the Manor today, Tommy. Really I am. You know us all so well.'

He smiled at her then. She saw the lines around his eyes and mouth. The two deep grooves alongside his nose, the greying of his hair. Time raced on with no regard.

She poured herself another drink and sipped it gratefully. 'It's funny, you know, Tommy, but a long time ago when Liselle was small I had a chat with one of the black girls in one of my houses. Nice girl she was and all. Real looker. She told me that a white-looking Negro could have children as black as night. We even had a black girl once with blue eyes. I think that's when I built up a wall in me mind about poor Liselle. If you don't think about it, it goes away. Well, it doesn't go away, that much was proved here tonight. Problems don't go away, mate, they just get bigger and bigger, and for the first time ever, I don't know the answer to this one.'

'You'll find the answer. You always do.'

Briony leant against him.

'I could never share anything before, not really. Not with a man. Not with you. I honestly never thought of you really, all those years ago. I didn't wonder what your reaction would be to anything, and it wasn't because I was selfish. At least, I don't think it was. I think it was because I didn't know how to be with a man. Not really. Not properly. Henry Dumas and me dad saw to that. Today was like a whole new world to me. I really loved it. Then all this happened.'

'Look, Briony, take a bit of advice. You can't take on

everything for everyone. No more than you can be everything to everyone. You need to keep a little bit of yourself for yourself. Does that make sense? You need to keep a little bit of all that love you've got back for yourself. For Briony Cavanagh.'

She nodded and sighed.

They stayed cuddled together in the firelight until the twins arrived home.

Liselle was quiet all the way back to her house. Boysie sat in the back of the car holding her to him, as if frightened she'd open the car door and run off. Daniel drove, his face hard and set. His granny had gone too far tonight. Her attitude when in drink had always left a lot to be desired, though they had laughed it off before. But this time she had really hurt someone.

Inside her house Boysie had made Liselle a strong cup of tea and they had sat with her, in their aunt's ornate lounge, and silently kept her company. No one seemed to know just what to say to her.

Finally, Liselle began to cry again. Quietly this time. She was held by the twins, both with an arm around her, both telling her not to worry, they'd sort it all out for her. And as they eyed each other over the top of her head, they both knew that that's exactly what they would do.

They'd find out who and what her father was. At least that way she'd know.

Upstairs Kerry slept the sleep of the drunk, unaware that her daughter's world had been shattered beyond repair.

Evander looked at Skip Paquale who smiled at him. Evander smiled back, but the smile, or grimace, didn't reach his bloodshot brown eyes.

He noted the other man's expensive suit, clean-cut good looks and flat, athletic stomach. Skip looked what he was, a ladies' man, from his well-cut hair and sweet-smelling skin to his handmade shoes. He was also a hood, a small-time Mafia man earning money from the numbers and a few other lucrative ventures. He was the great-nephew of Tommy Corolla, a big mob man who had his own family. At twenty-five Skip felt he wasn't getting the action he deserved so he was making a little action of his own on the side.

That was where Evander Dorsey came in.

He had been very drunk one night, working in a seedy bar, his gnarled hands playing him up. During his break someone had put a record on the juke box. It was one of Kerry's. He had sat back on the stool listening to her voice, looking down at the deformed fingers of his hands, when a guy beside him had asked him what he was thinking about. The guy was Delroy Burton, a black spiv who owned the club Evander was playing in. For some reason he had felt a great rage against Kerry, because she was big, a big star, famous, while he, Evander, was left broken down, working in dives because of her. He had told Delroy the whole story, having more and more drinks bought for him. The next night Delroy had been waiting for him, buying him drinks and getting names, dates, places, anything about his time in England. Then he had ignored him and Evander had just been sorry that the free drinks were not coming any more and forgot about Delroy.

Then one night a few months later Delroy had come to his house. Evander lived alone since the terrible 'accident' to his hands. Hands that were numb a lot of the time where they had been hastily set in Liverpool by a little black woman called Rula Demoinge. Hands that could still play music to a degree, but had lost the suppleness and eagerness of before. Hands that were getting weaker and more gnarled as the years wore on. Delroy had come to the little shanty where he lived with two white men. Italians. The men had been introduced and one had produced a couple of bottles of Wild Turkey and a hundred dollars. All they wanted was to hear the story of Kerry Cavanagh. Evander, eyes wide at the sight of the money and the booze, had welcomed them in with open arms and told them everything, embellishing the story as drunkenness descended. Later that night they'd left him, a hundred dollars richer and drunk enough to sleep.

He hadn't seen them for six months when they once more turned up, minus Delroy, and with the intention of 'helping him out'. They had taken him from Alabama back to New York, bought him new clothes, cleaned him up, watched his drinking, and now here he was, back in London, living in a nice place in Notting Hill Gate. Evander was to be the instrument of blackmailing Kerry Cavanagh. In return he would get back some money and self-respect, both the things that had been denied him when Kevin Carter and his henchmen had stamped their booted feet on his hands. It was a sweet revenge, a just revenge on the woman who had brought him this low.

But the child had thrown him, he had to admit that. He hadn't known about no child. A good-looking girl, more like an octoroon, like the whores in New Orleans. But she was his child all right. Looked like his sister Eulalie who'd had the same whitey look about her. His mama said she was the product of a sugar farmer, poor white trash. Well, Kerry wasn't poor white trash, Kerry was loaded, and he was going to see, with the help of Skip Paquale and his boys, that a few thousand dollars came his way. It was just and fitting, it was right.

Might even get enough to buy his own place. He wouldn't be playing the piano for much longer, the rheumatism had set in and his hands were getting to be less than useless.

He sat back in the chair contemplating his good fortune in meeting Delroy and Skip. Or 'Mr Skip' as he had to call him. Mr Skip to an Eyetalian! He smiled to himself at the thought. They were no better than him, they were just immigrants. His forefather had been in the States a mighty long time, longer than Paquale and his so-called family.

He knew the drink was making him aggressive and closed his eyes, once more seeing the creamy limbs of Kerry Cavanagh. She had been one hell of a loving woman.

She had also been his downfall, and he was looking forward to paying her back.

Skip looked at the big, bloated man sitting opposite him and hid his disgust.

'We move in tomorrow. You stop your drinking now, you hear?'

Evander opened one yellowing bloodshot eye and nodded. So tomorrow was the big day?

Big deal.

He drank the last of his whisky and, getting up unsteadily, made his way to bed.

Liselle woke up and looked out of her window. It was early December and in the night it had snowed. The snow already lay thick and quiet everywhere. It was just after five-thirty. She had only dozed. In her mother's room she heard the radio playing. Liselle pulled on a dressing gown and went in to her. Kerry lay on her bed still in the crumpled green wrapper, a glass of orange juice in her hand. Liselle sighed. Taking the drink from her mother she sipped it and raised her eyebrows.

Kerry laughed huskily.

'Ain't a drink to be found in the house. I take it you had a good hide up before you went to bed?'

Liselle had the grace to go red.

'It's snowing.'

Kerry laughed again.

'I know. I hate the snow meself. Always did. When we were kids, in the basements, snow could mean death. Honestly.' Her voice sobered. 'It was so cold in there anyway, damp and smelly. We woke up one morning and the whole inside of the room had a film of ice everywhere. Little babies froze to death that year. Little tiny babies. We used to have blue feet, navy blue feet, with big red sores on them.'

Liselle snapped at her, 'Stop it, Mum. For goodness' sakes!'

Kerry heaved a heavy sigh. 'I'm sorry, Lissy. It's just that I woke up thinking morbid thoughts. I have a feeling on me that something bad's going to happen. It's the snow, I think. I hate the solitude of snow. Even if you shout it somehow muffles your voice.'

Liselle shook her head.

'I think the trouble's already started.'

Kerry sat up in the bed and frowned. Liselle saw in the harsh light of day the veins beginning on her mother's cheeks from the drink. The deep hollows under her eyes that her make-up would make disappear, to leave her looking beautiful and young. Too young for this dark-haired girl to be her daughter. Yet unlike other mothers,

Kerry always told people about her daughter and never, ever lied about her age.

'What do you mean, love?'

'Last night there was murders round Auntie Briony's with me gran.'

Kerry laughed then in relief.

'There's always murders where your gran's concerned! Give her a drink and you've got a loony on your hands.'

Kerry's dismissive tone annoyed Liselle and she said nastily, 'Yeah, well, last night she informed the whole world and his wife that I should have been aborted. That having an illegitimate child was bad enough, but one like me . . . That's what she said, Mum. Those were her exact words.'

Kerry scrambled up so she was kneeling. 'Did she say anything else, girl? Did you say anything about me? About you as a baby?'

'Did she mention my father, you mean? No. But if it's not too much trouble, I wouldn't mind knowing who he was. After all, he is my dad! My father. The man who made me, if you like.'

Kerry's face blanched a sickly white. Liselle tried again, calmer this time.

'I have a right to know, Mum. I'm nearly twenty-two and no one seems to tell me anything. I don't know his name, nothing about him. I wonder, you know. I always have.'

Kerry licked her lips and stared at the beautiful girl in front of her. The girl she loved but who was a permanent reminder of what she had done, what she had been too cowardly to do. How many times over the years had she wished she had got on a boat and gone to find him? As she had wanted to. But she was a coward. It was easier to rely on the strength of Briony, to stay with her family, than to trek thousands of miles to a man who might reject her, who might have told her the truth about their relationship. Who had been beaten over her. Who must hate her for her part in his eventual downfall. That's why she refused down and out to sing in the States, or even to go there. It was still an open wound.

Now here was her child, the result of her union with Evander Dorsey, asking her for the truth. Could she say to her: 'I spoke to him yesterday, he rang me up. Your father's near, only I feel inside he's here to harm us. Not here to be welcomed with open arms by his old lover and his daughter.' No, she couldn't ever tell her that.

Instead she said, 'Why don't you let me worry about things, love? Your father was a nice kind man who left us. He didn't want to but he had to. Now leave it at that, and go and make me a nice strong pot of coffee. There's a good girl.'

Kerry's voice brooked no argument, Liselle had heard that tone many times over the years. Especially when she had asked about her father. Seething inside with anger, she flounced from the room, banging the door behind her. Kerry got up and lit herself a cigarette. Going to the window, she looked out at the white expanse of roofs and road. Blinking back tears, she smoked her cigarette in silence.

Out there somewhere was Evander Dorsey. It had been him yesterday, she would know that rich dark velvet voice anywhere. He was out there somewhere waiting for her and their child.

Boysie and Danny sat in Mrs Horlock's room with Cissy and Briony, listening to the story of Liselle's birth. They sat side by side on the bed, their sleek heads bowed as between them the three women told them the story from start to finish. When Briony got to the part about Kevin Carter's breaking Evander's fingers they both looked up and nodded, as if silently agreeing with his actions. It was the only time they moved. Mrs H watched them with shrewd rheumy eyes.

'That bloke went and we was all glad, it could only bring trouble to her, Kerry. She couldn't see that herself, not then. But then the child . . .'

Boysie shook his head.

'So Liselle is a half-chat then? Her dad was some soot piano player me Auntie Kerry was boffing . . .' He sounded disgusted. Somehow guessing something and finding out it was true were two completely different things.

Briony shook her head.

'Evander was a handsome man. If it had been today, who knows? Plenty of women have half-chats, as you call them, now. The Americans saw to that, son. But this was in the 1920s. It just wasn't done then. It just wasn't done.'

'But Auntie Kerry with a big soot!' Boysie's face was twisted with contempt.

Briony slapped his face, the crack resounding in the room. Danny stood up as if ready to fight her while Boysie rubbed at his smarting cheek.

Briony pointed at them and bellowed: 'That's my sister you're talking about. You wanted to know and we told you. Don't you get bloody lairy with me over the truth, I won't have it, you hear me? Liselle is your flesh and blood, boys. Why should anything change now? So her father was a soot. Big deal. He was a talented, handsome man as well.'

Danny stared at her and said quietly, 'If he was such a saint, why did you go to such lengths to get rid of him?'

'Because of this, the way you're acting. By Christ, I thought I'd brought you up a bit better than this. Your mother loved that little child when she was born. She doted on her. If you ain't inherited any care for people from me, I had hoped at least that my Eileen's tolerance would have rubbed off on you. You're like me mother. Everything has to be cut and dried. Well, the real world ain't like that. We never know where our heart's going to lie. You two have got to fall for someone yet, and believe me you don't know who it could be. It could be the biggest whore God ever put on this earth, but something could make you want her. That's real life, my loves.

'With my Kerry it was him. Black as night, handsome as the devil. He was like her, talented and beautiful. It was inevitable they'd fall in love. Only small-minded people like you two and me mother – and me, me as well – stopped them being together. Sometimes I look at her with the drink in her and it's like a knife twisting in me. I stopped her going to him, and the upshot's the fact that she's never known a happy day since. Not really. She kept Liselle and that's all power to her as far as I'm concerned.'

Boysie and Danny looked at Briony in shock.

'It's the thought of it, Mum . . . I mean, whoever's gonna want Liselle now?'

'Whoever gets Liselle will be a damned lucky fellow. That girl's worth fifty of others roundabout. Briony's right. Don't fall prey to small-mindedness, lads. It's a sin against God.'

Cissy's voice, normally good-humoured, was so vehement that the boys stared at her hard. Briony could have kissed her. It took good old Cissy, the funster, the woman the twins had always played pranks on and whom they loved in a haphazard, affectionate way, to put it all in perspective.

'She's still your cousin, who grew up with you, who you played with, who you always loved. She ain't changed because she has a bit of the tarbrush in her. It just makes her different to outsiders, that's all. Now, how about I make a nice pot of strong tea?'

Cissy made everything normal once more. Had taken the edge off the proceedings.

'I'll have a cup, me mouth feels like a buzzard's crutch.'

'Oh, Mrs H! You're disgusting.' Boysie's voice was overloud.

Cissy left to make the tea, Briony sat on the bed and sighed.

'Don't let Liselle know about all this. Let me tell her when the time's right. Don't treat her any differently, will you? Don't hurt her more than she's been hurt, and she's gonna be hurt.'

Danny nodded.

'Don't worry, Mum, we'll look after her. And if any of this does ever get out, well then, people can bastard well answer to us!'

The phone rang while Liselle was in the shower. Kerry picked it up hesitantly.

'Hello?' It was a question.

'Hello, Kerry baby. It's me, Evander.'

She closed her eyes as the feelings enveloped her once more. It was as if the past was there in the room with her.

'Kerry? Answer me, girl. Aren't you pleased to hear from me? I've seen my daughter. I've seen you, too.'

Kerry's mouth was dry.

'What do you want, Evander? Tell me?'

'I jus' want to see you again, for old time's sake. I don't want no trouble, girl. I had enough of that the last time.'

Kerry nodded, as if he could see her. 'When . . . When do you want to see me?'

'How about this afternoon? I know you're working tonight.'

Kerry didn't question how he knew this. Instead she said: 'Where? What time?'

'I've rented a little house in Notting Hill Gate. It's number sixteen Rillington Place. I'll expect you about two-thirty.'

Kerry nodded into the phone again, unable to speak properly.

Evander spoke once more, a worried tone in his voice. 'You are gonna come, girl? I'll be expecting you.'

'Yes . . . I'll be there.'

He laughed throatily. 'See you then.'

Kerry stared at the phone in terror. It was him. She had been right. And no matter how she tried to believe him when he said he was only here to see her for old time's sake, the frightened feeling inside her wouldn't go away.

Skip Paquale had sent his henchmen out for the rest of the day. Together he and Evander set up the front room of the little house ready for Kerry's visit. A tape recorder was hidden inside a box on the mahogany coffee table by the settee. They tested it three times before Skip was happy with it. Finally, placing a bottle of Wild Turkey and a bottle of vodka on the same table, with two glasses, he was satisfied.

'I'm warning you, Dorsey, don't get tanked up and ruin this or you'll be sorry. I want her right where I can really bleed her. You just reminisce with her, that's all, and find out about the girl. Get me?'

Evander nodded.

'That girl's a gold mine to us. A real gold mine. Without her we ain't gonna get a dime. Keep that in mind.'

Evander nodded again. In spite of everything, he had a sudden longing to see Kerry. Really see her. He found he was genuinely interested in the child. In his girl. Hearing Kerry's voice, after all this time, was something he had not been prepared for. He lit up one of his cheap cheroots and then his mind clouded again. Every time he looked at his hands it hurt him. Through Kerry he had lost his livelihood. His talent. He mustn't ever let himself forget that.

No one was worth the price he'd paid: years in dingy little dives, each day the crippling of his hands becoming more and more apparent. Each year the bitterness inside him growing. Until now. He was back in England once more, only this time he wasn't here to hit the big time and make a fortune. This time he was here to make blood money off the back of the woman who'd been like a Jonah to him from the day he had first laid eyes on her. She had had his child, his daughter, but that was nothing, he had to remember that. The child was his passport out of chocolate town and back into the real world where money cushioned everything. The colour of your skin, the roots you came from, even what friends you had.

With his own place he could be someone again. Evander Dorsey could once more hold his head up, could once more have a future.

Chapter Thirty-Seven

Liselle heard her mother come into the house at seven-thirty. She heard footsteps heavy on the stairs and knew Kerry had been drinking. She carried out her mother's clothes for the evening. She was singing tonight at The New Yorker as she did once a week whenever she didn't have concert dates. Victor had been on the telephone twice that afternoon, demanding to know just where her mother was. She had been supposed to meet him to discuss her recording contract and some dates for a European tour. Victor was livid to be stood up, and for the first time ever Liselle felt like telling him to piss off. One day she would. One day, good little girl Liselle would tell them all to piss off, her mother included.

'Oh, baby, I've had a lovely day. Such a lovely day.'

Liselle smiled as her mother came in. It was a forced smile and she hated herself for it.

'Tonight, after the show, I have a big surprise for you.'

'Good. Now how about getting in the bath and then getting dressed? We're late as usual.'

Kerry's face dropped at her daughter's flat voice. It was

because she'd been drinking. She shouldn't have drunk that vodka. But hadn't today been a celebration? Couldn't she have a celebratory drink?

She walked into the bedroom and began to run a bath, pulling off her clothes and dropping them on the floor. Well, she'd please her baby tonight. It had come to her in the taxi on her way home. Evander, her Evander, had wanted to see that she and Liselle were all right. All her worrying about trouble to come was unnecessary. He had just wanted to see her again. And as they had talked she had seen a shadow of the younger Evander emerge. The man who had attracted her. Well, in the cab it had dawned on her. She would take her daughter to see him. It would please Liselle so once she had met him, spoken to him, heard the full story, and it would please Evander. He had been touched that she'd named her after his mother. He had told her that three times. Sitting there with him had been like going back to her youth. Their time together was short but fruitful. Her baby girl, the result. Now it had come to her how she could right the wrongs she'd done to Liselle and Evander. She had told him how she'd wanted to go to him, how she'd nearly booked the passage but how she'd chickened out. If only she had gone! If only she'd followed her star! Things might have been so different. He was the father of her child and tonight she would give them both a big present.

She'd give them each other, father and daughter.

Skip had played the tape back five times. Evander sat quietly, listening to the husky, unmistakable voice of Kerry baring her soul.

'You did good, Evander, better than good even. That bitch ain't gonna know what hit her. This should be good for two hundred thousand dollars at least. There ain't no way she'll want all this common knowledge, it'll ruin her overnight.'

Evander's mouth fell open at that statement.

'And . . . Mr Skip, how much of that is mine?'

'How does twenty-five thousand grab you, black boy?'

Evander grinned. 'It grabs me OK.'

Greed was to the fore now. Listening to Kerry telling the world about their life together had been hard at first, he had felt like a snake in the grass, but the twenty-five Gs would soon put paid to that. He could buy a decent place for that. A decent place with decent acts and a good clientele. A good black clientele.

Skip's two henchmen let themselves in the house. Marty Duval and Kelvin Tomcola were young and not too bright. Exactly what Skip wanted in his heavies.

'Let's all have a drink to celebrate our good fortune. In a couple of days we'll be on our way back home, out of this godforsaken snowhole, and richer than we dreamed. What a Christmas present! The best part of it all is, we can bleed that bitch for years and years.'

Evander frowned at the words.

Then a large glass of bourbon was placed in his hands and he drank the toast with his so-called friends. But the words stayed with him.

At just after eleven a knock came on the front door. Skip looked out of the window and was amazed to see Kerry Cavanagh and her daughter on the doorstep.

'Jesus Christ! It's the broad and the kid. They're on the doorstep!'

Pushing the two other men from the room, Skip told Evander to let them in and play the game again.

This was working out even better than he'd hoped. As

he crept up the stairs to join the others he wished he had reset the tape recorder. This would have been better than ever.

Outside it was snowing again and Liselle looked at the shabby house and shivered.

'Mum, what are we doing here? What's this big surprise?'

Kerry, buoyed up with drink, pills and excitement, grinned, hugging her fur coat around her tighter.

'You'll soon see.'

Evander stood uncertainly behind the front door. This was not on the agenda, this was not supposed to happen. On the other side of that door was his child. If he met her, spoke to her, he would have to acknowledge her as such. Then he would have to cheat them both. Kerry was hard enough, but he figured she owed him. The child owed him nothing. He wished he hadn't had so much drink, or that he'd drunk more so he would be oblivious of all these feelings assailing him. Shame, guilt. And worst of all, much worse than the other two, longing. He was longing to see her now.

Kerry knocked again. From the landing came Skip's angry voice.

'Open the fucking door, black boy, what you waiting for? Christmas?'

The voice brought him back to earth and Evander opened the door. Kerry swept in, dragging the girl behind her, her red fox coat still glistening with flakes of snow. Her hair glossy and sleek on her head like a luxurious hat. He had to concentrate on Kerry because he was frightened to look at the girl with those deep brown eyes and that coffee-coloured skin.

Kerry, always the dramatist, held out Liselle's arm and said loudly: 'Baby, meet your father.'

Evander looked at his daughter then, full in the face. All he was aware of was the distaste he saw there, coupled with shock. Too late, he remembered he was in stockinged feet, his trousers unbuckled because they were tight, his shirt, clean on that afternoon, stained with drink and food. But it wasn't that that appalled her: it was the grey-tinged hands with their claw-like fingers.

Kerry looked at them both. Seeing Liselle's eyes riveted to Evander's distorted hands, she grasped her daughter by the shoulders and pushed her into the open doorway of the lounge. She closed the front door that was letting in a weak light from the street together with the freezing snow, and followed her daughter into the warmth.

'Yes, look at his hands. That was your Aunt Briony's work. Oh, she denied it, but she did that. Broke his fingers, every one of them, and his wrists, too. Smashed to smithereens in Briony's name. Now you know why I never told you. Was never going to tell you. Then he turned up here and I realised that you had to know. Especially after last night.'

Liselle still hadn't opened her mouth. She was staring in disgust at the man in front of her. He was fat, he was unkempt, this was not what girlish dreams were made of. This was not what she'd wanted. Deep inside herself she had known he was a black man, she admitted to herself she'd always known, but she had never really expected to have it thrust on her like this in a dingy little house in Notting Hill. It was laughable. That this man, with the huge belly and the clawed hands, could have been her reason for living! Nowhere in her wildest imagingings could she imagine him young and handsome and taking her mother, her beautiful mother, and giving her a child. Herself.

Evander looked at the girl with her silky blue-black hair and the high prominent cheekbones, her sensuous lips, and felt the enormity of what he'd done. What he had created. In the States she would have been aware of what she was from day one and would have adjusted accordingly. Brought up here, in this cold barren country, she wasn't remotely prepared for what life was going to dish out to her. Inside himself, he felt a cracking, breaking sensation. It was fear: fear of what she would think of him, fear of what was going to happen to this tall lithe creature who would draw men to her, who had such a beautiful, appealing exterior thanks to himself and his forefathers. Here in England she'd live in a no man's land, neither black nor white. Brought up white, she'd have no understanding of the black culture, of her people. Until she began to breed. Then she'd bear the legacy of her father and his father's father.

Kerry watched the two eyeing each other. Going to the table she poured out three stiff drinks. Handing one to Evander and one to Liselle, she sat on the settee, watching them warily now. It had not worked out as she had thought. It had all gone wrong. No one spoke a word for what seemed an eternity.

Kerry guzzled her drink, coughing at the unfamiliar taste of the raw cheap black market bourbon.

Evander stood silently with his drink in hand. He didn't want a drink now, when he should want one, when he should be gulping the precious liquid down to kill the pain inside him.

'Sit down, child. We need to talk.'

His voice was deep. Hearing it for the first time, Liselle was snapped out of her shock. Putting the drink on the mantelpiece untouched she strode past him, out of the room and out into the snow-filled night. Slamming the front door behind her she hurried away, slipping and sliding on the icy pavement.

That couldn't be her father. It couldn't. Not because he was black, but because he was so horrible. He was dirty-looking, he smelt of stale food and cheap Scotch. She came from better than that, she knew she did.

She made her way back to The New Yorker in a cab. Auntie Briony would know what to do.

She always did.

The twins were in one of their 'spielers', an illegal gambling club in Stepney. The place was packed out as usual. The twins were now treated like visiting royalty wherever they went in the East End. People went out of their way to be noticed by them. If they went into a shop, the cigarettes or whatever else they bought became 'gifts'. Stallholders made a fuss of them, shopkeepers kept on the right side of them. The twins, Boysie especially, loved this. Revelled in it.

The 'spieler' was approached through a large barred door, a small peephole was opened to establish who was there, and then they were duly let in, frisked, and allowed to get to the gaming tables and the bar. Prostitutes worked the clubs, generally married women out for a bit of adventure and a few quid to supplement the housekeeping. Nothing was organised in the twins' establishments unless they organised it themselves.

The place was buzzing tonight. The twins got themselves a drink and went through to the offices. They were waiting for a young Jew named Isaiah Lipman. He was twenty-five years old and one of the best 'longshoremen' in the business. The twins wanted to cultivate him.

The Jewish community and the Irish were similar in a lot of respects. They were immigrants, they were disliked by the majority, and Jewish men seemed much like the Irish in the fact that they either succeeded beyond imagination or they were wasters. Both cultures, though, had an inbred cunning. The Lane, or Petticoat Lane as it was better known, traded on a Sunday because of the Jews. Like the Irish they kept to their religion no matter what else they might do. And it paid off for them.

Longshoring was the term used for a particular scam. It involved renting cheap premises, getting headed notepaper printed up and then opening accounts with suppliers. For the first couple of months, while the business was supposedly getting on its feet, you paid for your goods as invoiced, with cash off the hip. Ready money. Gradually building up your credibility as a customer. Then one day you ordered fantastic amounts from your suppliers on credit, as usual. Then you disappeared off the face of the earth with up to one hundred thousand pounds' worth of stock. Usually electrical appliances or good clothes. Anything that could easily be sold on. This stock then found its way on to the markets, into shops and anywhere else it could be sold.

It was a very easy operation, it was patience that was needed. That was where Isaiah came in. Danny and Boysie wanted everything yesterday.

Boysie sipped his drink. 'That was a turn up, what The Aunt told us about Liselle. I guessed though. We both did. But hearing it like, that's a different thing.'

Daniel looked at himself in the mirror on the wall behind their desk. He patted down his hair and, licking a finger, smoothed one of his eyebrows.

'Yeah . . . We'll have to watch the rhyming slang now,

Boysie. Lemonade, spade. Macaroon, coon. Whistle me dog, wog. Sounds different when it's one of your family, don't it? If someone called Liselle that, I'd break their fucking necks. I'd rip their heads off with me bare hands. Yet I use those terms all the time.'

'That's because we ain't never known many blacks. I always liked Bessie, even as a kid. I liked that flowery smell of her when I was little . . . We'll have to stop saying front wheel skid and Yid, as well as a four be two, once old Isaiah becomes a part of the firm. Fuck me, we're going international, ain't we?'

Danny laughed. 'Yeah. I'm looking forward to meeting this bloke properly, though. He ain't a hardman, but he's got brains. Brains we can use to our advantage. Once we get him under our wing, we'll leave him to work on his own. He won't tuck us up.'

Boysie laughed as he left the room. 'He wouldn't dare, Danny Boy.'

Briony listened to Liselle's story with amazement tinged with annoyance. Only Kerry would pull a stunt like that! Anyone else would have done it gently, prepared the ground. But anyone else wouldn't have been under the influence of vodka and barbiturates. The way she felt now, if she saw Kerry she would be hard pressed not to slap her a ringing blow across the earhole.

'All right, love, calm down.'

'But you don't understand me! It wasn't that he was black. I knew that, I've always known that, though I couldn't admit it to myself. Now I know it's true, I don't care. It's him, the man himself. I can't believe he's my father. He smelt, Auntie Briony, of stale fags, booze and food. He was gross. He was so . . . so . . . tatty-looking.

That's what hurt me, that I could have sprung from him. And his hands . . . his hands were horrible. Then Mum said *you* had had that done to him. You got someone to break his fingers. But you wouldn't do anything like that, would you?' It was a plea.

Briony sat down in her chair and sighed. Outside the office was the sound of Bessie singing, the clinking of glasses, the buzz of conversation. If only they were out there instead of in here, trying to make sense of something that happened over twenty years ago. Something that should have stayed buried.

'Listen, my love. Your father was a big handsome man when he knew your mother. Really, he was like a big black Adonis if that's possible!' She smiled to take the edge off the words. 'He was talented, really talented. Together they could have conquered the world. When I got rid of him, and I did get rid of him, make no mistake about that, it was because twenty years ago . . .' Briony swallowed hard. 'Well, you have to realise, it was in the twenties. Mixed marriages were unheard of then. It wasn't like now when lots of girls marry their black GIs. It's a different world now, love. Then it would have ruined your mother and him. A black man seen with a white woman could cause murder to be done.'

Liselle sniffed, wiping her nose with the back of her hand. 'Your father looks like he does now because I sent someone to force him to leave. Well, the bloke, Kevin Carter, went too far. He broke his hands. I never asked him to, I take oath on that, Lissy. But I suppose that having his hands destroyed stopped Evander earning his living, doing what he did so well. He was a brilliant jazz pianist once, believe me, and I truly regret my part in putting an end to his career.'

Liselle nodded, trying to take in what her aunt was saying, trying to decipher her true feelings from amongst the sadness and shock that was enveloping her. Her aunt made it all sound so nice, so romantic. Her mother wanted the brilliant black man who could play the piano. Now, all these years later, Liselle was to be saddled with a man who'd been crippled because her aunt thought that getting rid of him was the best thing at the time.

'Shall I take you home?'

Liselle shook her head. 'Can I stay with you, please? I don't want to see me mum. Not for a while.'

Briony smiled and put her arm around the girl's slim shoulders. 'You can stay as long as you like, my darlin'. You know that.'

The twins had arrived at the club just after one-thirty. Briony had sent Liselle home with Tommy to look after her. She herself was determined to find Kerry. She was not at home, Briony had been ringing in ten-minute intervals, so they made their way to Rillington Place.

The twins had listened to Briony's explanation of the night's events in silence. Boysie shook his head in disbelief. His Aunt Kerry was a fruitcake. Poor old Liselle! They knew that their own mother hadn't been all the ticket, and now by all accounts Aunt Kerry was tipping herself over the edge. Well, they were finally going to meet the soot who had caused all this hag. They hoped for his sake he wasn't here to try and cause trouble.

Briony had voiced the opinion that it seemed funny, on reflection, for a man to turn up all these years later and rent a house. A tourist went to a hotel. Suddenly, it seemed very suspicious. Getting in touch with Kerry whose number wasn't listed . . . Who did he get it from? Who else knew he was here?

'Don't worry, Mum. If necessary we'll blast off every front door in the road but we'll find the right house. Stop letting it bug you.'

Boysie caressed a Beretta he kept with him at all times. Daniel smiled as he drove. In the boot was a shotgun that could kill a marauding elephant at a hundred paces. They'd find out the score all right.

In fact, he was quite looking forward to it.

After Liselle had left the house, Kerry got up to follow her. Then three men walked into the room. Kerry, in her usual drunken state, barely noticed. But when one man, whom Evander addressed as Mr Skip, pushed her back into her seat, it dawned on her that here was big trouble.

She looked at Evander with frightened eyes. 'What's going on here? Who are this lot?'

Skip laughed out loud.

'We are your biggest nightmare. Pour the lady a drink, Marty.'

Marty did as he was bidden and Kerry took it gratefully. But as Skip explained to her what they wanted, she gradually began to feel a numb fear.

Evander listened to Skip's gloating voice, wishing himself anywhere in the world but in this dirty little room. As he watched Kerry's eyes widen with fear and the realisation of what was happening, he felt sick inside himself.

Twenty-five thousand dollars was a lot of money. But was it really worth all this? When did this get so out of hand? When did it become so dirty, and so shaming?

As Skip had played back the tape Kerry's mouth had opened and shut, like a fish out of water, gasping for life.

Now she knew why he had asked her three times why she had named her child Liselle for his mother. Why he had repeatedly asked her about their life together. It was for this. Even in her drunken, drugged state she saw what a fool she'd been. She'd wanted to right wrongs when the biggest wrong was being done to her!

She started to laugh, a low chuckle at first. Then, as all became crystal clear, it turned into a full-throated belly laugh. Four pairs of eyes watched her in amazement.

'You can give this to anyone you like. The newspapers, anyone. I couldn't give a monkey's fuck!' Her voice was shrill. 'I ain't ashamed any more. I don't care. My baby knows now. She knows. Once she knew about this, it was blown wide open. You did all this for nothing . . . nothing!'

Skip gave her a stinging blow across the mouth. But still she laughed.

'Go on, beat me up! Nothing you can do to me can really hurt me, because I've been hurting all my life.'

But the laughter was gone from her voice now.

Skip, seeing his well-laid plans go awry, took her at her word. He began to lay into her with heavy fists. Evander stumbled across the room, his useless hands clawing at the man attacking Kerry. The two younger men watched with morbid fascination. Evander turned to them.

'You fools! She's famous . . . If you really hurt her, you'll all be finished.'

His voice persuaded the other two. They began pulling Skip off her, dragging him from the room as he hurled abuse at Kerry, at them and at Evander. They pulled him into the kitchen and tried to calm him down.

Evander went to Kerry. Her mouth and one eye were bleeding profusely. Her arms were crossed defensively.

Pulling her into his arms, he held her close, sorry to the core for what he had brought on her.

An hour later he saw the headlights of a car coming up the road. The curtains were back. He had opened the window to let in some air. Skip, calmer now, was still in the kitchen, trying to salvage part of his plan. Marty sat in the room with them, refusing to let either Kerry or Evander leave.

Kerry's face was swollen, her lip split, one eye black and blue. Evander was still holding her to him tightly. The shock of what had happened had counteracted the vodka and even the pills. Kerry was aware that they were both in great danger. Skip came into the room, calmer now.

'Listen to me, lady. I am gonna sell those tapes to the newspapers and whether you care or not, your career will be destroyed. Everyone will know what your daughter is and what you are. I have ten black men who will sign confessions saying they've slept with you. Had disgusting, perverted sexual relationships with you. Your name will be dirt, synonymous with every kind of filth, when I've finished. Unless you pay me what I want. Do you understand what I'm telling you?'

Kerry nodded painfully. 'How much?'

'Three hundred thousand pounds. I've upped the ante because I don't like mouthy broads, especially mouthy broads who sleep with niggers.' His voice was so vehement even Evander was shocked.

'I don't have that kind of money.'

It was Skip's turn to laugh now. 'Then my advice to you, little lady, is to find someone who does.'

The car Evander had heard was the twins' Aston Martin.

As they parked in the narrow road and got out, they

saw into the room of number sixteen. It was the only house still lit up.

'Wait here and keep down,' Danny ordered.

Creeping into the small front garden he looked in at the window of the lounge. The net curtains were about two inches too short for the window and he saw Kerry sitting on the settee opposite him, her face bloody. Beside her was the black man, Evander Dorsey; he was holding her hands in his. The three white men were sitting around the room watching them; one had a gun beside within easy reach of his hand. Daniel found his eyes riveted to his aunt and the man beside her. He glanced once more at the gun and went back to Boysie and Briony.

'They're in there all right, with three other men. One has a gun. Aunt Kerry's face is a mess, someone's roughed her up.'

'What?' Briony's voice was incredulous.

'That's the truth, the coon's sitting on the settee with Aunt Kerry. Something is happening here, Mum, and I don't know what. But me and Boysie will find out in about one minute.' He motioned to Boysie with his head. 'Come on, round the back. You sit in the car and wait. We'll open the front door when everything's sorted.'

Briony bridled.

'Excuse me, Danny . . .'

'Mum, please do as we ask – there's a shooter in there. Danny and me will sort it. Now sit in the car and wait.'

He took the Beretta from his coat and checked to see it was loaded.

Briony snatched the gun from him.

'Listen to me, you two will do as I say for once. I mean it. Get around the back. I'm going in the front. I'll sort out the geek with the gun once I'm in there.'

Boysie shook his head.

'Oh, leave it out, Mum . . .'

'No! You leave it out. That's my sister in there, and something's not kosher. Don't let's argue amongst ourselves out here. They'll let me in. I'll pretend I've come because of Liselle, because she's so upset. You two come in in five minutes, right? I don't want to hear any more about it.'

With that she walked away from them and up the pathway towards the front door. She turned and motioned to them to go around the back. As they disappeared down the alleyway that separated the house from the one next-door, she put her own Beretta into the pocket of her fox fur coat and knocked loudly on the door. Inside, everyone stood stock still as the hammering on the door reverberated through the house.

Skip slid off the table and picked up the gun.

'Stay here, I'll deal with this.' Pushing the gun into the waistband of his trousers and covering it with his jacket, he went out into the cold hallway. He opened the door to a tiny redhead and breathed a sigh of relief.

'Is my sister still here? My niece came home in a terrible state. Is Kerry here . . .' Briony walked into the house without a by your leave, pushing past the man to walk into the lounge.

Kerry's face and Evander's frightened eyes told her everything.

Turning to the man who had answered the door, she said in a shocked voice: 'What the hell is going on here?'

The man walked towards her, smiling nastily. As he opened his mouth to speak, Briony moved so fast he didn't have time to think. Nobody did. In a split second she was behind him with the Beretta digging into his kidneys.

'One move, big boy, and I'll splatter your guts all over this house!' She looked at the two other hoods, still sitting in the fireside chairs. 'Take out any weapons you've got and place them on the floor in front of you.' Skip started to put his arms down and Briony pushed the gun into his back once more.

'Don't even think about it! I'll just take you with me, boy. I'll take your gun myself, thank you.'

As she spoke Daniel and Boysie walked into the room. The sight of sawn-off shotguns gave all three prisoners a sinking feeling in their guts.

Boysie and Daniel, smiling now, were looking the three Americans over.

'Imagine leaving your back door open.'

'Especially in an area like this. It's a wonder you weren't burgled. Now I think we need a few explanations, and you three are going to provide them.' Danny's voice was soft as silk.

As Skip looked at the two young men and the tiny redhead he knew he would never see the outside of this room. Shaking his head in amazement, he resigned himself to that.

One thing Skip had always had in his favour: he knew when he was beaten.

Chapter Thirty-Eight

Briony listened with barely controlled emotion as Evander told the whole story. His voice was low, honest and without guile. He did not attempt to underplay his own role or justify himself, which did him some good with Briony and the twins. The East End had a saying: 'If you get a capture, hold your hand up.' When he said that Skip was related to Tommy Corolla, a Mafia don, the twins laughed out loud.

Boysie, always quick to joke, said to Skip, 'I couldn't give a fuck who your godfather was, mate, my godfather's bleeding Jonathan la Billière. You're dead as a frigging doornail, not because of what you done, but because of who you done it to. You so-called Mafia prats should find out just who you're dealing with before you start your little games over here.'

To prove his point he punched Skip in the head three times, knocking him to the ground. Boysie was losing that famous temper of his. Briony watched calmly.

'Leave it for a while, Boysie love. Let Evander finish.'

'He's a ponce, they're all ponces, that black bastard included!'

Kerry was crying softly. 'Look, leave it, please, I just want to go home now!'

Briony patted her arm and said loudly, 'What you want, Kerry, is a drink. Well, this is one time when you'll have to wait. We have to sort this thing out tonight, once and for all.'

Looking at Evander, she said, 'I take it you're sorry now, for all this?'

Evander looked at the ground. He nodded.

Briony stared at him. He was like a caricature of the man she'd known. Every time she saw his hands, she felt a flush of shame.

Making a decision, she stood up. 'Is there a phone here?'

Evander pointed to the hallway. 'Out there.'

'I'll phone up Tommy. He can take me, Kerry and Evander back to my place. You two can do what you like with these. They're pieces of shite and I don't care what happens to them.'

Going to Skip, she lifted his face towards her with one perfectly manicured finger. Looking into his eyes, she said, 'You made your big mistake when you touched my sister. No one, I don't care who they're related to, ever touches me or mine.'

Walking outside to the hall to telephone Tommy, it occurred to her that phoning him this way was just like old times.

It seemed the past was always there like a spectre, waiting to rise up and catch you unawares when you least expected it.

In the end Tommy had stayed to help dispose of the three Americans under fifty tons of concrete that was due to be poured into the footings of the new Ford plant at

Dagenham. Briony drove back to her house with a frightened Evander, his few belongings, and a shocked and subdued Kerry. When they got to Briony's house, Liselle had already gone up to bed and Briony was secretly grateful for this. It was four-thirty in the morning. The three new arrivals were wide awake, and quiet. Too quiet.

Kerry helped herself to a large neat vodka and Briony poured herself and Evander large brandies. She surveyed the man in front of her for a good while.

Evander looked like a beaten man, but Briony guessed he had looked like that for a long time. It was in his eyes, his stance, in those clawed and deformed hands that had trouble holding on to the balloon-shaped glass.

Finishing her drink silently, Briony took Kerry and tucked her up in bed. She had no fears about Evander running off, he would be easy enough to find. Kevin's overenthusiasm all those years ago would guarantee that.

She checked Kerry's face over and, satisfied it was just cuts and bruises, went back down to the room where she had left Evander. Pouring them both another drink, his in a tall tumbler this time, she sat opposite him and spoke.

'You realise those men are dead, don't you?'

Her matter-of-fact voice frightened Evander. She had changed, this Briony. He remembered her as softer, younger admittedly, but softer inside.

He nodded in answer to her question and Briony sighed loudly.

'In a way, I can see your point of view. I know you must have found it very hard over the years. I also realise that the offer of a large sum of money in your circumstances was very tempting. I did something bad once, a long time ago, and was paid a large amount of money. Once you get a stake, you can make it grow.'

'I wanted a little club of my own. Before it was too late.'

Briony nodded, as if understanding him, agreeing with him. 'But the reason you're here, Evander, is because my niece Liselle knows you exist, Liselle knows about you. No other reason. You understand me?'

He licked dry lips and nodded furiously.

'I will provide you with money, a car and decent clothes. Also a place to live. You, for your part, will make friends with your daughter, or at least try to. I want her to see you as you once were. If everything works out well, I'll give you enough to open a club. So my advice to you is, think long and hard about what I just said. The ball is in your court. I want my niece to have a few good memories to take her through her life. You will be one of them.'

To herself she thought, God knows she'll need them after these last few days.

It was the week before Christmas and the snow was piled high. It was a windowsill winter, as the wags said on the market stalls. The snow cleaned up London while it lay thick, and even the bomb sites looked picturesque.

Evander was now on relatively good terms with his daughter and Kerry was relieved that the trouble was over at last.

Briony, for her part, had pushed it all from her mind, concentrating on getting Evander and Liselle at least partly reconciled. She knew that they had talked a couple of times well into the night and this pleased her immensely.

If Liselle could get some idea of her background it would make her situation easier to bear. There was a marked change in her. She seemed quieter, more controlled. Her easy laugh had disappeared and Briony mourned for the innocent girl that was gone much as she loved the woman who was emerging. Molly was still getting what she termed the 'bum's rush' from everyone, and Briony hoped this taught her a lesson. Even poor old Rosalee was overlooked in the effort to make their mother pay for what she had done.

Evander seemed to have come into his own once he had money in his pocket and at least the appearance of independence. Bessie had whooped with delight at seeing him which pleased Liselle who didn't know Briony had arranged it. Bessie made Evander out to be the best thing since sliced bread and he sat back and accepted the accolade, unaware that Briony had talked Bessie through it.

Kerry, after the trauma, was drinking more than ever and unable to function at work. Briony had had to put the hard word on Victor through the twins, and unknown to Kerry herself, she was going into the clinic in Surrey after Christmas. Satisfied she had done all she could for her family, Briony concentrated on Tommy and Mariah and the businesses. But there were two further shocks awaiting her towards Christmas 1947 and the first happened while she was out shopping.

Coming out of Fortnum and Mason into a thick blizzard, Briony stood under the canopy waiting for Boysie and the car. As she turned round she came face to face with Isabel Dumas and Benedict: a grown-up Benedict carrying a young boy in his arms. Briony knew immediately this was her grandson and the rush of blood to her head made her feel faint.

Seeing his mother's face, Benedict frowned. Then, looking at Briony fully, he wondered where he had seen her before. She looked familiar. Very familiar. He smiled at her hesitantly. Briony looked into the face so like her own and smiled back, her heart thumping in her breast like the band of the Coldstream Guards. The boy in Benedict's arms had the green eyes and red hair of his grandmother, though today Briony's hair was hidden under a large hat.

'Hello, Isabel.' Briony spoke carefully, pronouncing her words properly.

'Why, Briony. How are you?' Isabel's voice was strained and Benedict looked from one to the other in consternation.

'I don't think we've been introduced?' His voice, soft and musical, was like a dream to Briony.

'This is Miss Briony Cavanagh. Miss Cavanagh, *my* son, Benedict Dumas.'

Briony nodded to him.

'And this little scallywag is my son, Henry. Henry Dumas.'

Briony put up a gloved hand and stroked the plump cheek lightly.

The child had a toy gun. He pointed it at her and said, 'Bang!'

Briony smiled widely. The child was exquisite. Was beautiful. Was her grandchild. She felt like blurting out the truth there and then. But Isabel, seeing her expression, shook her hand quickly and hustled the others off, away from her. She watched them disappear into the snow-filled street, her heart breaking. She had seen her boy, her son, and her grandson.

She could see the twins in that child, the same shape of head, the same build. She smiled bitterly. He even had a gun.

Boysie drove up with the car and was shocked to see she had been crying.

Benedict waited until they were home before he spoke.

'Who was that Miss Cavanagh we met? I feel I know her somehow.'

His father choked on his cup of tea and Benedict slapped his back hard.

Isabel shook her head and said dismissively, 'Oh, she's a madam, to be honest. Did a lot of charity work in the war. Couldn't ignore her after that. But she really isn't to be encouraged.'

Benedict nodded. But there was something else about the woman, something so familiar it preyed on his mind for the rest of the day.

The next shock for Briony that year was even more serious.

Molly was beside herself with annoyance, continually telling poor Rosalee exactly what she thought of Briony and her gang, as she referred to her daughters and grandchildren. Mother Jones was bad again, and Molly's time was taken up with looking after her. Unlike previous illnesses, this one was serious enough to have the doctor visit daily without being asked. Mother Jones had picked up a flu virus and it was really knocking her out. Molly was single-handedly taking care of the old woman who was now bedridden and incontinent of both bladder and bowels. Consequently, Molly was very busy and for this reason didn't notice Rosalee's unusual quietness. When she finally did, she was grateful for it. But Rosalee was ill herself. Unable to tell anyone exactly what was wrong with her, she just sat passively, feeling worse by the day.

*

'What are we doing about Gran? Is she coming here for Christmas?' Boysie, always the first to calm down after an argument, wanted to see her now, and his Auntie Rosalee for whom he had bought a beautiful brooch as a Christmas present.

Kerry shrugged. 'To be honest, Boysie, I thought she'd have been in touch by now. I sent Mother Jones a basket of fruit. Abel's really worried about her. I expected me mother on the doorstep before now, moaning about looking after her.'

Briony bit her lip thinking about this for a second. 'Tell you what, how about me and you pop round and see the old girl tonight? That way me mother can either act as if nothing's happened, or she can start her antics. Either way we gave her a chance. But I ain't begging her. No way. This last turn out was all her fault, and if she does come for Christmas she ain't drinking. Kerry's bad enough.'

Boysie laughed. 'Fair enough. Danny should be in soon, we'll all go.'

Briony looked at the big man in front of her and grinned. 'You're missing your old gran, ain't you? Big as you are.'

He smiled good-naturedly. 'She's a pain in the arse at times, but she ain't really a bad old stick. It's Christmas Eve tomorrow. We'll go tonight and see how the land lies. I want to see Auntie Rosalee anyway.'

Briony smiled again. The twins loved poor old Rosalee. Other children might have been ashamed of her, but not them. They doted on her.

They were all missing Rosalee in their own ways, herself included. It was a sad fact that her mother and Rosalee went hand in hand. In fact it was one of her mother's saving graces, the way she looked after her. Yes, they would have to go. For Rosalee's sake, if for no other reason.

Bernadette watched her husband closely.

'Why the change of clothes at lunchtime, Marcus? That shirt was clean on this morning.'

He turned from the elaborate mirror on their dressing table and chucked her under the chin.

'I've got to see an important client today. As you know, Briony has expanded her clientele and now I have to deal with some very important people. I have to look respectable.' His voice had the evasive quality she hated.

'You looked respectable this morning, Marcus.'

He rolled his eyes and sighed loudly. 'Look, Bern, I am getting a bit sick of all this questioning. I'm only changing my shirt, not having a bath to meet a fancy woman. Now will you just leave it?'

Bernadette bit back the retort that was on her lips and kept her peace. Fifteen minutes later he left the house without kissing her goodbye. That was her punishment for questioning him. Walking into her daughter's bedroom she absentmindedly smoothed the quilt on a bed and straightened up already perfectly straight pictures. The girls were too old to take up all her time now, she admitted that fact to herself. Which was why she had too much time to think. Think about Marcus, and his increasing handsomeness.

Why was it a man could father fifteen children, a hundred children, and still look untouched? Whereas a woman like herself paid the price for her children's birth in every stretch mark, in the sagging of her stomach muscles, in the spreading of waist and hips. Going into her own bedroom she picked up the shirt her husband had discarded and held it to her nose, breathing in the smell of him. His soap, his sweat, and, thank God, for once no smell of perfume. Cheap perfume. That smell had been there a lot lately.

She had known for many years that Marcus was a philanderer. He liked women and was in a job where he was surrounded by them. Beautiful women. Until now it had only bothered her periodically, knowing that as the mother of his children she held the upper hand. That was until about six months ago when she had first noticed the distinctive smell of cheap perfume. The same smell had lingered on a lot of his shirts since then. A cloying, orangey fragrance, a whore's smell. Only this whore was still in attendance six months later and that worried her.

One-night stands she could cope with, they were more or less an occupational hazard with Marcus's job. But a permanent woman was a different kettle of fish. That meant commitment of some sort, it meant he was having regular conversations with her, maybe about Bernie herself and the children. It meant that Marcus was enamoured enough to see the same girl again and again. Maybe fancy himself in love with her. It meant a threat to Bernadette, her children, and their idyllic homelife.

It meant big trouble.

She put the shirt into the washing basket and sat on the bed. The house was exceptionally quiet. The girls were both round at friends' houses, her cook and cleaner had the day off. Alone and troubled, she sat on the bed observing herself in the large gilt mirror opposite, finding herself sadly lacking in any attractions that might snare a wandering husband. The tears came then. Seeing her face in the mirror, screwed up with misery, only made her feel worse.

But the Cavanaghs were fighters. All the Cavanagh women were, and by Christ she had more to fight for than most.

She wiped her eyes, dragging at the lids with her fingers, enjoying the pain she caused herself.

She would fight all right.

Molly was cooking a small capon, braising it in a thick gravy so Mother Jones could just suck at it, when she heard the car pull up outside the house. She smiled to herself. So the buggers had come at last. She'd resigned herself to waiting out Christmas and maybe New Year until she saw her family. She put in a small shake of salt and tasted the bubbling gravy before she deigned to answer the knock on her front door.

Rosalee, sitting by the fire, saw her nephews and made a snorting noise with delight. Boysie and Daniel, striding past their granny, went straight to her, talking loudly as they always did, even though she wasn't in the least deaf, and making a big fuss of her.

'Hello, Auntie Rosalee, how are you, darlin'?'

Briony stepped in at the front door and nodded at her mother.

'Mum.'

Then walking to Rosalee she too made a fuss of her. Only unlike the boys she stared at her sister for a long while first.

Molly pursed her lips and went back to her cooking. Well, she mused, at least they came, even if it was just to see Rosalee.

'That smells handsome, Gran.' Boysie as always was the first to make a friendly overture.

Molly suppressed a grin and said sternly, 'Well, sit yourself down then! There's plenty to go round.'

Daniel and Boysie sat at the scrubbed table and Briony sat with her sister on the fireside chairs. She lit herself a cigarette.

'How's Mother Jones?' Her voice was neutral.

Molly shook her head and said truthfully, 'I'll be surprised if she lasts the Christmas, Bri. She's bad this time, God love her. The priest is coming tonight.'

'We'll go in after the boys have eaten.'

Molly nodded and the room was quiet once more. Finally she swallowed her pride and said, 'How's Liselle and Kerry?'

Briony pulled on her cigarette. If her mother asked that, she was admitting responsibility for what she had done. It was something they all knew but no one alluded to.

'They're fine, Mum. Great in fact. Liselle's father is over here actually, visiting her.'

Briony took great pleasure in seeing her mother's face whiten. The wooden spoon clattered to the floor.

'What did you just say?'

'I said, Evander Dorsey is over for a visit, from the States. Liselle is very pleased finally to know him, as a matter of fact.'

Briony berated herself inwardly for enjoying saying all this to her mother, but God himself knew, she'd asked for what she got.

'I wouldn't be surprised if she went over for a visit next year.'

Molly stooped down to pick up the spoon. Running it under the tap, she said, 'Jesus, Mary and Joseph! Would you credit that?'

Boysie and Daniel laughed, enjoying their gran's discomfiture.

'He's nice bloke, Gran, me and Boysie really like him.' Daniel rubbed salt into the open wound with glee.

Molly, cute enough to know that the joke was on her, kept her peace. Now they were all here in front of her, she realised just how much she had missed them all, especially the twins. 'I'm glad the child has met her father. It must be a great load off her mind. How did she take it?'

Boysie laughed out loud then. His gran was not only eating humble pie, she was chewing it in big lumps and swallowing it without water.

'Oh, better than we expected, Gran. Much better.'

Molly nodded and began dishing out broth, cutting large lumps of soda bread, hot from the oven, for the twins. She placed the food in front of them and they attacked it with relish.

'Rosalee looks rough, Mum, has she been all right?' Briony's voice was low and concerned.

Molly flapped a large hand and shook her head. 'Oh, you know what she's like. She's been off her food a couple of weeks, that's all. It's all the upheaval with Mother Jones. You know how she hates change of any kind. And she's missed you lot.' The last was a barb aimed at them all, and it met its mark because all three felt ashamed.

Molly, satisfied she'd paid them all back for their earlier jokes at her expense, felt happier.

Rosalee guessed she was being talked about, and whimpered. Her fat cheeks were white and her eyes a flat grey. Briony took one pudgy hand in hers and squeezed it gently.

Well, we're here now. I thought you might like to come for Christmas, Mum, you and Rosalee?'

Her sister whimpered and took her hand from Briony's. Holding it to her side, she rocked herself in the chair.

'Is her hand hurting, Mum? Has she knocked it?'

Molly shrugged.

'Not that I know of, but come to think of it, she's been holding it like that for a while. I looked her over last week and I can't find anything wrong there. No broken bones anyway. I think it's the snow. She hates the cold. All she wants to do is sit in front of that fire and keep as warm as toast.'

Molly bent down to her daughter and smiled widely. 'Don't you, darlin'?'

Rosalee smiled and nodded, her face devoid of any real expression.

'We'll try and come for Christmas but with Mother Jones as she is . . . Well, I can't leave her, can I?'

'I suppose not.'

Molly put the kettle on for tea and said nonchalantly, 'Will that . . . Will Liselle's father be there for Christmas like?'

'Yes. He will. We're all having dinner at my place.'

Briony frowned to herself. She was treading a fine line at the moment with Evander and Liselle. The girl felt that her father's disfigurement was all Briony's fault, and in reality it was. But it was all a long time ago, and in her youthful ignorance Liselle couldn't understand different circumstances and different times.

'What's he really like then? This . . . Liselle's father?'

Daniel and Boysie looked at their gran and felt sorry for her. She couldn't even bring herself to say his name.

'He's all right. Ain't he, Danny? He loves Liselle, Gran. He really does. I think it's done her good meeting him. She seems more grown-up somehow. More sure of herself.'

Molly made the tea and kept her peace. A little while

later she went into Mother Jones with a small bowl of broth and some soda bread. Briony and the twins joined her.

Rosalee sat by the fire, the pins and needles in her arms beginning to fade a little now. But the pain across her chest, as if a great weight was lying across it, was still there.

Kerry wasn't singing, in fact she wasn't really doing anything except drinking. The shock of what had happened to her had affected her more than she would admit. The cuts and bruises had faded. She had told Liselle she'd had a fall, and Liselle had upset her by not questioning that, assuming her mother was drunk. The injuries had gone but the reason for them was still fresh in her mind. Evander had been trying to blackmail her. He had taken her trust and abused it. She had been a fool. A complete and utter fool.

Now, seeing him and Liselle together was like a knife inside her gut. Twisting and turning for the maximum pain. And three men were dead, she was sure of that. The twins would have taken care of them. Kerry wondered what Eileen would have thought of the two boys she had entrusted to Briony. Eileen, the sister with a goodness of spirit lacking in the others. Eileen who was too kind for this world and its harsh realities. Eileen whom they all missed, each and every day. What would she have made of her boys, her babies, taking people and making them disappear?

Briony didn't even care. She didn't care what they did as long as they were all right. As long as the family survived whatever was thrown at it.

Kerry couldn't admit to herself that she was jealous of Evander now, of his need for his child and her need for him. That Liselle was picking up his ways, his expressions. Was gradually blanking her out and welcoming her father in. Even though he had tried to destroy her, destroy them both.

Briony said she wasn't ever to tell Liselle the truth of the situation. That she should only know her father as a kind man, the man he had been twenty years ago, before he was embittered by years of hardship. What about *her* years of hardship, knowing that she had a child who was destined for sorrow? Knowing that she had to live with that fact. Knowing she hadn't been woman enough to follow her star when she should have, when it would have been right to follow it.

Each day the closeness developing between Evander and Liselle made her more aware of the distance widening between herself and her child. She found it hard to forgive Evander for what he had attempted to do. She found it harder to face the fact her child now had a foot in two different worlds.

Well, she consoled herself, he was leaving for the States in the New Year. Only a few more weeks and she could wave him goodbye and get back on to her old footing with her daughter.

But deep down inside she knew the footing would never return. Liselle and Kerry were worlds apart now, divided by skin colour, and by deep-seated prejudice. But she couldn't allow that thought to surface just yet. She wasn't drunk enough to forget it immediately afterwards. She wasn't drunk enough even to admit it.

Not yet.

Chapter Thirty-Nine

'That tree looks a right picture, Bri, even if I say it meself.'

Briony smiled at Cissy's happy face.

'It's not half bad, is it? How's Mrs H? Do you think we'll get her down tomorrow for a bit of dinner?'

Cissy snorted through her large nose. 'She wouldn't miss Christmas with them lads for nothing. Though I must admit, Bri, I think this'll maybe be her last one.'

Briony sighed.

'What with Mother Jones going, and she's going hard by all accounts, and Mrs H catching up with her, we're gradually shrinking, aren't we?'

Cissy nodded.

'Well, the lads have yet to marry, and Liselle. Not to mention young Becky and Delia. We'll soon swell the numbers up again! When you get old you're not frightened of death. Well, not as frightened of it as you are when you're young. Put it this way, Mrs H has had a good innings. She's ready to meet her maker. She told me that herself.'

Briony knew Cissy was talking for effect. Over the years

they had become very close, like mother and daughter. Closer in fact than most family. This fact touched Briony deeply. Cissy had been a workhouse child, Mrs Horlock was the only individual to give her a pleasant word. All Cissy had known until then was the back of someone's hand and their curses.

Briony placed the last few presents under the tree, smiling wryly at the present for Evander. It was indeed a lovely tree, and it was going to be a lovely Christmas. She would make sure of that personally. It was Liselle's twenty-second birthday.

Christmas Eve had always been a magical time to Briony. Even in the days when there was no guarantee there'd be even an orange in her stocking. It was the very feel of Christmas Briony loved. The fact of being part of something the whole world was involved with. Knowing that millions of children all over the world were experiencing the same feeling of anticipation as she was. That feeling had never left her, ever. Which was why she donated so much money each year to the welfare organisations. Boots for Children was all well and good, she always gave to that particular charity, but her favourite was the Catholic Church's annual Christmas present rout. Where every child, no matter what its religion, got a present, a few sweets and a piece of fruit. The thought of all those happy faces cheered her.

She had bought Rosalee a brightly coloured coat as she did every year. A thick warm wool coat that would please her immensely. She caressed the silver wrapping paper, looking forward to seeing Rosalee tear it to pieces.

It was going to be a good Christmas.

*

Evander was feeling closer to his daughter by the day. After a particularly difficult beginning they were finally getting to respect and trust each other. He knew she found it hard to look at his hands, and could understand that. He still found it hard to look at them himself. They were now next to useless. His piano playing was laboured and he found it painful. But he also found it extremely difficult to stop playing, which was the bug bear. The music was in him day and night. Hearing a beat or a few notes brought back his longing, and this made him either resentful of whoever was playing, or depressed because he knew he'd never play like that again.

He also found it hard to face Kerry. If only he could make it right with her, he would be happy. But Kerry was finding it hard to forgive him, and in the same circumstances he would have felt the same.

Liselle watched the changing expressions on her father's face. Father. The word seemed strange to her, alien. Yet she knew it was the truth. This man with the deep brown voice and the claw-like hands had been the reason for her existence. It was so hard to visualise him as a young man, with handsome good looks, a way with women, and her mother's heart held firmly into his then perfect hands. Now she knew, it didn't really affect her any more.

She had known she was different since childhood, had guessed she was part-coloured. Admitting it had taken a burden from her. A great burden. Over the years she had been asked out numerous times. But she had always put the man off. Perhaps because deep inside she didn't want the heartache she knew the relationship might bring. Her only wish now was that she was a little darker so there could be no mistake about her parentage. This lightness, this illusion of whiteness she gave out, would always cause her the most trouble. With white people anyway. She knew now that Bessie and the band had always known about her, not just because of Evander but because they had known half-castes all their life. Only their half-castes in America were from black women and white men. Her mother, as usual, had done it the other way round.

This thought made her smile. She felt an enormous respect for her mother now because she had kept her child against the opposition of her own mother and family. Kerry, as weak as she could be, was strong enough to brave the world for her. For that alone, she deserved every ounce of respect Liselle had inside her and she would get it.

She had felt the estrangement between her mother and father and was sorry, desperately sorry, because she had seen her mother's happiness at bringing them together. But something had happened to change that, and Liselle would dearly love to know what it was.

She sipped her cold coffee and grimaced. Evander smiled at her. He looked at her all the time, and far from embarrassing her, she quite enjoyed it. It was the look of a man who really knew her for what she was.

'Why is my mother so against you now?' Her voice was low, with the same huskiness as his. Evander thought hard. Should he tell her?

'I think I've a right to know.'

It could have been Kerry, all those years before. Wanting to be told about his family, his mother, his life.

'Listen, child. Your mother and I . . . Well, all I can say is I did something bad to her. Real bad. If I tell you, then you might look at me differently.'

'I need to know. My mother has been there for me all my life. I know she drinks, and she can be selfish at times, but I really need to know everything. Everything to do with the three of us. It's the only way I can ever really be myself.'

Evander nodded, seeing the logic of what she said. She was wise, this child of his. She had the same candour as her mother, and just a hint of his own mother, a woman who had brooked no nonsense from her big sons and even bigger, more aggressive, husband.

'It's a long story. It began when I got back to the States.'

He told her quietly and calmly about the life he'd had there, leaving out some of the least savoury parts but not ducking the truth either. He told it like it was. Until Liselle, in her imagination, could smell the dirt, feel the heat. Could feel the decline of this once proud man as he tried to pick himself up in a country where his colour was burden enough without being crippled. She could feel the stale enclosed atmosphere of each chocolate town he drifted to, his hands growing stiffer, his piano playing more laboured. His life descending on to a plane of poverty most English people only heard about. When he got to the part where he met Skip he faltered and Liselle poured him a glass of Scotch, waiting patiently while he sipped it, gathering himself together.

All the time he spoke she was silent. She watched him, his hands moving unconsciously, face paling, growing grey and bleak. Body sagging in the big plush seat, he told her everything except the part where her twin cousins disposed of the Americans. He knew instinctively that was another part of the story he should keep from her. Like the parts where he played piano in cheap brothels to whores full of syphilis and cheap whisky. Some things were best left unsaid, even if they were the truth.

When he finished, Liselle stared at him for a short

while. Her face held no hint of her thoughts at all. Her mind was like a closed book to him. Just as he wondered whether she was going to get up and walk out on him, away from him forever, she moved.

Kneeling in front of him she put up her sad, beautiful face. He saw what was inside her then, all the love and the need. She put her arms around his waist voluntarily, the first daughterly embrace. She put her forehead on to the rough broken hands he held in his lap and he felt the hot salty tears running over them. Awkwardly he gathered her to him, kissing the sweet-smelling hair, feeling his child for the first time, her delicate bones pulled against his heavy body.

Looking over her head as he held her, he felt his own tears then. For his daughter, for himself, and for Kerry. His beautiful Kerry who had taken everything he had to offer without a thought for herself or what her love could bring to her door. Yet he had brought her more trouble than she deserved. More trouble than she could ever have anticipated.

Yes, most of all he cried for his Kerry, the girl she had been, and the woman she had become. He had helped shape both, and he wasn't proud of what he had created.

It had all started in that dirty room in Stepney. It ended here in a plush hotel in Mayfair.

His child knew it all, and still she wanted him.

Bernadette watched as Marcus walked out of the house in Hyde Park with the blonde. The girl, and she was only a girl, nineteen at the most, was tall and willowy, with thick heavy hair, cut in a page boy style, and startlingly long slim legs. Even wrapped up in a fur coat, Bernie knew she'd have big breasts. Bernie watched from a taxi as Marcus unlocked the passenger door of his car and the blonde caressed his arm as she spoke to him. Bernadette bit on her lip, feeling the rage building up inside her.

So this was the competition, was it? Well, it was competition she could well do without. Miss Bathing Belle 1947 was even more beautiful than she had dreamed and a tiny part of her could see what her husband was so attracted to. If she was working in the Hyde Park house she was an expensive brass. A very expensive, very young brass, but a brass all the same. She slept with men for money. Except Marcus, of course. He wouldn't pay for a woman, he wasn't the type. He was too bloody good-looking for a start.

The taxi driver rolled himself another cigarette and coughed loudly, annoying her.

'You finished here yet, love?'

Bernadette snapped at him, 'No, I bloody well ain't. I'm paying you, so just shut your trap and wait till I tell you where I want to go.'

The taxi driver, used to getting all sorts in his cab, just shrugged.

'All right, love, no need to get out of your tree.'

Bernie fumed silently. If she was the tall blonde the cabbie would be wetting himself with excitement. He wouldn't talk to Miss Long Legs Strawberry Blonde like that. He'd sit here till bleeding doomsday if she was in the cab.

Two-faced bastard! They were all two-faced bastards. Especially Marcus. Oh, especially him. The futility of her anger made her more annoyed. The snow-covered streets annoyed her. The fact that the tall blonde bitch was even breathing annoyed her.

'Take me back home. NOW!'

The girls were due in. Presents had to be wrapped. What a Christmas Eve this was turning out to be. As they drove she thought about Marcus and the girl. Sorry now she had seen the competition because she wasn't sure what to do about it. How could a woman in her forties hope to compete with that? She might be the mother of Marcus's children, might run his house, might share his bed. But she knew that as far as sex went, and she meant real sex, the kind of sex they had enjoyed those first years before the children had arrived, that was long gone. Now he lay on her for a while, told her he loved her, disposed of his seed inside her, always hoping she would get pregnant and give him a son, then he was snoring gently, no doubt dreaming about the strawberry blonde with the long, oh so long, legs.

Bernadette paid the taxi man without giving him a tip. She paid him and waited for her change, enjoying the feeling of having something over him. He pushed the change into her gloved hand roughly, giving her large house a final sneering appraisal as he drove away. She knew what he was thinking. Living in that place and not even a tip on Christmas Eve! She knew it would be his Christmas story up the pub with his mates, and at home with his wife and family. The house would get bigger with each telling until everyone thought he'd dropped her off at Buckingham Palace.

She walked up her drive, depressed, deflated, and more than anything ashamed of her actions towards the cab driver. It was Christmas Eve and she should have given him a tip. But it was Christmas Eve and she was forty-two and her husband was strupping a young girl.

That was the difference.

She opened the front door of her house to pandemonium. Rebecca and Delia were fighting in the hallway. Delia, always the volatile one, had Becky's hair in her hand and was yanking it. Overcome by her day, Bernadette swiped the two of them with her large black leather handbag. She swiped them mercilessly, their tears and screams barely reaching her.

Holding the bag up menacingly, she shouted, 'Get out of my sight now, the pair of you.'

Delia opened her mouth to argue and got another painful swipe from her mother's bag.

Bernie took off her coat, hat and gloves and dumped herself into a seat. The tree was glaring at her and she felt an urge to get up and drag it from its pot and destroy it. Destroy it and everything in the house that was remotely connected with Christmas.

The dinner was nearly ready to be served and Briony and Tommy poured drinks for the assembled family. Everyone was there, and Molly, a subdued Molly, watched the black man, as she still thought of Evander, sitting with Liselle and chatting amiably to her. She shuddered every time she looked at him. It weren't natural, she kept telling herself. But she kept her peace, knowing she was there on sufferance.

The twins chatted to Tommy and Marcus, business talk that seemed just about acceptable at the gathering as far as Molly was concerned. Kerry was drinking heavily and alone, barely bothering to answer Bernadette when she spoke to her. Delia and Becky sat on the floor like a pair of young foals, all long legs and ankle socks. Molly wished Abel was here, but he had to watch his mother. Mrs H was coming down to dinner the next day, but Molly decided she might go up for a visit before that. The drinks in this house were stingy this year. Hers was like cat's piss.

Rosalee sat beside Briony, a weak rum punch in her hand. Briony noticed she had difficulty in holding the glass and took it from her gently, holding it to her lips. Rosalee sipped it and Briony smiled at her.

'All right, Rosalee?'

'Bri . . . Bri . . .'

Her voice was lower than usual. She held her right arm to her chest, her expression pained.

Briony decided that as soon as Christmas was over she was taking her sister back to the Mile End Hospital and getting her the once over by Dr Matherson. He liked Rosalee and was good with her. She wasn't right, and Briony wondered if maybe her sister was getting her change. Maybe it was coming early? She seemed to sweat an awful lot lately, as cold as it was out, and she seemed to be bloated around the face though she was losing weight. Her arm seemed to pain her as well. There was something not right with her.

Briony kissed her face gently and Rosalee smiled, looking more like her old self.

Briony's eyes strayed to Tommy, her own personal present. Together they made one hell of a team. There was a knock at the front door and she got up to greet Mariah. Now everyone was here they could sit down to eat.

'Come in and get your coat off. We're eating soon. Have you been to the houses, is that why you're late?' Briony raised an eyebrow and Mariah laughed.

'Well, let's just say I had a quick peep! It's always a busy night and I thought I'd give the girls a bit of moral support.'

'You're coming to Midnight Mass, I take it?'

Mariah slipped off her coat and displayed a white and gold evening dress that was gaudy and tight and much too young for her. 'Of course. If Mary Magdalene was good enough for old JC, I'm sure I am.'

Briony laughed at the blasphemy, though she wouldn't have if anyone else had said it.

Bernadette was quiet and Briony found her eyes straying to her throughout dinner. She hardly ate anything, and there was a tracery of fine lines around her eyes that was more pronounced than usual. She wished Bernie would smarten herself up. It wasn't as if she had no time, everything was done for her. She could spend time on herself if she wanted to.

She watched Bernie watching her husband. Putting two and two together, she sighed. Marcus had played away from home for years. Bernie knew, she had discussed it with Briony on more than one occasion. But it had never really bothered her until now. She had always been sure she was the main recipient of his affections and that had been enough. Briony had once offered to put the hard word on him and Bernie had laughed. Marcus was too damned good-looking for his own good, she had said. It was natural women would want him, and that was OK with her as long as he stuck to the brasses and was discreet. Briony had admired her sister then. She wondered what had changed and decided to keep her eye on Bernie. If she could help, then she would.

The twins were chatting with Evander. Briony watched them. It was funny, but the more they saw of him the more they liked him. They could listen to his tales of America for hours. Probing for details about the country, about the way of life there, the cars and the clothes. The States fascinated them.

At ten the dinner was nearly over, with just dessert, coffee and brandy to be served. Briony was pleased with the way the meal had gone, but troubled by the different undercurrents. Tommy caught her eye and winked and she winked back saucily.

Bernadette saw the exchange and it depressed her beyond

measure. Everyone treated her with contempt. Everyone.

It was just so unfair. She had tried to be respectable, she had tried to be good, and what had it got her? Nothing, that's what. Her husband was having sexual gymnastics with a girl young enough to be his daughter, her sister, a sister who was a madam of all things, had her old beau back. Even that drunken Kerry, Miss Golden Voice, was sitting around the table with a bloody great black man who had fathered her child. Her illegitimate child at that! Now he was treated like visiting royalty and Bernie was overlooked as usual. Overlooked and made to feel like a joke. All of them, Rosalee included, had made a hash of their lives in one way or another, were not even respectable, and here she was, the only one to be wedded lawfully, and she had all this on her plate!

The old Bernie was resurfacing with each passing second. The Bernie who was jealous of everyone – her sisters, her friends, anyone. Who wished bad on the whole world.

St Vincent's church was jam packed as it was every Christmas Eve. Most Irish men did what they called their devotion, Christmas, Easter and the Apostle Saints days, and without fail Ash Wednesday and All Souls.

In the front pew Briony held Rosalee's hand and pointed out to her, as she did every year, the wooden pieces of the nativity. Rosalee listened with the same rapt attention as she did every year. When the priest finally arrived, all the grubby altar boys were in place, some smelling suspiciously of cigarettes.

The Mass began. The twins and all the Cavanaghs took it seriously. A calm fell on to the church that was to Briony's mind a little piece of heaven on earth.

Beside her, Rosalee was gasping and Briony held her hand gently. The Mass was long as always on Christmas Eve, and the number attending Communion was great. Rosalee was asleep against Briony's arm. Rather than wake her sister, she got Tommy to take her weight while she took Communion herself.

He looked down on her, and as he did, his face blanched. Her head rolled to the side, and her eyes, half-closed, saw nothing. He realised immediately she was dead. Putting his arms around her he pulled her against his coat. He sat like that until the end of the Mass, holding back a great urge to cry for the woman who had known nothing of malice, of the world, who was still an innocent.

Just after the final blessing Father Tierney asked the congregation to listen to his last few words with serious attention. He then cleared his throat.

'In church this evening we have a woman who has been with this community since a child.' Everyone looked at Briony. 'Well, she's always been pretty free with her money, as we all know.' There was scattered laughter at this and Briony felt her face burning. 'Now this same women and her two nephews, the terrible twins as I called them when they were my altar boys . . .' He looked at the twins in a mock stern way over his pince nez glasses and there was more laughter. 'Well, the fact is, these three have donated over twenty thousand pounds to my orphans' fund.' He paused for the intake of breath he knew would be forthcoming and wasn't disappointed. 'So I wanted to thank them publicly and to make a point of acknowledging the respect I have for them all. Firstly as good Catholics, and secondly as very, very good and kind people. The Cavanaghs.'

His Irish voice rose on the last two words and the

church went wild. The clapping was loud and long.

Briony and the twins sat stunned at what the priest had done. Not one of them had expected it. Father Tierney came down and made the sign of the cross in front of the altar and then shook hands with the twins and Briony, thanking them once more.

Tommy sat supporting Rosalee, his terrible secret still untold. He waited until the church began to empty before he crooked his forefinger at Boysie and whispered the secret for the first time. He looked at Rosalee in Tommy's arms and, kneeling down, put a hand gently to her face. Then, to the amazement of the priest, he began to sob, loud sobbing that caught the attention of everyone around him. Kerry, drunk as she was, took in the news quicker than anyone else. She sat crying silently alone until Evander, still smarting over the shock he had caused to the congregation, put his arm around her and tried as best he could to console her.

Briony was stunned. She sat beside her sister while the priest held the purple stole to her and whispered the prayers for the dead.

Her Rosalee was dead.

Her Rosalee whom she had loved all her life. Had cared for, fed with frozen fingers in the basements. Had played with and crooned to. Whom she had loved as Rosalee. Just Rosalee, her sister and her friend. She was gone forever.

Poor Rosalee, people had always said. They had never realised just how rich she was.

Chapter Forty

'I don't care if it is Christmas, I don't care if Christ himself is coming here to gamble, I want me money, Davey, and I want it now.' Boysie's face was dark with anger.

Davey Mitchell was terrified, but made a good show of hiding this fact.

'Look, Boysie, I borrowed the money and you're charging me interest on it. I'll pay it, right. It'll be paid.'

Boysie clenched his fists and held them up in front of his face.

Davey felt a thrill of terror.

'Don't mug me off, Davey, don't even think about mugging me off. You borrowed a grand, now you owe two and a half. I want that by New Year's Eve or I'll hurt you. Really hurt you.'

The last was said low and Davey swallowed hard. 'You'll have it.'

He looked all injured innocence and Boysie began to breathe heavily through his nose. Davey Mitchell annoyed him beyond measure. He was so cocksure. He had borrowed a thousand pounds to open his own spieler,

Boysie and Daniel had lent him the money in good faith. They knew, from whispers on the street, that the spieler was doing very well, so where was their money? The interest was rolling up by the day, but that had not deterred Davey in the least. He still gave them a load of old fanny every time they sent someone to pick up what was their money after all. Now Boysie had visited personally and he was annoyed. Deeply annoyed. Davey Mitchell had best watch that big Yid mouth of his, and that cocksure attitude, because he needed putting down a peg and the mood Boysie was in, he would be the man to do it. No trouble.

Boysie poked him in the chest, hard.

'I'd better have it, Davey, or your guts will be strewn all over fucking Bethnal Green. Right?'

Davey nodded. But he still didn't look as if he was really bothered and Boysie fought down an urge to smash him in the face.

He left the little office and walked through the games room. As he left the club and climbed into his car he took a few deep breaths to calm himself. He sat still for a couple of minutes and decided he would make arrangements with Davey after the New Year for a larger cut of his takings. He might even just take the club from him. That would teach the bloody ponce a lesson he wouldn't forget in a hurry!

Smiling grimly now, he pulled away from the kerb. His next stop was a man called Liam O'Docherty, a bookie. Liam owed them over two grand. He was a good payer usually, but that didn't deter Boysie. He would go and tell him he wanted his money, and quick.

He had to do something, and this was as good a something as anything else he could think of.

Unlike Daniel, who was still ensconced in his bedroom

moping after Rosalee's death, Boysie needed excitement. He needed action. And by Christ he would find it if it killed him!

Briony and Tommy were sorting out the final arrangements for Rosalee's funeral. The coffin was chosen, the shroud was a delicate pink and white, the rosary in her hands of olive wood brought from Jerusalem and given to Briony by the priest. It had been blessed by the Pope himself.

As Briony sorted out food and other arrangements she fought an urge to scream. Every time she thought of Rosalee in that church, dead and silent, she wanted to scream. She was to be buried beside Eileen, which helped. At least they would be together. All the Cavanaghs would be together in the end.

Tommy saw Briony's haunted face and kissed her gently. Briony put her arms around him. She was exhausted from lack of sleep and he pulled her close. Oh, what would she have done without him? He had been like a rock for her. Had held her up when she thought she would just collapse, because somehow all her strength seemed to have drained out of her. That phenomenal strength that was her trademark, that made her the woman she was, seemed to have disappeared overnight until now she found it hard even to pick up a phone. Mariah had told her to take things easy, leave everything to her, and Briony was grateful. Even work had lost its usual appeal. Was not enough to take her mind off her sister's death. Rosalee had been such an integral part of her life. It was hard to imagine life without her.

The doctor said her heart had given out on her. Just given up. She had had a massive heart attack which accounted for her holding her arm; he said she had probably had pain along her arms and her chest and couldn't communicate that fact. Briony berated herself for not taking her sister to a doctor immediately. For not realising that she was really ill. For not taking enough interest in her.

Tommy had ordered strong hot coffee, and as he poured Briony out a steaming cup she once more blessed him for his support. How on earth had she done without him all these years? How could she have let him go?

It amazed her to think she could ever have contemplated living her life without him.

Davey Mitchell was in The Volunteer in Barking, drinking with two brothers called McCain. They were both men well respected in their own right as hard men, but also well liked because they were jokers. Both had a great sense of humour and they told jokes non-stop, each vying with the other to be the funnier. They worked for the twins, and were happy to do so. They had been friends of Davey Mitchell's for many years. Davey sat at the bar drinking large Scotches and laughing at their jokes.

Pete McCain was telling one as usual.

'So this bloke goes in the hairdresser's and says, "I want me hair cut with a large hole on top of me head, scissor marks all around the sides, and a fringe that's five different lengths." This big poofy hairdresser says, "I can't do that, sir!" And the bloke says, "Why not? That's how you fucking cut it last time!" '

Jamie McCain busted up with laughter as did Davey, Pete McCain, and half the bar.

Davey ordered another round of drinks as Jamie McCain said, 'How about this then? This bloke is at the funeral of an eighty-year-old man, and there's loads of young girls around the grave crying. Right? So this young bloke like, he says, "What they all crying for?" And the undertaker he says, right, "Well, the old boy was a really good lover, see. All the young girls liked him." So this bloke says, "Get out of it, you're mucking me about!" And the other undertaker says, "He ain't, son, I had to give him a wank to get the coffin lid on!" '

Davey and half the bar busted up with laughter again. Maisie, the large barmaid, served them their drinks tight-lipped and Jamie grabbed her hand.

'Sorry, Maisie, that one was a bit near the mark.'

'You just remember there's ladies in here, Jamie McCain.'

Davey pushed a five-pound note over the bar and said, 'Fucking ladies? I don't see no ladies in here, love.'

Maisie snatched the money from the bar and put his change in a puddle of beer deliberately.

Davey looked at the soaking wet money and Maisie smiled at him sarcastically.

Davey poked a finger in her direction and said, 'You pick that money up and you sort it for me. Now.'

Pete and Jamie sighed loudly.

'Leave this to us, Maise. Give it a rest, Davey. You're out of order.'

He turned on Jamie and sneered. 'Don't you tell me when I'm out of order, mate. Just because you work for those pair of Cavanaghs, the nancy boys. Don't you get fucking lairy with me!'

Pete stepped towards Davey and Jamie held him back, both serious now. All their laughing and joking gone.

Jamie poked a finger at Davey and said quietly, 'You're pissed so I'll forget what you just said, Davey boy. Get yourself off home.'

The bar was quiet now, people watching the proceedings with eager eyes.

Davey was very drunk and all caution was gone as he said in a high girlish voice, ‘What’s the matter, boys? You scared that pair of fucking paper hats the Cavanaghs will hear what I said about them? Are we scared they might get their aunties after me? Oh, they can’t get all their aunties, can they? The big fucking nutty one died the other day! Good job and all. I wish they’d died with her. Fucking bits of kids telling me . . . ME . . . Davey Mitchell, what to do! I worked this town when they were still a twinkle in their father’s fucking eye!’

The whole bar was silent now and Jamie shook his head. ‘You must be out of your mind.’

‘What, you gonna tell them what I said then? Run and tell them, go on. See if I care!’

Peter McCain pushed Davey hard in the chest. ‘We won’t have to, you stupid bastard, the whole fucking pub heard you! What you on, Davey, eh? A fucking death wish?’

Davey walked unsteadily to the door of the pub. Looking at all the faces around him, he laughed out loud.

‘Bollocks to the Cavanaghs! They don’t scare me.’

Tommy heard about Davey before the twins and it bothered him. He had wanted to speak to Briony about them for a while, but the time never seemed right. Now he knew that Davey Mitchell was dead. That was a certainty. Boysie and Daniel would not take such public humiliation. And Davey Mitchell, drunk or sober, should have known that.

But the twins had to be made aware that you didn’t just kill people willy-nilly. They were far too violent for the wrong reasons. Even a small debt was called in with a violence that was astounding to the hardened men of London. A few hundred pounds and Boysie or Daniel would have arms or legs broken. They had crippled someone over seventy quid. It wasn't as if there was any rhyme or reason to it. People who owed them hefty amounts of wedge were just left, then one day Boysie called the debt in. No warning, nothing. It was ludicrous. That sort of thing would be their downfall.

He would talk to them. For Briony's sake, it was the least he could do. Because if she lost those boys, it would finish her. They were her boys, her babies, no matter what they did to anyone. However big they became, to her they were her Eileen's children, and she would never see any wrong in them. No matter what they did.

Briony was heading for a fall, and deep inside Tommy knew no matter how hard he tried, he couldn't even hope to catch her.

Boysie went into the Chapel of Rest. Daniel was already there, sitting by the open coffin. His face was pale, his eyes dead. He put out a hand to his brother and Boysie grasped it, holding it tight.

'Poor old Auntie Rosalee. Look at her, Boysie. She never done no one a day's harm.'

'Nah. I know that. The Aunt's taken it really bad.' Boysie's voice was low. He looked at Rosalee in the coffin for a few seconds and then said, 'I thought I might find you here, Danny boy. I came earlier today, after I saw that slag Mitchell. I suppose you've heard?'

Danny's face darkened in anger. 'I heard.'

'So what do you say we pay him a little visit?'

Danny turned in the chair and squeezed his brother's

hand till it hurt. Then he half smiled as he said, 'What do you think?'

The twins locked identical blue eyes for what seemed an age. Then Boysie laughed deeply.

'I thought you'd say that. Let's go.'

Mariah came to Briony's just after six. She kissed her friend gently on the cheek, nodded to Tommy, and then after she had been given a brandy, spoke what was on her mind.

'Listen, Bri, I know you've got a lot of hag at the moment but I must talk to you.' She paused. 'It's about the twins.'

Briony raised an eyebrow and Tommy looked down at his drink, grateful to Mariah for doing what he should have done. He knew, he knew exactly, what she was going to say.

'What about the boys, Mariah?' Briony's voice was neutral.

'That prat Davey Mitchell slagged them off this afternoon in The Volunteer. I mean, really slagged them off. He made remarks about Rosalee as well.'

Briony frowned. 'Go on.'

Mariah took a large gulp of her drink.

'The word on the street is that the boys are after him, rooting for blood. You've got to stop them. I had a whisper today from an Old Bill at Bethnal Green. They want them, Briony. They want them badly. If they touch Mitchell, they're banged up. Over with, finished, done, and there's nothing we can do about it. All our judges and politicians will do no good. Murder isn't something they want to get involved with.'

Tommy was impressed with the way Mariah just laid it on the line for Briony. She didn't dress it up as he would have done. She just told it like it was.

Briony silently digested what Mariah said to her.

'They're out of control, Briony. I've said this to you before, you must put the hard word on them. Now. Before it's too late. If they top Mitchell, they'll put themselves away, and all the donations to charity and all the good feeling from the East End won't mean a tinker's fart.'

'What did Mitchell say about Rosalee?'

Mariah waved a hand at her and said dismissively, 'Oh, a load of old crap. He was pissed out of his head. Anyway, what does it matter? Words can't hurt her. Nothing can hurt her, Bri . . .'

Briony stood up and put down her glass. She lit herself a cigarette slowly, drawing the smoke deep into her lungs before blowing it out.

Mariah sighed heavily. 'For Christ's sake, Tommy, you tell her, will you? If she won't listen to me, she might at least listen to you.'

'Mariah's right, Briony. You have to try and stop them from going near Mitchell. It's the talk of the streets. If they touch him they're away. Pure and simple. I was going to talk to them myself, I wasn't really sure what to do.'

Briony nodded slightly, her eyes far away as she said, 'You leave the boys to me.'

Bernadette was sitting in her kitchen eating a large slice of cake. Bernadette was a comfort eater, she knew that, and the knowledge annoyed her. She would balloon in weight if she wasn't careful. The house was as quiet as the grave. The girls were at her mother's; Mother Jones was on the mend and demanding all sorts. The girls enjoyed helping their gran, and Molly enjoyed their company. Liselle was still hardly speaking to her and this thought made Bernadette laugh.

Liselle was like something from a novel. She really thought she was it. Just because she was young and her mother was famous, she thought she was something special. Well, all she was was a half-chat!

Bernadette knew she was being vindictive and nasty, and knew she was ashamed deep down, but, oh, it did feel good. Who the hell did they think they all were anyway?

They were nothing; none of them was anyone of importance. Not Briony or Kerry or Liselle or that long-legged tart who was even at this moment with her husband – the two-timing two-faced git!

Finishing the last piece of cake, Bernadette poured herself another large whisky. She drank it straight down and the wooziness made her want to laugh. She looked bleary-eyed around her pristine kitchen and then, pulling herself from her chair, walked over to a long wooden shelf that held an assortment of teapots, her lovely teapots that she had collected over the years and which had miraculously escaped the Blitz. With one swipe of her hand she destroyed them. They smashed to the floor, their shattered pieces scattering to all corners of the large room.

Stepping through the mess carefully, she went out of the kitchen and through the hallway to her drawing room. There she took her wedding photos down and stamped on them. She looked at Marcus's face smiling up at her and ground the heel of her shoe into it with every ounce of strength she had.

A little while later she walked unsteadily up her neatly polished stairs and went into her bedroom. Then she opened Marcus's big heavy wardrobe and began pulling out his clothes.

*

Boysie and Daniel were shocked to see Briony walk into their gambling club in Canning Town.

'Hello, boys. Surprised to see me?'

Boysie stood up and offered her his chair. Briony sat down, her body leaden with fatigue.

'I hear you're both looking for Davey Mitchell? He mouthed off about you and a few other choice things in The Volunteer.'

Daniel lit a cigarette and passed it to his aunt. Briony took it gratefully.

'He's out of order. He needs a few lessons in good manners.'

She nodded. 'I agree totally. But not yet, boys. You're burying Rosalee tomorrow. I don't want any cloud over her funeral. Get that, the pair of you. There'll be no violence before her funeral or after it. It's a mark of respect.'

Daniel opened his mouth to speak but Briony held up her hand.

'I ain't here to argue, boy, I'm here to tell you. No violence, nothing. Let's get this funeral out of the way first.'

Both boys looked at the desk. The scratched wooden surface suddenly seemed fascinating as they digested what their aunt had said. Briony watched them both, feeling sadness at the way they had turned out, yet no real surprise. They were of her blood, they had the same wants and needs as her. They were indeed more her children than Eileen's. After what Tommy had told her tonight, she was sorry for this. Heart sorry.

It seemed they were able to terrify the very life out of people and that was wrong. That kind of violence was mindless, and totally against anything she had ever taught them. If she told them about the police being on the alert she knew they would want to take out Davey Mitchell more than ever. They would pit their considerable wits against the police, she knew that as sure as she knew who her own mother was. She also knew it would be their downfall. As Mariah said, where murder was concerned, none of their 'friends' would come near them. The carefully nurtured judges, the bent politicians, would leave them out in the cold. And Briony admitted to herself that that was how it should be.

Davey Mitchell was a fool of the first water, what he had said about Rosalee was foolish in the extreme, but it didn't warrant death. Throughout her life she had dealt with people from every walk of society, and one crucial lesson she had learnt was this: you never did anything unless it gained you something. Useless violence gained you nothing but bad feeling and hatred. She had used violence many times, over the years, but only as a last resort. That was real life. But her boys, her darling boys as she always thought of them, used their muscles and their paid muscles for all the wrong reasons.

She had known deep inside the first time they had asserted themselves that they were gone from her. She only hoped she still held enough weight with them to make them listen to her now.

'Well? Have you listened to anything I've said?'

Boysie looked from the desk to Daniel and their eyes locked. Briony watched them as she had so many times when they were children. Sometimes she thought they communicated without words. That they could see into each other's minds. They both nodded simultaneously.

'I mean it, I want no trouble to mar my Rosalee's passing. No trouble at all. If you defy me now on this, I'll never forgive either of you.'

Daniel smiled, one of his winning smiles, and took hold of her hand gently.

'We won't defy you, Mum. Don't worry. It'll all be sweet as a nut.'

Briony nodded, feeling a surge of relief go through her veins.

But to himself Danny was thinking: He'll keep. Davey boy will keep. For a few weeks anyway.

Marcus was with Davinia in one of the best 'rooms'. The house wasn't busy yet so they were taking advantage of the lull in her regular customers. As she sat on the edge of the bed and brushed her hair, he watched her. Once the Berwick was up and running properly, she would be one of the star attractions, and what an attraction she was. Five feet ten inches tall in her stockinged feet a forty-two-inch chest and a hand's span waist. Her legs were so long. He had never seen legs that length in his life. Her hair was dyed, that was the only imperfection so far as he was concerned. Her skin was flawless.

He dragged deeply on his cigarette and smiled as she faced him. Her eyes were a bright blue, with deep brown arched eyebrows that gave them a mysterious appearance. Her mouth was a perfect pout in repose and he felt a stirring inside himself once more.

Davinia, real name Sally Jenkins, looked down at him and smiled lazily.

'You're feeling very energetic tonight.'

Her voice was low, a controlled sexiness underlying all her words.

Marcus laughed. He knew every wile a whore possessed, but he had to admit Davinia was really good at her craft. It annoyed him sometimes that she played him like a john, like a customer. It wasn't that he was in love with her or anything like that. It was the principle of it. He wasn't paying her, so she should behave herself. It was that simple. But he had noticed over the years that a lot of the girls didn't know when to stop acting. Even her cries of delight had turned into practised moans of ecstasy lately. She had been with him six months, longer than any of his women in the past, and as delectable as she was, her days were numbered. But he wouldn't let on to her, not just yet anyway.

Bernadette was like some kind of automaton lately. He knew she was upset about her sister, and he also knew, but wouldn't admit it outright, that he should have been with her tonight. But Davinia was here, and he was here, and the house was quiet. He justified himself every way he could. He noticed that his earlier interest was gone and lit himself another cigarette from the butt of the previous one.

'I saw a lovely flat today. I'm thinking of renting it.'

Marcus drew on the cigarette again. This time he looked down at the gold and green bedspread.

'I can't really afford it, but it is lovely. So dinky!'

Marcus blew out a swirl of smoke and then looked at her again. She was still brushing her hair, looking at herself in the many mirrors strategically placed around the walls. He could see about twenty Davinias, from all angles.

'Is that right, Davinia? It must be expensive if you can't afford it.'

She looked at him then, fully.

'We could be together there, more often. Without all the other girls knowing about it.'

Marcus cleared his throat and looked around for the ashtray. He put his cigarette out and stood up, his body still lean and firm, even at his age.

'Listen, Davinia love, I don't want a permanent relationship, I told you that at the outset. I have a wife and two children . . .'

Davinia walked to him, her breasts wobbling seductively. She put her hands on to his shoulders and looked into his eyes.

That was when pandemonium broke out.

They both heard the screaming and shouting and looked at one another in shock and consternation. Marcus made a grab for his trousers, thinking one of the customers or the girls was getting out of order, when the bedroom door banged open.

Marcus had never felt so shocked in all his life as when he saw Bernadette standing in that room with two suitcases. She looked at him and then at Davinia. He was in the process of putting on his trousers and stood there with them half up his legs, his mouth open in astonishment.

Dropping the cases, Bernadette pulled herself straight. Looking at the two of them, she said loudly, 'You want him, darlin', you can have him. Washing and all!'

Behind her women and girls of all shapes, sizes, colours and creeds watched the show with glee.

Giving Marcus and Davinia one last look of contempt, Bernadette walked from the room, pushing through the assembled women with every ounce of dignity she could command.

The day of Rosalee's funeral dawned cold. It had begun to snow again during the night, and the streets were covered with a glistening whiteness, which hid the black greasy slush beneath. As they all stood around the graveside, Briony looked at her family and felt a chill of apprehension.

She looked at her mother and Abel, both white-faced and tight-lipped. She knew Rosalee would be missed by her mother, missed dreadfully.

She looked at Kerry, flanked either side by Evander and Liselle, her face, even at this early hour, showing the signs of drunkenness. Well, Kerry was going away in the New Year whether she liked it or not. She would drink herself to death otherwise. Briony guessed shrewdly that once Evander returned to the States Kerry would be happier. It had all worked out wrong for her. The knowledge of his real reason for arriving on her doorstep had broken her. Liselle, though, seemed happier to have her father nearby. She had spoken of going out to see him in America.

She looked at Cissy's big moon face, tears still shining on her red-veined cheeks. Poor Cissy. They had been through a lot together over the years. She felt a huge surge of emotion as she looked at her friend. Then her eyes strayed to Bernadette and Marcus. A rather quiet and shocked Marcus. Briony was pleased to see them together again. Their two daughters cried quietly for their aunt and Briony studied them. Two more Cavanagh girls, with the same looks and mannerisms. It seemed that the Cavanagh looks were hard to stamp out. All her nieces and nephews had the unmistakable look of the family, even Liselle. They were strong women and men. Mustn't forget the Cavanagh men.

The twins were broken-hearted. Briony watched them with a detachment she would have thought impossible a few days before. But some of the things Tommy had told her had changed her towards them. Oh, she knew she would get over the shock of learning about their sadistic ways, their vindictive assaults. They were her boys, no matter what they did. But she would like to think she could influence them enough to see the errors of their ways. She could try to change them.

Jonathan stood with the twins, his face grave. It had been good of him to fly over from Hollywood for the funeral. He had been a good friend over the years, and would continue to be for a long time.

She stared at the coffin, seeing Rosalee in her mind's eye, smiling and clapping her hands, all those years ago in the basements, her chubby feet blue with the cold. Briony had sold herself to take them out of there, to give them all a better life, and the result was Eileen dead, Rosalee dead, and the new generation inheriting problems that were far worse than mere cold and hunger.

Was it all worth it?

It was a question she couldn't honestly answer. Not now while her heart was laden down with this unhappiness, this terrible destructive unhappiness.

Only the future could answer that question. Only hindsight could give her even a glimmer of an answer. She would wait.

She had been waiting all her life for something, her natural son for one thing. A few more years wouldn't make much difference.

Book Four

In trouble to be troubled is to have your trouble doubled.

– *The Further Adventures of Robinson Crusoe*
Daniel Defoe, c. 1659–1661

Chapter Forty-One

1968

Delia smacked her daughter's chubby leg hard. A deep red handprint appeared in the skin as if by magic.

'You touch that once more, Faith, and I'll hammer you.'

Faith looked at her mother and, lips trembling, put back the brightly coloured ashtray on Briony's coffee table.

Briony put her arms out to the child and she climbed on to her lap, starting to cry now she had a bit of sympathy.

'Auntie Briony, you ruin her!'

Briony laughed out loud.

'What else are children for? She's only three, Delia, she doesn't really understand right and wrong yet. Give the child time!'

It was said lightly but Delia was aware of her aunt's controlled anger. She couldn't bear to see a child smacked, it completely threw her. Delia wondered how Briony would have been if she had had to live as Delia did, in a high rise flat with a man who was no good whatsoever.

She stifled this thought. They had all warned her about Jimmy Sellars and she should have listened. Now, after refusing all their offers of help, she was tied to a man whose sole occupation in life was getting stoned, listening to Hendrix, and having sex, preferably with everyone else but her. The worst of it all was she still loved him. Was, in fact, besotted by the bugger. This fact never ceased to amaze her. Knowing what he was, she still wanted him.

So much for this new permissive society.

Her old Auntie Briony was more permissive, what with her bloody 'houses' and her other nefarious businesses. She loved her Auntie Briony though, she did. Even at her advanced age, in her sixties now, Briony still looked good. Her hair did not have to be dyed, which amazed everyone; her face, lined as it was, still looked youthful. Her slim figure had not an ounce of spare fat on it. Delia looked down at her own overweight body and sighed. It wasn't fair really. Even her own mother looked better than she did, but she had had her face done. Face and breasts, at her age! It was embarrassing.

She watched Briony kiss Faith and smiled. The child was so loved by everyone. She was glad. Briony took the child's little hand in hers and kissed the fingers greedily, making Faith laugh. Then Delia saw her aunt frown. Pushing up the child's cardigan, she revealed a large purple bruise.

'How the hell did she come by that?'

Delia heard the outrage in her aunt's voice and shook her head dismissively. 'You know what children are like, she caught it in the bars of the cot.'

'It's about time you put her in a bed then, Delia! Christ, that looks painful.' Briony looked at the little girl on her lap and said sweetly, 'Is my baby hurting, my poor little Faithey?'

Faith grinned her best grin and Briony kissed her once more, hugging her tight. Delia relaxed. That had been a close one all right.

Too close for comfort.

Boysie and Daniel were visiting their gran. She still lived in Oxlow Lane and they made a point of calling in often. She was alone now, Mother Jones passing away in 1950, and Abel dying of cancer in 1966. Molly was in her eighties, and though she now lived on the bottom floor of her house, finding the stairs too difficult, was still alert, still fiercely independent, and wanting to stay in her own home no matter how often Briony tried to persuade her to come and live with her.

She made the twins a large pot of tea and sat listening to their chatter. They were still her boys. Her favourites. Their reputation was now legendary in London but every time Molly looked at them she saw her gentle daughter who had died birthing them. Her eyes misted over. More and more lately she was thinking of the people who had died. Abel, Mother Jones and even Mrs Horlock. The dead seemed more real to her than the living. Except for her grandsons. They were her whole existence rolled into two large men. They had taken over many of Briony's clubs, and had also taken over the houses. They owned everything from used car lots to large plant hire firms. They had fingers in every pie and Molly was as pleased as punch with them.

She began to doze in her chair, the fire roaring even in the late-spring sunshine.

Boysie and Danny looked at her and grinned at one another.

'Gran . . . Gran . . . Before you nod off I want to tell you me news,' Boysie said.

Molly sat upright in the chair. 'I wasn't asleep, you cheeky young bugger! I was thinking!'

Boysie laughed. 'Well, think about this then. I'm getting married.'

Even Daniel laughed at the shocked look on her face.

'What, to that Emerald bird?'

Emerald was a high-class call girl Boysie had been seeing for about a year.

He shook his head. 'Nah! I'm marrying a girl called Suzannah Rankins. Her nan used to run the bingo down at the church. Remember her?'

He was talking loud and slow and Molly slapped his arm.

'I ain't in me bleeding dotage, you know. I still have all me faculties! 'Course I remember Jessie Rankins. We was good mates. She's in a home now, poor old bitch.'

'Well, I'm marrying her granddaughter, Jessie's son's girl. Remember Jessie's son, Frankie Rankins?'

Molly looked at Danny and shook her head. 'Will you explain to this bleeding numbskull that I can hear him all right? I ain't at the end of the street.'

Danny laughed. 'All right, Gran, keep your hair on.'

'How old's this Suzannah then?'

Boysie looked shamefaced.

'Twenty-one, Gran.'

'Good bit younger than you then.' She paused. 'Bring her around on Sunday at five-fifteen, I'll tell you what I think then.'

'I'll bring him personally, Gran, all right?'

The twins climbed into their white Rolls-Royce and drove away, oblivious of the stares of the other tenants in the road. They were sponsoring a boxing tournament for under-fourteens in Wapping, and were dressed up ready to have their photos taken for the local papers. They both looked the part: neat black suits, slicked-back hair and plain grey ties, their practised smiles coming now without any effort on their part. Big, powerful men, both physically and mentally.

They thought they were untouchable.

'What time are you meeting Suzannah?'

Boysie shrugged.

'About seven. I'm seeing her mum and dad tonight, about the wedding like.'

Danny laughed. 'It seems funny, thinking of you married.'

Boysie laughed too. 'I want a family, Danny Boy, a family and a nice house and a nice wife. A decent type of bird. I've had me eye on Suzannah since she was at school. She's a good kid.'

'Yeah, the emphasis on "kid"! She'll wear you out, mate, before you know it you'll be draped in nappies and smelling of piss and sick!'

Boysie rolled his eyes in ecstasy.

'I can't bleeding wait!'

Danny punched him on the arm, none too gently.

'Well, just so you know and don't get soft.'

Boysie stopped laughing and said seriously, 'Don't worry, I won't.'

They had had a small confrontation and both knew it. Daniel wasn't happy that his brother was marrying. It was like splitting them up. But he would allow it, as long as nothing else changed. Their business partnership would stay as it was, Boysie had confirmed that.

Detective Inspector Harry Limmington looked into the face of the man sitting opposite him in the interview room.

'You're going down for a twelve stretch, my son, and

I'll laugh my head off as they pass sentence.'

Larry Barker was rolling a cigarette and Limmington saw his hands shaking. He smiled to himself. He had him worried all right. Really worried. They had had him in the station for twenty-eight hours and he hadn't slept once. He had been interrogated continuously, with only a cup of coffee now and again to relieve the pressure. He was ready to crack.

'How many kids you got, Larry? Five, is it?'

He nodded. 'Yes, Mr Limmington. Five boys.'

Limmington laughed scathingly. 'Another crowd of fucking thugs growing up! What is it with you villains, why don't you have many daughters?'

Larry lit his thin roll-up with trembling hands. 'I don't know, Mr Limmington.'

Limmington stood up and smashed a closed fist on to the table. ' "I don't know, Mr Limmington. Yes, Mr Limmington." I want results, boy, and I want them now! I'm losing me patience!'

With that he clubbed Barker a stinging blow across the side of the head, sending him flying off the wooden chair and on to the floor.

The young PC standing in the corner of the room kept his eyes straight ahead.

Larry was dragged up from the floor roughly and shoved back on to his seat. The lack of food and sleep, the overdose of nicotine and the blows, had all taken their toll. He was indeed broken.

'Now, Barker, you tell me all you know about the Cavanaghs and I'll take you to a nice clean cell, get you a bit of egg and bacon, and let you have a lovely long sleep.' Then he bellowed: 'So don't wind me up, boy! I know they was behind the blag, or at least a party to it in some way. I want answers and I want them now or I'll kick you from one end of this station to the other!'

Larry wiped a grubby hand across his sweating forehead, leaving a long black stripe.

'I ain't got nothing to say about the Cavanaghs, Mr Limmington. Nothing. With respect, sir, you can scare me, you *do* scare me, but not half as much as the Cavanaghs. You'll have to go somewhere else to get them grassed. I'd rather do me twelve years alive and kicking than get off with it all and be dead.'

Limmington sighed deeply. He knew now as sure as eggs was eggs that Barker wouldn't crack. But it had been worth the try.

He wanted the Cavanaghs, he wanted them desperately. The twins and that bloody dragon Briony.

They were a taint on the earth, they were scum, and he wanted them out of the ball game for good.

Kerry watched the woman warily as she put a sandwich and a glass of milk on to the table in front of her.

'Come on, Miss Cavanagh, get this down you, you'll feel much better.'

Kerry smiled half-heartedly and took a bite of the ham and tomato sandwich to placate her. Then she picked up the milk in an exaggerated gesture and sipped it, holding it up first as if toasting the woman before her – with her great muscled arms and harshly cropped hair.

'You're a card, Miss Cavanagh, and no mistake.'

The woman, Betty Bradley, shook her grey head and walked from the room. Kerry pushed the tray from her and looked once more out of the window.

She needed a drink desperately.

She could cheerfully kill for one.

But Briony, Briony the wonder woman, the marvellous sister who knew everything and was practically omnipotent, had seen fit to supply her with a large, obviously lesbian, minder. Betty Bradley watched over her day and night. It was sickening.

Kerry sagged visibly in her seat, her show of defiance leaving her drained.

She had not worked since 1949. She had not sung in public since then, and only rarely in private. She had sunk into a world of booze and drugs after Briony, wonderful Briony, had seen fit to send her to that place where they had dried her out.

Well, they had dried her out in some ways. But not the way they wanted.

Six months later she had emerged from the beautifully kept grounds of Fairhaven in Surrey, slim, bright-eyed, and dead inside. It had shown in her performance and it had also shown in her face. She had lost it all, the need to sing, the love of music, she had lost everything that had made her special in that place, thanks to ECT.

Within a year of being home she was on every kind of drug imaginable, she was into heroin, barbiturates, hashish, anything she could lay her perfectly manicured nails on. The last doctor she had seen had told her the same as all the others: she was self-destructive.

Then why the fuck didn't they just let her destroy herself.

Suzannah Rankins was dressed in her best. She wore a short dress of white broderie anglaise, her legs in skin-tone tights and her make-up minimal. She had not worn much makeup because her dad didn't like it. Her dad didn't like anything, least of all her relationship with Boysie

Cavanagh, and that was a big part of his attraction. Boysie was the main man, and when he had singled her out she had felt so special, so grown-up – yet so in awe of his fine clothes and cars and jewellery she had wanted to die of happiness. She really liked him as well. She wouldn't go so far as to say she loved him, but as good as. Now he was marrying her, and she was glad she had taken her mother's advice. If she had slept with Boysie, she knew he would only have used her. It was her virginity that attracted him, and her freshness. Well, soon she'd be married as she had always dreamt she would be, in a nice church in a big expensive dress with a rich husband beside her.

It was a dream come true all right.

Then, as Mrs Boysie Cavanagh, she could do what the hell she liked. No worrying about playing her records loud and at all hours, no worrying about what time she was in. No more hassles from her mum and dad, she would be a respectable married woman.

Briony and Tommy were visiting Mariah. She now lived in aged splendour in a small but expensive ground-floor flat in Hampstead. She was surrounded by rock musicians, models and other well-off but unconventional folk, and loved every second of it. Her face, still plastered with make-up, looked garish, the thick green eyeshadow and painted red lips emphasising each of the considerable creases on her face. She held large, loud parties, and the twins and all the children doted on her. She was especially close to Delia, Bernadette's younger daughter. Rebecca was married to an accountant and living in Brighton, an old married woman years before her time. Delia on the other hand was full of life, unconventional, and generally preferred by everyone, Bernadette and Marcus included.

Bernie often wondered aloud how the hell they had got Rebecca, so prim, proper, and tight-lipped.

Molly always said Rebecca was like Eileen, she didn't need the excitement of the world like all the others, she was a respectable girl. Everyone rolled their eyes when Molly started her ramblings but her great age guaranteed she was listened to respectfully.

Briony sipped her drink and looked with pleasure around her friend's small garden. The young couple above Mariah had their windows open and the sound of heavy rock music was blaring. Mariah, to the amusement of Briony and Tommy, was tapping her foot in time.

'So how's the Berwick these days?'

Briony sipped her glass of white wine and sighed. 'The twins have done well with it. It's mainly a gambling place really, the girls are all dispersed around London and the home counties. They're raking the money in, though.'

Mariah laughed.

'Good, that's what I like to hear. As long as they don't forget their old Auntie Mariah and her ten per cent of the profits!'

Tommy laughed.

'As if they could ever forget that! Have you heard Boysie's getting married?'

'No! What, Boysie? The most eligible bachelor in town! Who to?'

Briony answered her. 'To a young, very young, lady called Suzannah Rankins. She's only twenty-one but seems like a really nice kid. The big do's in June. Boysie can't wait.'

'I bet he can't if she's that young! Horny old devil. How's Danny Boy taking it?'

'Better than we expected, to be honest. I thought there

would be hell to pay. I mean, they were both confirmed bachelors, but Boysie's besotted with this little girl, and I for one am heartily pleased. He wants children, a nice house, the whole works.'

'Not before time either. Him and Danny are so close, too close at times.' Mariah nodded to herself. 'He was always a strange one, Daniel. Very deep.'

Briony put down her glass of wine with a bang on the ornamental ironwork table and said tartly, 'Well, there's no law against that, is there?'

Mariah sat up in her chair and laughed.

'You'll never change, Briony Cavanagh, not while there's a hole in your arse! Them boys are grown men, big grown men, they don't need you looking out for them, they're quite capable of looking out for themselves. And stop seeing bloody slights everywhere. It's getting harder and harder to talk to you lately! It's your bleeding age catching up with you!'

Briony shook her head and sighed. 'I'm sorry, Mariah.'

'So you blinking well should be. Now let's change the subject. How's all the other houses going along?'

Tommy launched into a long conversation with Mariah about the different houses and Briony sat quietly, watching the two of them talking, her mind troubled.

The boys were once more getting too big for themselves and it worried her. She had had word off the street that the Cavanaghs' days were numbered. They were being watched, being monitored by the tax man, and they still were flying dangerously close to the wind. They thought they were indestructible. Well, she knew from experience that no one was indestructible. No one.

The worst of it was there was absolutely nothing she could do about it.

Tommy's voice brought her back to the present. 'What? sorry, Tommy love, I was miles away.'

'We'd better make a move if we're to get to Kerry's in time for tea.'

'Oh, yes, I forgot we were due there.'

As they said their goodbyes and walked out to their car, Briony saw as if for the first time the stooping of Tommy's shoulders and the hair that was now all grey. As he held the car door open for her she wondered when he had got so old-looking, and why she hadn't noticed it before.

Doreen Rankins was beside herself with pleasure at having Boysie Cavanagh inside her house. Every time she thought of his Rolls-Royce outside her front door she felt a thrill inside her eighteen-hour girdle.

'Have another sandwich, Boysie.' She said his name timidly, shyly.

He took another cucumber sandwich and bit into it. 'Best sandwiches I've had in yonks, Mrs Rankins.'

Doreen patted her newly permed and treated hair and giggled like a schoolgirl.

'Oh, call me Doreen. We don't stand on ceremony in this house.'

Suzy raised disbelieving eyebrows at her mother's complete change of character. But Boysie had that effect on people.

'We're over the moon at your news, Boysie. Our little girl has made us very happy, hasn't she, Frank?'

Doreen looked at her large silent husband with an expression of desperation on her face.

Frank nodded. 'Oh, yes, son. We're over the moon.'

Boysie grinned and winked at Doreen saucily before taking another slice of walnut cake.

'May I be so bold as to ask for another cup of your excellent tea, Mrs . . . I mean, Doreen?'

'Of course you can. We went to Spain last year, and they have a saying there: "My casa your casa". Something like that. It means . . .'

'My house is your house.'

'Oh, Suzy, isn't he clever? Imagine knowing Spanish.'

Boysie and Suzy laughed.

He liked the old bird Doreen, she was all right. The father was a bit weird, a bit too quiet. But as long as they had no objection to the wedding, he wasn't bothered.

'We're booking St Vincent's for the wedding, Doreen, my Aunty Briony is seeing to that for me. She'll be in contact soon, so you can decide along with Suzy what you want. I hope you won't be offended, Mr Rankins, but I would like to insist from the start that I shall be paying for the wedding, and there will be no expense spared.'

Suzy watched her father's face. It looked almost pleasant now. He absolutely hated spending money. His favourite saying was: 'A penny earned is a penny saved.'

Frank Rankins leant forward in his seat and picked up his pipe.

'Please, son, call me Frank,' he said happily.

An hour later Boysie was at Suzy's front door kissing her goodbye before going off for an evening of business.

'Well, that went all right, love.'

'Oh, Boysie, I can't wait!'

He kissed her cool clean lips and grinned. 'Neither can I, love. Neither can I!'

[illegible]

[illegible]

[illegible]

[illegible]

[illegible]

[illegible]

[illegible]

[illegible]

[illegible]

Chapter Forty-Two

Jimmy Sellars woke up feeling drained. He had been tripping for most of the previous day, but now he'd come down with a vengeance, from the feeling of paranoia to the quick 'rushes' that kept making his heart beat a violent tattoo in his chest. He could hear Delia's soft breathing beside him and Faith's low crying coming through the thin wall from the bedroom next door. It was the crying that had woken him. He gritted his teeth. The kid got on his nerves. This whole set up got on his nerves.

Leaning off the mattress that was on the floor, he picked up half a joint from the overflowing ashtray and lit it, taking the cannabis deep into his lungs and holding it there for a good while before letting it out slowly. He felt the rush hit his brain and tried to relax.

He let his eyes roam around the room, settling for split seconds on the posters and paintings all around. He looked at his favourite poster, a back view of a girl dressed in a short white tennis dress, holding a racquet in one hand. With the other she scratched a perfectly tanned buttock. She had no underwear on. Feeling himself getting hard, he allowed his usual sexual scenario to run through his head. The girl turned to face him and lifted the front of the dress, giving him the come on.

He turned over in bed and looked at Delia. Her breasts were spilling out of the covers in the early-afternoon light, the stretch marks visible, blue-grey. He felt his erection deflate and wished he was still tripping. He could handle Delia then. Sexually he couldn't bear her any more. He wondered briefly why he'd ever taken up with her. Since the birth of Faith she was a pain in the arse. Correction, he told himself, she had always been a pain in the arse. But she had been good in the sense she'd had money. She'd always had money. And with Purple Hearts going at £60 a thousand in Piccadilly, she had supplied him the capital to start his own business.

Now they lived in the council tower block, and she didn't take money from her family any more. She relied on him to keep her and the kid. That was the most annoying thing of all. All that lovely money going to waste, and that crying bastard in the other room.

He glanced at his watch. It was just after one-fifteen and that bitch was still asleep. The kid should have been fed hours ago, no wonder she was crying. Sometimes the child went to bed at five after only being up three or four hours. He elbowed Delia in her ribs none too gently and she woke with a start.

'What was that for?' Her eyes were ringed with mascara and kohl pencil, her hair a mass of backcombed knots.

'Get up and see to the fucking kid, will ya? It ain't been fed for ages.'

Delia turned on to her back and let out a long breath. 'Give us a toke first.'

Jimmy passed the roach to her and as she pulled on it

she burned her fingers. Jumping up in bed, she flicked the red hot flakes off her chest.

'Serves you right, you fat bitch. Now make me a cuppa and get that kid sorted out.'

Delia got out of the bed, her large cumbersome body heavy with the LSD and cannabis of the night before. Jimmy closed his eyes so he wouldn't have to look at her.

Delia pulled on a dressing gown, none too clean, and he heard her bare feet padding out of the bedroom.

Jimmy waited, tense in the bed. He heard the short slap and the child's heartrending cry. Leaping off the mattress, he stamped into the child's bedroom. Faith was standing up in the cot that was too small for her, a red handprint on her cheek. Her nose was running snot and her eyes were obliterated by tears.

He grabbed hold of Delia's hair and slapped her across the face three times, back-handed slaps that sent her head this way and that with the force of the blows. Holding her chin in one big grubby hand, he pressed his face close to hers.

'One of these days, Delia, I'm gonna tell your precious family about the way you treat that kid. I'll tell them all about your little act, good old Delia, mother of the year. Now feed the child, for fuck's sake, and let me get some peace. I've work to do this afternoon.'

She looked into the long-haired, bearded face before her and bit her lip to stop the tears.

She knew what his work was this afternoon, what it was nearly every afternoon. Hanging around the 'Dilly trying to look like he was somebody, selling a bit of this, trying a bit of that, and ending up in bed with some little tart in a cheesecloth top with no bra.

Gathering up all the spittle she could in her drug-coated mouth, she spat into his face.

Then the fight really started.

Detective Inspector Limmington was sitting in the offices of the Home Secretary. His hands were nervously picking at bits of lint, real or imagined, on his good black suit, which last saw the light at his son's funeral. His only son had died during National Service, one of those freak accidents that mean nothing to anyone but the victim's parents and the people who witness it.

A woman of indeterminate age smiled at him from behind a large desk and said, 'You can go in now.'

Harry Limmington walked through the doorway to the right of him and closed the door quietly. The large man behind the desk offered him a seat and Harry sat down, listening to him finish his telephone call.

'OK . . . Yes . . . OK then, I'll be there at about eight-thirty . . . Yes, usual place, the Lords' Bar.'

He broke the connection and smiled widely at the tall, grey-haired man before him. Standing up he held out a large hand, not a gentleman's hand, more a workman's. That first impression stayed with Limmington.

'Sorry to keep you, old chap, a bit of urgent business. Now, can I offer you a drink? Coffee, tea, something stronger?'

Limmington smiled. 'Tea would be good, thanks, sir.'

The man pressed a button on his telephone and said: 'Tea please, Miss Pritchard, for two.'

Limmington wondered how often he had tea for one when he had appointments. The man in front of him, despite all his good-humoured camaraderie, looked capable of it. For that reason Limmington was glad he was on the right side of him. He'd seen him on television countless times and now he was with him, was even more aware of the power that emanated from him.

They chatted about nothing till the tea was served to them, a weak brew in paper-thin cups that Limmington was not sure he really wanted to hold. Then, when Miss Pritchard shut the door, the man before him grinned.

'You want the Cavanaghs, I want the Cavanaghs. I think we could help one another there.'

Limmington raised one eyebrow and sipped his tea to give himself more time before answering. All the time he was thinking, Why pick on a DI? Why me? He could smell a dead dog before it was stinking.

The man before him seemed nonplussed at his lack of response. Harry Limmington enjoyed the sensation he was creating.

'I want you to give everything you collect on them to me, me personally. I think that between us we can nail them.'

'You do?' The two words were spoken low.

The man smiled now, happy to have a response.

'I certainly do. I think you should know, though I have a shrewd idea you already do, that the Cavanaghs have ears in all departments. They know everything, or at least their aunt does, before you can say knife. To catch them we will have to get up very early in the morning, very early indeed. But you look like an early riser to me.'

Limmington smiled back then. A slow smile.

'I think I get your drift, sir.'

The man rubbed those large hands together and smiled back. 'All their big friends are getting cold feet these days, you know. The Cavanaghs are making a lot of enemies and now their so-called friends want them off the streets almost as much as we do. But it has to be done diplomatically, which is where you come in.'

Harry Limmington settled back in his chair then. Even his fear of breaking the porcelain tea cups deserted him. He knew what he was here for now, and the knowledge was like balm to him. He didn't care how many big, well-heeled arses he had to save in his quest to get the Cavanaghs. He wanted them so badly he could taste it. Now it seemed they were within his reach.

Henry Dumas had expired at the select Sunnyside Nursing Home in Torquay, his wife and son with him. Albeit not so much from choice as for appearance's sake. Now Benedict and his wife sat in the lawyer's office with his mother, waiting for the final reading of the will.

Isabel, looking younger since her husband's death, sat with her hands clasped in her lap, wishing this was all already over.

Mr Otterbaum the solicitor looked at the three of them over his pince nez and took a deep breath.

'This will was made in 1951. It's short and to the point. Your husband was never a man of many words, Mrs Dumas, as I'm sure you know.'

Isabel nodded slightly, thinking, Get on with it, you silly old fool. Before it occurred to her the man was younger than she was.

'"I, Henry Dumas, being of sound mind and body, leave everything I possess to my natural son Benedict. He can see to his mother as he sees fit."'

The three people sat up straight in their chairs, outraged expressions on their faces.

'"As his mother is Miss Briony Cavanagh, I expect he will make his own mind up about that. My wife, however,

Isabel Dumas, gets nothing, her father having left her well provided for." '

Mr Otterbaum looked at them with a pained expression.

'I can only tell you what your husband put down. I can't begin to express my sorrow at the contents. It was drawn up by my father . . .'

His voice trailed off.

Isabel had closed her eyes tightly.

'The bastard! The dirty rotten stinking bastard!' The words were whirling around her head. She had not realised she had said them out loud.

Benedict looked at his wife, then his mother, with a stunned expression on his face.

'What the hell is going on here?'

Isabel grasped his hand and shook her head. Then the tears came.

An hour and a half later, Benedict had been told the true story of his birth, and such was Isabel's rage at her departed husband, she told it with the same cold callousness she knew he would have used. Benedict listened gravely to the story of a young girl giving birth at thirteen years old and felt the rainbow trout he had eaten for lunch rising up inside his stomach.

Now he knew why he had never liked his father, why he'd always felt a distaste for him. Now he knew why his father had never been to him as other fathers were to other sons. The truth of his life was laid bare and Benedict, not having the hardness or strength of his natural mother, cried.

Fenella Dumas, his wife, listened to the story with detachment. There was one thing in Fenella's favour. No matter how much Isabel disapproved of her otherwise, nothing threw her. Nothing at all.

She was quite looking forward to telling the children. Natalie especially, being a golden sixties child, would absolutely love this. Their real granny was a tart of the first water. It was like something from the *News of the World*.

Benedict, however, had different thoughts on the subject.

Briony, Kerry and the twins sat drinking weak coffee and talking about the wedding. It was the first time Kerry had shown a spark of interest in anything for years. She wanted to know where it was, what they were wearing, what they were going to eat. She wanted to know every detail. Her face was animated and Briony detected something of the old Kerry then, the live wire Kerry of her youth, and this spark saddened her.

Boysie sipped his coffee and took a large bite of a cheese sandwich. 'I was wondering, Auntie Kerry, would you sing for us? In the church like. I know that Suzannah would love that.'

Briony watched Kerry's face close. 'Oh, I don't know . . .'

'Come on, Kerry, we can't have a marriage and you not sing. You always sing at everything.' Briony's voice was light.

Kerry lit a cigarette and shook her head. 'I ain't sung properly for years, Bri . . . I don't even know if I still can.'

Briony gripped the arms of her chair and laughed out loud. 'I'll tell you what, let's have a go. Me and you. I'll help you. We'll practise every day, see how it goes. What do you think, boys?'

'I think Boysie's wedding won't be the same without his favourite aunt singing for him. Come on, Auntie Kerry, you can pick the number yourself. We'll get Bessie's old band, they're still going strong. Last I heard they was at Ronnie Scott's. What do you say? Bessie will be going anyway.'

Kerry began to feel a thrill of enthusiasm surging through her body.

'Well, I can give it a try. I heard a great number the other day actually . . . It was on the wireless . . .' Her voice trailed off. 'I don't know, boys, I don't know if I can still hack it.'

Boysie and Daniel grinned at her, identical grins, showing identical teeth.

''Course you can. Us Cavanaghs can do anything!'

Kerry smiled and took another deep drag on her cigarette. Some of the Cavanaghs can do anything, she thought. But not all of them.

Not me.

'Is Evander coming over for the wedding?' Her voice was light.

Boysie's face sobered instantly.

'Would you mind if he did? If you don't want him there he won't be invited. Lissy will understand.'

Kerry sighed. 'I don't mind, Boysie. You have whoever you want, my lovely, it's your day after all.'

Boysie kissed her cheek gently. She could smell his lemony aftershave and the remnants of the Scotch he had drunk at lunchtime.

Her mouth watered.

One drink, that's all she needed, and she'd sing like a blasted canary. The wedding would be laden down with booze and they couldn't watch her continuously.

Not even the Cavanaghs could do that.

'Did I tell you the BBC were after your aunt to sing on

one of their shows?' Briony told the boys proudly. 'Since "Miss Otis Regrets" has been used for that perfume ad, she's become quite famous again.'

Daniel shook his head.

'Why don't you go for it, Auntie Kerry? I've heard you singing to yourself and you sound OK to me. You'd probably be a guest on loads of programmes. Might even get on Simon Dee's.'

Kerry laughed nervously.

'Look at me, Danny Boy, I'm an old woman. Who'd be interested in me?'

Briony tutted loudly. But what Danny said had given her an idea.

'Be ready at nine-thirty tomorrow, Kerry. Me and you are off out for a while.'

'Where to, Bri?' Kerry's voice was suspicious.

'You'll find out in the morning. It's a surprise.'

Marcus and Bernadette listened to their daughter with shock and anger registering on their faces.

Delia played her trump card by lifting up her grubby tie dyed tee shirt and showing them the bruises on her chest and shoulders.

'He really gave me a hiding, but I took it to stop him touching the little one.'

All eyes went to Faith who sat on the settee eating an iced cake.

Marcus felt a great rage in his chest and instinctively put up his hand to stem the erratic pounding of his heart. 'You mean, he's been beating up you and the child?'

Delia nodded, her eyes big and round with self-pity.

'And you never told a bleeding soul about it?' Marcus's voice was high with disbelief. Not at his daughter's story, but at the fact she had taken it all this time without telling a soul.

'That's why I never wanted you up the flat, see? Jimmy had people there all the time, drug dealers, all sorts . . . He made me keep you away. Then, today, he really went off his head. I thought he'd surely kill me or little Faithey.'

Bernadette swallowed hard. Her maternal instincts were telling her to protect her child and her grandchild, but her womanly instincts were telling her that her Delia, whom she had loved dearly even with all her faults, was a blatant liar. It was one of her less appealing traits but she had been like it since a child. She embroidered everything, eventually believing the story she had created. Bernadette's eyes flickered to her husband who was now pacing up and down the room, his hands clenched into fists.

'If Jimmy was beating you and the child, love,' she asked, 'why didn't you ever tell us before? You stayed here for two weeks a while ago when you and him had the last bust up. Why didn't you tell us then? We never even had an inkling that anything was going on.'

Bernie watched her daughter's eyes flicker and her face colour up. Delia was floundering. She hadn't expected anyone to question her. Marcus saved her when he bellowed:

'For fuck's sake, Bern. The girl was obviously terrified of him! Can't you see that?'

Bernie held up a hand.

'All I'm saying is, she had plenty of occasions to tell us, frightened or not frightened. I mean, think about it, Marcus! She don't exactly come from a family that scares easily, does she? What with you as her father, and Briony and the boys. This Jimmy Sellars must be some kind of prat if he thought he could get away with all she reckons!'

Delia jumped from her seat, her voice hysterical.

'That's why I never said nothing, Dad, because she always takes his side. Always. I knew she wouldn't believe me.'

She stamped across the expanse of the lounge and dragged Faith up.

'Well, if I ain't welcome here, I'll go somewhere else, but I ain't going back to that bastard to get me face smashed in.'

Marcus went to her and took the terrified child from her arms. Then, cradling Faith to his chest, he said to Bernadette: 'I don't believe you, Bernie, sometimes you bleeding well amaze me! Your daughter is standing here bruised from head to foot and your granddaughter with a black eye, and you stick up for that piece of scum! Jesus wept, woman, when you had your last face lift they must have cut into your sodding brain by accident!'

He turned to his tearful daughter. 'You stay here, my love, and you leave that ponce to me and your cousins. He won't be hitting anyone for a long time. Now, is he still at the flat?'

Delia sniffed loudly for maximum effect.

'He ain't there now, but he will be tonight. Late tonight.'

'Then me and your cousins will go and sort him out. Now you take little Faithey and get her upstairs. If you need any money for anything, see me later. All right?'

Delia nodded. Taking her daughter, she left the room, giving her mother a last smouldering glance over her shoulder.

Marcus shook his head in disgust. 'I don't believe you, Bernadette!'

She shrugged lightly. 'Obviously not. You believe her though, I take it?'

'Sodding right I do! That long-haired beatnik has raised his fists once too often. Tonight he gets his comeuppance. No one touches me or mine without they answer to me personally.'

Bernadette allowed herself a little laugh.

'I'm delighted to hear it, but listen to me, Marcus, and listen good. Our little girl is a fucker, and a lying fucker at that. Take it from me, mate, I know her better than anyone. So think long and hard before you go round and see that lad. He ain't as black as he's painted. Christ himself knows there's been times when I've wanted to hammer the cow myself!'

Marcus looked at her, disgusted.

'Where did the bruises come from then? Answer me that?'

'I ain't disputing he cracked her one, Marcus, all I'm saying is, she might just have deserved it. She could make the Archangel Gabriel get the hump when she starts her antics.'

Marcus shook his head at his wife and stormed from the room.

Bernadette sighed loudly.

She loved her daughter, she did. She loved both her children. And as big a bugger as Delia could be, she was her favourite. But Bernadette had always called a spade a spade, it was one of her few saving graces. And Delia could try the patience of a saint.

Upstairs, Delia put Faith on to her old bed and stroked the child's red hair. Jimmy had left her after the fight, telling her he wanted her out by the time he returned. He had told her she was a fat ugly bitch and he wanted nothing more to do with her. He had told her she was soapy, like a great big smelly unwashed whale. That's what had really hurt her. That and the fact he meant every word he said. He also told her that he had been seeing Olivia Sands for six months, her so-called friend. Well, he was going to get a big shock, because no one, no one at all, spoke to her like that and got away with it.

Least of all an acid head like Jimmy Sellars. And a two-timing acid head at that!

As Faith dropped off to sleep her mother stroked the fiery red hair inherited from her Auntie Briony and smiled down at her child, wincing painfully as she looked at her black eye.

She had better not touch her here, her mother would suss it immediately.

A little while later she went into the bathroom and had a long soothing bath. She eyed herself critically in the mirror opposite the bath and felt the sting of tears as she surveyed her heavy body. Since the birth of Faith she had lost the battle with her weight and it showed.

What she would do now she was back home was stick to amphetamines and lay off the cannabis. The cannabis made her hungry, but the amphetamines would kill her appetite. Before she knew it, she'd be back to her old self again.

Humming happily, she washed her hair and shaved her legs with her father's razor, blunting it.

She wished she could see Jimmy's and Olivia's faces when her father turned up that night with the twins. It really would be something to see!

The bathroom looked like a bomb had hit it when Delia finally left it. Bernadette picked up her daughter's soiled underwear, her clothes and the towels she'd used.

She looked at the thick scum around the bath itself, and sighed.

Delia was home all right.

Daniel and Boysie were like raving lunatics. Every word Marcus said fired their tempers and they sat then, three big, powerful and dangerous men, planning their course of action. Marcus enjoyed the feeling of their combined wrath. It was so real, it was positively electric. And it would see that Jimmy Sellars would never again hurt his daughter or his granddaughter. Or indeed any woman. If he survived the night, he would only do so half a man, and that thought, more than anything, calmed Marcus's soul.

Ten minutes later they were driving to the high-rise flat in Plaistow where their quarry awaited them.

As they pulled into the car park that surrounded the monstrous block of flats, a crowd of youths with motorbikes and long straggly hair watched them. A white Rolls-Royce was not par for the Plaistow flats. Not by a long chalk.

Boysie and Daniel looked at them scathingly, disgusted at their clothes and their attitude. A tall boy with long blond hair and watery blue eyes looked back.

'What you looking at then?' Daniel's voice was hard. In the dim lights from the streetlamps he saw the boy flinch in recognition.

'Nothing. Nothing, Mr Cavanagh.' All his bravado gone now he knew who they were.

'You just shut your trap and watch my motor. One little dent in it and I'll personally have each and every one of your hearts. Get that?'

They all nodded in wide-eyed fear.

The three men walked into the entrance to the flats.

Both lifts were open on the ground floor and they stepped gingerly into the one that took them to the even-numbered flats. Boysie wrinkled his nose at the smell of urine, human and canine, and the stench of unwashed aluminium.

'Lovely place this, ain't it? No wonder Delia never let no one visit her here.'

Boysie pressed the button for the tenth floor and the doors shut clumsily, the machinery's cranking and groaning the only other sound in the lift itself. All three men were silent with a combined anger and lust for revenge. The lift clanged to a halt, dropping a couple of inches down as it hit the tenth floor. The doors opened and they all walked out, simultaneously letting out breath held while the lift rose through the dirty tower block. They stood in the small lobby, glancing to either side for the number of Delia's flat. Looking in at a door to the left of them, they were surprised to see a small black child of about eight playing five stones on the concrete floor. The sounds of Janis Joplin blared out of the flat opposite, where Delia had lived, and a blasting reggae number came from an open front door which was obviously the black child's home.

The little girl watched them with dark sombre eyes. No fear there, nothing except childlike curiosity.

Picking up her five jacks and a stone, she stood up and went into the hallway of her house. Crouching down on her hunkers, she watched the three men.

Daniel banged on the front door of Delia's flat.

There was no answer.

He banged on the door again, this time harder.

A young white woman of about twenty-five came out of the flat opposite. Seeing the men, she pulled the little girl into the flat and shut and bolted the front door.

Boysie moved back and then gave the door an almighty kick. It sprang open immediately.

Holding up his arms as if for applause, he led the way into the foul-smelling hallway.

At the first banging on the door, Jimmy had gone out to the hall and looked through the spyhole in the front door. As soon as he had seen who was there he had telephoned the police.

Just as he put the phone down, Boysie kicked the door in. Now Jimmy stood in the front room, with its ragged nets and brokendown settee, his head clear for once, fear making the cannabis recede inside his mind, and he waited for the good hiding that he knew was coming.

'Hello, Jimmy son, I hear you've been a very busy boy?'

Daniel's voice was low, conversational. He pulled out from under his coat a large pickaxe handle, carefully wrapped with green insulating tape, the type electricians use to bind live wires.

Jimmy's eyes were riveted to the pickaxe handle as if glued there.

'I never hardly touched her, I swear.'

Boysie laughed. 'What about little Faithey then, and her battered eye, you ponce?'

He clubbed Jimmy with a large meaty fist.

Jimmy spun with the force of the blow and landed on the settee. He held his cheekbone with a trembling hand. 'I cracked her, I admit, but I never touched that child. That was her ma, that was Delia. That's what the bloody fight was over!'

'You lying bastard!' Marcus's voice was shrill and then he began kicking Jimmy, using every ounce of force he could muster. A few minutes later, Boysie joined in with

Daniel. The first crack of the pickaxe hit Jimmy Sellars on the back of his head.

Jimmy thankfully lost consciousness. He would never regain it. The last voice he heard was Janis Joplin singing his favourite song: 'Take another little piece of my heart.' He died three hours later on the operating table of King George's Hospital.

The police had arrived five minutes after the three angry men had left the block of flats. Miraculously, no one had seen or heard anything. But the police hadn't expected anything else.

Limmington looked at the broken body being taken into the ambulance and gritted his teeth. He would get those Cavanaghs. He would get them, and he would put them away for good.

Chapter Forty-Three

'I hope you're pleased with yourself, young lady? I hope you realise just what you bloody well caused?'

Delia's face was white and stricken. Her mouth was moving, but she couldn't seem to make any sound. Jimmy dead? Jimmy, her Jimmy, dead?

'Your father could be up on a murder charge because of you! Your father and your cousins. And do you know what really gets to me, Delia Dowling? The fact that that boy never asked for what he got. You wanted him taught a lesson. You. Now this is the upshot!'

Delia sat up in bed. 'You mean he's dead, Mum, Jimmy's really dead?'

'As a bleeding doornail, and your father and the twins were pulled in not an hour ago. I just had a call from their brief. I warn you now, girl, if anything comes of this *I'll* be up on a bleeding murder charge. Yours! Now get out of that bed, it's nearly lunchtime, and at least try and act like the grieving girlfriend, for your father's sake if not your own!'

With that Bernadette slammed from the room.

Delia lay in the bed, shocked into wakefulness. Jimmy was dead, her Jimmy. Her father had killed him. She heard a steady drumming noise and realised it was her heart beating in her ears.

Sweet, sweet Jesus, what had she caused?

Downstairs, Briony and Bernadette sat together, both worried and both furious with Delia. Faith was sitting on Briony's lap, her eye still purple and blue. She smiled at Briony with pretty even teeth. Bernadette knelt on the floor and took the child's hands into hers.

'Tell Nanny, darlin'. Tell Nanny what happened to your little face.'

Faith, at three, was a diplomat already. She licked rosebud lips and grinned, making a deep chuckle in her throat.

'No!' her little voice piped.

'Come on, sweetie, tell Nanny and she'll give you a big bar of chocolate. Just for Faithey. No one else.'

Faith's face straightened. Her eyes were bright and alert. She absentmindedly rubbed at her blackened eye, the unconscious movement of many battered children who don't feel pain as acutely as a child who is rarely smacked, let alone punched.

'A big chocolate? For me?' Her eyes opened wide as she spoke the words and Bernadette and Briony held their breaths.

'Did your daddy smack you, darlin'? Tell Nanny.'

Faith decided to tell the truth and shame the devil. Though she didn't quite put it like that to herself. She decided to say what had happened because she sensed that there was a desperate need in her granny to know. This coupled with the promise of a big bar of chocolate decided her.

'Daddy smack Mummy.' She pronounced smack 'mac'.

Bernadette nodded furiously.

'I know that, baby, but who smacked your poor eye? Was that Daddy as well?'

Faith shook her head, shy now. She pushed her face into Briony's bosom.

'No . . . Daddy didn't smack you, Faithey? Who did then, darlin'? Tell Auntie Briony.'

Faith looked at Briony, then at her granny.

'Mummy smacked me.' Her lip trembled for a few seconds before she finished. 'Hard!'

Briony looked at Bernadette and their eyes were sad but alive with malice.

'I'll murder that bitch, Bri, I take oath on that.'

Briony held the tiny child to her and kissed her springy hair. 'Calm down. Nothing will be gained if you lose your rag. What we have to do is think, girl. Think long and hard.'

She bit her lip, tasting the thickness of her Max Factor lipstick.

'But I promise you this, Bernie, if they go down over that little mare, *I'll* break her neck. You won't even be in the running for that pleasure.'

Bernadette felt her sister's animosity then, and despite her own temper, and her real worry for her husband, a thin trickle of fear ran down her spine. Delia had pushed the wrong people too far this time.

Harry Limmington could not believe his luck as he sat in the canteen of Barkingside Police station.

The twins had left not only fingerprints, but also the bloodstained pickaxe handle in the boot of their Rolls-Royce. He had them right where he wanted them.

Sipping at his cup of steaming tea, he grinned to himself, a wide, pleased as punch kind of grin.

They had played right into his hands. It was a great feeling. Jimmy Sellars was the scum of the earth, a drug dealer, a lazy good for nothing who had never done an honest day's work in his life. But his death had not been in vain. No, by Christ. His death had been the big stick that Harry was going to beat the Cavanaghs' arses black and blue with. Oh, he was sure of that.

He sipped his tea again, as if it was expensive champagne. After all, this was a celebration.

Ruby Steinway was a corpulent Jew of uncertain age and temperament. He was now in Barkingside Police station with the twins and Marcus, causing his usual rumpus.

He had been their lawyer for many long years, was quick, intelligent, and best of all as bent as a two-bob clock.

Ruby waved heavily beringed hands. Diamond and rubies glittered in the fluorescent lighting.

'Listen to me, my boys, I have everything in hand. They will keep you overnight, but I should have things under control by the morning. Obviously your prints are in the flat. After all, you have visited it on many occasions.' He raised thick heavy eyebrows as he said this, and the three men smiled and nodded, understanding him immediately. 'It's just the matter of the murder weapon, and I have a feeling that that will all come right in about twelve hours. So keep your heads down, be cool and calm, and most of all,' he glanced at Daniel and Boysie, 'don't lose your tempers.'

He stood up then, his heavy briefcase banging against his short fat leg. He rubbed his thigh absentmindedly.

'I'll bid you goodnight.'

Without bothering to shake hands with them, he bowed his head once and bustled from the room.

Limmington heard about the three suspects seeing their solicitor all at the same time and hit the roof.

'You're telling me they were allowed to see their brief together? They're on a murder charge, for Christ's sake!'

The smaller man, the desk sergeant, shrugged his shoulders, and said: 'Who gives a toss? I was following orders from the Chief Constable himself, Mr Limmington. I thought you knew about it.'

Limmington bit his lip and turned away abruptly. The Chief Constable, eh? Well, the Home Secretary would have to know about that. But a little voice in the back of his mind told him that, somehow, the Home Secretary already knew.

He made his way down to the interview rooms with a stony expression on his face. He had a feeling on him that his little celebration had been premature. He had made the usual mistake most people made with the Cavanaghs.

He had counted his chickens well before they had hatched.

'Hello, Mr Limmington. Any chance of a cup of tea?'

Boysie's face was so open and ingenuous that despite himself Harry Limmington smiled. Of the twins, he had always liked Boysie. Even as a young tearaway, he'd had a way with him. Unlike his twin brother who was a different kettle of fish altogether.

'I'll arrange some tea, Boysie, don't fret. I wanted to have another word with you, on your own like.'

Boysie sat back on the wooden chair and crossed his

arms over his chest, his eyebrows raised as if listening intently. Harry Limmington sat opposite him and, motioning for the young PC to leave the room, he smiled. His best smile.

'You realise that you're going down for a long time, don't you, Boysie? A long, long time. Murder is a serious charge. Now I won't beat about the bush, I'll be straight with you. I know your brother is a very strange individual. I know more about you two than you think. Now your uncle is getting on a bit, he won't do the stretch as easily as you two. More'n likely he'll die inside, in some prison hospital, without his family around him.' He paused to let this sink in.

'I think that between us we could come to some arrangement. Your cousin Delia has been sporting bruises, so has her nipper. Oh, I can find out anything if I want to. I can make it look like you and Danny boy went round there to see him friendly like and it just got out of hand. But I need your signature on a piece of paper to do that. You could save yourself, your uncle and a lot of people grief by keeping your head down, putting your hand up and carrying the can. What do you say, Boysie?'

Boysie looked at the man opposite him with a cold glare. He uncrossed his arms slowly. His voice low and even, he said, 'Why don't you get me a nice cup of tea, Mr Limmington, and then why don't you piss off? You're getting on my nerves now. Me and my brother and my uncle were nowhere near that flat and you know it. You're trying to fit us up. Well, you picked on the wrong people this time.'

Limmington opened his eyes wide as he said nastily, 'You trying to threaten me, Boysie?'

He looked around the empty room, his face showing an

expression Limmington had not seen before. It was almost feral.

'What do you think? You don't scare me, mate, you don't even enter my thoughts. You're nothing, a tiny speck on the arsehole of the world. Don't sit there with your poxy newspaper advert suit and your good brown brogues and try and get one over on me or mine. You're just an Old Bill. You're dirt on the bottom of my shoes. You're nothing. Get that? Nothing. I could see you off the face of this earth if the fancy took me, so don't push me, mate. Just don't push me. Now call in your little friend and let's forget this conversation ever took place.'

Despite himself Limmington felt afraid. Boysie Cavanagh had just told him in no uncertain terms that his life could be in danger. That he was ready to extinguish him as he would a cockroach or a beetle. Harry Limmington saw for a brief second his wife Violet mourning him as she had her only son.

It was only then, in the small interview room, face to face with the least fearsome of the Cavanagh twins, that he realised, really understood, just what he had taken on.

PC Dillinger was a rather skinny man with large, obtrusive ears. He was thirty-six years old, unmarried, and had been a policeman for over ten years, never aspiring to be anything more than plain PC. He was at this moment in possession of the blood-stained pickaxe handle that was the main evidence against the Cavanaghs. It had been removed from the locked cupboard in the evidence lab by another policeman, a DC called Rushton, and had been given to him in the car park of The Oaks in Ilford half an hour earlier. He was now sitting in his black Zephyr on the London Road at The Chequers, Dagenham, waiting for someone to pick it up and dispose of it. He would be five hundred pounds better off afterwards and he had already planned exactly how he was going to spend the money.

His first stop would be Berwick Manor, where he would pick up a nice girl and play roulette. Then he would put a bit aside for his mother, and fifty pounds towards his sister's wedding.

He was startled out of his reverie by a tap on the window of the car. He got out, passed over the parcel, took the envelope with the money in and, getting back in his car, pulled away immediately. No words were exchanged.

Smiling to himself, PC Dillinger turned left and made his way towards Rainham, Berwick Manor and the good life.

Briony burnt the pickaxe handle herself, watching it until all that was left were a few cinders. Then she smiled tightly at the man in Ford's furnace room, slipped him a monkey, and walked back to her car where Jimmy Nailer drove her silently back to Manor Park and Bernadette.

Delia had not emerged from the bedroom, had neither eaten nor spoken to anyone. Bernadette had left her there, frightened of what she would do to her daughter if she spoke to her for any length of time. When Briony returned, Bernadette ran out to the hallway, beating a white-faced Cissy to the front door.

'Is everything all right, Bri?'

Briony smiled. Her first real smile of the day. 'It's OK now. Everything done. We should have them back in the morning.'

She pulled off her light coat and slung it over the banister.

'Cissy love, stop staring and make a cuppa, strong and sweet. Where's Delia, Bernie?'

Cissy rushed off to make the tea, her nervousness apparent to anyone. Bernadette followed Briony into the drawing room and stammered, 'She ain't been down. I can't go up to her, Bri, I'll muller her. I've never been so frightened or so annoyed in all me life.'

Briony nodded, understanding.

'Where's Faithey?'

'She's asleep, bless her heart. I put her down about an hour ago.'

'I'll go up to Delia. She has to know what to say. The Old Bill could be here again any time with a warrant for her arrest. They'll want to question her about the fight with Jimmy. I want her word perfect when they see her.'

Briony practically ran up Bernadette's shining staircase and burst into Delia's bedroom.

She jumped with fright as she saw her aunt at the bottom of her bed like an avenging angel.

'You've caused some trouble, my girl, but I'm pleased to say I have sorted it all out.' Briony's voice was low and hard, nothing like the usual tone she used with her niece, and Delia felt the prickle of fear getting bigger until it enveloped her whole body.

'Oh, Auntie Bri . . .'

Briony cut her off with a wave of her hand and sat on the bed heavily.

'Shut up, Delia, I ain't interested in explanations, not yet anyway. I want you to listen to me carefully, very carefully. The police have already been here looking for you.' She saw Delia's eyes open wide. 'Your mother sent them away with a flea in their ears, but they'll be back. She told them you was sedated with shock. They believed her, but as I say, they'll be back. Now you tell them that you had a fight with Jimmy, right. But afterwards you left the flat and you were here, with your cousins and father, all day and all night. Me, you and your mother will be the alibi. Cissy's staying here as well. She will say she served dinner here. If we all stick to the same story, they can't do a thing, get it?'

Delia nodded, her eyes wide open.

'Now listen to me, Delia, this is serious, very serious, and if the boys go down and your father too, there'll be hell to pay. Do you understand what I'm telling you? You caused all this and it's up to you to help salvage as much as we can from it.'

Delia nodded, her eyes wide and frightened. Briony knew, looking at her, that she would be the one they had to watch. She could be the fly in the otherwise perfect ointment. The evidence was gone, disposed of. That would cause a stir, but all the same, without it the police had nothing. The boys' fingerprints would be in their cousin's flat, that was only natural. So that evidence was negligible. Jimmy Sellars was a known drug dealer, anyone with a grudge could have killed him, anyone he owed money to or supplied. If they all stuck together, the three men would be home in the morning. Ruby was already working on a writ accusing the police of harassment; this would be served if they tried to carry on their investigation in the wake of the loss of evidence. Everything pertaining to the pickaxe handle was now in Ruby's possession. All the files had been lifted, everything. Tommy had seen to that. Briony herself would dispose of them when the time came.

Other than Delia, the cause of all the aggravation, it was all well under control.

She poked a slim finger at her niece.

'I know for a fact it was you who hammered Faithey, not Jimmy. That boy died because you're a trouble maker.

I never thought I'd say this to you, Delia, never, but in future you give me a wide berth. You keep a distance between us because I don't know yet what I'm capable of where you're concerned. Do you understand me? The twins will be told the truth of what you done, that's only fair. You used them, and you don't ever use family. Think on that.

'You were the instigator of your own child's father's death. You was also the cause of your father and your cousins being locked up and charged with murder. I for one won't forgive that fact lightly. Neither will your mother or your father, or indeed your cousins. So take my advice, girl, get your act together, and soon. Think on what I said, and tell the police exactly what I told you. Act dumb, in shock. Tell them that Jimmy was a dealer with many enemies. He was always tucking people up. Only you can get your father out of the shit you dropped him in. Only you. Right?'

Delia nodded, her eyes fearful and full of tears.

Briony felt no compassion for her whatsoever. In fact, it wouldn't have taken much for her to give Delia a blow that would leave her ears ringing for days after.

She didn't trust her niece. That fact, on top of everything else, saddened her more than anything.

'What do you mean, the evidence has gone walkabout?' Limmington's voice was high with disbelief.

'What I say, Mr Limmington sir. The pickaxe handle is gone. The back of the Rolls-Royce has been scrubbed clean as a nun's tits, and that's that.'

'What do you mean, that's that?'

Limmington was beginning to wonder if the young man in front of him had lost a few marbles.

The young detective sighed. He had not wanted this job, knew he would have to take the flak, and it annoyed him.

'You know the pickaxe handle, sir? The one used by the Cavanaghs to murder Jimmy Sellars?'

Limmington nodded.

'Well, at some time between late last night and early this morning, it disappeared from the evidence cupboard. Along with all the records and files. It's as if it never, ever existed. We have no pickaxe, no records, we have nothing on the Cavanaghs whatsoever. Or Mr Dowling for that matter.'

'But I personally put that pickaxe into evidence myself. I ain't having this. I'm going to see the Super!'

The PC nodded imperceptibly as if expecting this. 'He's waiting for you, sir.'

Harry Limmington stormed through the building, his whole body tense with shock and disbelief. He walked into the Super's office without knocking, something he had never done in his life.

'Ah, Limmington, in you come.' Chief Superintendent Christopher Whiteside's voice was friendly and calm. 'Sit yourself down, man. Bad business this. A very bad business. I'm looking into it personally, you can be assured of that.'

Harry Limmington felt his heart sink down to somewhere in the region of his clean nylon socks.

'I placed that pickaxe into evidence myself, sir. I signed for it. I feel we can still charge the Cavanaghs with murder. I am quite willing to take the stand myself and explain their skulduggery to whoever happens to want to listen.'

Christopher Whiteside knew this was a veiled threat and grinned. The grin was similar to Boysie Cavanagh's and

Limmington felt the same fear. Only this time it was tinged with disgust.

'I have in my possession a writ, a copy of a writ actually, which is to be served on yourself as a matter of fact. It states that on sixteen different occasions you have harassed the Cavanagh twins, the culmination being a charge of murder that could not be corroborated.

'Now let's look at this rationally, shall we? We have no evidence at all, we have a writ with sixteen different times you have allegedly harassed the Cavanaghs. The papers would have a field day! I have it on good authority that the *News of the World* are very interested in it already. You're a good policeman, Limmington, one of the best in fact. But if you pursue this, you're heading for a fall from a great height, in fact. Leave it. Let's just keep our eye on them and wait our chance.'

Limmington felt his body sag. It had all been for nothing. He felt physically sick.

'So you're letting them go then?' His voice was low, barely audible.

Whiteside smiled, a 'we're all boys together' smile.

'They were discharged from custody two hours ago.'

Harry turned and left the room.

He walked back to his office like a man already beaten. He picked up the telephone and dialled a number. The Home Secretary was unavailable to take his call, he was told.

Harry had a feeling he would be unavailable for a long while yet.

Boysie had gone straight to Suzannah's house, to reassure her everything was all right. Marcus and Daniel went home to Manor Park.

Bernadette and Briony were so pleased to see them the two men were overwhelmed with kisses and hugs. Cissy, bursting into tears, began to cook them a breakfast the likes of which they would never see again in their lives.

Drinking a cup of tea, they listened with troubled faces as Bernadette and Briony explained the truth about Sellars. Marcus was devastated. Daniel on the other hand was so angry Briony thought he was going to walk up the stairs and commit another murder there and then.

'She what?'

'It's true, Danny Boy.' Bernie's voice was ashamed. 'Jimmy never touched the child. He hit Delia because of her treatment of Faithey. Delia told us the whole of it last night. She wanted Jimmy taught a lesson. He'd been batting away from home, told her to get lost. She was getting her own back.'

'So you're telling me I spent the night in an Old Bill shop because that little mare wanted to get even with her bloke? I nearly had a murder charge hanging round me neck, and The Aunt's been running round like a blue-arsed fly sorting it all out, and it was all because that little slut wanted Jimmy Sellars to get a good hiding. Jesus wept! We could all be doing a ten stretch now, and all because that fucking drug head wanted her boyfriend given a slap! I don't believe I'm hearing this. Where is she?'

Briony held his arm, digging her nails in with the force of her grip.

'Calm down, Danny, calm down. Losing your rag is what got you into this. If you take a bite out of her now, she'll crumble. Believe me when I say she's learnt her bloody lesson. She knows what she's done. You shouting and hollering at her ain't going to achieve anything.'

Marcus spoke for the first time.

'It's funny, you know, I always had a soft spot for Delia, more so than Rebecca. But at this minute I could cheerfully break her neck, I could. I could snap it like a twig when I think of what she's caused!'

'Calm down, Marcus. It's as Briony said. Delia isn't very stable at the moment. If you go hammering her, there's no telling what she'll do. I never thought I'd say this but that girl is trouble.'

Delia had heard the raised voices coming from below and her heart was beating a tattoo in her chest.

The worst of it all was not so much the fact that Jimmy was dead, though she was very sorry about that, but the loss of face. The being found out for what she was. And the more she thought about what she was, the more she needed something to take the edge off it. Danny and Boysie and her father were now aware that she was a liar, a troublemaker and, worst of all, a child beater. Her mother had already informed her that the child was never leaving the house with her again. Well, she wasn't too trashed about that. Faithey was a nice enough kid, but she did rather cramp Delia's style. All she had been was a way to get Jimmy Sellars, and she had done that much.

Now Jimmy was gone and Delia had blotted her copybook, she had to look for a new life.

Boysie was pleased at his reception from Suzannah who had literally thrown herself into his arms. Boysie picked her up on her front step and Doris Rankins stood at her window and nodded to herself with glee.

Her girl had picked wisely.

Boysie kissed Suzy fervently, feeling her hard little breasts squeezing against his chest.

'I knew you couldn't have done that terrible thing, Boysie. I told me mum and dad that!'

'It was all a big mistake, darlin'. Now how about me and you go for a little drive and plan that wedding of ours?'

Suzy grinned as he placed her on the ground gently.

'That would be lovely, Boysie.'

He took her to Hatton Garden where he bought her an engagement ring that was staggeringly expensive and inordinately showy.

Suzy, pleased that her man was back home and the wedding was still on, looked at it with both pride and fear.

Now she was owned by Boysie, irrevocably and forever. In fact, a little voice told her, she was owned by the whole of the Cavanagh clan.

But she swallowed the feeling down and kissed Boysie full on the lips in front of the aged jeweller. She couldn't wait to flash this ring in her friends' and relatives' faces.

Chapter Forty-Four

'So where have you been then, Boysie? You just march out of here without a by your leave, and stay out all night. I wanna know where you've been? And more to the point, Boysie Cavanagh, who you've been with?'

Suzy's voice was shrill. It seemed that in the year since they had married her voice had taken on a strident quality, frighteningly similar to that of a pantomime dame.

Boysie tried unsuccessfully to put his arms around his wife's swelling belly.

'Don't you touch me, I don't know where you've been.'

Boysie gritted his teeth together and then said, as quietly as his anger would allow, 'Suzy darlin', I have been out on a bit of business. That's all. I never discuss my business dealings with you, love. The less you know, the better. Now, shut your trap and get me a bit of brekky, will you? I'm starving.'

Suzy knew by the inflection in Boysie's voice that she had pushed him as far as she could. Knowing when to retreat, she gave him a cold stare for a few seconds before she went into the kitchen and began cooking eggs and bacon. Her face was closed now, but she was still fuming.

She lived in a large imposing house, it was furnished to her taste, she had more money than she knew what to do with, and she was having a baby. Her husband, she knew, doted on her. So why wasn't she happy? Why did she cause this ruckus every time she felt like it?

Because, she told herself, you hate every second of it. You have hated it since the novelty wore off and you got a real inkling of what your life was going to be.

She could not go out alone or with friends. She went out only with her husband, normally to clubs he owned or pubs where he was more than welcome. His aunts were frequent visitors to her house, and she was expected to visit them frequently.

Boysie watched her like a hawk. The friends who still visited were given the silent treatment by him, who said he had nothing to say to a gang of young girls.

Well, she was still a young girl, wasn't she?

She wanted a life of her own but even her music had to be turned down because Boysie couldn't stand loud noise.

Even the novelty of being treated like visiting royalty in shops and around the markets had long worn off. In fact it got on her nerves. The day before she had gone into the grocer's and he had stopped serving someone to serve her. She had seen the naked hatred on the other girl's face, as she looked at Suzy's new clothes, her packed purse, and the deferential manner bestowed on her by the shopkeeper.

Suzy had felt like screaming at her: 'You wouldn't want to be me, love. It all looks nice but it's not. My life is like a caged bird's. I can't move but there's six people asking me where I'm going, what I'm doing, and why I'm doing it.'

Even his bloody granny, Granny Moll as he still called her, was like another appendage of him. Always round the house, poking her beak in where it wasn't wanted. His Auntie Briony listened to him with rapt attention, the same as she listened to that little brat Faithey. Faithey! What a stupid name.

Suzy flung three rashers of best bacon into the frying pan. The fat was so hot it spat at her immediately, hitting her on her cheeks. The stinging sensation brought tears to her lovely china-blue eyes.

She hated being pregnant, and she hated being married. Married to a man who treated her like some kind of doll, to be picked up and played with when it suited him, and then cast back into the toy cupboard until he wanted to play with her again.

She placed his breakfast in front of him ten minutes later and, pouring out two cups of tea, sat and watched her big fine husband eat the lot.

It occurred to her then, that she was beginning to hate him.

Bessie and Liselle helped Kerry dress for her television appearance. After appearing on the *Music Show* on BBC2, at Briony's instigation, Kerry had enjoyed a little of her former fame. Now, a year on, she was taking on quite a few engagements. Liselle was over the moon at the turn events had taken. She was now her mother's manager, which cut down the number of visits to see her father in New York but which nevertheless pleased her immensely.

'This deep green suits you, Mum, it brings out the highlights in your eyes. You'll look well on camera.'

Kerry sighed slightly.

She didn't care that much about her looks, she was

more interested in getting in the green room before the show and having a quick snifter of vodka. She made the effort and smiled though.

'Thanks, darlin'. I think I'll shock quite a few people this time with my choice of song. I mean, me on the Old Grey Whistle Test! At my age.'

Her laughter was genuine.

'Listen, Mum, John Peel knows a good thing when he hears it. There's a big jazz revival that's been going on since the late-fifties. It was only a matter of time before you were remembered. You were one of the best blues and jazz singers of your day. You were singing the blues when most of the singers today weren't even thought of! I'm not surprised you're back on top again. You deserve it.'

Kerry smiled at her daughter's words. Lissy, as she still thought of her, was one hell of a daughter in some respects. Her absolute belief in her mother's talent being one of them. Liselle, no matter what, had always had a great respect and regard for her mother's voice, and now she managed her with an iron will. No one would knock Kerry Cavanagh while her daughter was there. No one.

In some respects she reminded Kerry of Briony. She had the same single-mindedness her aunt possessed when she wanted something badly enough. Briony had kept her promise a year ago, albeit a few days late. She had taken Kerry out, dressed her from head to toe, and had arranged for Kerry to appear on the *Music Show*, taking her there herself and giving her two large neat vodkas to calm her nerves. Kerry had sung 'Miss Otis Regrets', clearly and hauntingly, gathering all her old fans to her once more, and quite a few new ones. Young fans who looked through old seventy-eight records on the markets to hear her old songs. In the last twelve months her life had taken on some surprising new angles, but at least she was enjoying it again.

Today, she would have two large vodkas before her performance, and the few snifters she could sneak herself. Liselle had come to terms with the fact Kerry needed a drink to sing. It was that simple. If they monitored her drinking, they could get a performance from her which pleased Kerry, Lissy, Briony and the audience. She had already guested at Ronnie Scott's and Bessie had sung with her at other venues around London.

Kerry was drinking again, but she was drinking in a constructive way that even the Harley Street doctor, bought and paid for by Briony, couldn't find fault with. As he had said himself, many people had a couple of large drinks every day. It took the edge off stressful work situations, and from otherwise claustrophobic marriages.

Kerry liked Dr Montgomery. He was her kind of doctor. She hadn't told anyone that he was the kind of guy who also administered shots of demerol for forty quid a time. After all, no one had asked her about that, had they? So why spoil a good thing?

Briony and Tommy sat in the studio with the whole of the family around them. Briony watched Boysie and his wife sitting at the end of the row. She sighed inwardly. There was trouble there, she'd lay money on that. Daniel sat beside her, his current amour Christabel – what a Godawful name that was – chattering to him nineteen to the dozen. Briony smiled grimly to herself. She wouldn't last long.

Bernadette sat with Marcus and her face, the skin stretched over the bones like parchment, was heavily made-up. Since Rosalee's death and Marcus's misbehaviour at that time, Bernie had taken an inordinate interest in her appearance. She now spent a small fortune on cosmetic surgery, and any other paraphernalia she could lay her hands on to keep her young-looking. Well, poor old Marcus was too old for his philandering now. Bernie should come down to earth with the rest of the mere mortals and start looking a little more her age.

Beside Bernie and Marcus sat Rebecca and her husband John. Briony saw the thin-lipped look of husband and wife and suppressed a smile. They even looked alike these two, with their dark hair, their almond-shaped eyes and Roman noses. Rebecca had on a fur coat even in the heat of the studio lights and Briony guessed correctly it was new. Second hand, but new to Rebecca. It was her way of showing them John was doing all right. Strangely, this fact pleased Briony. Rebecca was doing all right, and she was glad. If she wanted to go it alone, without the help of the family, all the more power to her.

Briony's eyes clouded a little as she looked at Delia. She sat with another one of the great unwashed, which was the family's terms for Delia's boyfriends. She sat quietly though. Unlike her old self, unlike the girl she was before all the trouble with Jimmy. Her pupils were dilated and Briony wondered what shit was pulsing through her system tonight. It was strange how drugs and drink seemed to play a big part in the Cavanagh women's lives. There was Kerry and her drinking and her drug taking. Now Delia. It was a crying shame really. How could they be so weak?

It amazed Briony, who could never understand that not everyone was as strong as herself, could cope with life as she did. It was one of the things everyone else knew and admitted to themselves except Briony. Because she was such a strong personality, she abhorred weakness in others.

She shifted her eyes to her mother, then grinned at Tommy who shook his head and smiled. Molly was sitting between her two grandsons, her beaver lamb coat sending out a powerful whiff of mothballs and lavender toilet water. She was a great age and a great woman, Briony accepted that fact now, all the old animosity buried. At the end was Cissy, hankie already out for when she started crying. Cissy, love her heart, cried at the drop of a hat.

The studio lights were warm and Briony settled herself into her seat. All around her were people who, young or old, had one thing in common. They wanted to hear Kerry Cavanagh sing. Briony felt so secure as she sat there, so invincible, it was like a warm invisible cloak wrapped tightly around her. They had weathered so much, this family. There was nothing more that could befall them. Or so she thought.

John Peel came out and began talking to the camera and the studio audience.

'Tonight we have a woman who has sung for nearly five decades. After a lull in her career of nearly twenty years she's back, proving that she is still one of the greats. Miss Kerry Cavanagh!'

The lights came up at the back of the stage to show Kerry and her backing group. The applause was deafening and took three minutes to settle down. When the studio was quiet, Kerry spoke to the audience in her sing-song voice.

'Thank you. Thank you one and all. Tonight I'm going to do a few of the old numbers, but first I want to sing a song I heard a few years ago which touched me deeply, and which I hope you all enjoy.'

A young man began to play an acoustic guitar, then Kerry stepped to the microphone, and taking it in her hand, she beat her foot in time for a few seconds. Then she began to sing 'Me and Bobby McGee'. The audience sat stunned, listening to the clear tones, to the breadth of her talent. Then of one mind they relaxed and enjoyed the song.

The lone guitarist was joined by two men on electric guitars, a drummer and a pianist. The blues beat picked up and Kerry belted out the chorus in a voice that was loud and clear, singing that freedom only meant you didn't have anything left to lose.

Briony sat stunned as she listened to her sister's voice, belting out the Janis Joplin number in her old inimitable style. This proved not only to Briony, but to everyone who heard Kerry, that she could indeed carry on singing till she dropped. She was over sixty years old yet she gave the song a new dimension, a new angle, and the band, who were all playing now as if their lives depended on it, were all feeling privileged to be in on this miraculous fact.

As she finished the number, the audience stood up and clapped the gaunt woman on stage who could still sing like an angel. The ovation was electric. John Peel came out and clapped with them. The place went wild. Even the cameramen were clapping.

Briony looked at Cissy and was not surprised to see she was crying.

Happier than she had been for a long time, Briony sat back in her seat and grasped Tommy's hand. She squeezed it tightly. He leant towards her and brushed her cheek with his lips.

'She can sing, Bri, no one can take that away from her, love.'

And Briony nodded at him furiously. Tommy was right. No one could ever take that away from her. Not even Kerry herself, and Christ himself knew she had tried.

Briony was humming the tune to herself all the next day. It seemed to her as if it was imprinted on her memory. She had heard it many times, but it had just sounded like a noise to her, a record for the young. Now it was a song for everyone.

Briony was humming it as she walked out of her house to her car. She felt light of spirit and light of foot. She felt quite youthful herself. This thought made her laugh. Tommy had gone to the dog track with Boysie, Daniel and Marcus, a pastime that was both recreational and profitable seeing as the twins owned it. She was driving over to see Kerry and Liselle. At least, that was what she'd planned until she saw the man standing on her drive.

The sun was in her eyes and she blinked furiously, walking over to the dark-coated figure. He seemed familiar to her somehow even though she couldn't see his face. As she approached him, her heart stopped dead in her chest.

The man saw the reaction his presence caused and instinctively put out a hand to steady her. Briony grasped it as if she was a drowning woman, feeling the warmth of her son's hand for the first time in many years.

'Miss Briony Cavanagh.' It was a statement not a question.

Briony felt a sensation in the pit of her stomach, a burning as if she had swallowed a bottle of acid.

'Benedict.'

As soon as she uttered the word Benedict Dumas knew that it was all true. He had watched her for a year, following in her footsteps, observing her. He had hired private detectives to find out all about her business interests and still his thirst for knowledge had not been quenched. No matter how bad the news about her, how terrible she seemed, she had fascinated him. He had to know about her. Now he had to speak to her.

A mixture of contempt for her mingled with curiosity. She was his natural mother, she had borne him.

'Come inside . . . Come into the house . . .' Briony was finding it difficult to talk. He had sought her out, as she had always prayed. He had sought her out and he was here, on her doorstep, and the joy in her knew no bounds. He followed her silently into the house.

Cissy took one look at the man with Briony and her jaw dropped with shock. It was like looking at Briony. He had the same green eyes, the same shaped face, he even had a reddish tinge to his hair. This was Briony's son, come home.

Briony shut the door and gestured for Benedict to take a seat. He sat down carefully, as if he might break the chair. Briony went to the drinks cabinet and poured two large brandies.

He accepted his without a word.

They surveyed one another for long, long minutes. Both acknowledging the likeness. Both wary, and yet greatly interested in the other, and both loth to show this fact. Finally, after what seemed an age, Briony broke the silence.

'Who told you?'

'My father.'

Briony savoured the sound of his voice, as she might have a delicious pastry or a longed-for drink of cool clean water.

'Henry? Henry told you?'

Benedict shook his head. 'He died last year. He mentioned it in his will. I never knew, never had any idea . . .'

Briony heard the hurt in him then, the hurt and the unpleasant shock the knowledge had apparently given him. It was a revelation that he hadn't enjoyed, that much was evident.

'It was a long time ago. Over fifty years actually, but you'd know that of, course.'

'You were a child, a child prostitute . . .'

Briony heard the words and the effect they had on her was like a blow. Her head was reeling. The way he had said them! And then anger came to her. It spewed into her head, and came out of her mouth like molten lava.

'Listen here, Benedict Dumas, I was thirteen when you were born, thirteen years old! My father sold me to your father, it's as simple as that. It was a business arrangement. My elder sister Eileen had gone to him first, God rest her, she never got over it. She died because of Henry Dumas, she died out of her mind!

'Now you listen to me and you listen good. Your mother bought you from me. I was a kid, that's all. I didn't know what life had in store for me, I knew nothing, yet thanks to your father I knew everything! I bore you and I loved you, God help me, I loved you more than anything in the world, but circumstances were such that I had to give you up. It was another of the Dumas business deals.

'Your father was incapable of sleeping with a grown woman, he liked little girls with no breasts and no knowledge of men. He bought and paid for them as other men would a grown prostitute. I'm sorry to shatter your illusions about him, but facts are facts. He shaped my life, Henry Dumas, he shaped it and left me half a woman who felt nothing for years.

'Not a day has gone by since but I've thought of you, Ben. The only child of my body. I'm sorry if I don't fit the bill, but that's another thing I can't do anything about.'

Benedict looked into her face and what he said didn't really surprise her.

'I hated Henry Dumas all my life. It's funny, but my mother's . . . my adopted mother's . . . father was the only man I ever cared for. Yet now I know he was nothing to me really, no blood relation at all.'

Briony was sorry for her outburst, but this big handsome well-spoken man frightened her, even while she loved to look at him and hear his voice. He frightened her because she knew he was looking down his nose at her. Knew he would be ashamed of her, *was* ashamed of her and what she was. The knowledge made her want to cry.

'Why did you come here? Why did you want to see me?'

She asked the question even though she was terrified of the answer.

'I had to know you, I had to see you and talk to you. I had to know what stock I had come from, I had to know if you were as low as I had been told . . .'

Briony laughed then, a heartrending little sound that was nearly crying.

'And am I?'

Benedict finished the brandy in one gulp and looked into the face so like his own.

'Yes, you are.'

With that he stood up and left the room.

Briony heard his footsteps as he walked to the front door, she heard the crunch of his expensive boots as he walked across the gravel of the drive and away from her.

Then the tears did come and with them the burning heat of humiliation and shame.

He was her son, her boy. She still loved him with every ounce of her being.

Benedict walked from his mother's house and down the drive in a state of terror and shock. He had seen her, spoken to her. He had sat in her house. The biggest impression she had made on him was the fact she looked the same age as him. They could have been brother and sister.

As he pulled open the door of his car and got into the driving seat, he felt his heartbeat begin to slow down. His pulse was not so erratic now and he took long deep breaths to calm himself.

She was so young.

Brother and sister.

The thoughts swirled around in his head, making him dizzy. He saw her then in his mind's eye as a young girl, a very young girl of ten or eleven. He saw his father as he had seen him in countless old photos, taking the young girl as a grown man might a woman. Taking her as his right. After all, he had paid for her. He saw the frightened face, her crinkly red hair and those huge green eyes. The scene before his eyes sickened him, and the way he had hurt her sickened him more. But, oh, he had wanted to hurt her, that girl-woman who had borne him. He had wanted to make her hurt as he had been hurting for the last year.

But hadn't she been hurting for fifty years? Over fifty years in fact. Since she had first come into contact with his father? Hadn't he wanted to hurt her because she had abandoned him, given him to Isabel and Henry Dumas, when she was his flesh and he was hers. When they were mother and son?

Hadn't he wanted to hurt her for every hurt inflicted on him by a father who couldn't stand the sight of him, who had wickedly tortured the young boy in his care because he was the product of Briony Cavanagh and for no other reason but that? Because his mother had been a young girl, a young child, and Henry's wife Isabel had bought his son from her because she wanted a baby so desperately?

And with the clarity of adulthood and hindsight Benedict realised that he himself had also been a stick to beat Henry Dumas with. A hold over him. Something Isabel could use to get her own back for the barrenness of her marriage and her life.

Wasn't that why he had hurt the woman back in that house? No other reason but that? Because through her he had been hurting all his life?

And now through his meeting her, and what he had just done to her, he would carry on hurting, only this time the hurt would be tinged heavily with shame and guilt.

Yet, through her, now he had it all. A good education, a good marriage, two healthy children, more money than he could ever hope to spend, and a place in society that had culminated in his inheriting his grandfather's peerage. Benedict Dumas, now Lord Barkham. He smiled a twisted smile at he thought. Lord Barkham begotten by a man's twisted desire for young children.

It was a heavy burden to carry around with you day after day, and yet he knew he would have to. For his own children's sakes.

He felt an urge to run back to that house and into that

woman's arms, to cry on her shoulder and hear that deep husky voice tell him everything would be fine. Instead, he started up his Daimler and drove home to Fenella and Natalie and his son Henry Dumas the second. Home to his real life, that wasn't really his life, had never been his life.

At over fifty years old he felt like an orphan, and strange as human nature can be, after the revelations of last year, that felt quite good.

Delia was in the Jack of Spades, a small club in Soho that played jazz music, served warm beer, and turned a blind eye to the smoking of cannabis. She looked at the youth with her, about nineteen, with a three-day stubble on his chin. Already she wished she had never met him.

He loved the thought that she was related to Kerry Cavanagh. The name Cavanagh haunted Delia. Jimmy Sellars had loved the fact she was related to all those people whom he admired, the twins most of all. It was just a pity Delia herself didn't garner the respect her cousins and her aunts did. Then she might be a bit happier.

She accepted the tiny piece of blotting paper from Andy and looked at it for a second before putting it on her thickly coated tongue. It had a little smiling face printed on it. The LSD was called California Sunshine and was about as good as you could get. She felt the need for the rush tonight, a deep inner need that had nothing to do with Andy, her aunts or her cousins.

This was between her and her brain.

The thought made her smile.

Everywhere she looked were Jimmy Sellars lookalikes. All smoking dope, dropping uppers and downers and acid. The smell of chemicals should be coming out of their pores by now, she reckoned. But she did miss Jimmy Boy, missed him a lot.

An hour later she was smashed out of her skull. The room had taken on rosy edges, faces were swimming before her eyes, faces that were like plasticine models. She lifted an arm and watched the strobing. Fifteen arms moved in perfect harmony together. She smiled to herself. All around her she could see a blue heat coming from the bodies. Bodies that were entwined, were moving with perfect clarity, and yet were not moving at all. Let's hear it for California Sunshine, she thought to herself then. For being out of your box and still able to think.

Andy thrust a drink into her hand and she gulped at it gratefully, feeling the warm bubbles of lager as they made their way through her body. Every nerve was alive, every pore in her body could feel. That was what she loved most about LSD. Only when tripping could she really feel that aliveness, that being present feeling that deserted her when she was straight. When real life was just a bummer. When her feelings were deadened and frustrated by lack of chemicals. Whoever invented LSD should get the peace prize, should be fêted and adored. Whoever made this synthetic feeling of happiness should be rewarded.

Such was Delia's thinking when she bumped into the guy with the long black hair and the crooked grin.

Before she knew what was happening she was out of the club, was in a car then in a flat in Ilford, with Pink Floyd on the stereo and her own voice talking above it.

She was telling him all about her life, her child, and the death of her child's father.

The man listened gently, prompting her now and then or asking her questions.

Delia, in her drugged innocence, answered everything he asked her. Truthfully. Without a shred of nervousness.

Later on he made love to her.

That bit, as far as she was concerned, was the best bit of all.

Chapter Forty-Five

Tommy watched Briony as she pushed her food around her plate. He watched her closely, taking in everything about her, from her hair, piled high on her head to reveal her slender neck, hardly creased with age, to her coral-painted fingernails. Dressed as she was in a deep green three-quarter length dress with matching sandals, she looked every bit the lady to him. Her eyes were expertly made up. The fine lines around them made her look more interesting than old.

He wished with all his heart that she would tell him what was ailing her. Whatever it was it had been on her mind for over a week. She had lain beside him, pretending to sleep, but with the knowledge of someone who has spent countless nights beside her, he knew she was faking.

'Come on, Bri . . . Tell me what's up. We've never kept things from one another, have we?'

Briony looked startled. Her eyes glanced into his and he saw first the hurt, then the confusion.

'I think that whatever's on your mind, girl, should be shared. Just talking about a problem can automatically make it seem less gigantic.' He smiled as he said that.

Briony half smiled. Tommy was shrewd enough to know that whatever was wrong with her was big. Was enormous. Otherwise she would have sorted it herself.

But should she tell him?

Should she open up to him and tell him all the demons that were plaguing her day and night? About the guilt and the fear, yes, fear, because she was frightened of her son, frightened of what he thought of her. What he felt about her.

She closed her eyes and shook her head.

'I'll tell you soon, my love, I promise you.'

'Is it very bad?'

Briony heard the hurt in his voice and was sorry. 'It's bad enough. It's a family problem.' Well, that was true anyway.

'It's not about me then?'

Briony did smile now. 'No, Tommy Lane. It's not about you. It's about something that happened a long time ago and has come back to haunt me.'

Then Tommy knew.

There was only one thing in her past that could rise up and have this effect.

Her son.

Nodding his understanding, he carried on eating the excellent steak and kidney pudding cooked by Cissy.

He made a mental note to find out about Benedict Dumas. If that little bugger was causing hag, then he wanted to know about it. It wasn't until dessert that he realised the epithet 'little bugger' was completely wrong. Briony's son was only thirteen years younger than she was.

This thought stayed with him all night. Suddenly he saw again a beautiful young girl, dressed in blue velvet.

And, being a gentleman, he told himself she hadn't changed a bit.

Daniel combed his hair in the hallway mirror of Boysie's house. He could hear Suzy's voice coming from the lounge and closed his eyes. She was one mouthy cow, that Suzy. If she was his old woman he'd give her an almighty slap, shut the bitch up.

'So I've got to stay in all night on me own then, is that it, Boysie Cavanagh? Is that this evening's plan then? You fuck off out and I stay here bored out of me brains?'

Boysie stared at his little wife and sighed.

'I've got a bit of business, Suzy, I'll try not to be late . . .'

She interrupted him.

'Oh, don't you worry about me, Boysie, or should I say us? Me and the baby. *Your* baby by the way. We'll sit in here and watch telly. Like we always bleeding well do. You go out and enjoy yourself!'

Boysie picked up his jacket from the back of the settee and quickly left the room.

Suzy, though, wasn't letting him get off that lightly. She followed him. Bursting out into the hallway, she launched herself at him, nails and hair flying.

'You big gormless bastard! You walk out of this house and that's it, the finish! I mean it!'

Boysie grabbed at her wrists and held her away from him.

'Enough!' Daniel's voice was scandalised. 'I ain't never heard anything like it in my life!'

Boysie and Suzy stared at him. He had come through the front door as Suzy's mother had left. He'd been waiting in the hall for the fight to finish before showing himself. Now, however, he had listened to enough from Suzy Rankins, as he still thought of her.

'Listen here, darlin', you married a fucking man. Ever heard of one of them, have you? If you wanted a nine to fiver, love, you should have spent your time down at the Ilford Palais or some other dive full of civil servants and insurance brokers. You wanted the excitement of being Mrs Cavanagh. Well, you've had your day, darlin'. Most dogs get one, you know. So shut your fucking trap up and give us both a bit of peace!'

Suzy stood stock still, the naked hatred in her brother-in-law's face enough to stem any further words from her.

She looked at Boysie, expecting him to defend her, but he stared at her, eyes like flint. She knew that this humiliation in front of his brother would cut deep, and felt a prickle of fear then at what she had done. Her breathing was erratic in her chest. Pain constricted her windpipe, made her eyes water. Fear emanated from her in waves. Looking at her, Boysie wondered why he couldn't smell it. It was acute, almost tangible.

So great was his temper, his feeling of complete humiliation at his brother witnessing his domestic strife, he could easily have wrung her neck.

'Boysie . . .' It was a plea.

Turning from her abruptly, he walked from the house. Danny shook his head at her and poked a finger into her chest.

'You'll push him too far, girl, then you'll be sorry. But if ever I hear you carry on like that again, you'll have *me* to deal with and all. Just remember this. He raised you, darlin', when he married you, and he could cast you back down any time he wanted to.'

*

DC Sefton sat before DI Belling dressed in his straight gear. His long hair was tied back in a ponytail and his earring had been removed. He accepted the proffered cup of coffee and sipped the scalding liquid cautiously.

'So, Sefton, what's the buzz on the streets?'

He shrugged.

'The usual really. I've put in my report the names of the dealers, the suppliers, and also some of the addicts. Only the ones we'll get info from though. Most of them are two sandwiches short of a picnic.' He paused so Belling could give his perfunctory laugh, then continued. 'There's something I've found out though, sir, that isn't in the report. I thought I'd have a word with you about it.'

Belling nodded. 'Go on.'

'Well, sir, I've picked up a girl. Delia Dowling actually. Well, she's a known face around the clubs, she can introduce me to a lot of people. Her cousins are the Cavanagh twins and her father is Marcus Dowling.'

He heard the sharp intake of breath from Belling and was gratified.

'The thing is, while under the influence of LSD, she told me about the death of a certain Jimmy Sellars. It seems her father and the Cavanagh twins murdered him, but they all stuck together to protect them. I get the impression she's rather out of favour with the family as a consequence of this. I think, reading between the lines, she set Sellars up. It's definitely preying on her mind. Sellars is, or rather was, her child's father.'

Belling frowned.

'I know about that. Limmington is an old crony of mine, we go way back. You did right not to put it in the report, son. Do you think she might spill the beans if pushed? If we had something on her like?'

Sefton grinned. 'To be honest, I think if you gave her the edge, she'd do anything. She's one of those people who have to be in the centre of a drama. You know the type. If there ain't one, she'll create one. You get the picture. I think she'd grass up her own granny if the price or the time was right.'

'I'm telling you, Mr Cavanagh, that's what he said.'

Vince Barlet was frightened of Boysie, but he had to tell the truth, didn't he? He had to make sure that Boysie knew it wasn't anything to do with him. He wiped a dew drop from the end of his nose with a grubby fist, and seeing Boysie's disgust at his action, hastily wiped his hand on the jacket of his mohair suit.

Vince watched the changing expressions on the other man's face and sighed. Why did he always get the shit jobs?

'So what you're saying is, Vince, Pargolis is inching in on our territory. Who's the stooge?'

'That's just it, Mr Cavanagh, I don't know exactly. But I heard a word on the street that he's been seen with Mitchell, Davey Mitchell.'

There, it was out, he had said it, and Boysie Cavanagh could do what he liked with the information.

'Piss off, Vince.' This was said calmly, almost nicely, and Vince, never one to overstay his welcome, left the room in double quick time.

Boysie watched the man leave. He looked like a snotty-nosed ferret, made Boysie feel sick. Silversleeves, they called him behind his back. He was disliked, hated even, but he knew his scam and so for that reason the boys put up with him. He was a grass, but he was too frightened to grass them. He didn't have the guts.

Mitchell, now, he was a different kettle of fish

altogether. He had disappeared off the face of the earth after Rosalee's funeral, which was just as well because for all the twins' promises to their aunt about not touching him, they would have decapitated the ponce on sight, such was their temper with him. Well, they'd had a few scores to settle with him, and now they had a few more. With all the trouble and aggravation at home, and now this as well, Boysie was practically enjoying the thought of getting it all out of his system.

Limmington had spoken to Belling and was feeling on top of the world.

If what Belling said was true, they could nick the Cavanaghs this time good and proper. It was like a dream come true. Delia Dowling was unreliable in as much as she was a drug user, but she also knew better than anyone what her family was capable of. If she could be a credible witness . . . He savoured the thought to himself like a pools win. It was too good to be true.

The Cavanaghs had eluded him before, he knew they batted with the big boys. Well, even the big boys got their comeuppance. Eventually, they would make a mistake and he would be waiting for them.

A young PC walked into the room and smiled at him.

'There's a lady to see you, sir, rather old, small, says she wants to talk to you about something important.'

'Who is she? Do I know her?'

'I don't think so, but she seems on the level. She reckons you'll be interested in what she has to tell you. It's about Briony Cavanagh. Her name is Heidi Thompkins.'

'Send her in.'

Limmington had a feeling he was on to something

interesting. Briony Cavanagh, the madam, the aunt and foster mother of the twins.

He watched in amazement as the woman walked into his office. The stench of poverty permeated the room. She was small and dressed in a collection of outlandish garments that had obviously been given to her at some kind of hostel. After smelling cider he guessed correctly that she was an Embankment maiden – the polite euphemism for the drunken women who slept under the arches. But the most surprising thing about her was her eyes. She blinked constantly. It made him feel dizzy to look at her.

Getting up, Limmington helped her into a chair and then opened the window behind him. He sat down and gave him most encouraging smile, hoping her story was not a long one.

Her voice when it came was phlegmy from years of smoking Capstan and drinking neat alcohol. She smiled hazily and Limmington found it was getting very difficult to keep his own smile tacked into place.

'I'm after a bit of money, Mr Limmington, and a friend of mine told me you might be the man to provide it.'

'With respect, Miss Thompkins, why should I provide you with any funds?' His voice came out harsher than he'd meant it to, but he wasn't in the mood for this.

Eyes blinking overtime now, she said, 'Because, mate, I can finger Briony Cavanagh on two murders committed many years ago. You see, as a girl I worked for Miss Cavanagh as a tweenie in her house in Hyde Park. Well, I was young, but I was much shrewder than they ever dreamt. Maybe you've heard of Willy Bolger? He was a pimp, and he cut and killed one of Briony's girls, Ginelle. Her and Tommy Lane caused him to top himself and on the same night they took out Ronnie Olds. I knew everything that went on. Kids do. I also know that Briony Cavanagh has a child by a Mr Henry Dumas. The kid's nurse was a friend of mine. Sally and me still keep in touch. So you see, I can tell you an awful lot, Mr Limmington.'

He was finding it hard to contain his excitement. 'How do you know she murdered anyone?'

Heidi grinned. 'Because I made it my business to find out. I saw Ginelle's body in the crate the night it was delivered to us. She was well messed up. Briony said in front of me, "Bolger's dead." Later he was supposed to have shot himself, but I don't think he did, do you?

'Then there was a lot of talk about Olds. Her and Tommy took over as Barons in the East End for a while after his murder. They went to Victoria Park and topped him there. I'll stand up in court and say the lot.'

'You will?'

Heidi's eyes began their strange dance once more before she said: 'For a price. In fact, I'll say I saw the lot, Mr Limmington. I'll say whatever you want me to say. Because let's face it, they have an answer for everything. And sometimes, to catch a thief, you have to be one yourself.'

Limmington sat back in his chair and relaxed. This woman had a point. He could nail Cavanagh like Christ on the cross. This woman could be told what to say, carefully coached. She could put the Cavanagh woman away for a long time. He was disgusted with himself for the thoughts he was having, but the desire, the absolute need, to put away the twins and their aunt was stronger than his innate honesty.

'When did these murders take place?'

'In the twenties. I was a girl then. I'm younger than Cavanagh, believe it or not, but I ain't had the advantages she's had, have I? I never was a girl who would flog me arse for a price.'

The last was said with an air of righteousness that made Limmington want to say: 'Anyone who'd pay to have sex with you would have to be mentally unstable!'

But he didn't. Instead he smiled kindly.

He sat forward and grinned. 'Would you like a cup of tea, Miss Thompkins?'

'I would, and a few sandwiches and all if you can arrange it. I'm so hungry I could eat a scabby horse between two mattresses.'

Limmington felt his smile sliding once more and tried valiantly to keep it in place. 'We're fresh out of horse. Would ham and tomato be all right?'

The old woman laughed then.

'Anything, my lovely. Long as it's edible. Then me and you can get down to business.'

Isabel Dumas was knitting. She seemed to spend her life knitting or embroidering. It seemed to her she would be lost without something in her hands. Her grand-daughter Natalie was due at five, and she wanted to get the back of the cashmere jumper finished by then.

She glanced at the clock and sighed. It was just after one. Her eyes turned to the telephone and she itched to pick it up and ring Benedict, but didn't. The atmosphere was strained between them these days. The past was always there. Always.

She heard the tap on her door and called out: 'Come in, Catriona.'

A woman of uncertain years entered the room and bobbed a small curtsy.

'There's a lady to see you, mam, says to give you her card.'

Isabel took the small white card and as she looked at it she blanched.

'Show the woman in, Catriona.' The maid walked from the room, puzzled. The lady was very well dressed but her speech was at odds with her appearance. She sounded a low sort.

'Hello, Isabel.'

She looked at Briony and was half pleased to see her. The effect of age, she mused. Faces from the past were welcome. Only she couldn't welcome Briony, she couldn't.

'What do you want?'

Briony shook her head as Isabel barked out the words.

'What do you think?'

Walking towards the other woman, Briony was amazed at her changed appearance. Gone was the bigness she remembered, and the nut brown hair. Gone was every reminder of youth. Briony guessed shrewdly that Isabel had been old long before she needed to be. Had worn her years like a banner demanding respect.

'Ben won't see you, Briony,' Isabel declared.

The voice was cold, without emotion. Briony felt a second's sorrow for this woman who had lived a second-hand life. Who was still trying to hang on to the remnants because they were all she had left. Knowing this, Briony felt the awkwardness lift from her. Felt almost light. She had the edge, after all these years she had the edge, and it was a good feeling.

Sitting down in the chair opposite, she said, 'I've already seen him.'

She saw Isabel's mouth drop open. She also saw fear, naked and unadulterated, in the heavily powdered face before her.

'He came to me a while ago. He was very upset.'

Isabel sagged in her chair.

'How was he, when you saw him?' she capitulated.

Briony sighed. 'Unhappy, very unhappy. That bastard Henry saw to that.'

Isabel nodded.

'He was a difficult man, Briony. As you yourself know. I often wonder, sitting here, what I would have done had I been a girl today? It would have been so much easier. But then, you married and that was it.'

Briony spoke what was really on her mind. 'Ben came to my house, and it was difficult. He seemed set on disliking me, and yet so curious to see me. Understandable, I suppose. I wondered if you had said anything?'

Isabel shook her head.

'Not a word. I didn't even know he had visited you. He doesn't speak to me now. He hasn't for a long while. The children are beginning to notice. Fenella, his wife, understands. She's a good girl. She was all for telling the children the truth, but thank God Benedict stopped her.'

Briony grinned mirthlessly. The last few words, spoken so offhandedly, made her see red. Is that all this woman thought of her? Of what had happened?

'Oh, yes, thank God! We mustn't let them know the stock they come from, must we? We mustn't hurt them by letting them know they were the product of a sick man and a child, we mustn't ever let on about that, eh? That their father's mother is only thirteen years older than him? We must never let on about that.

'It seems to me, Isabel, that your hiding of the truth over the years is what's caused all this. Your fear of everyone knowing the truth about your husband and your life. You stole my son from me really, you stole him with kindness and love. I respected you so I let you take him, and you were quick to do that, weren't you? If I remember rightly, he was taken from the house almost as soon as the birth was over. Then you had no more need of me, did you? You couldn't wait to take him away from me, in case I tainted him somehow.

'Well, the taint's there, whether you like it or not. I gave birth to him and now he knows the truth. Any unhappiness is because you thought your elaborate charade would last forever. Well, it didn't.'

Briony felt the anger spewing from her and was loth to stop it. She had wanted to say these words so many times over the years. How many times had she lain in bed, going through this scenario in her mind? Except in her mind's eye she had walked in and taken her child with her. Only her child was now a grown man, with children of his own, and all this had come too late. Far too late for any of them.

'I loved him, Briony, more than you know. I worshipped that boy. Anything I did, I did for him.'

Briony shook her head slowly.

'You loved him? I loved him as well you know, and what you did wasn't for him really, Isabel. Be honest. It was all done for yourself.'

Briony realised then that this visit had been a waste of her time and Isabel's. She'd gathered her bag up from the floor ready to leave when Isabel put a hand on to her arm. It was a wrinkled hand, but the strength in it was surprising.

'Listen, Briony, let's try and make something good come out of all this. Through you I could get my son back . . . You could make him understand . . .' Her voice was so low, desperate.

Briony shook the hand off roughly.

'Through you I lost him, through you I'll never have him. What makes you think I would help you now? My God, you've got a nerve, woman. You've got some neck!

I wanted to see you one last time, because I know that after today we'll never see one another again. And do you know something? I'm glad, heartily glad, because you disgust me, Isabel Dumas. You lived a lie, here in your ivory tower. Well, now the lies come home to roost and I'm glad I'm not the only one hurting.'

Daniel listened to all that Vince had said with a face like flint. Boysie finished the story and Daniel nodded slowly.

'You know what this means, don't you, Boysie? It means we have to take them all out of the ball game. And I can tell you now, mate, with me hand on me heart, that slag Mitchell is mine. All mine.'

Boysie nodded.

'I think we'd better start making a few enquiries around the place. We have to find out their stamping ground. Then we can plan our attack.'

'We'll take them all out together, Boysie. It'll be a regular blood bath. I ain't having that cunt Pargolis mugging me off. Not him nor that prat Mitchell. I could kill someone now this minute, I'm so incensed.'

Daniel clenched his hands into large fists. The knuckles whitened with the pressure.

'First things first, Danny Boy. I'll get on the blower to Vince. That little ponce will grass us everything we need within the next few hours. Then we can plan properly.'

Danny stood up and lit himself a Dunhill cigarette. 'I think we should call a few of the team leaders in. If Pargolis has been putting his boat around the place, I think we should know why we ain't had it reported back to us. Maybe he's bought himself a few little friends, eh . . . Maybe he wants to come and live in our fucking house and all! I know, how about we just make out a will leaving everything to him? The ponce, the bloody Greek ponce! He wants what we've got, does he? He wants my life's work? Well, let's see how far he gets with no fucking legs!'

'Calm down, Danny Boy, for Christ's sake!'

'Calm down, you say? Has that fucking Suzy eaten up the little bit of brain you had to start with, has she? Remember the old joke, Boysie. I do the thinking, and you don't! Remember that, mate. I am the main man here, me, Daniel Cavanagh. I call the long shots and I am calling them all in this night. We're gonna get tooled up and we're gonna take that bastard and his cronies out, once and for all.'

'Thanks a lot, Danny, thanks for telling me what a prick I am. I really needed that tonight.'

Daniel looked into the face so like his own, except softer, smoother, and felt ashamed.

'I'm sorry, Boysie. Honest, mate. It was temper. I'm in a temper.'

Boysie laughed.

'And I'm not, I suppose? I ain't annoyed in the least, me, am I? I'm too thick to be annoyed, me . . . You and Suzy should set up house together. It's a shame to waste two houses between ya! Both of you seem to think that mugging me off is a great pastime.'

Daniel grabbed his brother's shoulders and shook him gently. He looked into his eyes.

'I was out of order, Boysie. I couldn't function without you, bruv. Me and you, well, we're one really. We function as one. Without you I'd be nothing, mate. Nothing. There's only two things important to me in this life, you and The Aunt.'

Boysie bit his lip, then of one mind the brothers embraced.

'We'll get the fuckers, Danny Boy, me and you. We'll find them, we'll hunt them down, and we'll blow them off the face of the earth.'

Peter Pargolis stood in The Two Puddings in Stratford with a large brandy in one hand and a large woman named Cynthia Malling in the other. Cynthia was a speciality brass. She could do things with her huge breasts that defied not only most people's physical capabilities but also the imagination of even the most dedicated porn lover. Davey Mitchell had provided her for his good friend's evening entertainment.

Davey watched Pargolis as he sipped his drink fastidiously. Say what you liked about the bubbles, they were a good crew if you was in with them. He knew that Pargolis was intent on taking over some of the East End businesses of the Cavanaghs and reckoned he had a good chance of fulfilling his dream. Davey was to get a nice little slice of the action himself, otherwise he wouldn't have bothered with the Greek.

Full of beer and good-humoured camaraderie, he looked around the small pub and saw one of the Cavanaghs' henchmen, Dicky D'Arcy, standing watching them with another man, a black man he'd never seen before. Seeing his chance to bring himself up more in the estimation of Pargolis, he began to bait D'Arcy. Mitchell's big mouth always was his downfall.

'Oi, D'Arcy! Where's the twins tonight then? At home with Mummy, are they? Fucking pair of slags . . . How's Boysie then? His new wife looks right fucked off. Found out the twins are stuck up each other's arses, has she?'

Pargolis and his men laughed. Cynthia didn't, she had

too good a knowledge of the Cavanaghs to be seen laughing at their expense.

Dicky D'Arcy lifted two fingers at Mitchell.

'Why don't you shut your mouth and give your arse a chance, Mitchell? What's wrong? Had a large shandy, have we and can't take it?'

Mitchell was serious now. He pointed at D'Arcy with a thick tobacco-stained finger.

'You tell them two pricks that their days are numbered. They don't scare me, mate. The pavement stinks of them, it stinks. Well, soon those pavements will be ours. Tell them that from me.'

D'Arcy made a big deal out of shaking. He said in a high falsetto voice: 'What's that noise?' Then looking round the pub he said. 'I do believe I can hear my knees knocking! Get real, Mitchell, you're dead meat when Danny Cavanagh hears about tonight. Dead fucking meat!'

Turning his back on Mitchell he carried on drinking and talking as if the other man did not even exist.

Mitchell walked towards him but Pargolis held him back. 'In time, Davey, in time. Soon they'll all be singing a different tune.'

Cynthia Malling picked up her bag and hitched up her heavy breasts in one movement.

'Where you going?' Pargolis's voice was high.

Cynthia smiled at him nastily. 'As far away from you lot as possible, mate. That's where. If I wanted a ruck with the Cavanaghs, I wouldn't have one over the likes of you.'

With that she walked from the pub, hailed a cab and went home without a penny piece earned that night, but with the sweet knowledge her departure had been witnessed. No way was she getting involved with all that. No way.

Vince followed her from the pub, whistling through his teeth. He wanted to get back in touch with the twins before they heard the lot from D'Arcy and half the clientele of The Two Puddings.

They had promised him a pony and he wanted it.

Chapter Forty-Six

'What you going through all them old records for?'

Limmington grinned and waved the DC away with his hand. 'Just idle curiosity, son, that's all.'

He watched the young man leave the room then carried on with his reading. The Cavanaghs had eluded him once. Well, this time he would sew them all up good and proper. When he went for Miss Briony Cavanagh and Mr Tommy Lane he would go armed and dangerous. With the case sewn up. And through her he would get the twins.

He felt a tingling of excitement at the thought. As they closed the doors on those two he would do a dance of happiness all over the East End.

He had heard a whisper that they were to hit Pargolis. Well, let them. Pargolis was just another carbuncle on the face of the earth. The twins could hit him and good luck to them, then Limmington would have them right where he wanted them. It seemed Davey Mitchell was back in town and shouting his mouth off in the pubs and clubs. Well, he mused, the Cavanaghs would soon put a stop to his gallop and all.

He scanned the papers in front of him. It seemed Mr Ronnie Olds was found in Victoria Park, in a marquee of all things, with his entrails in his hands. Yes, it sounded like a Cavanagh had had a hand in that. Bolger was found in a back garden with his brains splattered all over the place. Could have been suicide, of course, or it could have been the work of Miss Briony Cavanagh and Mr Tommy Lane.

He had also pulled all the newspaper cuttings on Henry Dumas. It seemed he'd been a force to be reckoned with in the twenties. He'd liked little girls and all, from what Limmington had gleaned from Heidi. If he had made Briony pregnant, then she was only thirteen at the time of the birth. A flicker of distaste appeared on his face. Shame the man was dead. He could have had a little word with him, the father of Briony Cavanagh's child, a child that was adopted by Dumas' wife Isabel. Now this Isabel was a different kettle of fish all together. A peer's daughter, if you please, and the spawn of Briony Cavanagh was now Lord Barkham, a respectable and influential businessman. Limmington wondered if he knew the stock he really came from. That was a poser. He'd have to tread warily here, but tread he would or his name wasn't Harry Limmington!

Heidi Thompkins had a point. If he couldn't make the charges stick, then he would have to play around with the evidence to suit himself. He was quite willing to do that to ensure they all got banged up once and for all. The ends justified the means in Harry Limmington's book. As far as he was concerned, all the Cavanaghs were scum.

Briony was tired out. It seemed she was always tired lately. She brushed out her hair, looking at herself critically in the mirror of her dressing table. It was a strange feeling, seeing herself. She still looked in the mirror expecting to see herself as she had been when young. But Christ knew, she felt old lately. She'd felt old since she had seen her son. Her true son. But, she admitted to herself, she'd felt a lot better since she had seen Isabel. That was something she had needed to do for many a long year, and she had enjoyed it in a funny sort of way. Isabel had been the cause of great sadness, Isabel and Henry.

She smiled ruefully. Now she had a grandson named Henry Dumas. Strange the way life snuck up on you, without you even realising it. Strange and disturbing. She wondered how Henry had felt seeing her image before him day after day, because Benedict was her double, like the spit out of her mouth as an East Ender would say. It must have galled him, seeing Benedict and knowing there was nothing he could do. She guessed, correctly, he had made the boy's life difficult. Well, she'd expected that. Henry hated to be bested and Isabel had certainly done that much. It would not have made for a good relationship between them. But then, that's exactly what Isabel had wanted, wasn't it?

Yet who had taken the brunt of it all? Briony herself. Her son now felt a rage towards her that would not be assuaged by anything she could do. It was this fact, this terrible fact, that had brought on the tiredness, the feeling of lethargy.

All her life she had hoped and prayed to be reunited with him. Now her hopes were dashed, she had nothing else to look forward to. Her eyes stung with unshed tears, and she dragged the brush through her hair, pulling it till her scalp ached.

The bedroom door opened and Tommy came in. Briony watched him in the mirror. He seemed so chirpy today. How she wished at that moment she could tap his energy and channel some of it into herself.

'Come on, Bri, get your finger out. It's not like you to be a lieabed!'

Something in his voice, in his words, said so lovingly and kindly, sent her over the edge. The tears sprang from her eyes and blurred her vision. Her shoulders shuddered with sobs.

Tommy realised she was crying and rushed to her. Pulling her round to face him, he held her to him, raining kisses on her face and neck.

'Come on, darlin', for goodness' sake. Tell me what's ailing you?'

Briony leant against his shoulder, breathing in his smell and feeling the strength of his body. She needed his strength today, oh, she needed it. Only Tommy could make her feel right. It had always been that way since they were children.

Slowly, haltingly, the story came out. Tommy stroked her back gently and listened to her silently, feeling rage at Benedict engulf him, rage at the unfairness of life. That she should have been taken like that, sold like that, and now all these years later have to pay for something she'd had no control over! 'Life's a bastard' was one of his mother's expressions and it fitted this situation perfectly. Life was indeed a bastard sometimes.

Picking her up, Tommy carried her to the big bed and placed her on it gently. Then he lay beside her and murmured to her. They spoke of the trouble in hushed tones as lovers do. Tommy brought out all her grief and bore it himself. He listened to her anguish, to her heartfelt sadness at the unfairness of life. Then, when her sobs were fading, he kissed her long and hard, gradually undressing her with practised fingers.

Briony watched him above her, his hair all grey now, no sign of the shiny blackness of yesteryear, but that was how she still saw him in her mind's eye.

Together they spanned the years, making love like youngsters, with a sharp abandon, a poignancy, that only the knowledge of age can bring about.

Tommy, for his part, saw the girl in the blue velvet dress, with her startling red hair and green eyes. The girl he had met every afternoon on a park bench. Today Briony was that girl again, though she had always stayed young to him.

They made a long slow loving that crept into the afternoon, and afterwards they held one another tightly, whispering of the old days, laughing at their shared memories of people long gone now and times well past.

They spoke only of the good times. It was a healing, and they both knew that.

Briony slept for a while in his arms, to wake later in the day refreshed and without a shadow of the tiredness she had felt earlier. She awoke to see Tommy looking at her with love and tenderness in his eyes, and suddenly that was enough for her.

Jimmy Granger checked his shotgun.

'So we go in now then?'

Daniel looked at him. 'That's about the strength of it, yeah. But remember, *I* want that slag Mitchell, *I* waste him first. You all got that?'

He scanned the faces of the men in the car and each of them nodded once.

Boysie laughed low.

'Then I take out Pargolis. You lot just look and listen, keep your eyes peeled on the people in the pub. If any of

Pargolis's blokes try anything, blow them away. That goes for anyone drinking in the pub too. If you think they're a threat, just blow them away, simple as that.'

Boysie was repeating himself with nerves and excitement. Two minutes later Daniel gave the signal and they all got out of the Rolls-Royce. Six large men, with shotguns underneath their coats and murder on their minds.

Inside The Two Puddings, Davey Mitchell was holding court, telling jokes to Pargolis who laughed a little too loudly. The manager of the pub was surreptitiously watching the door, all the while serving drinks and holding conversations with the punters. The pub was only half full, the atmosphere charged. Conversations were loud and in some cases aggressive. The clientele was a mixture of workmen and local bully boys, young up and coming villains who wanted a bit of the reflected limelight being seen with the likes of the Cavanaghs or Pargolis could give them.

As Daniel and Boysie walked into the pub, their four minders fanned out in the bar area itself, having been let in by the barmaid as arranged.

One look at Daniel and Boysie and the pub went quiet. Unnaturally quiet. Men moved towards the sides, out of range of the shotguns, drinks still firmly in their hands, excitement heightened by alcohol. This was news, this was big news and they were to witness it.

'Hello, Davey, not like you to be quiet. Normally your mouth's going like the clappers.' Daniel's voice was friendly, conversational. He placed his shotgun on the end of the bar, facing away from Pargolis, Davey, and the three men with them.

Davey swallowed hard, his eyes riveted to the gun. Pargolis watched everything in shock. His head was reeling at the sight of the twins.

'Don't worry, Davey boy, I ain't gonna shoot you, son.'

Walking towards him, Daniel opened his coat and brought out a long-handled eighteen-inch blade. It was more like a machete than a knife. At a signal from Daniel, two of his men pinned Davey Mitchell to the bar by his arms.

'Look, let's talk about this . . .' Pargolis's voice was a croak. This was not supposed to happen. This was what they were going to do to the twins. This was wrong, all wrong. He had been buying the twins' men, been setting the scene himself. He was Peter Pargolis, he was a big man.

Boysie laughed out loud, as if reading Pargolis's thoughts.

'That's the trouble with you bubbles, you talk too much, like your friend here. Never heard of the early bird then, I take it? You have to get up before your clothes are on, mate, to get one over on us.'

'Danny . . . Danny Boy, don't do this thing . . . Let's try and talk about it at least . . .' Mitchell was stuttering with fright. The bright blade was catching the light as Daniel held it up, bringing it slowly towards his mouth.

'I'm going to shut you up, Davey, I'm going to shut you up permanently, like I should have when you shot your trap off when me auntie died . . . Remember that, do you, you ponce!'

Pushing the blade lengthways into Mitchell's open mouth he pushed with all his might, slicing through the soft skin of his cheeks and jowl. The scream was loud and frightened, the man's voice gradually trailing off as Daniel pushed upwards, bringing the blade out once more and then upwards again, pushing the tip through the roof of his mouth and up into his brain.

Daniel nodded to the minders and as they let go of his arms, Davey Mitchell dropped to the floor. Finally Daniel dragged the blade free and stood with blood dripping on to the floor as he wiped it off on Davey Mitchell's good suit.

Pargolis watched the scene in morbid fascination. Then he saw Boysie walking towards him with the shotgun poised, aimed at his stomach, and knew, totally and irrevocably, that he would never see his wife or his children again.

Briony was woken by the loud knocking on her front door. Tommy got up and looked out of the bedroom window, half asleep.

'Who is it, Tommy love?'

'It's the Old Bill.'

She sat upright in the bed then, her face pale with shock. 'The Old Bill? What on earth could they want?'

She leapt from the bed and pulled on her dressing gown. She could hear the flapping of Cissy's slippers as she went to open the front door and, charging out on to the landing, she collided with Daniel.

'It's the police, Danny Boy. What have you been up to?' He smiled good-naturedly and shrugged.

'I ain't done nothing, Mum, I swear.' He smiled down at her and she watched as he belted up his dressing gown and walked nonchalantly down the stairs.

Briony and Tommy followed him. Briony had a sick feeling on her that grew as she saw the number of policemen in her hallway. 'What is going on here, please? Why are you here at this time of the morning?'

Her voice was surprisingly steady. She glared at the gaunt detective in his old, well-worn raincoat.

Limmington smiled, and took off his hat in a courtly gesture.

'Miss Cavanagh, I'm sorry to get you out of bed. It's your nephew we're after.' He turned to Daniel who was watching him with a closed expression on his face.

'Daniel O'Malley, I arrest you for the murder of one David Mitchell. You are not obliged to say anything, but anything you do say will be taken down and may be used in evidence against you. Do you understand what I have just said?'

'Yeah, I understand, and me name's Cavanagh, mate. Get it right.'

Limmington looked at the big, handsome man before him and couldn't restrain a smile. He'd said he'd get them, he had promised himself that. But in the end the two Cavanagh boys had simply taken themselves out of circulation. They couldn't hope to get away with this night's work. No matter how many high-powered friends they possessed. He had witness statements, and he had fingerprints, bloody fingerprints from the knife blade. Daniel had given it to one of his men to dispose of. He should have done it immediately instead of leaving it in the back of his car. He had them all bang to rights. Soon he'd be visiting this house a second time, and then he would arrest the woman in front of him, standing with her hand held to her mouth and those deep green eyes wide with innocence. Well, she would have a murder charge on her and all.

Handcuffing an unprotesting Daniel, he took him out to the waiting car and they made their way back to the station. Briony watched the policemen leave. They had obviously been expecting a fight and they were disappointed.

Tommy took hold of her hand and held it tightly. Then, picking up the phone, he dialled. He would find out the score of last night's work, see what he could do, if he could salvage anything.

It was two-thirty. By three o'clock he told Briony everything.

Suzy watched in disbelief as her husband was dragged, protesting from the house. Unlike Daniel, Boysie was not coming quietly. He was making a racket that woke up the whole street, and caused more than a few curtains to twitch. Looking at the large imposing house opposite his own, the owners two respectable doctors, Boysie shouted at the window: 'Had your fucking look, have you? You nosy pair of bastards!'

Then, dragging his arms away from the policemen restraining him, he took a swing at the young uniformed man nearest him and caught him a stunning blow on the temple. The boy went down and Boysie kicked him in the head with slippered feet.

Standing in his drive, he looked around at the twenty other policemen. Fists clenched, he was ready for a fight.

'Come on then, come on, you ponces. I dare you to come and take me.'

Then he laughed out loud, head back, teeth exposed.

'Come on then, what's the matter? Your mummies told you not to play with the naughty boys, did they?'

DI Canningfield shook his head in amazement. This boy was a lunatic. He should be put away where he belonged.

Boysie walked slowly down his drive, arms still up, fists still clenched.

'Come on then . . . What's the fucking matter with

you? You've got an audience, ain't you? Show the public what hard nuts you are.'

Then he was running down the road, the police in hot pursuit. As he approached the end of it, he saw the road block. They had come prepared.

He swerved away and ran down a neighbour's drive. She watched in fascination as he scaled her side entrance. He ran the hundred and fifty feet of her back garden, stepping through her ornamental pond, his trousers heavy now with water and dirt. He launched himself at her back fence, repeating the run through the garden backing on to it. He burst from this over a large wooden back gate and out into the street parallel to his own. As he ran full pelt down the street, he bounded out on to the main road, the men behind him shouting and hollering for him to stop.

Laughing once more, he catapulted himself on to the main road, where he was hit full on by a police car.

Boysie was seen by the policeman following him to rise about fifteen feet into the air before landing with a sickening thud on the pavement on the other side of the road. His head was bent to the right in a grotesquely unnatural position.

As the police all surrounded him he looked up at them. He opened his mouth to speak and a trickle of blood slid slowly down from his nose and into his open mouth.

He mouthed the word 'Bastards' before a shuddering passed through his body and he died. A young PC watched his legs twitching in the final throes of death and put his hand over his mouth to swallow the sickness engulfing him.

The DI pushed his way through the men and, smiling to himself, kicked Boysie Cavanagh as hard as he could in the stomach, lifting him off the pavement with the force of the blow.

The young PC watched his superior, silent and nauseated.

'That's one piece of shite removed from the face of the earth. Timpkins, get an ambulance.'

With that, the man walked back to the squad car and lit himself a cigarette.

Boysie Cavanagh lay on the cold pavement, dead but with a twisted smile on his face. It seemed even in death the Cavanaghs had got one over on them.

Daniel had not said a word since he had been told the news of his brother's death.

Limmington, against all his instincts, actually felt sorry for him. Knowing how close they were, how they were together continually and had stuck by each other through thick and thin, he couldn't help but feel sympathy for the large man before him.

'Drink your tea, son . . . Come on. It'll do you good.'

Daniel looked at the tea and then at the old man before him. Picking up the paper cup, he stared at the hot liquid for a few seconds before he flung the entire contents into Limmington's face. Limmington put up his hands instinctively, then Daniel was up and fighting. He grabbed hold of Limmington's jacket, raining punches on the man's face and head.

It was all over in seconds. The officer in the room raised the alarm and then five men were holding Daniel down, kneeling on him to contain him. His face was pressed against the coldness of the floor. Then, to the absolute amazement of the other men in the room, he began to cry, big bubbles of snot mingling with tears that seemed inexhaustible. His shoulders shuddered violently as he sobbed, mouthing his brother's name over and over.

The enormity of death hit him with the force of a twenty-pound hammer. His Boysie, his other half, was gone. Gone, never to return. They had been together since birth, had shared, had planned, had dreamed together, with never any real thought for anyone but the other. It was all gone, Boysie was gone. Daniel wished he could have died with him.

Limmington straightened his clothes and knelt on the floor. He pushed back Daniel's hair from his face and, taking a hankie from his pocket, wiped his face and nose.

'Come on, son, calm yourself down. We're very, very sorry.'

PC Dawson looked at Limmington and felt an enormous surge of respect.

'Don't bother putting this in any of the statements. He reacted as any of us would have under the same circumstances. I'll ring for the quack, get him a shot. He ain't in any condition to be questioned. What we have to say to him will keep.'

With that he stood up and left the room, his jacket still crumpled up and his eye beginning to swell.

Outside Briony and Tommy sat in the waiting room. Briony was cold inside. It was a strange feeling. As if something inside her had died along with Boysie.

Tommy held her gently, his arm around her shoulders protectively, his own face grey and mottled.

All Briony could see in her mind's eye was two little scraps of humanity lying in the bed with their gentle mother. A mother who would have loved them to distraction, and done a damn' sight better job of raising them than the woman to whom she had entrusted them.

Briony had identified Boysie's remains, his wife being, in no condition to do the job herself. She had stood and stared down at the lifeless body of the man who had been a son to her. Who had been cared for and loved, oh yes, loved. She had always done that, even when they were at their worst.

But she had never really had any control over them, she knew that now. They had always gone their own way, their combined personalities and resources making that inevitable.

Now the upshot was one dead, one arrested for a bloody and senseless murder. Even with her own past, her own way of life, she could not find it in herself to condone, or indeed even understand, an act of such callousness and absolute lunacy as the twins had committed that night. They had barbarically murdered in cold blood, in front of witnesses, two men who were well known, albeit well disliked. To do something like that in public you had to be either mentally unstable or a lunatic of the first order. The twins, it seemed, had been both these things. Now Daniel at least would have to pay the price. She couldn't hope to help him out of this.

Even if she had wanted to.

It was this that saddened her more than anything: she didn't want to help Daniel. She guessed, shrewdly, that it had been his big idea to kill them in The Two Puddings in Stratford, in front of everyone. It had his mark of showmanship about it. Oh, that was Daniel's way all right. It had been a calculated move by him, to guarantee total autonomy in the East End. To guarantee they would never be challenged again. Well, Boysie, God love him, was dead, Daniel had seen to that. Now Daniel would have to take the can.

It amazed her how they had even dreamt they could get away with it. It was 1969, not the days of the Wild West. Daniel's exceptional brain should have made him aware of that, but he had a kink in his nature, brought about by God knows what, that made him think they were invincible. And they had been, until that final act of folly.

She pushed her face into Tommy's coat, savouring the feel of him.

Limmington watched them as he passed through the front of the station. He mistook Briony's demeanour for sorrow at their getting caught; sorrow at losing her boys. He couldn't have been more wrong if he had tried.

It was sorrow all right, but sorrow tinged with guilt and wonderment. Like many a parent before her, she was wondering just where the hell she had gone wrong.

Liselle looked at the headline on the front page of the *Daily Mirror* and felt a tightness in her chest: BLOODBATH IN EAST END. She saw a picture of the twins with an airbrushed rip so the photograph was in two ragged pieces. Her eyes scanned the page.

> Last night in Stratford two local businessmen were murdered in cold blood. Mr Peter Pargolis was shot twice with a sawn-off shotgun, in the stomach and the legs, and fatally wounded.
>
> David Mitchell was slaughtered with a long-bladed knife.
>
> The Cavanagh twins, Daniel and Dennis, were arrested for the two murders late last night after a major police operation. Dennis Cavanagh, better known as 'Boysie', died while attempting to evade police capture.

Liselle closed her eyes tightly. She had heard nothing from her Aunt Briony about this, nothing at all. This fact hurt her, while at the same time she wondered uneasily how her mother would be affected by this catastrophe and the newspaper coverage of the family.

Liselle leafed through the paper with trembling hands. Sure enough, there were pictures of her mother, herself and all the family, taken by the local *Barking and Dagenham Post* over the years.

Emblazoned across the top of the centre pages was a large headline reading: GOODNIGHT LADY.

Underneath was the story of Briony's houses in London and Essex. A picture of Berwick Manor showed Briony and Kerry standing in the doorway, smiling. Liselle began to read again, taking in every word, her eyes seeking for her own name and her mother's.

> The Cavanaghs were born in Barking where their mother Eileen died shortly after their birth and they were given over to the care of her sister, Briony Cavanagh. Briony was a celebrated madam who ran many establishments with her friend and associate Mariah Jurgens. Her career began nearly fifty years ago, her first house bought when she was just fifteen years old. She is a well-known figure around London's East End, and is generally described as a fair and generous woman. Many of the people we interviewed, including her parish priest, had nothing but good to say about the Cavanagh family, the twins included.
>
> Kerry Cavanagh, sister of Eileen and Briony, is a well-known jazz singer who recently enjoyed a revival of her career when her recording of 'Miss

Otis Regrets' was chosen to accompany a prestigious perfume advertisement.

Less widely known is the fact that Kerry gave birth to an illegitimate child forty-three years ago, the father being the black pianist Evander Dorsey, who now owns the celebrated Jazz Club in New York.

Liselle put her hands to her face. She wept as she looked at the photograph of Boysie, then, pulling herself together as best she could, she went to the telephone to ring her Auntie Bernadette. That's where the family would be gathering. That's where she and her mother would be expected to go.

As always, the Cavanaghs felt better when they were all together. It was as if their strength could ward off any trouble.

Only this time, it seemed to Liselle, the trouble was just too big, and too public.

Delia was lying in bed, her eyes red-rimmed from crying. The knock at her front door made her heart stop in her chest. She was straight, completely straight, which was why her mind was going over and over the events of her cousin's death. She was reminded of Jimmy. It brought it all back.

She went to the front door and opened it, peering out through the gap allowed by her security chain. It was her mother. Taking the chain off she opened the door wide, allowing her mother in.

Bernadette walked in the tiny flat and her face screwed up with distaste at the stench. She hadn't brought Delia up to live like this! To live like a bloody hippy! She bit back the words that were in her mouth and said instead: 'You've heard about your cousins, I take it?'

Delia nodded, biting down on her lip to stop the tears.

'Oh, stop the act, Delia, I ain't in the mood!' Bernadette's voice was harsh and Delia felt the full force of her anger.

'You've been knocking off a bloke called Dave, ain't you?'

Delia watched her mother warily as she walked through to her tiny lounge. She watched her mother's eyes scan the dirty room and felt a prickle of shame. The place was filthy.

'What if I have?' There was defiance in her tone now, brought on by humiliation at her mother's obvious disgust for her living conditions.

'Well, your dad had a call about him. As if we ain't got enough bloody trouble on our plates as it is! It seems he's an Old Bill, CID. That was clever of you, wasn't it? But then, you always found trouble, Delia, didn't you? Well, let me tell you something, girl, if my sister ever finds out about the conversations you had with him about Jimmy's murder, there'll be another one done. Do you get my drift?'

Delia watched her mother's eyes. They scanned her face with no glimmer of maternal sorrow at what her daughter, her beautiful talented daughter, had been reduced to. Gone was the loving smile that told Delia she would put up with her no matter what. Instead there was open animosity, and it frightened Delia.

'I . . . I've not said a word, Mum . . . I swear!'

Bernadette poked her daughter in her ample breasts.

'Shall I tell you something, Delia? You was always my baby. You. Not Becky, poor Becky, who was always second best. Remember how we all used to laugh at her, at her posh ways and her posh voice? We all knew Becky would chase respectability, and deep inside I was glad. But you, miss, you was my baby, the favourite. Not any more. Not after the turn out with Jimmy and little Faithey. You don't care a penny piece for that little girl, I'm bringing her up for you. Your dad's her dad, he dotes on her. She don't even bother to ask where you are any more. And I *will* look after her, I promise you that, young lady.

'But I want to get something clear here today. If you cause any more trouble to this family, Briony won't be in it, mate. *I'll* break your bleeding neck, snap it with me bare hands, I take oath on that. Because you're a slut, a mouthy, dirty little slut! And I'm ashamed to admit I bore you.'

Delia stared at the floor, unable to meet her mother's eyes. 'You'd better take in what I'm telling you, girl, this is your last chance with me, I mean it. You get rid of that bloke. I don't care if you destroy yourself, that's up to you, but this family's got enough on its plate without you causing more hag.'

With that, Bernadette made to leave. Delia's voice stayed her.

'I'm sorry, Mum. Truly, I'm sorry about everything, about Jimmy, about Faithey . . .'

Bernadette turned at the door and looked back at her. They stared into one another's eyes for long moments before Bernadette answered.

'Save your sorry for when you really mean it. Sorry's an easy word to say, but that don't automatically get you forgiveness. That's like respect. You have to earn it. And judging by the way you live, it'll take you bloody years!'

With that she left the little flat and shut the door behind her. As she walked down the stinking staircase, strewn with used condoms and old chippy papers, dirty syringes and circulars, she held her breath. Then she walked out into the weak sunshine and breathed in deep gulps of fresh air to cleanse her herself.

Chapter Forty-Seven

Briony looked around the room with keen eyes. Since the shock of Boysie's death had worn off, her survival instinct had come to the fore. She wasn't interested in Daniel any more, felt he had had all the help she could give him. She was more interested in protecting the rest of the family. Her mother for a start.

Molly sat hunched in a seat by the fire, a large hot rum in her hand. Every so often she wiped away a tear with a crumpled tissue, shaking her head as if in wonderment. Every so often she would read the newspaper accounts of her grandsons' lives. Even with one of them dead and the other locked away awaiting trial for murder, she still enjoyed reading about them.

Bernadette was white-faced and quiet. Her two nephews had been a big part of her life. She would miss them genuinely and acutely. Briony loved Bernie for this fact.

Delia was not there, conspicuous by her absence, as was Suzy, Boysie's wife, who was too busy selling her story to anyone who would pay for it: MY LIFE WITH GANGLAND MURDERER.

Scheming little bitch! She'd better not bother to attend Boysie's funeral because, baby or no baby, Briony would take great pleasure in slapping her face for her.

Kerry sat alone on a small stool, hands around a glass of vodka, her face bereft of make-up and expression. Liselle sat beside her, kneeling on the floor, sad and quiet.

The men, Marcus and Tommy, were closeted in Bernadette's kitchen. The daily woman and the cook had not turned up for work, which surprised no one. Photographers and reporters were camped outside on the pavement like vultures.

Mariah had turned up dressed in her loudest clothes and plastered with make-up and had stood out on Bernadette's drive for a full twenty minutes while they took photos and she answered questions.

'No,' she had said, 'I can't believe any of the things the papers are saying about the twins. They were hard-working businessmen who gave a great deal of money to charity.'

One reporter had asked cheekily if it was true she had been a celebrated prostitute in her day. Mariah had answered him just as cheekily.

'If you've got five crisp new twenty-pound notes, son, you can find out!'

This had gone out on the nine o'clock news to the merriment of the whole East End population.

The Cavanagh trial was going to be big business for the newspapers and television. The twins had somehow captured the imagination of the whole country, and the newspaper headline GOODNIGHT LADY was everywhere Briony looked. Her past was dragged up and embroidered so she looked like some kind of monster. Even Joshua O'Malley had been found and had sold his story to the

News of the World, saying how his sons were brought up by Briony Cavanagh because she had threatened to kill him unless he gave them over to her. This had caused another sensation. Briony was made to look like Lucrezia Borgia.

The photograph taken outside St Vincent's on the day of the twins' christening all those years ago appeared regularly in the papers, Jonathan la Billière, herself and all the family smiling out at the world. Who would have thought then that those two innocent little children would one day cause all this?

The worst thought of all, though, was the thought of Benedict reading it all. Reading about her being a madam, a whoremaster. The papers made her sound so hard, so evil, even though many of her girls had in fact come forward to say that she had looked after them extremely well. That story did not appear. It wasn't what the papers wanted to hear.

Stories about Berwick Manor before the war, when it had been frequented by politicians and other well-known people, were appearing in the papers every day. Hints of scandals involving government ministers and diplomats were given prominence. Most of the stories held a grain of truth, but they were written primarily to shock, to sell newspapers. They were written for people who wanted to believe it all; wanted to believe that the rich, the famous, and the people in charge of their country ran around naked with young girls beside a warm swimming pool. One paper had even hinted at an international scandal involving the Russians, like the Profumo scandal earlier in the decade.

There was an awful lot Briony could have said, but she didn't. It would help no one.

*

Daniel was being treated like visiting royalty in Wormwood Scrubs. Even the screws deferred to him, made conversation with him, and called him 'Mr Cavanagh'. He had a man to do his slopping out, a man to deliver his meals to him, he even had his own cell.

This treatment soothed him. He was on remand and once the trial was over, was convinced he would be a free man.

He felt a shadow pass over his face and looked up from the letter he was reading.

A tall man stood before him. He was thin to the point of emaciation.

'I wondered if you fancied a bit of company?' The voice was high, a thin falsetto.

Daniel looked at the man for a few seconds, unable to believe the utter neck of the obviously homosexual individual before him.

'If I was so hard up for company, mate, that I had to resort to you, I'd fucking top meself!' He got up from his bed angrily as the man ran from the cell in blind panic.

Back in his own cell Bernard Campion, better known as Gloria, sat on his bunk shaking. His cell mate and long-time confidante Ian Snelling, known as Pearl to his friends, shook his head in annoyance.

'I told you not to go, didn't I?'

'Well, you can't blame a girl for trying!'

Gloria sat daydreaming of what it would have been like to have had the protection of Daniel Cavanagh. In this place it was as good as money in the bank.

Daniel couldn't calm himself after Gloria's visit and put the letter to one side.

A bloody shirtlifter coming on to him! The more he thought about it, the more it annoyed him.

Lying there in the six by eight cell, the silly encounter began to grow out of proportion in his mind. He began to see it as an affront to him as a man of means and position. He was Daniel Cavanagh. He and his brother were the undisputed Kings of London, the Big Boys. They were the two most feared individuals since Jack the Ripper, and that long streak of paralysed piss thought he would make out with him! The more he thought about it, the bigger the insult became in his mind.

Finally, he got up and walked from his cell. He marched along the landing kicking open cell doors and looking for the tall thin man who had not only invaded his personal space, but had also insulted his very manhood.

He found Gloria and Pearl sitting on their bunks. Gloria's face shone hopefully at the sight of him, convinced he had changed his mind about the offer. This was soon proved wrong as Daniel dragged the screaming man from the cell and began to belabour him with a long leather belt, used with the buckle end for maximum effect.

Men came out of their cells to watch the drama being enacted. It broke up the day, added a charge to the semeness of their existence.

Later on the screws reported that Bernard Campion had been taken to the prison hospital after falling down the stairs from the top landing.

Such was life on remand at Wormwood Scrubs. It suited Daniel Cavanagh right down to the ground. It was just what he needed after his brother's death and his own arrest. Somewhere he could still be the main man. Could sit out his time given the respect he deserved and expected, until such time as he was let loose on the world once more.

*

Limmington had taken the statements made by Heidi Thompkins to the Home Secretary himself. He wanted this done properly, without any mistakes whatsoever. The Home Secretary gave him the go ahead to arrest Briony Cavanagh and Thomas Lane for two murders. Heidi Thompkins was going to swear in a court of law that she was at the house where Bolger died and that she saw Briony Cavanagh and Thomas Lane put the gun to his head. She was going to swear also that she had been present when they had discussed the murder of Ronald Olds, how Tommy Lane had ripped his belly open with a double-bladed boning knife. As long as he kept her away from the Cavanaghs, off the drink, and promised her a good few pounds, she was as sweet as a nut.

Limmington stood now, in full view of the photographers and reporters, outside Bernadette Dowling's house, the warrant for their arrest clutched firmly in his hand.

Cissy, with eyes red and swollen from crying, let him in. He walked into the drawing room with two officers, and was amazed by the number of people he saw.

Briony stood up and greeted him with a nod. 'What can I do for you, Mr Limmington?'

He was struck by the sadness in her husky voice. In the wake of her nephew's death she seemed to have aged considerably, and looking at her, so tiny, so diminished in her grief, he felt a moment's shame at what he was about to do.

Willy Bolger had been nothing but a dealer in porn and child prostitution, not exactly a pillar of the community. But Limmington's deep-rooted desire to take this women off the streets overrode the moment of compunction.

'Miss Briony Cavanagh and Mr Thomas Lane, I have a warrant here for your arrests . . .'

Briony's eyes widened. She heard Tommy's voice as if from a distance.

'What the bleeding hell are you arresting *us* for?'

'For the murders of William Bolger and Ronald Olds.'

Tommy laughed outright. 'Fuck me, couldn't you go back no further? Why don't you chuck in the murder of Abel and all while you're about it!'

Limmington smiled. 'If you'd both like to accompany me to the station?'

Tommy shot out his arm and grabbed him.

Two DCs grabbed him in his turn, expertly forcing his arms behind his back.

Briony sighed.

'Come on, Tommy, we'll be home before the day's over.' She looked at Limmington with hooded eyes.

'I've never heard so much old bollocks in all my life. You're living in a fantasy world, Mr Limmington, and you'll find out soon enough what happens to people who annoy me. I'll sue you and the police force for every last halfpenny you possess. I hope for your sake you're ready to take us on, because I can tell you now, we'll have cast-iron alibis.'

Limmington watched her warily as she went out to the hallway for her coat.

'I have everything I need, Miss Cavanagh.'

Briony faced him and smiled.

'Shall I tell you something, Mr Limmington? A lot of people have tried to get one over on me, an awful lot. But I'm still here.'

Limmington smiled back.

'Yes, but for how much longer?'

Before Briony could answer, Molly was shouting her head off.

'You fuckers of hell! You dirty bastards! My grandson's not cold and you're haunting the rest of me family.'

Bernadette took her mother in her arms and gave her a kiss.

'We'll be home before you can say knife!'

Limmington watched the scene and said in a low voice: 'Would that be double-bladed boning knife by any chance?'

James McQuiddan was supposed to be the best as far as barristers went. Or so Briony had been told. She sat in chambers with Tommy as the man argued their case for bail.

McQuiddan was enormous. Even the man's hands were huge, and he had an undeniably menacing presence.

The Judge, Mr Justice Melrose Deakins, listened to McQuiddan's lightly accented Scottish voice attentively.

'Your Honour, we have here two people of the highest repute. And yet today they stand accused of two murders committed over forty years ago.

'One of the so-called murder victims is in fact on public record as having committed suicide. How can you *not* grant these two people bail? Briony Cavanagh is an esteemed member of her community, she has been an active charity fundraiser, a businesswoman widely respected. Thomas Lane is similarly regarded. Neither has ever been in trouble with the police. How my learned friend here can oppose bail . . .'

'Mr McQuiddan, I have listened to you with interest, and all I can say to you is, Miss Cavanagh and Mr Lane, pillars of the community, fundraising charity workers and otherwise exemplary citizens notwithstanding, are here charged with murder, not traffic offences. Murder is a heinous crime, and not one to be taken lightly. In view of the gravity of the charges, I have no alternative but to refuse them bail.'

Briony's face dropped, and Tommy closed his eyes tightly.

McQuiddan shook his head dramatically and stood up once more, his black robes billowing around him.

'Your Honour, I really must protest . . .'

Mr Justice Deakins held up one scrawny hand for silence. 'I think we have heard quite enough protesting from you for one day, Mr McQuiddan.'

Outside, when the news was broken, DI Limmington smiled and chalked the first round up to himself.

Briony walked into Holloway Prison in a daze. She had been so sure she was going to get bail, the decision of the judge had shocked her to the core. As she sat in the prison van between two policewomen she felt a plummeting inside herself. The bang of the steel doors behind her as she entered through the side door of the prison reverberated in her head.

The elder of the policewomen helped her down from the van. 'Come on, love.'

Briony smiled woodenly. She would not show them that she was frightened. If they put her away for a long time . . .

She swallowed down the terror and walked unsteadily through to the prisoners' reception. This room was dark, a window letting in the minimum of light due to its reinforced glass. She felt a pair of arms divest her roughly of her fur coat. Without it and her handbag she felt suddenly very vulnerable. This couldn't be happening to her. This was all some kind of mistake.

A woman called Marilyn, a prison officer for twenty years, grinned at her nastily.

'Come on, darlin', let's get you stripped, washed, suited and booted. Then we'll escort you to your cell. You're sharing with two bitches who should suit you right down to the ground.'

Briony drew herself up to her full height, five foot, and said coldly: 'Let's get something straight here, shall we? I am not your darling. In fact, the thought of it makes me feel physically sick. You may be big and you may be ugly, but it'll take more than that to put the frighteners on me.'

Marilyn looked down at the tiny old woman – and she was old, there was no mistaking that – and felt a great rage.

'No one talks to me like that!'

Briony, her old self back to the fore now the shock had worn off, said scathingly. 'Up yours, darlin'. I've dealt with bullies all my life, one more won't make much difference. Now then.' She looked at the assembled screws. 'Let's get this over with, shall we? Where do I shower?'

A younger officer called Tracy took her arm.

'I'll take you through to the showers just as soon as we've signed you in.'

Marilyn catalogued Briony's possessions in silence, the diamond rings and necklace patently annoying her. As Briony walked away with Tracy in tow she said to the other girl: 'That one needs knocking down a peg.'

'And you're the woman to do it, I suppose?'

Marilyn stared at the girl and nodded, a twisted smile on her face.

Briony had showered, been disinfected, and was now dressed in a skirt and blouse, her wet hair plastered to her head. Devoid of make-up she still looked good, which surprised Tracy. As she was walked across the landing to A wing, Briony took in everything around her. She was put in a cell on the top landing, and as the door opened a stench of stale cigarette smoke and urine hit her full in the face. She hesitated a few seconds at the door. Tracy, feeling the woman's discomfort, pushed her gently over the threshold.

'In you go, love. We eat tea at five-thirty, you'll be out for that.'

Briony stood in the cell as the door banged behind her and, taking a deep breath, stared at the two faces before her.

A tall black girl, no more than nineteen, stood up and held out her hand.

'Hello, love. My name's Letitia and this here is Marla.' Marla was small, plump and blonde, in her forties.

'Sit down, we've been expecting you. Would you like a roll?'

Letitia's face was open and friendly. Briony nodded and sitting on the bottom bunk, accepted a thin rolled cigarette.

'Tracy will bring you round a cuppa in a minute. Everything's been taken care of, Belinda has seen to that. You'll see her at teatime. It's only a sandwich but force it down, you won't get nothing else till the morning.'

Briony allowed Marla to light her cigarette and tried desperately to relax.

The walls of the cell were too close, the place stank, and nice as the two women were being to her, Briony would rather be anywhere in the world than here, in a small cell in Holloway prison.

Marla smiled, sensing her thoughts.

'Listen, love, it's a shock the first time. I know that

from experience. But I'll give you a bit of advice. When you walk out of this cell, walk like you own the fucking place. You're a name, a big name. Your reputation's preceded you. There's plenty of little tarts in here who'd love to be the one to do you up. Get my drift?'

Briony took a deep pull on the match-thin roll-up.

'I know what you're saying, Marla, and don't worry about me. I can more than take care of myself.'

Something in the little woman's demeanour, her tone of voice, even the way she held her head, told both women she was speaking the truth.

Marla grinned.

'Get the feel of the place. It stinks, it's full of arseholes, but you get quite attached to it, as hard as that may be to believe. I'm waiting to go off to an open. Cookham Wood will do me lovely!'

Briony relaxed. 'What you in for?'

'Clipping. Prostitution and fraud. Me usual. Now our Letitia here is in for the big M like yourself, so you two should get on well!'

Letitia laughed.

'I'm on remand, there ain't no one proved I done it yet!'

Briony smiled. These two women, whom she would normally have avoided like the plague, had made her welcome in their own way and she was inordinately grateful.

'Who are you accused of topping?'

Letitia grinned.

'My pimp. His name was Delroy Lafayette, believe it or not.'

Briony took another drag on her cigarette. 'With a name like that, he deserved to be murdered!'

Letitia and Marla screamed with laughter.

'You'll fit in here lovely, Miss Cavanagh. Just lovely.'

Briony laughed, her old self.

Tracy, outside on the landing bringing them three cups of tea, heard the sound with approval. Briony Cavanagh was settling in. If she could laugh she could do her time, whatever it was going to be. Mariah Jurgens had slipped her a quick grand through a mutual friend to see that Briony had whatever she wanted while she was a guest, and Tracy had every intention of seeing that she carried out her part of the bargain to the last letter. Putting a packet of Strands on to the tray with the tea, she entered the cell.

Belinda, or Big Belinda as she was called, watched out for the new arrival as they were let out of their cells at teatime. She stood leaning nonchalantly on the top landing, her keen eyes scanning the faces around her. She saw a mass of red hair between Letitia and Marla and walked towards them slowly. Belinda was in for aggravated burglary. She was big and fat, and had the most beautiful face Briony had ever seen on a woman.

As Belinda pushed her way through to Briony, people moved instinctively out of her way.

She smiled and held out a soft pudgy hand. 'Belinda Crane, pleased to meet you.'

Briony shook the proffered hand and grinned.

The four women walked down to the canteen together, Briony aware of the glances she was gathering from the other inmates. As they entered the canteen she saw a girl being dragged from the queue by her hair, then her face was slammed into the side of one of the wooden tables. No one took any notice. The prison officers in the room looked the other way.

Belinda smiled and said. 'That's Mary Molinero, she's in for drowning her baby.'

Briony watched as the girl crawled to a chair and pulled herself on to it, her face bleeding and her sobs audible.

'She gets fucking tortured over it. She held its face in boiling water. Can you understand people like that?'

Briony shook her head.

Belinda carried on talking as if the scene had never happened.

'Mariah Jurgens has seen to it that you got a good reception committee, and I'm part and parcel of it. I run this wing. If you want to take on any of the action, just say and I'll cut you in immediately. But you're only on remand at the moment and you might get a court date any time, so I'd wait till you're sentenced before going in for the big scams. There ain't no one gonna say a dicky bird to you, your reputation's guaranteed that, plus I've put the word out. There's some right fucking nutters in here, cut their own granny up for the price of a packet of fags! So watch your back all the same, we all have to do that.'

Briony took a mug of tea and a plate of spam sandwiches to a back table. From there they had a grand view of the whole canteen. The noise was deafening. Briony drank in everything around her, and now the enormity of what had happened had begun to wear off, she realised she had to assert herself.

'Belinda, let me eat me sandwich. I want to think, all right?'

Belinda nodded, looking askance at the two other women at the table. Briony bit into the dry as dust sandwich and made a face. What Belinda had said had worried her. 'Wait until you're sentenced.' It was as if everyone had already found her guilty. She took a sip of the hot sweet tea and that made her feel better. It was the stewed tea of her childhood. A reminder of home. She felt a lump rise in her throat as she thought of what she had come to. Hastily swallowing it down she said: 'Who is Mariah working through? That Tracy the screw?'

Belinda nodded.

'Then tell her I want a message out of here today. I want to see my brief, and quick.'

Belinda nodded once more. The sheer force of the little woman's attitude and her commanding presence hit home.

Gradually conversation started up between them and they chatted amicably until the bell rang for them to go back to their cells. It was as they walked up the stairs to their landing that the trouble started. Marilyn, the most hated screw in Holloway, stood arms akimbo in front of Briony. The buzz of conversation on the landing died out in seconds. Blank faces were swiftly averted. Briony felt the hair on the back of her neck rise as she looked into the hard face before her. Other screws were standing with the inmates, waiting to see the result of this confrontation.

'I don't like you, lady.' Marilyn's voice dripped venom.

Briony raised her head slightly to look her in the face.

'You got the "lady" right, anyway. Now get out of my way.'

Even Belinda moved back as Marilyn's arm came up. Briony grabbed at her uniform front and, jerking it as hard as she could, swung her body and turned, sending Marilyn careering down the iron stairs. Briony walked down after her slowly. Then, kneeling on the floor, she said in a whisper: 'I don't like you, fat girl, I don't like you at all. You push me too far and I'll see you dead. That's a promise.'

Standing up, she tidied her hair and walked sedately back up the stairs and on to the landing. The buzz of conversation started up again as soon as she was safely inside her cell.

The prison was as quiet as it was ever going to be. The hollow sounds of people coughing, and others moaning in their sleep, could still be heard.

Briony lay in her bunk, her face white and strained. She had to get out of here, she had to get away!

Today had been a nightmare. There was so much contained violence around her. And yet she was in here as Miss Briony Cavanagh, aunt of the twins, lover of Tommy Lane. She had her creds. Even her sister being a famous singer was thrilling to the average inmate, and her notoriety thanks to the papers had guaranteed her a place in the prison hierarchy that would be her protection. But Briony wanted none of it. She wanted to be at home in her bed, with Tommy beside her.

Before she slept, she saw Benedict's face. He would have heard everything by now. It would go out on the evening news. What would he be thinking?

Please God, she prayed, please dear God in heaven, help me.

Tommy awoke to the sound of shouting. He rubbed his eyes wearily, stifling a yawn.

'Shut up!' His cell mate Timmy Carlton punched his pillow in temper. 'I can't stand that bleeding racket any longer, first thing in the morning I'm going to drown that ponce in his own slop bucket!'

Tommy laughed softly.

'He's only a kid, Timmy. He's scared.'

'He'll be scared in the morning. I'll give him something to shout about mate!'

'Oh, stop being such an arsehole and give me a fag.'

Timmy took a tin from under his pillow and gave Tommy a roll-up.

Tommy lit it in the dark, saying, 'Can't you get these any thinner? It's like smoking a match!'

'Smoke it will ya! Gordon Bennett, Tommy, a fag's a fag. If you hadn't given all your Strands to that little ponce shouting his head off we'd be quids in!'

Tommy grinned.

'Timmy and Tommy, we sound like a bloody double act.'

Timmy took a deep drag on his own cigarette and said seriously, 'Ain't you trashed at all, Tommy? I mean you could get the big one.'

Tommy shook his head in the dimness. 'I ain't worried, Timmy, as long as my old woman gets a result. That's all I'm worried about.'

Timmy scratched his short cropped hair.

'I remember her from years ago. A right looker she was.'

'She still is as a matter of fact, Timmy.'

Timmy laughed. 'My old woman looks like the back of a bus, but she's a good sort. Always visits like, brings the kids to see me. I like seeing the kids. But they took their toll on old Gabby. She's half the size of a house these days. Used to be a right nice bit of stuff and all.'

Tommy laughed again. 'You've got some kids and all ain't you? How many at the last count?'

'Nine. Five boys and four girls. My eldest girl Susan is doing ever so well. Works in an office up West. The boys take after me, got one in the 'Ville for malicious wounding, one on the island for armed robbery and the other three won't go to school for love nor money. When I get out I'm gonna take the buggers in hand. Give me girls any day of the week. You ain't got any kids have you?'

'Nah. I'd have liked them though. But me and Briony, well the time was never right.'

Timmy kept quiet.

'Sometimes, like now, I wish I had a boy of me own like.'

Timmy heard the yearning in his friend's voice and made a noise in the back of his throat.

'Let me tell you, mate, they're nothing but bleeding hag.'

Tommy turned over in his bunk to sleep. 'Goodnight, Timmy.'

As Timmy began to snore softly, Tommy thought about his life with Briony. He had forfeited children for her. He had given up a lot. The question in his mind was, was it all worth it? As the sun came up, bringing a few rays of light through the window of his cell he grinned to himself. He didn't have to answer that question. Every time he looked at her, he had his answer. He'd gladly do any amount of time for her, he loved her deeply and abidingly.

The young man started shouting again in his sleep. His fear of prison made his nightmares terrifying.

Tommy closed his eyes tightly and tried to sleep. He was getting too old for all this.

Chapter Forty-Eight

Briony and Mariah hugged each other tightly.

'Oh, Briony, how are you, love?'

Briony sat down at a table in the visiting room and shrugged. She had been in Holloway a week, and this was her friend's first visit.

'It's not too bad in here once you get used to it, Mariah. But I wouldn't say no if someone asked me to leave, know what I mean?'

Mariah laughed delightedly.

'I knew you wouldn't let all this get you down.' Her face sobered as she said, 'We tried everything to get you out for Boysie's funeral, you know.'

Briony nodded.

'Listen, Mariah. I want you to do something for me. I want you to pull in a few favours . . .'

Mariah grinned and cut her off.

'I know what you're going to say and I'm here to tell you it's all in hand. Today, while we speak, more than one person is going to get a big shock. The main person being that slag Heidi! Imagine that little bitch turning out to be the fly in the ointment, eh? I can't believe it. Well, she's at a safe house in North London and she's getting a little visit today that should make her change her statement quick smart. Also a few of our more illustrious customers are getting the bad news. Before I forget, Jonathan's coming to see you tomorrow. He's in a right state. Well, it can only look good for you. He's still news because of his knighthood in the New Year's honours. So don't you worry, by hook or by crook you'll be out of here soon.'

Briony laughed out loud.

'I should have known you'd have it all in hand!'

Mariah grabbed her friend's arm and said softly, 'We go back a long way, Bri.'

Briony nodded sadly.

'We're the old breed, Mariah. In here, in just a week I've been offered more drugs than I'd know what to do with. I'm in with women me and you wouldn't piss on if they burst into flames in front of us, and I've met young girls who make Ma Baker look like Little Red Riding Hood!'

'But you're holding your own, I take it?' Mariah's voice was low now, worried.

'Oh, I'm holding me own all right, never fear about that, and I've you to thank for me reception commitee! Now how's my Tommy? What's the news? How're the family?'

Mariah settled back in the uncomfortable chair and regaled Briony with all the news.

Both women were happier now, knowing that something was being done.

Peter Hockley was in a state of nervous prostration. Standing in front of him was a woman, a frightening woman, and in her hand he had photographs of him in full drag together with a young friend called Percy Parkinson.

Bernadette smiled as she spoke.

'My sister is going to make a full statement about an event in the twenties when you and a Mr Rupert Charles were responsible for a young man losing his life during an orgy. These photographs of you and your current amour will more than lend credibility to the story. Mr Jonathan la Billière is also willing to say he was there when your father paid a vast sum of money to hush everything up. Briony says, if she goes down, everyone goes with her.'

Peter's voice came out a low throaty croak.

'But what can *I* do?'

Bernadette put the photographs on the desk and said in friendly fashion: 'You can keep these, I have plenty of copies. Now, what do I want you to do? I want you to go and see your cousin, the Lord Chief Justice, who happens to be closely related to the Home Secretary through marriage. A brother-in-law, isn't he? What a coincidence. I want you to tell him that these photos are going in the *Daily Mirror*, and the *News of the World*, the *People*. In fact, anywhere I can get them that will do you all the most damage. Do you get my drift, Peter old chap!'

He felt the sting of tears. He was himself, nowdays, the Member of Parliament for Rochford East and Shadow Defence Secretary, yet these few photos could blight his life and bring disgrace on his family. Briony Cavanagh was willing to bring up all the old trouble that he had so conveniently forgotten after his father had bought him out of the biggest scrape of his life.

He watched the woman walk to the door. As she turned she said as an afterthought: 'Before I forget, you've got forty-eight hours.'

With that parting shot, Bernadette left the room,

leaving Peter with his photos and his conscience. And a clear picture of a young man bound and gagged and with his throat slit like an animal's.

Heidi, scrubbed now from head to foot and wearing a tweed skirt and a scratchy sweater, looked in shock at the woman before her. Mariah looked so out of place in this little room with its electric fire and nylon curtains. She looked too big and far too outrageous to be in a place so conservative.

Mariah spoke again.

'So what you're telling me is you came for a bit of trouble like, is that it? You thought you'd quickly make a couple of bob and fuck off? But you didn't have what Limmington wanted so he made a point of doctoring your statement to suit him?'

Heidi nodded fearfully.

'That's about the strength of it, yeah. I was so hard up, Mariah. I had nothing . . .'

She put up her hand for silence.

'Don't give me all your old fanny. You could have come to me or Briony, we'd have seen you all right, we always see our old girls all right. Well, you're going to tell a lot of people about Limmington's skulduggery, and you're going to be well paid for doing it.'

Heidi's eyebrows shot up with interest.

'Yeah, that's right. You're going to get a good drink. Enough to keep you pissed for the rest of your natural. But one stipulation. You disappear once it's all over.'

'Oh, don't worry, I will. All this is getting on my tits now.'

Mariah looked down at her own ample breasts, straining to escape from a lurex dress, and grinned.

'Not half as much as it's getting on mine!'

*

Sir Geoffrey Dance, the old man of the House, and a very respectable businessman, was biting his perfectly manicured nails, a habit he had given up in the throes of adolescence. His six daughters and his wife stared out from a photograph on his desk. In his hand he held another photograph. It had been taken three Christmases ago at Berwick Manor at a Christmas theme party, with all the men dressed up as Santa's gnomes. But even with the long false beard, no one could doubt it was indeed Geoffrey. On his lap sat a young girl of about seventeen, in a Santa Claus costume. On her long slim legs, which were wrapped around his waist, she wore fishnet stockings. The photograph had been taken from the side, and as he had nothing on the bottom half of his body, anyone could make anything they wanted from the photo. It was clear, from the pink buttocks on his lap, that the girl was devoid of briefs.

He felt a sinking sensation in his chest. The Manor had always been so private. They had never had a moment's worry about anything being leaked. The upstairs function room had always been a place where men like himself could go and indulge themselves in anything that took their fancy without the slightest fear of its ever coming back to haunt them. That was what the large amounts of money guaranteed, and he had paid huge sums over the years. Now with Briony Cavanagh and Tommy Lane about to be brought to court, many secrets would be spilt. Not just his, but an awful lot of other people's too.

The last thought cheered him.

He looked at the photograph again and saw in the background, as plain as day, the current Chancellor of the Exchequer. This made him smile as he picked up the receiver.

He was in the shit all right, but then so were a lot of other people.

Fenella Dumas went into the den, as Benedict called the office he used when working from home. Placing a cup of coffee on his desk, she said: 'I think you should be ashamed of yourself, Ben, I do really.'

Benedict wiped a dry hand over his face and sighed heavily. 'Give it a rest now, Fen.'

Fenella sniffed through her Roman nose. 'She is your mother, whether you like it or not. I can't understand why you're so set against her. Think about it. She was a girl, just a little girl. Every time I think about your father . . .' her voice trailed off. 'I know now why your mother never left him on his own with Natalie. Your father was a twisted, perverted man, yet you're allowing yourself to be taken over by his petty mindedness. I'll tell you something for nothing: I'd rather be related to Briony Cavanagh than Henry Dumas. There, I've said it now.

'She needs you, Benedict. That woman really needs you. You don't have to visit her in public, but you can talk to a few of our friends, try and make it a bit easier for her . . .'

He shouted at the top of his voice, 'Oh for crying out loud, Fen, leave it!'

Fenella bit on her bottom lip to stop the tears. She had lived with and loved this man for many years. They had brought up two children and she had thought she knew him, really knew him. But since the revelation about his real mother, he had gradually died inside, been eaten up with the knowledge. Now she had a man on her hands whose innate kindness and gentleness were gradually draining away, and she didn't like it, couldn't cope with it.

'I'm telling you, Benedict, this is 1969, not the bloody Dark Ages. Legally you're Henry's and Isabel's, no one can take anything away from you. Not your title or your money. But you'd have had none of that if that poor little girl who gave birth to you had decided to keep you. Think about it. Maybe she did what she did to make sure you had the best that life could give. She never came knocking on our door for anything, did she? She never tried to get money from you . . . Oh, you're making me so cross!'

Benedict had rarely heard his wife this upset. It was as if she had already taken Briony Cavanagh into her heart and home. No matter what was written about her in the papers, Fenella just ignored it. Blood meant a lot to Fen, and as far as she was concerned, Briony Cavanagh's blood ran through her children's veins so she couldn't be all bad.

He tried to smile.

'I can remember her, you know, Fen. She used to come to Regents Park where I went with my nanny every day. I can remember her hair. She still has got the same hair, crackling and so red. It was like looking in the mirror, only I couldn't see it then. But now, when I look at Nat and young Henry, I can see her in them. I can see her in me every time I look in the mirror. I can't believe she's my mother. She looks my age, for Christ's sake! She looks just like my bloody sister!'

Fenella put a slim hand on his shoulder and squeezed it.

'She is your mother, no matter how she looks. Try and see it from her point of view. Try and understand.'

Benedict laughed softly.

'I've been trying to do that since the day I found it all out. I think the worst thing of all is the fact my so-called father could have waited all that time to hurt me and Isabel. It's sick.'

Fenella sniffed loudly.

'He was a sick man. I thought we'd already established that much. He was rotten with his own hatred. Don't you go and make the same mistake.'

Benedict sat forward in his chair. 'I don't hate her, Fen, that's the trouble.'

Fenella sighed and said gently, 'Drink your coffee, Ben, before it gets cold.'

Briony lay in her bunk listening to the chatting of her cell mates. Marla was speaking in a low voice and Briony felt a deep sadness as the women spoke.

'My daughter's still in care now. I was homeless, see, so they took her off me. I was lodging with this right spiv in Canning Town. Well, he took me rent and done a moonlight, only he don't really own the drum, see. Some other geezer does, a Pakistani called Pardel. Well, he had me removed, bag and baggage. So the Welfare came and took her off me. That was nine years ago. I was picked up the next night at King's Cross for soliciting, so when we got to court, they'd made her a ward of court, saying she was in moral danger with me! I was only soliciting to get the money for a meal and a bed like. I was hardly an old hand at the game. I mean at my age, I ask you? Anyway, I just give up after that. This is about my seventh time in here. I'm hoping to get a result and go to an open to finish me sentence. They'll bring me girl if I get an open, see.'

Briony asked softly, 'How old is your daughter now?'

Marla sighed in the darkness.

'Just on twelve. She's lovely, beautiful, like her father. He was a West Indian. She's half-caste.'

'I bet she is beautiful and all. My niece Liselle is very attractive.'

'That's your sister's daughter, isn't it? The singer. You're a very famous family really, aren't you? What with Jonathan la Billière being close and your sister being a famous singer. The twins . . .'

Briony heard the jolt in Marla's voice and said, 'My boys, and they were my boys, weren't really bad. They were just . . .'

Marla's voice came out of the gloom. 'Go on?'

Briony cleared her throat and said, 'Never mind. Forget it.'

But the twins stayed with her for the rest of the night. She saw them at every age, with their ready smiles and their constant demands.

Harry Limmington was at home eating a ham sandwich and having a cup of tea while he watched *Z Cars*. He heard a deep voice and dragged his eyes from the screen to look towards the hall of his council house.

'What did you say?' He heard his wife cry out.

A uniformed police officer pushed past her and came into the room.

'Mr Harry Limmington, I am arresting you for tampering with a witness's statement and attempting to pervert the course of justice.'

Limmington stood up in shock, his sandwich and plate falling to the floor.

'Is this some kind of joke?' His voice was incredulous.

The grey-haired man said sadly, 'No joke, mate. You've been tumbled. Get your coat and let's have this over with.'

Five minutes later Harry Limmington was sitting in the back of a panda car on his way to Barkingside police station.

*

Briony kissed Marla and Letitia goodbye. As she walked along the landing she was hugged by Belinda who said gruffly, 'Don't forget us lot now, will you?'

Briony laughed out loud. 'As if I could.' She followed Tracy off A wing, and as the door was locked behind her, sighed with relief.

She was leaving the place, and the thought gave her a thrill. Soon she would be outside in the filthy London air and she'd breathe it in gratefully. Soon she would be with her family, and with Tommy, her Tommy. Then she could put all this in the past.

Twenty minutes later she was dressed, had signed for her belongings and stepped outside Holloway to a blaze of photographers and newsmen. She felt an arm on hers and turned to see Bernadette.

'Come on, Bri, we've a car here for you. Let's get you home, girl. Marcus is picking up Tommy.'

They pushed their way to a waiting Rolls-Royce and, slamming the door behind them, Briony began the journey back to her family.

'How you feeling, Bri?'

'Great, Bernie, really great. I tell you something, I have never been so pleased to see anyone in my life before! Now all I want is a bath to get the smell of that rathole off me.'

Bernadette laughed.

'The whole family is waiting at home for you.'

Briony grinned.

'I had a feeling they might be.'

Briony walked into Bernadette's house to see Cissy crying, her mother drinking, and Kerry and Liselle popping champagne corks. Jonathan had flown over for her homecoming. As she kissed his cheek, and felt the family envelop her in their love, she knew, finally and irrevocably that she had indeed come home.

Mariah came out of the drawing room to greet her and the two women hugged.

'Welcome home, Bri. We beat the fuckers! I told you we would, didn't I?'

'We did that. Mariah. Now I want a large brandy and a nice fag. Then I want to have a bath and wash me hair!'

Mariah poured her a brandy in a large balloon glass.

'Cheers, everyone.' Briony drank the burning spirit straight back. Then, sitting in a chair, she grinned.

'By Christ, it's nice to be home.' Her voice broke then and everyone stood in amazement as she cried her eyes out. Molly finally went to her daughter and cuddled her.

'Come on now, darling. Once we get your man out, Daniel, we'll all be together again.'

Briony was saved from answering as Marcus and Tommy came through the front door.

Briony was swept up into Tommy's arms and kissed hard on the mouth.

'I've missed you, Bri. Oh, but I've missed you, girl!'

Then, in excitement and happiness, the homecoming party started in earnest.

Briony and Tommy lay in bed together, the aftermath of energetic lovemaking leaving them both warm and pleasantly tired.

'Oh, Tommy, I've dreamt of this. Being with you again. I really thought me and you were going to go down and they would throw away the key.'

Tommy pulled her closer to him.

'I'll tell you something, Briony, I was shitting meself. But Mariah came up trumps. She put pressure on the right people. She knew who would be the most vulnerable, and the most helpful.'

'You know, Tommy, I never thought Harry Lammington would have stooped to doctoring a statement. I always had him down as straight as a die. I know it sounds crazy, but him being bent, it's upset me!'

Tommy laughed low.

'I don't believe you, Briony! He was after putting us away for the rest of our natural and you're upset because he's a little bent! I hope he gets ten years, the ugly ponce!'

She snuggled into his arms.

'I never want to go inside again, Tommy. I think I'll retire now.'

He laughed again, louder this time. 'I'll believe that when I see it.'

'Believe it, Tommy Lane. I'm too old to be banged up!'

Tommy looked down into her green eyes. 'You'll never be old to me, Bri. You'll always be the girl in the blue velvet dress.'

Briony kissed him again. 'You're an old bullshitter, Tommy Lane, but I love you.'

'And I love you, Briony, more than you know.'

They were quiet for a while, just enjoying each other's presence, then Tommy said: 'What are we going to do about Daniel?'

Briony took a deep breath.

'What can we do? There's no way we can nobble for him, is there? It's too big. Me and you were on charges so old they were practically entered in the Domesday Book! But Danny boy, they've got him bang to rights. He committed a grisly murder in a packed pub. He went too far, Tommy. He went over the top. For all we ever done, we never enjoyed any of it. To me and you it was always a means to an end. But Danny and Boysie, God love them, they enjoyed the killing. Especially Daniel.

'They made the cardinal mistake. They really thought they were above the law. We both tried to tell them over the years, and this is the upshot. I have no intention of lifting a finger to get Daniel out. I'll get him a brief and that's that.'

Tommy stroked the erratic red hair he loved so much and said truthfully, 'I'm glad.'

She sighed.

'Are you? I'm not. I wonder what my Eileen would have thought of the way those two boys turned out? She entrusted them to me and I ruined them. I made the mistake I've always made. I loved them too much.'

Tommy pulled her to him and held her close.

'You can never love anyone too much, Bri.'

But she didn't answer him.

Briony opened the front door herself. It was early afternoon and everyone had eaten lunch. The doorbell rang as she was coming out of her kitchen with a large tin of cakes freshly baked that morning by Cissy for Tommy, who still ate as often as possible. Briony put the cake tin on the hall table and opened the door with a smile on her face, expecting it to be one of the bevy of reporters camped outside her house. She sent them out tea at intervals and they always thanked her politely.

She opened the door and the smile froze on her face.

'Hello. I hope I'm not intruding?'

Briony felt a wave of heat wash over her body as the rich voice spoke to her. She stood stock still, her eyes boring into those of her son.

'Benedict?' It was a question.

The two stood looking at one another for long moments before Tommy came bowling into the entrance hall. One look at the man at the door told him everything. He saw the same green eyes, the same heart-shaped face, the same finely boned features. Even the man's hair had a red tint.

'Benedict? Bloody hell, Bri, he's like the spit out of your mouth!'

Tommy's incredulous voice broke the tension. Benedict felt himself being pulled over the threshold and into the warmth of his mother's home.

Briony stared at her son from head to toe. She had to crane her neck to look up into his face, he was so tall. As big as Tommy. The two men shook hands, Tommy grabbing her son as if frightened Benedict was going to run away.

'This is indeed a pleasure. I'll go inside and keep everyone contained.' He laughed. 'I expect you two would like to see one another for a while in private?'

Benedict smiled as the big jovial man went back into the dining room and left them alone.

'Come through to the drawing room, Benedict. We can talk there.'

He followed her. She looked amazingly youthful from behind. She had the same easy carriage that his own daughter had, along with the deep red hair and green eyes.

Inside the drawing room, Briony turned to face him.

'I hope you've come in friendship, Benedict.'

She looked so small standing there, hands clasped in front of her like a schoolgirl, her brilliant eyes lowered. He felt as if someone had pushed a knife into his chest, so great was the pain. Then over her shoulder he saw a photograph of himself in a heavy silver frame. His childish face was smiling. The photograph was faded with age.

'Sally took me to have that photograph taken, I can remember it as if it was yesterday. I realise now she worked for you as well as my family.'

Briony licked her dry lips.

'I knew everything there was to know about you, Benedict, I got it all from her. Second hand, of course, but you'll never know how much it meant to me. I never forgot you. Not a day has gone by but you've been in my mind. You have to believe that.'

'It's funny, but I do believe you. I know you loved me dearly. I'm sorry for the way I acted before . . .' His voice faltered. 'It was finding out the way I did.'

Briony dismissed it with a wave of one jewelled hand.

'What can I do for you, Benedict?'

He smiled crookedly and shrugged his shoulders. Taking all his courage into his hands, he said, 'You can start by filling me in on your life. Then, if you want, I'll tell you about my wife Fen, and my children Henry and Natalie. Your grandchildren.'

Briony felt as if her chest was burning, so intense was the moment.

Of one mind they stepped towards one another and then Briony felt herself being pulled into the arms of her son, her flesh and blood. She could smell his aftershave, and a mingled scent of leather and tobacco. For the first time ever she was being held by her son, her big handsome son whom she had thought hated her, had been disgusted by her. It was a homecoming for both of them.

'Oh, my son, my son. I've waited so long for this. A lifetime.' Her words were thick with emotion and for long minutes they held one another, the only sound the deep steady ticking of the long case clock in the corner of the room.

Eventually Briony pulled her face from his coat. Smiling, she looked up into the face that mirrored her own.

'Why? What made you come to me after all that's happened in the last few weeks?'

Benedict smiled.

'Because, Mother, you're my blood, as silly as that may sound. You're my mother. My reason for being. Your blood runs through my veins and the veins of my children.' He grinned. 'Do I sound pompous?'

Briony shook her head, unable to talk for the sheer enormity of what was happening to her.

'I knew it that day. I had known about you for so long, but I couldn't admit it to myself. Then my wife, dear Fen, pointed out to me what I had known myself all along. You are me, and I am you really. I wanted to come back that day and say I was sorry. I was paying you back for the hurt I was feeling over my father's will. Over finding it all out like that. So cold-bloodedly. I can't ever tell you how sorry I am.'

Briony grasped his hand and held it to her cheek.

'You're here now, Ben, that's enough for me.'

'I tried to help you. I put pressure on more than a few of my friends and colleagues.'

This statement pleased her enormously. She looked at him again, as if frightened he was going to disappear as quickly as he had come.

'Thank you, Benedict. Thank you.'

As they stood there Molly burst into the room, her aged eyes still piercingly sharp.

'What's going on here then?' Her voice was loud, distrustful.

Briony smiled. 'Benedict, I'd like you to meet your maternal grandmother.'

She went to her mother and, taking her arm, walked her to Benedict and said proudly: 'Mum, this is my son, Benedict Dumas.'

Molly smiled crookedly and said, 'I've got eyes in me head. You look like two peas in a bleeding pod! Come here, son, give your old granny a kiss.'

Benedict kissed her on her papery cheek, feeling her frailness as he embraced her. Then the room seemed to be full of people. He was surrounded by his family, all smiling and looking at him curiously. He saw Bernadette and Kerry; saw his own children in these women, in their jawlines, in the movement of their heads.

Yes, indeed, this was his real family. He held on to his grandmother and his mother, relishing the contact with people who were a part of him.

This was his family. Whether he liked it or not, this was the stock he came from. Then they were all touching him, wanting to get to know this big son of Briony's, this extension to their large close-knit family. He was accepted immediately and at face value, something he had never experienced before in his life.

With all her troubles of the last weeks, with all her heartache over Boysie and Daniel, Briony still felt as if she led a charmed life.

The one thing she had wanted all her life, above everything, had now come about. After over fifty years of trouble, strife and heartbreak, when every family gathering had been bitter-sweet because one crucial person was always absent, always missing, the mainstay of her life was here now.

Benedict was in the fold.

Her son had come home to her.

*

Briony sat opposite Daniel in Wandsworth Prison. He was sitting with his legs crossed, his handsome face dour. She was listening intently to what he had to say.

'Then, once I'm out, I'm going to go after the fucking lot of them. I'm going to tear the East End apart if needs be, but I'll find them all. Every last one of them.'

Briony sighed softly. It was always the same.

'As for that cunt Limmington, I heard he just got a slapped wrist. Well, I'll fucking pay that slag out and all for my Boysie. You see if I don't.

'And did you see that ponce on Friday, did you? Telling the court how I pushed the knife into Mitchell's mouth. I know that shite, I know his name and address. I'll torture him and his fucking kids. I'll torture his kids in front of him . . .'

Briony held up her hand.

'Enough! For Christ's sake, Daniel, that's enough! You know the old saying, don't you? "If you can't do the time, don't do the crime." You made a big mistake. You thought you could do what you wanted. Well, you can't. I've got you McQuiddan and he's good, but you're going down, Danny boy. You'd best get used to that fact.'

Danny's face twitched.

'You and Tommy never went down, did you? You two got a result.'

Briony nodded. 'We were charged with a very old crime, Danny boy. I know about violence, all right. But we were violent in the twenties and believe me when I say you had to be violent then. You had to take what you wanted. It wasn't like today, when the working classes can get an education, can follow their stars. I had the choice between looking after myself and my family, or going under, like me Mum had to.

'You don't know the first thing about real violence. Oh, you hurt people, you shoot them. But you have no inkling of real poverty, and that's where real violence is bred. The survival of the fittest. Me and Tommy came from an era where eating regularly was a result, where keeping warm was a major occupation. You grew up with everything anyone could want. I even sent you two to Ampleforth and what for, eh? What the hell for? You even take pleasure in keeping your East End accent. I take the blame for you two – I should have knocked you down a peg when I had the chance; but being me, I loved you so much I couldn't see your faults. I made excuses for you and in reality there were none. You were just a vicious little bastard and this is the upshot. I never hurt anyone for fun, for recognition. People had to tread heavily on my toes before I retaliated and that's why I'm sitting here and you're sitting there.'

Daniel sneered at her. 'The voice of Briony Cavanagh. Shall I tell you something? We used to laugh at you and Tommy behind your backs. You was a joke to us. Me and Boysie, we had them there.' He held out his palm. 'We had them there, and would have kept them there and all. It was grasses who tucked us up and they'll pay, believe me.'

Briony shook her head in sorrow. 'Can't you see anything, Danny? Can't you see we're living in a different world now? The days when you could walk into a pub with a shooter and expect everyone to turn a blind eye are long gone. You made the mistake of making too many enemies. The big I am, were you? Well look where it's got you. I couldn't give a monkey's whether you laughed at us behind our backs, because at the end of the day, Tommy Lane is worth fifty of you, a hundred. That man deserves your respect. If you'd had any sense you'd have emulated him. Fifty years on and he's still respected, still liked and what's more, still outside on the street. The way you're carrying on you won't see the light of day until the year two thousand.'

'Well, now we both know where we stand, don't we?'

Briony nodded. 'We do. I blame you for my Boysie, he followed you in everything. I'll give you a last bit of advice, my son: keep your head down and do your bird. No more outbursts in court threatening all and sundry, it just makes you look a prat.'

Danny's eyes were blazing. 'You know it all, don't you? You're not sitting in the dock. You and Tommy walked out your nicks and now you're coming on to me like some kind of saint!'

Briony leant across the table and said through gritted teeth, 'I told you, Danny, we were the old style of villain. You and Boysie could never understand us. Shall I tell you something? In all honesty, I never really wanted any of it. None of it. But I made my bed, as me mother would say, and I think we can safely say I lay down in it. For over fifty years. You two never *had* to do what you did, you chose it. You decided to be what you are.'

Daniel's face was still twisted. Getting up, he said: 'I ain't listening to this shite. I'm better off in me cell. It's Saturday, and on Saturday we can listen to our radios and have a laze about. Come to think of it, that's what we do most days. But you'd know all about that, wouldn't you? So if you'll excuse me? I have better things to do.'

Briony sat stone-faced as he went to a prison officer to be taken back to his wing. People were staring at them, their last exchange having been overheard. Standing up she walked with as much dignity as she could out of the visiting room.

She had done her best.

Mr Justice Martin Panterfield stared at the man in the dock before him. He wiped his mouth with a spotlessly clean handkerchief before delivering his judgment to the packed but hushed courtroom.

'Mr Daniel O'Malley, you have been found guilty of a vicious murder. Never before have I listened to such grisly accounts of barbaric and unnecessary violence. You took a knife and cold-bloodedly executed David Mitchell in full view of a packed public house. You and your twin brother terrified the East End of London, and were involved with a number of illegal businesses. You were a wicked and callous murderer who thought you could do what you wanted. You are the frightening result of this so-called permissive society. I would be failing in my duty to the public if I did not impose the maximum penalty the law dictates.

'I hereby sentence you to life imprisonment with a recommendation you serve at least thirty years. Have you anything to say?'

Daniel stood up, hands clasped in front of him, face devoid of expression. Then he looked the judge in the eye and said clearly: 'Yes, I have, mate. The name's Cavanagh!'

The judge shook his bewigged head. Looking around the court, he said: 'Take him down.'

Molly stood up then. Her face streaming tears, she screamed: 'You dirty bastards, that's my boy. My Boy! Danny, son, Danny.' Her voice reverberated around the courtroom as Daniel was escorted from the dock by two burly policemen. On his way down to the holding cells he held up his arms in a victorious gesture and shouted:

'That's it, Gran! I'll be back, I'll be back!' His voice was lost as he disappeared below.

Limmington looked at Briony and their eyes locked. She nodded at him almost imperceptibly. It was a job well done.

Chapter Forty-Nine

Suzy looked around her mother's front room, breathing in the scent of Airwick and furniture polish. She placed her hands roughly on her stomach, repressing the urge to scream. Her mother popped her head around the door and said; 'Shall I make you a drink, love? How about a cuppa?'

'I don't want anything, leave me alone.'

The woman walked into the room and tried to take her daughter's hand. Suzy shrugged her off.

'Oh for crying out loud, leave me be, woman!'

Doreen sat down on a chair and said softly, 'I know you're hurting, love, but you must try and keep yourself together; that child will take a lot of looking after – children do. I know you're upset over Boysie, God knows I am myself.' She dabbed at the corner of a heavily made-up eye with a tissue. 'I loved that boy as if he was me own, God rest him.'

Suzy raised her eyes to the ceiling, then, leaning forward awkwardly, she said through gritted teeth. 'Cut the act, Mum, there's no one here to see it but me. As for this bloody baby, I don't want it. I can't stand being pregnant, and I hate living here.' She bit her bottom lip to stem the trembling and said brokenly, 'I'm glad he's dead, I hated him. I hated everything about him.'

Doreen sat back in her chair. Then, without warning her hand shot out and she slapped Suzy a stinging blow across her face. 'You little bitch! Let words like that get out and there'll be trouble, my girl. You broke your frigging neck to get up that aisle and don't you forget it. When I think of the shame we've had to endure because of your association with them Cavanaghs, I could cheerfully throttle you, and that little child you're carrying can't be blamed. My God, I wonder at times just what you think you're playing at, madam, with your butter wouldn't melt look and that scheming brain. Let his Aunt Briony hear talk like that and you'll be singing a different tune.'

'Oh go away, Mum!'

'No I won't. You left that lovely house, all that nice furniture. Me and your Dad would have moved in there and looked after you, but no, not you. You had to come running home here like a baby.'

Suzy felt a moment's triumph as they reached the nub of her mother's annoyance. Doreen saw herself in the big detached house, bringing up her grandchild, guaranteed a good allowance and the property. Suzy had sussed that out in no time. 'You'll never live in that house, Mother, get that straight now.'

Doreen's lips moved back over her teeth, and she said, 'You're a little bitch, Suzy Rankins, a bitch. When I think of how I brought you up, gave you the best . . .'

Doreen's tirade was interrupted by the doorbell.

Suzy smiled grimly. Saved by the bell. If her mother knew how much she had been paid for her interview with the paper she'd have a fit, but there was a method in her madness. Once she was delivered of this child she would go away and make a fresh start. The name Cavanagh, which had excited her so much when she had first met Boysie, disgusted her now. She was pointed at, stared at and gossipped about every time she walked down the street.

Her heart stopped as she heard her mother's voice: 'Oh, hello, Briony, come away in. I was just making a cup of tea.'

Briony rustled into the room. 'Hello, Suzy, love.'

Suzy forced herself to look at the little woman. 'Hello, Briony.'

Doreen, overcome with awe as usual, left the two and went to make the tea.

Briony sat down on the chair Doreen had vacated and smiled.

'How you feeling?'

Suzy lit a cigarette and smiled wanly, blowing out the smoke in a large cloud around her head. 'All right I suppose.'

Briony patted her hand and the action so startled the girl she flinched. 'Calm down, Suzy! Anyone would think you had something to be frightened about.' Briony's voice was sad. 'I know you must be devastated about Boysie, we all are. He was a good boy, my Boysie. A good kind boy. I miss him so much.'

Suzy took another drag on her cigarette and kept silent.

'Have you seen the doctor about Junior?'

'I'm fine. I just wish I could get it over with.'

'I can understand that, but it will be over sooner than you think.'

Doreen bustled in with the tea and began chattering.

'I've told her she should go back to her own home, there's no room here for a baby. I've offered to go with her, like. After all, it is her house now, isn't it?' Doreen's voice was innocent and Briony closed her eyes for a few seconds.

'Yes it's her house, Doreen, but maybe it brings back too many memories, eh, Suzy?'

Suzy made herself look into the older woman's eyes and smile gratefully. 'That's right. I never want to go in there again. I can't face the neighbours, after what happened . . .'

Briony sipped her tea and nodded understandingly. 'I was wondering if you'd like to come to me until the baby arrives.'

'No! No really, I want to be here with me mum. I don't want to go anywhere else . . .' Her voice was rising in panic.

'All right, Suzy, calm down. It was only a suggestion. Everyone wants their own around them in times of upset. I can understand that. Only you are carrying all that's left of my Boysie, see. It's like my grandchild, I always thought of the twins as my own sons, as you know. Heard anything more from the reporters? I wondered if they'd asked you why you didn't attend the funeral.'

Suzy stared down at her cup, unwilling to answer the question.

'If you wanted money so badly, Suzy, you should have come to me. Especially with the baby coming. As long as I see the child regularly, you'll be amply provided for. I've booked you in a private clinic, that way you won't be mobbed by press when your time comes. I don't expect you want to have the child in a blaze of publicity do you?' Opening her bag, she took out a small white card. 'This is the clinic's address and phone number. Ring up and arrange your check-ups with them. I'll pay the bill so don't worry about expense. They delivered Princess Margaret's children, nothing but the best for my Boysie's baby, eh?'

Standing up, she kissed Suzy's cheek softly. 'Look after yourself love, you'll see me again soon.' Suzy stared down in her cup, her eyes riveted to the tea leaves floating on the bottom.

She was never going to get away from the Cavanaghs.

Briony walked into her house with a heavy heart. She wished she could get on with Suzy, could like her. She had to if she wanted to see the child.

Tommy was on the phone in the den; she smiled as she heard him laughing. His back was to her as she stood in the doorway.

'Don't worry, love, I'll be there. Briony watches me like a hawk, but she can't watch me all the time!' He laughed again.

Briony felt as if someone had punched her in the solar plexus; all the air seemed to leave her body in a split second. She stepped out of the doorway and back into the hall. Tommy's voice drifted out to her.

'I'll see you then, all right. Yeah, you too.'

Gathering up her strength she walked into the den.

'Who was that, Tom?' Her voice was brittle, over bright. Tommy smiled at her widely. 'Hello, Bri!' He walked across the room and hugged her tightly. 'How's it go with Suzy?'

Briony disengaged herself from his embrace. 'All right. Who was that on the phone?'

Tommy flapped a hand at her.

'Oh, Fat Peter. I'm doing a bit of business with him. You're back early.'

'Yeah, I gave Bernadette a miss. I'll see her later.'

'I dropped Danny Boy a line this morning, I'll post it on me way out. He's moved to the Island tomorrow so I thought a letter might cheer him up until he gets acclimatised.' Tommy looked at his watch. 'I've got five minutes before I have to go out, fancy a quick cuppa?'

The phone rang again and Tommy rushed to answer it. 'Hello . . . Oh hello, Bern, hang on she's here.' He handed the phone to Briony and, kissing her on the cheek, went out of the room, leaving Briony more unsettled than ever.

'I'll ring you back, Bernadette.'

She bit her lip. Since when had he called Fat Peter love?

Bernadette was lying in her darkened bedroom with a cold flannel across her eyes. 'Oh Bri, this is torture.' She spoke through her teeth.

'Well if you have a facelift you have to expect a bit of pain, don't you?' Briony's voice held no sympathy whatsoever. 'He's cut right through your skin to the bone . . .'

'Oh shut up Bri, I feel sick as a dog!'

'Well why didn't you stay in the clinic then?' You've been home a week and you haven't stopped moaning!'

'You know why. I wouldn't leave that Marcus for longer than five minutes. You know what he's like.'

Briony didn't laugh, as usual, but said seriously, 'Is he still batting away from home then?'

'Not that I know of, but I won't give the bugger a chance. They're all the same, men – a flash of teeth, a pair of tits and they're undone.'

Briony's voice was cold. 'Not all men are like that.'

Bernadette laughed softly. 'Ain't they? Then why have you built a fortune on your houses? Most men play the field; it's just some are cleverer than others. As for my Marcus, even Pan's People on the telly have him riveted to his seat! I tell you what, if dick was brains he'd been another Magnus Pike!'

'Tommy wouldn't do it to me.'

Bernadette took the flannel off her forehead and raised herself gently on her shoulders. 'Who said anything about Tommy?'

Briony shrugged. 'No one, I'm just saying he wouldn't do it to me, that's all.'

'Well,' Bernie said grudgingly, 'he seems all right. I mean you think about it, Bri, he's no children, nothing, has he? He gave up a lot for you if you could only see it. That man's a diamond and you've never really appreciated that fact.'

'Well, I wouldn't go through all you do, no man's worth that pain.'

Bernie grinned painfully. 'In another week, I'll look the dog's gonads, as Boysie used to say. Then it'll all have been worth it.'

'Boysie also used to say that one day you'd come out of the clinic with a beard and your belly button on your forehead!'

Bernadette sighed heavily. 'I thought you was going to cheer me up! Instead you're sitting there taking the piss!'

Marcus walked into the room and saved Briony from answering. 'Cissy's just rang, your Mum's up and looking for you, Bri.'

Briony stood up and, saying goodbye to a subdued Bernadette, she walked down the stairs with Marcus. 'Can I ask you something personal, Marcus?'

'Course you can.'

'Do you still play around?'

Marcus laughed and the laugh turned into a heavy smoker's cough. 'Chance would be a fine thing! I ask you, Briony, at my age?'

Briony smiled and left the house. She was taking her mother to church and she quickened her step. She was looking forward to Mass this afternoon.

'Are you sure you're not coming, Tommy? Only your name's on the visiting order as well. This is the second visit you've missed this month.'

'Honestly, Bri, I feel rough, the ferry crossing will knacker me. You go with Delia and give Danny my best.'

'All right then. I'm picking Delia up on me way. See you later if you're in!'

With that she marched from the house and got into her car, wheelspinning it out of the drive. Tommy shook his head and Cissy tutted. 'You're heading for a fall trying to get one over on her, Tommy Lane.'

'Be fair, Cissy, it'll be the first time ever if I do! Did it ever occur to you that I might want a bit more out of life than what I've got? That I might want a woman who belongs with me, who has my name?'

'Well, it's not bothered you up to now has it? Christ, you and Briony have been an item for the last five decades, that's longer than most marriages!'

'Yeah well maybe it's not enough!'

'She'll go spare.'

'Well, we'll see about that won't we.'

Delia was quiet, watching the other people on the ferry. The children laughing and joking around. The women in their catalogue coats and home perms calling them to order.

'Have you seen anything of Faithey?'

Delia nodded. 'Yeah, I popped round yesterday. Me

Dad's been looking after her while me Mum had her op. Honestly, Auntie Briony, my Mum's embarrassing. She looks better than I do!'

Briony looked her niece over from head to foot and said scathingly, 'Cissy looks better than you do. You could at least have made an effort. You're getting enormous again!'

Delia looked out of the ferry window, took a deep breath and said, 'That's because I'm pregnant again.'

'You're what!'

'Four months. I've got to tell me Mum.'

'Who's the father this time?'

'Ray Stockyard. He wants to marry me.'

'Oh he does, does he? And what does this Ray do? Another drug pusher is he?'

'He's unemployed. Look I ain't happy about this either, but I can't have another abortion, the doctor's already told me that.'

Briony shook her head sadly. Give her a good honest working girl any day of the week, rather than this fat individual beside her.

'I don't know what's happened to this family. Boysie's dead, Danny's banged up, and now on top of it all you're pregnant. One child with your mother because you couldn't look after her, and now this! Another poor innocent on the way. I hope you've knocked the drugs on the head, girl. If you harm that baby I'll murder you.'

They were quiet for the remainder of the journey. Briony had enough on her plate with Tommy's erratic behaviour and Suzy's attitude towards her. It seemed trouble was determined to dog her family and she was getting too old for it.

*

Molly and Briony were sitting by the fire. Molly was drinking her habitual hot rum toddy and Briony was nursing a scotch.

'Where's Tommy tonight?'

'He popped out, he said he won't be long.' Briony glanced at the long case clock as it chimed the hour. It was eight o'clock and he'd been gone over two hours.

'Sure he's never in these days! How's Bernadette now?'

Briony shrugged. 'Over the shock. The boyfriend's another of the great unwashed. Marcus went garrity. Honestly, Mum, I don't know what happened with all the kids.'

Molly laughed. 'Every parent says that at some time. Get the telly on, I don't want to miss Kerry.'

Briony got up and switched the television on.

Molly sighed with contentment. 'I love Morecambe and Wise. Kerry said she'd get me their autographs!'

Briony heard Tommy's key in the door twenty minutes later and went out to the hall. 'You're back then?'

Tommy laughed. 'I am! Now how about making me a Scotch and soda, I could do with one.'

'Tommy, where have you been?'

Tommy slipped his coat off and grinned. 'I've been out, Briony, with a mate. Now are you going to interrogate me or are you going to let me in to watch Kerry on *Morecambe and Wise*?'

Briony stood her ground. 'I want to know where you've been, Thomas Lane, and I want to know now!'

'I just told you, Briony, I've been out! You're sounding more like a wife every day. What's it you've always said? You don't want to be married, you don't need a piece of paper to prove to the world who you are with . . . Marriage is outdated . . . So stop sounding like a harping wife and let me in to watch Kerry. I came back especially to see her.' He pushed her gently out of the way and went into the lounge.

'Hello, Molly, love. Have I missed her?'

'No, Tom. She's not been on yet.'

'Good, want a refill, Moll?'

Briony stood in the hallway and felt an urge to cry. She walked slowly upstairs and went into her bedroom. All her life Tommy had been there as and when she wanted him, now all of a sudden she wasn't sure of him. She felt a subtle shifting in position. It occurred to her that she needed Tommy Lane a lot more than he needed her.

It was a frightening thought.

Kerry's voice was loud. 'Will you hurry up, Briony, Liselle will be here in a minute to pick us up.'

'All right, Kerry, keep your hair on. I don't see why you want me there anyway!'

Kerry rolled her eyes at the ceiling. 'Let's not start all that again, please! You know how nervous I am when I'm doing TV. We'll be in and out in no time.'

Briony brushed her hair, looking at herself critically in the mirror.

'You look lovely, Briony.' The two sisters smiled at one another.

'I don't know why you're so worried about how I look, you're the one going on telly!'

'Quick, put your hat on, I can hear Lissy sounding the horn.'

Briony pushed her hat on her head and they rushed down the stairs.

Inside the car Lissy smiled. 'You two look lovely.' She

pulled out of the drive. 'That Delia's a cow, isn't she? You know Bernie's taking on this child as well?'

Briony nodded. 'In fairness to Bernie, as silly as she can be, she looks after Faithey brilliantly. If Delia was my daughter I'd have got her done with the cat!'

Liselle laughed. 'Delia's all right really, she's just a bit scatty.'

Briony sighed heavily. 'I don't know where we got her from. Look at Becky, she's all right and they come from the same stable . . . Hold on, you're going towards Barking!'

'I promised Gran and Cissy I'd pick them up from Mass first.'

'You're cutting it a bit fine, ain't you?'

'Stop worrying, we've all the time in the world.'

As they approached St Vincent's church, Briony looked at Kerry and said, 'What's going on here today? Look at all these cars.'

They pulled up in a space right outside the church.

'There's Tommy!' Briony got out and stared at the people outside the church, all dressed in their Sunday best. Mariah was there, her mother and sisters, nieces, Cissy, crying as usual. She saw women who had worked for her years before, bouncers from her clubs. Bessie Knight and the Velvetones. Even Jonathan La Billière was there, with his usual posse of press photographers. It was as if her whole life had risen up before her eyes.

Tommy walked towards her and grinned. 'You got here then?'

Liselle opened the boot of her Daimler and took out a posy of flowers. She gave them to Briony and kissed her on the cheek.

Briony stared down at the flowers and opened her mouth to speak but no sound came out.

'For once in your life, you're lost for words!' Taking her none too gently by the arm he led her towards the church.

Briony staggered along beside him, looking at the sea of faces around her, all smiling and laughing. As she walked into the lobby of the church, Benedict was waiting for her. He held out an arm.

'I'm going to give you away, Mother.'

Tommy brought a black velvet box from his pocket, took out the choker he had bought her years before and tied it gently around her throat.

'I hope you're not going to say "I won't", Bri. This little lot was murder to arrange and cost a small fortune.' She looked up into his face and saw the uncertainty there. She shook her head.

'I can't wait to become Mrs Thomas Lane. Let's do it!' She walked proudly down the aisle on her son's arm, her face glowing with happiness.

At sixty-five years old she finally understood what life was all about.

Tommy kissed her gently on the lips. 'I love you, Bri.'

Briony snuggled into him in the warmth of the bed. 'I love you, too, only I never realised how much.'

He cupped her breast gently and Briony slapped his hand away. 'Do you mind, Tommy Lane? I'm a respectable married woman now!'

Tommy laughed out loud. 'I was really scared you know, Briony. I thought, if she knocks me back now, in front of everyone . . .'

Briony looked up into his face. 'I thought you had someone else, I did.'

'I know, I let you think it and all. Be fair, Bri, you've

never let me look after you really, have you? And I wanted to. I admit that over the years I stepped in to help you, but without you knowing about it. You're a hard woman to love, Bri, you are so self-possessed, so strong! It's like living with a bloke at times!'

Briony kissed his chest. 'After all the trouble with the boys, my Boysie dying, Danny going away, I realised that I needed you more than anything. No matter what's happened in the past, we have had each other. If that's what marriage is, then I want it.'

Tommy kissed her again.

'How did you arrange it all without me guessing?'

'You can thank Mariah, Cissy and the whole family for that. It was hard, I can tell you.'

'Well, I'm glad you did. I think it was the nicest thing that ever happened to me.'

Tommy pulled her tightly to him and said, 'Come here, wife!'

Briony started laughing. 'You've called me a few things over the years, but I never thought to hear you call me that!'

They both laughed.

'You realise one thing though, Thomas Lane: you got me by default!'

'How'd you make that out?'

'I was in shock!'

'You'll be in shock in a minute if you don't stop rabbiting. Now get your nightdress off!'

'Respectable married women sleep with their nighties on!'

Tommy laughed throatily. 'Not in this bleeding house they don't.'

Chapter Fifty

1970

Kerry stood waiting to be announced, feeling the euphoria induced by vodka fighting with her nervousness. She could hear the muted sounds of conversation coming from the audience. She felt Liselle take hold of her and squeezed her daughter's hand gently.

'All right, Mum?'

Kerry nodded, unable to form any words. It was always like this until she walked out into the lights, to the sound of the music. Then something took her over. Something came down over her mind and wiped away the nervousness, the fear, leaving a feeling of peace and a desire just to make the audience enjoy themselves, enjoy her. Tonight, though, it was more acute than it had ever been. She had travelled a long way to do this show and she was glad, in a funny sort of way, to be doing it now after all the events of the last year. It seemed right somehow. Right and fitting.

It was Briony who had told her to go, who had made her realise that they were getting too old to nurse grudges for any length of time. They were old and wise enough, surely, to chase their own ghosts?

Which was what Kerry was going to do tonight.

The ghost was Evander Dorsey, and after all those years, all the trouble with him and through him, she was going to sing in his club in America. CBS Television was out there waiting for her, she was going to be seen from coast to coast. 'Kerry Cavanagh the Legend' they called her these days. The twins had given her career a bigger boost than she had ever dreamed possible. After Daniel's trial her records had been recut and she had been inundated with offers to sing, star in shows, be interviewed. It had frightened her. But Briony, dear Briony, and Bernadette had told her, 'Use whatever you can, girl. If you're making a bigger comeback as a result of Boysie's death and Daniel's misfortune, then at least we can all be glad that some good came from it all.' So she had taken up the offers, she had gone on the talk shows and the music shows, she had toured the country and sang in just about every auditorium there was in Britain.

Now she was on New York's east side, in Evander's Jazz Club. There was a packed audience waiting for her, and Evander himself was going to introduce her.

In the week since she had arrived they had regained a little more of their old footing. It was inevitable when they shared a common bond, their child.

Kerry heard her cue and swallowed nervously. Her throat was dry, her eyes felt hot.

Liselle kissed her on the cheek and smiled widely. 'Go on, Mum, get out there and show them what a Cavanagh can do!'

Kerry heard Evander's voice, that deep brown voice that she had loved so much all those years ago. And as she listened, her ears tuned to it, her mind chased down the years until she could picture the handsome lover he had been.

Evander stood on stage, dressed in a dinner suit, looking dapper and confident. The hands that clutched the microphone were wearing black silk gloves.

'Ladies and gentlemen, I give you the woman they call The Living Legend, the woman who can sing like an angel, and the woman I have respected, deeply and sincerely, for far more years than either of us cares to remember!'

He swept out his arm in a dramatic gesture: 'Miss Kerry Cavanagh.'

The place went wild.

Kerry walked out on to the stage, a tall slim figure dressed in a silver evening dress cut high on the hip to expose a long shapely leg, her black hair piled high on her head, her stage make-up making her look younger, softer, than she really was.

There was an audible gasp from the audience. Kerry took the microphone from Evander and as he made to leave the stage, grabbed his arm, holding him there with her.

'First, I would like to thank you for your welcome. New York has been very kind to me.' She smiled as she waited for the cheering and the catcalling to die down. 'Secondly, I would like to thank this big handsome man standing beside me. He gave me something precious, something that has made my life complete. He gave me the gift of a child, our child, Liselle.'

She looked to the side of the stage and gestured for Liselle to join them both on stage.

She walked out into the bright lights, her eyes misting

over, her heart full to bursting. She stood between her mother and father as the audience clapped, and the band played the first few bars of Kerry's opening number.

Then Evander kissed her gently on the lips and, taking Liselle's hand, walked proudly from the stage.

Kerry laughed, that deep, husky laugh so like Briony's, and said, 'Now for some singin'! This is a song I have loved for many years and I sing it tonight for all my family, both here in the States and at home in England.'

The band played louder, the lights were dimmed and her voice was husky as she began to sing the first number of her set, 'I Love You So Much It Hurts'.

Liselle and Evander stood watching Kerry. She took the audience and held them in her hands. Then she gave them everything she had, and a little bit more.

As Evander watched her, he realised the quality of the woman who had borne his child, whom he had taken down, and whom he now watched with a mixture of love and deep respect.

She was indeed a living legend, and he felt deeply honoured to be allowed once more to be a part of her life.

Briony lay in the dark, Tommy's breathing beside her regular and even. She envied him his capacity to sleep. She put a hand to her heart, reassured by the regular beating that seemed to be keeping time with Tommy's breathing.

Her heart bothered her sometimes. The twins were in her mind tonight. She had thought Daniel getting put away for so long would have made her ill, but instead it gave her a feeling of peace.

He had pushed his luck and his violent streak too far. He had had to pay the price. Thirty years. She would likely be dead by the time he got out.

Tommy turned over in his sleep and she felt his arm creep around her waist, holding her gently. Her husband. It still seemed strange to call him that. He snuffled into the pillows, sounding ridiculous and so normal she felt the sting of tears once more.

'Oh, Eileen,' she whispered into the darkness. 'You gave me the gift of your children, and I tried to do the best I could by them. I really tried.'

She saw Henry Dumas in her mind's eye, with his ridiculous large moustaches. Through him she had been given the most important thing in her life: her son. And later Henry had inadvertently brought them together again, brought them close. This thought pleased her more than anything because she liked to think that somewhere Henry Dumas was spinning in his grave, distraught with the knowledge the two of them had come together again through his folly.

'Henry, you bastard,' she whispered once more into the blackness of her bedroom, 'I bested you in the end. You were the cause of every unhappiness that befell me and mine, but I am the victor. With all my troubles the victor.'

With that she closed her eyes and thought of the twins as boys, her boys. How she would always think of them.

Boysie's daughter Deidre, born fatherless and in a blaze of publicity, was asleep in the next room.

Suzy was quite happy for her to stay with Briony and Tommy at weekends. It was her way of trying to make amends for the way she'd acted after Boysie's death. Briony put up with Suzy so she could see the child.

A new generation was growing. Faithey and Deidre were both fatherless, both cursed with mothers who were no good at all. It seemed that they needed Briony and Bernadette and even Kerry to look out for them.

Molly wouldn't last much longer, Boysie's death and Daniel's prison sentence had finished her. She had lost the will to live now, had become old overnight, really old and decrepit. Briony snuggled against Tommy's back.

Age was creeping up on them all, but while they had the children they had life and a reason for living.

She wondered how Kerry was getting on in America and smiled then, a genuine smile. At least some good had come out of all the troubles of the last few years. Kerry was back on top. She was still drinking, but at her age, what could anyone really do? At least she was enjoying her life. She was a big star again. Briony hoped she took America by storm, and being a Cavanagh, that was probably exactly what she would do.

A Cavanagh. Even Daniel had insisted, right at the last, that he was a Cavanagh. She would write to him tomorrow. His mind was deteriorating rapidly, but the prison psychiatrist said that was delayed shock at his twin's death. He was being sent to Broadmoor next week, so instead of the monthly trek to Parkhurst, on the Isle of Wight, they would have to go to Berkshire. Daniel still thought he was somebody of renown, but then, she supposed, in prison he was. They would never release him. He had already attacked two other prisoners for imagined slights. The psychiatrist said he was a psychopath. She had felt like saying to him: 'Tell me something I don't know.'

She felt her eyes getting heavy with sleep and was glad. Finally, Briony slept, only to be woken a few hours later by Deidre crying. Briony settled her on her lap and rocked her to sleep, happy now she had a child in her arms. Deidre made up for the loss of the two babies she had loved too much. She was to see Benedict the next day.

He visited regularly. She hoped that he would one day

bring his children with him. But it was something they had not discussed yet. They were still feeling the way, building the love and trust between themselves.

She rocked the little girl gently, crooning softly to her. Briony kissed the downy forehead and said softly: 'Who knows what the future holds, my lovely? For me, for you, for any of us.'

The child was the living image of Boysie, she was wholly his daughter.

Yes, the Cavanagh genes were very strong. Too strong, perhaps? Who knew?

Briony carried on rocking the child, making plans for her in her mind. As always, Briony's mind was on the future. A future, she knew from experience, which would be shaped by the past.

Epilogue

Therefore my age is as a lusty winter, frosty, but kindly.

– *As You Like It*
William Shakespeare c. 1564–1616

1989

'Do you think we should wake her?'

The blonde nurse nodded and smiled. 'I think she'd be very cross if we didn't. She's been looking forward to seeing you all day.'

The man came into the room and the others followed. He went to the bed and gently shook the woman beneath the covers. She opened one eye, to show a flash of vivid green, then the other eye opened quickly.

'Is it that time already?' Her voice had the querulousness of great age and the man laughed.

'We're all here, Gran.' As he spoke, a boy in his late teens looked over his shoulder and grinned.

'Come on, Granny, it's not like you to be a lie-abed.' The words brought a stinging sensation of tears to her rheumy eyes. That was an expression of Tommy's.

'Come here, me lovelies, and give me a kiss.'

One by one they kissed her. Faithey first, her own two children following. Then Deidre with that startling red hair so like her own. She had a young man with her, Briony noticed, and smiled at him. Then came Becky, her children and grandchildren. Then came Delia with her son Daniel, a fine strong boy, nothing like his mother at all. Though he had a look of Marcus, his grandfather, about him. Briony swallowed heavily. Bernie's dying had been a great blow; she had died five days after Marcus had had his coronary. Briony wondered if Bernie still didn't trust him, she'd followed him so fast. It seemed all the old people were disappearing, but that was how it should be. Though she didn't particularly want to leave them all, not yet.

Then Liselle was kissing her heartily. Briony squeezed her hard. Nearing seventy, Liselle was still as sprightly as a girl. She had inherited the Jazz Club on her father's death ten years before; Kerry had sung there the night she died. It was hard to believe at times that her Aunt Briony was the only one of the sisters left.

'Let Lissy sit down, will you, she's getting on.'

This was said seriously and Lissy smiled at the people in the room. Briony always forgot her own age.

Then came Natalie, Briony's grandchild, and her two boys. A pair of buggers if ever there was, Briony thought. They kissed their granny with real affection. They thought she was absolutely great. They loved bragging about her and being a part of her. Briony grabbed their cheeks tightly in her jewelled hands.

'You two need watching, my lads! You've too much of the Cavanagh in you.'

Everyone laughed.

Then came her favourite, the one she had least expected to steal her heart. He stood with his father, smiling at her. Benedict's face glowed as his son wrapped his granny in a long embrace and kissed her. He had a deep love for his granny, and his two daughters and his son all stood round the bed waiting their turn.

It always amazed Briony that a man called Henry Dumas could kiss her like that and she feel nothing but love. The love she bore her grandson. The name was exorcised for her, it meant nothing but happiness now.

She swept Henry's children into her sweet-smelling embrace and said, 'Next year, we'll all go away together. I thought we might get a big house out in the country and have a holiday there.' She saw them all smiling around her, none of them wanting to say what they were really thinking. So Briony, being Briony, said it for them:

'I know what you're all thinking – that I might not be here next year. The thought had crossed my mind. But let's look at it like this.' She paused, eyes bright. 'There's a fifty-fifty chance I'll be dead . . .' She paused again and looked around her, at her family, at her blood, and then she said craftily: 'But there's also a fifty-fifty chance I just could still be here, alive and kicking!'

'You will be, Bri, God willing.' Tommy's face came down on hers and he kissed her gently on her lips.

'Me and you, Tommy Lane, we seem to go on and on!'

Hard Girls

Martina Cole

HARD LIVES. HARD LESSONS. IT'S MURDER ON THE STREETS.

Danielle Crosby had a body to die for. A body she sold to the highest bidder. But she ended up paying for it with her life.

When a prostitute's body is found lifeless, mutilated and brutally raped, DCI Annie Carr has never seen anything like it and never wants to again. Kate Burrows, retired DCI and now consultant, has plenty of experience when it comes to murder – after all she caught the Grantley Ripper and broke the biggest paedophile ring in the South East. She is determined to help put the killer behind bars. But whoever it is won't be easily caught. And when another girl's body is found, even more horrifically disfigured than the last, it's clear the killer is just warming up . . .

In a ruthless world where everyone's out for themselves, Annie and Kate must dig deep if they hope to catch a callous serial killer who knows no limits and makes no mistakes. For some, prostitution is seriously big business. But how many people will pay the ultimate price?

Utterly riveting, HARD GIRLS is a gripping and disturbing thriller that will have you hooked until the very last page.

'Cole is brilliant at portraying the good among the bad, and vice versa, so until the very end we never quite know who to trust. This is the very stuff that makes her so compelling' *Daily Mirror*

978 0 7553 2870 3

headline

Dangerous Lady

Martina Cole

DANGEROUS LADY is an explosive thriller of corruption and violence from one of the most original voices in fiction today.

No one thinks a seventeen-year-old girl can take on the hard men of London's gangland, but it's a mistake to underestimate Maura Ryan: she's tough, clever and beautiful – and she's determined that nothing will stand in her way. Which makes her one very dangerous lady.

Together, she and her brother Michael are unbeatable: the Queen and King of organised crime, they run the pubs and clubs, the prostitutes and pimps of the West End. With Maura masterminding it, they pull off an audacious gold bullion robbery and have much of the Establishment in their pockets.

But notoriety has its price. The police are determined to put away Maura once and for all – and not everyone in the family thinks that's such a bad idea. When it comes to the crunch, Maura has to face the pain of lost love in her past – and the dangerous lady discovers her heart is not made entirely of stone.

Praise for Martina Cole's sensational bestselling novels:

'Distinctive and powerfully written' *The Times*

'Martina Cole pulls no punches, writes as she sees it, refuses to patronise or condescend to either her characters or fans' *Independent on Sunday*

'Her gripping plots pack a mean emotional punch' *Mail on Sunday*

'An author who knows intimately the world she writes about' *Daily Express*

978 0 7553 7406 9

headline